PUNK ROCK KARAOKE

BIANCA XUNISE

VIKING

ACKNOWLEDGMENTS

Punk Rock Karaoke is a book about community, and in bringing this story to life, I had a huge lesson in the importance of having one. Thanks to my agent, Linda Camacho, my editor, Aneeka Kalia, and the art team at Viking (Kate Renner and Lucia Baez!) for believing in this story. Thanks to Sage Coffey and Hank Jones for their coloring help. A huge thanks to the 3Arts/Bodies of Work Residency Fellowship for weekly tear-filled check-ins and constant cheerleading as I reached the finish line. And a special thanks to Shelly Ghost for doing it all, from building a faux punk dive bar in our living room during the lockdown so I could get over writer's block, to making me unforgettable carne asada tacos when I would forget to eat, to stepping up to be my copilot in every part of the process. There's a bit of your genius on every page.

  This book couldn't have been possible without all of you. Thank you from the bottom of my heart. (ﾉ●ヮ●)ﾉ*:･ﾟ✧

VIKING

An imprint of Penguin Random House LLC, New York

First published in the United States of America by Viking,
an imprint of Penguin Random House LLC, 2024

Visit us online at PenguinRandomHouse.com.

Library of Congress Cataloging-in-Publication Data is available.

ISBN 9780593464502 (hardcover)

1 3 5 7 9 10 8 6 4 2

ISBN 9780593464526 (paperback)

1 3 5 7 9 10 8 6 4 2

Manufactured in China

TOPL

Edited by Aneeka Kalia

Design by Lucia Baez & Kate Renner

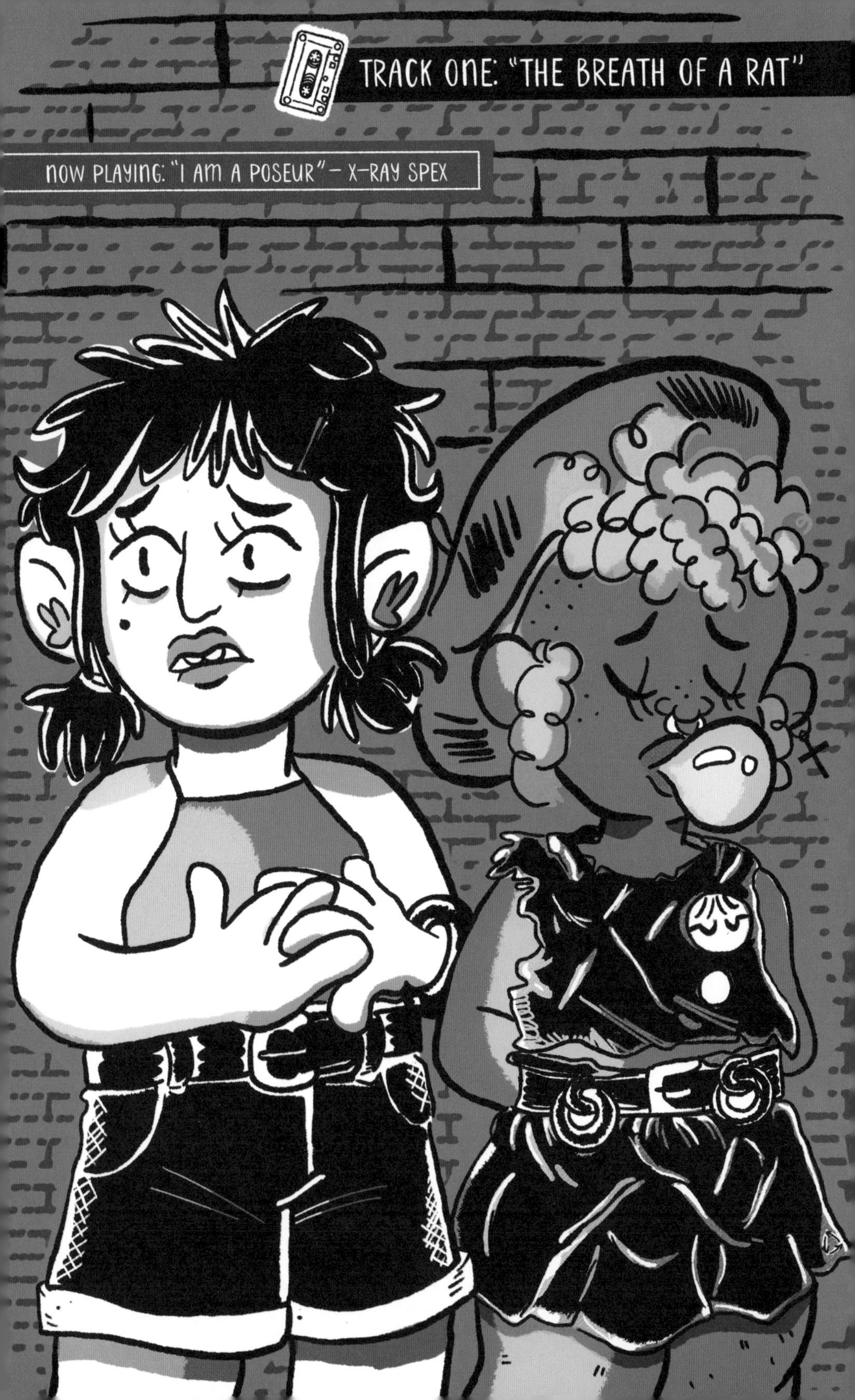
TRACK ONE: "THE BREATH OF A RAT"
NOW PLAYING: "I AM A POSEUR" – X-RAY SPEX

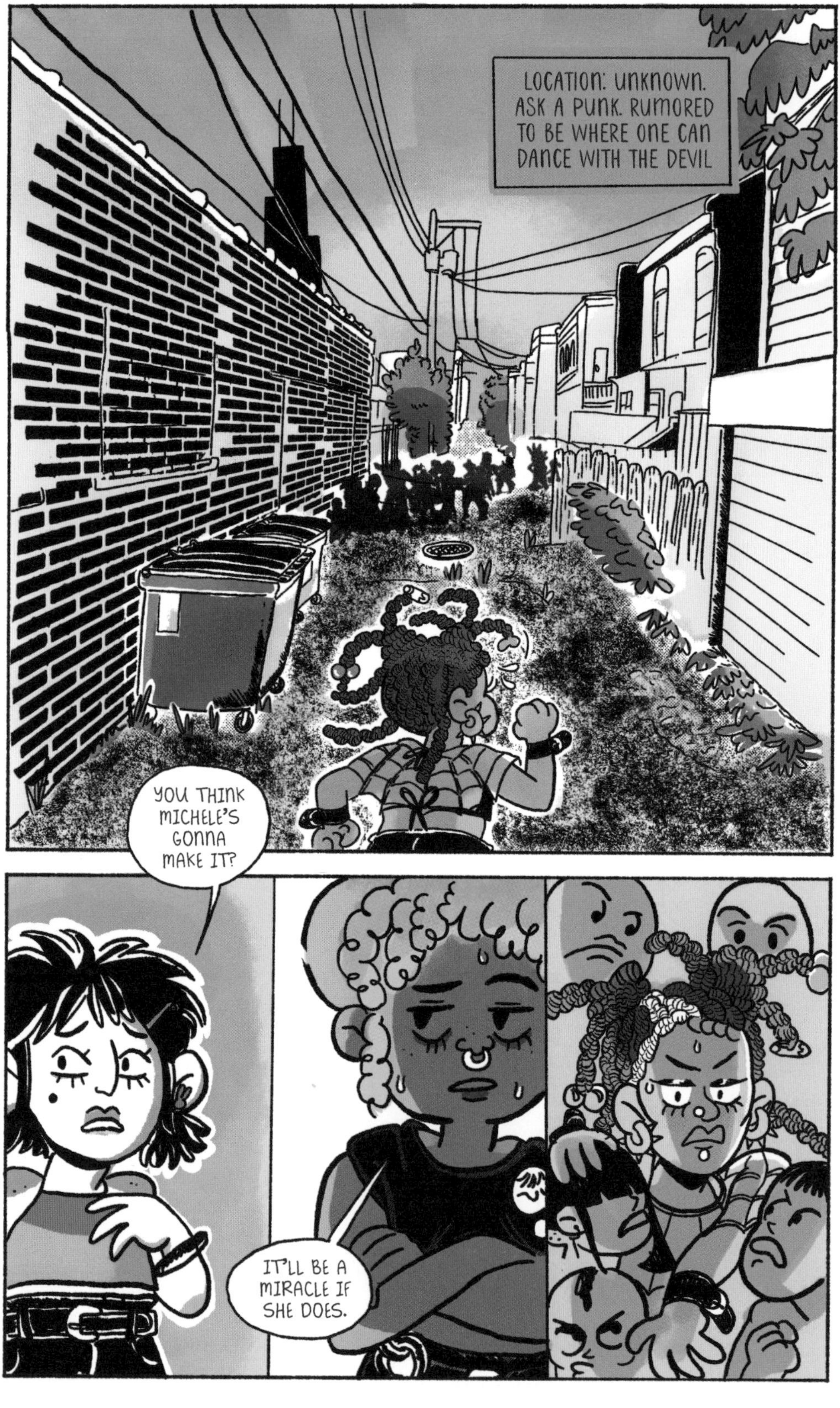
LOCATION: UNKNOWN. ASK A PUNK. RUMORED TO BE WHERE ONE CAN DANCE WITH THE DEVIL
YOU THINK MICHELE'S GONNA MAKE IT?
IT'LL BE A MIRACLE IF SHE DOES.

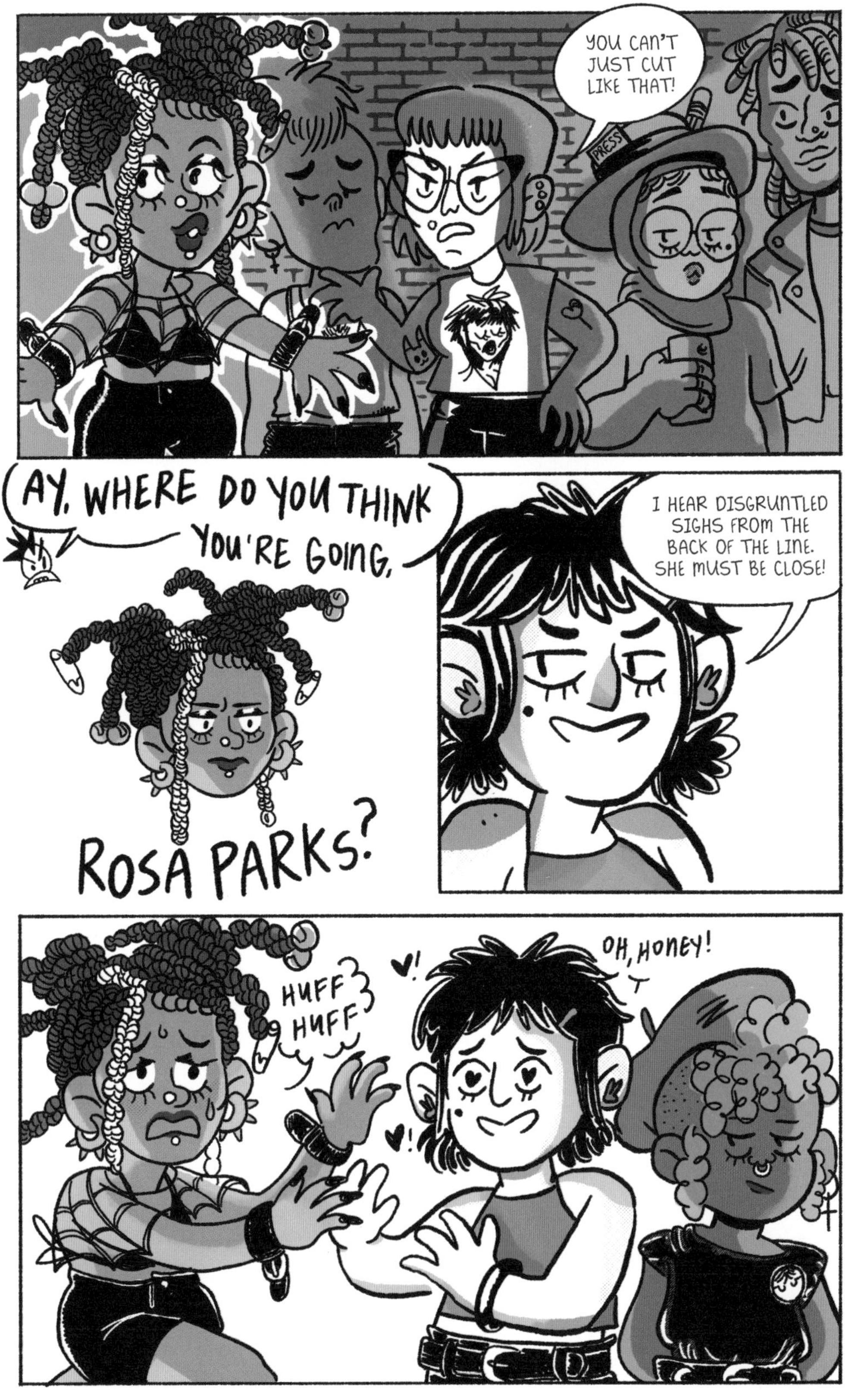
YOU CAN'T JUST CUT LIKE THAT!
PRESS
AY, WHERE DO YOU THINK YOU'RE GOING, ROSA PARKS?
I HEAR DISGRUNTLED SIGHS FROM THE BACK OF THE LINE. SHE MUST BE CLOSE!
HUFF HUFF
OH, HONEY!

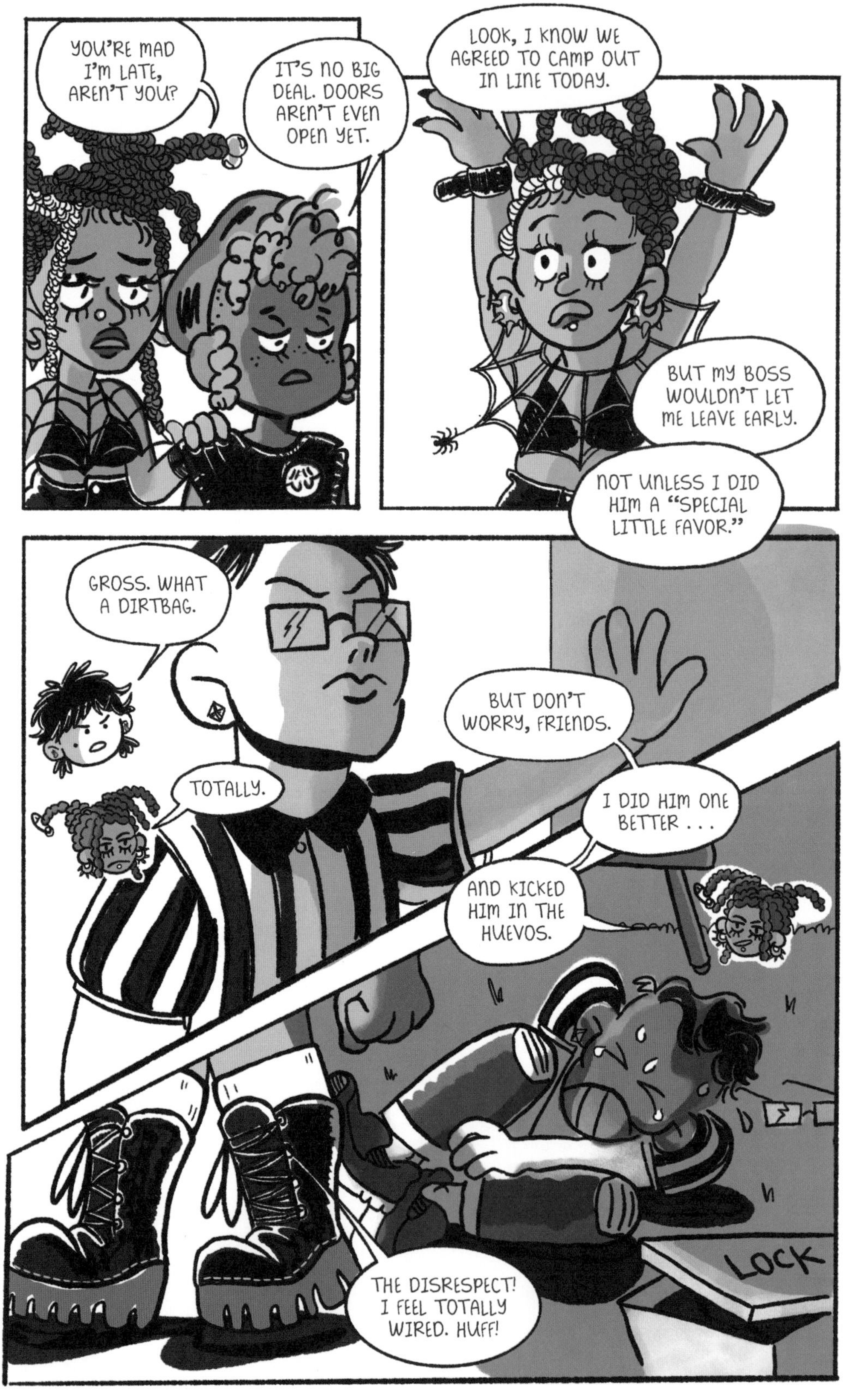
YOU'RE MAD I'M LATE, AREN'T YOU?
IT'S NO BIG DEAL. DOORS AREN'T EVEN OPEN YET.
LOOK, I KNOW WE AGREED TO CAMP OUT IN LINE TODAY.
BUT MY BOSS WOULDN'T LET ME LEAVE EARLY.
NOT UNLESS I DID HIM A "SPECIAL LITTLE FAVOR."
GROSS. WHAT A DIRTBAG.
TOTALLY.
BUT DON'T WORRY, FRIENDS.
I DID HIM ONE BETTER . . .
AND KICKED HIM IN THE HUEVOS.
LOCK
THE DISRESPECT! I FEEL TOTALLY WIRED. HUFF!

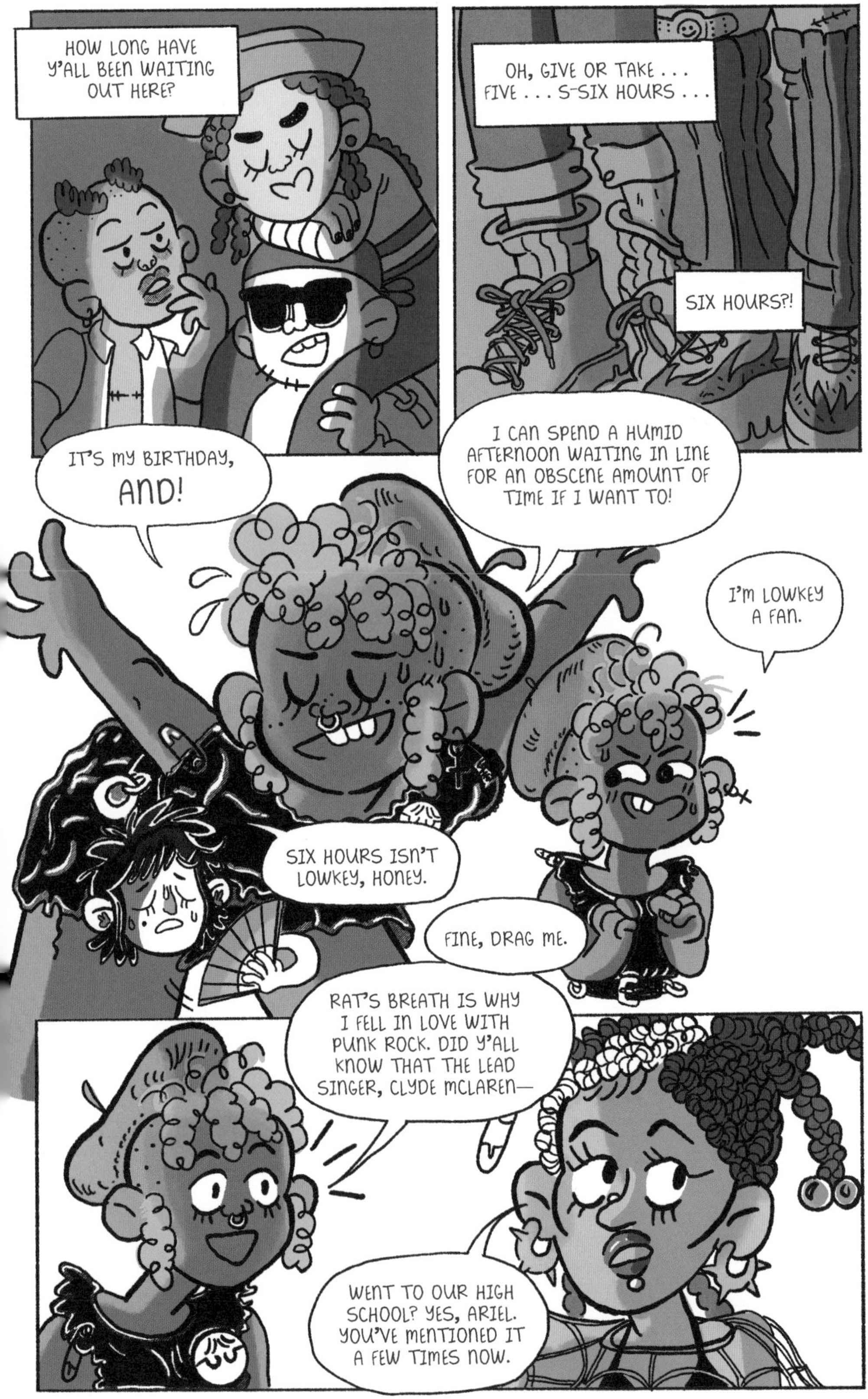
HOW LONG HAVE Y'ALL BEEN WAITING OUT HERE?
OH, GIVE OR TAKE . . . FIVE . . . S-SIX HOURS . . .
SIX HOURS?!
IT'S MY BIRTHDAY, AND!
I CAN SPEND A HUMID AFTERNOON WAITING IN LINE FOR AN OBSCENE AMOUNT OF TIME IF I WANT TO!
I'M LOWKEY A FAN.
SIX HOURS ISN'T LOWKEY, HONEY.
FINE, DRAG ME.
RAT'S BREATH IS WHY I FELL IN LOVE WITH PUNK ROCK. DID Y'ALL KNOW THAT THE LEAD SINGER, CLYDE MCLAREN—
WENT TO OUR HIGH SCHOOL? YES, ARIEL. YOU'VE MENTIONED IT A FEW TIMES NOW.

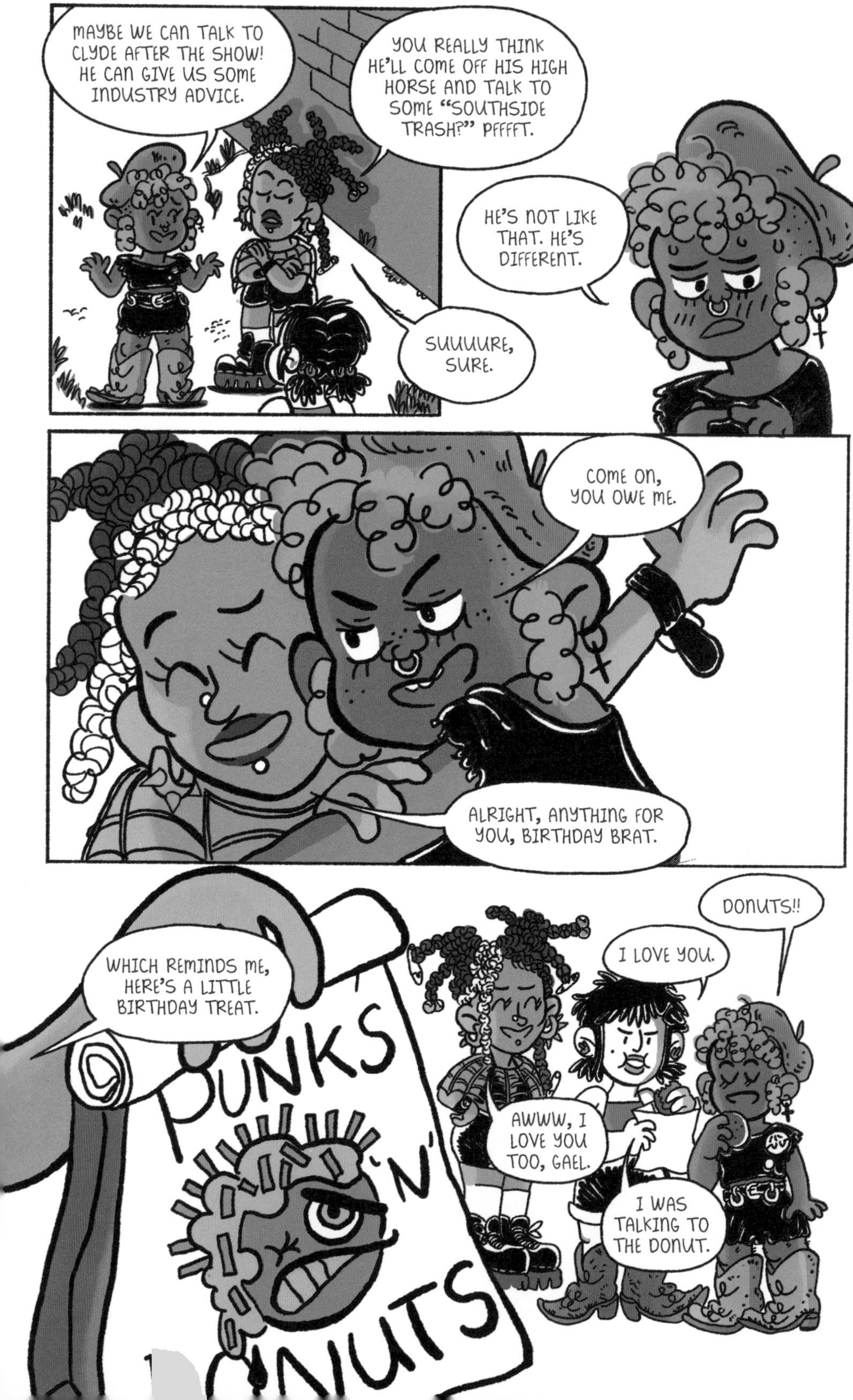
MAYBE WE CAN TALK TO CLYDE AFTER THE SHOW! HE CAN GIVE US SOME INDUSTRY ADVICE.
YOU REALLY THINK HE'LL COME OFF HIS HIGH HORSE AND TALK TO SOME "SOUTHSIDE TRASH?" PFFFFT.
HE'S NOT LIKE THAT. HE'S DIFFERENT.
SUUUURE, SURE.
COME ON, YOU OWE ME.
ALRIGHT, ANYTHING FOR YOU, BIRTHDAY BRAT.
WHICH REMINDS ME, HERE'S A LITTLE BIRTHDAY TREAT.
PUNKS 'N' DONUTS
I LOVE YOU.
DONUTS!!
AWWW, I LOVE YOU TOO, GAEL.
I WAS TALKING TO THE DONUT.

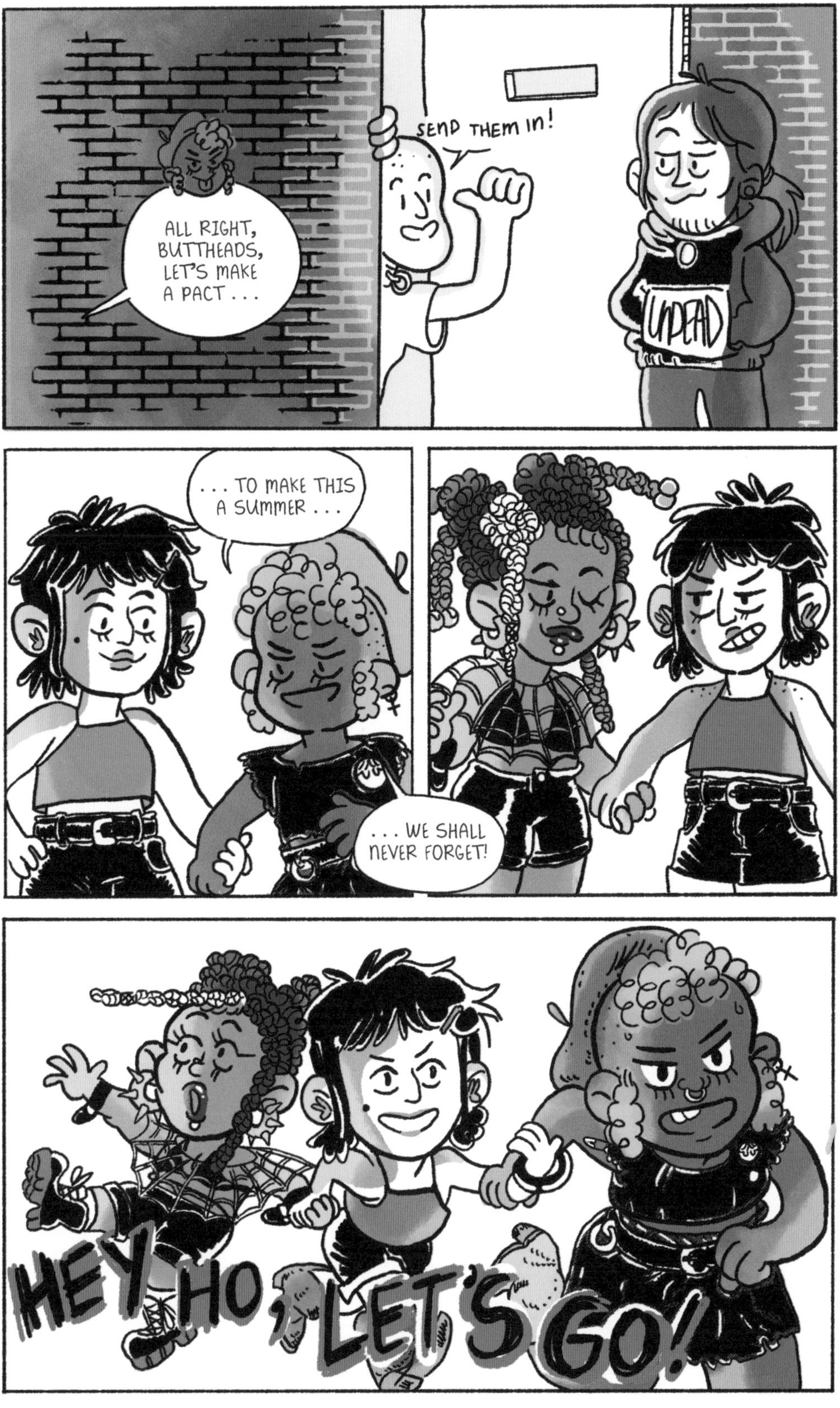

ALL RIGHT, BUTTHEADS, LET'S MAKE A PACT . . .
SEND THEM IN!
UNDEAD
. . . TO MAKE THIS A SUMMER . . .
. . . WE SHALL NEVER FORGET!
HEY HO, LET'S GO!

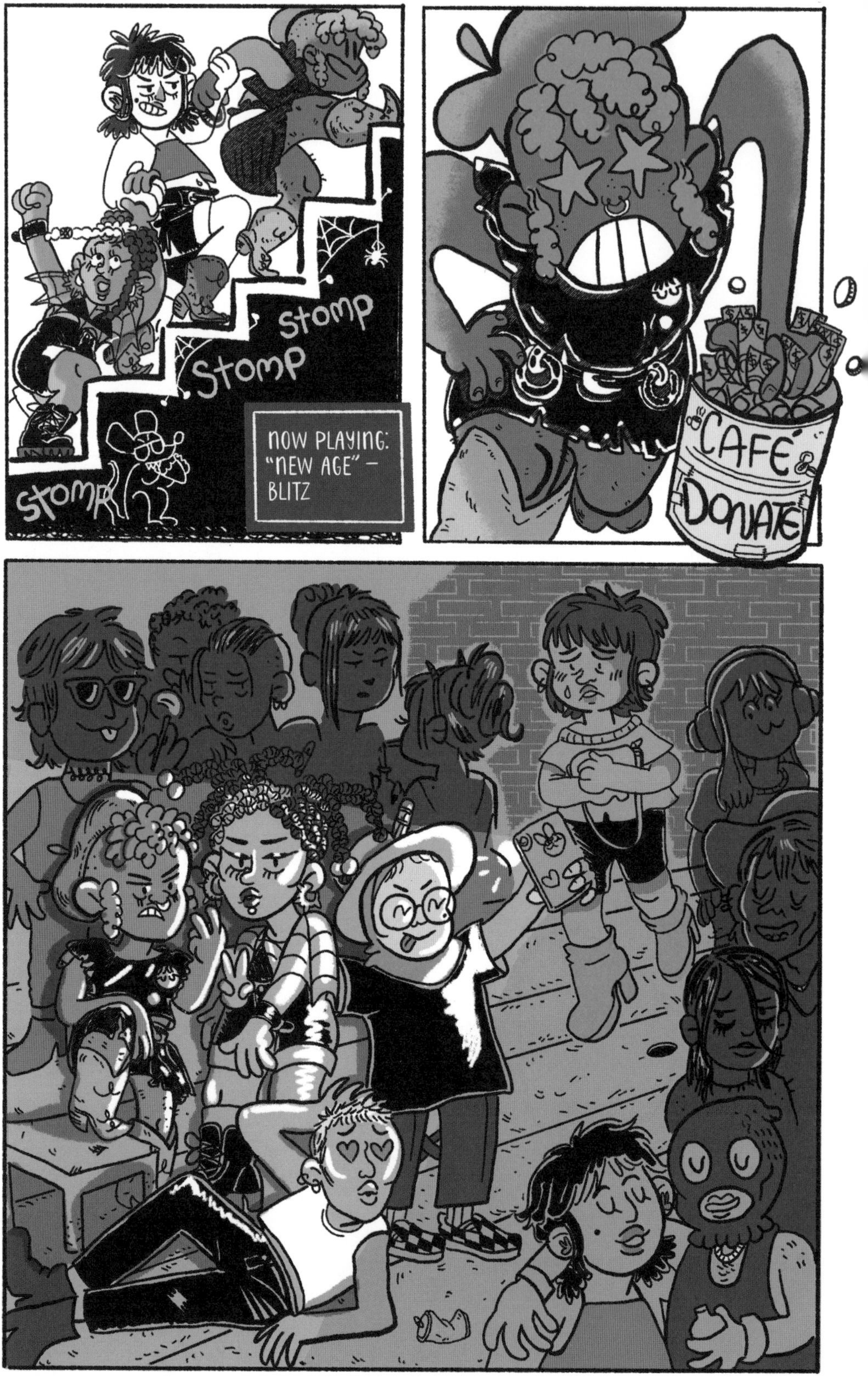

stomp
Stomp
stomp
NOW PLAYING: "NEW AGE" — BLITZ
CAFÉ
DONATE

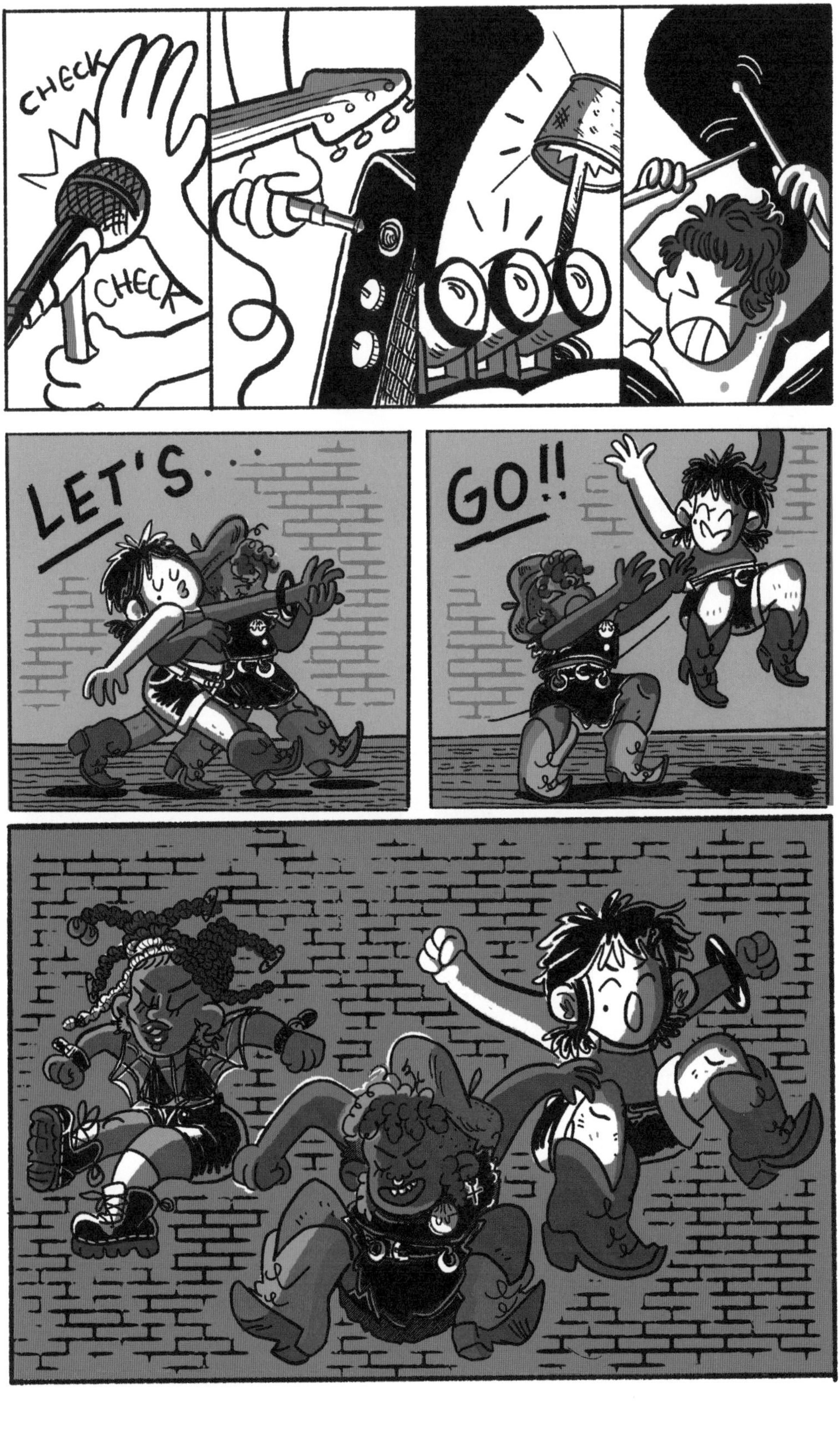
CHECK
CHECK
LET'S...
GO!!

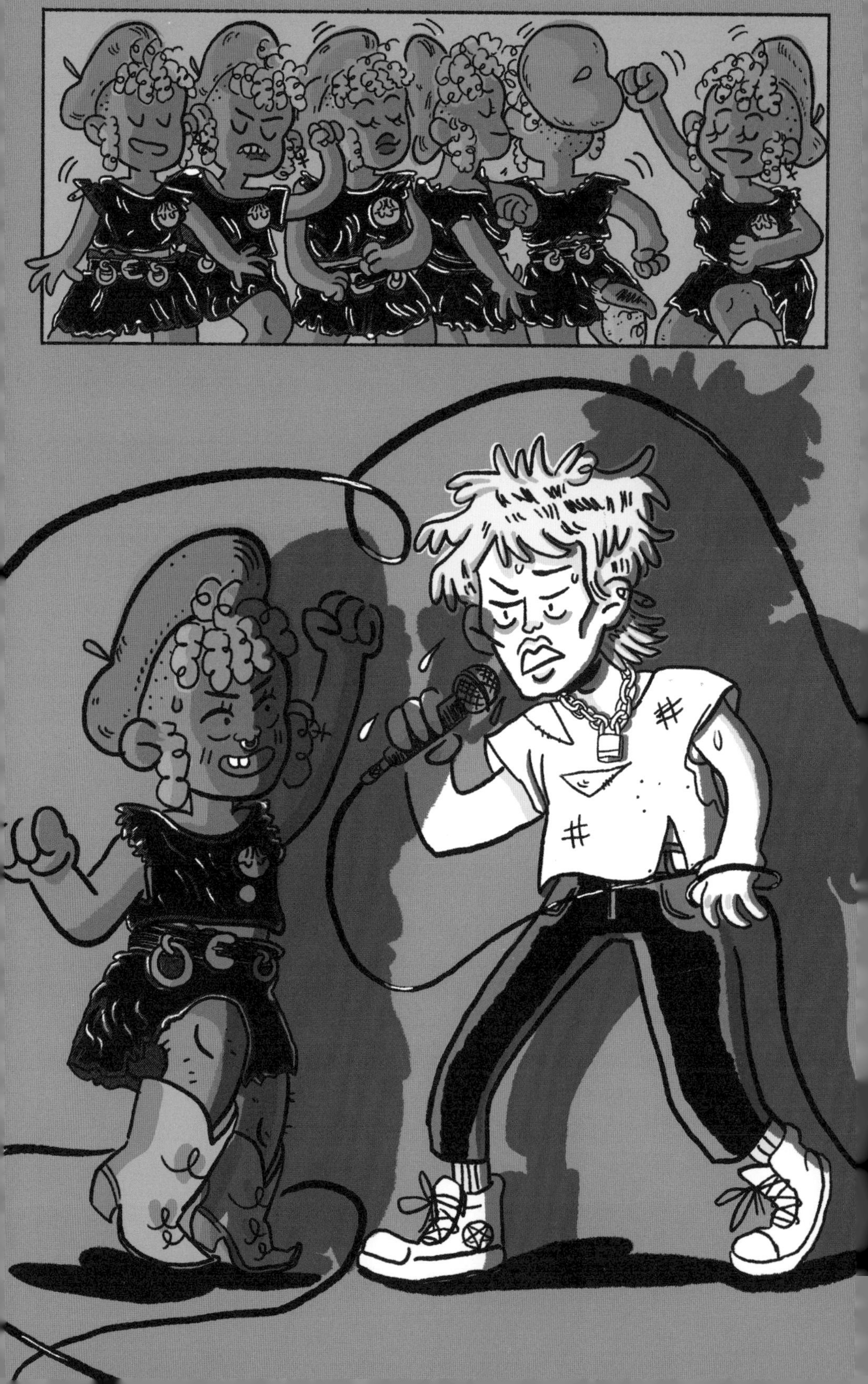

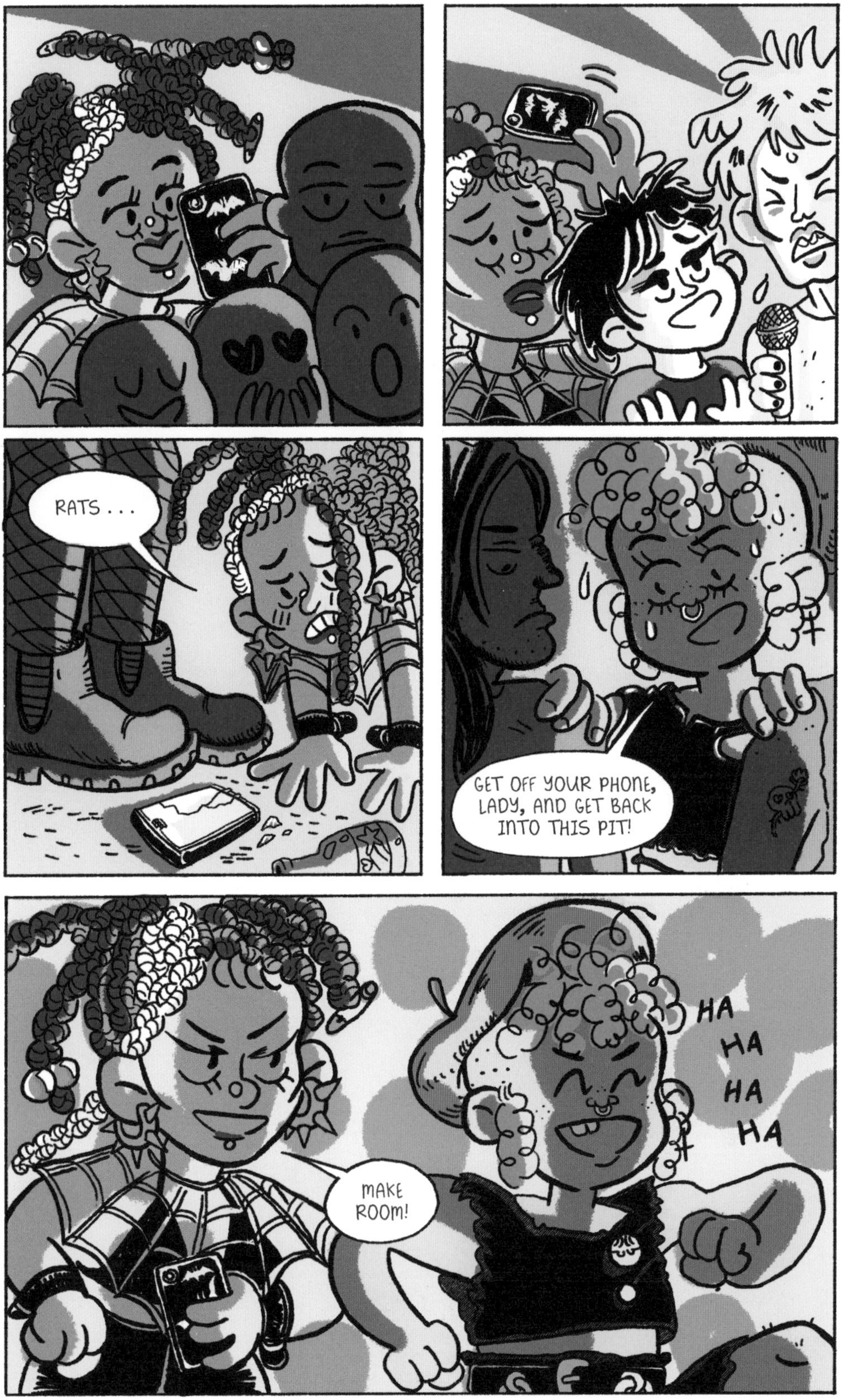
RATS . . .
GET OFF YOUR PHONE, LADY, AND GET BACK INTO THIS PIT!
HA HA HA HA
MAKE ROOM!

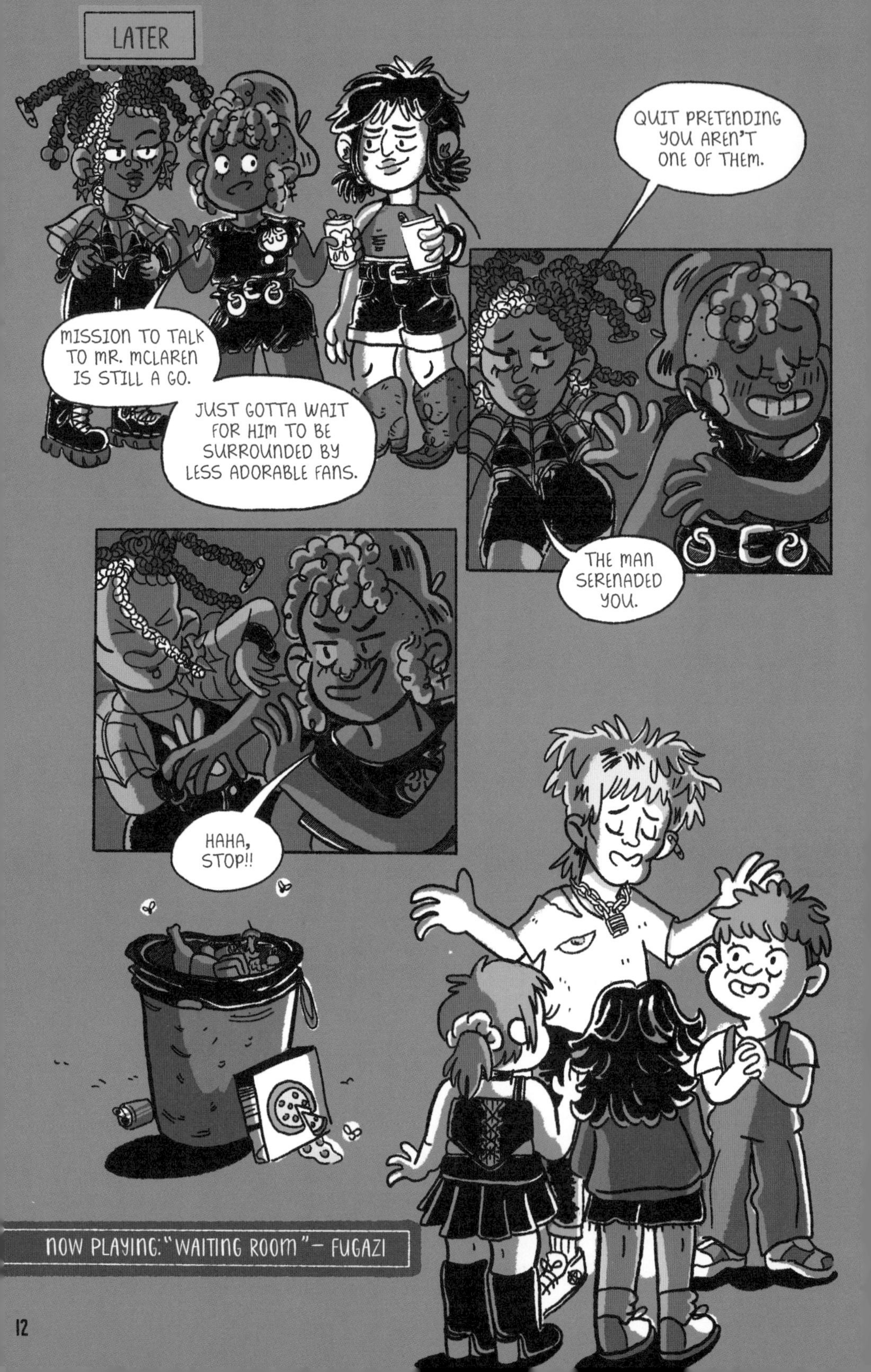
LATER
MISSION TO TALK TO MR. MCLAREN IS STILL A GO.
JUST GOTTA WAIT FOR HIM TO BE SURROUNDED BY LESS ADORABLE FANS.
QUIT PRETENDING YOU AREN'T ONE OF THEM.
THE MAN SERENADED YOU.
HAHA, STOP!!
NOW PLAYING: "WAITING ROOM" – FUGAZI

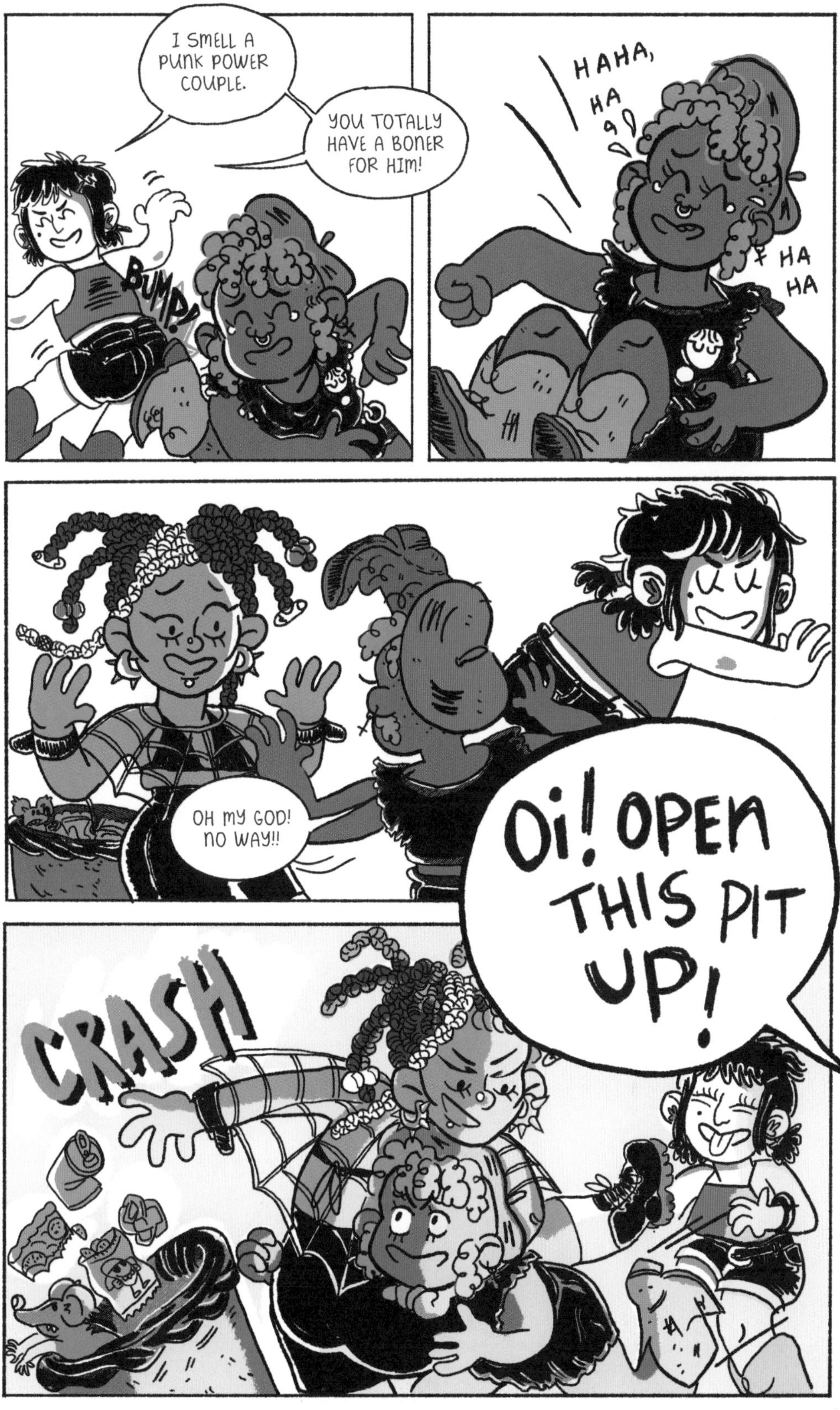
I SMELL A PUNK POWER COUPLE.
YOU TOTALLY HAVE A BONER FOR HIM!
BUMP!
HAHA, HA HA
HA HA
OH MY GOD! NO WAY!!
OI! OPEN THIS PIT UP!
CRASH

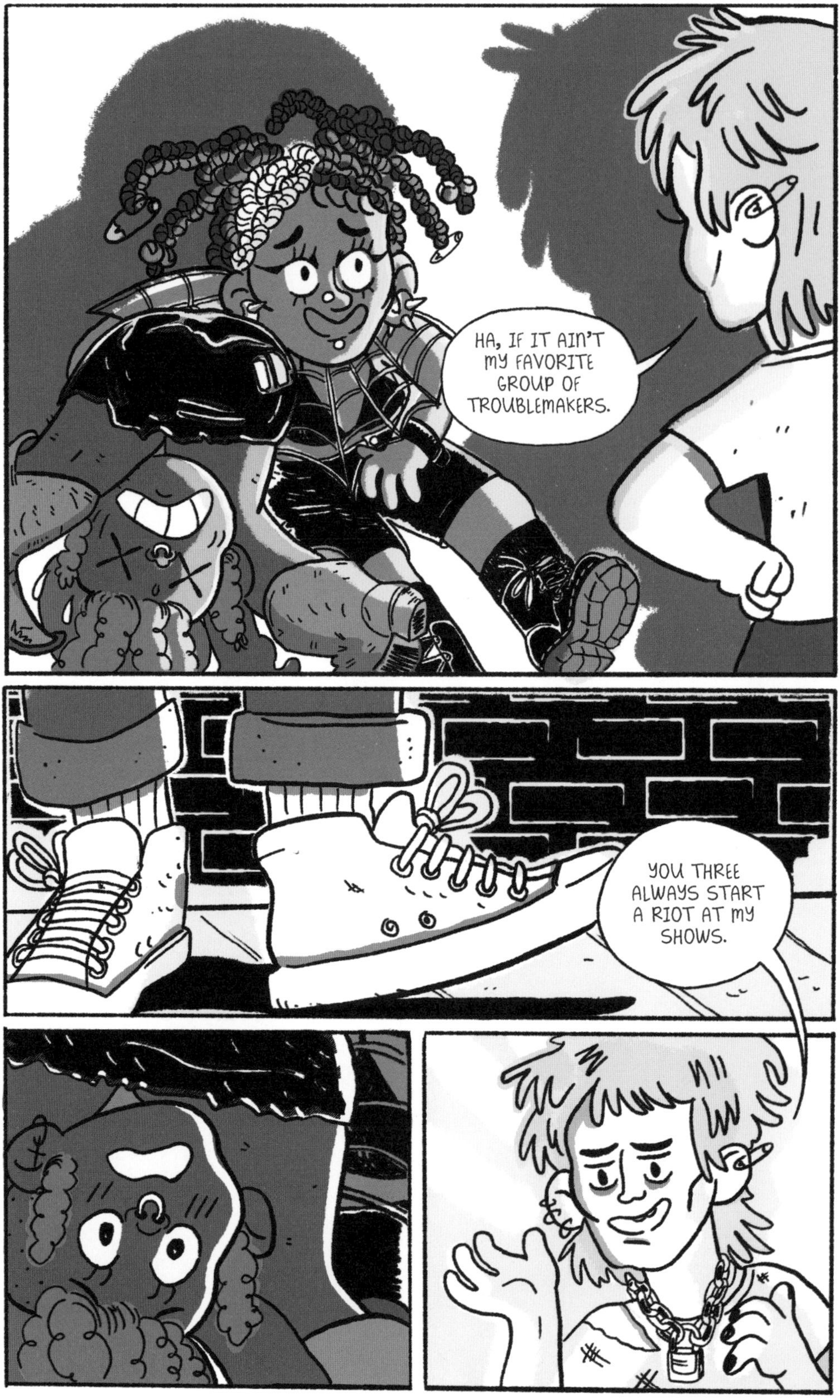
HA, IF IT AIN'T MY FAVORITE GROUP OF TROUBLEMAKERS.
YOU THREE ALWAYS START A RIOT AT MY SHOWS.

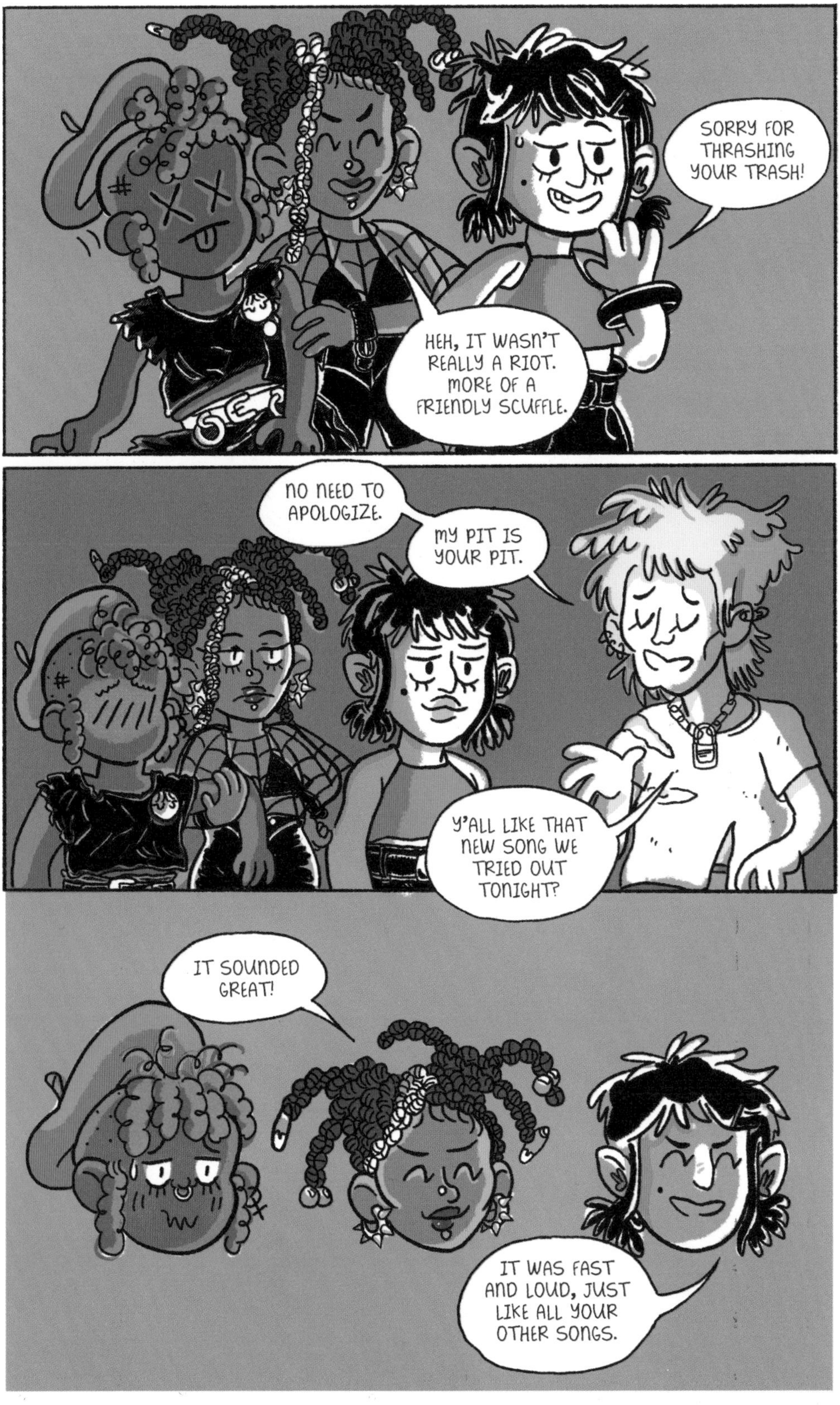
SORRY FOR THRASHING YOUR TRASH!
HEH, IT WASN'T REALLY A RIOT. MORE OF A FRIENDLY SCUFFLE.
NO NEED TO APOLOGIZE.
MY PIT IS YOUR PIT.
Y'ALL LIKE THAT NEW SONG WE TRIED OUT TONIGHT?
IT SOUNDED GREAT!
IT WAS FAST AND LOUD, JUST LIKE ALL YOUR OTHER SONGS.

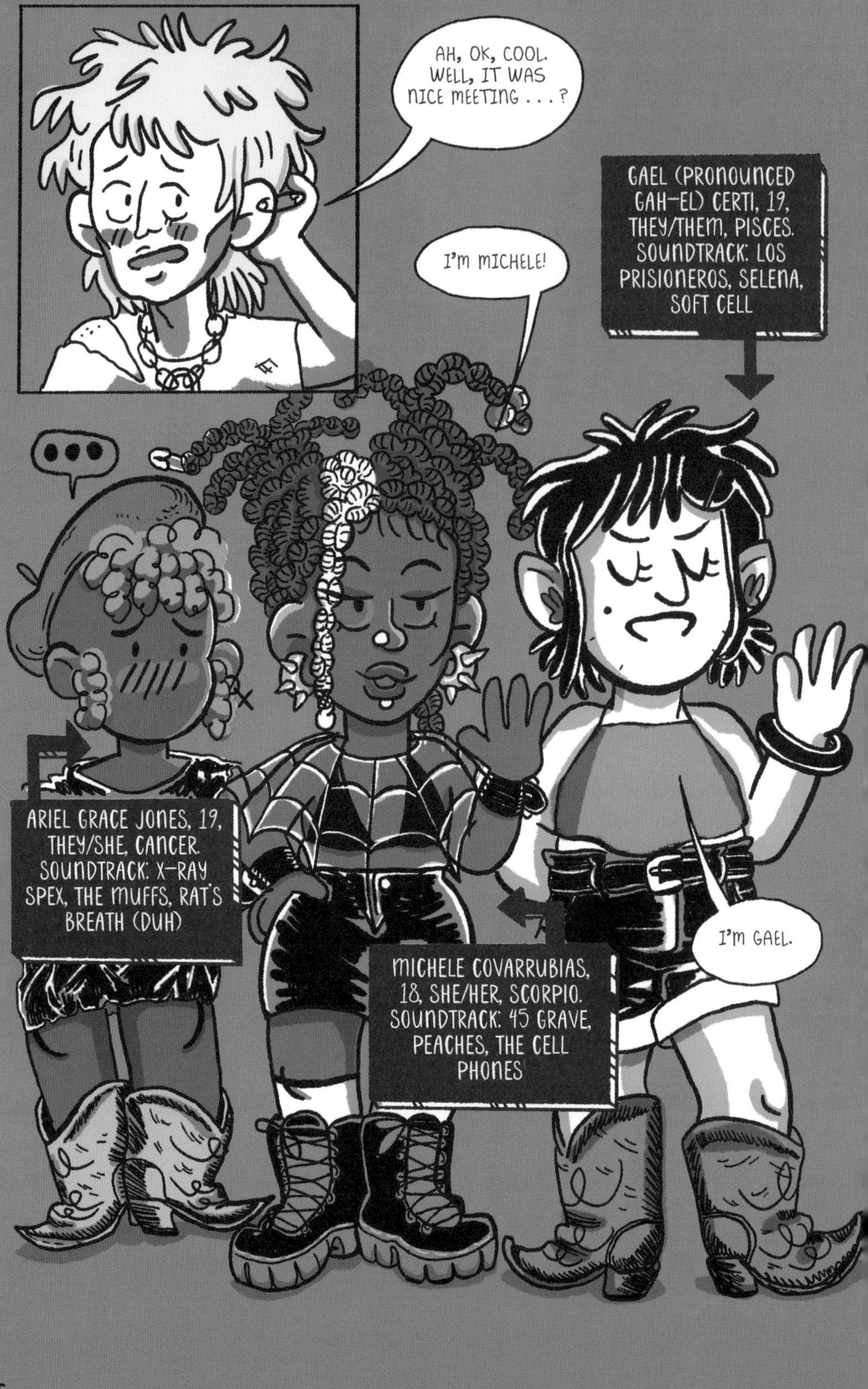
AH, OK, COOL. WELL, IT WAS NICE MEETING . . . ?
GAEL (PRONOUNCED GAH-EL) CERTI, 19, THEY/THEM, PISCES. SOUNDTRACK: LOS PRISIONEROS, SELENA, SOFT CELL
I'M MICHELE!
•••
ARIEL GRACE JONES, 19, THEY/SHE, CANCER. SOUNDTRACK: X-RAY SPEX, THE MUFFS, RAT'S BREATH (DUH)
MICHELE COVARRUBIAS, 18, SHE/HER, SCORPIO. SOUNDTRACK: 45 GRAVE, PEACHES, THE CELL PHONES
I'M GAEL.

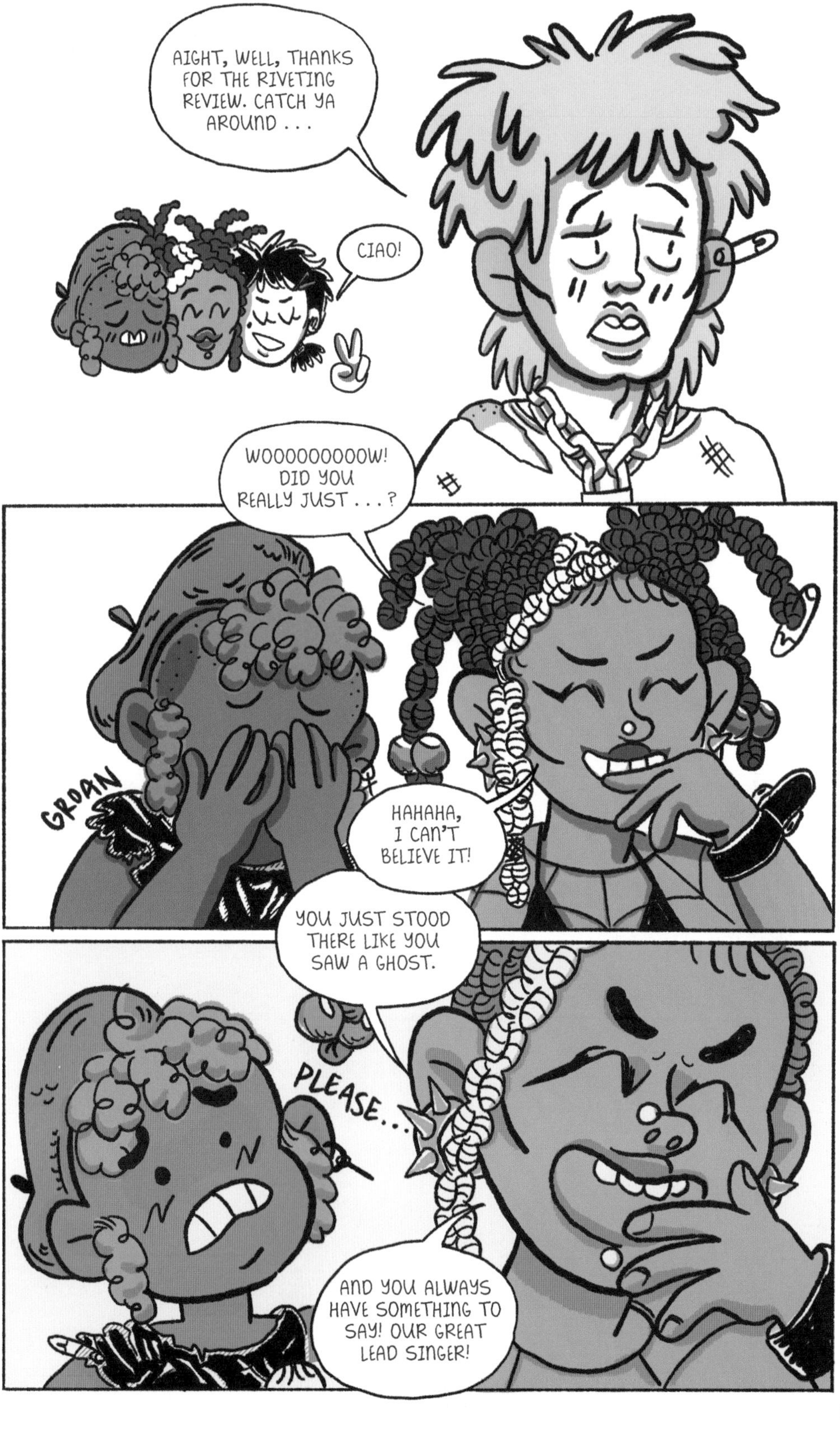
AIGHT, WELL, THANKS FOR THE RIVETING REVIEW. CATCH YA AROUND . . .
CIAO!
WOOOOOOOOOW! DID YOU REALLY JUST . . . ?
GROAN
HAHAHA, I CAN'T BELIEVE IT!
YOU JUST STOOD THERE LIKE YOU SAW A GHOST.
PLEASE . . .
AND YOU ALWAYS HAVE SOMETHING TO SAY! OUR GREAT LEAD SINGER!

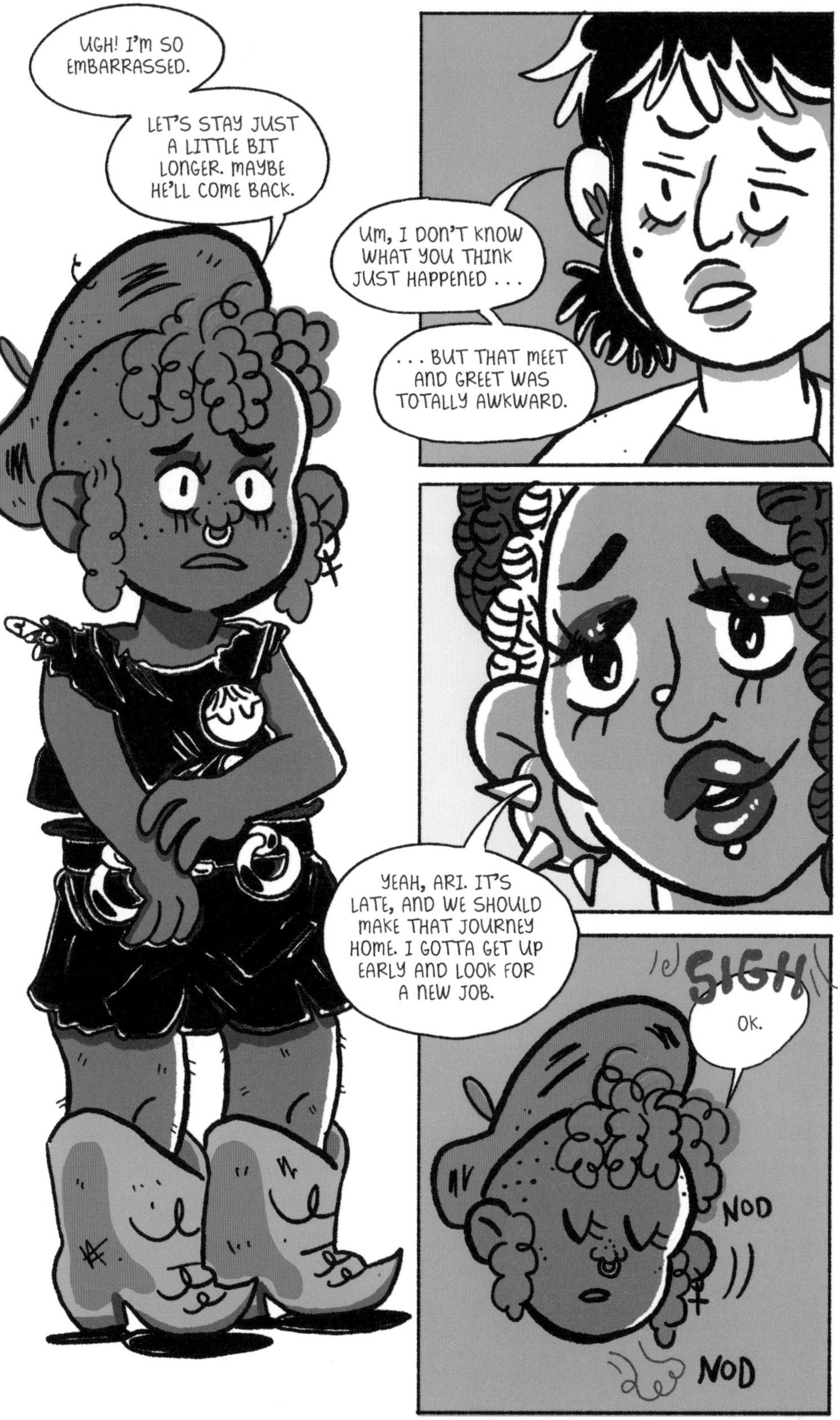
UGH! I'M SO EMBARRASSED.
LET'S STAY JUST A LITTLE BIT LONGER. MAYBE HE'LL COME BACK.
UM, I DON'T KNOW WHAT YOU THINK JUST HAPPENED . . .
. . . BUT THAT MEET AND GREET WAS TOTALLY AWKWARD.
YEAH, ARI. IT'S LATE, AND WE SHOULD MAKE THAT JOURNEY HOME. I GOTTA GET UP EARLY AND LOOK FOR A NEW JOB.
SIGH
OK.
NOD
NOD

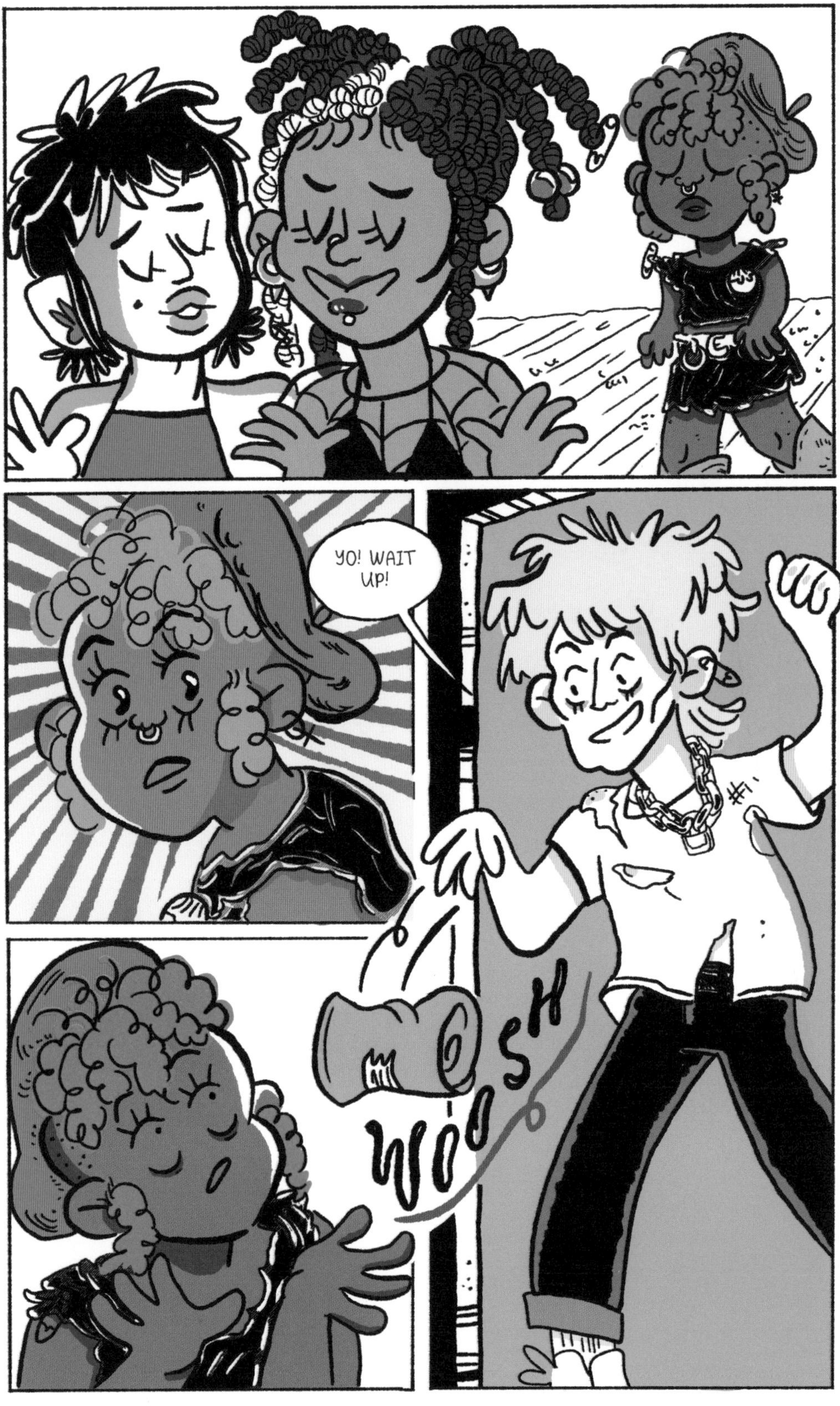
YO! WAIT UP!
WOOSH

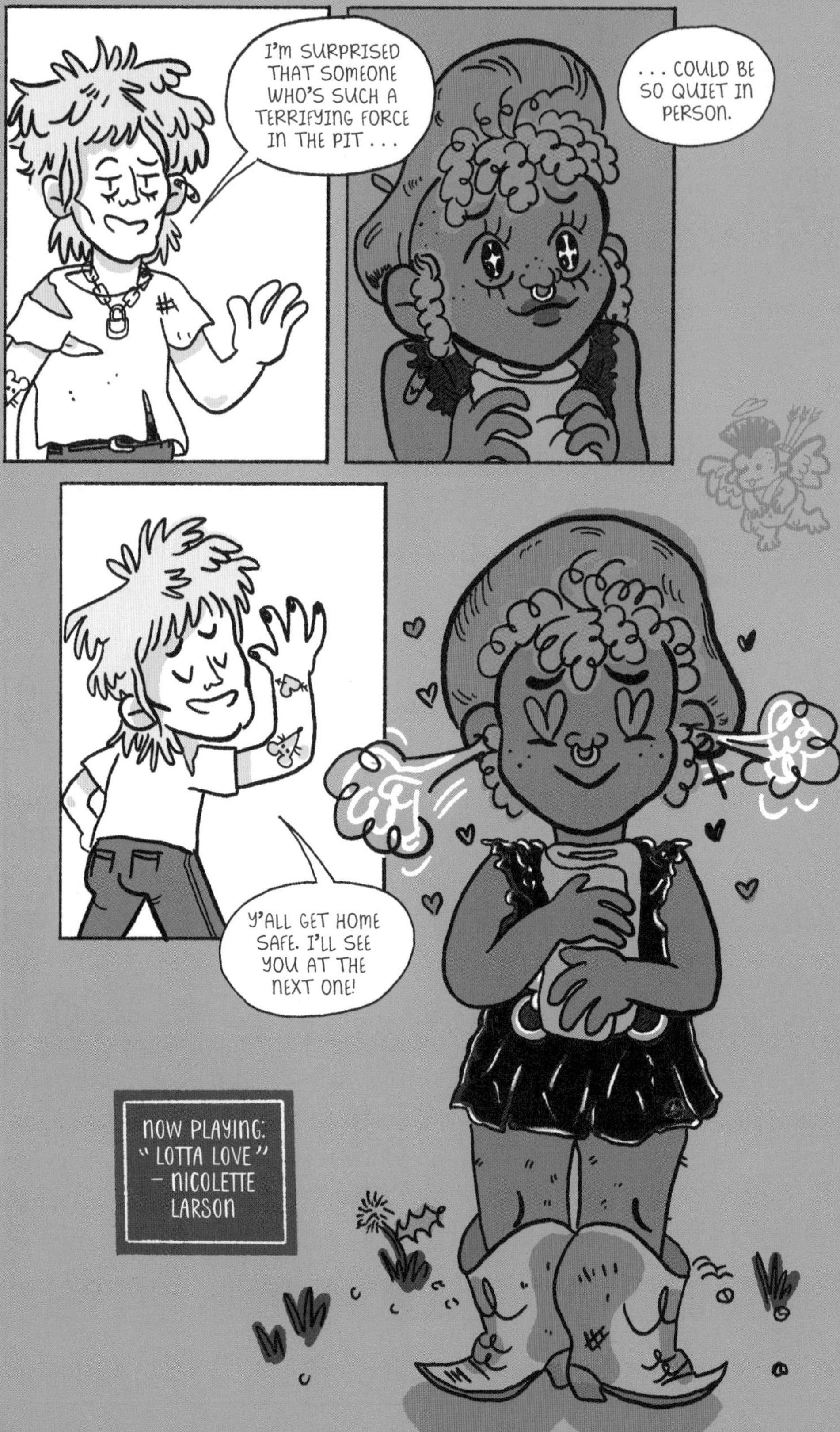
I'M SURPRISED THAT SOMEONE WHO'S SUCH A TERRIFYING FORCE IN THE PIT . . .
. . . COULD BE SO QUIET IN PERSON.
Y'ALL GET HOME SAFE. I'LL SEE YOU AT THE NEXT ONE!
NOW PLAYING: "LOTTA LOVE" – NICOLETTE LARSON

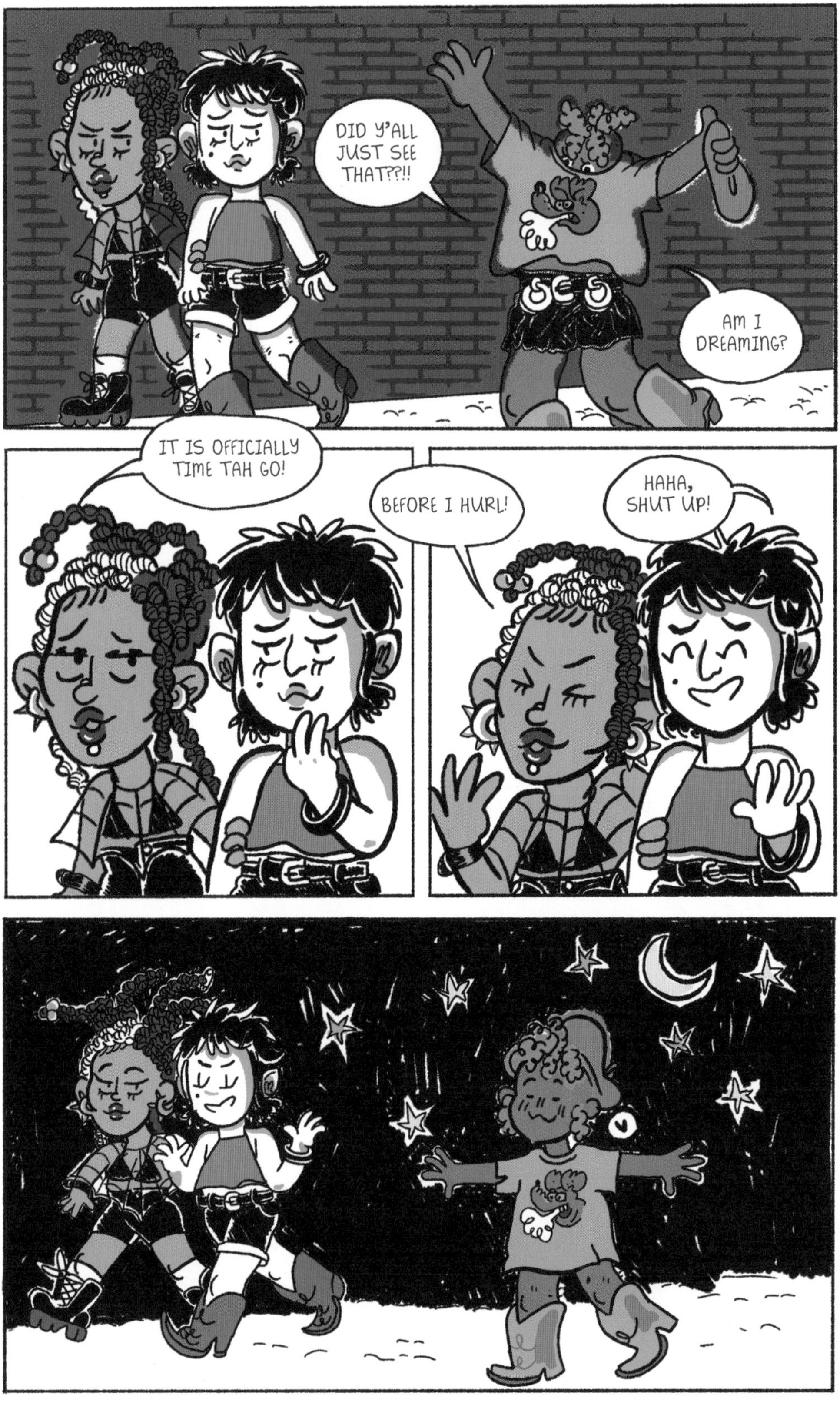
DID Y'ALL JUST SEE THAT??!!
AM I DREAMING?
IT IS OFFICIALLY TIME TAH GO!
BEFORE I HURL!
HAHA, SHUT UP!

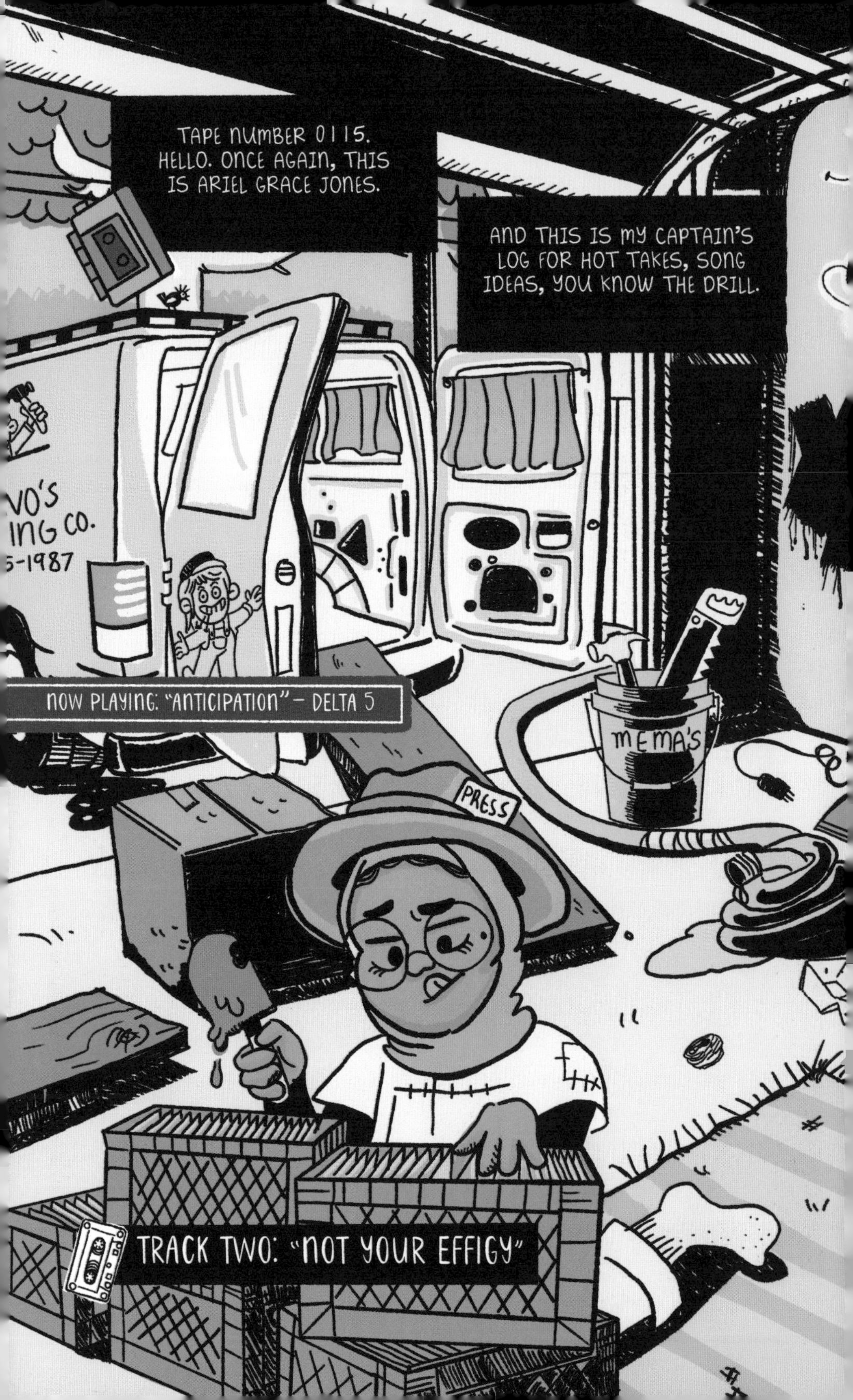
TAPE NUMBER 0115. HELLO. ONCE AGAIN, THIS IS ARIEL GRACE JONES.
AND THIS IS MY CAPTAIN'S LOG FOR HOT TAKES, SONG IDEAS, YOU KNOW THE DRILL.
NOW PLAYING: "ANTICIPATION" — DELTA 5
PRESS
MEMA'S
TRACK TWO: "NOT YOUR EFFIGY"

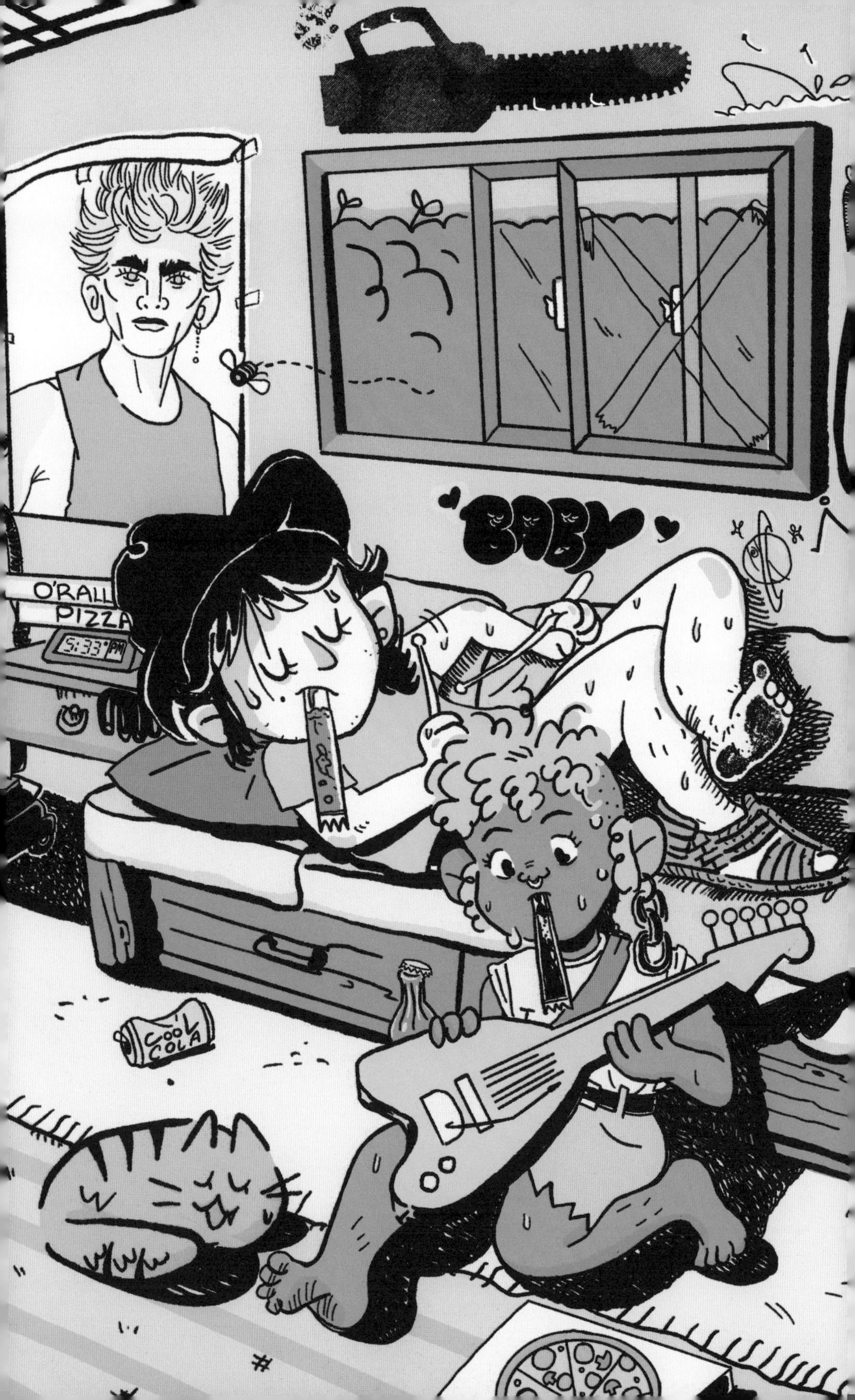
O'RALL
PIZZA
5:33 PM
BABY
COOL COLA

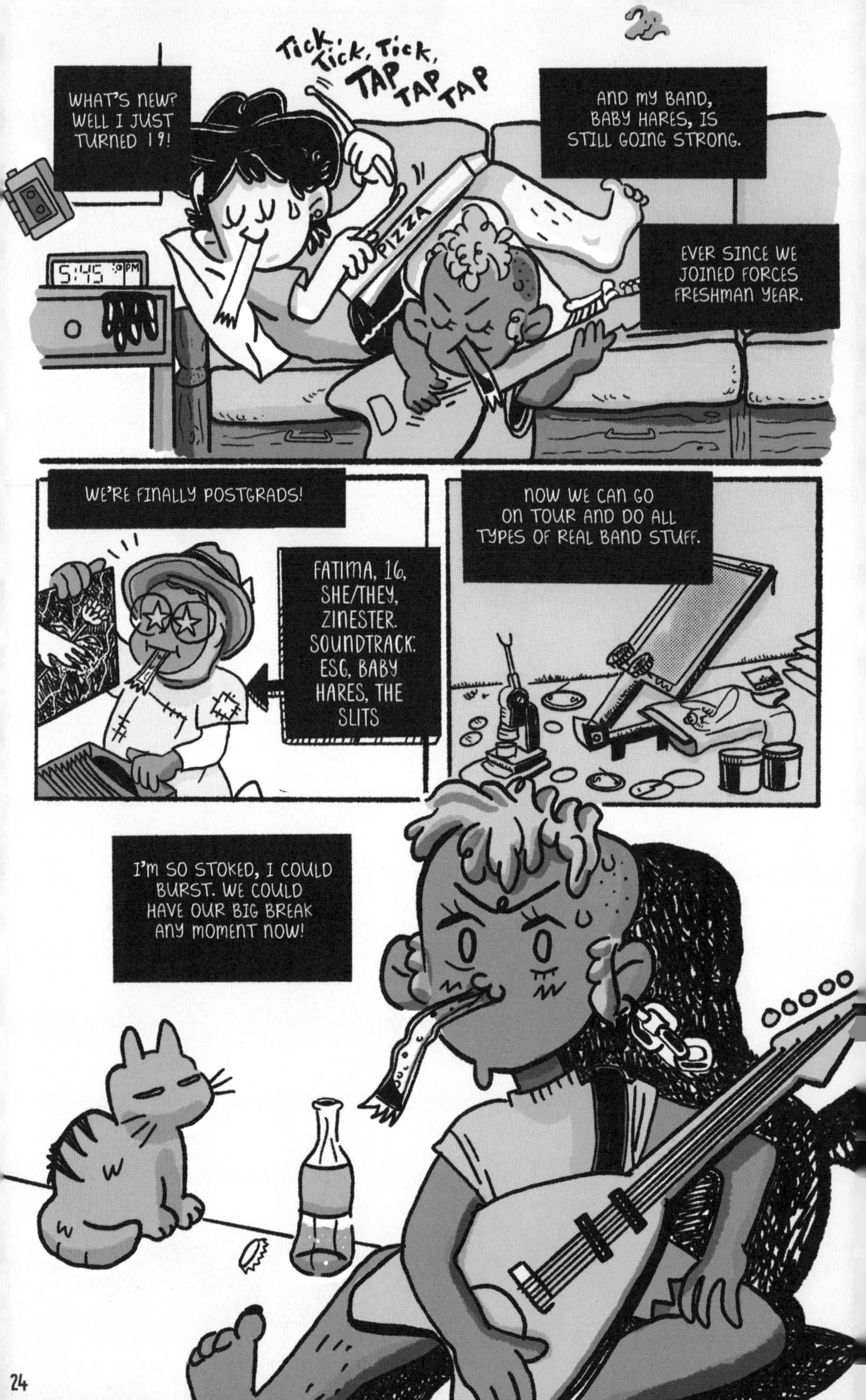
TICK, TICK, TICK,
TAP TAP TAP
WHAT'S NEW? WELL I JUST TURNED 19!
AND MY BAND, BABY HARES, IS STILL GOING STRONG.
PIZZA
EVER SINCE WE JOINED FORCES FRESHMAN YEAR.
WE'RE FINALLY POSTGRADS!
FATIMA, 16, SHE/THEY, ZINESTER. SOUNDTRACK: ESG, BABY HARES, THE SLITS
NOW WE CAN GO ON TOUR AND DO ALL TYPES OF REAL BAND STUFF.
I'M SO STOKED, I COULD BURST. WE COULD HAVE OUR BIG BREAK ANY MOMENT NOW!

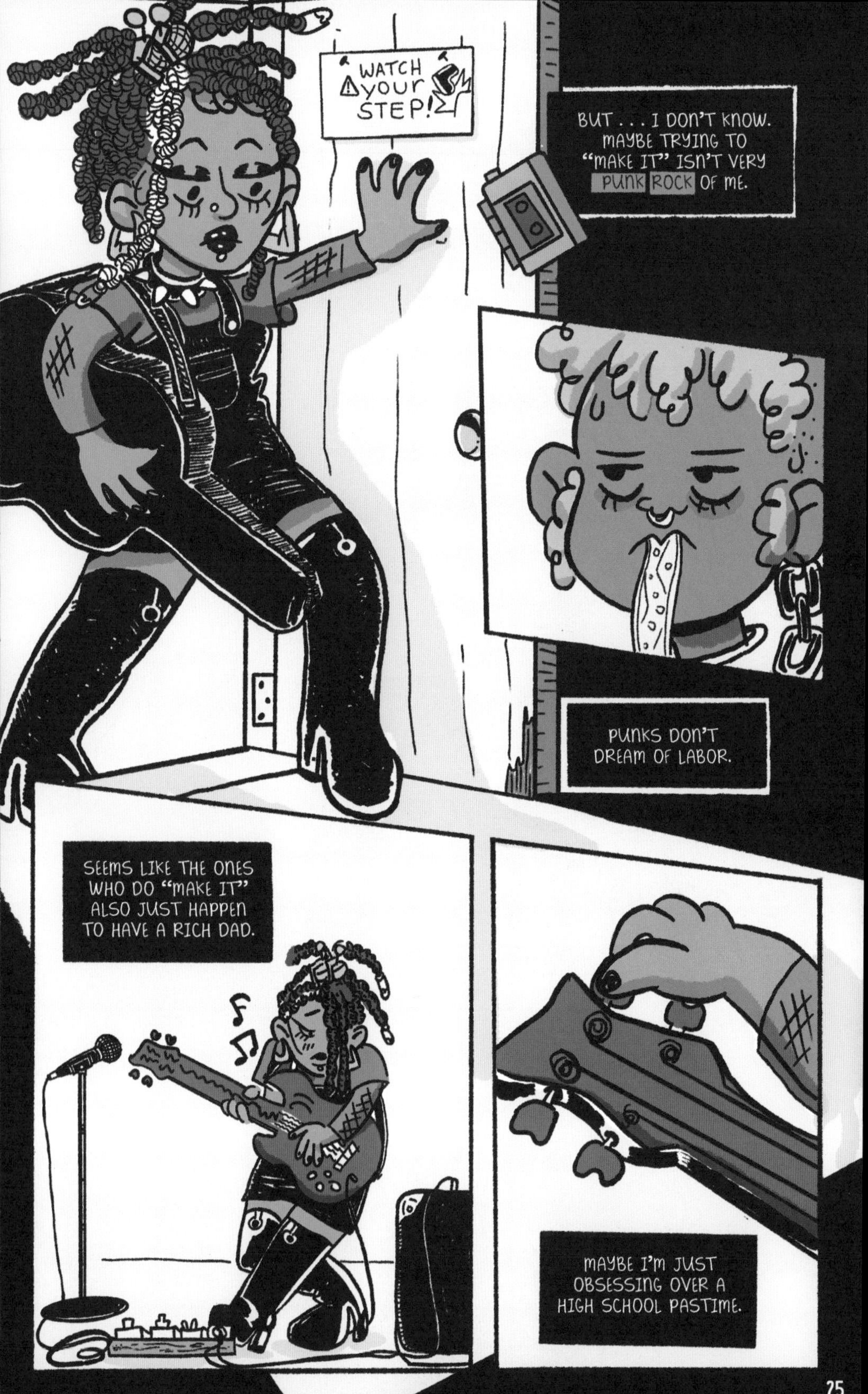
WATCH
⚠ your
STEP!
BUT . . . I DON'T KNOW. MAYBE TRYING TO "MAKE IT" ISN'T VERY PUNK ROCK OF ME.
PUNKS DON'T DREAM OF LABOR.
SEEMS LIKE THE ONES WHO DO "MAKE IT" ALSO JUST HAPPEN TO HAVE A RICH DAD.
MAYBE I'M JUST OBSESSING OVER A HIGH SCHOOL PASTIME.

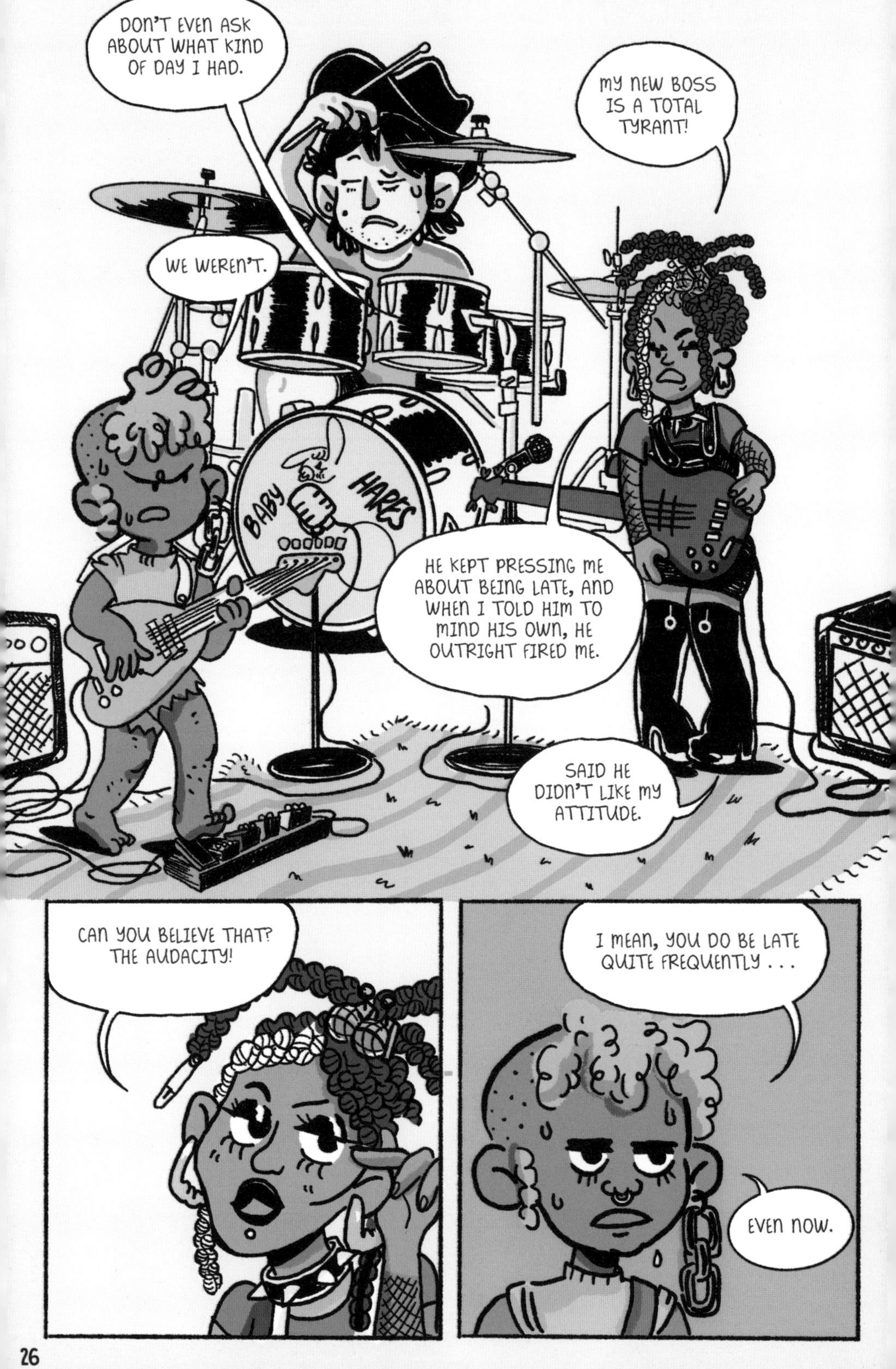
DON'T EVEN ASK ABOUT WHAT KIND OF DAY I HAD.
WE WEREN'T.
MY NEW BOSS IS A TOTAL TYRANT!
BABY HARES
HE KEPT PRESSING ME ABOUT BEING LATE, AND WHEN I TOLD HIM TO MIND HIS OWN, HE OUTRIGHT FIRED ME.
SAID HE DIDN'T LIKE MY ATTITUDE.
CAN YOU BELIEVE THAT? THE AUDACITY!
I MEAN, YOU DO BE LATE QUITE FREQUENTLY . . .
EVEN NOW.

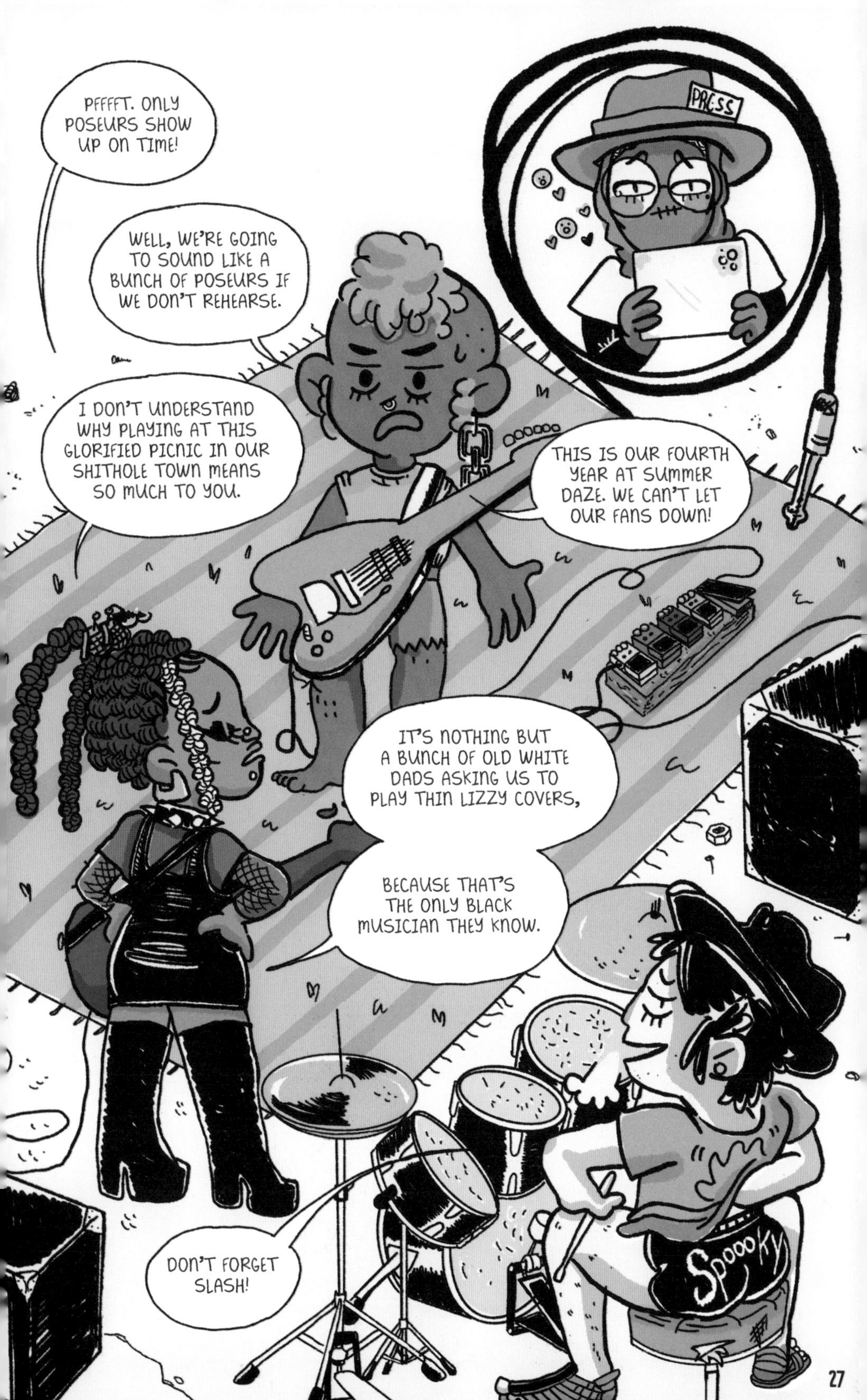
PFFFFT. ONLY POSEURS SHOW UP ON TIME!
PRESS
WELL, WE'RE GOING TO SOUND LIKE A BUNCH OF POSEURS IF WE DON'T REHEARSE.
I DON'T UNDERSTAND WHY PLAYING AT THIS GLORIFIED PICNIC IN OUR SHITHOLE TOWN MEANS SO MUCH TO YOU.
THIS IS OUR FOURTH YEAR AT SUMMER DAZE. WE CAN'T LET OUR FANS DOWN!
IT'S NOTHING BUT A BUNCH OF OLD WHITE DADS ASKING US TO PLAY THIN LIZZY COVERS,
BECAUSE THAT'S THE ONLY BLACK MUSICIAN THEY KNOW.
DON'T FORGET SLASH!
Spooo ky

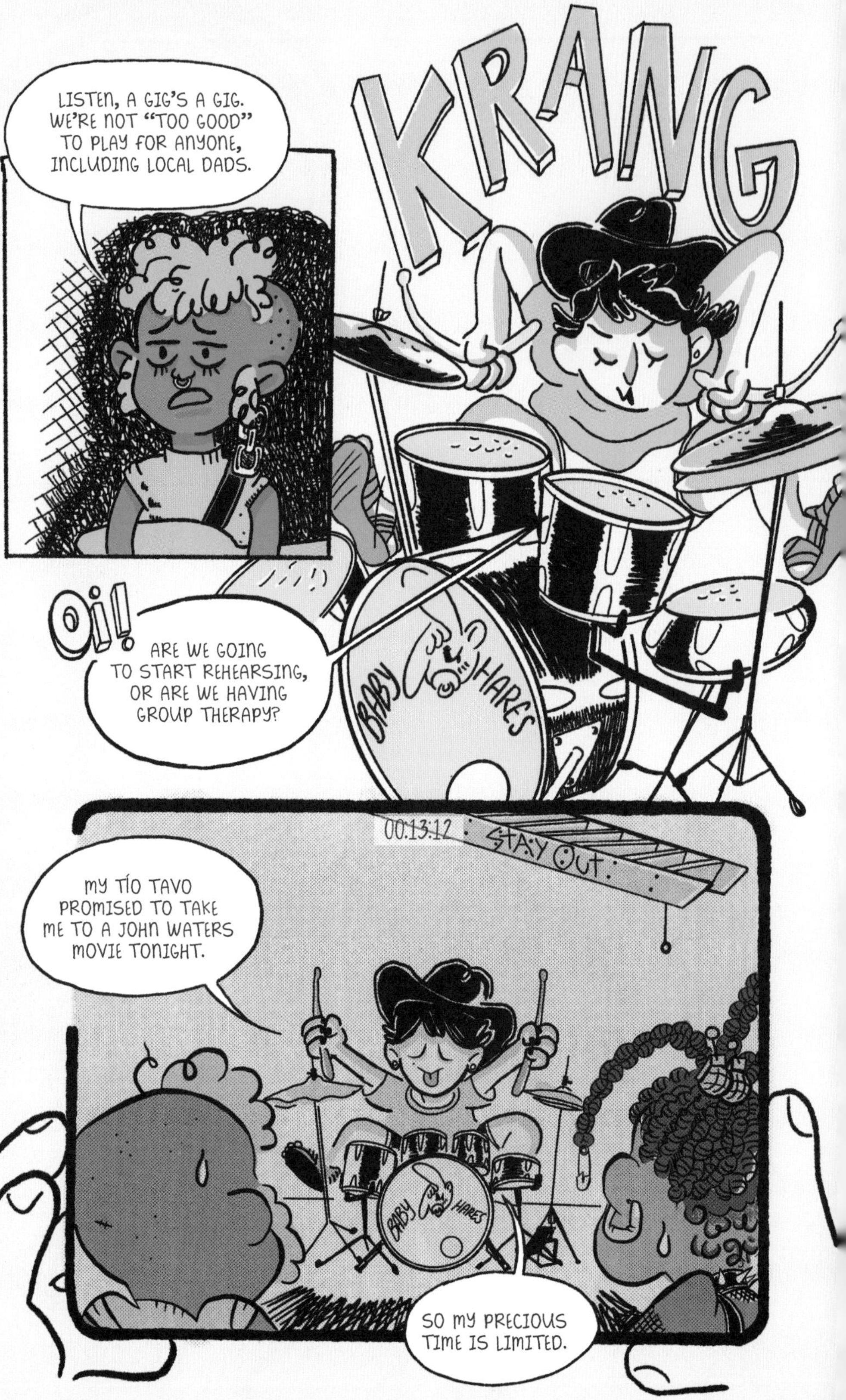
LISTEN, A GIG'S A GIG. WE'RE NOT "TOO GOOD" TO PLAY FOR ANYONE, INCLUDING LOCAL DADS.
KRANG
OI!
ARE WE GOING TO START REHEARSING, OR ARE WE HAVING GROUP THERAPY?
BABY HARES
00:13:12
STAY OUT
MY TÍO TAVO PROMISED TO TAKE ME TO A JOHN WATERS MOVIE TONIGHT.
BABY HARES
SO MY PRECIOUS TIME IS LIMITED.

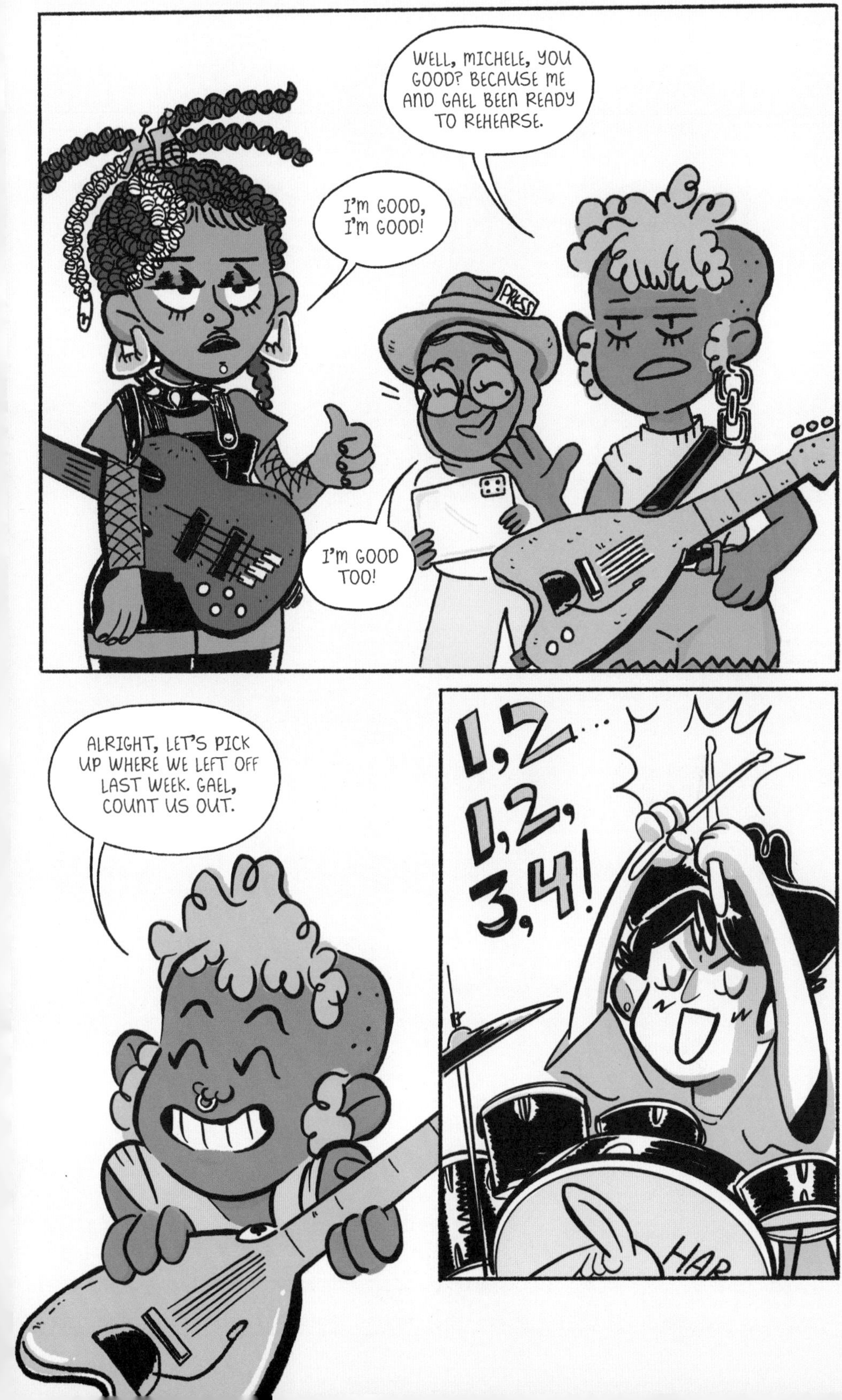
WELL, MICHELE, YOU GOOD? BECAUSE ME AND GAEL BEEN READY TO REHEARSE.
I'M GOOD, I'M GOOD!
I'M GOOD TOO!
ALRIGHT, LET'S PICK UP WHERE WE LEFT OFF LAST WEEK. GAEL, COUNT US OUT.
1,2... 1,2, 3,4!

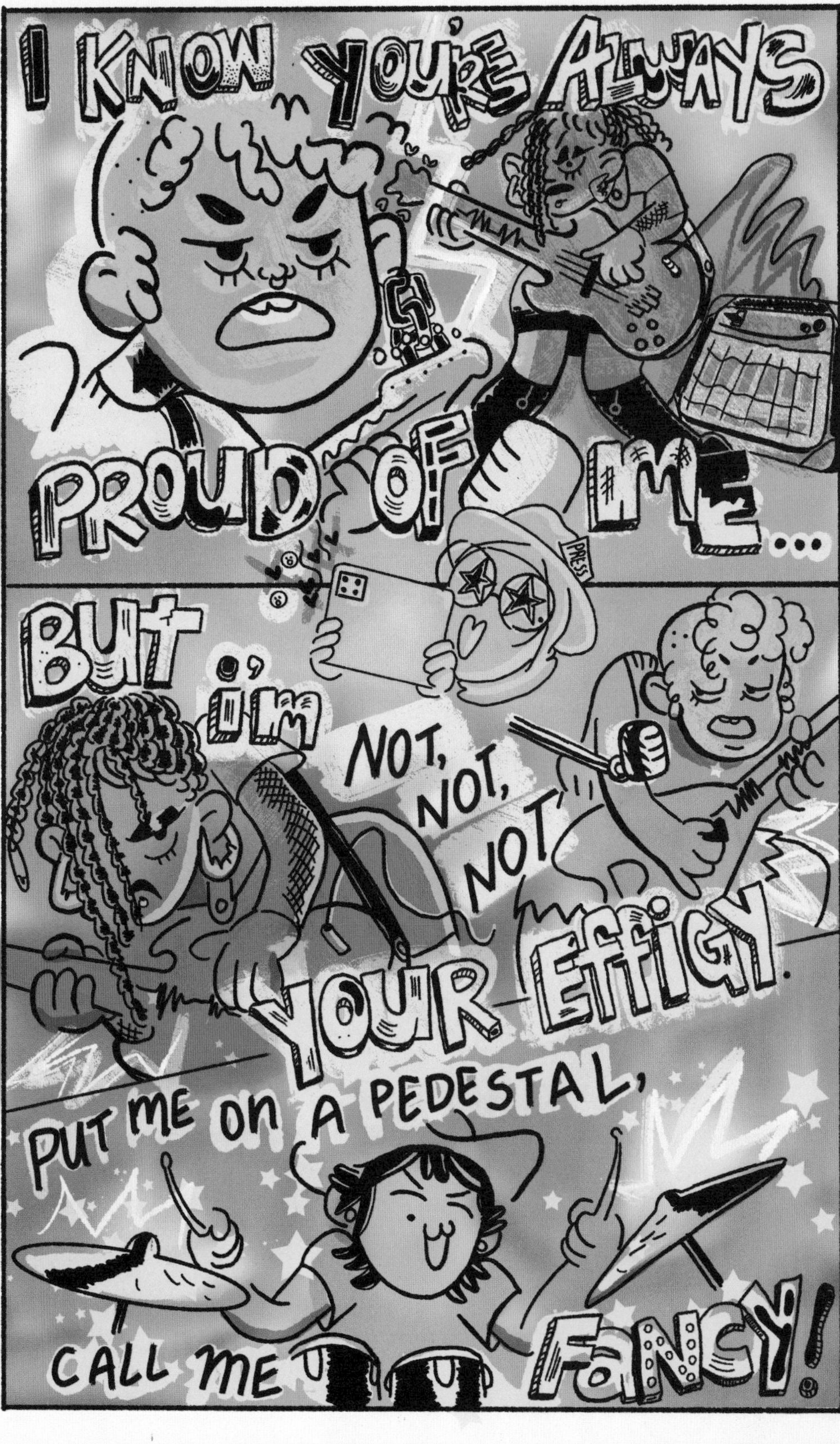
I KNOW YOU'RE ALWAYS
PROUD OF ME...
PRESS
BUT I'M
NOT, NOT, NOT
YOUR EFFIGY.
PUT ME ON A PEDESTAL,
CALL ME FANCY!

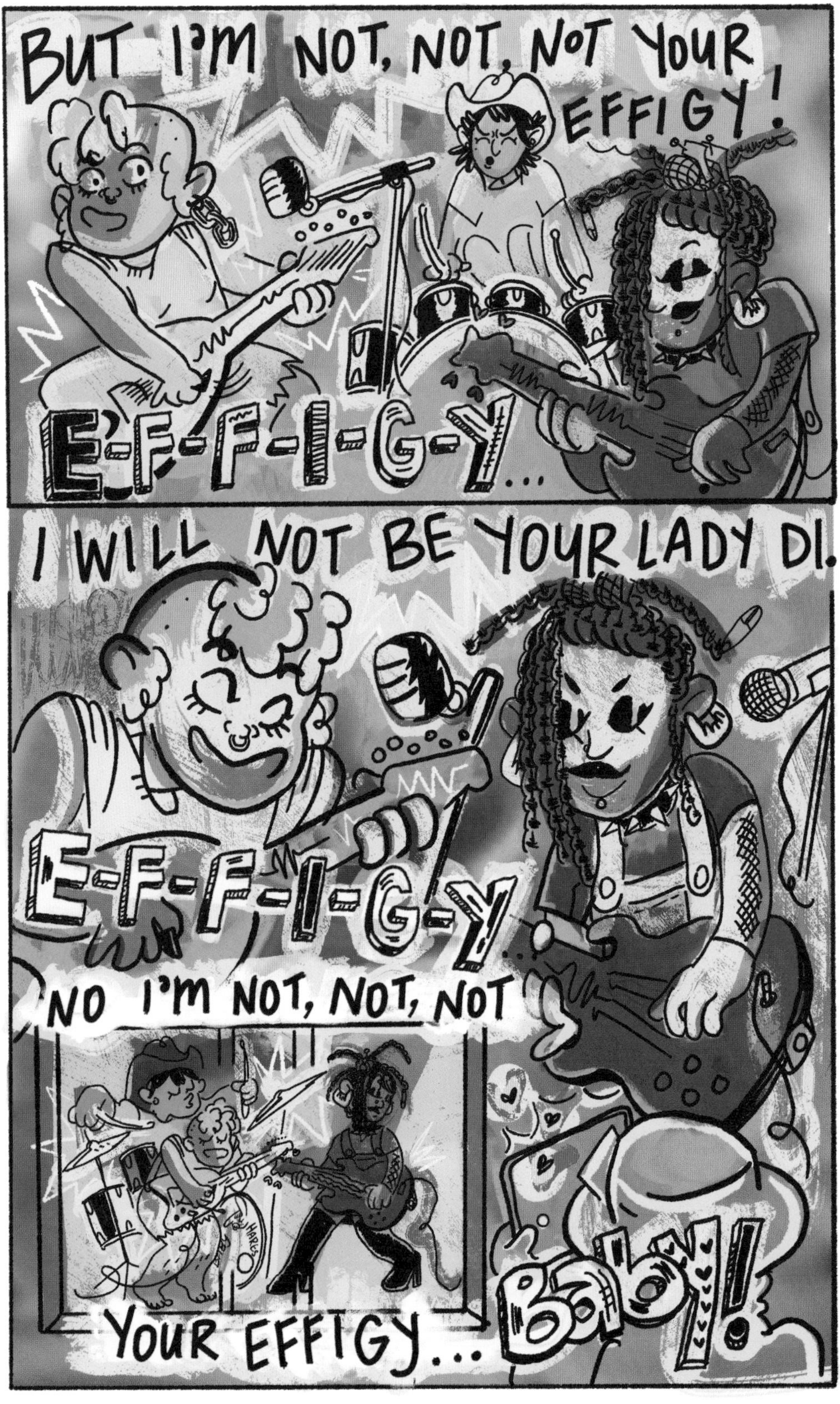
BUT I'M NOT, NOT, NOT YOUR EFFIGY!
E-F-F-I-G-Y...
I WILL NOT BE YOUR LADY DI.
E-F-F-I-G-Y...
NO I'M NOT, NOT, NOT
YOUR EFFIGY... BABY!

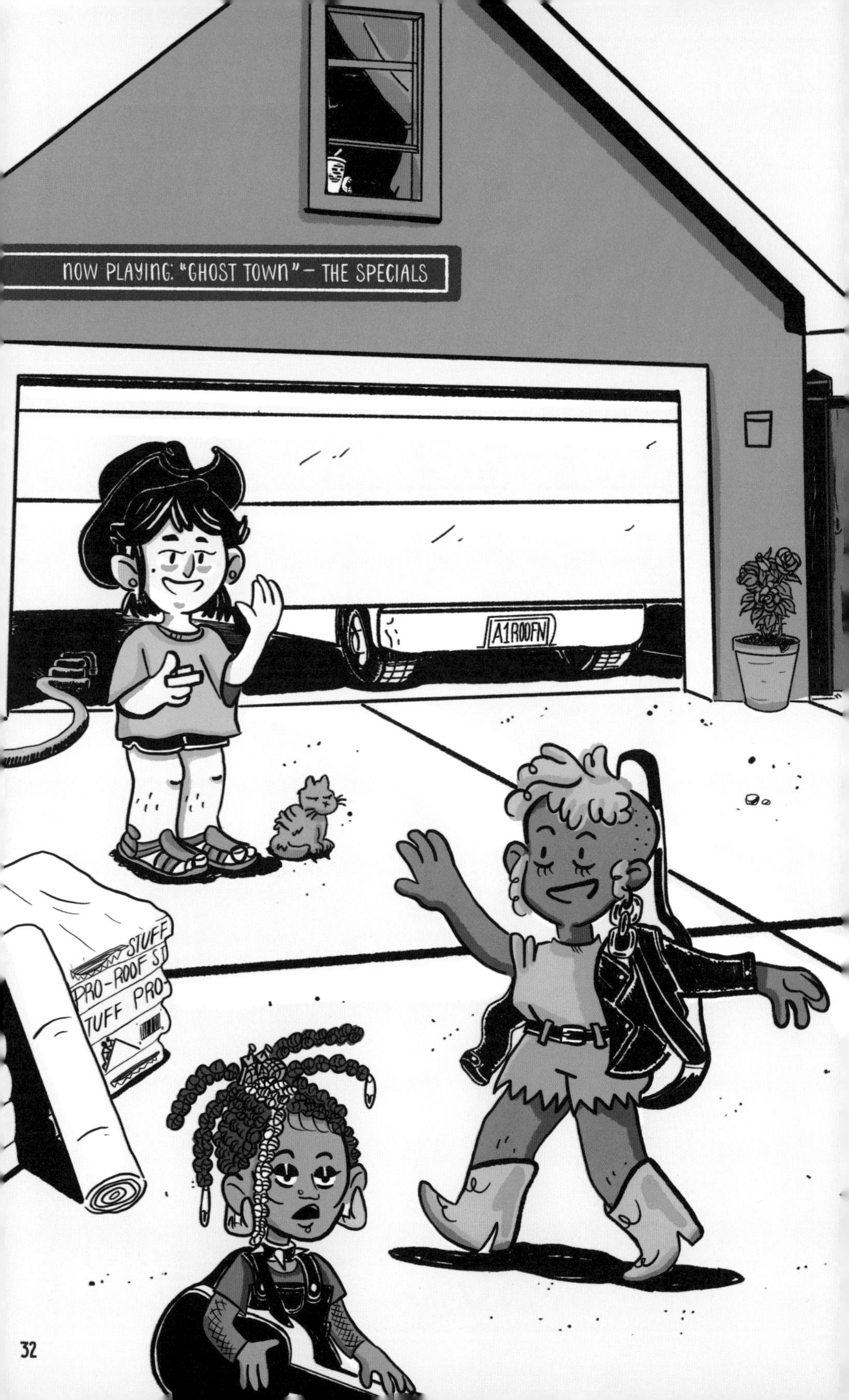
NOW PLAYING: "GHOST TOWN" – THE SPECIALS
A1ROOFN
STUFF
PRO-ROOF ST
TUFF PRO-

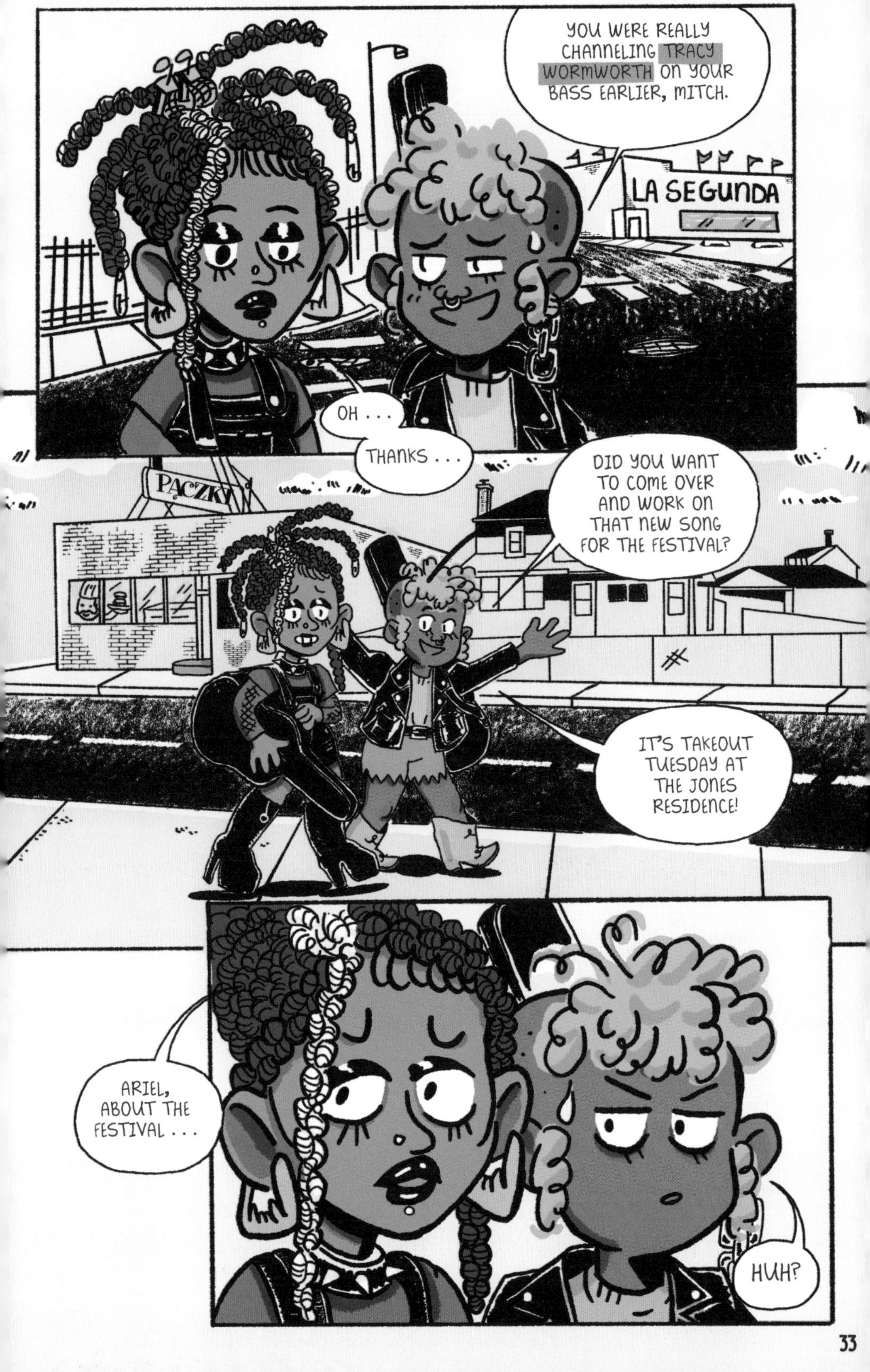
YOU WERE REALLY CHANNELING TRACY WORMWORTH ON YOUR BASS EARLIER, MITCH.
LA SEGUNDA
OH . . .
THANKS . . .
PĄCZKI
DID YOU WANT TO COME OVER AND WORK ON THAT NEW SONG FOR THE FESTIVAL?
IT'S TAKEOUT TUESDAY AT THE JONES RESIDENCE!
ARIEL, ABOUT THE FESTIVAL . . .
HUH?

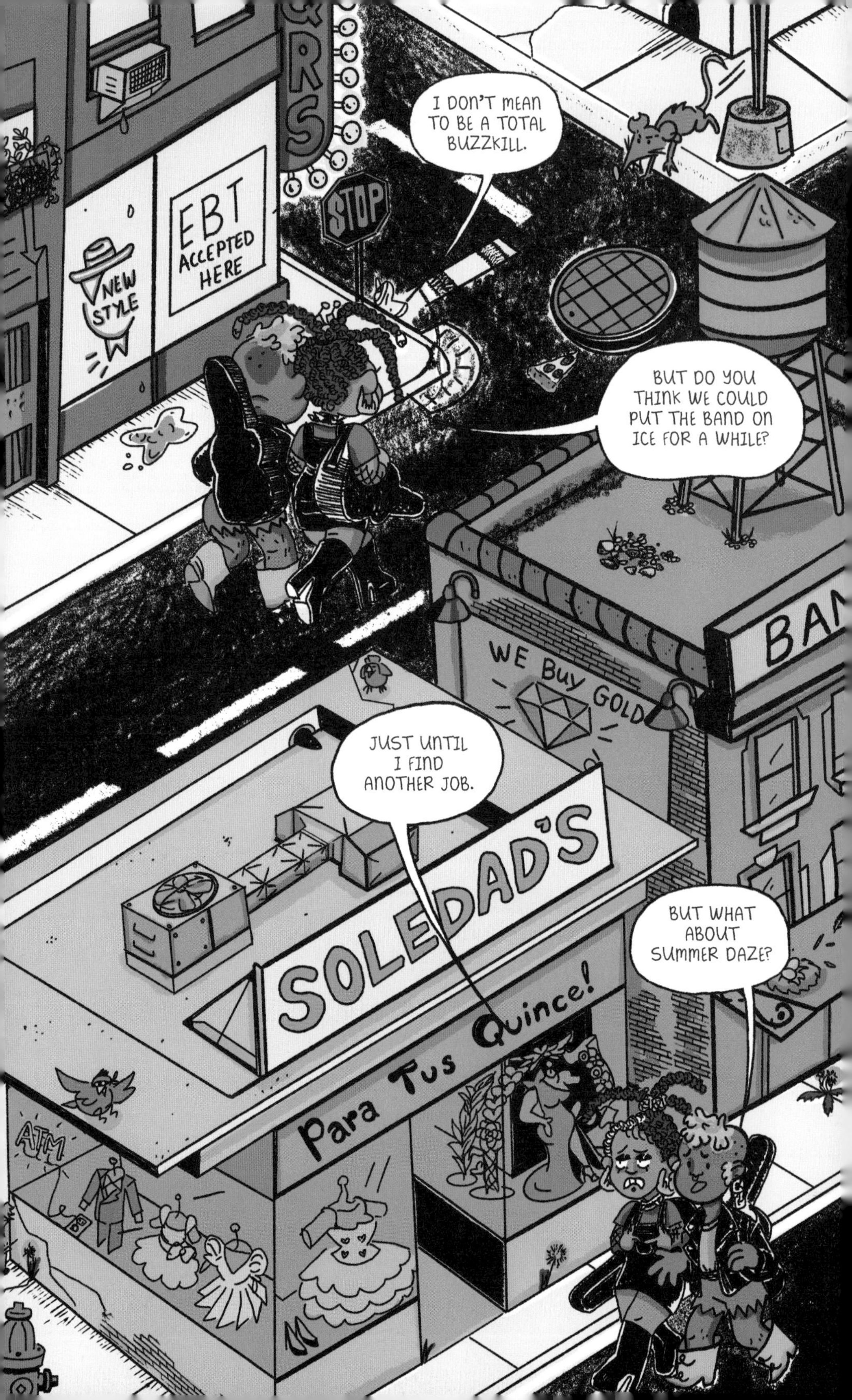

I DON'T MEAN TO BE A TOTAL BUZZKILL.
BUT DO YOU THINK WE COULD PUT THE BAND ON ICE FOR A WHILE?
JUST UNTIL I FIND ANOTHER JOB.
BUT WHAT ABOUT SUMMER DAZE?
STOP
EBT ACCEPTED HERE
NEW STYLE
WE BUY GOLD
SOLEDAD'S
Para Tus Quince!
ATM

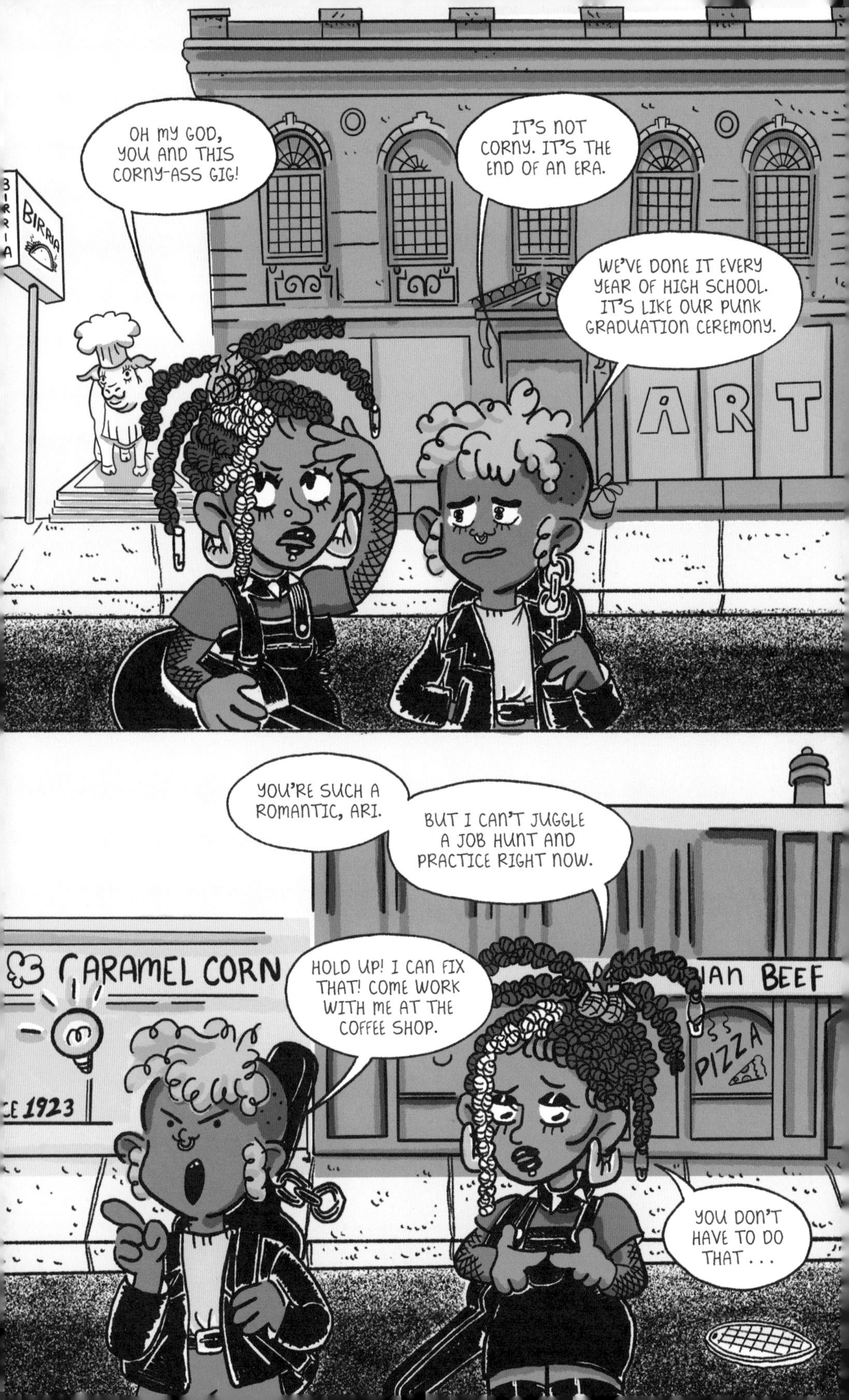
BIRRIA
BIRRIA
OH MY GOD, YOU AND THIS CORNY-ASS GIG!
IT'S NOT CORNY. IT'S THE END OF AN ERA.
WE'VE DONE IT EVERY YEAR OF HIGH SCHOOL. IT'S LIKE OUR PUNK GRADUATION CEREMONY.
ART
YOU'RE SUCH A ROMANTIC, ARI.
BUT I CAN'T JUGGLE A JOB HUNT AND PRACTICE RIGHT NOW.
CARAMEL CORN
CE 1923
HOLD UP! I CAN FIX THAT! COME WORK WITH ME AT THE COFFEE SHOP.
IAN BEEF
PIZZA
YOU DON'T HAVE TO DO THAT . . .

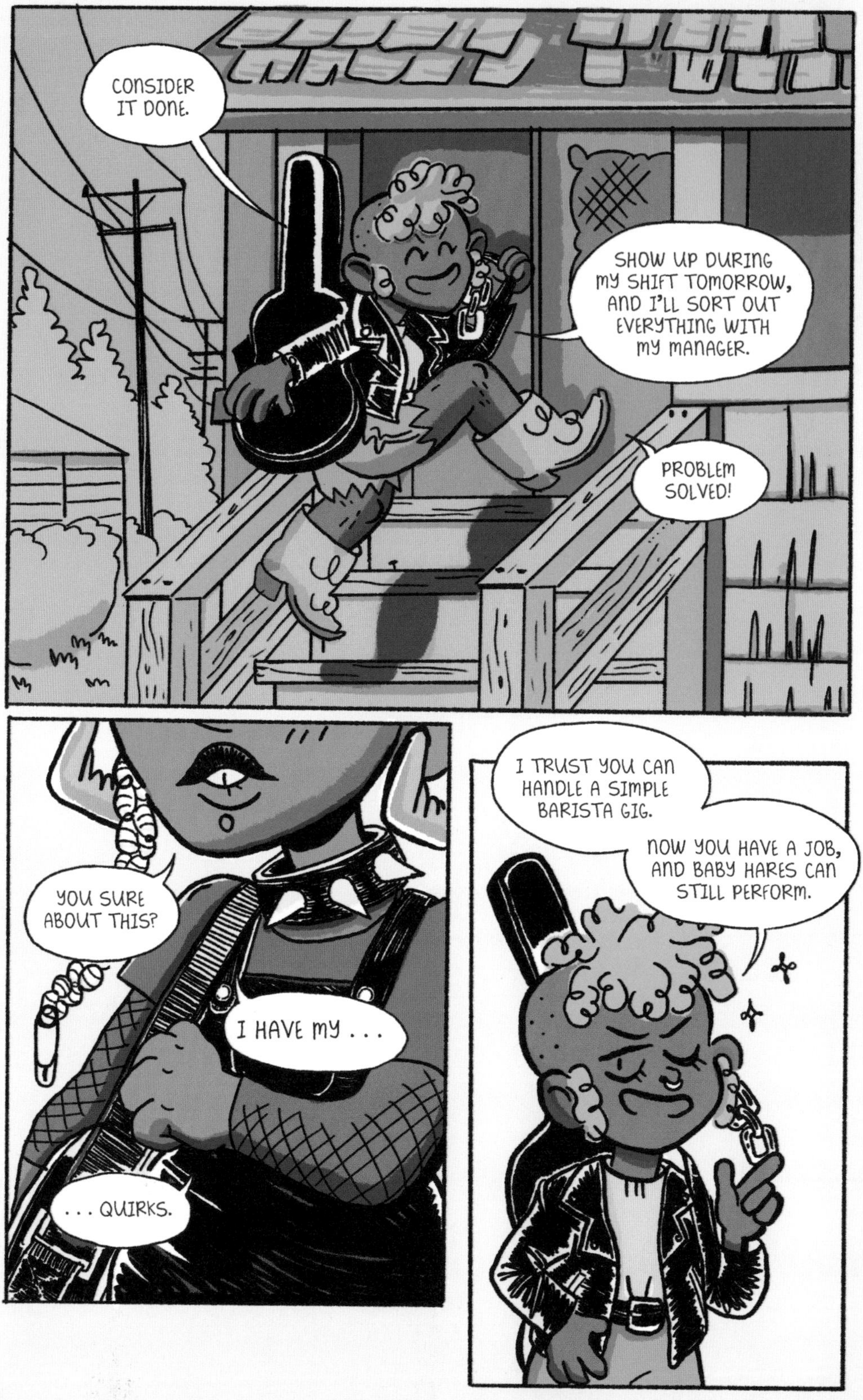
CONSIDER IT DONE.
SHOW UP DURING MY SHIFT TOMORROW, AND I'LL SORT OUT EVERYTHING WITH MY MANAGER.
PROBLEM SOLVED!
YOU SURE ABOUT THIS?
I HAVE MY . . .
. . . QUIRKS.
I TRUST YOU CAN HANDLE A SIMPLE BARISTA GIG.
NOW YOU HAVE A JOB, AND BABY HARES CAN STILL PERFORM.

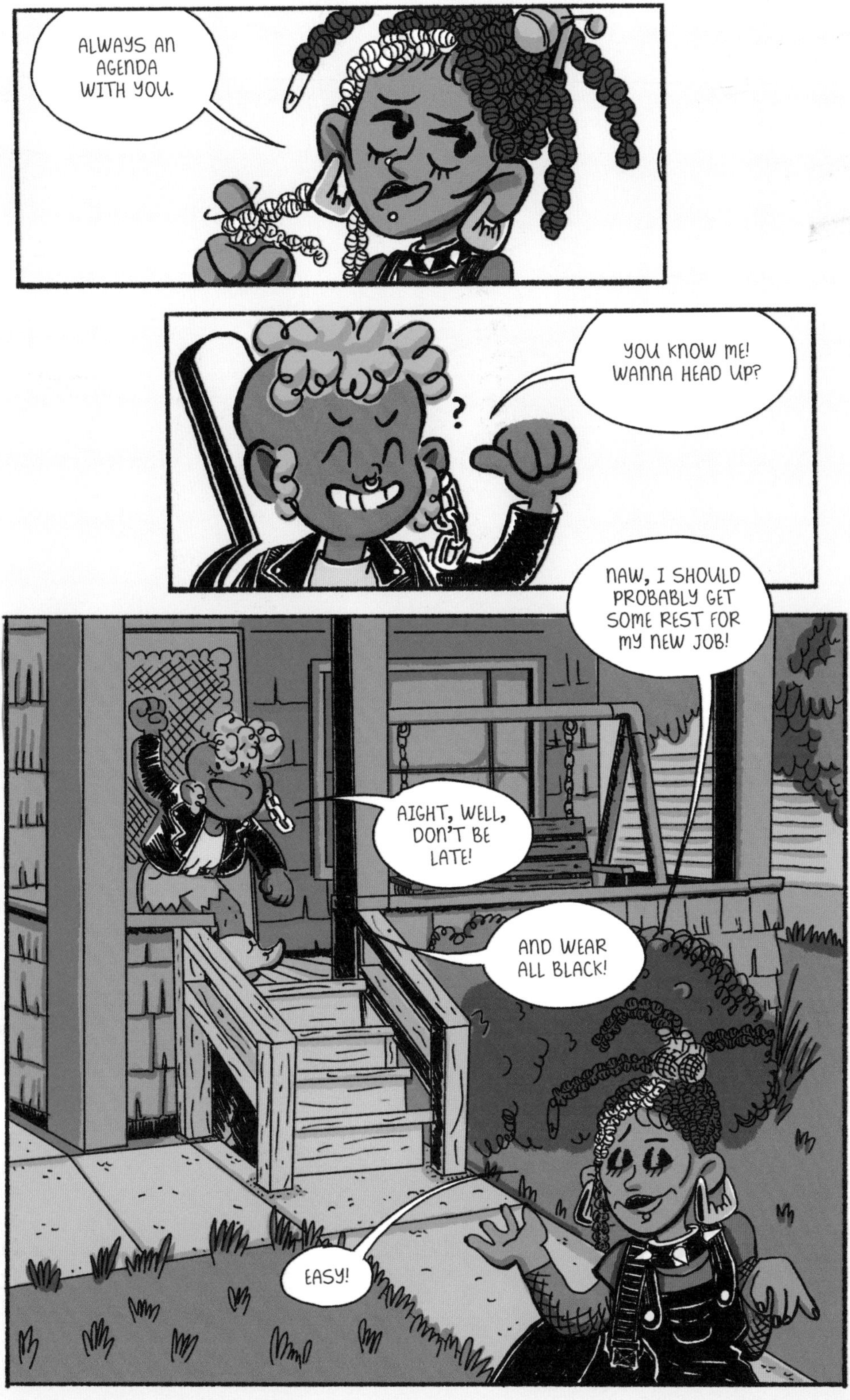
ALWAYS AN AGENDA WITH YOU.
YOU KNOW ME! WANNA HEAD UP?
NAW, I SHOULD PROBABLY GET SOME REST FOR MY NEW JOB!
AIGHT, WELL, DON'T BE LATE!
AND WEAR ALL BLACK!
EASY!

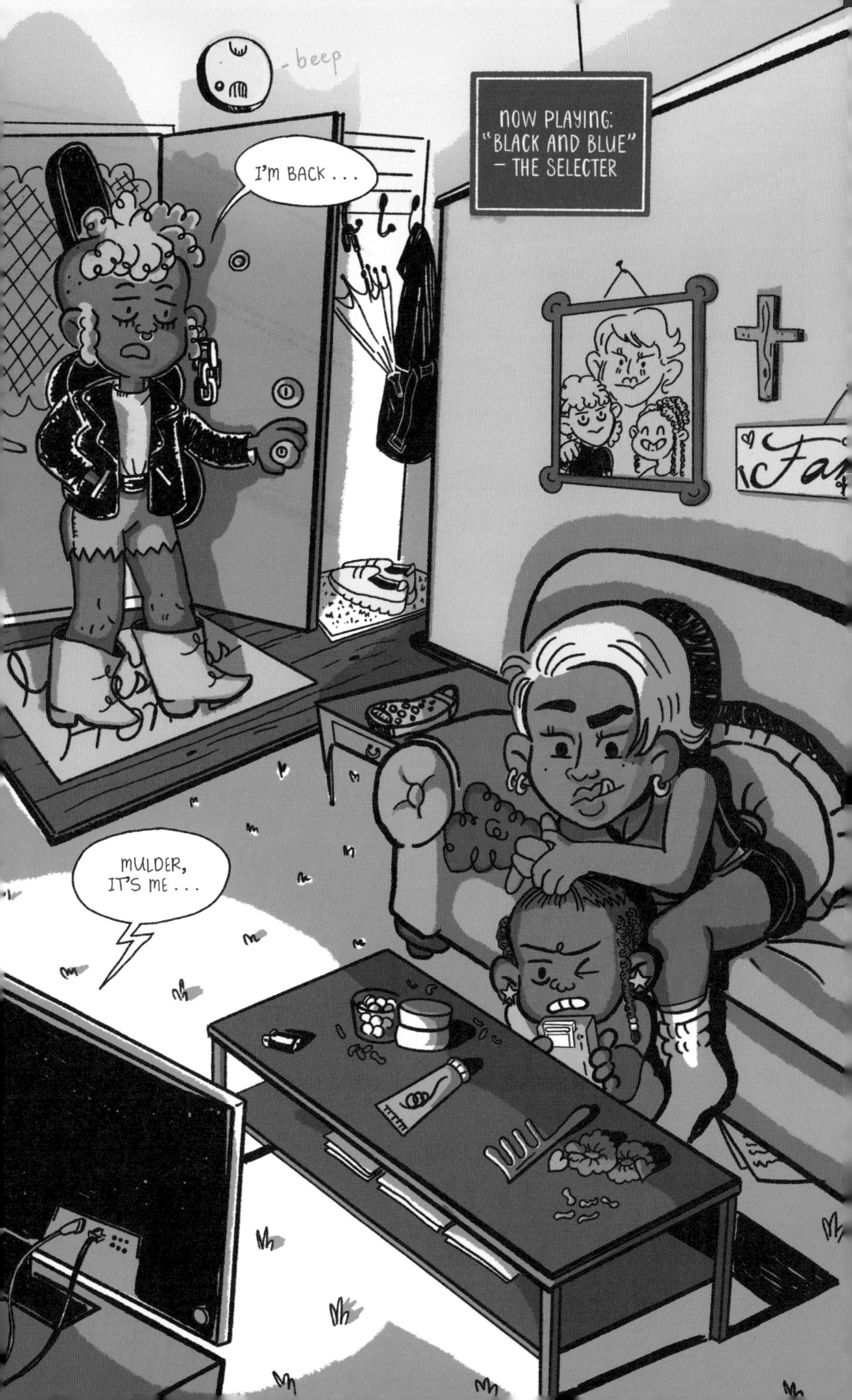
-beep
NOW PLAYING:
"BLACK AND BLUE"
– THE SELECTER
I'M BACK . . .
MULDER,
IT'S ME . . .

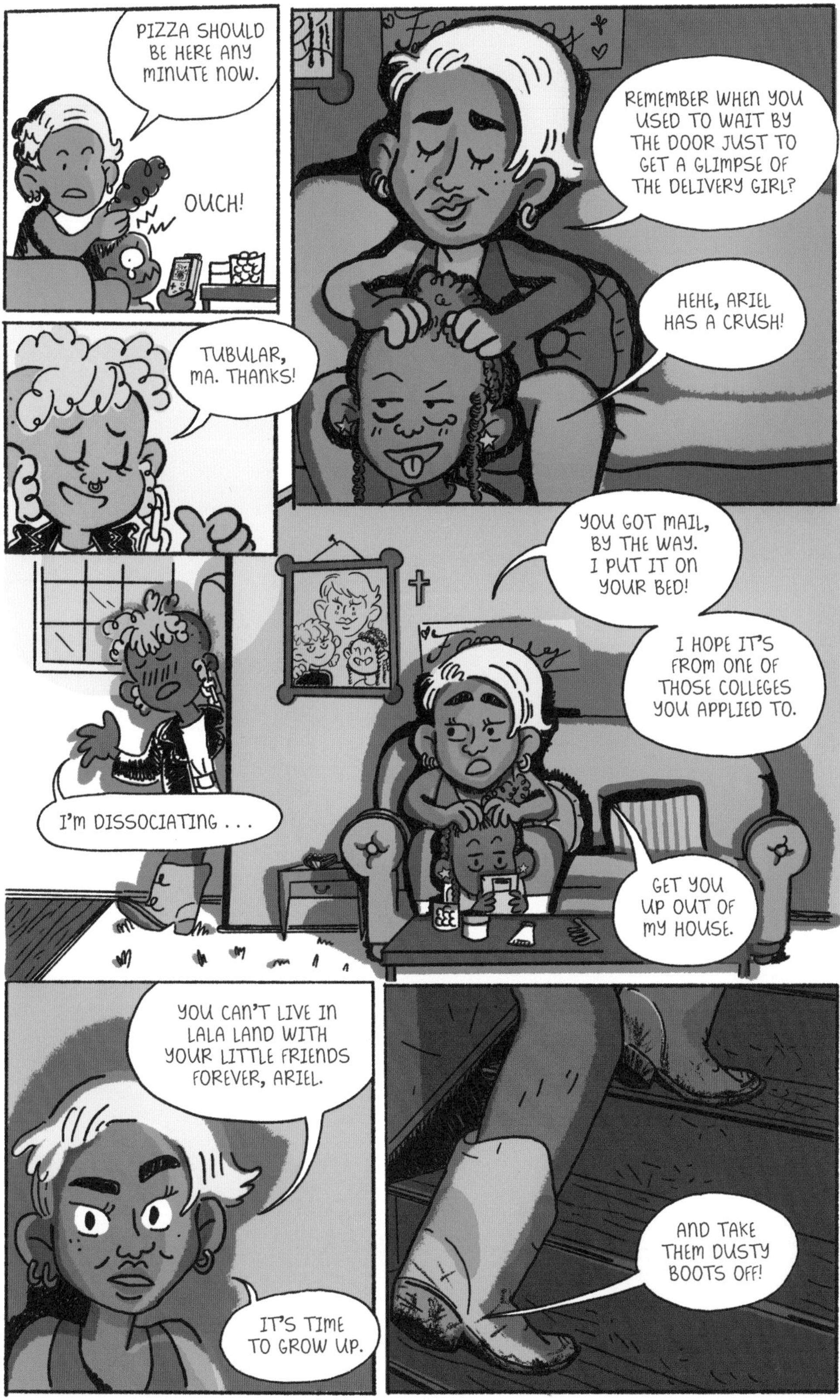
PIZZA SHOULD BE HERE ANY MINUTE NOW.
OUCH!
REMEMBER WHEN YOU USED TO WAIT BY THE DOOR JUST TO GET A GLIMPSE OF THE DELIVERY GIRL?
HEHE, ARIEL HAS A CRUSH!
TUBULAR, MA. THANKS!
YOU GOT MAIL, BY THE WAY. I PUT IT ON YOUR BED!
I HOPE IT'S FROM ONE OF THOSE COLLEGES YOU APPLIED TO.
I'M DISSOCIATING . . .
GET YOU UP OUT OF MY HOUSE.
YOU CAN'T LIVE IN LALA LAND WITH YOUR LITTLE FRIENDS FOREVER, ARIEL.
IT'S TIME TO GROW UP.
AND TAKE THEM DUSTY BOOTS OFF!

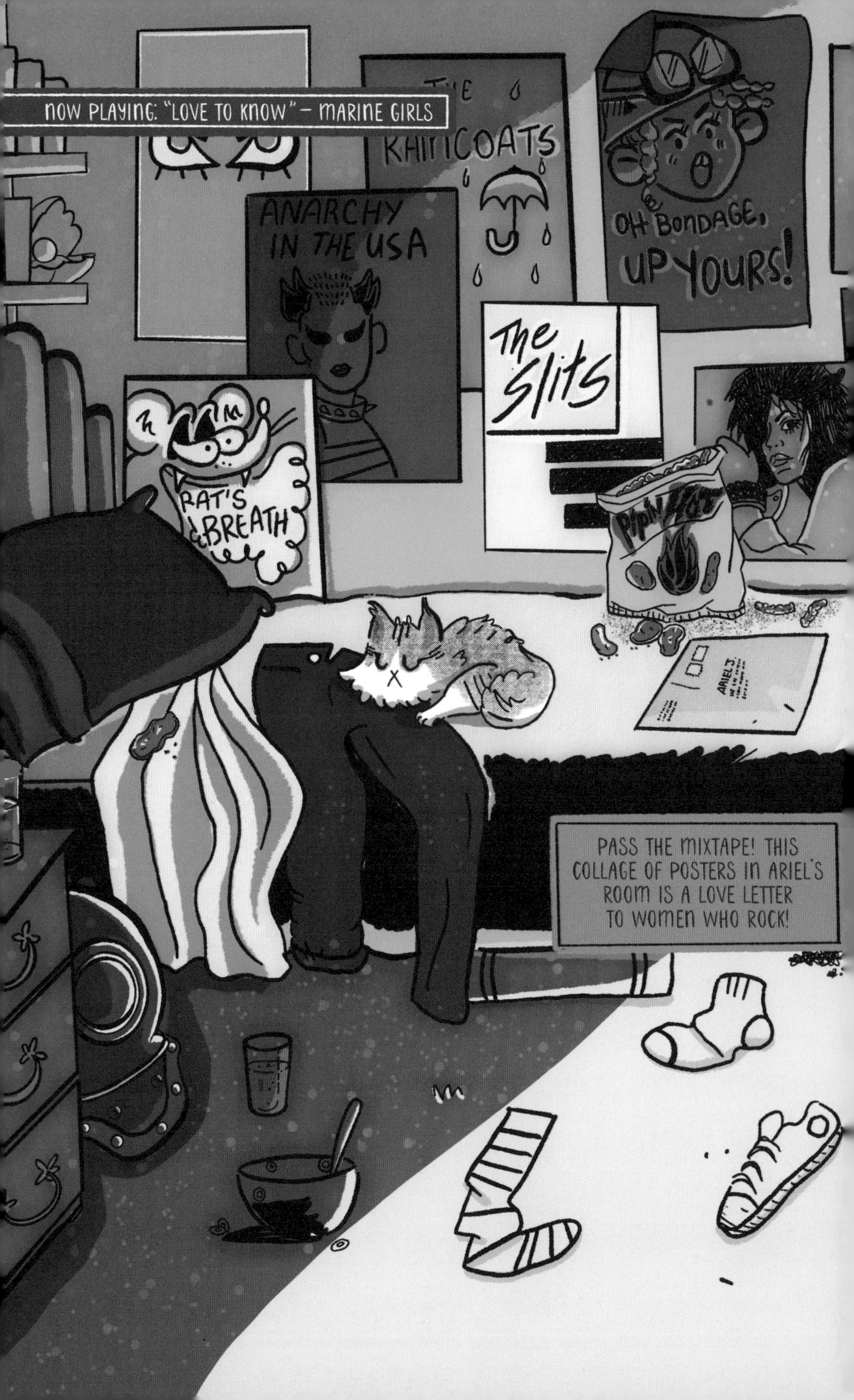
NOW PLAYING: "LOVE TO KNOW" – MARINE GIRLS
ANARCHY IN THE USA
OH BONDAGE, UP YOURS!
The Slits
RAT'S BREATH
ARIEL J.
PASS THE MIXTAPE! THIS COLLAGE OF POSTERS IN ARIEL'S ROOM IS A LOVE LETTER TO WOMEN WHO ROCK!

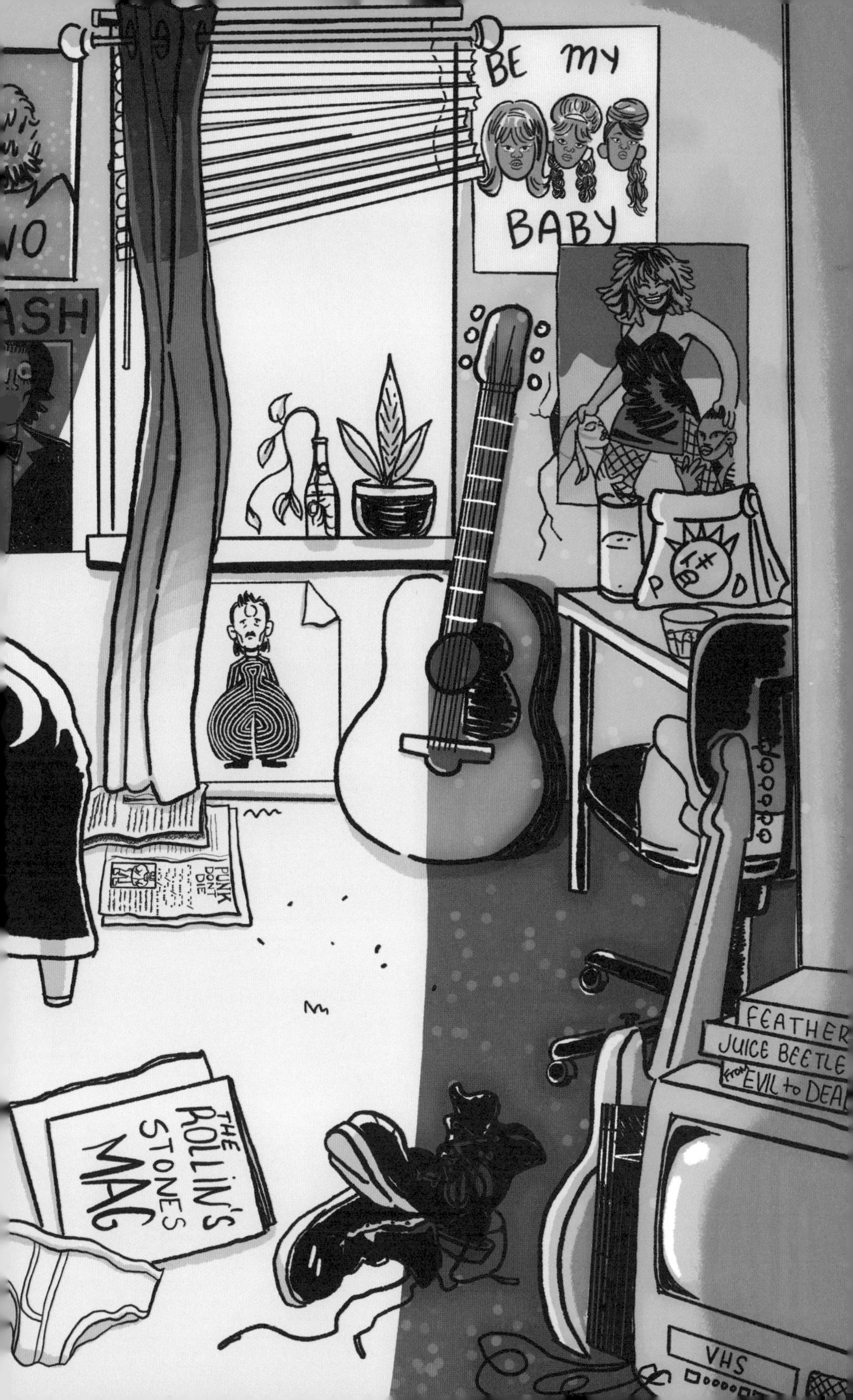
BE MY BABY
PUNK DON'T DIE
THE ROLLIN'S STONES MAG
FEATHER
JUICE BEETLE
FROM EVIL to DEA
VHS

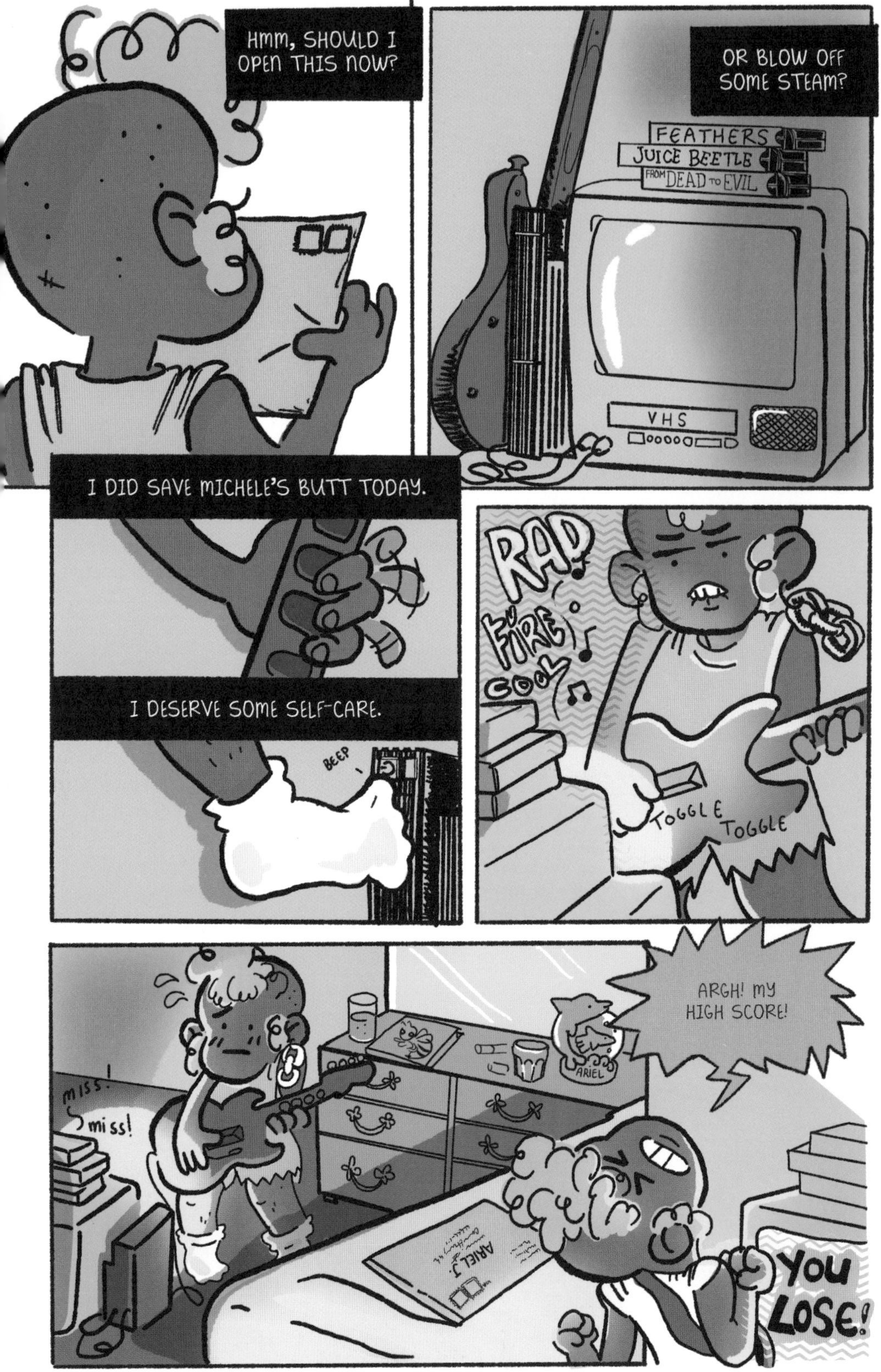

HMM, SHOULD I OPEN THIS NOW?
OR BLOW OFF SOME STEAM?
FEATHERS
JUICE BEETLE
FROM DEAD TO EVIL
VHS
I DID SAVE MICHELE'S BUTT TODAY.
I DESERVE SOME SELF-CARE.
BEEP
RAD
FIRE
COOL
TOGGLE TOGGLE
miss!
miss!
ARIEL
ARGH! MY HIGH SCORE!
YOU LOSE!

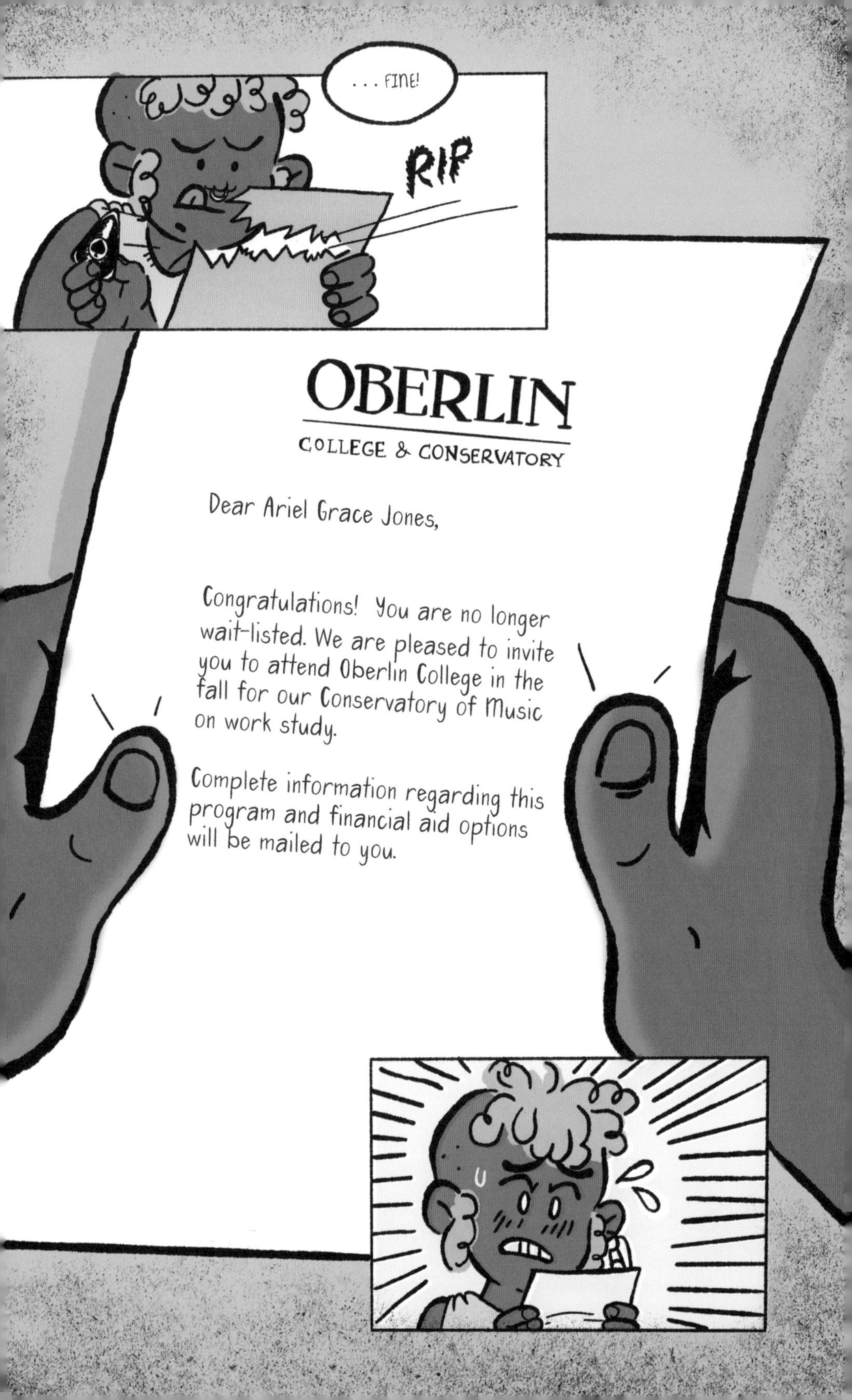
. . . FINE!
RIP
OBERLIN
COLLEGE & CONSERVATORY
Dear Ariel Grace Jones,
Congratulations! You are no longer wait-listed. We are pleased to invite you to attend Oberlin College in the fall for our Conservatory of Music on work study.
Complete information regarding this program and financial aid options will be mailed to you.

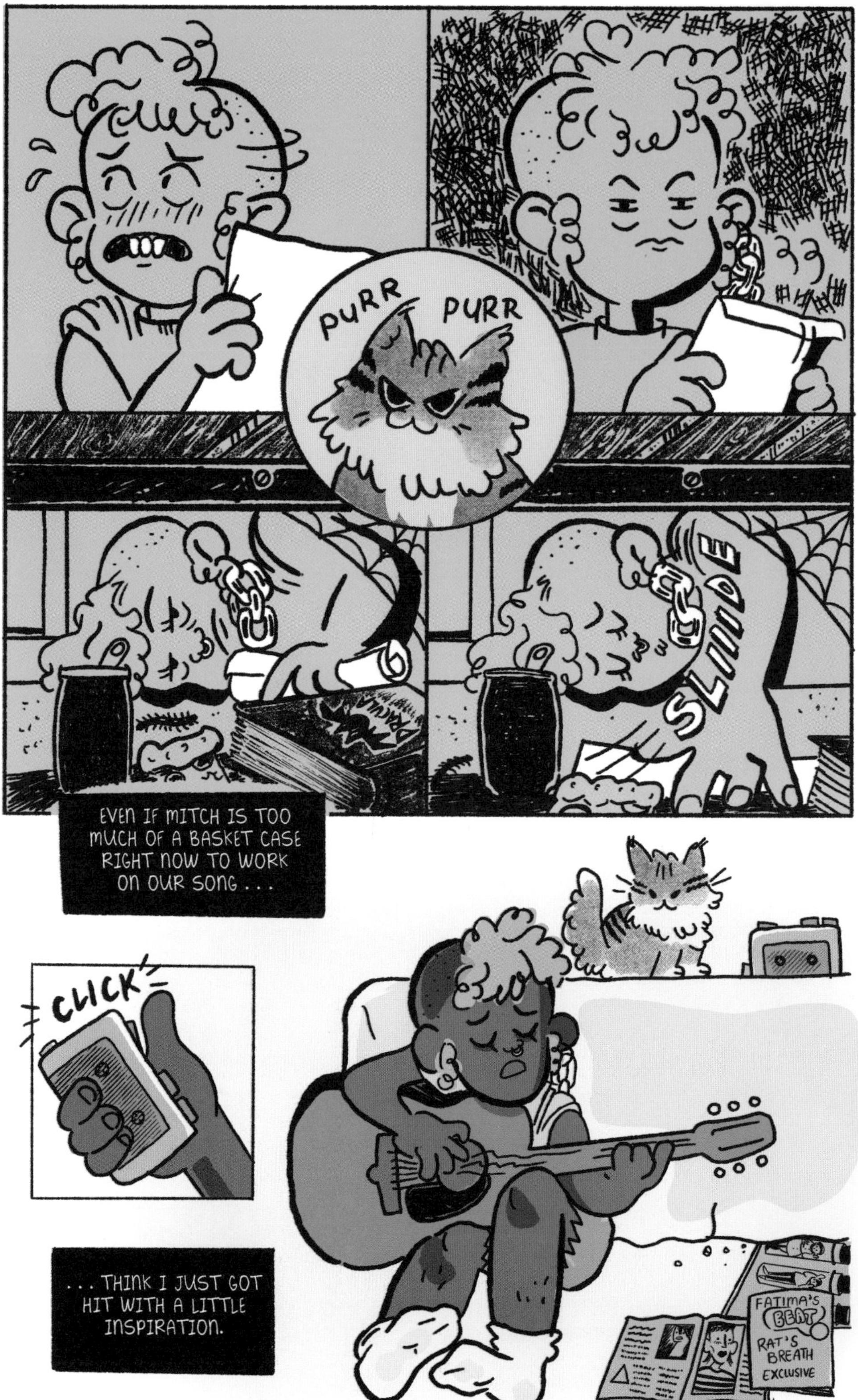
PURR PURR
SLIIIDE
EVEN IF MITCH IS TOO MUCH OF A BASKET CASE RIGHT NOW TO WORK ON OUR SONG . . .
CLICK
. . . THINK I JUST GOT HIT WITH A LITTLE INSPIRATION.
FATIMA'S BEAT
RAT'S BREATH EXCLUSIVE

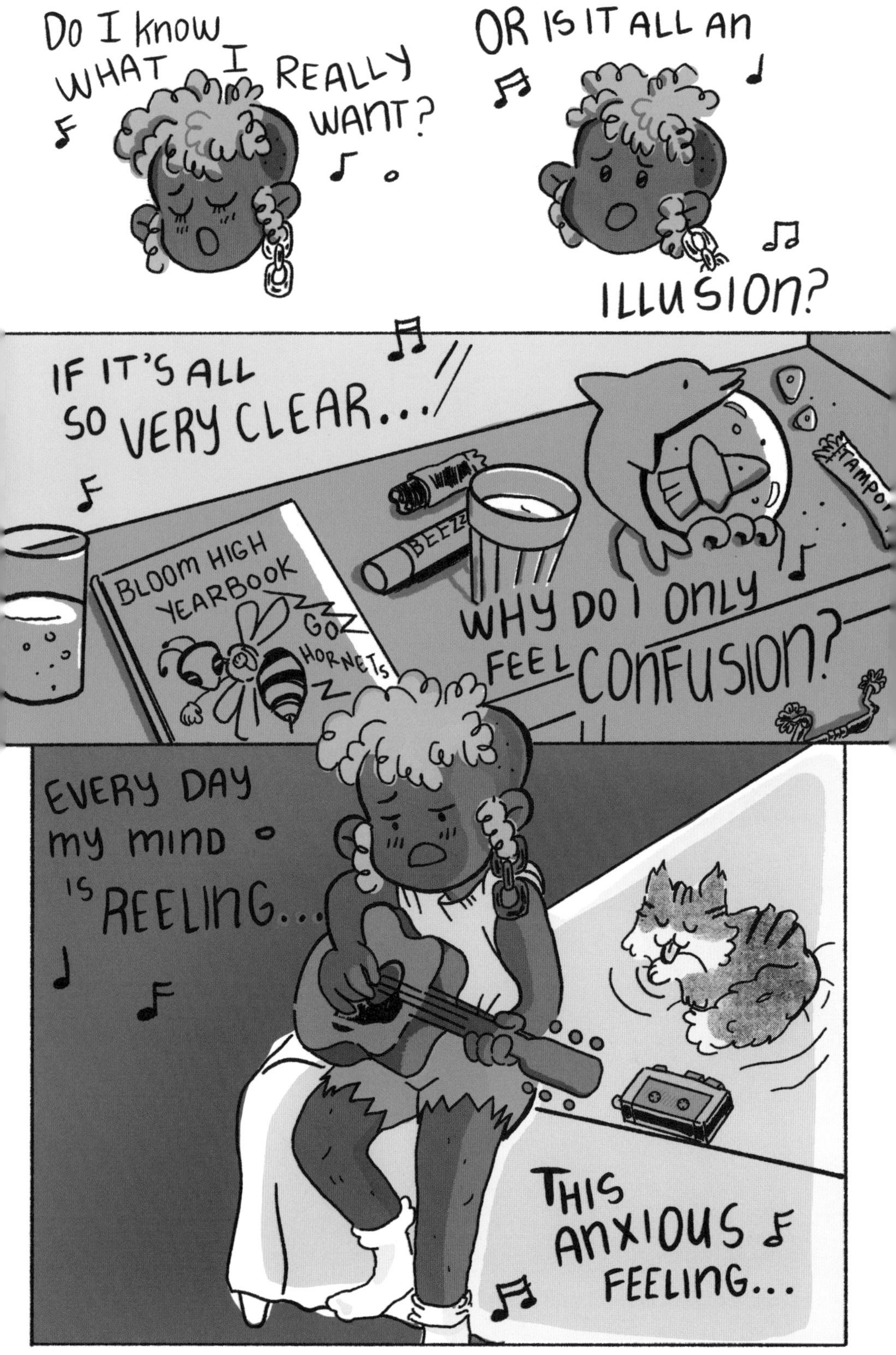
Do I know WHAT I REALLY WANT?
OR IS IT ALL AN ILLUSION?
IF IT'S ALL SO VERY CLEAR...
BLOOM HIGH YEARBOOK
GO HORNETS
BEEZ
WHY DO I ONLY FEEL CONFUSION?
EVERY DAY my mind is REELING...
THIS ANXIOUS FEELING...

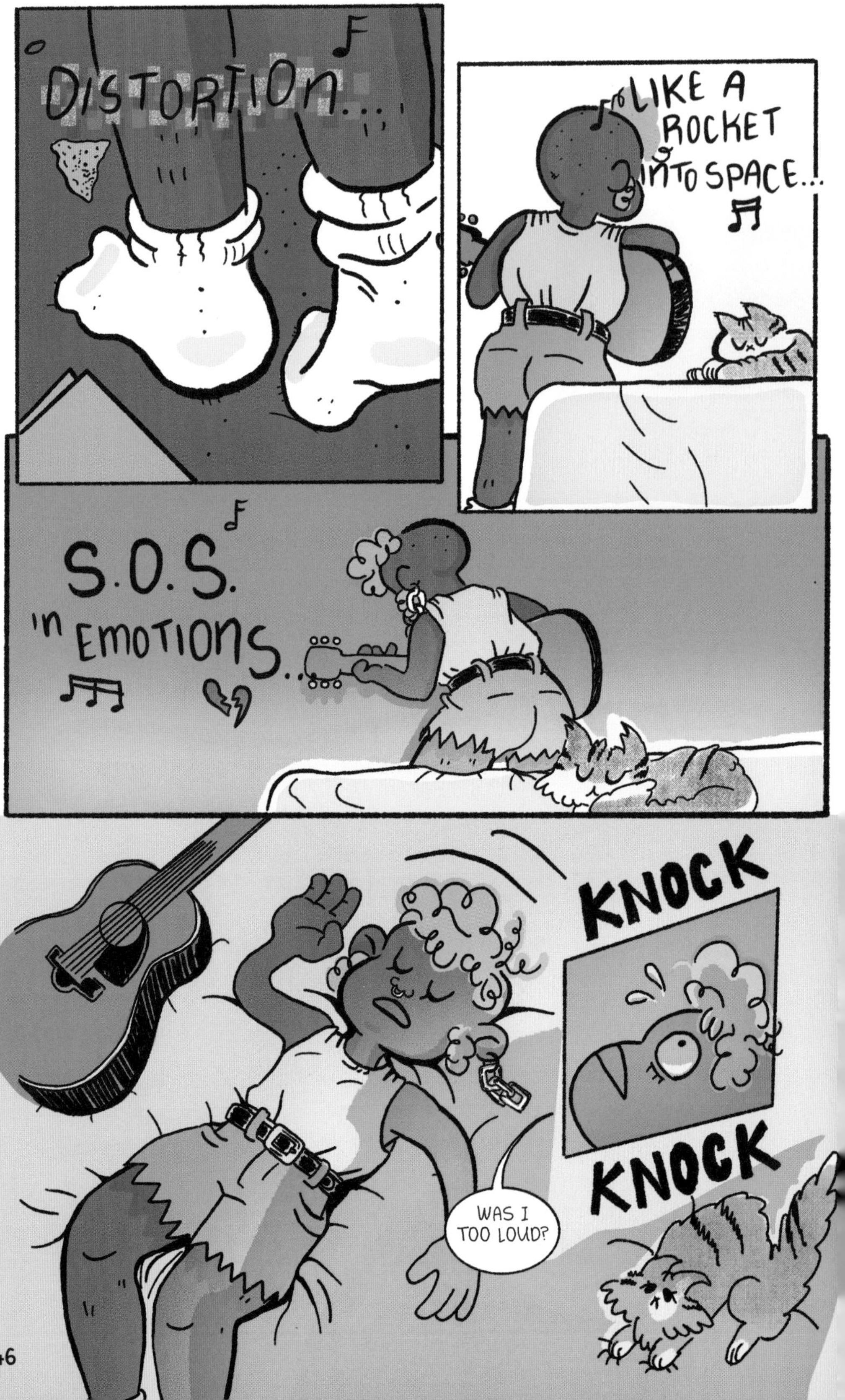

DISTORTION...
LIKE A ROCKET INTO SPACE...
S.O.S. 'n EMOTIONS...
KNOCK
KNOCK
WAS I TOO LOUD?

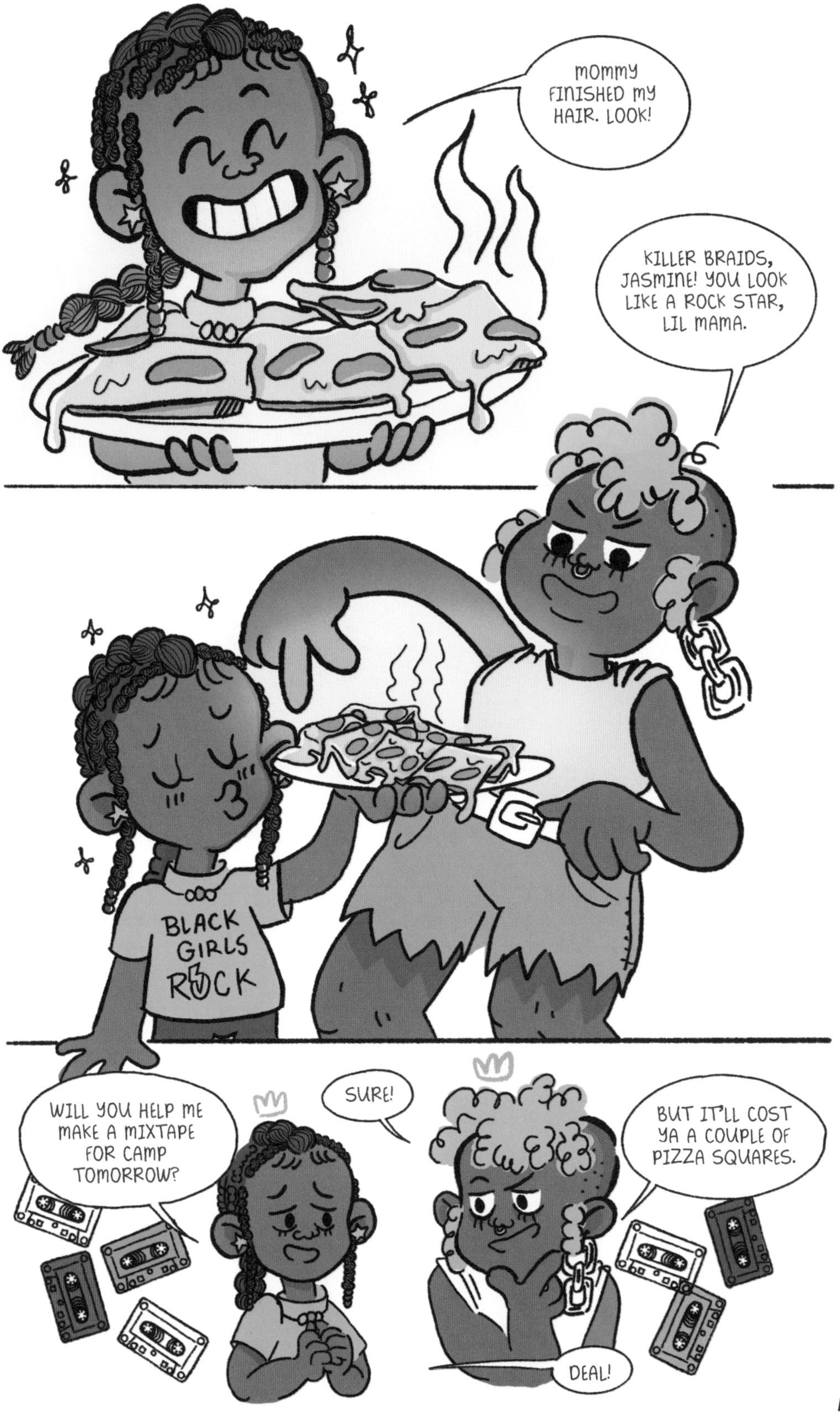

MOMMY FINISHED MY HAIR. LOOK!
KILLER BRAIDS, JASMINE! YOU LOOK LIKE A ROCK STAR, LIL MAMA.
BLACK GIRLS ROCK
WILL YOU HELP ME MAKE A MIXTAPE FOR CAMP TOMORROW?
SURE!
BUT IT'LL COST YA A COUPLE OF PIZZA SQUARES.
DEAL!

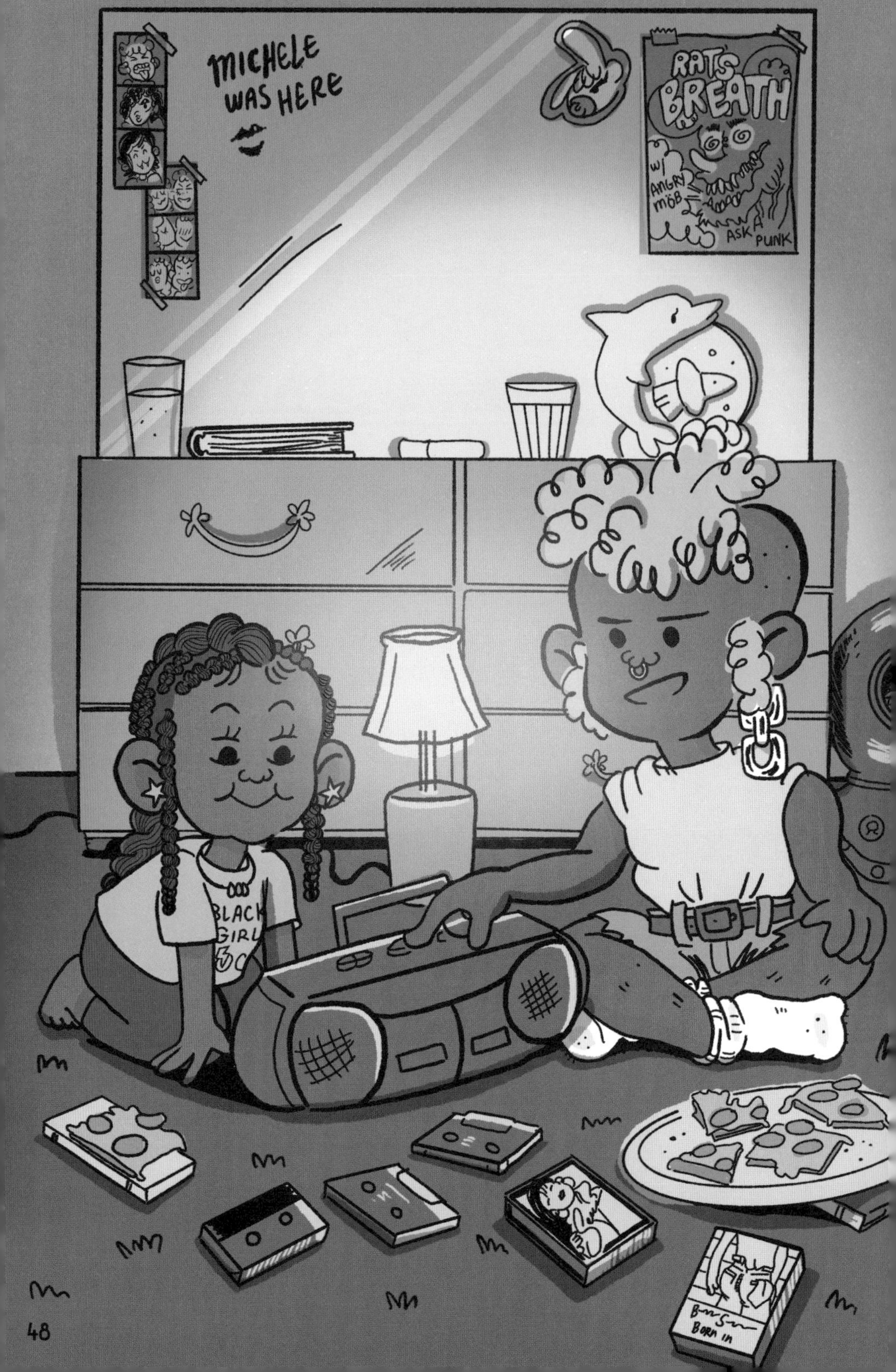
MICHELE
WAS HERE
RATS BREATH
W/ ANGRY MÖB
ASK A PUNK
BLACK GIRL

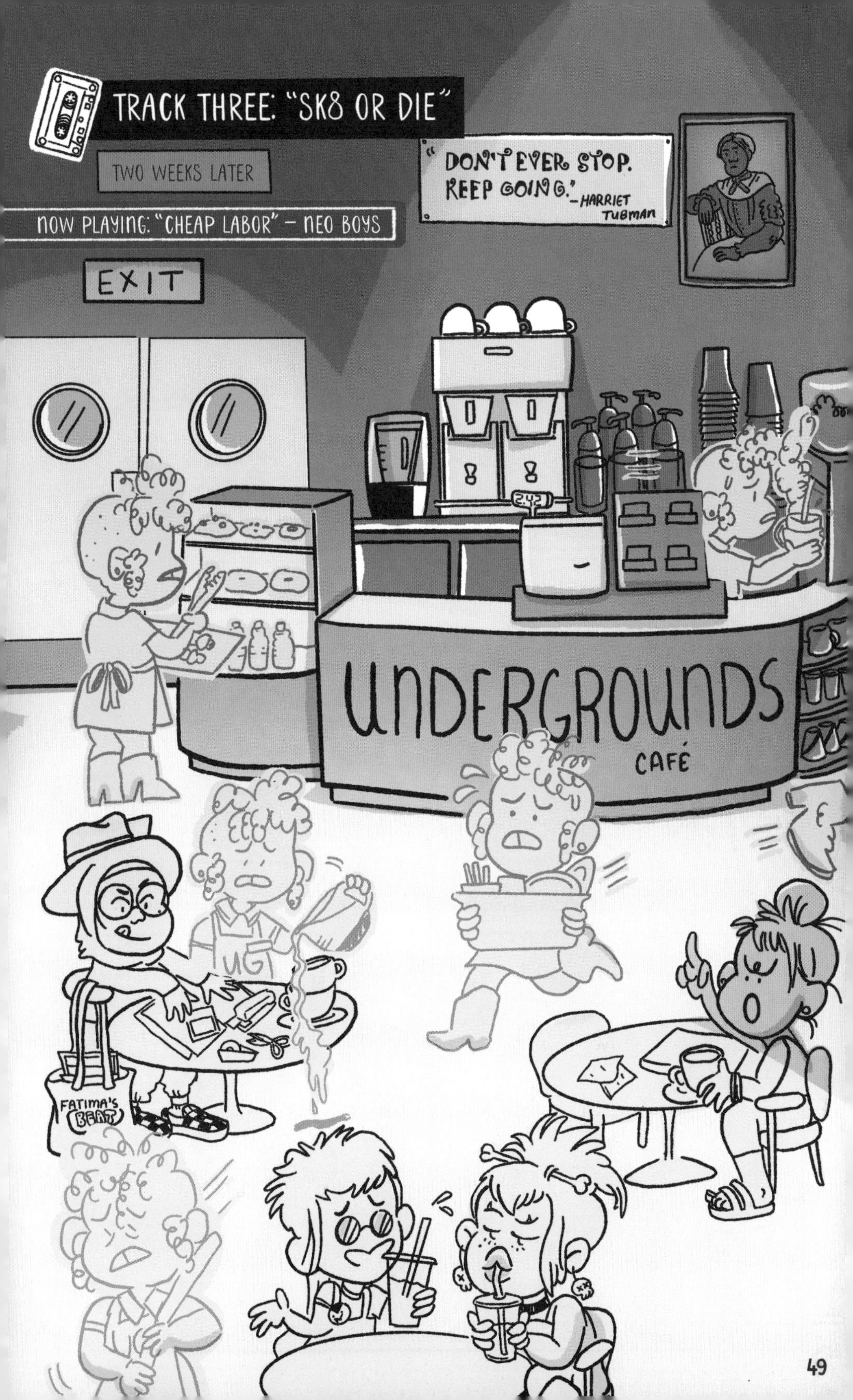
TRACK THREE: "SK8 OR DIE"
TWO WEEKS LATER
NOW PLAYING: "CHEAP LABOR" – NEO BOYS
EXIT
"DON'T EVER STOP. KEEP GOING." – HARRIET TUBMAN
UNDERGROUNDS
CAFÉ
UG
FATIMA'S BEAT

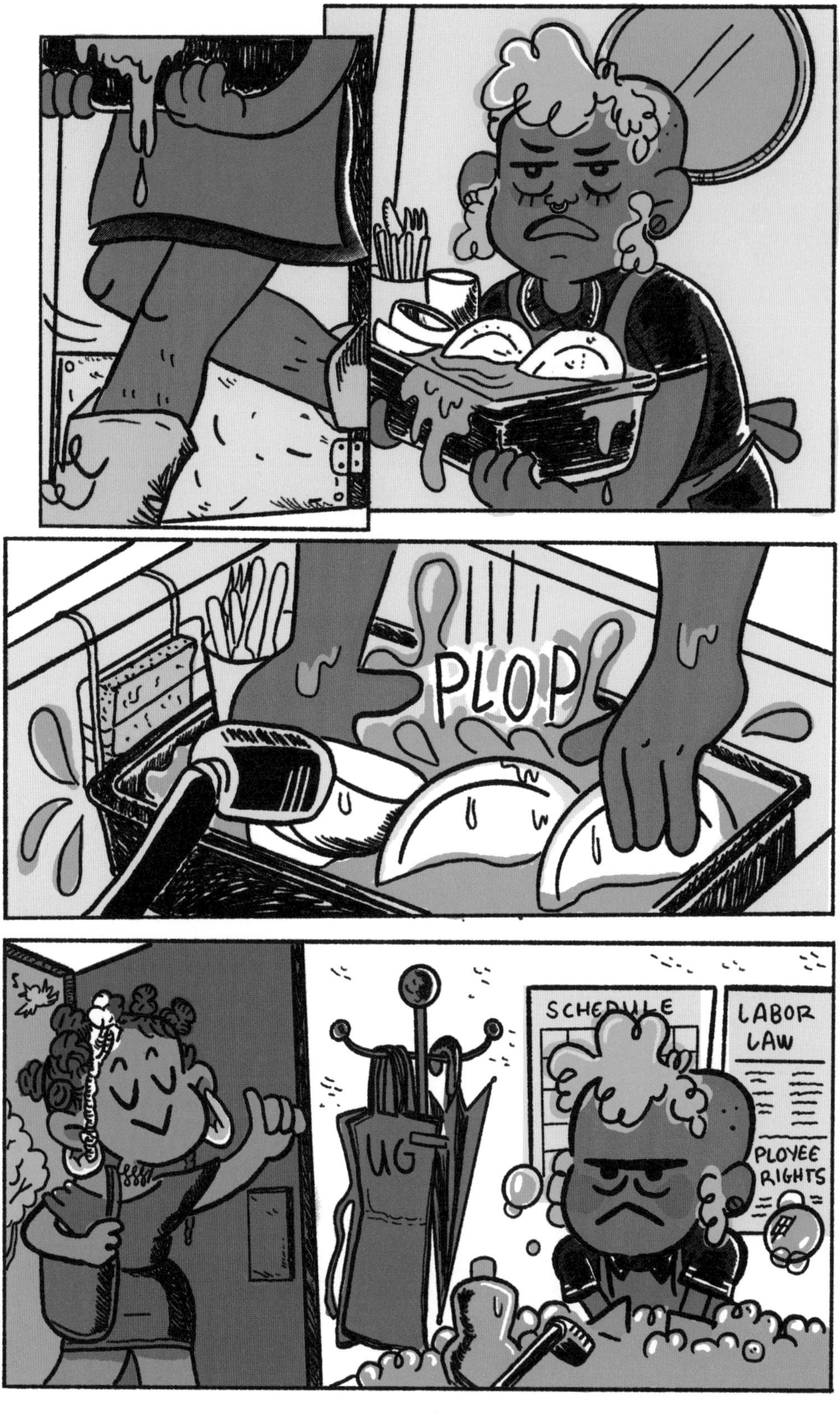
PLOP
SCHEDULE
LABOR
LAW
PLOYEE
RIGHTS
UG

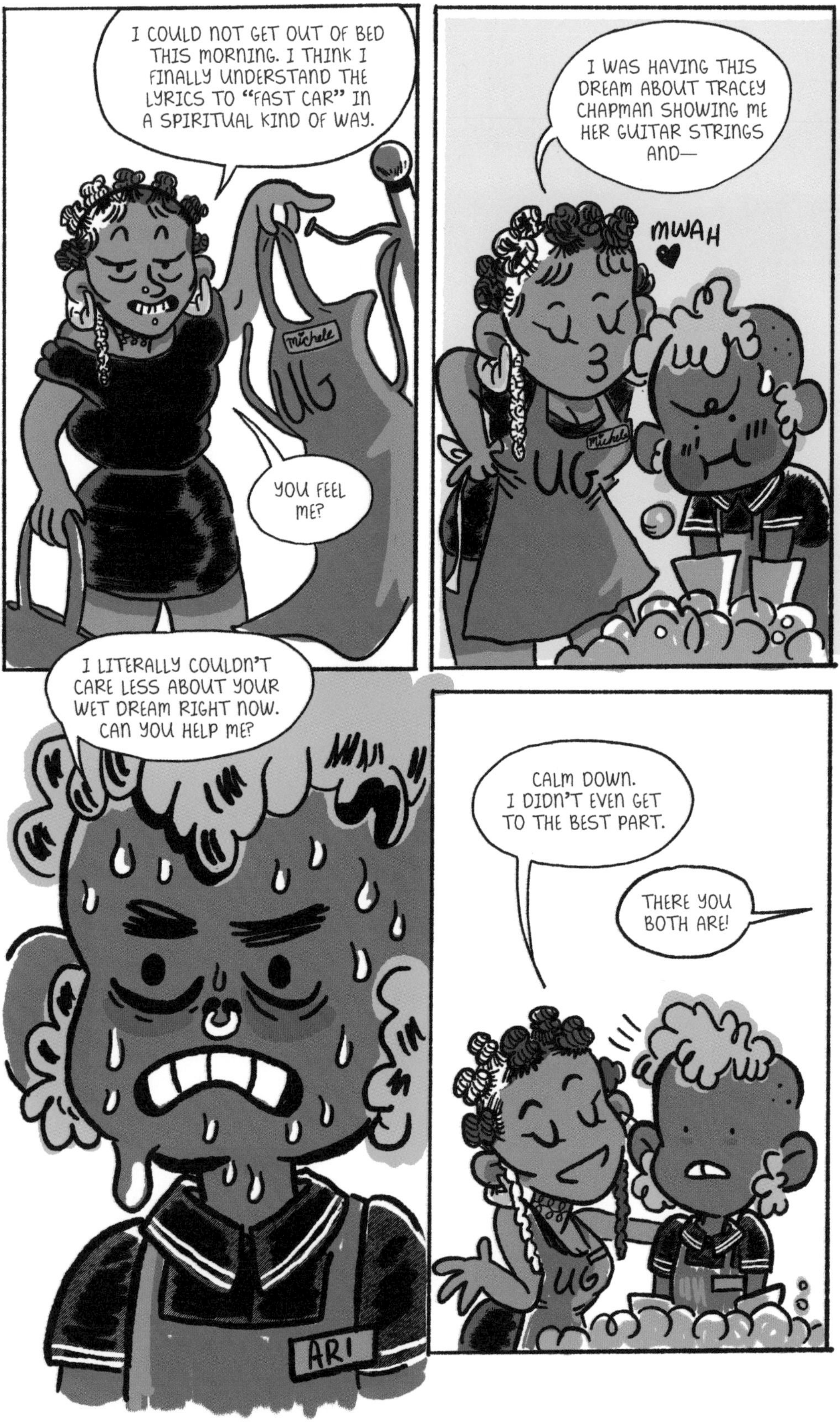
I COULD NOT GET OUT OF BED THIS MORNING. I THINK I FINALLY UNDERSTAND THE LYRICS TO "FAST CAR" IN A SPIRITUAL KIND OF WAY.
Michele
UG
YOU FEEL ME?
I WAS HAVING THIS DREAM ABOUT TRACEY CHAPMAN SHOWING ME HER GUITAR STRINGS AND—
MWAH
Michele
UG
I LITERALLY COULDN'T CARE LESS ABOUT YOUR WET DREAM RIGHT NOW. CAN YOU HELP ME?
ARI
CALM DOWN. I DIDN'T EVEN GET TO THE BEST PART.
THERE YOU BOTH ARE!
UG

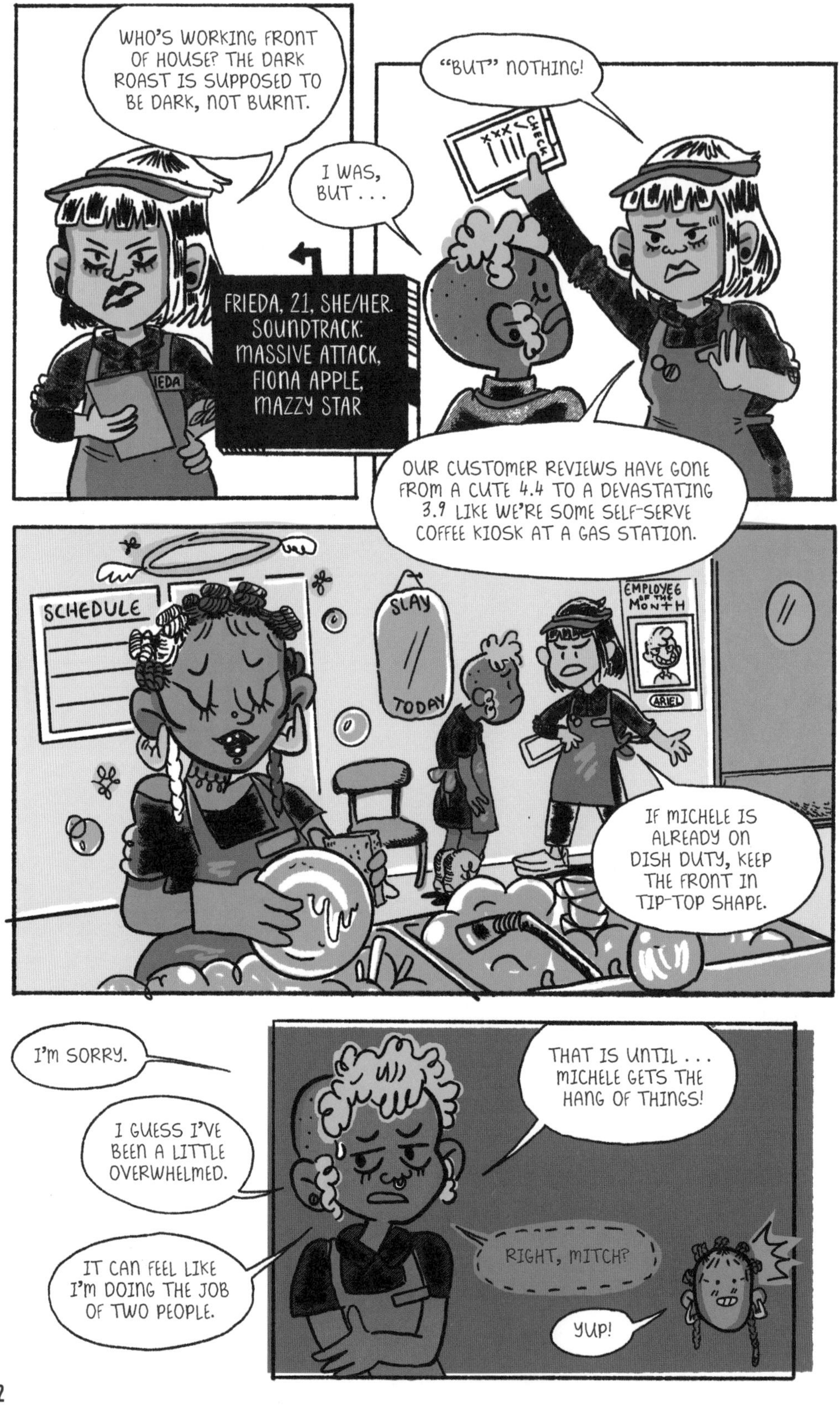
WHO'S WORKING FRONT OF HOUSE? THE DARK ROAST IS SUPPOSED TO BE DARK, NOT BURNT.
I WAS, BUT . . .
FRIEDA, 21, SHE/HER. SOUNDTRACK: MASSIVE ATTACK, FIONA APPLE, MAZZY STAR
IEDA
"BUT" NOTHING!
CHECK
OUR CUSTOMER REVIEWS HAVE GONE FROM A CUTE 4.4 TO A DEVASTATING 3.9 LIKE WE'RE SOME SELF-SERVE COFFEE KIOSK AT A GAS STATION.
SCHEDULE
SLAY TODAY
EMPLOYEE OF THE MONTH
ARIEL
IF MICHELE IS ALREADY ON DISH DUTY, KEEP THE FRONT IN TIP-TOP SHAPE.
I'M SORRY.
I GUESS I'VE BEEN A LITTLE OVERWHELMED.
IT CAN FEEL LIKE I'M DOING THE JOB OF TWO PEOPLE.
THAT IS UNTIL . . . MICHELE GETS THE HANG OF THINGS!
RIGHT, MITCH?
YUP!

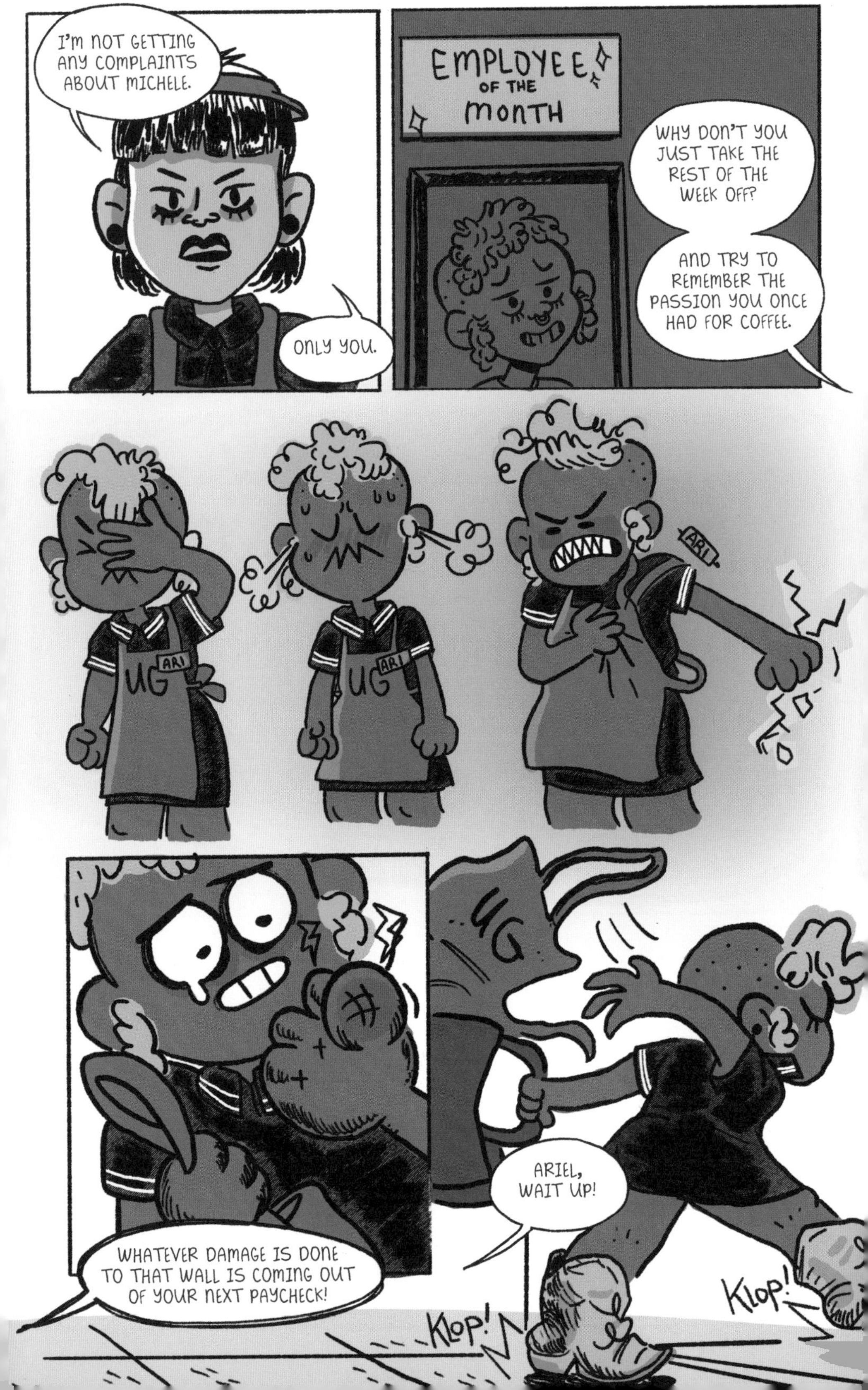
I'M NOT GETTING ANY COMPLAINTS ABOUT MICHELE.
ONLY YOU.
EMPLOYEE OF THE MONTH
WHY DON'T YOU JUST TAKE THE REST OF THE WEEK OFF?
AND TRY TO REMEMBER THE PASSION YOU ONCE HAD FOR COFFEE.
ARI
ARI
ARI
UG
UG
UG
WHATEVER DAMAGE IS DONE TO THAT WALL IS COMING OUT OF YOUR NEXT PAYCHECK!
ARIEL, WAIT UP!
KLOP!
KLOP!

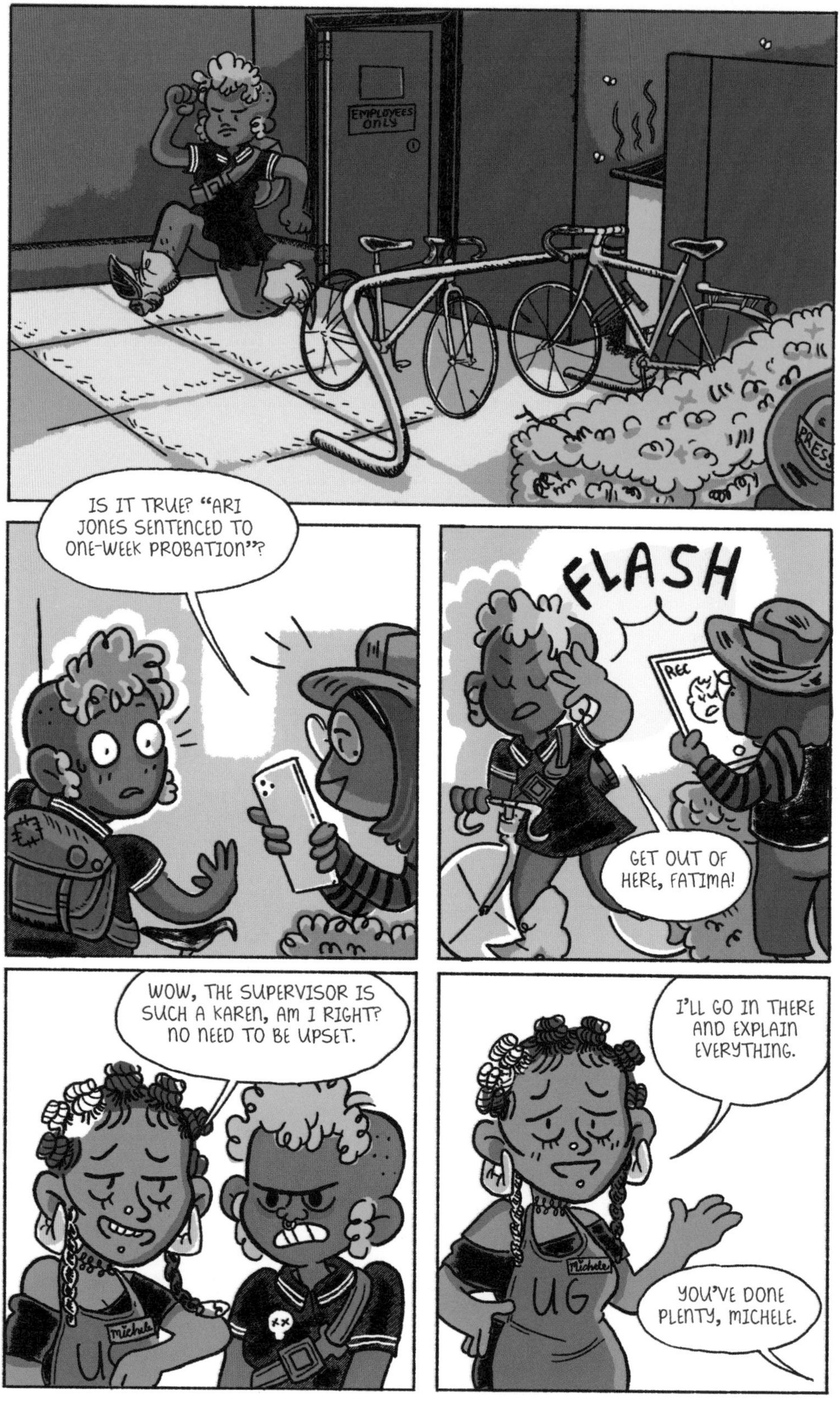
EMPLOYEES ONLY
PRESS
IS IT TRUE? "ARI JONES SENTENCED TO ONE-WEEK PROBATION"?
FLASH
REC
GET OUT OF HERE, FATIMA!
WOW, THE SUPERVISOR IS SUCH A KAREN, AM I RIGHT? NO NEED TO BE UPSET.
Michele
I'LL GO IN THERE AND EXPLAIN EVERYTHING.
Michele
UG
YOU'VE DONE PLENTY, MICHELE.

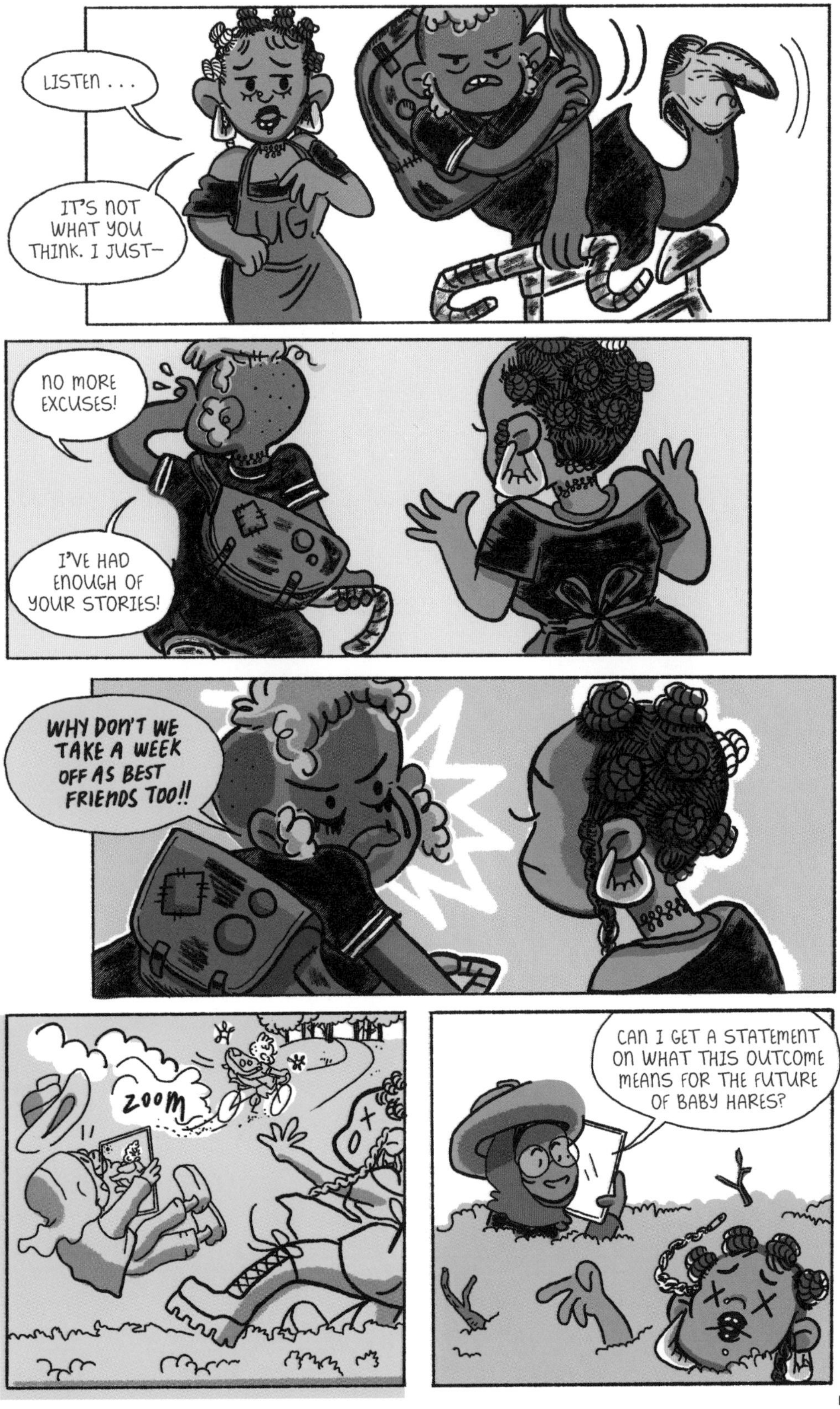
LISTEN . . .
IT'S NOT WHAT YOU THINK. I JUST—
NO MORE EXCUSES!
I'VE HAD ENOUGH OF YOUR STORIES!
WHY DON'T WE TAKE A WEEK OFF AS BEST FRIENDS TOO!!
ZOOM
CAN I GET A STATEMENT ON WHAT THIS OUTCOME MEANS FOR THE FUTURE OF BABY HARES?

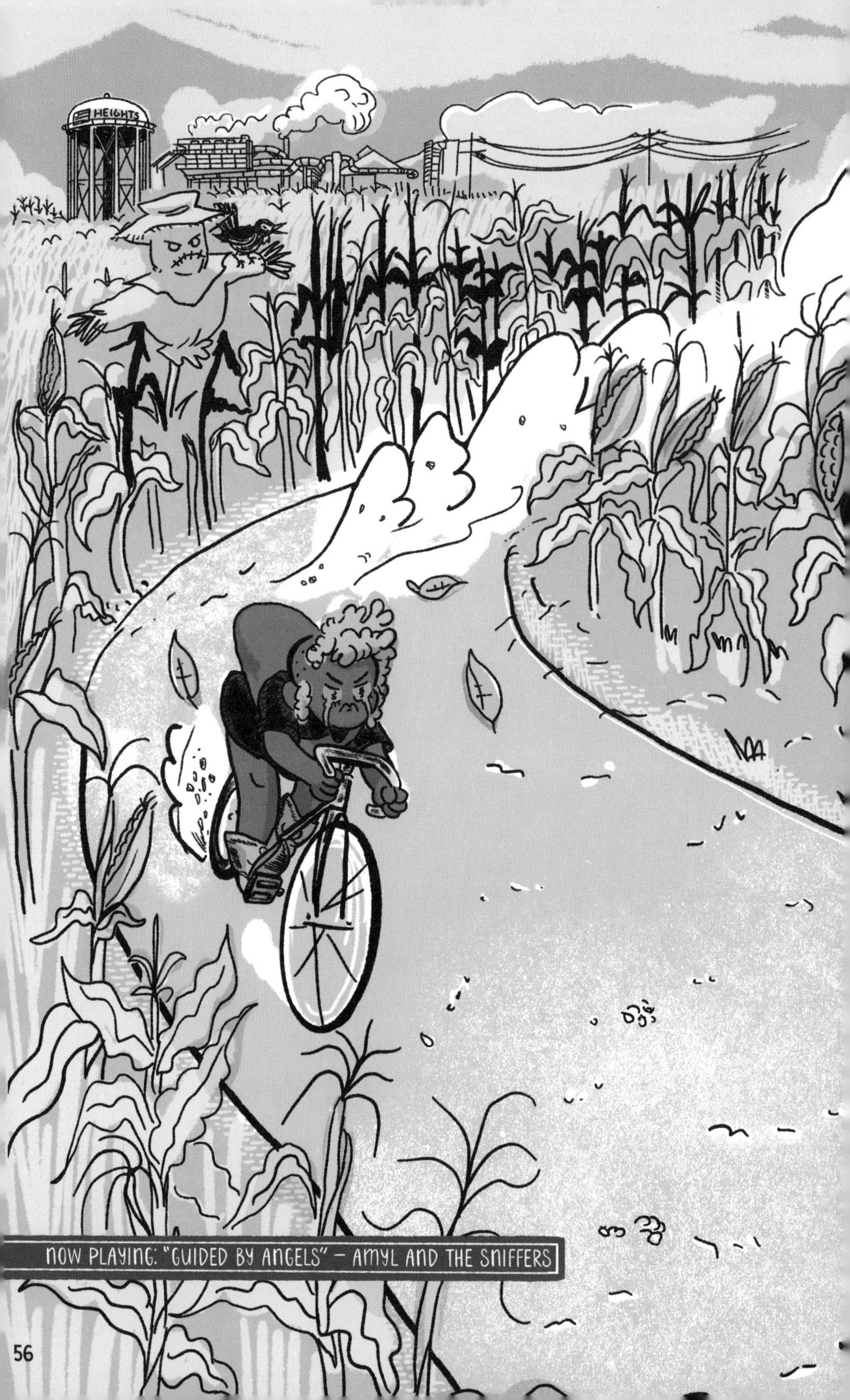
HEIGHTS
NOW PLAYING: "GUIDED BY ANGELS" – AMYL AND THE SNIFFERS

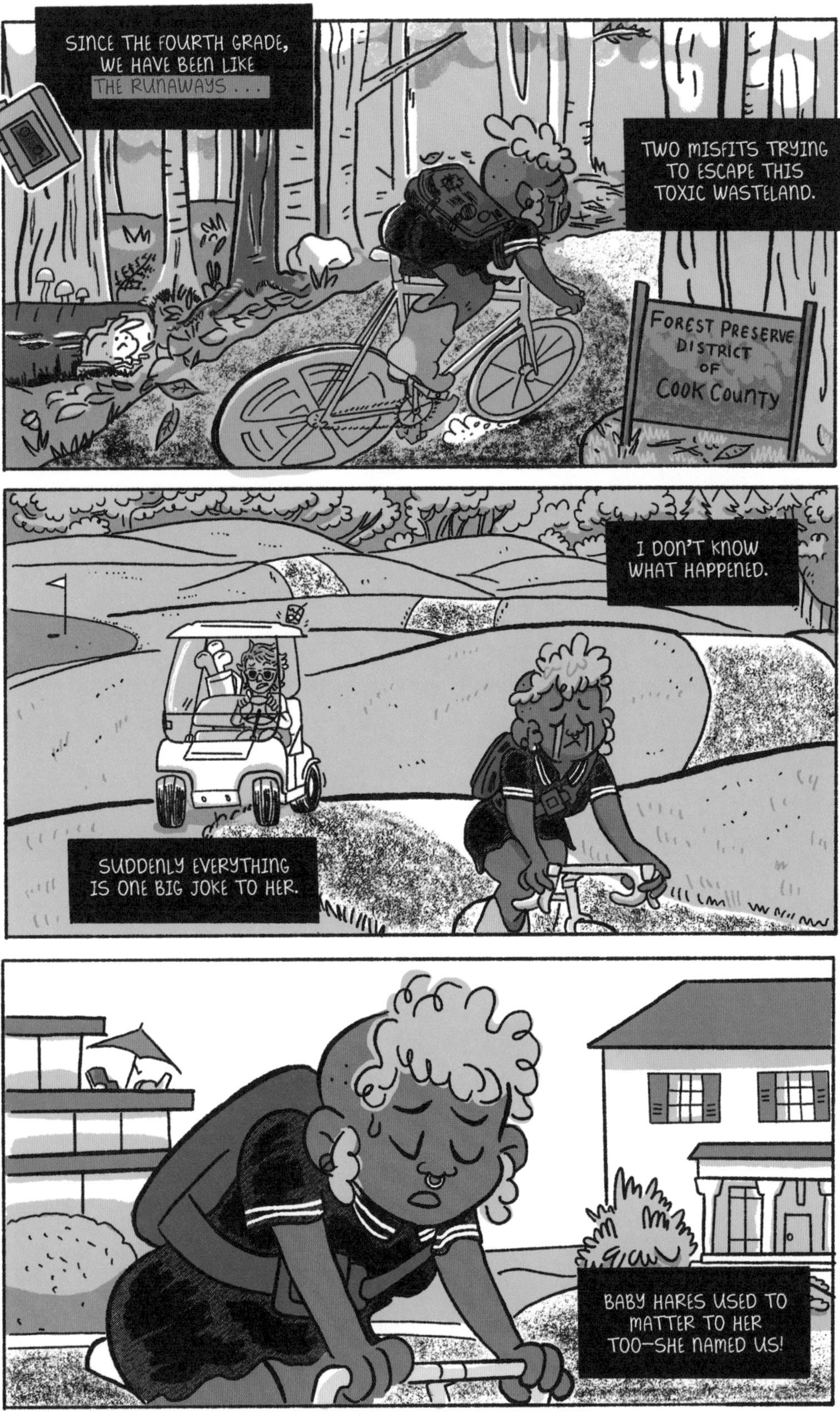
SINCE THE FOURTH GRADE, WE HAVE BEEN LIKE THE RUNAWAYS . . .
TWO MISFITS TRYING TO ESCAPE THIS TOXIC WASTELAND.
FOREST PRESERVE DISTRICT OF COOK COUNTY
I DON'T KNOW WHAT HAPPENED.
SUDDENLY EVERYTHING IS ONE BIG JOKE TO HER.
BABY HARES USED TO MATTER TO HER TOO—SHE NAMED US!

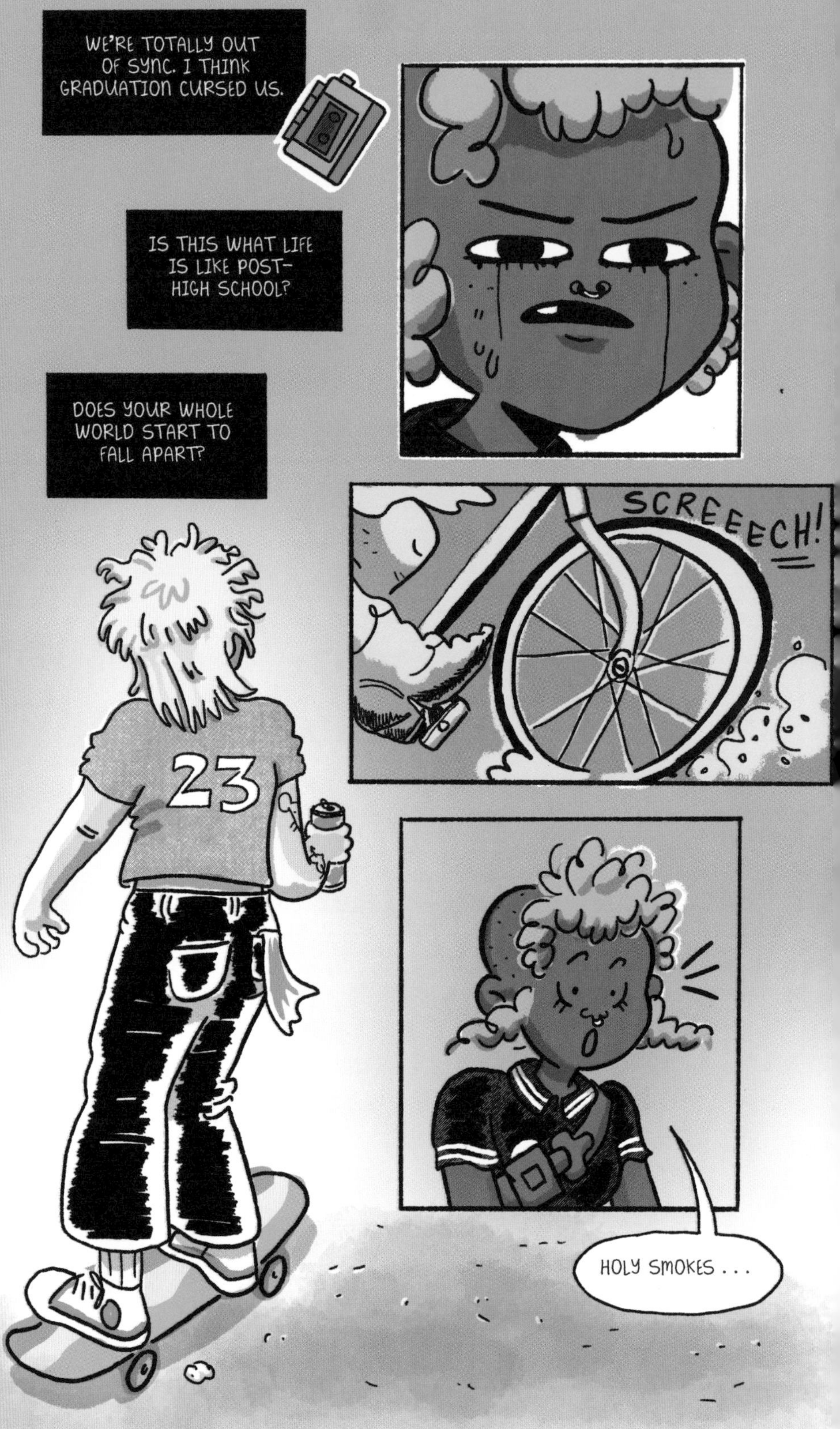
WE'RE TOTALLY OUT OF SYNC. I THINK GRADUATION CURSED US.
IS THIS WHAT LIFE IS LIKE POST-HIGH SCHOOL?
DOES YOUR WHOLE WORLD START TO FALL APART?
SCREEEECH!
HOLY SMOKES . . .

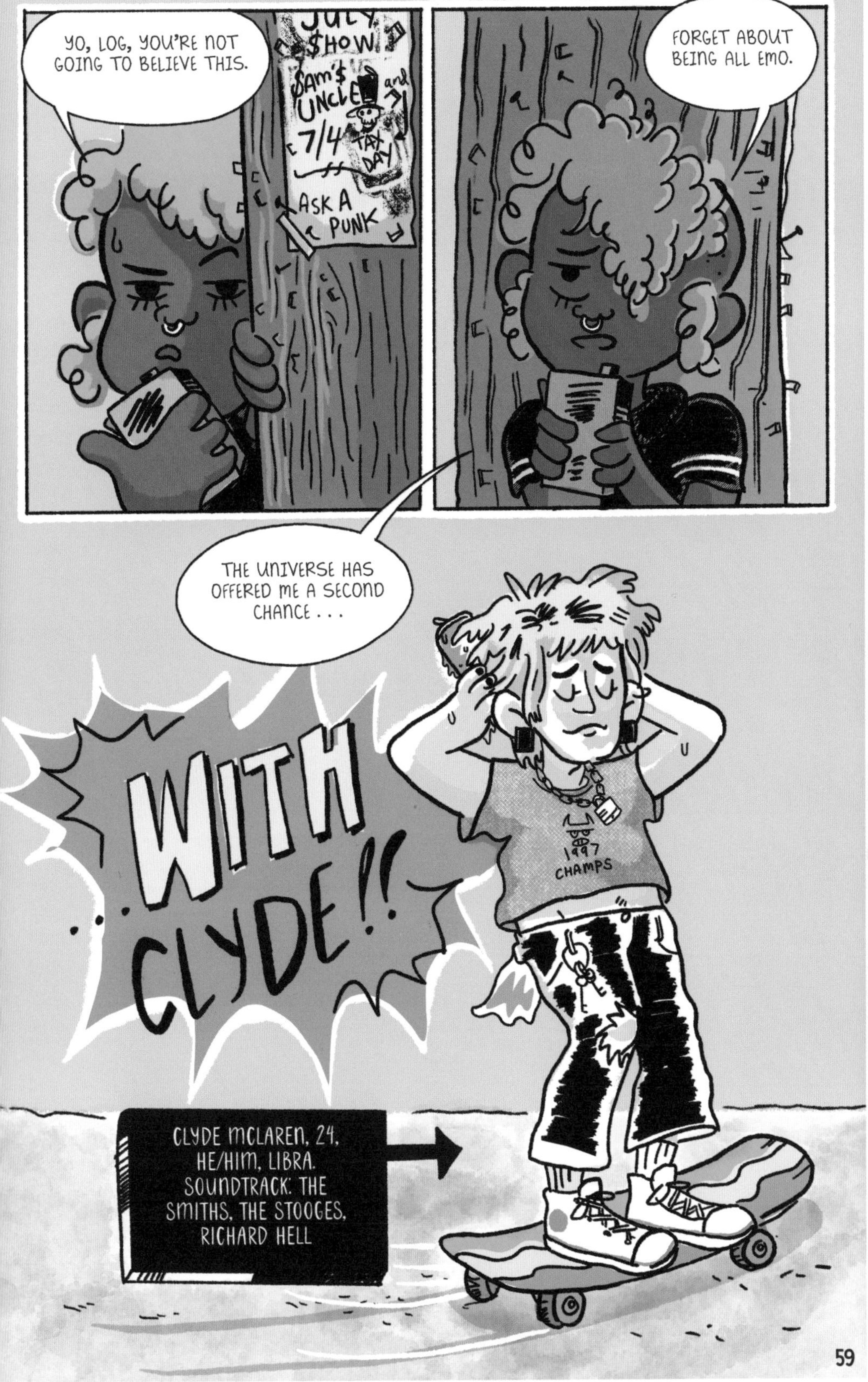
YO, LOG, YOU'RE NOT GOING TO BELIEVE THIS.
JULY $HOW
AM' UNCLE and
7/4 TAX DAY
ASK A PUNK
FORGET ABOUT BEING ALL EMO.
THE UNIVERSE HAS OFFERED ME A SECOND CHANCE . . .
WITH CLYDE!?
1997 CHAMPS
CLYDE MCLAREN, 24. HE/HIM, LIBRA. SOUNDTRACK: THE SMITHS, THE STOOGES, RICHARD HELL

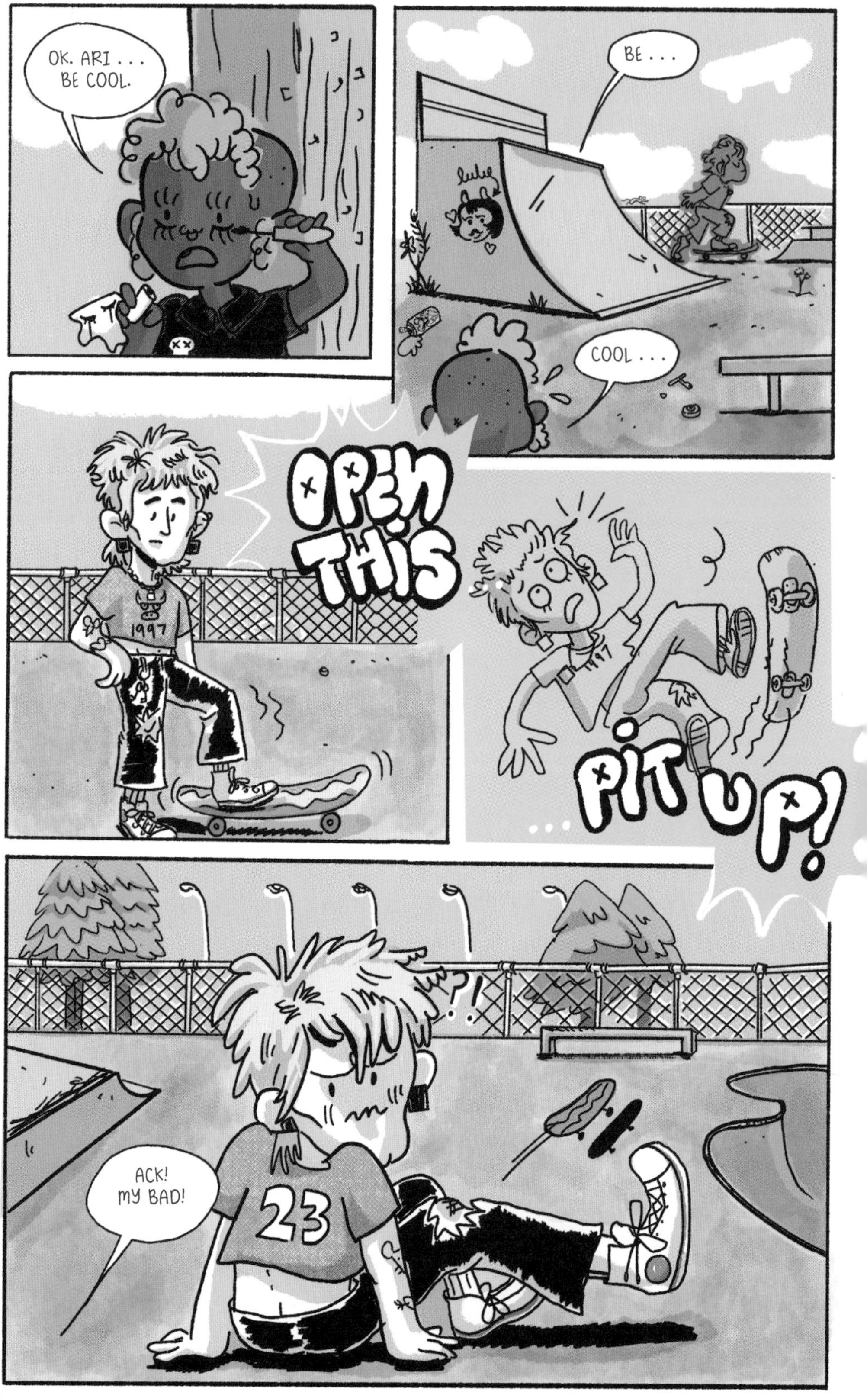
OK. ARI . . .
BE COOL.
BE . . .
COOL . . .
OPEN THIS
. . . PIT UP!
?!
ACK!
MY BAD!

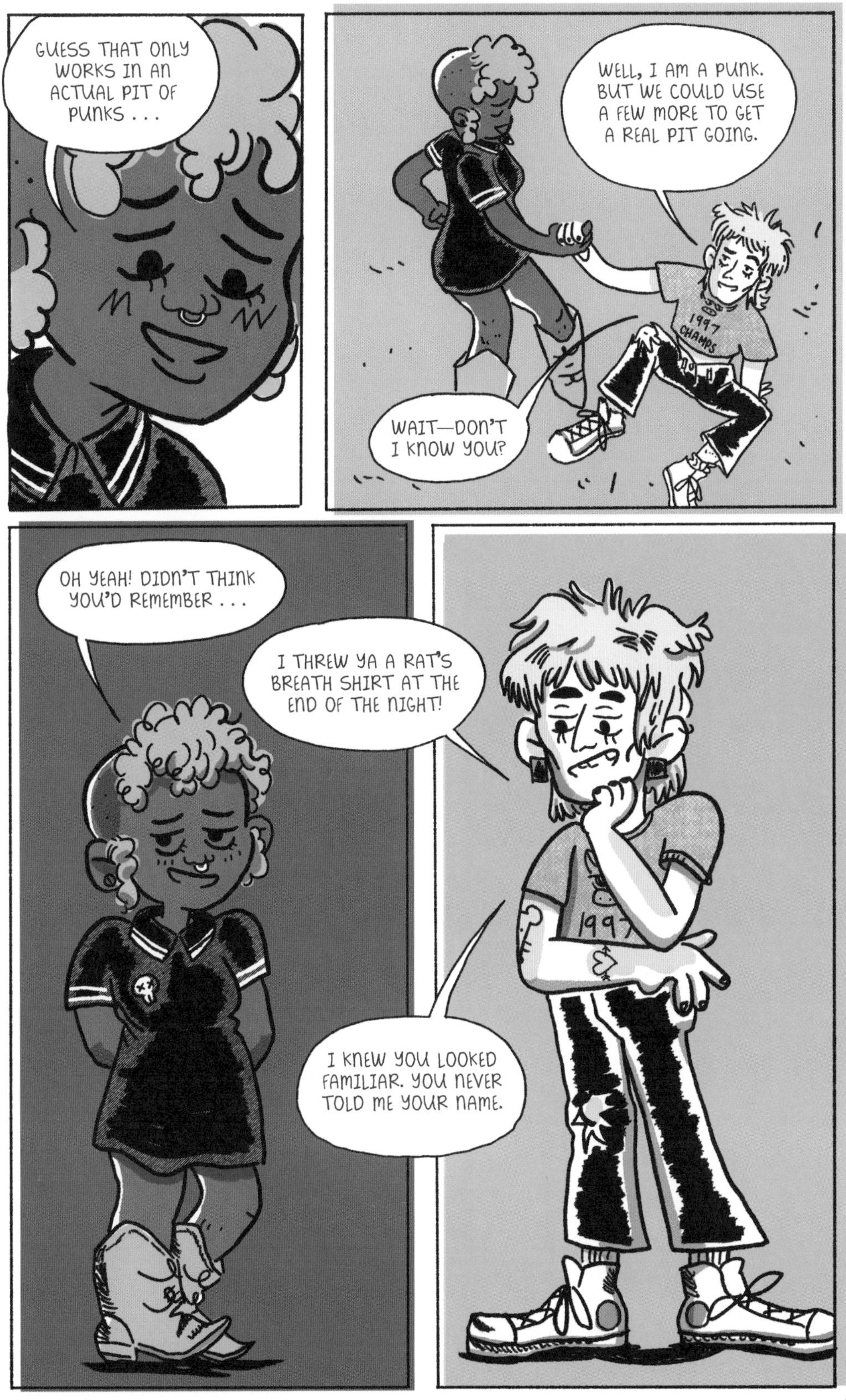
GUESS THAT ONLY WORKS IN AN ACTUAL PIT OF PUNKS . . .
WELL, I AM A PUNK. BUT WE COULD USE A FEW MORE TO GET A REAL PIT GOING.
1997 CHAMPS
WAIT—DON'T I KNOW YOU?
OH YEAH! DIDN'T THINK YOU'D REMEMBER . . .
I THREW YA A RAT'S BREATH SHIRT AT THE END OF THE NIGHT!
I KNEW YOU LOOKED FAMILIAR. YOU NEVER TOLD ME YOUR NAME.

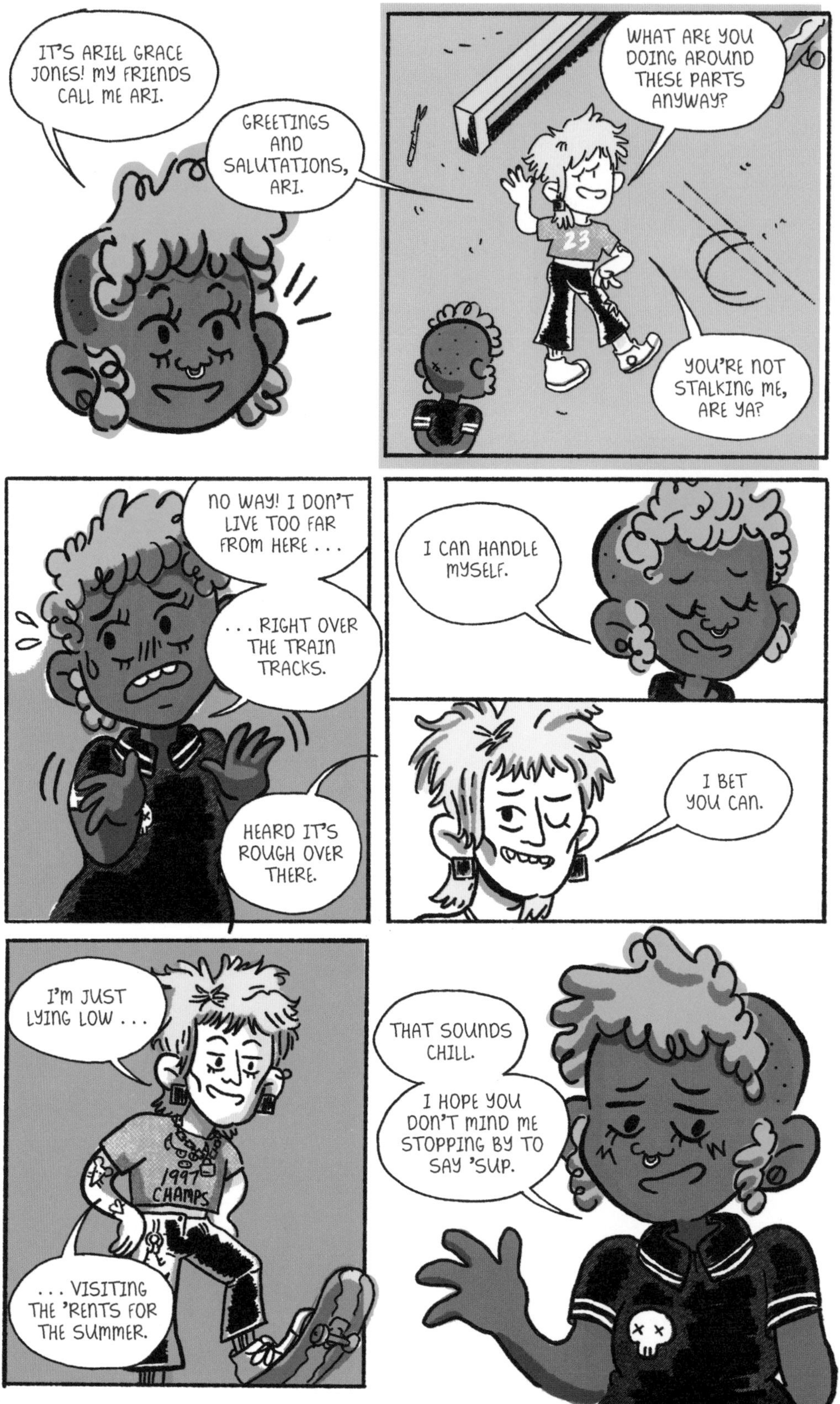

IT'S ARIEL GRACE JONES! MY FRIENDS CALL ME ARI.
GREETINGS AND SALUTATIONS, ARI.
WHAT ARE YOU DOING AROUND THESE PARTS ANYWAY?
YOU'RE NOT STALKING ME, ARE YA?
NO WAY! I DON'T LIVE TOO FAR FROM HERE . . .
. . . RIGHT OVER THE TRAIN TRACKS.
HEARD IT'S ROUGH OVER THERE.
I CAN HANDLE MYSELF.
I BET YOU CAN.
23
I'M JUST LYING LOW . . .
. . . VISITING THE 'RENTS FOR THE SUMMER.
1997 CHAMPS
THAT SOUNDS CHILL.
I HOPE YOU DON'T MIND ME STOPPING BY TO SAY 'SUP.

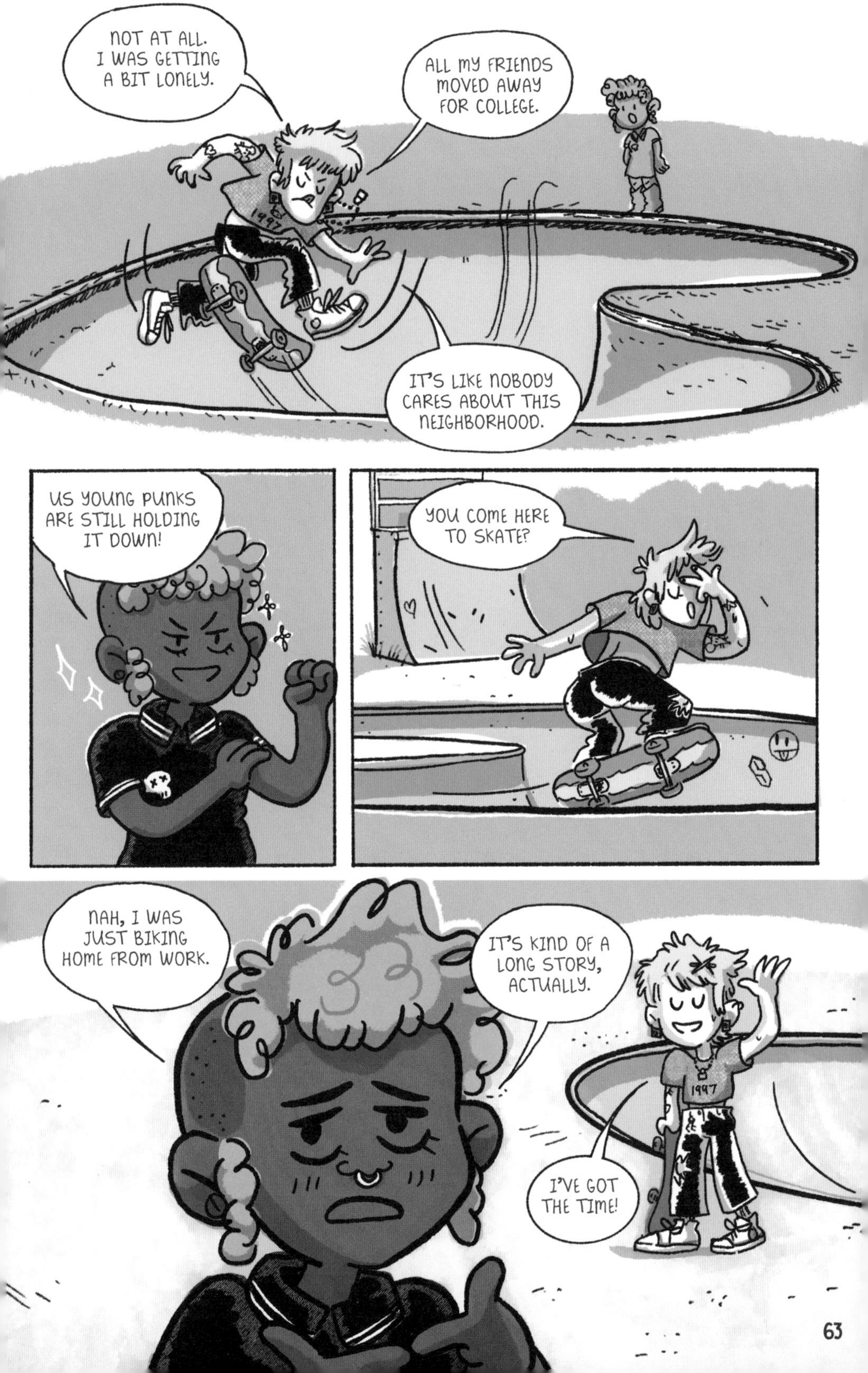
NOT AT ALL. I WAS GETTING A BIT LONELY.
ALL MY FRIENDS MOVED AWAY FOR COLLEGE.
IT'S LIKE NOBODY CARES ABOUT THIS NEIGHBORHOOD.
US YOUNG PUNKS ARE STILL HOLDING IT DOWN!
YOU COME HERE TO SKATE?
NAH, I WAS JUST BIKING HOME FROM WORK.
IT'S KIND OF A LONG STORY, ACTUALLY.
I'VE GOT THE TIME!

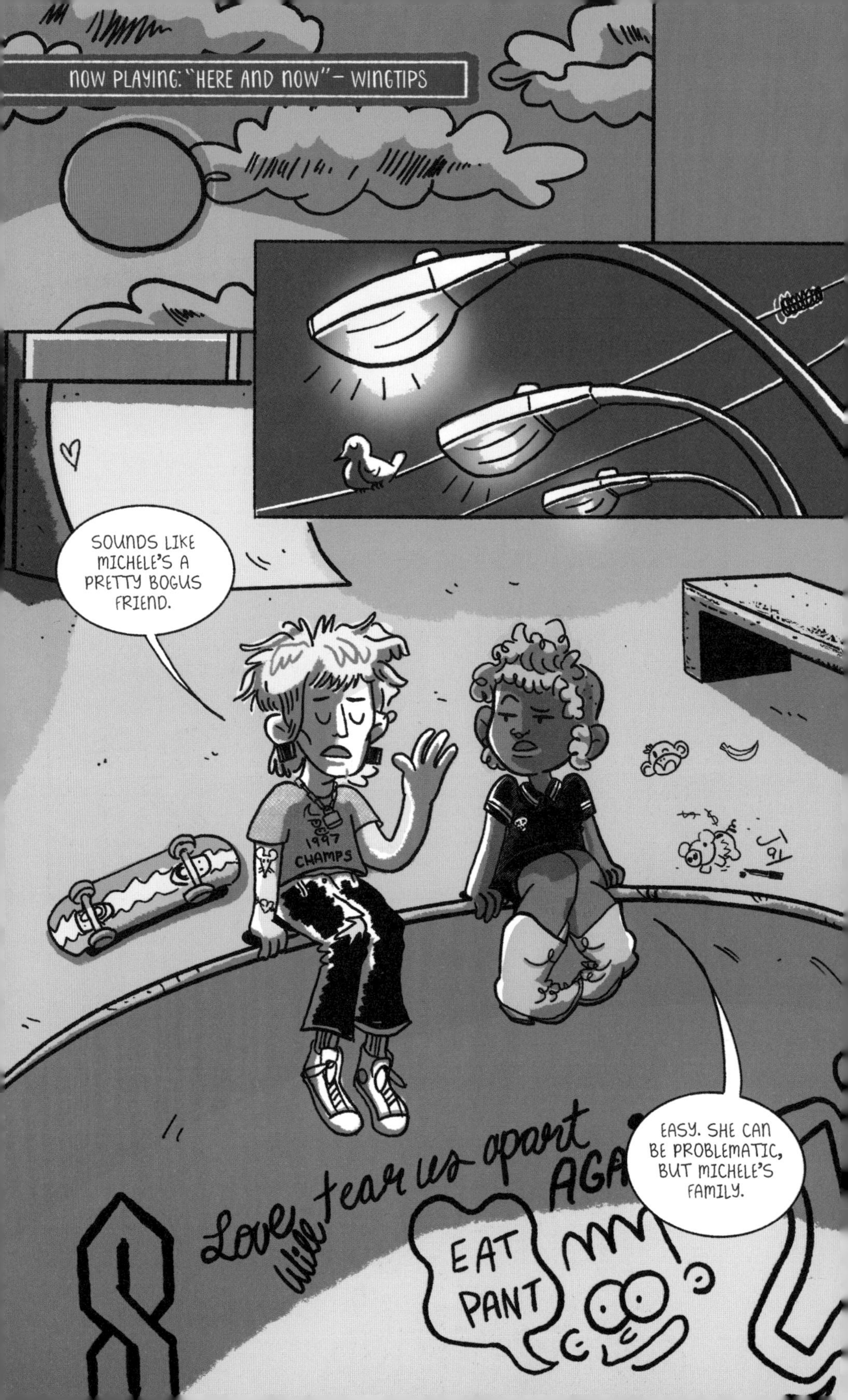
NOW PLAYING: "HERE AND NOW" – WINGTIPS
SOUNDS LIKE MICHELE'S A PRETTY BOGUS FRIEND.
EASY. SHE CAN BE PROBLEMATIC, BUT MICHELE'S FAMILY.
1997 CHAMPS
Love will tear us apart
AGA
EAT PANT

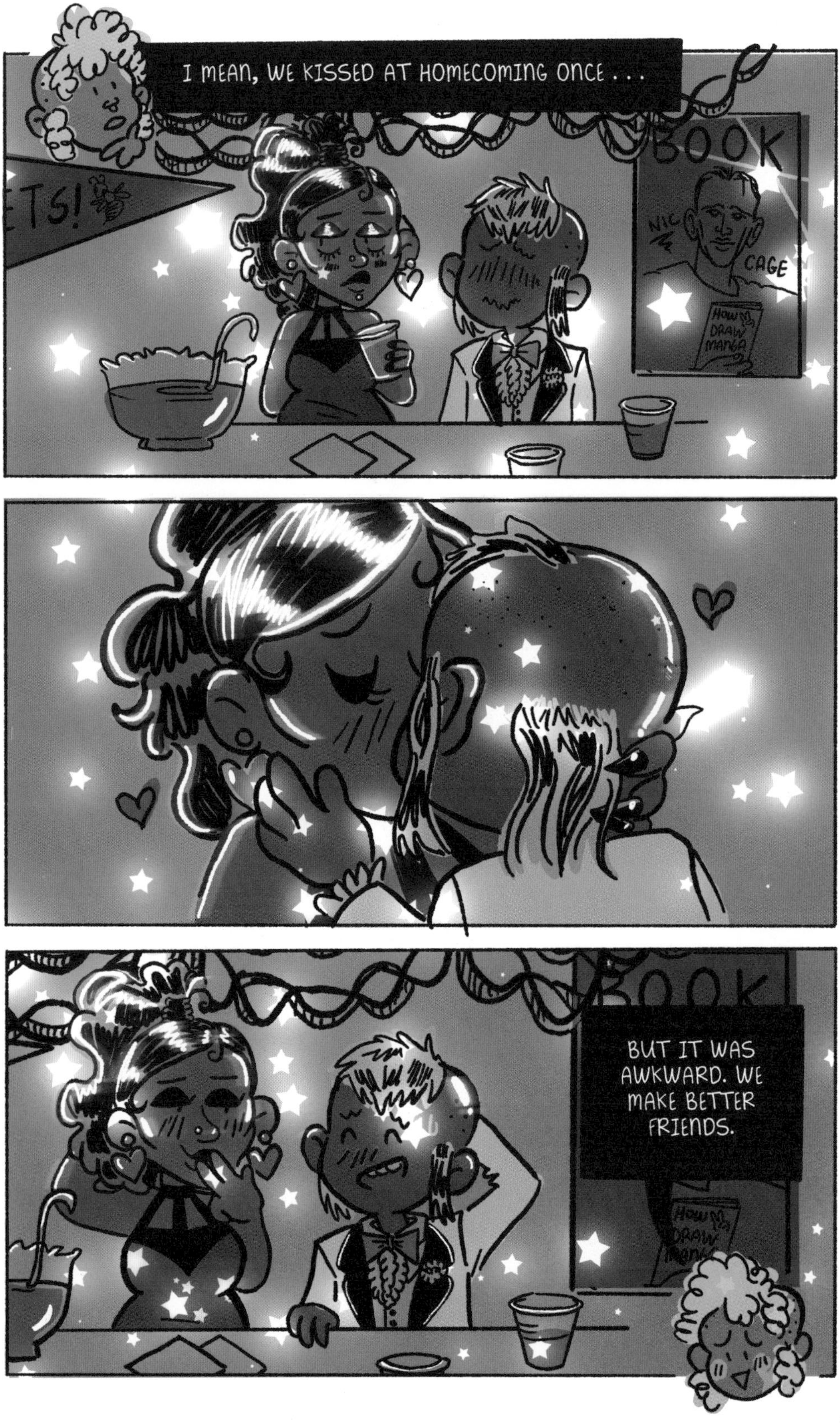
I MEAN, WE KISSED AT HOMECOMING ONCE . . .
BOOK
NIC
CAGE
HOW DRAW MANGA
BUT IT WAS AWKWARD. WE MAKE BETTER FRIENDS.

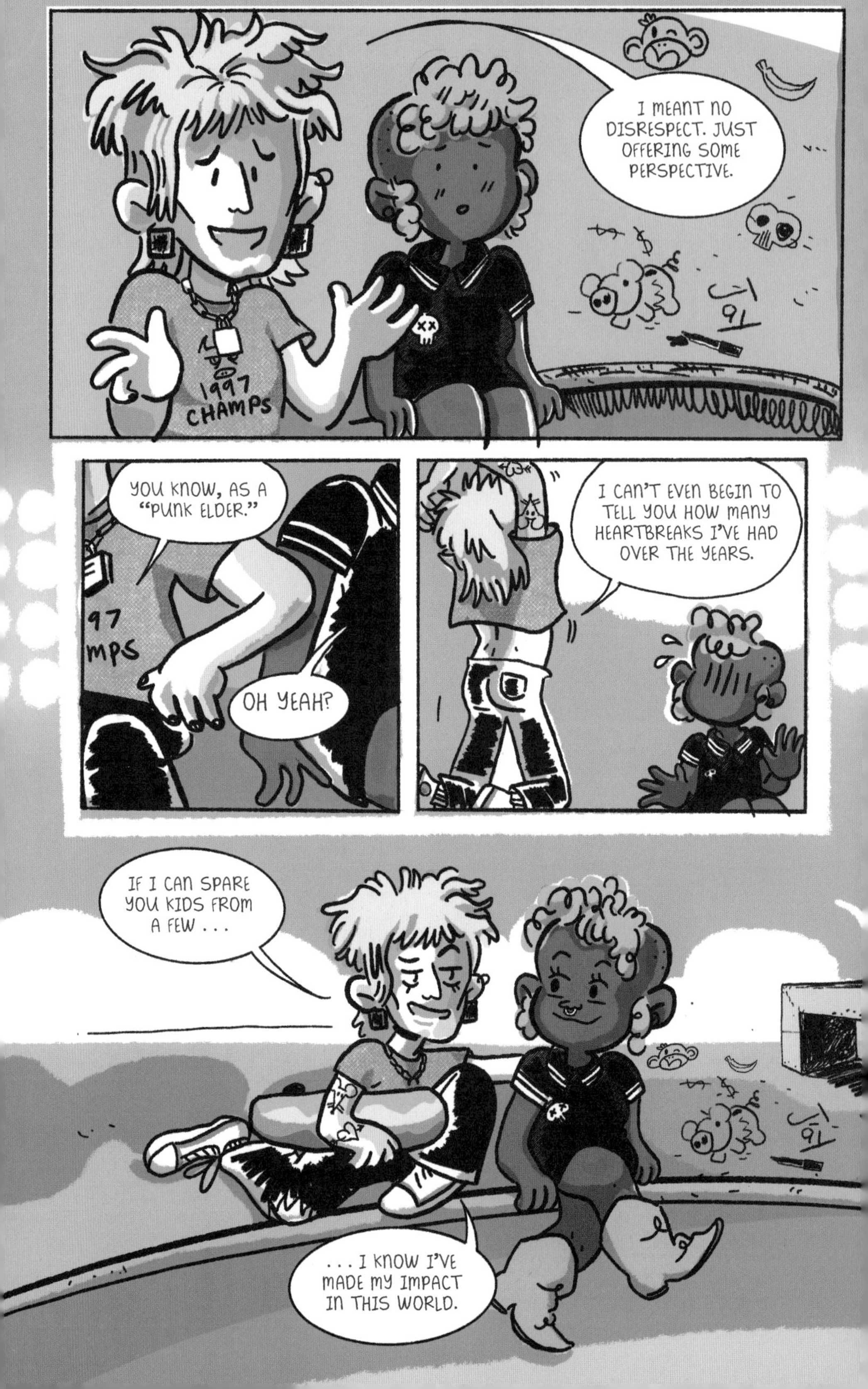
I MEANT NO DISRESPECT. JUST OFFERING SOME PERSPECTIVE.
1997 CHAMPS
YOU KNOW, AS A "PUNK ELDER."
OH YEAH?
I CAN'T EVEN BEGIN TO TELL YOU HOW MANY HEARTBREAKS I'VE HAD OVER THE YEARS.
IF I CAN SPARE YOU KIDS FROM A FEW . . .
. . . I KNOW I'VE MADE MY IMPACT IN THIS WORLD.

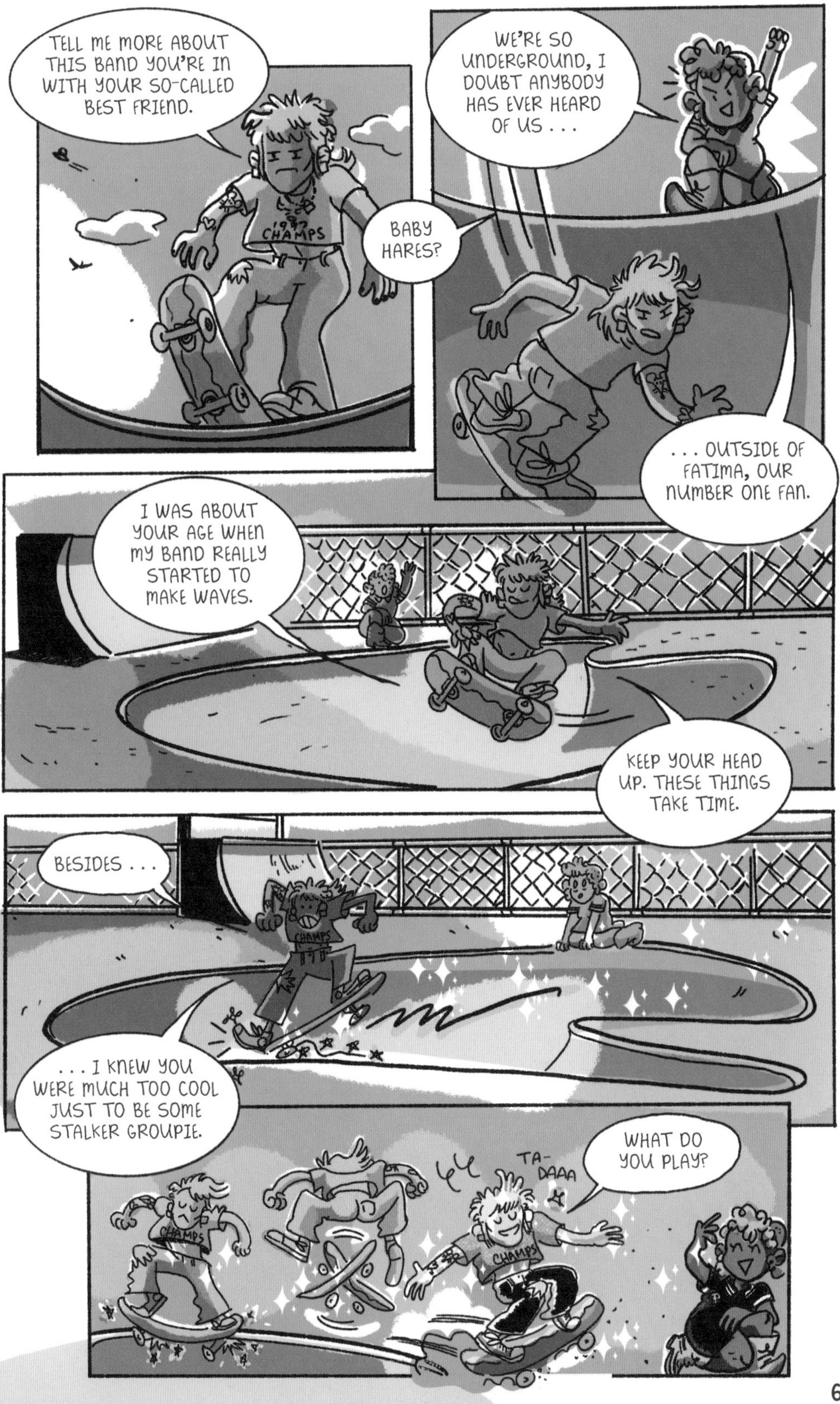
TELL ME MORE ABOUT THIS BAND YOU'RE IN WITH YOUR SO-CALLED BEST FRIEND.
1987 CHAMPS
WE'RE SO UNDERGROUND, I DOUBT ANYBODY HAS EVER HEARD OF US . . .
BABY HARES?
. . . OUTSIDE OF FATIMA, OUR NUMBER ONE FAN.
I WAS ABOUT YOUR AGE WHEN MY BAND REALLY STARTED TO MAKE WAVES.
KEEP YOUR HEAD UP. THESE THINGS TAKE TIME.
BESIDES . . .
CHAMPS
. . . I KNEW YOU WERE MUCH TOO COOL JUST TO BE SOME STALKER GROUPIE.
CHAMPS
TA-DAAA
CHAMPS
WHAT DO YOU PLAY?

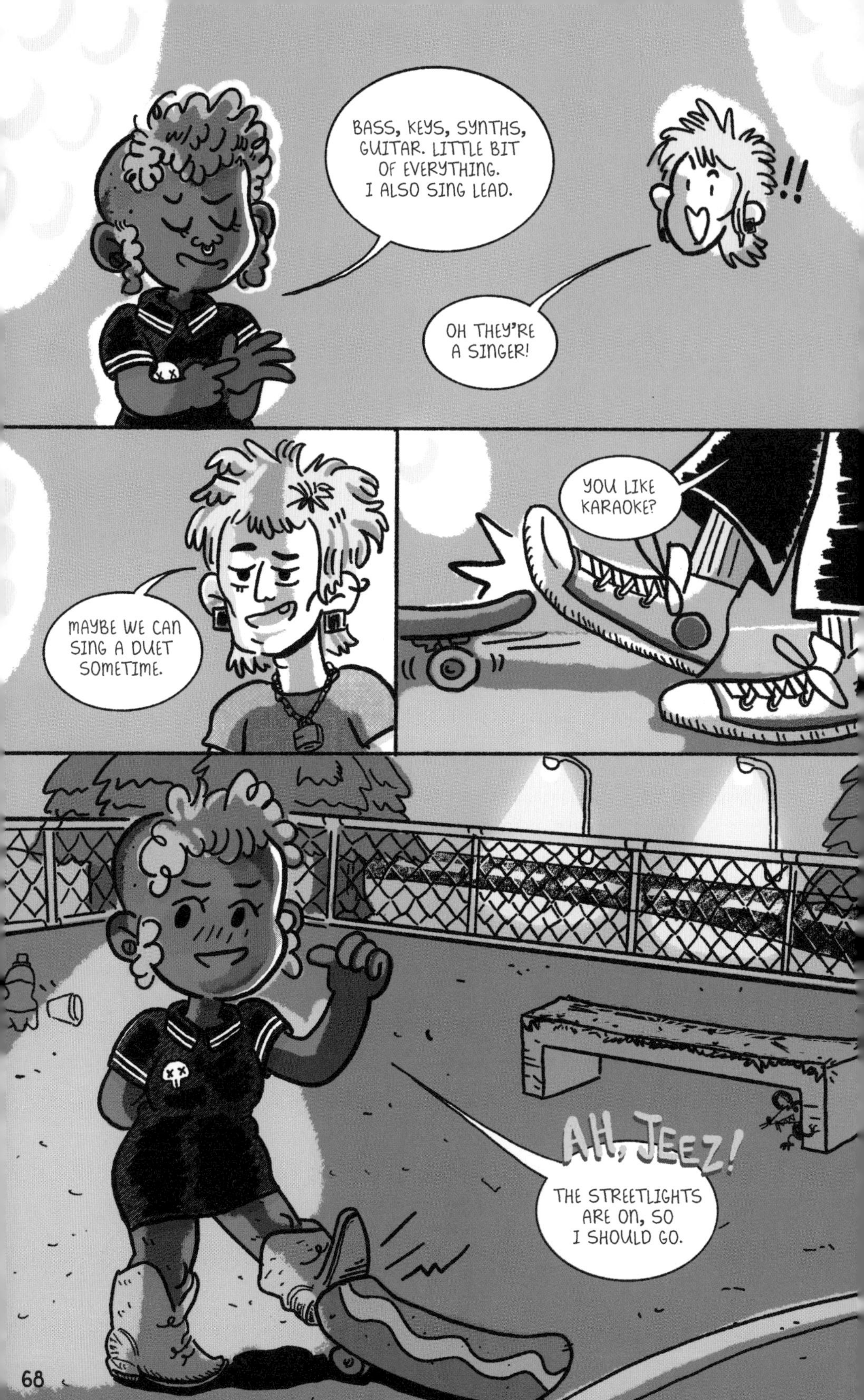
BASS, KEYS, SYNTHS, GUITAR. LITTLE BIT OF EVERYTHING. I ALSO SING LEAD.
!!
OH THEY'RE A SINGER!
MAYBE WE CAN SING A DUET SOMETIME.
YOU LIKE KARAOKE?
AH, JEEZ!
THE STREETLIGHTS ARE ON, SO I SHOULD GO.

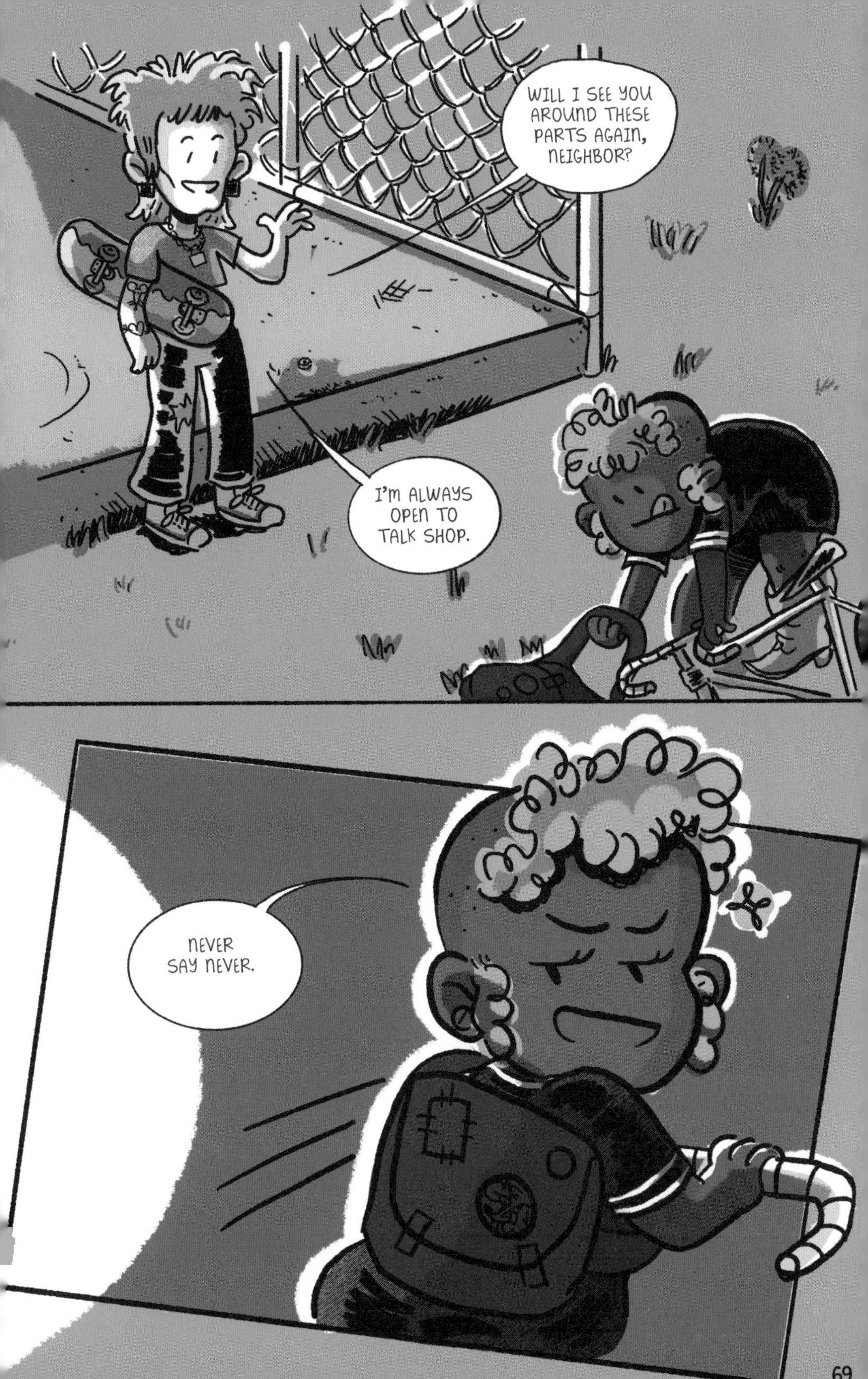
WILL I SEE YOU AROUND THESE PARTS AGAIN, NEIGHBOR?
I'M ALWAYS OPEN TO TALK SHOP.
NEVER SAY NEVER.

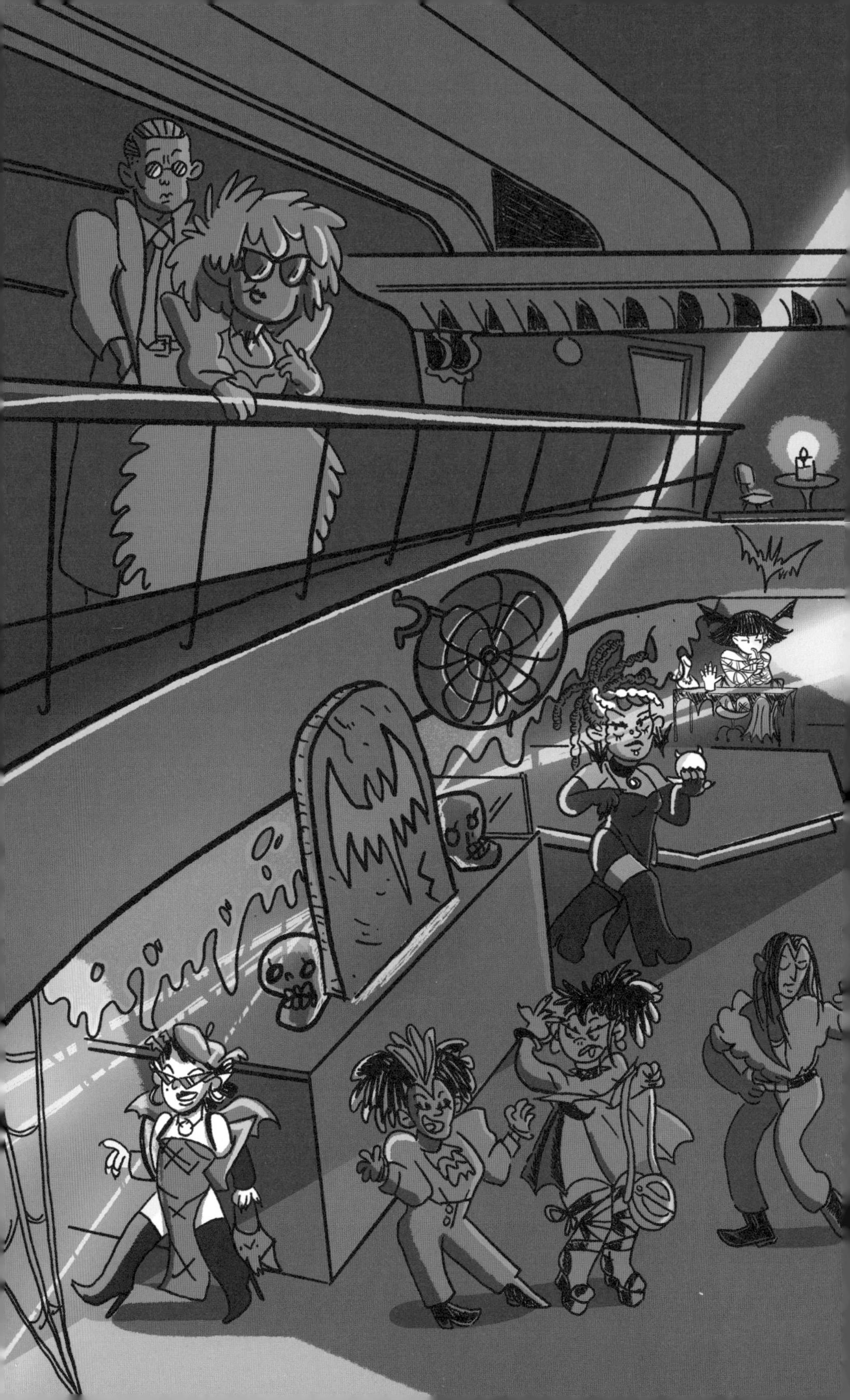

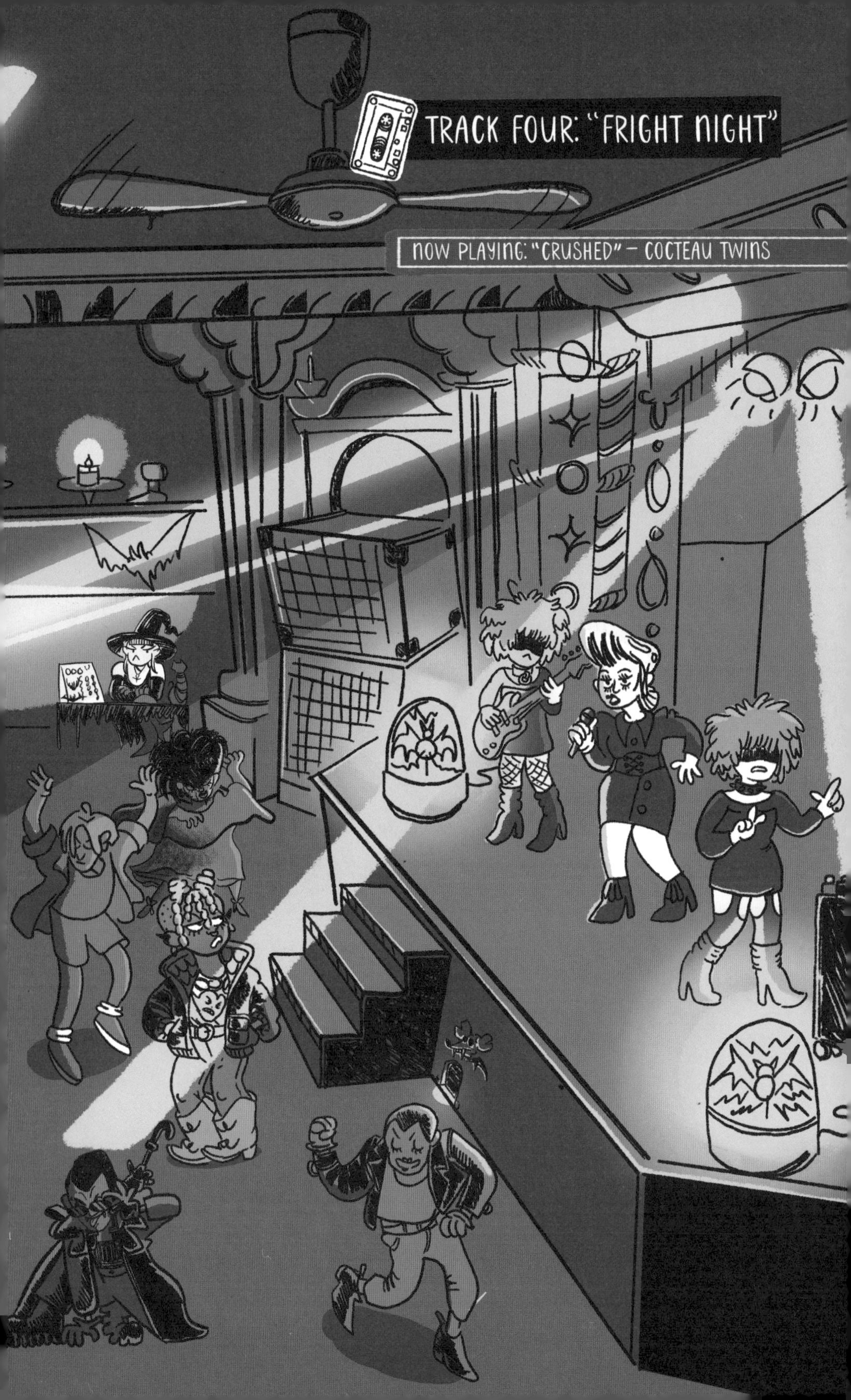
TRACK FOUR: "FRIGHT NIGHT"
NOW PLAYING: "CRUSHED" – COCTEAU TWINS

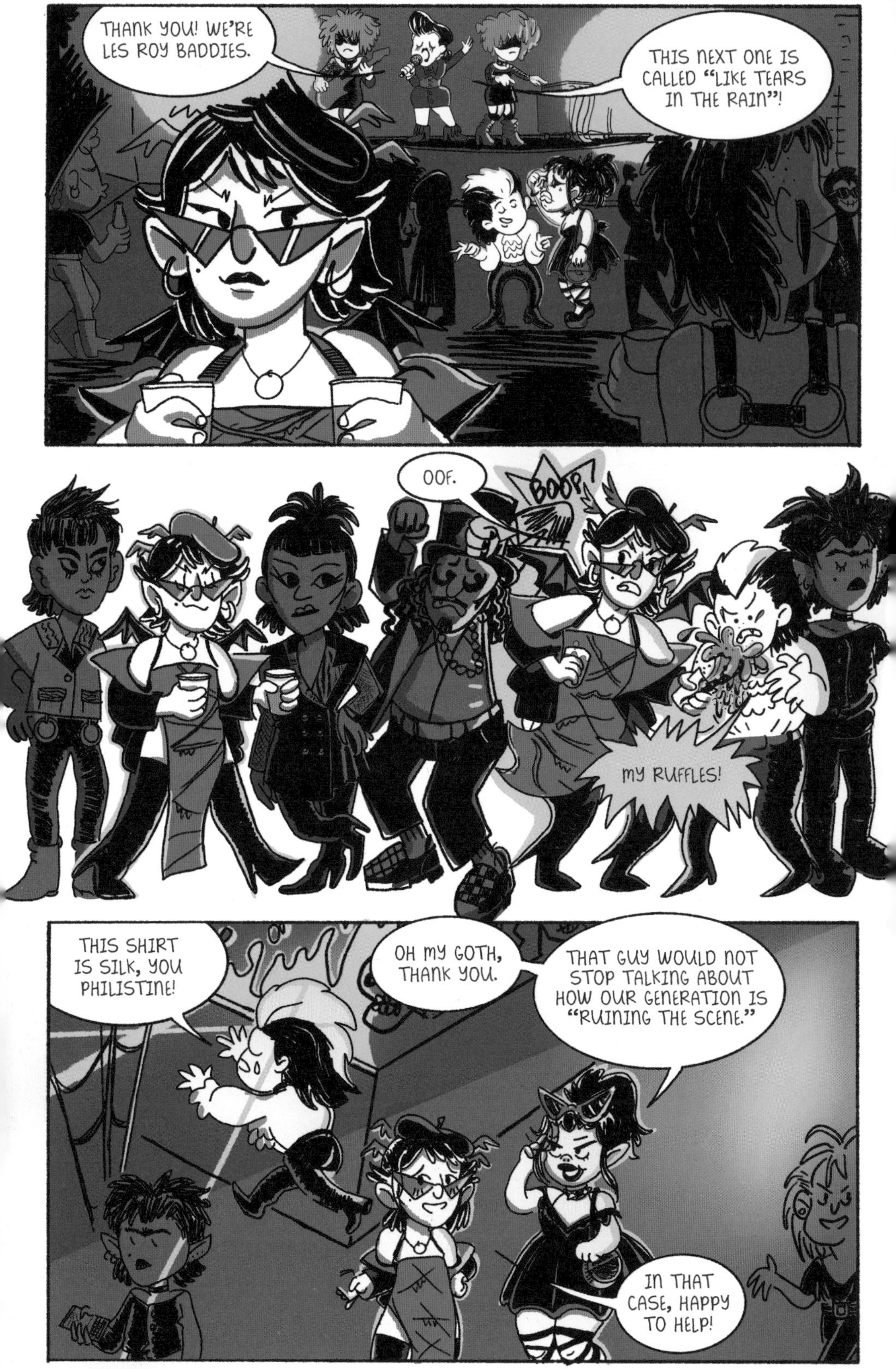
THANK YOU! WE'RE LES ROY BADDIES.
THIS NEXT ONE IS CALLED "LIKE TEARS IN THE RAIN"!
OOF.
BOOP!
MY RUFFLES!
THIS SHIRT IS SILK, YOU PHILISTINE!
OH MY GOTH, THANK YOU.
THAT GUY WOULD NOT STOP TALKING ABOUT HOW OUR GENERATION IS "RUINING THE SCENE."
IN THAT CASE, HAPPY TO HELP!

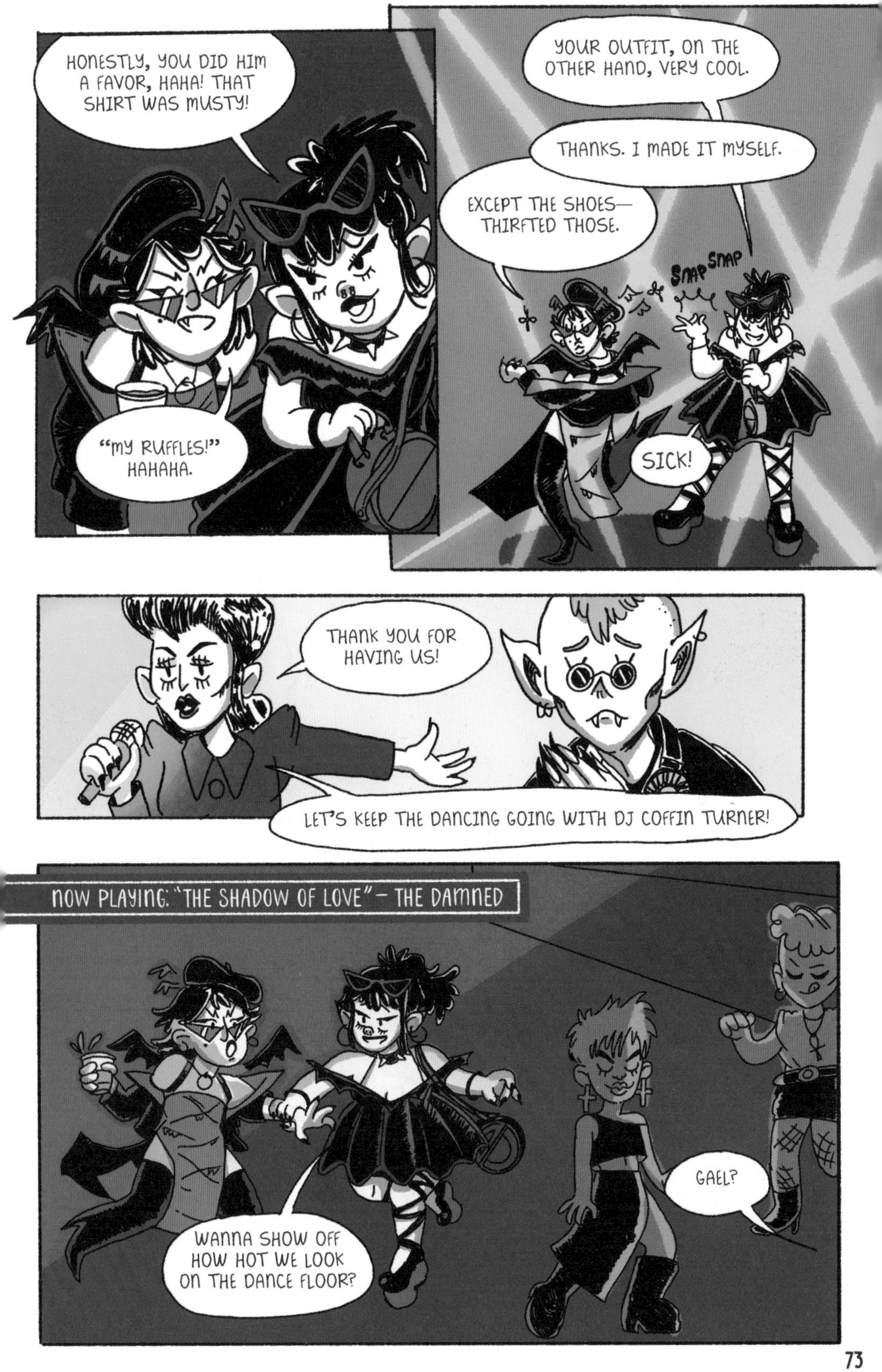
HONESTLY, YOU DID HIM A FAVOR, HAHA! THAT SHIRT WAS MUSTY!
"MY RUFFLES!" HAHAHA.
YOUR OUTFIT, ON THE OTHER HAND, VERY COOL.
THANKS. I MADE IT MYSELF.
EXCEPT THE SHOES— THIRFTED THOSE.
SNAP SNAP
SICK!
THANK YOU FOR HAVING US!
LET'S KEEP THE DANCING GOING WITH DJ COFFIN TURNER!
NOW PLAYING: "THE SHADOW OF LOVE" – THE DAMNED
WANNA SHOW OFF HOW HOT WE LOOK ON THE DANCE FLOOR?
GAEL?

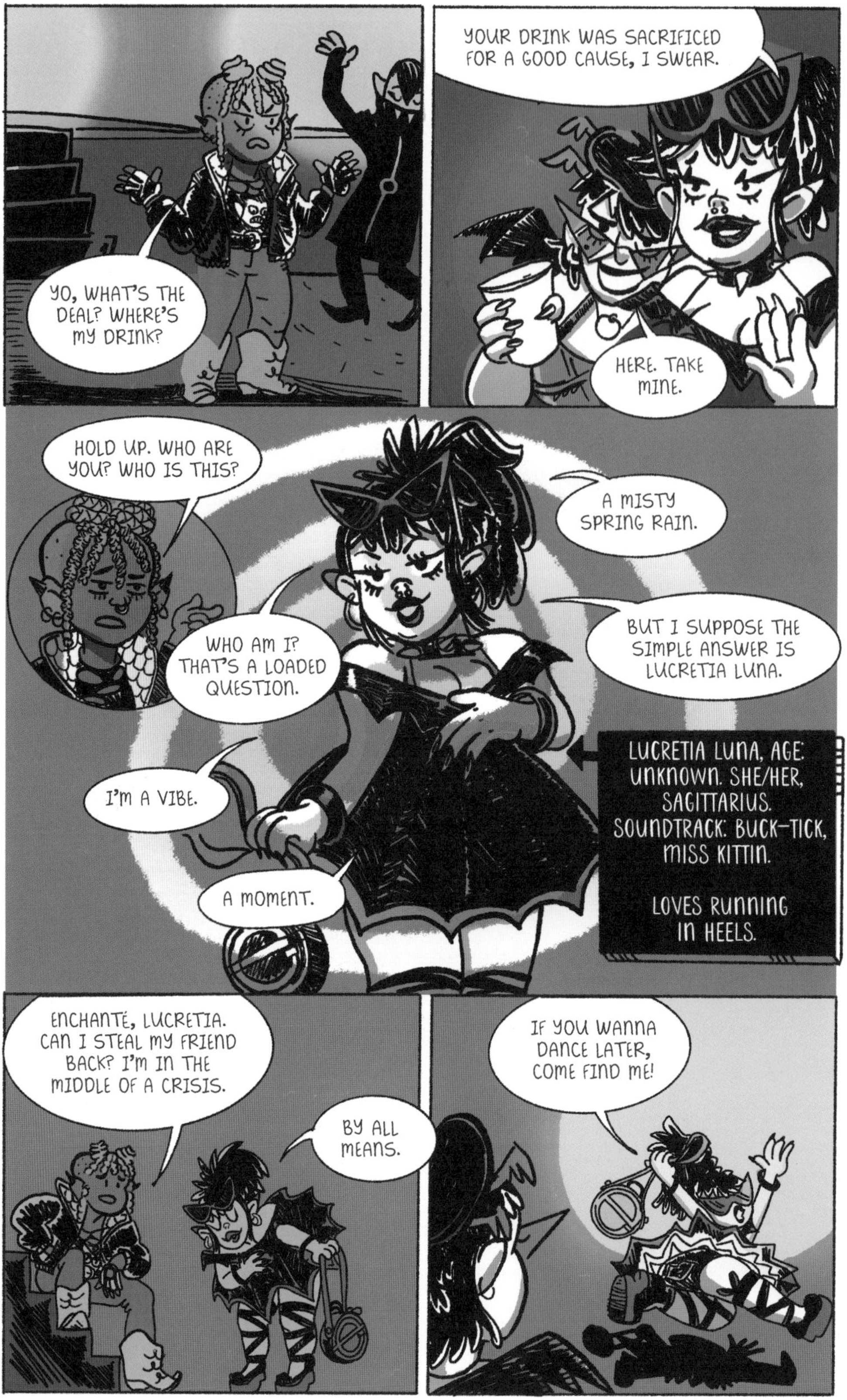
YO, WHAT'S THE DEAL? WHERE'S MY DRINK?
YOUR DRINK WAS SACRIFICED FOR A GOOD CAUSE, I SWEAR.
HERE. TAKE MINE.
HOLD UP. WHO ARE YOU? WHO IS THIS?
A MISTY SPRING RAIN.
WHO AM I? THAT'S A LOADED QUESTION.
BUT I SUPPOSE THE SIMPLE ANSWER IS LUCRETIA LUNA.
I'M A VIBE.
A MOMENT.
LUCRETIA LUNA, AGE: UNKNOWN. SHE/HER, SAGITTARIUS. SOUNDTRACK: BUCK-TICK, MISS KITTIN.
LOVES RUNNING IN HEELS.
ENCHANTÉ, LUCRETIA. CAN I STEAL MY FRIEND BACK? I'M IN THE MIDDLE OF A CRISIS.
BY ALL MEANS.
IF YOU WANNA DANCE LATER, COME FIND ME!

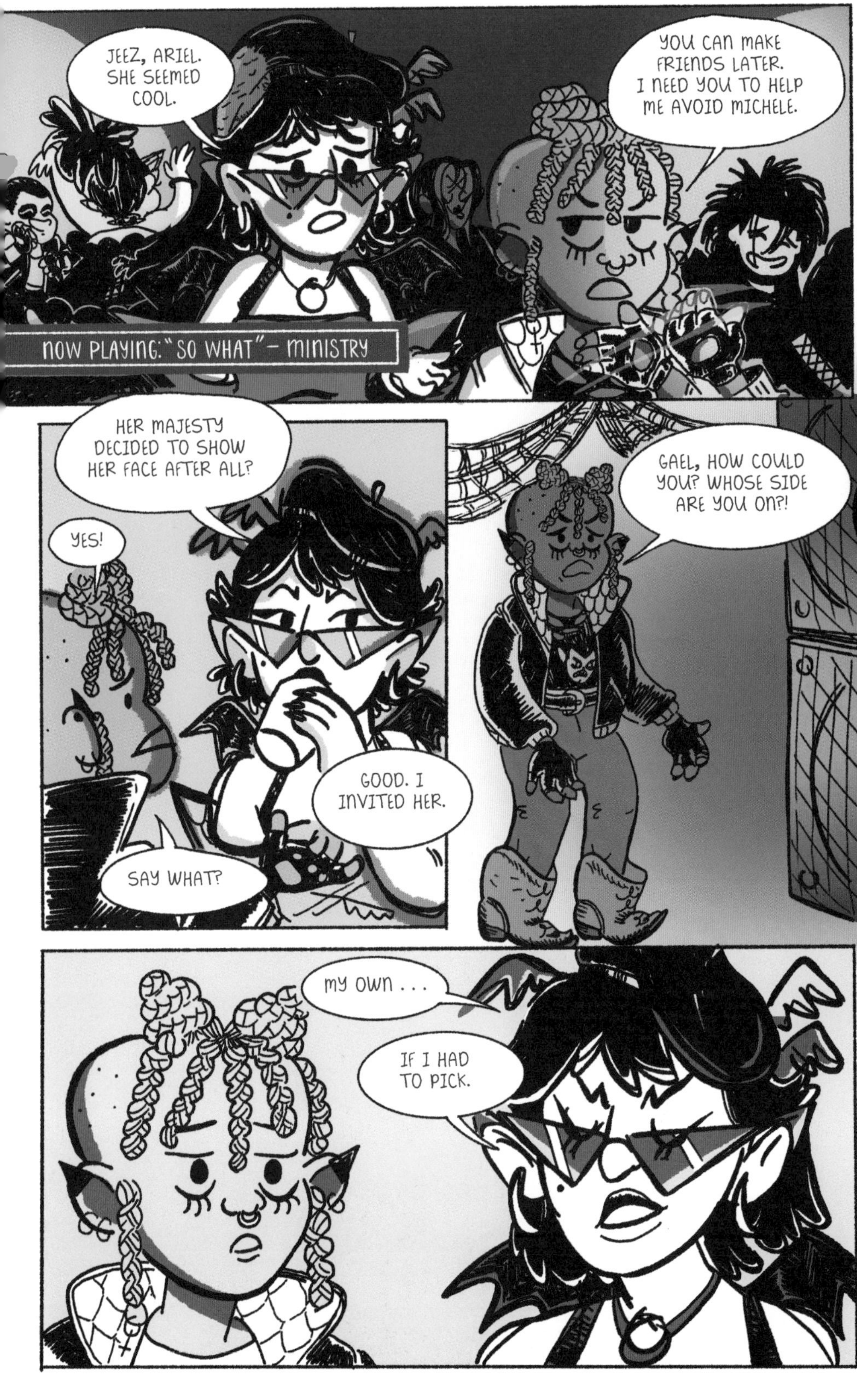
JEEZ, ARIEL. SHE SEEMED COOL.
YOU CAN MAKE FRIENDS LATER. I NEED YOU TO HELP ME AVOID MICHELE.
NOW PLAYING: "SO WHAT" – MINISTRY
HER MAJESTY DECIDED TO SHOW HER FACE AFTER ALL?
YES!
GOOD. I INVITED HER.
SAY WHAT?
GAEL, HOW COULD YOU? WHOSE SIDE ARE YOU ON?!
my own . . .
IF I HAD TO PICK.

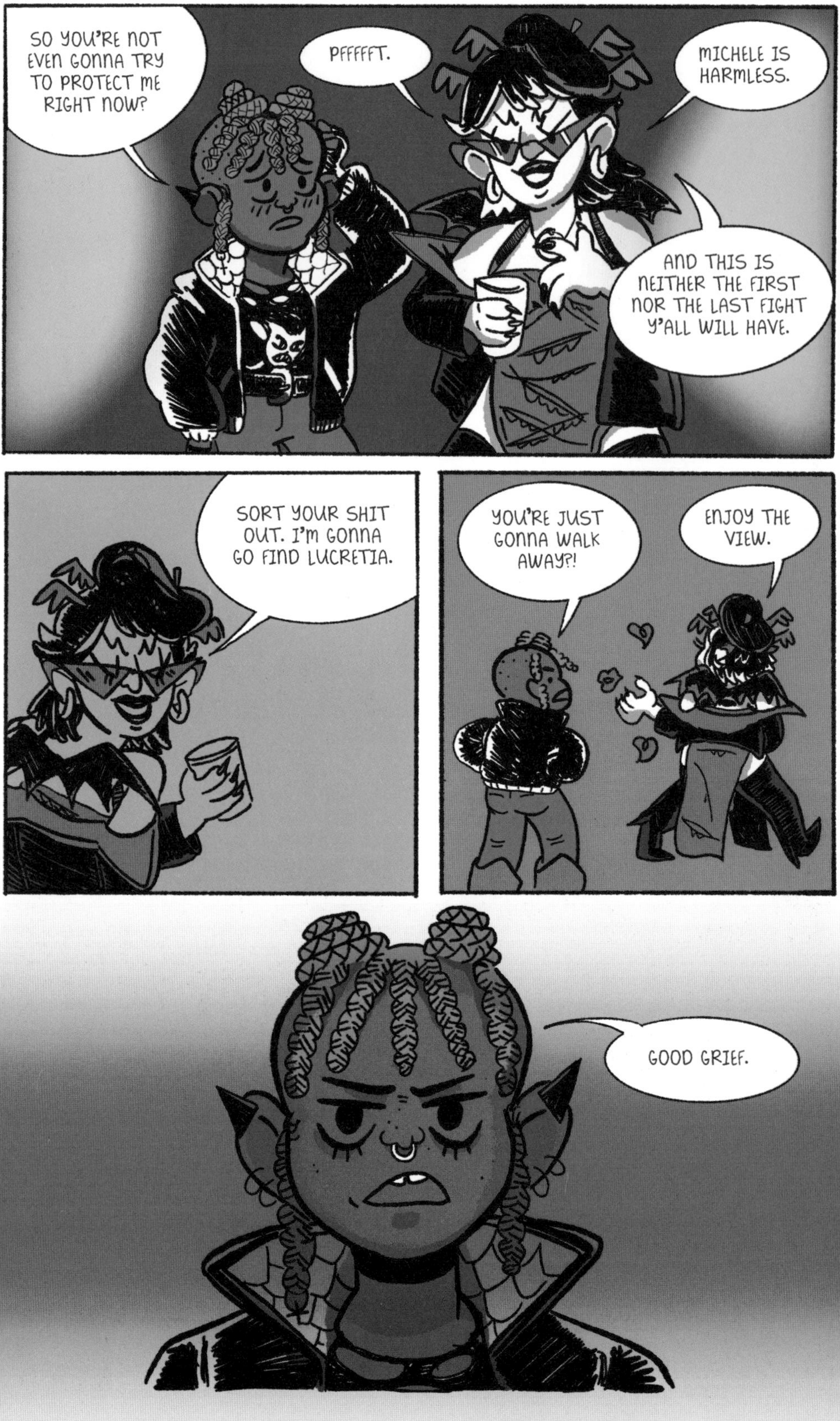
SO YOU'RE NOT EVEN GONNA TRY TO PROTECT ME RIGHT NOW?
PFFFFFT.
MICHELE IS HARMLESS.
AND THIS IS NEITHER THE FIRST NOR THE LAST FIGHT Y'ALL WILL HAVE.
SORT YOUR SHIT OUT. I'M GONNA GO FIND LUCRETIA.
YOU'RE JUST GONNA WALK AWAY?!
ENJOY THE VIEW.
GOOD GRIEF.

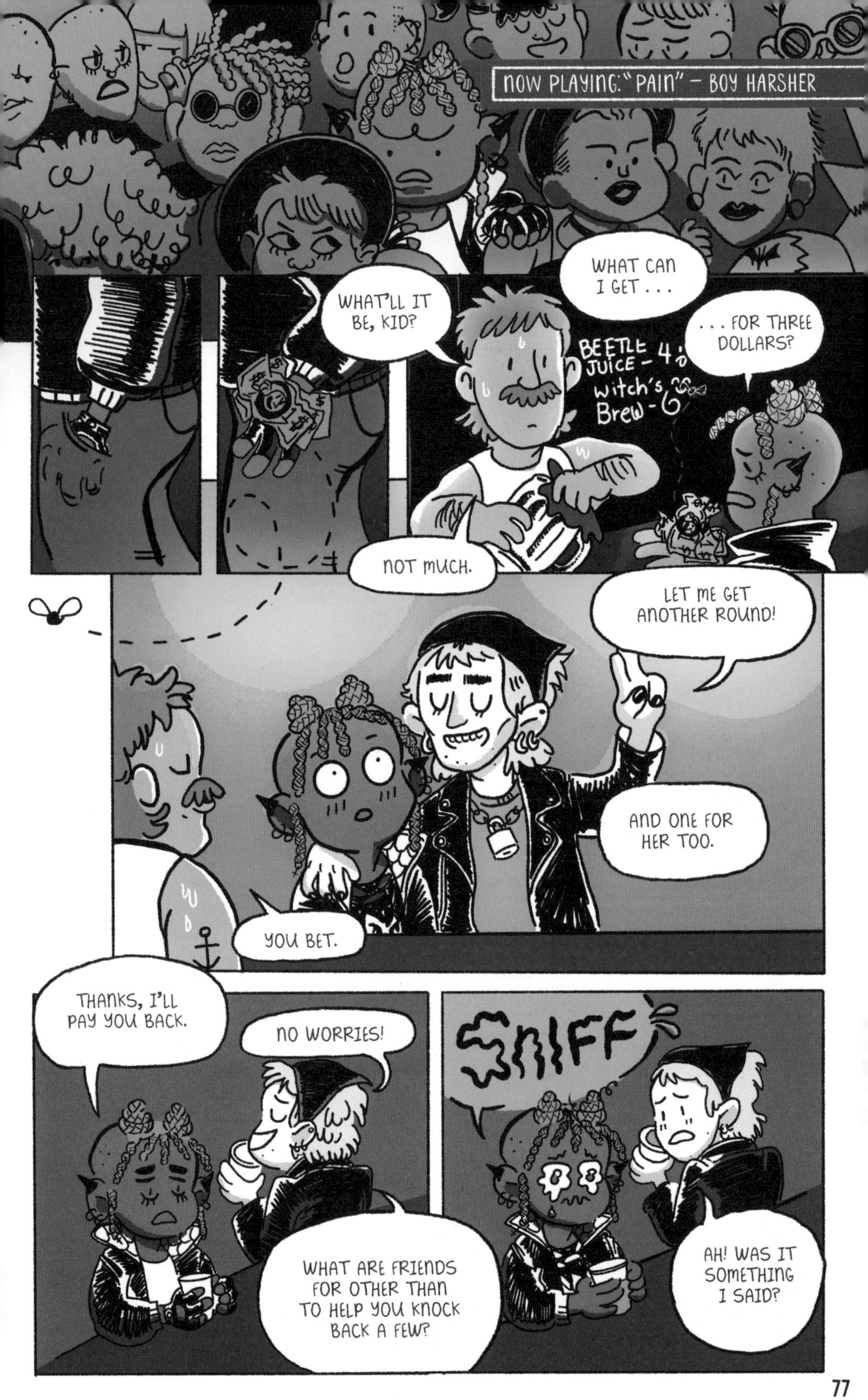

NOW PLAYING: "PAIN" – BOY HARSHER
WHAT'LL IT BE, KID?
WHAT CAN I GET . . .
. . . FOR THREE DOLLARS?
BEETLE JUICE – 4
Witch's Brew – 6
NOT MUCH.
LET ME GET ANOTHER ROUND!
AND ONE FOR HER TOO.
YOU BET.
THANKS, I'LL PAY YOU BACK.
NO WORRIES!
WHAT ARE FRIENDS FOR OTHER THAN TO HELP YOU KNOCK BACK A FEW?
SNIFF
AH! WAS IT SOMETHING I SAID?

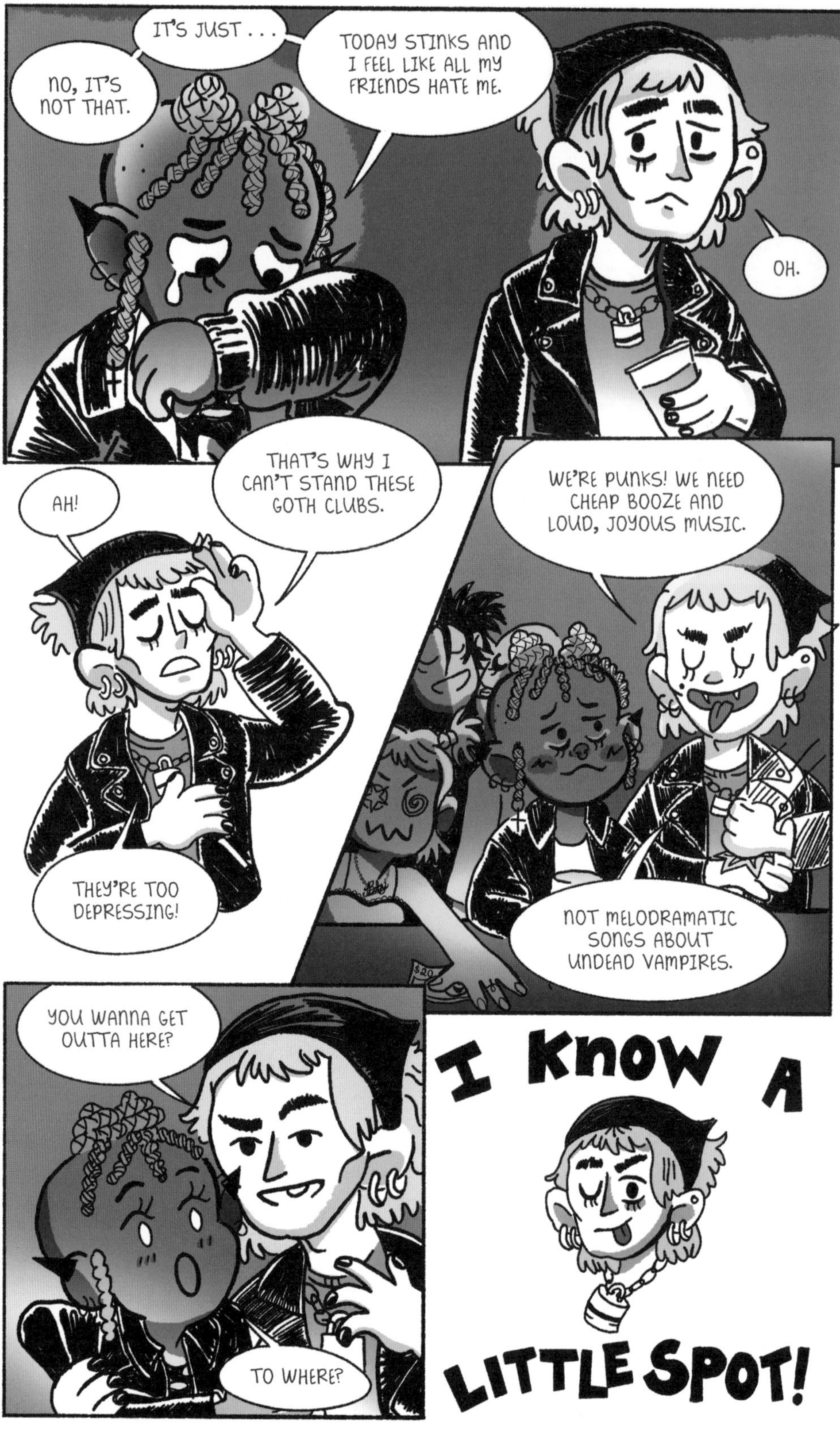
NO, IT'S NOT THAT.
IT'S JUST . . .
TODAY STINKS AND I FEEL LIKE ALL MY FRIENDS HATE ME.
OH.
AH!
THAT'S WHY I CAN'T STAND THESE GOTH CLUBS.
THEY'RE TOO DEPRESSING!
WE'RE PUNKS! WE NEED CHEAP BOOZE AND LOUD, JOYOUS MUSIC.
NOT MELODRAMATIC SONGS ABOUT UNDEAD VAMPIRES.
YOU WANNA GET OUTTA HERE?
TO WHERE?
I KNOW A
LITTLE SPOT!

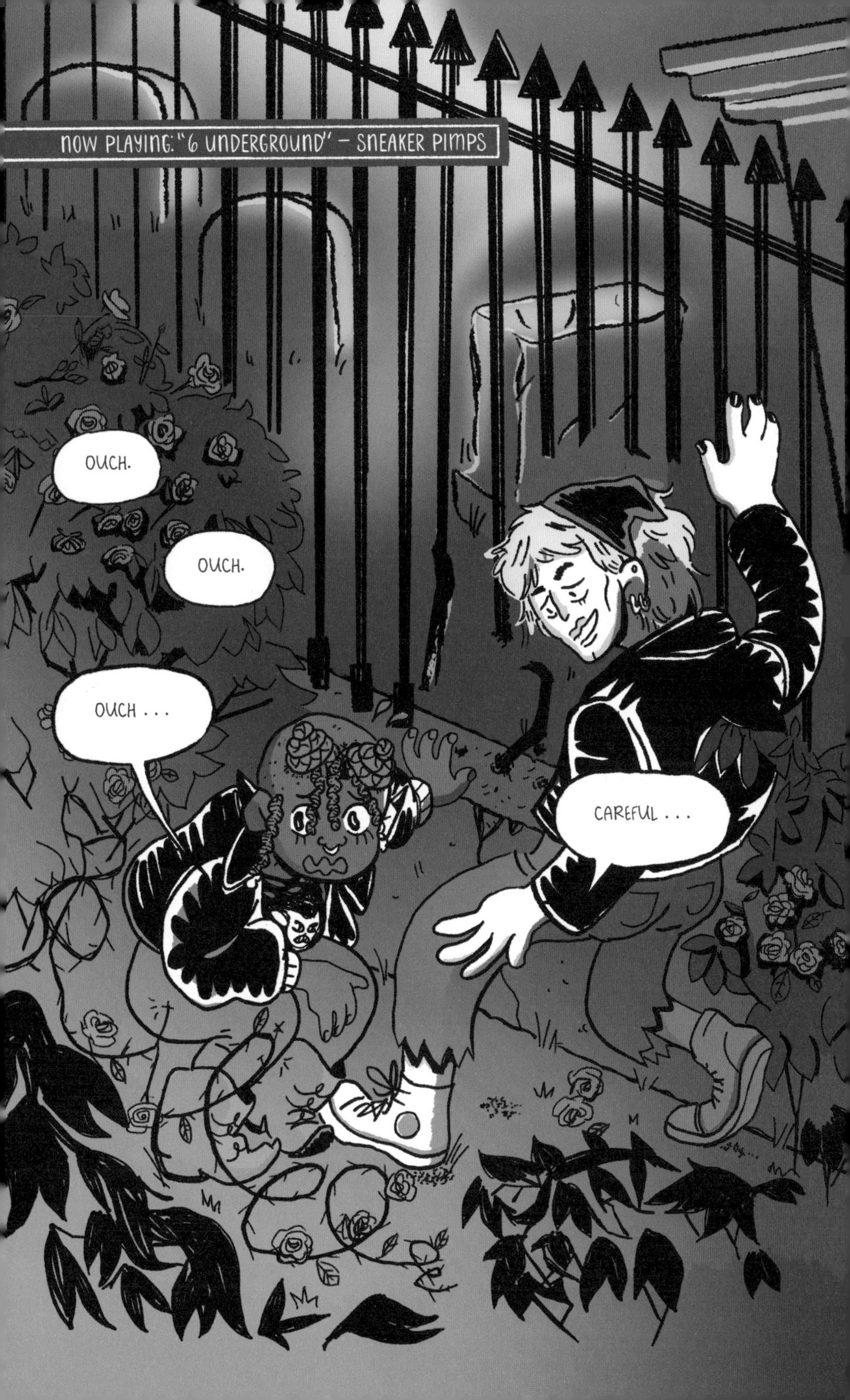
NOW PLAYING: "6 UNDERGROUND" – SNEAKER PIMPS
OUCH.
OUCH.
OUCH . . .
CAREFUL . . .

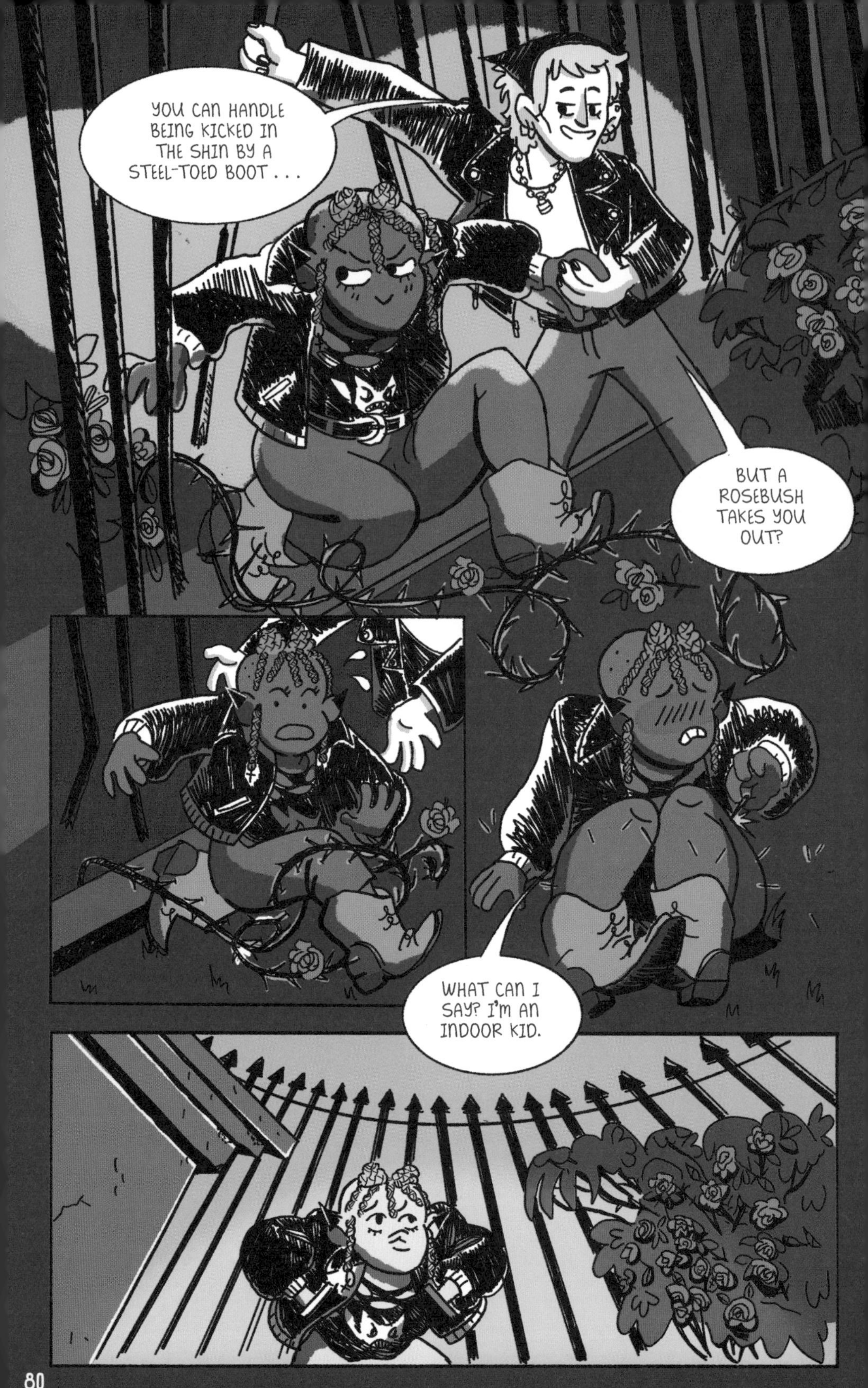
YOU CAN HANDLE BEING KICKED IN THE SHIN BY A STEEL-TOED BOOT . . .
BUT A ROSEBUSH TAKES YOU OUT?
WHAT CAN I SAY? I'M AN INDOOR KID.

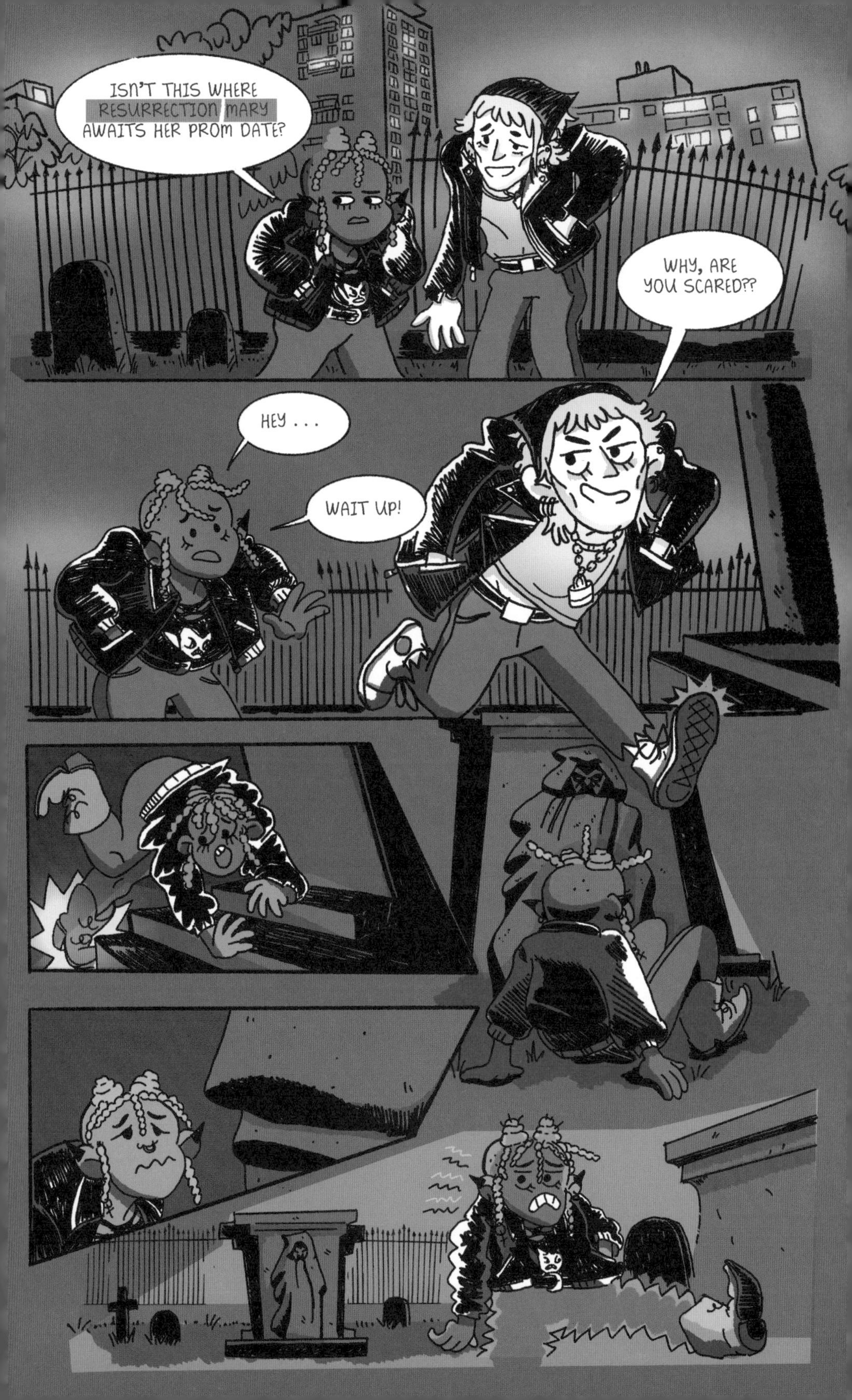
ISN'T THIS WHERE RESURRECTION MARY AWAITS HER PROM DATE?
WHY, ARE YOU SCARED??
HEY . . .
WAIT UP!

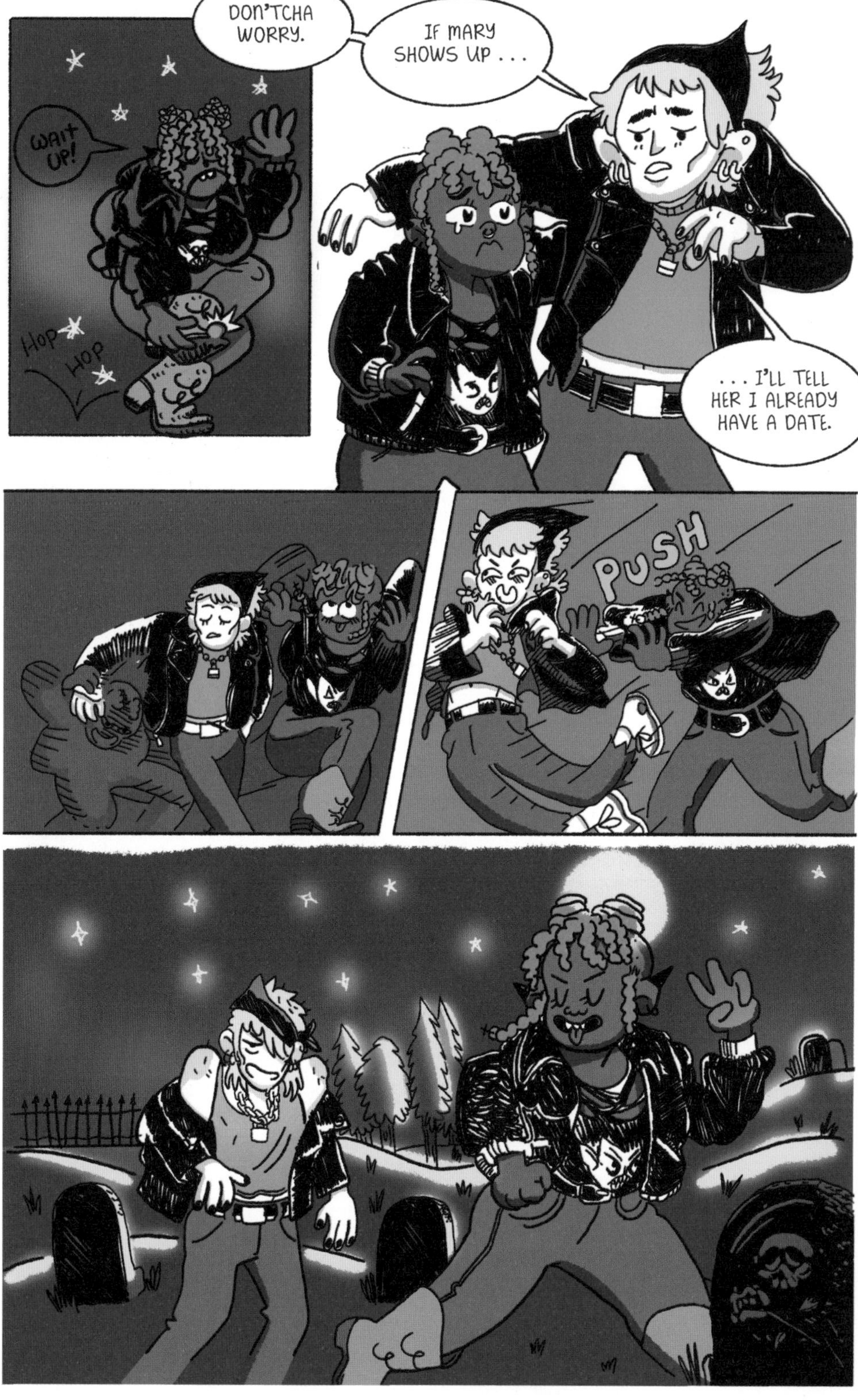
WAIT UP!
HOP HOP
DON'TCHA WORRY.
IF MARY SHOWS UP . . .
. . . I'LL TELL HER I ALREADY HAVE A DATE.
PUSH

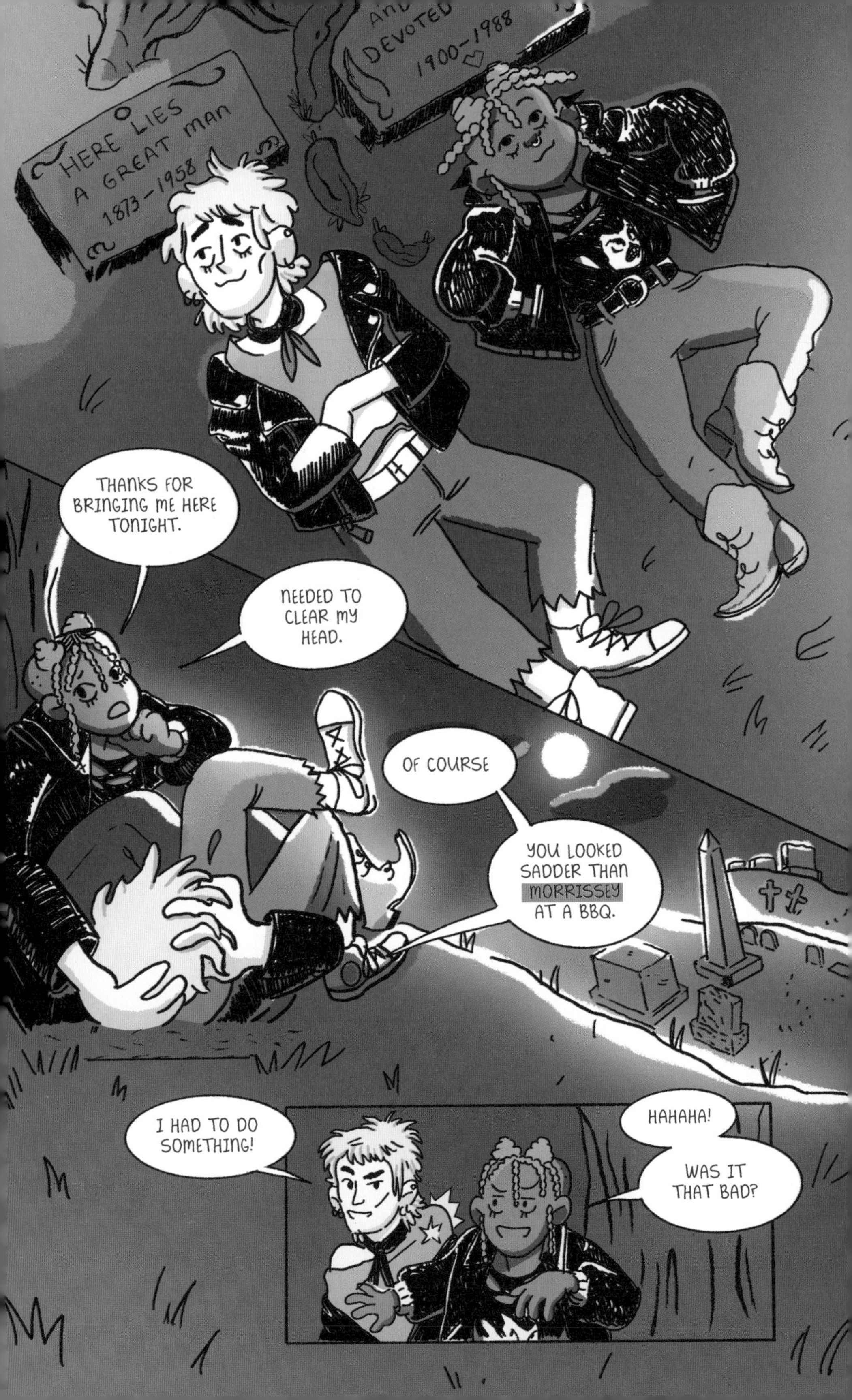
DEVOTED 1900–1988
HERE LIES A GREAT man 1873–1958
THANKS FOR BRINGING ME HERE TONIGHT.
NEEDED TO CLEAR MY HEAD.
OF COURSE
YOU LOOKED SADDER THAN MORRISSEY AT A BBQ.
I HAD TO DO SOMETHING!
HAHAHA!
WAS IT THAT BAD?

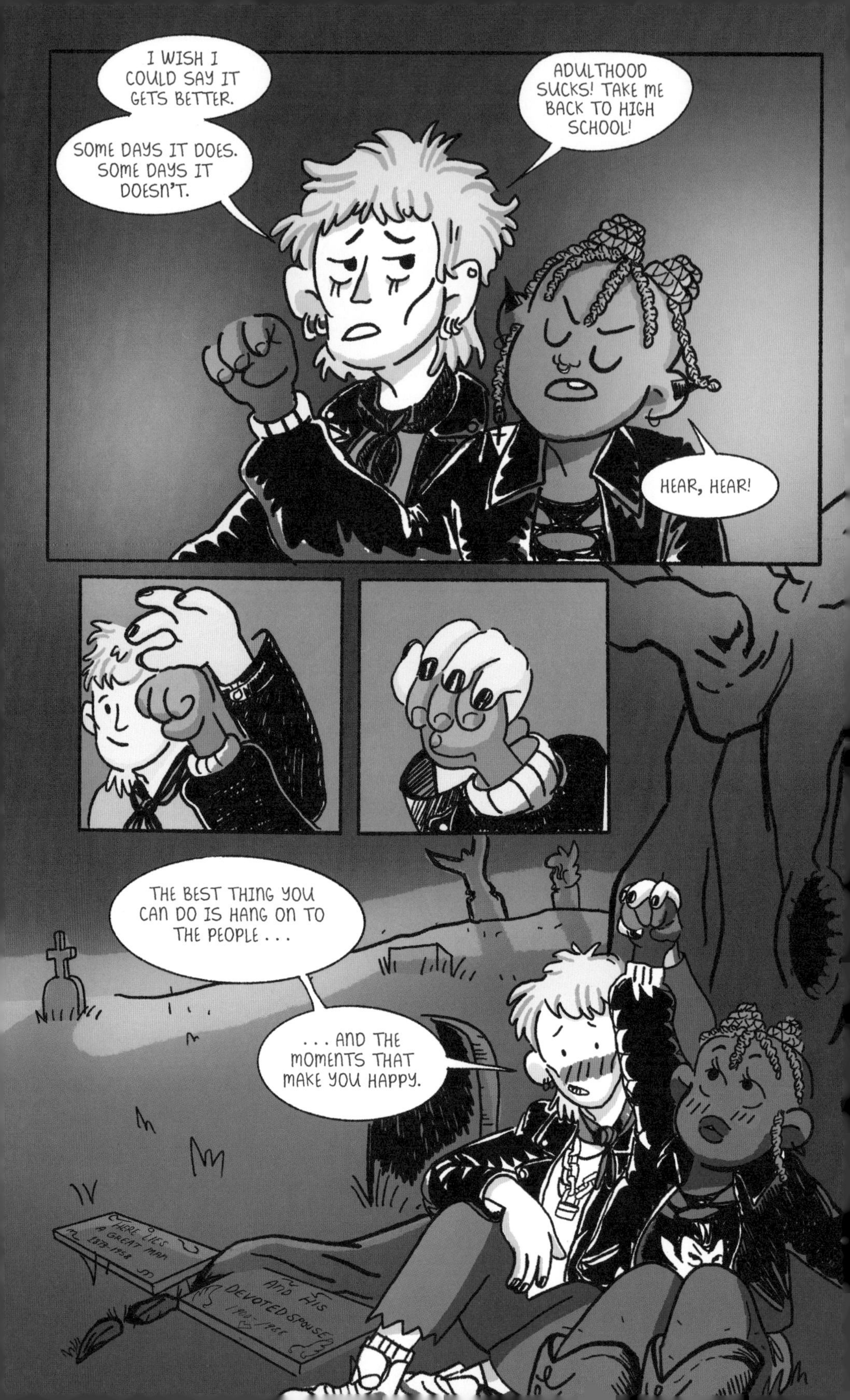
I WISH I COULD SAY IT GETS BETTER.
SOME DAYS IT DOES. SOME DAYS IT DOESN'T.
ADULTHOOD SUCKS! TAKE ME BACK TO HIGH SCHOOL!
HEAR, HEAR!
THE BEST THING YOU CAN DO IS HANG ON TO THE PEOPLE . . .
. . . AND THE MOMENTS THAT MAKE YOU HAPPY.
HERE LIES A GREAT MAN
AND HIS DEVOTED SPOUSE

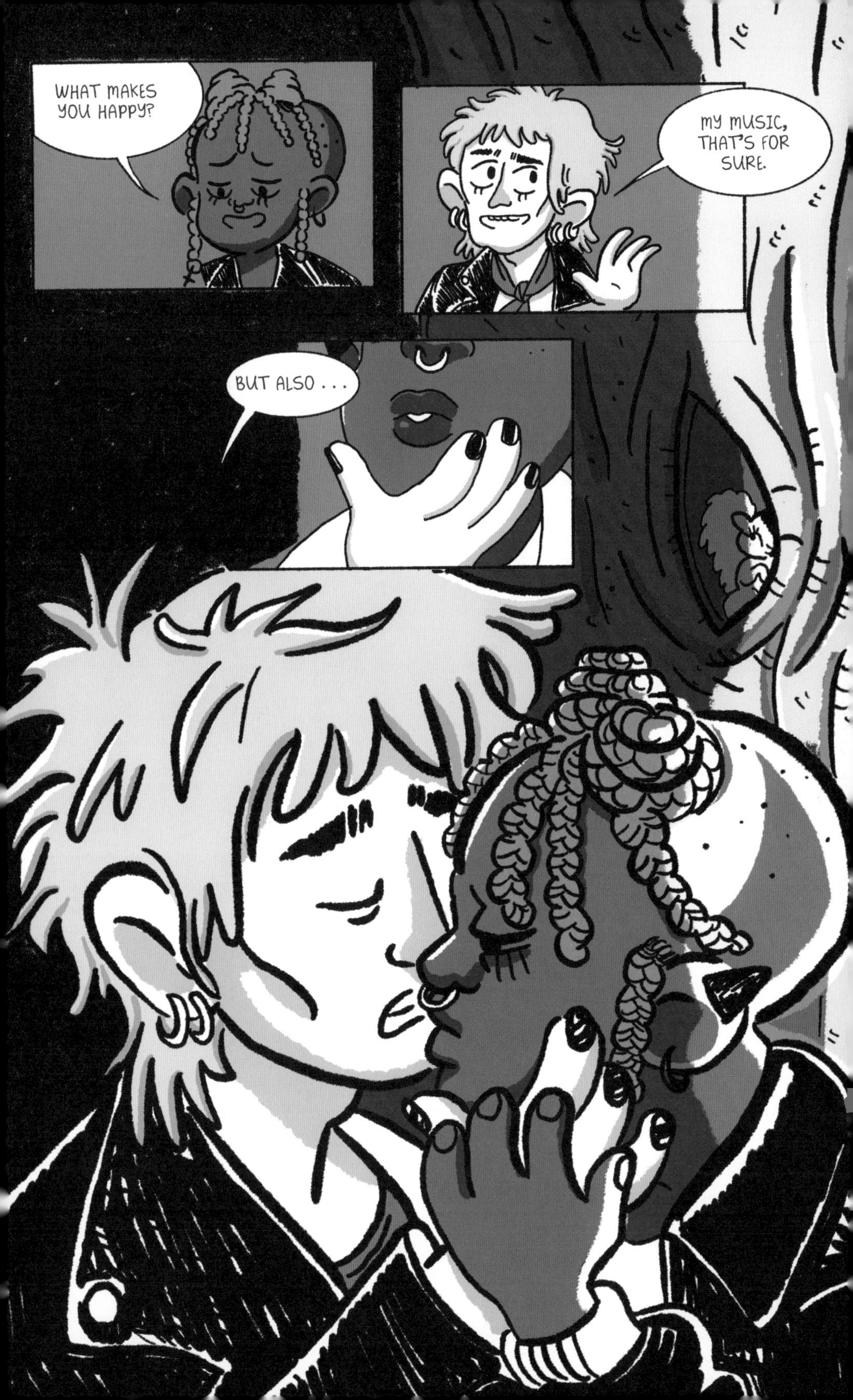
WHAT MAKES YOU HAPPY?
MY MUSIC, THAT'S FOR SURE.
BUT ALSO . . .

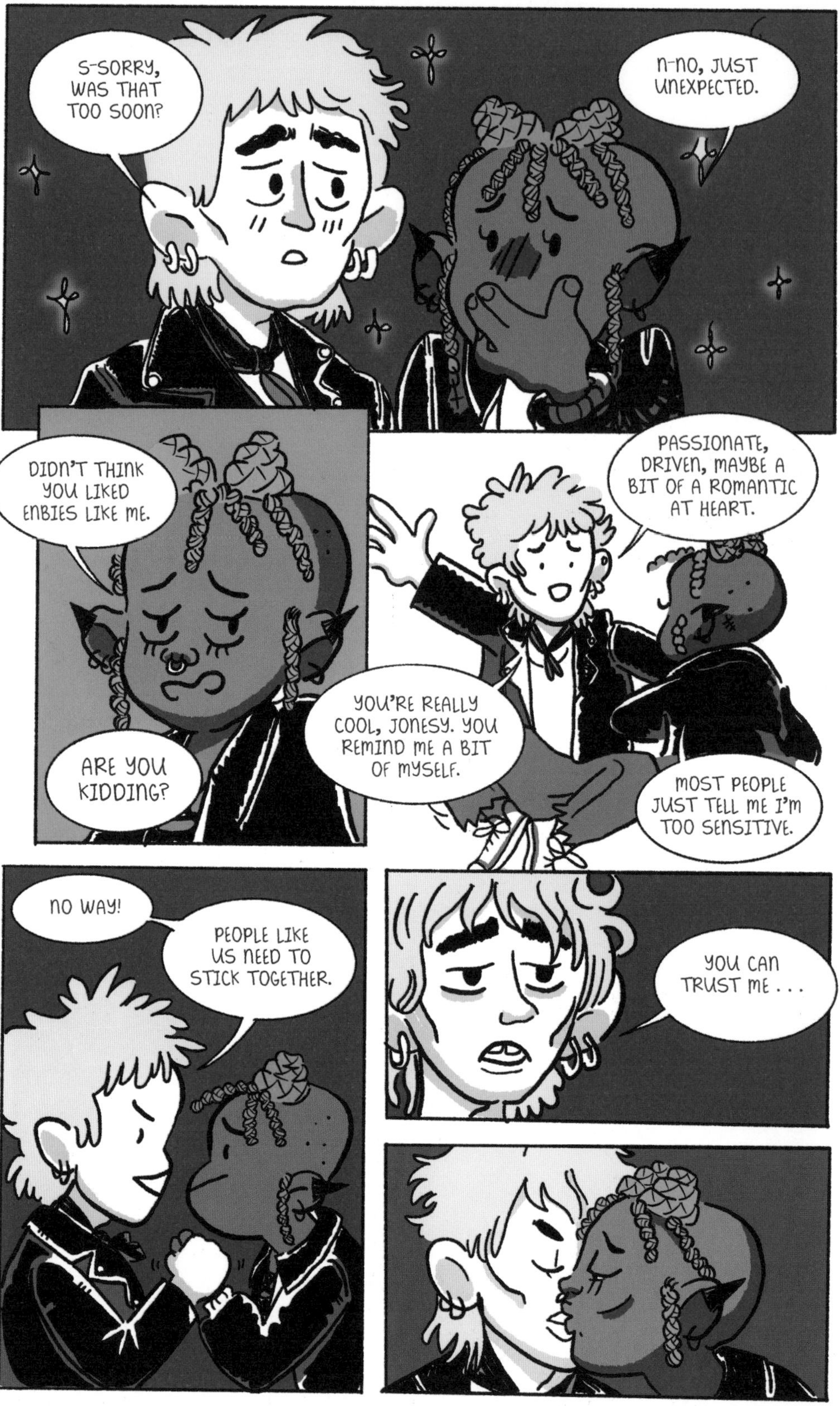
S-SORRY, WAS THAT TOO SOON?
N-NO, JUST UNEXPECTED.
DIDN'T THINK YOU LIKED ENBIES LIKE ME.
PASSIONATE, DRIVEN, MAYBE A BIT OF A ROMANTIC AT HEART.
ARE YOU KIDDING?
YOU'RE REALLY COOL, JONESY. YOU REMIND ME A BIT OF MYSELF.
MOST PEOPLE JUST TELL ME I'M TOO SENSITIVE.
NO WAY!
PEOPLE LIKE US NEED TO STICK TOGETHER.
YOU CAN TRUST ME . . .

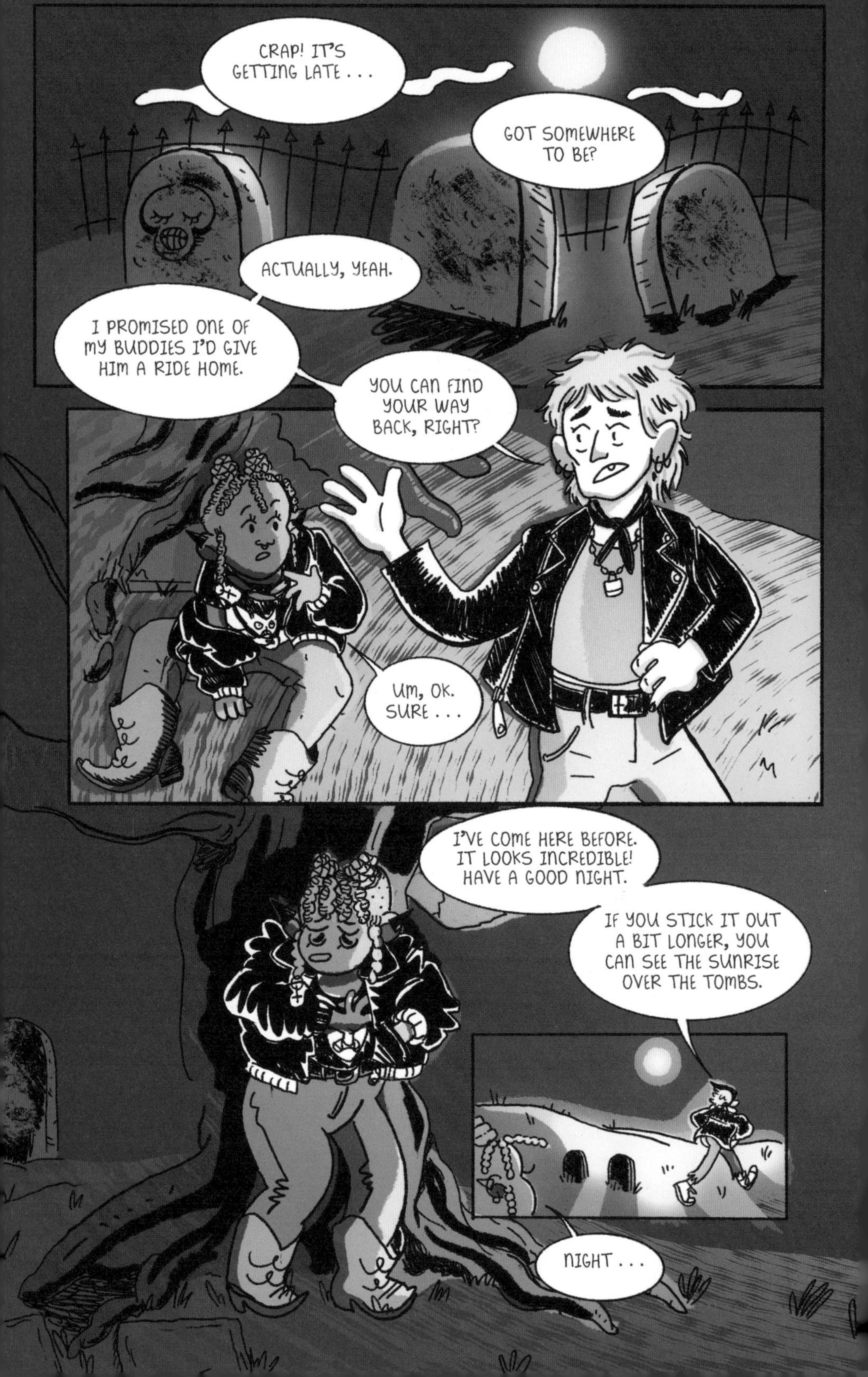
CRAP! IT'S GETTING LATE . . .
GOT SOMEWHERE TO BE?
ACTUALLY, YEAH.
I PROMISED ONE OF MY BUDDIES I'D GIVE HIM A RIDE HOME.
YOU CAN FIND YOUR WAY BACK, RIGHT?
UM, OK. SURE . . .
I'VE COME HERE BEFORE. IT LOOKS INCREDIBLE! HAVE A GOOD NIGHT.
IF YOU STICK IT OUT A BIT LONGER, YOU CAN SEE THE SUNRISE OVER THE TOMBS.
NIGHT . . .

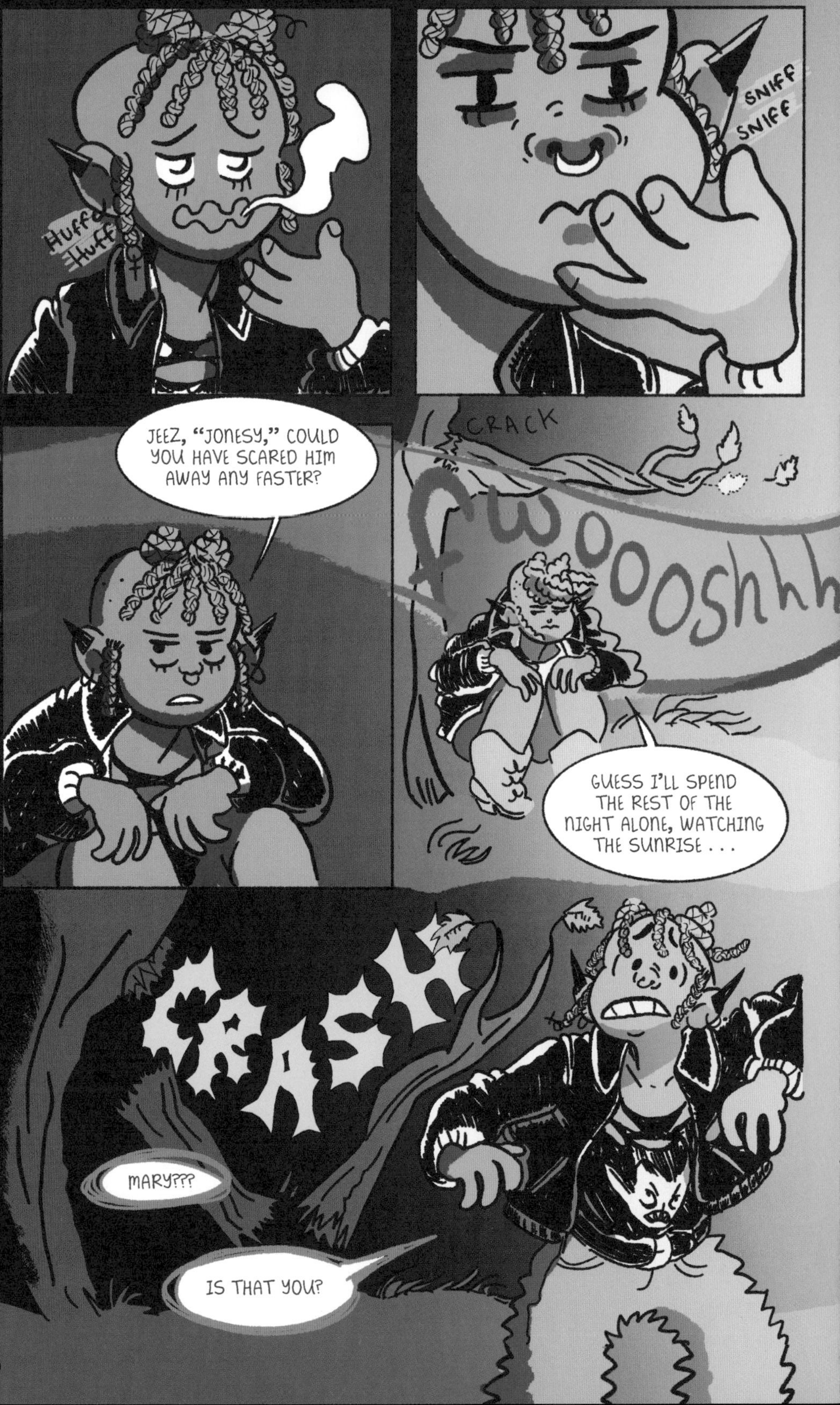
HUFF
HUFF
SNIFF
SNIFF
JEEZ, "JONESY," COULD YOU HAVE SCARED HIM AWAY ANY FASTER?
CRACK
FWOOOSHHH
GUESS I'LL SPEND THE REST OF THE NIGHT ALONE, WATCHING THE SUNRISE . . .
CRASH
MARY???
IS THAT YOU?

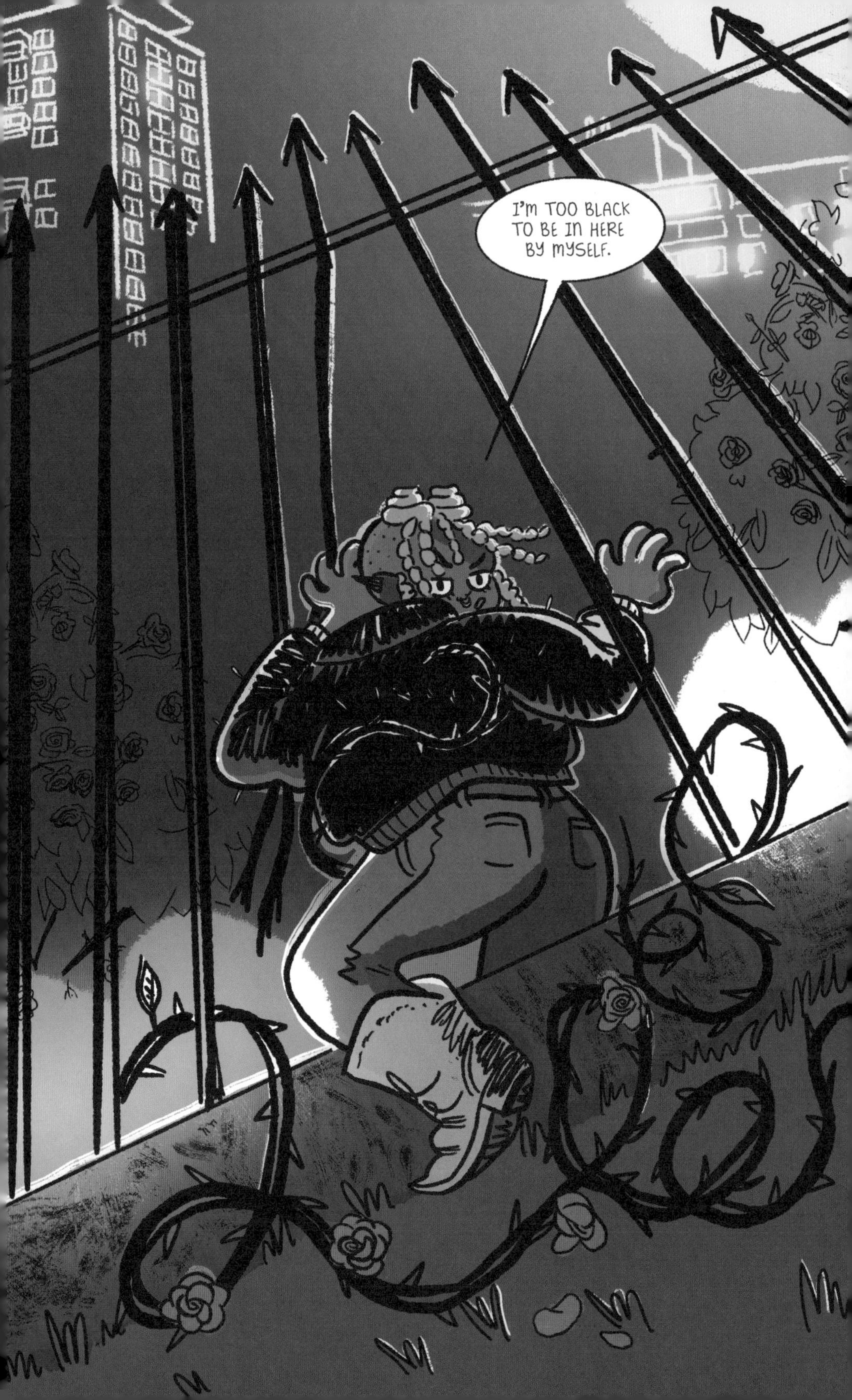
I'M TOO BLACK TO BE IN HERE BY MYSELF.

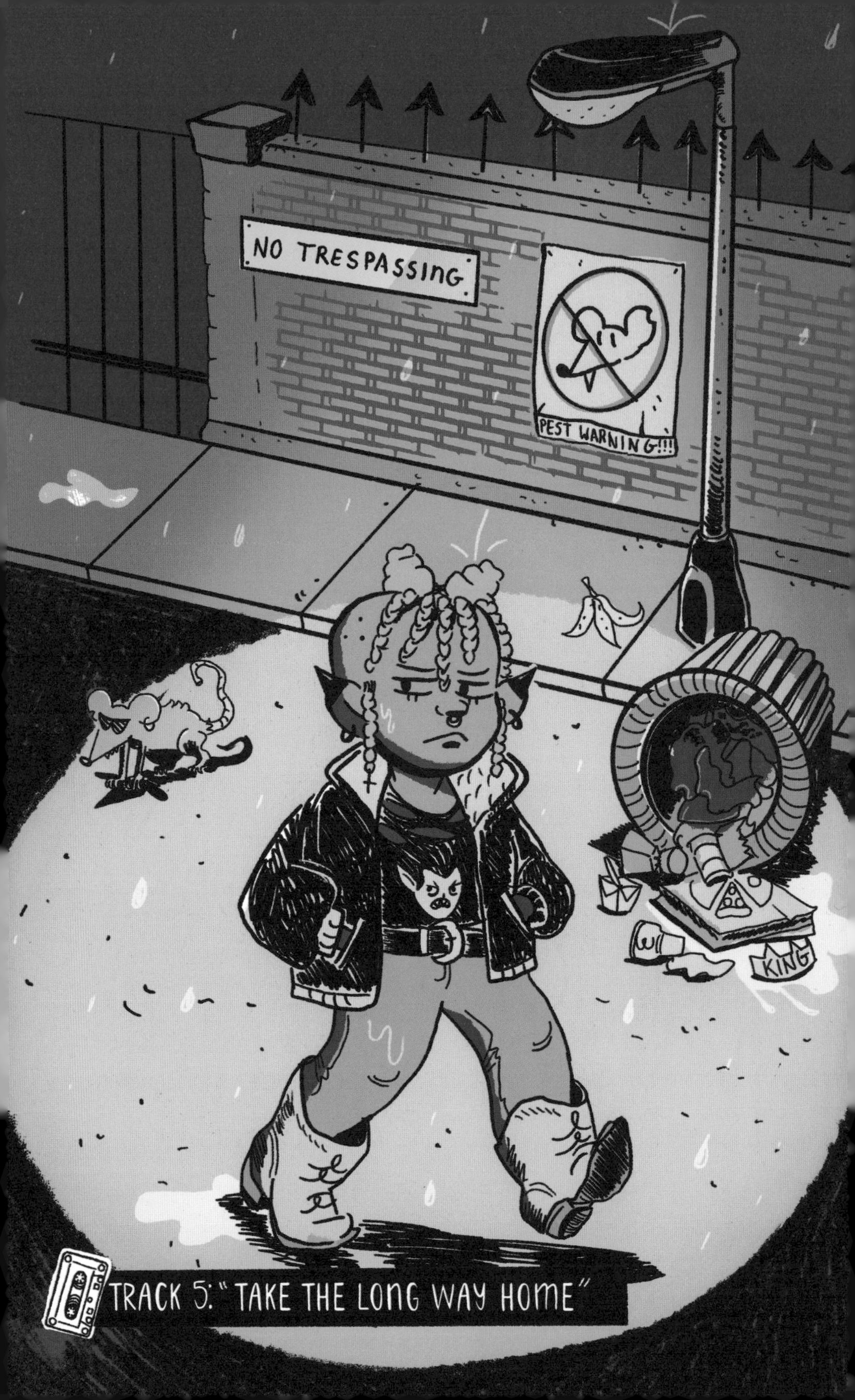
NO TRESPASSING
PEST WARNING!!!
KING
TRACK 5: "TAKE THE LONG WAY HOME"

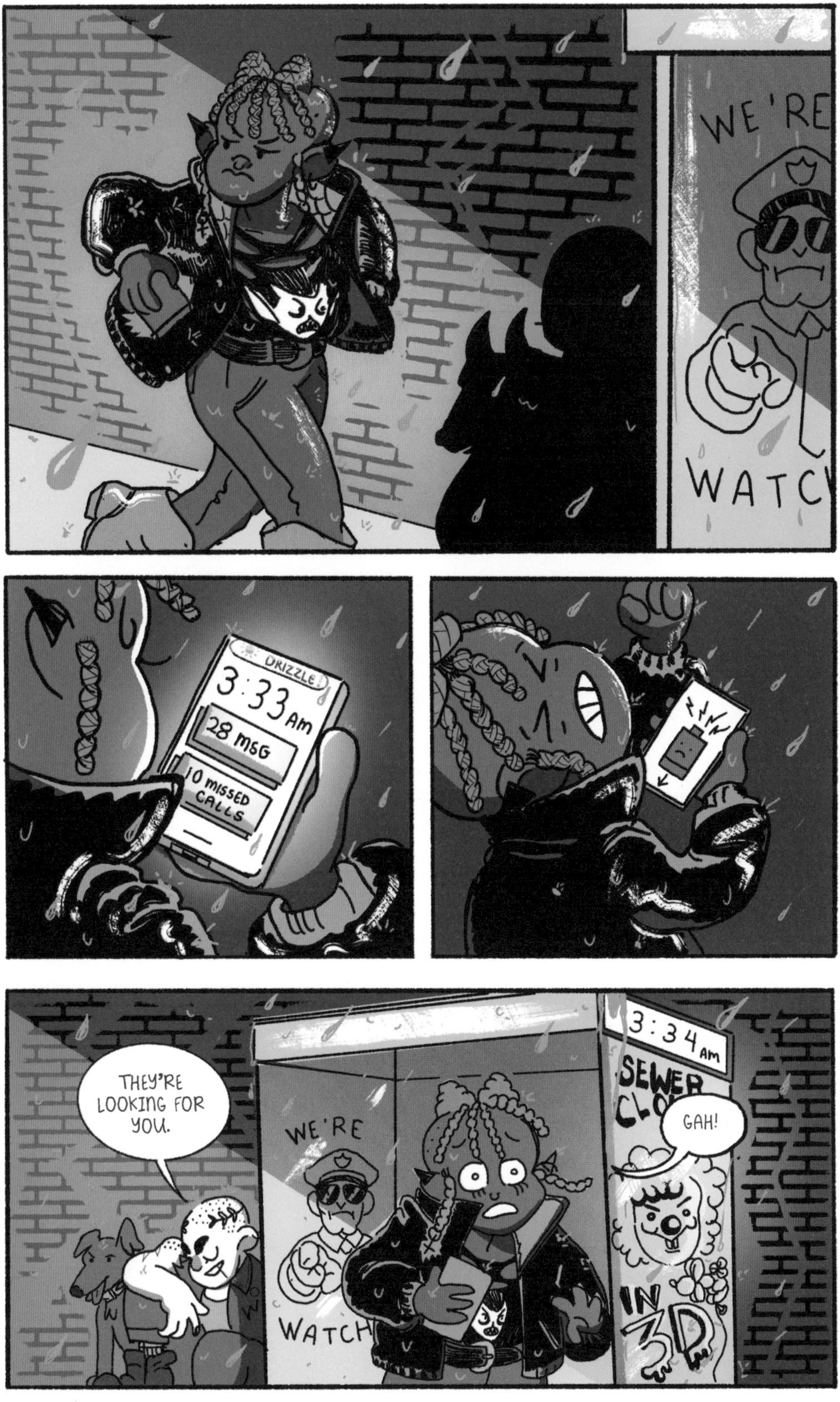
WE'RE
WATC
DRIZZLE
3:33 AM
28 MSG
10 MISSED CALLS
THEY'RE LOOKING FOR YOU.
WE'RE
WATCH
3:34 AM
SEWER CLO
GAH!
IN 3D

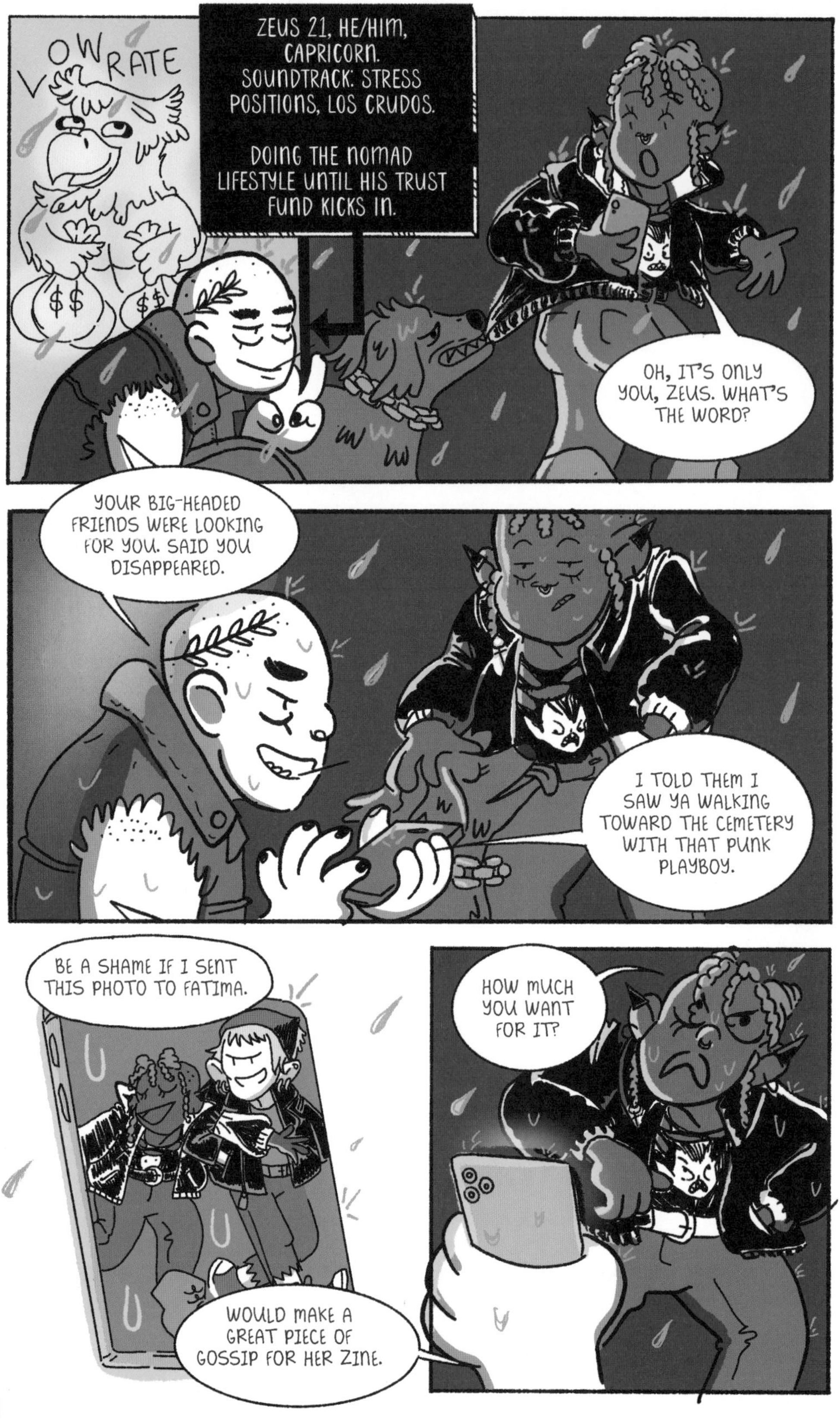
LOW RATE
$$
ZEUS 21, HE/HIM, CAPRICORN. SOUNDTRACK: STRESS POSITIONS, LOS CRUDOS.
DOING THE NOMAD LIFESTYLE UNTIL HIS TRUST FUND KICKS IN.
OH, IT'S ONLY YOU, ZEUS. WHAT'S THE WORD?
YOUR BIG-HEADED FRIENDS WERE LOOKING FOR YOU. SAID YOU DISAPPEARED.
I TOLD THEM I SAW YA WALKING TOWARD THE CEMETERY WITH THAT PUNK PLAYBOY.
BE A SHAME IF I SENT THIS PHOTO TO FATIMA.
HOW MUCH YOU WANT FOR IT?
WOULD MAKE A GREAT PIECE OF GOSSIP FOR HER ZINE.

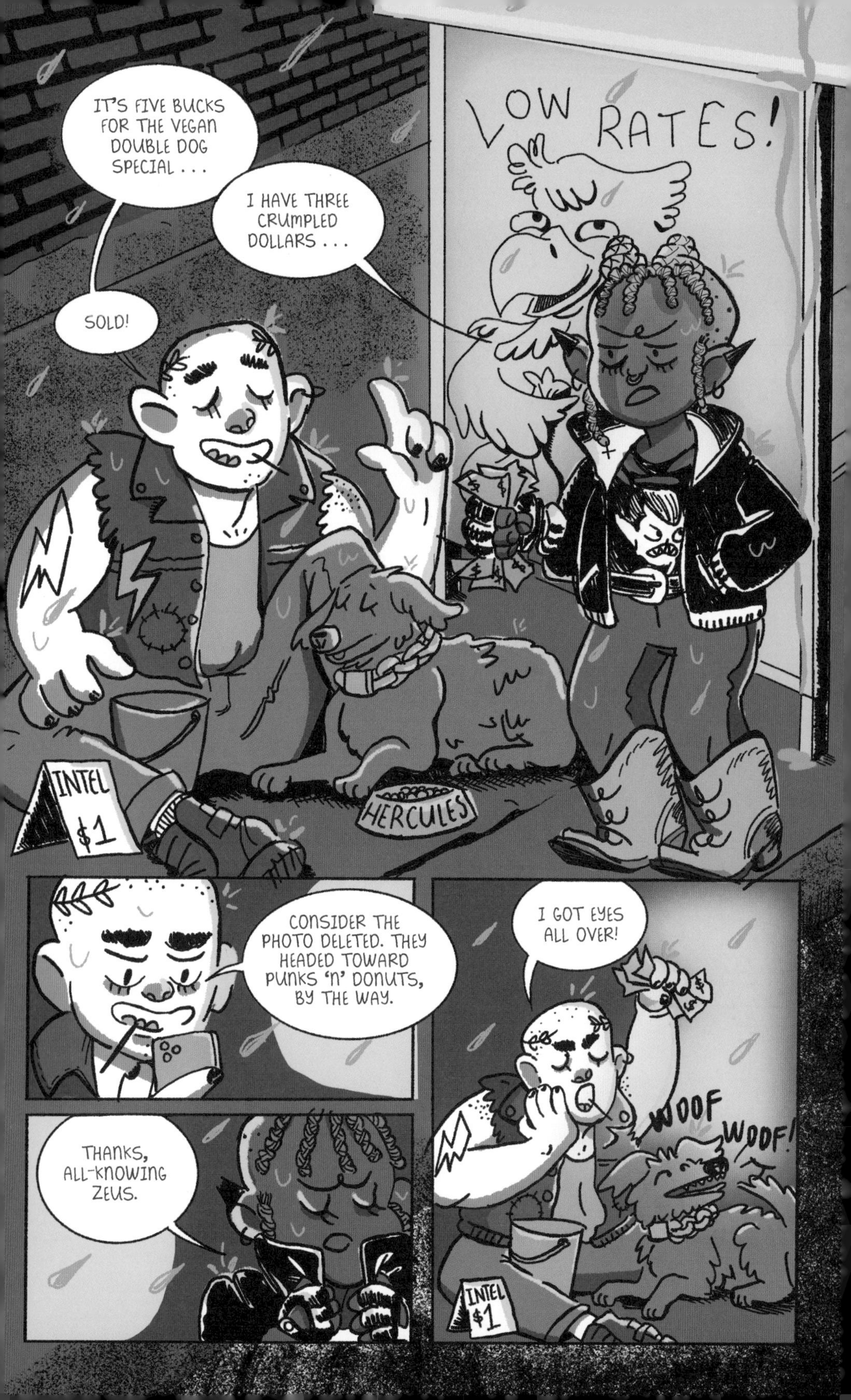
LOW RATES!
IT'S FIVE BUCKS FOR THE VEGAN DOUBLE DOG SPECIAL . . .
I HAVE THREE CRUMPLED DOLLARS . . .
SOLD!
INTEL $1
HERCULES
CONSIDER THE PHOTO DELETED. THEY HEADED TOWARD PUNKS 'N' DONUTS, BY THE WAY.
I GOT EYES ALL OVER!
WOOF
WOOF!
THANKS, ALL-KNOWING ZEUS.
INTEL $1

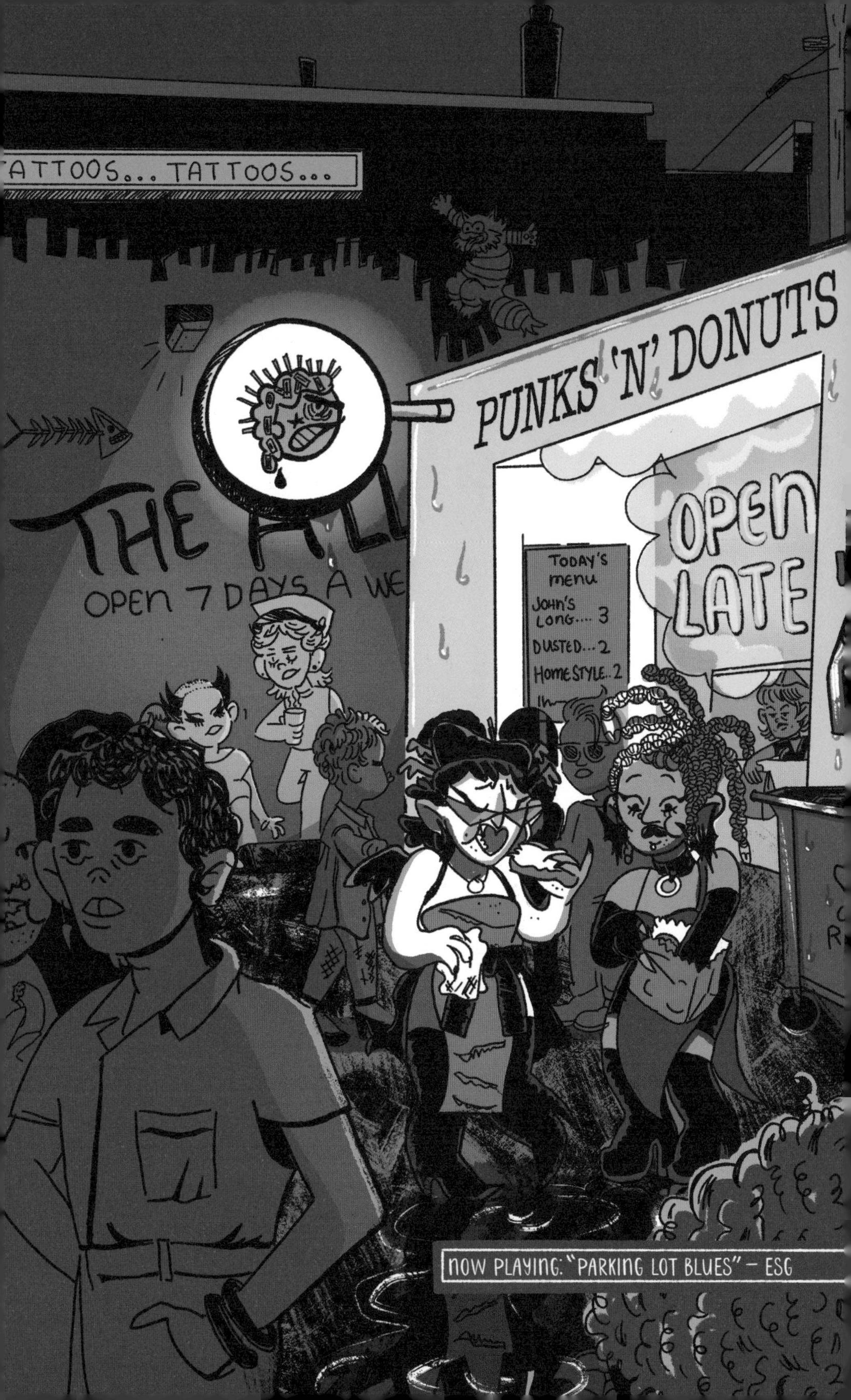
TATTOOS... TATTOOS...
PUNKS 'N' DONUTS
OPEN LATE
TODAY'S menu
JOHN'S LONG.... 3
DUSTED... 2
HOMESTYLE.. 2
THE
OPEN 7 DAYS A WE
NOW PLAYING: "PARKING LOT BLUES" – ESG

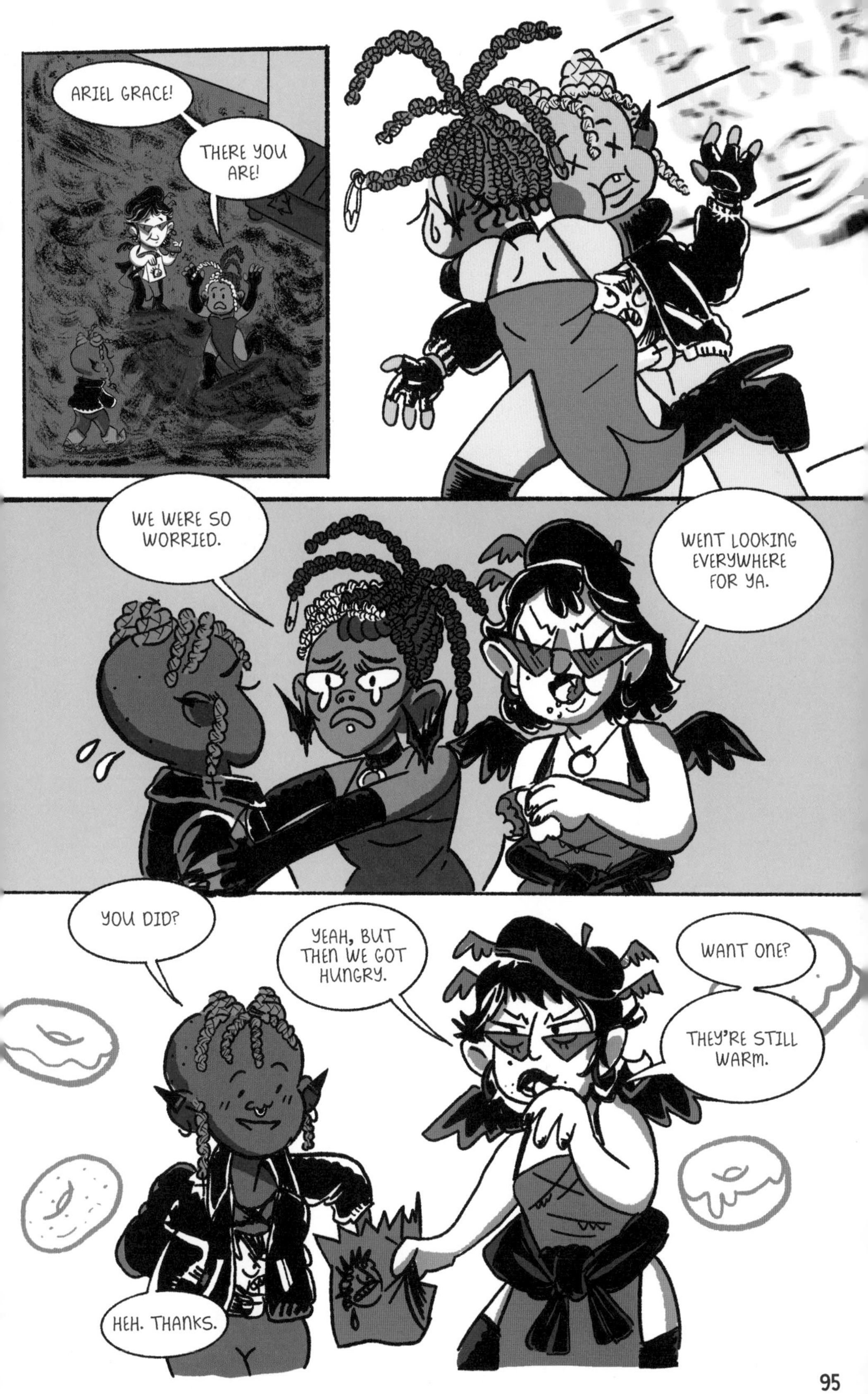
ARIEL GRACE!
THERE YOU ARE!
WE WERE SO WORRIED.
WENT LOOKING EVERYWHERE FOR YA.
YOU DID?
YEAH, BUT THEN WE GOT HUNGRY.
WANT ONE?
THEY'RE STILL WARM.
HEH. THANKS.

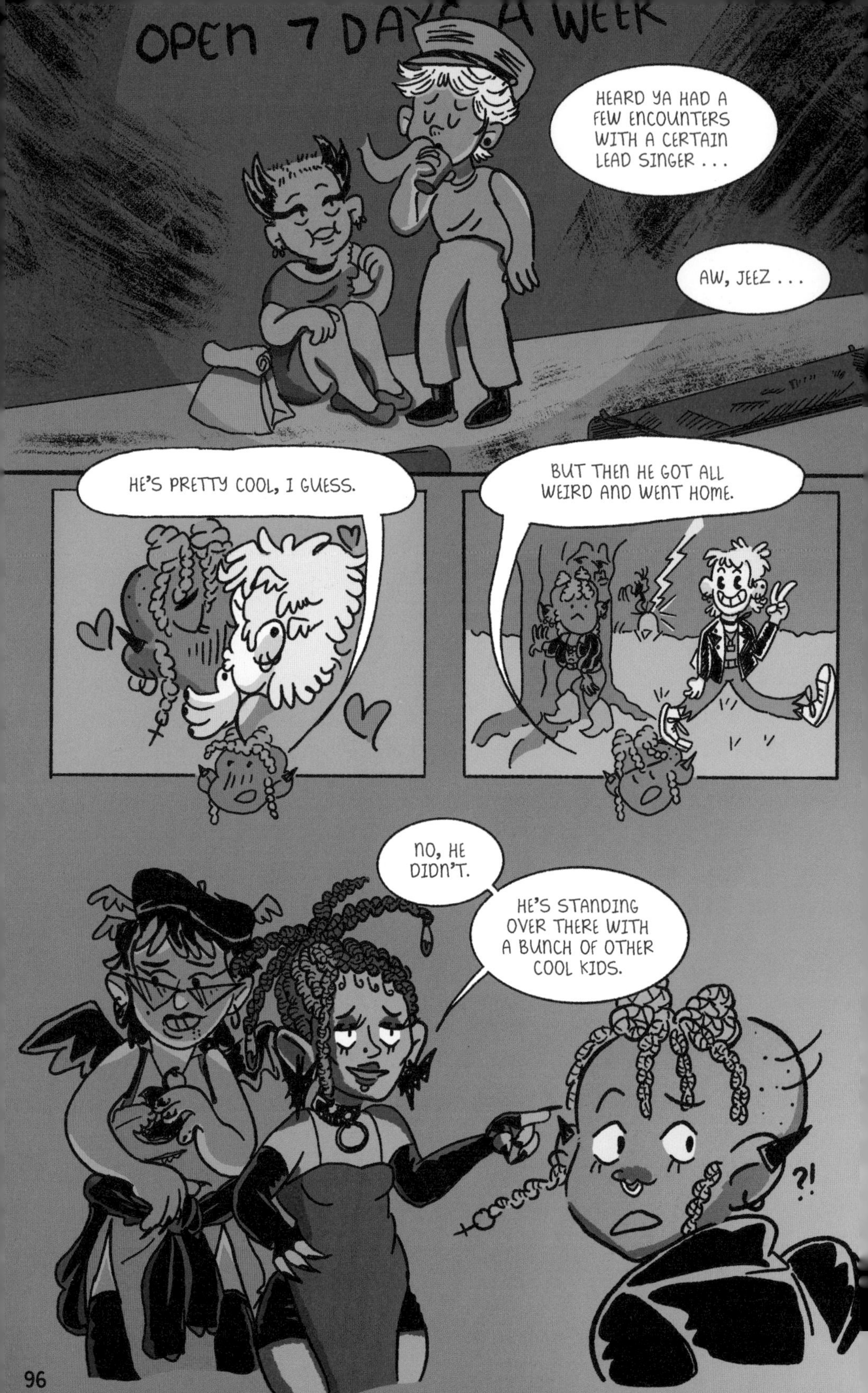
OPEN 7 DAYS A WEEK
HEARD YA HAD A FEW ENCOUNTERS WITH A CERTAIN LEAD SINGER . . .
AW, JEEZ . . .
HE'S PRETTY COOL, I GUESS.
BUT THEN HE GOT ALL WEIRD AND WENT HOME.
NO, HE DIDN'T.
HE'S STANDING OVER THERE WITH A BUNCH OF OTHER COOL KIDS.
?!

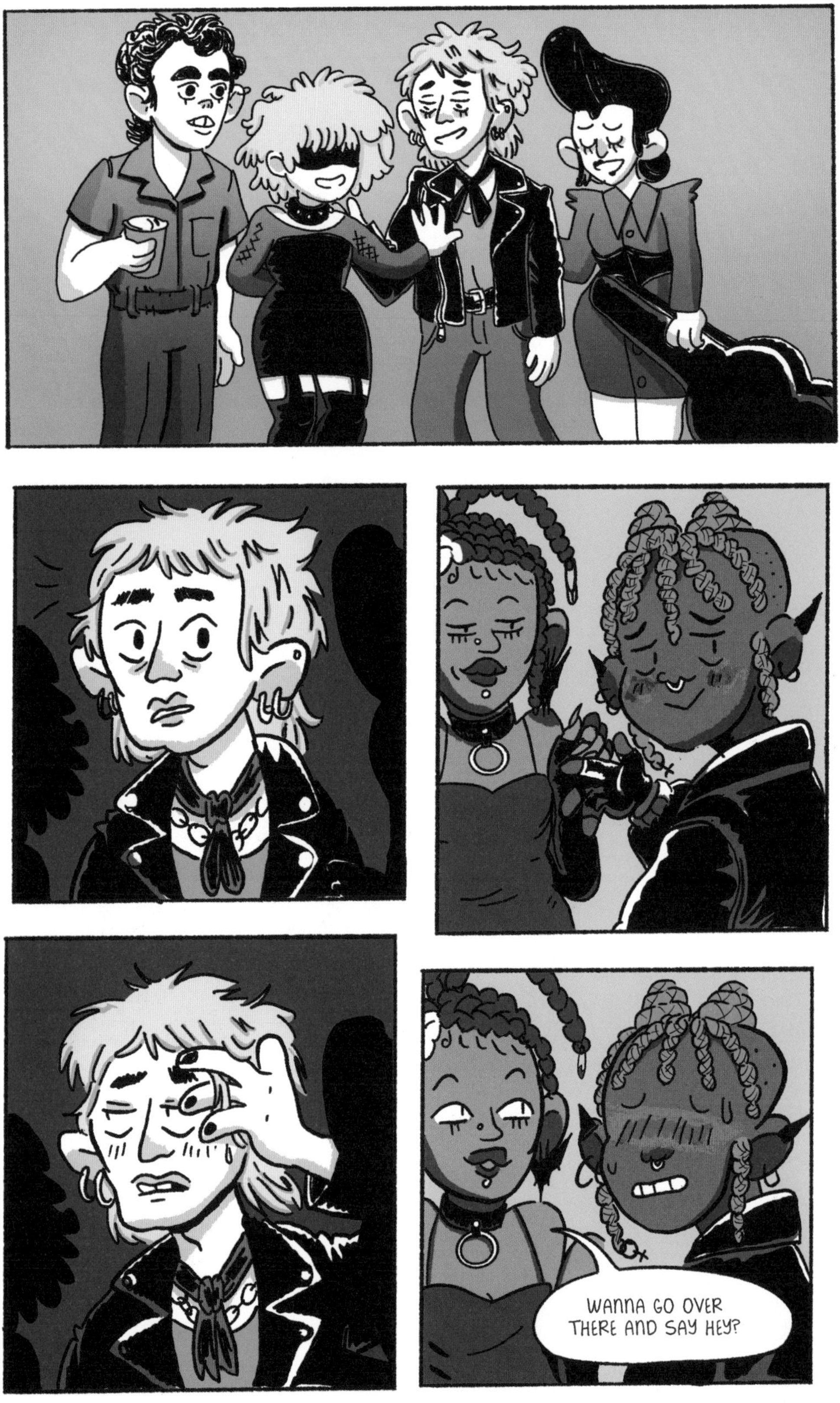
WANNA GO OVER
THERE AND SAY HEY?

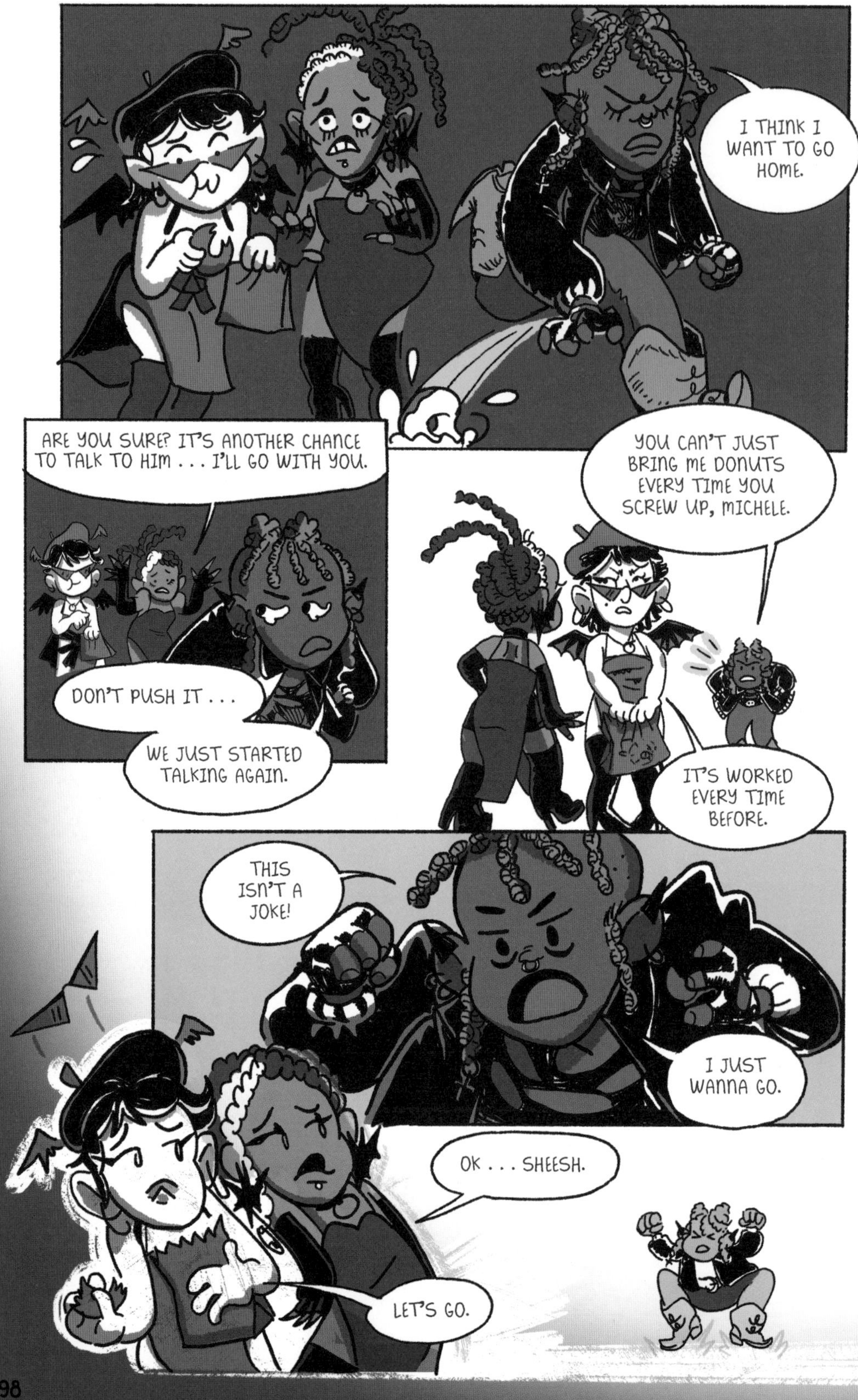
I THINK I WANT TO GO HOME.
ARE YOU SURE? IT'S ANOTHER CHANCE TO TALK TO HIM . . . I'LL GO WITH YOU.
DON'T PUSH IT . . .
WE JUST STARTED TALKING AGAIN.
YOU CAN'T JUST BRING ME DONUTS EVERY TIME YOU SCREW UP, MICHELE.
IT'S WORKED EVERY TIME BEFORE.
THIS ISN'T A JOKE!
I JUST WANNA GO.
OK . . . SHEESH.
LET'S GO.

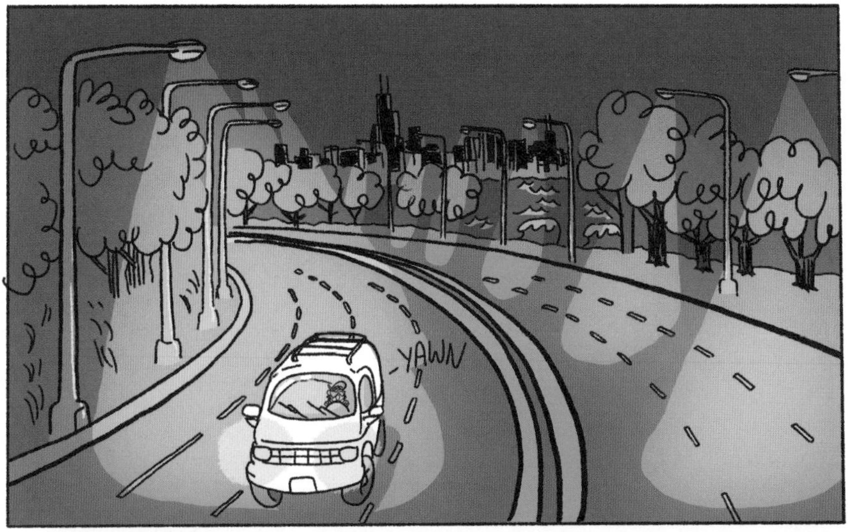
YAWN

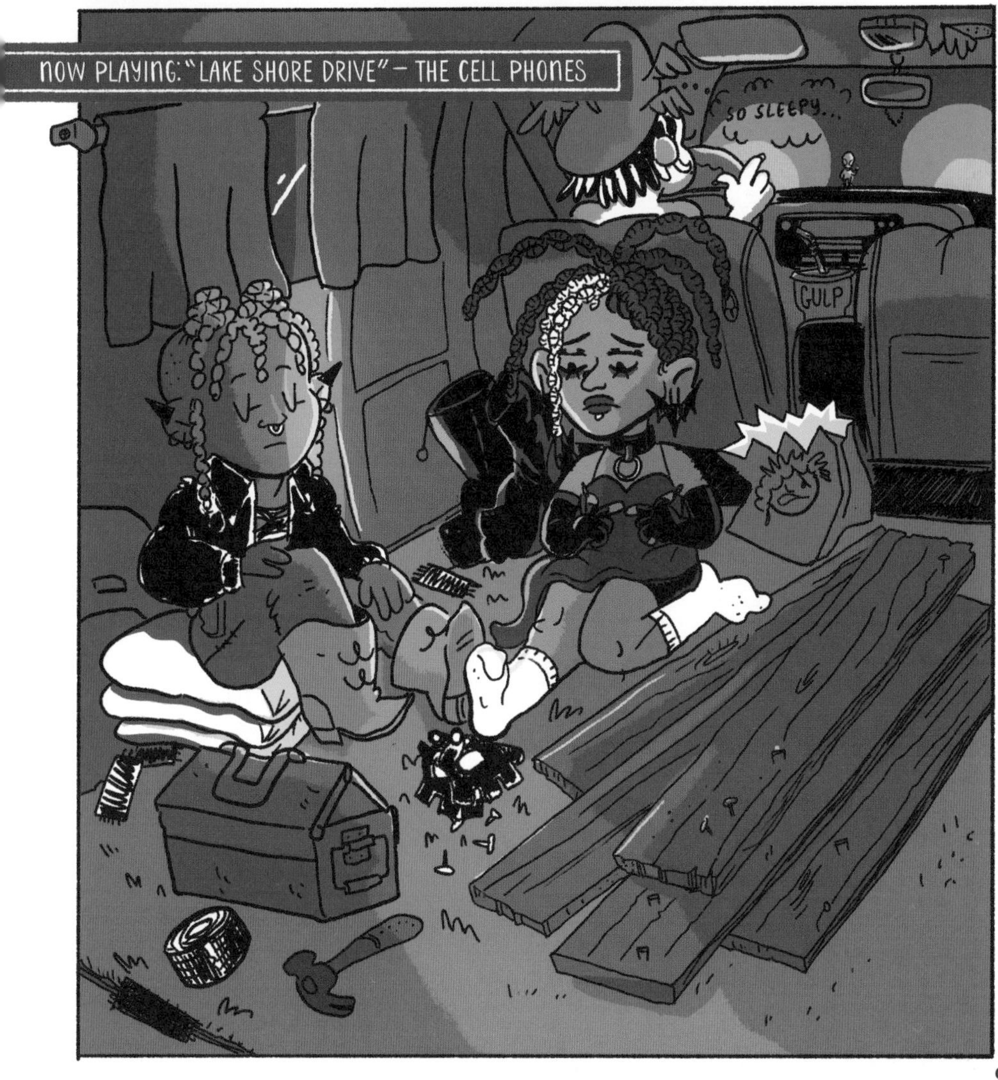
NOW PLAYING: "LAKE SHORE DRIVE" – THE CELL PHONES
SO SLEEPY...
GULP

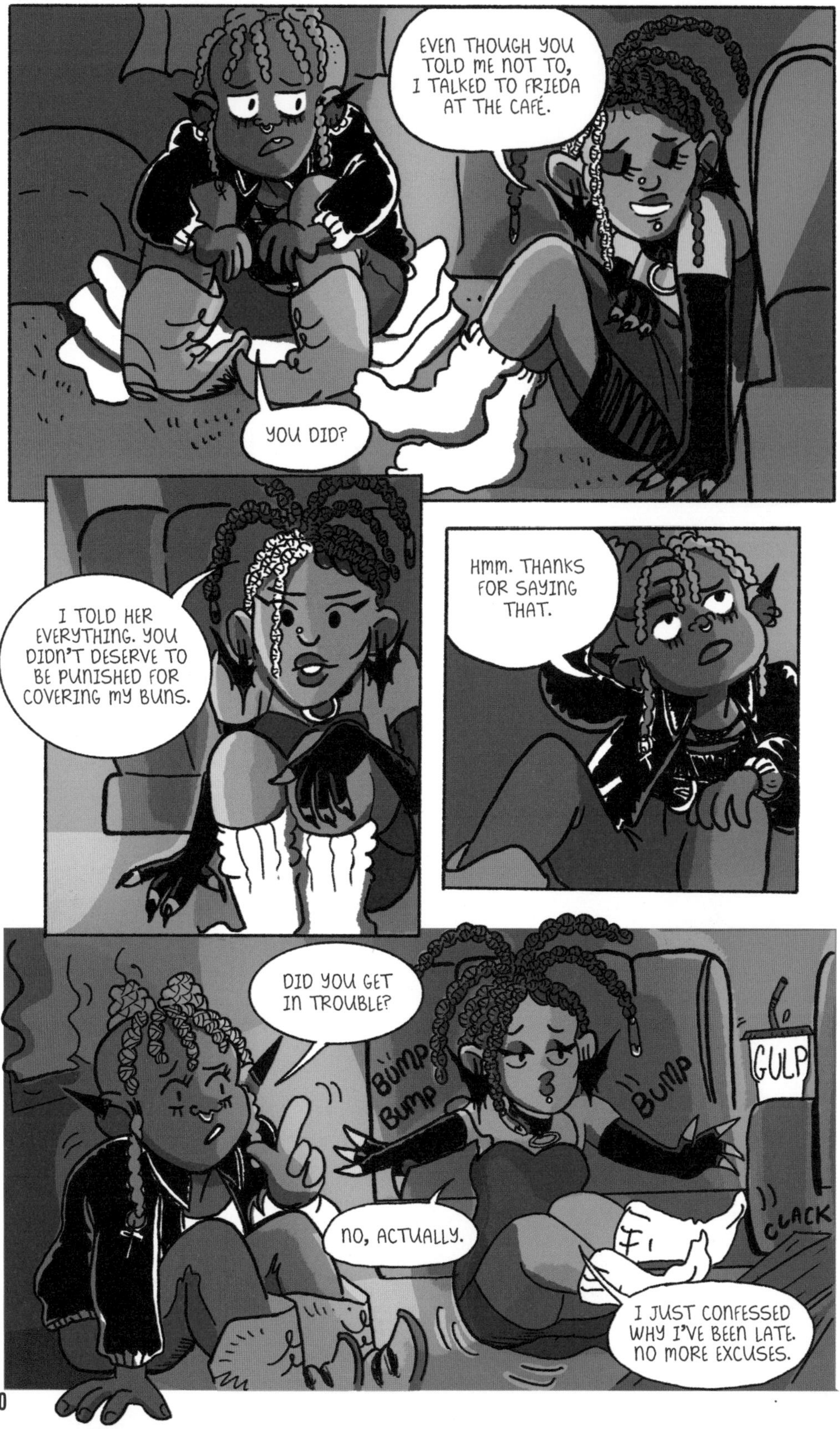
EVEN THOUGH YOU TOLD ME NOT TO, I TALKED TO FRIEDA AT THE CAFÉ.
YOU DID?
I TOLD HER EVERYTHING. YOU DIDN'T DESERVE TO BE PUNISHED FOR COVERING MY BUNS.
HMM. THANKS FOR SAYING THAT.
DID YOU GET IN TROUBLE?
BUMP BUMP
BUMP
GULP
NO, ACTUALLY.
CLACK
I JUST CONFESSED WHY I'VE BEEN LATE. NO MORE EXCUSES.

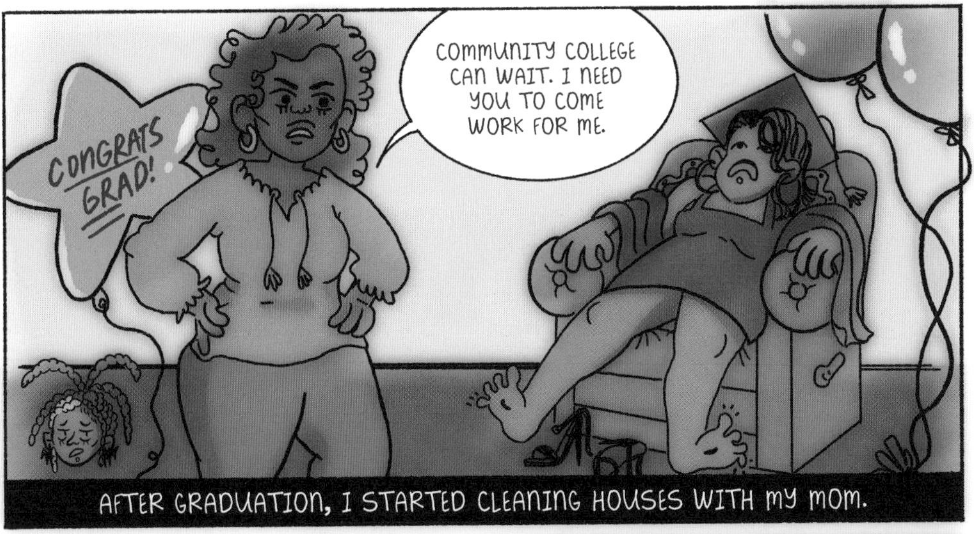
CONGRATS GRAD!
COMMUNITY COLLEGE CAN WAIT. I NEED YOU TO COME WORK FOR ME.
AFTER GRADUATION, I STARTED CLEANING HOUSES WITH MY MOM.

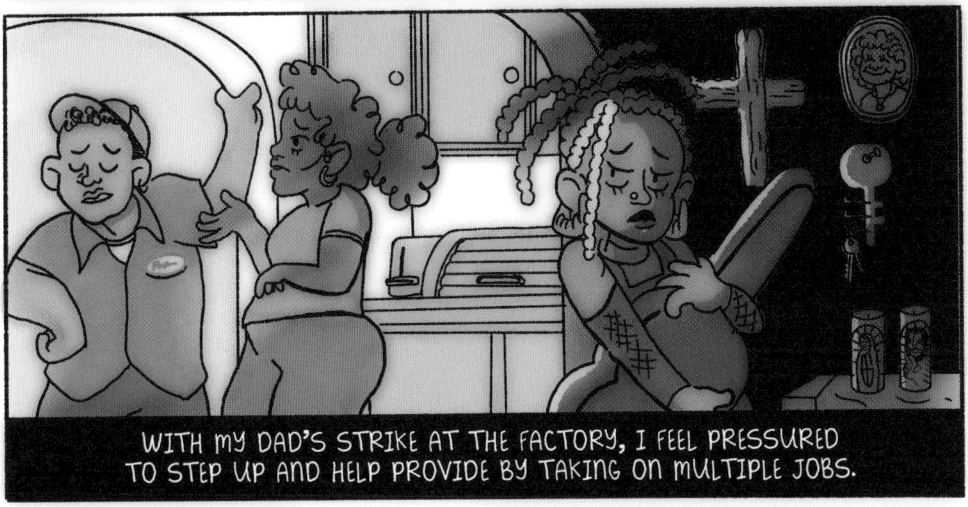
WITH MY DAD'S STRIKE AT THE FACTORY, I FEEL PRESSURED TO STEP UP AND HELP PROVIDE BY TAKING ON MULTIPLE JOBS.

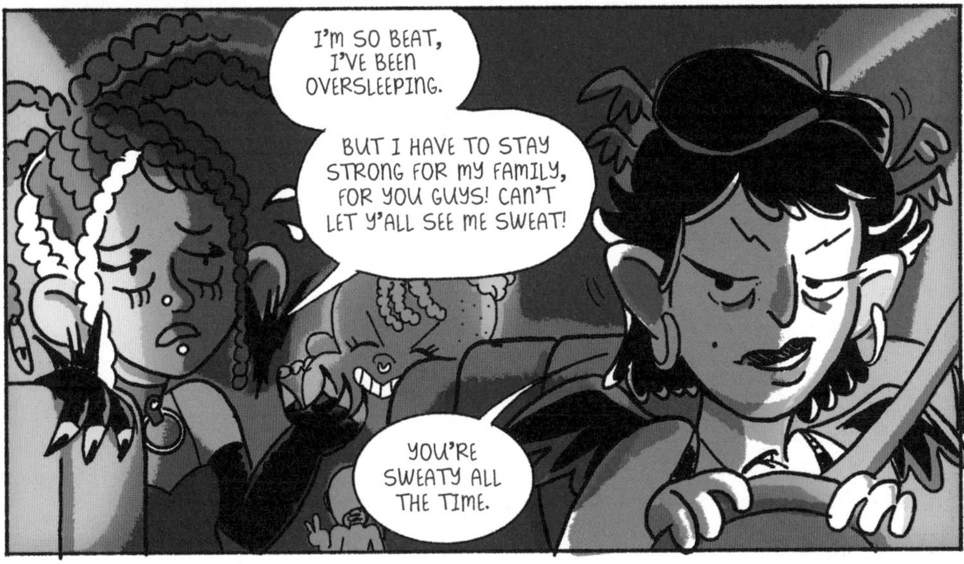
I'M SO BEAT, I'VE BEEN OVERSLEEPING.
BUT I HAVE TO STAY STRONG FOR MY FAMILY, FOR YOU GUYS! CAN'T LET Y'ALL SEE ME SWEAT!
YOU'RE SWEATY ALL THE TIME.

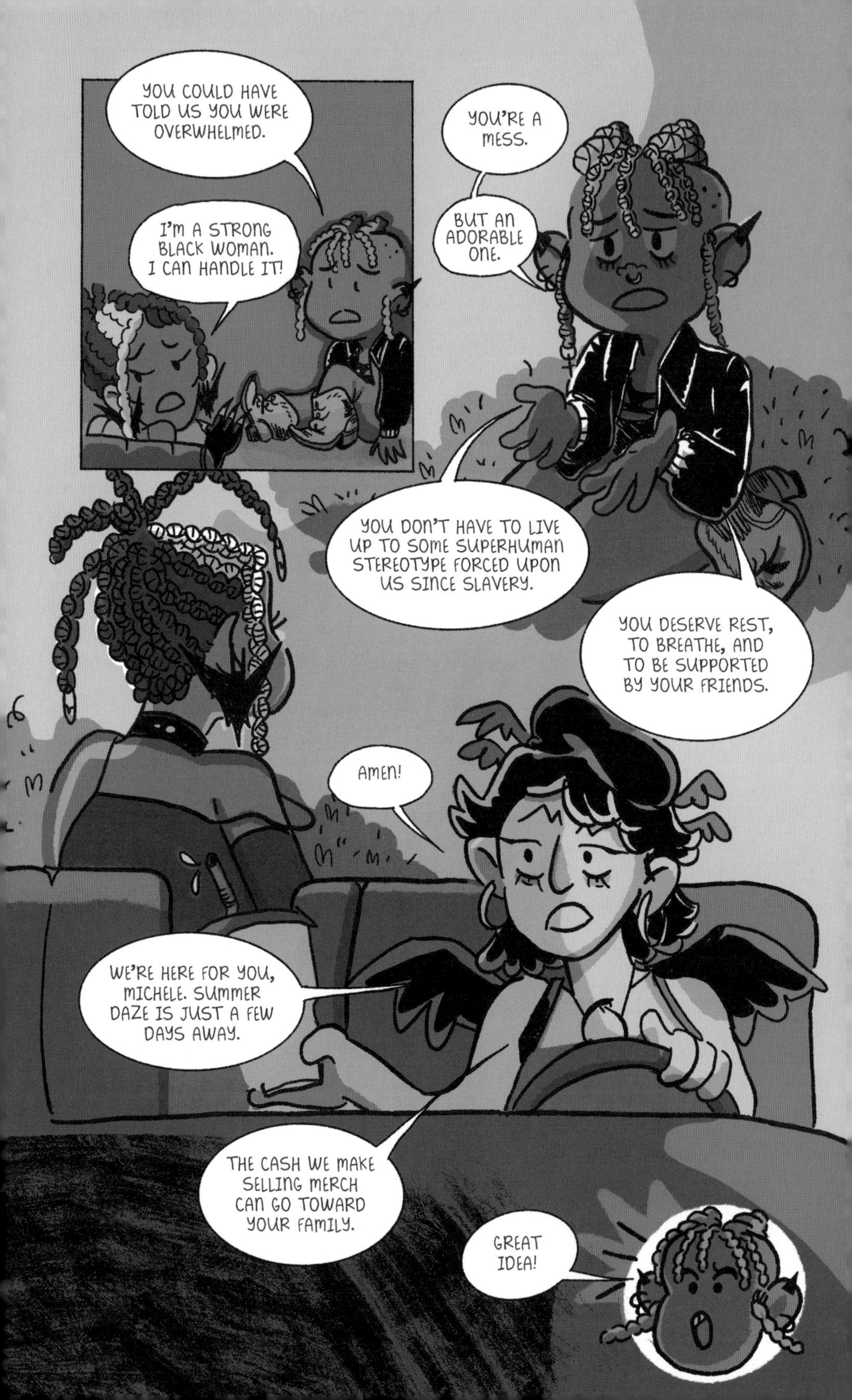

YOU COULD HAVE TOLD US YOU WERE OVERWHELMED.
I'M A STRONG BLACK WOMAN. I CAN HANDLE IT!
YOU'RE A MESS.
BUT AN ADORABLE ONE.
YOU DON'T HAVE TO LIVE UP TO SOME SUPERHUMAN STEREOTYPE FORCED UPON US SINCE SLAVERY.
YOU DESERVE REST, TO BREATHE, AND TO BE SUPPORTED BY YOUR FRIENDS.
AMEN!
WE'RE HERE FOR YOU, MICHELE. SUMMER DAZE IS JUST A FEW DAYS AWAY.
THE CASH WE MAKE SELLING MERCH CAN GO TOWARD YOUR FAMILY.
GREAT IDEA!

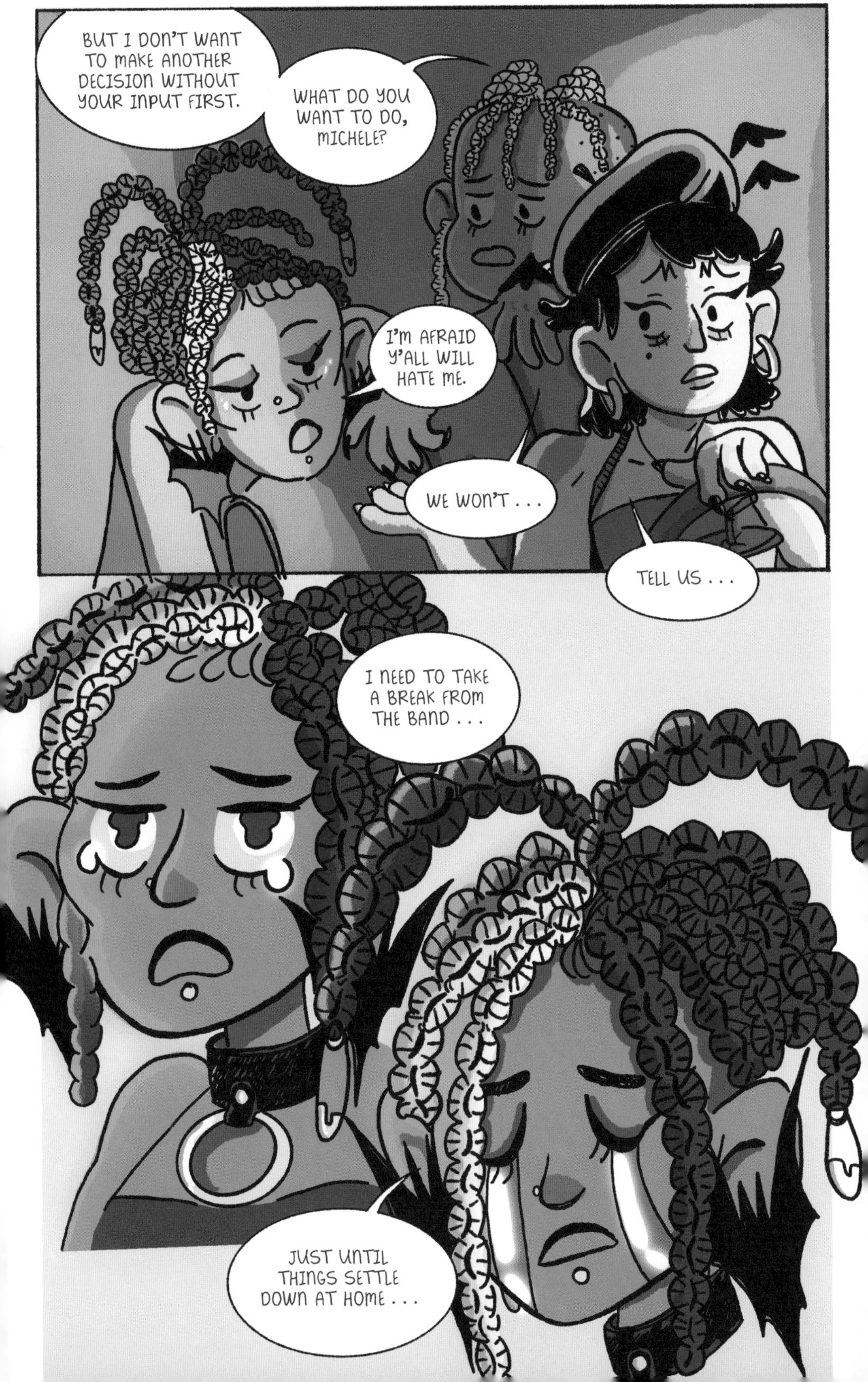
BUT I DON'T WANT TO MAKE ANOTHER DECISION WITHOUT YOUR INPUT FIRST.
WHAT DO YOU WANT TO DO, MICHELE?
I'M AFRAID Y'ALL WILL HATE ME.
WE WON'T . . .
TELL US . . .
I NEED TO TAKE A BREAK FROM THE BAND . . .
JUST UNTIL THINGS SETTLE DOWN AT HOME . . .

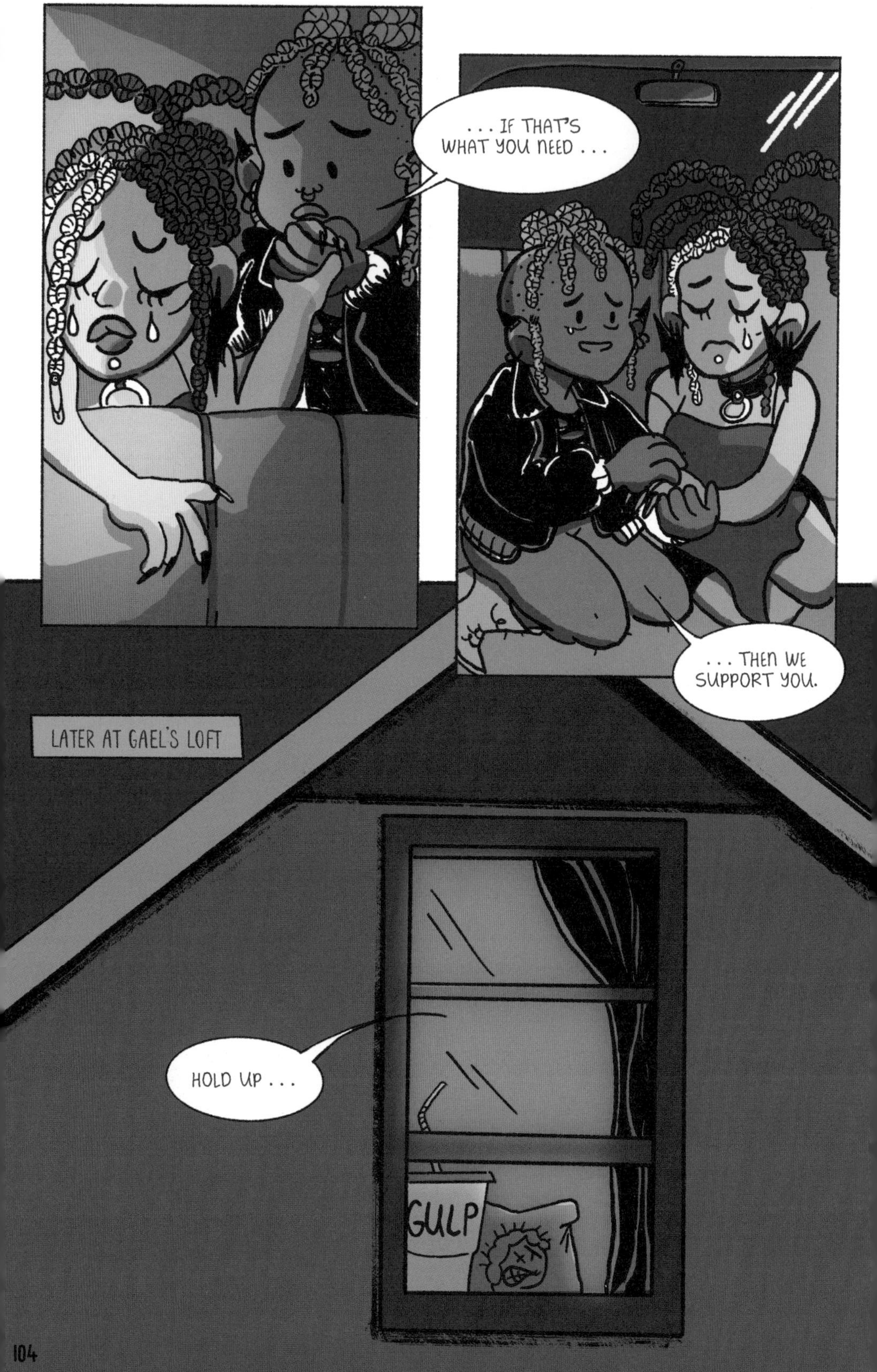
. . . IF THAT'S WHAT YOU NEED . . .
. . . THEN WE SUPPORT YOU.
LATER AT GAEL'S LOFT
HOLD UP . . .
GULP

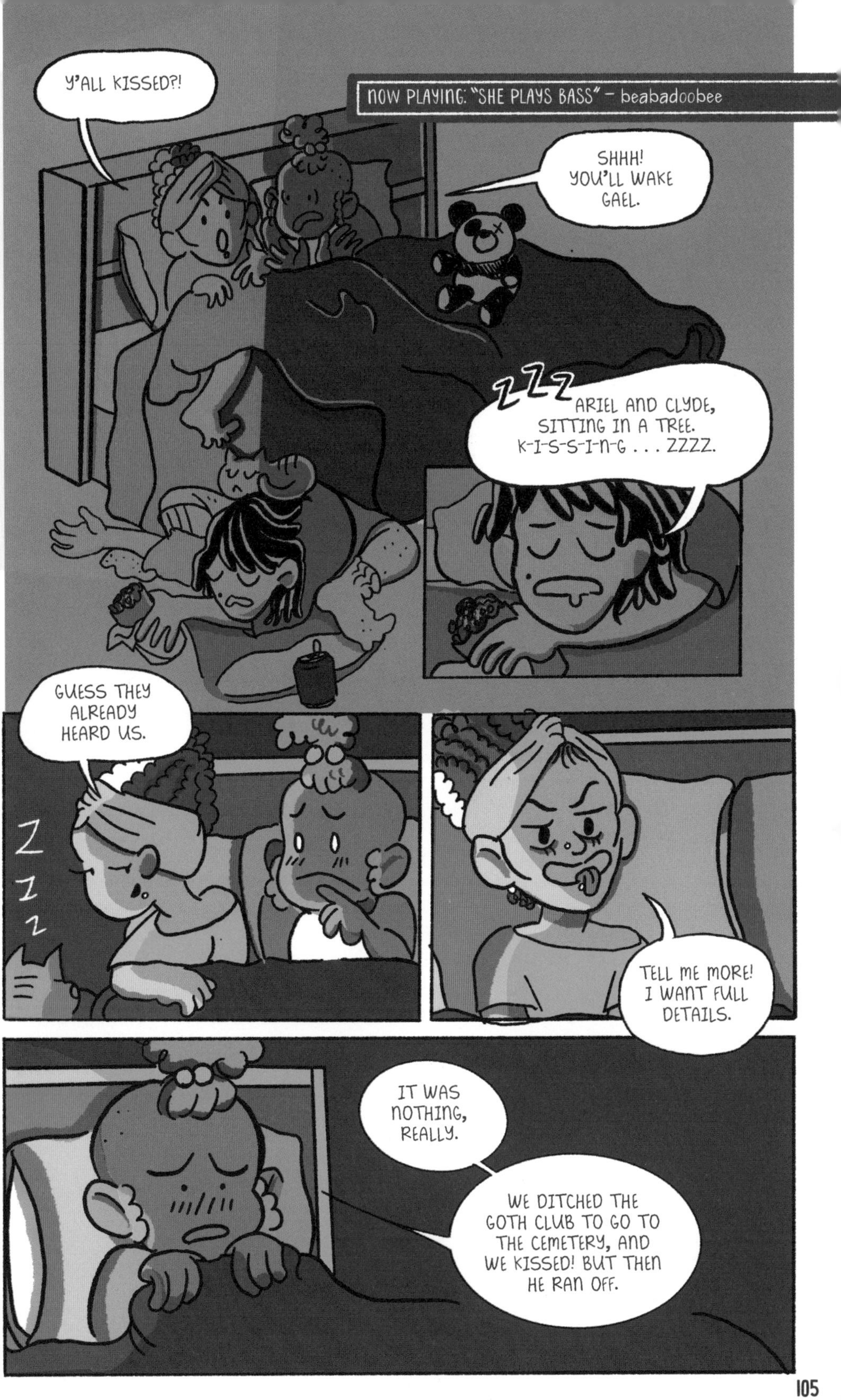
Y'ALL KISSED?!
NOW PLAYING: "SHE PLAYS BASS" – beabadoobee
SHHH! YOU'LL WAKE GAEL.
ZZZ ARIEL AND CLYDE, SITTING IN A TREE. K-I-S-S-I-N-G . . . ZZZZ.
GUESS THEY ALREADY HEARD US.
Z Z Z
TELL ME MORE! I WANT FULL DETAILS.
IT WAS NOTHING, REALLY.
WE DITCHED THE GOTH CLUB TO GO TO THE CEMETERY, AND WE KISSED! BUT THEN HE RAN OFF.

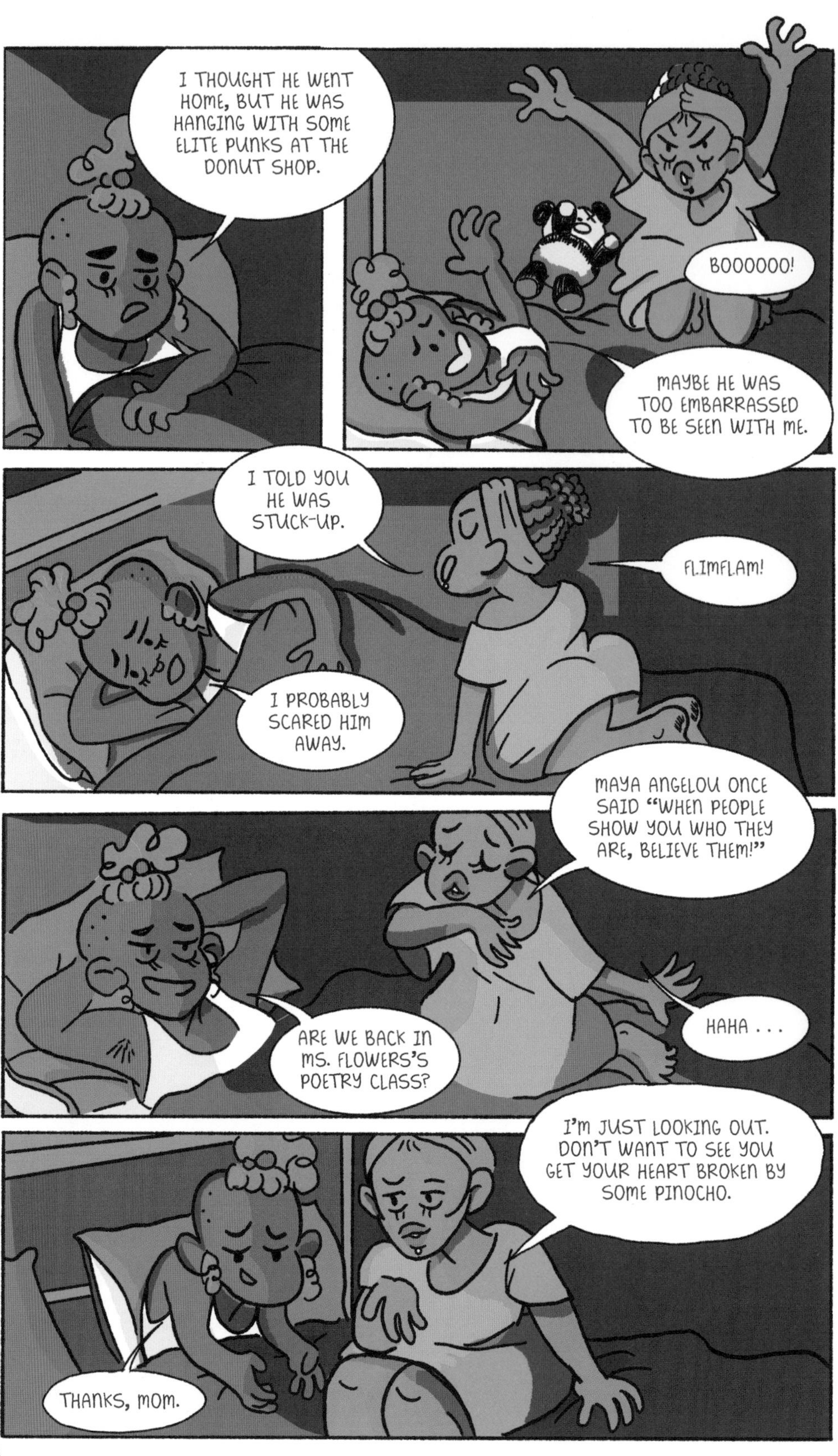
I THOUGHT HE WENT HOME, BUT HE WAS HANGING WITH SOME ELITE PUNKS AT THE DONUT SHOP.
BOOOOOO!
MAYBE HE WAS TOO EMBARRASSED TO BE SEEN WITH ME.
I TOLD YOU HE WAS STUCK-UP.
FLIMFLAM!
I PROBABLY SCARED HIM AWAY.
MAYA ANGELOU ONCE SAID "WHEN PEOPLE SHOW YOU WHO THEY ARE, BELIEVE THEM!"
ARE WE BACK IN MS. FLOWERS'S POETRY CLASS?
HAHA . . .
I'M JUST LOOKING OUT. DON'T WANT TO SEE YOU GET YOUR HEART BROKEN BY SOME PINOCHO.
THANKS, MOM.

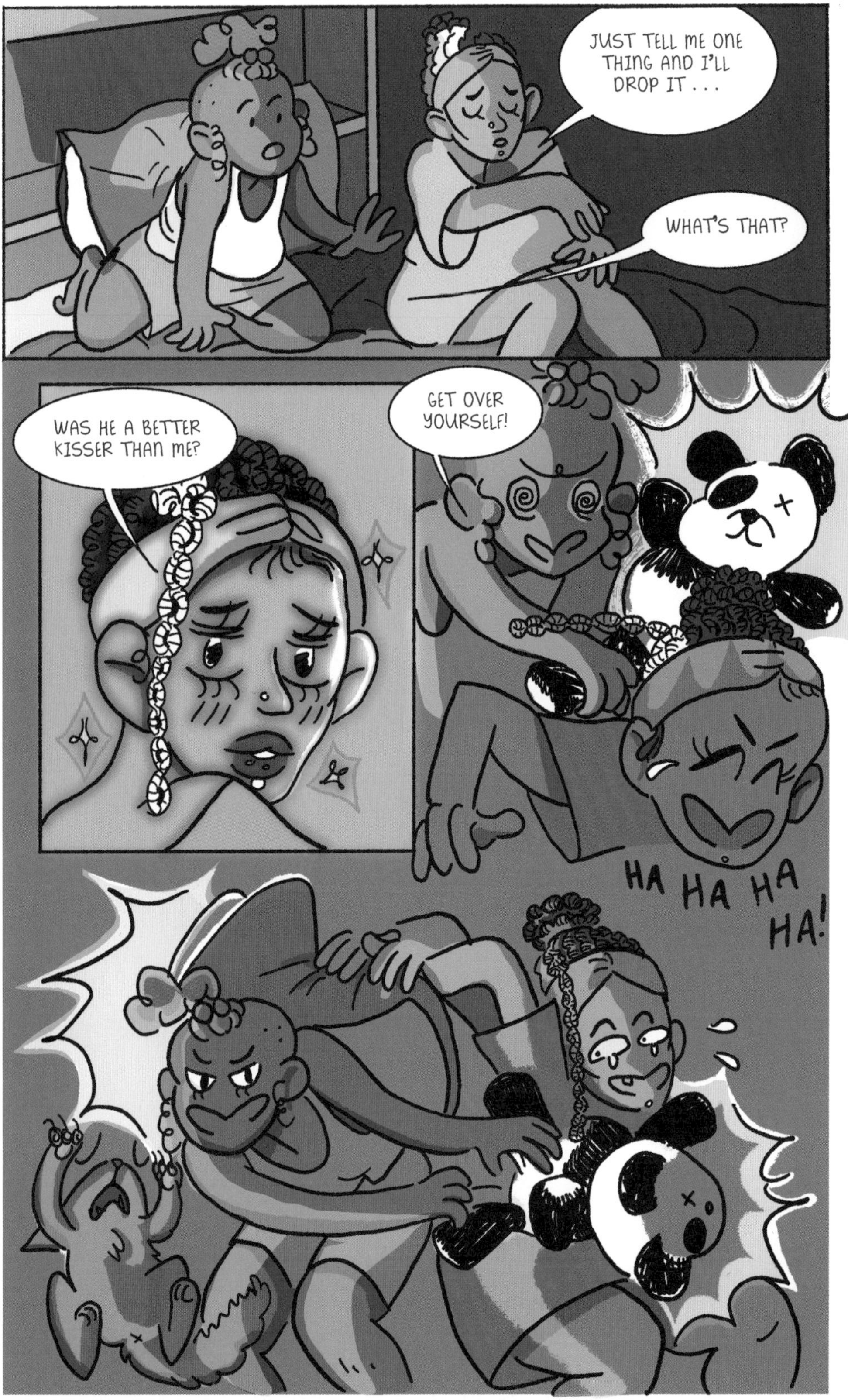
JUST TELL ME ONE THING AND I'LL DROP IT . . .
WHAT'S THAT?
WAS HE A BETTER KISSER THAN ME?
GET OVER YOURSELF!
HA HA HA HA!

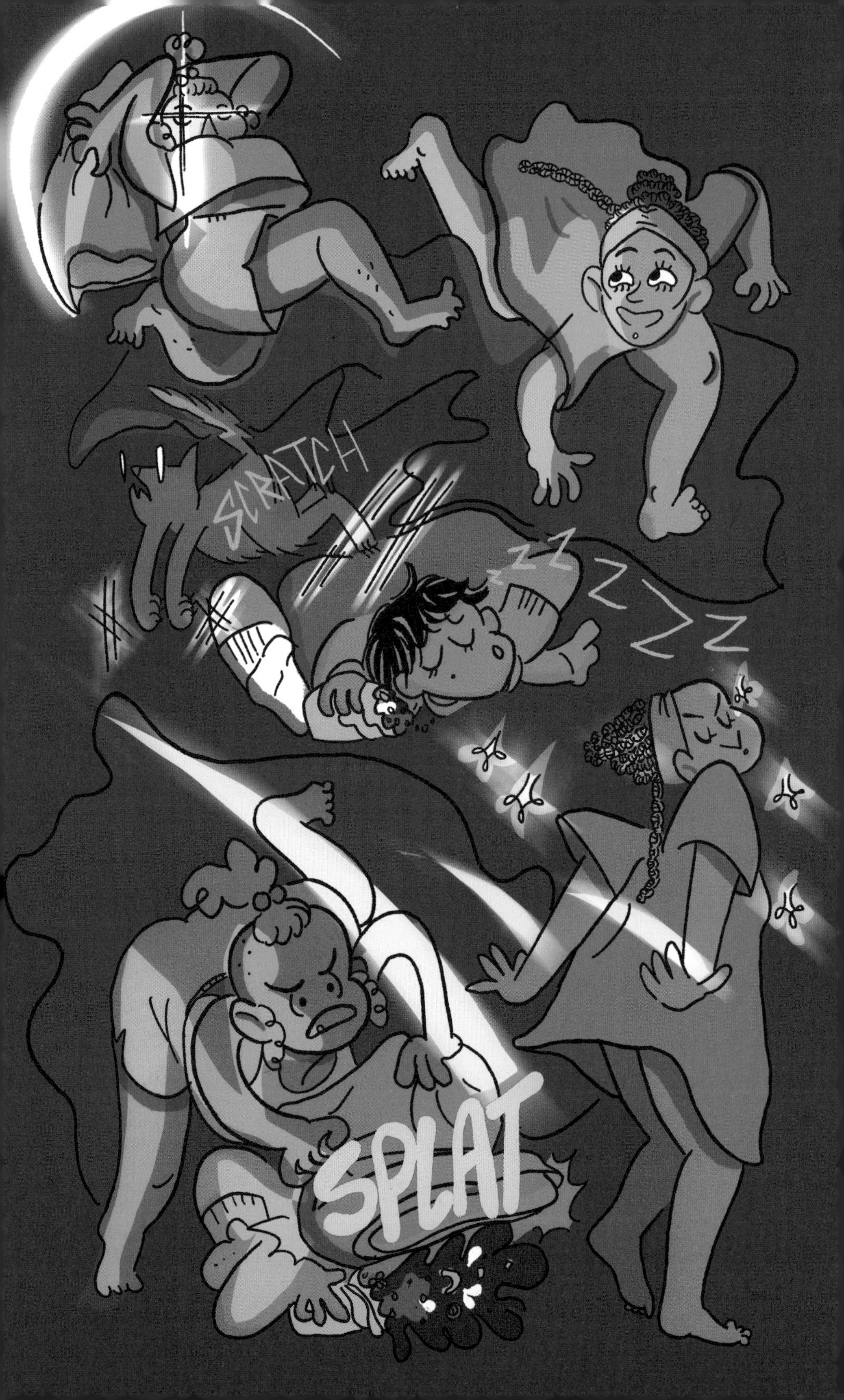
SCRATCH
zZZ ZZ
SPLAT

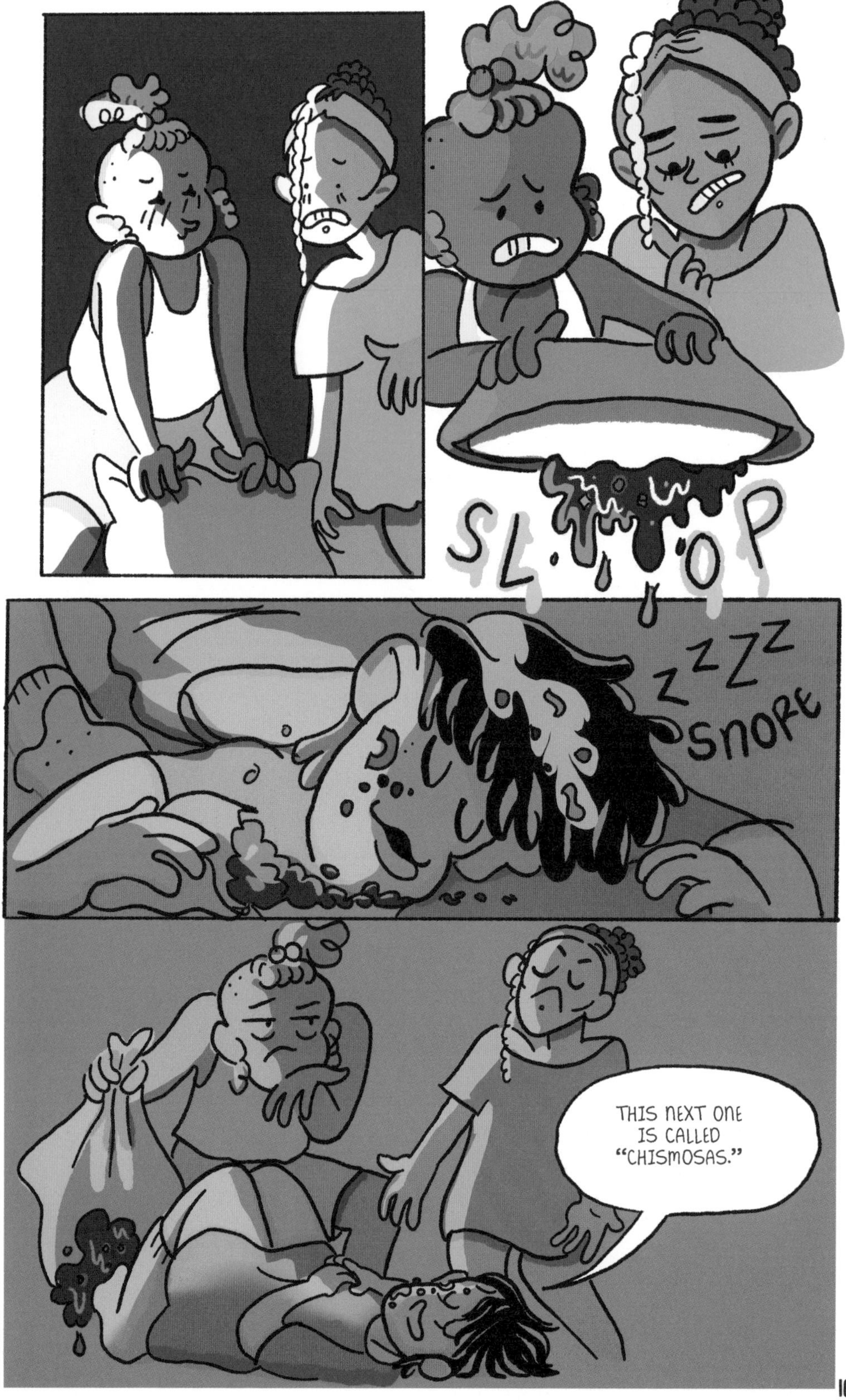
SLOOP
ZZZZZ
SNORE
THIS NEXT ONE IS CALLED "CHISMOSAS."

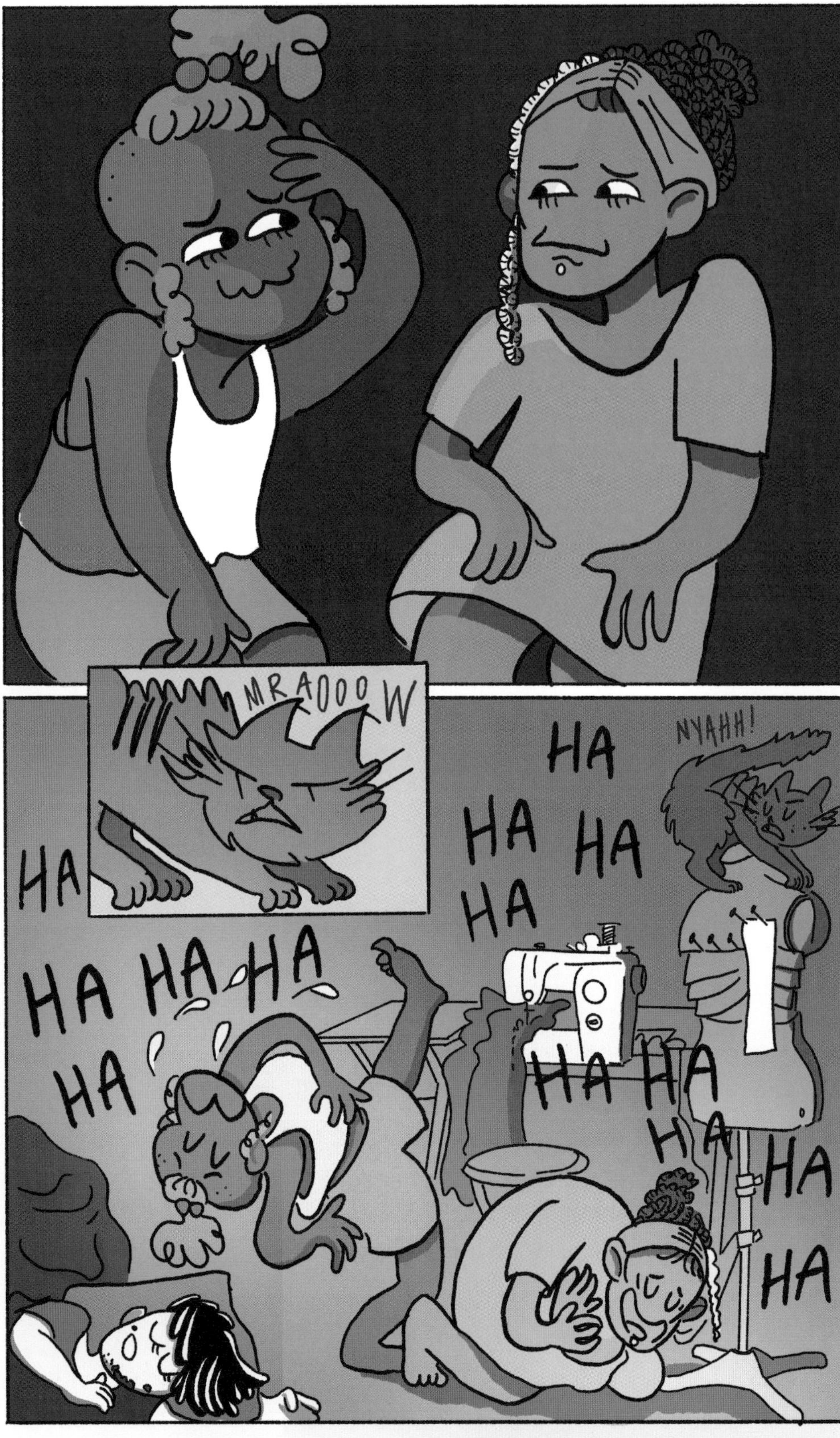
MRAOOOW
HA
HA
HA HA
HA
NYAHH!
HA HA HA
HA
HA HA
HA
HA
HA

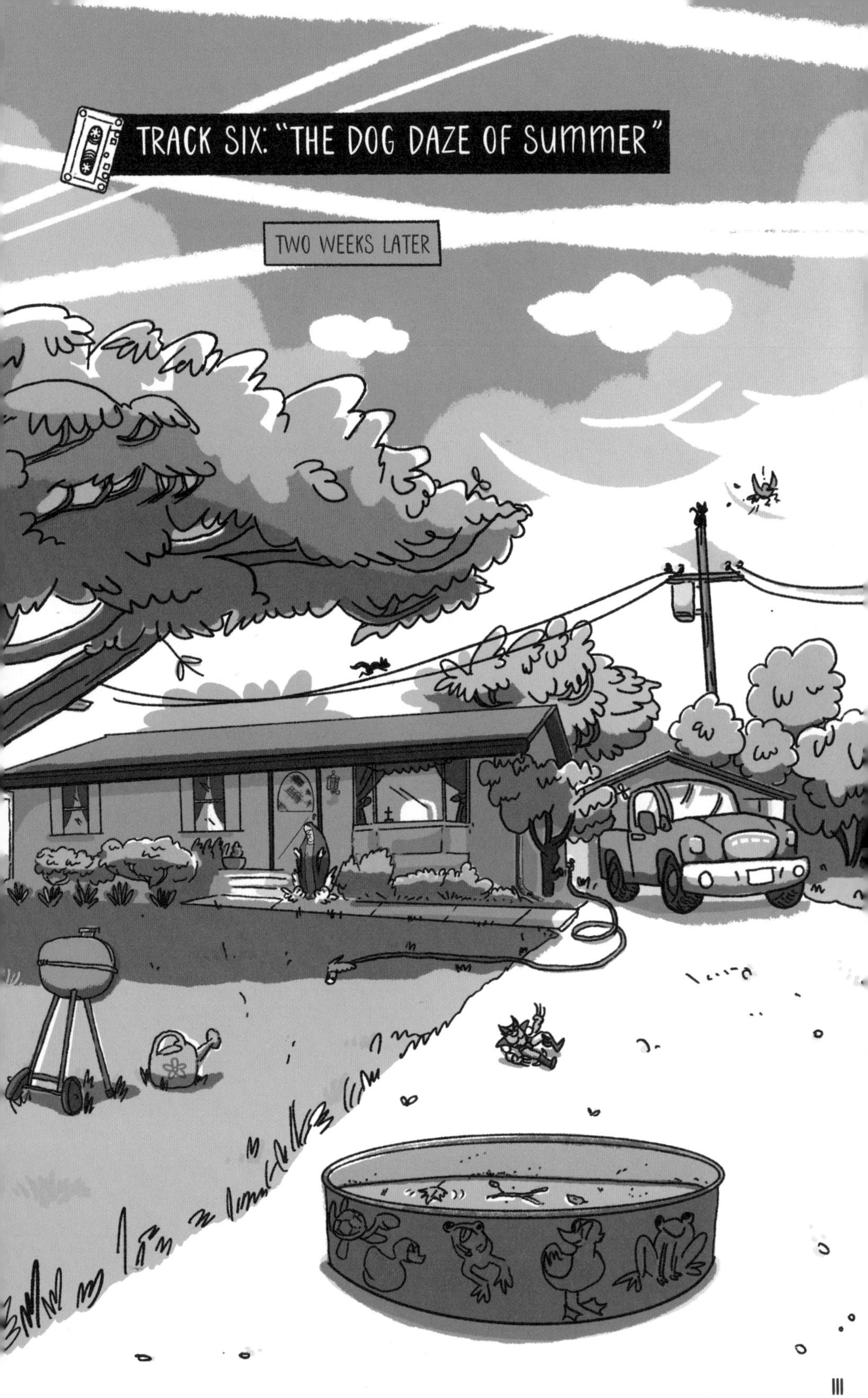

TRACK SIX: "THE DOG DAZE OF SUMMER"
TWO WEEKS LATER

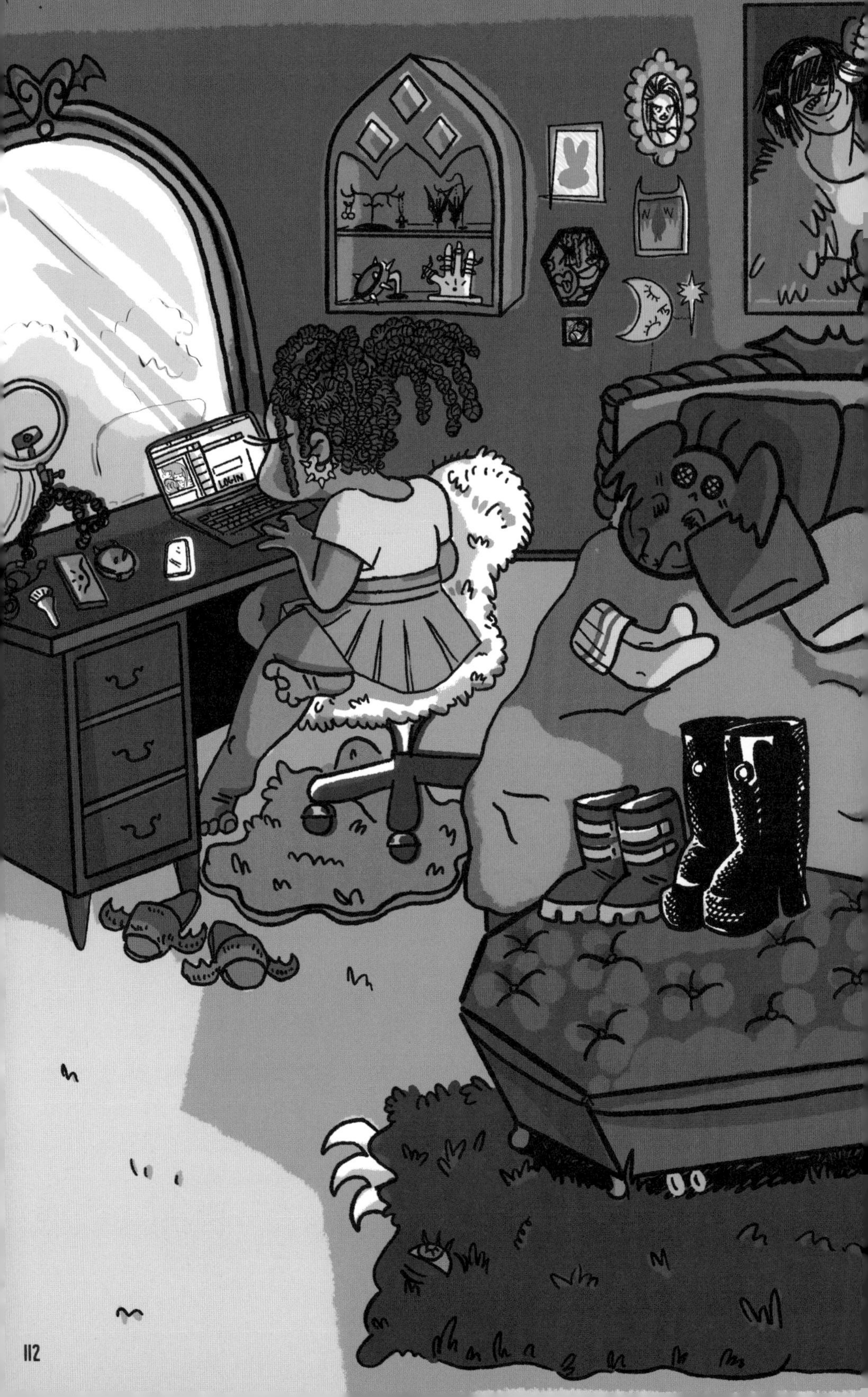
LOG-IN

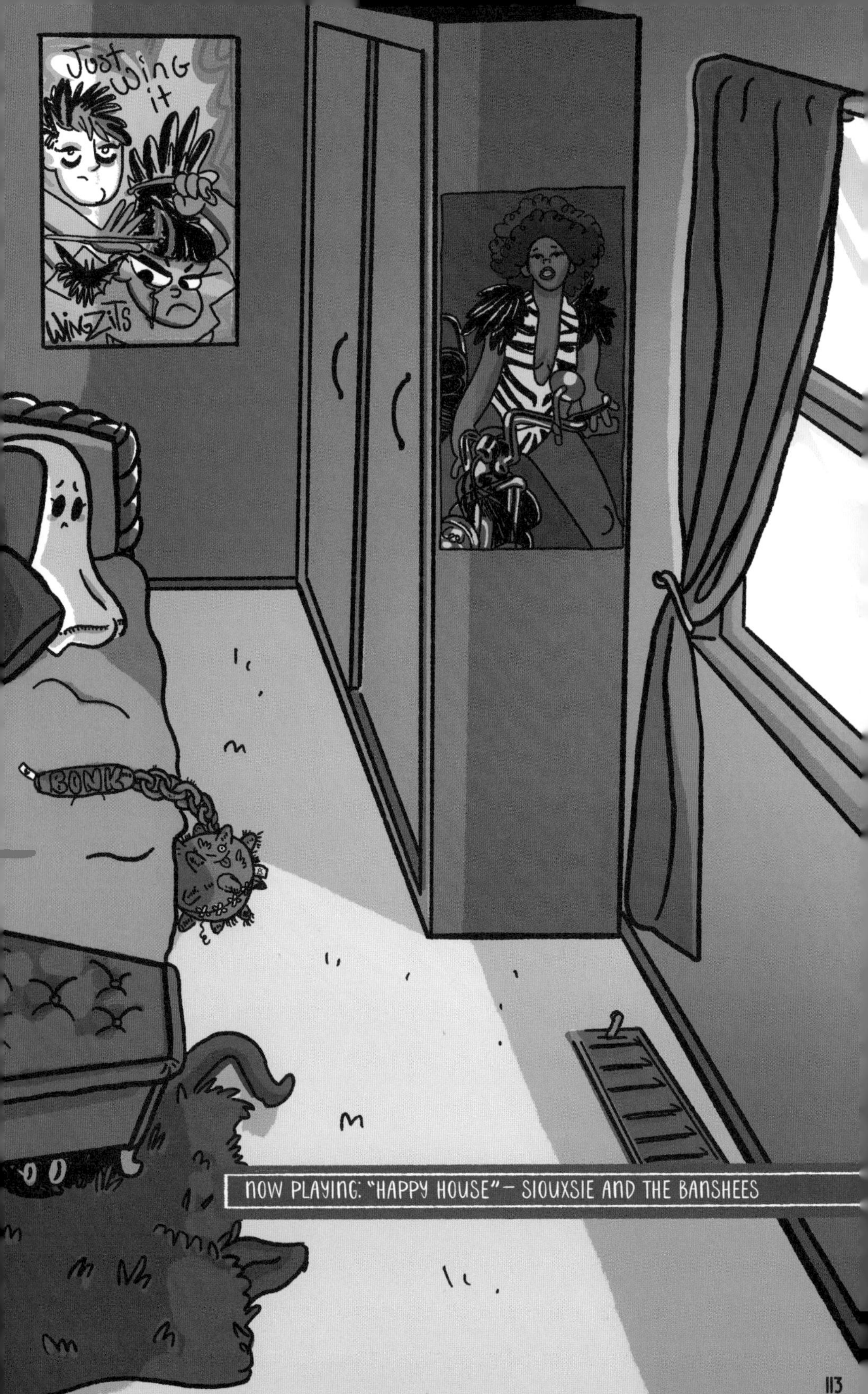

Just Wing it
WINGZITS
BONK
NOW PLAYING: "HAPPY HOUSE" — SIOUXSIE AND THE BANSHEES

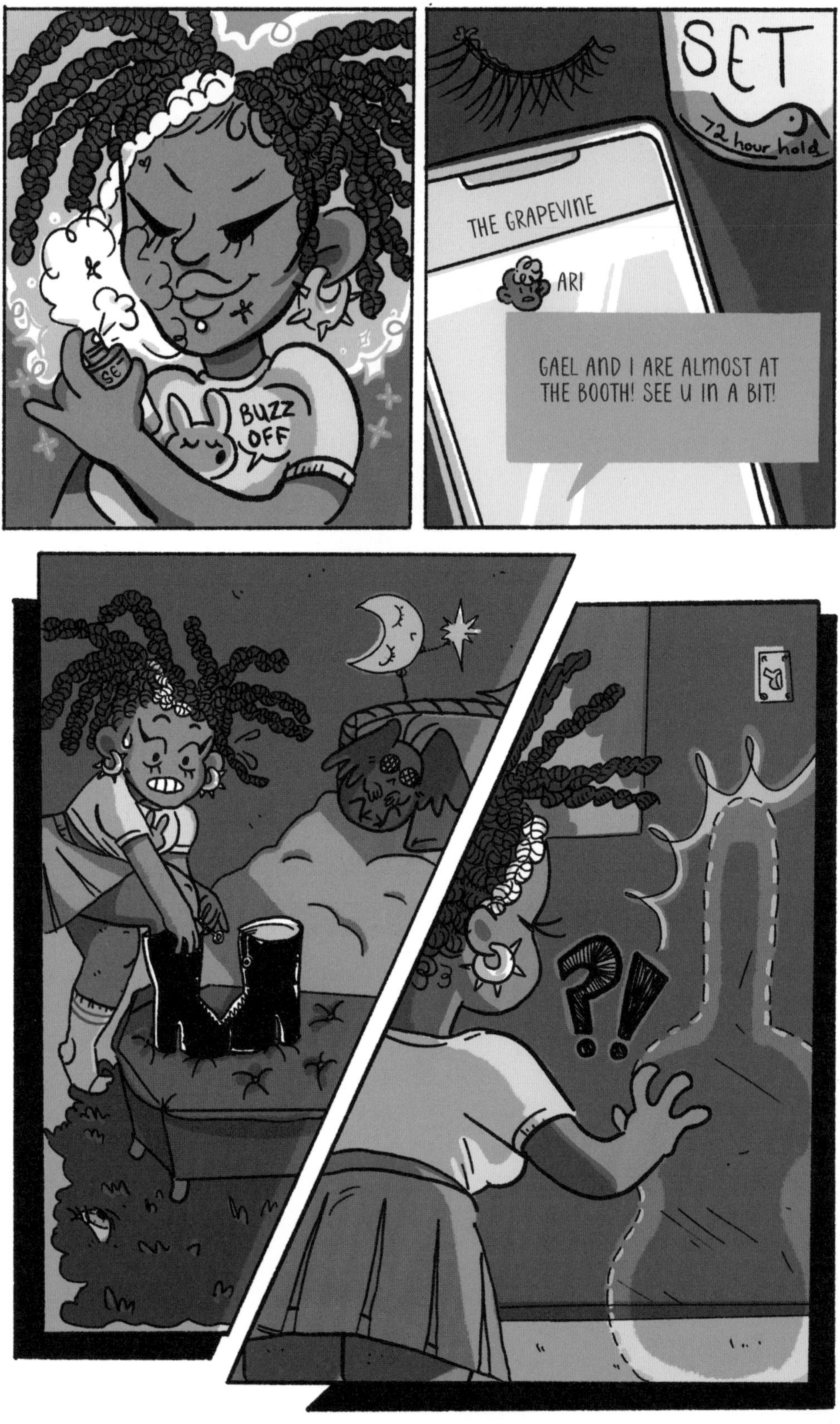
BUZZ OFF
SET
72 hour hold
THE GRAPEVINE
ARI
GAEL AND I ARE ALMOST AT THE BOOTH! SEE U IN A BIT!
?!!

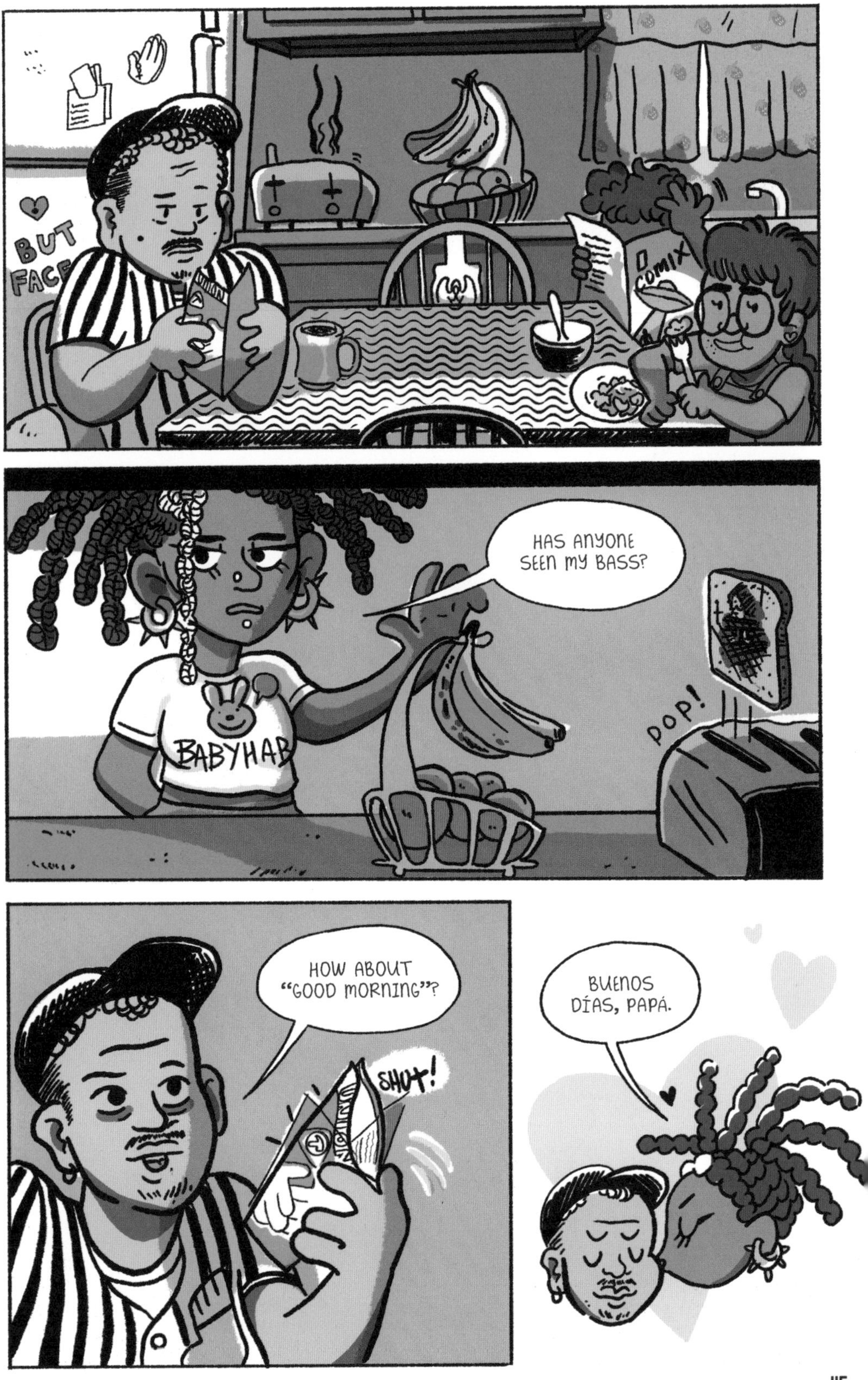
BUT FACE
COMIX
HAS ANYONE SEEN MY BASS?
BABYHAB
POP!
HOW ABOUT "GOOD MORNING"?
SHUT!
BUENOS DÍAS, PAPÁ.

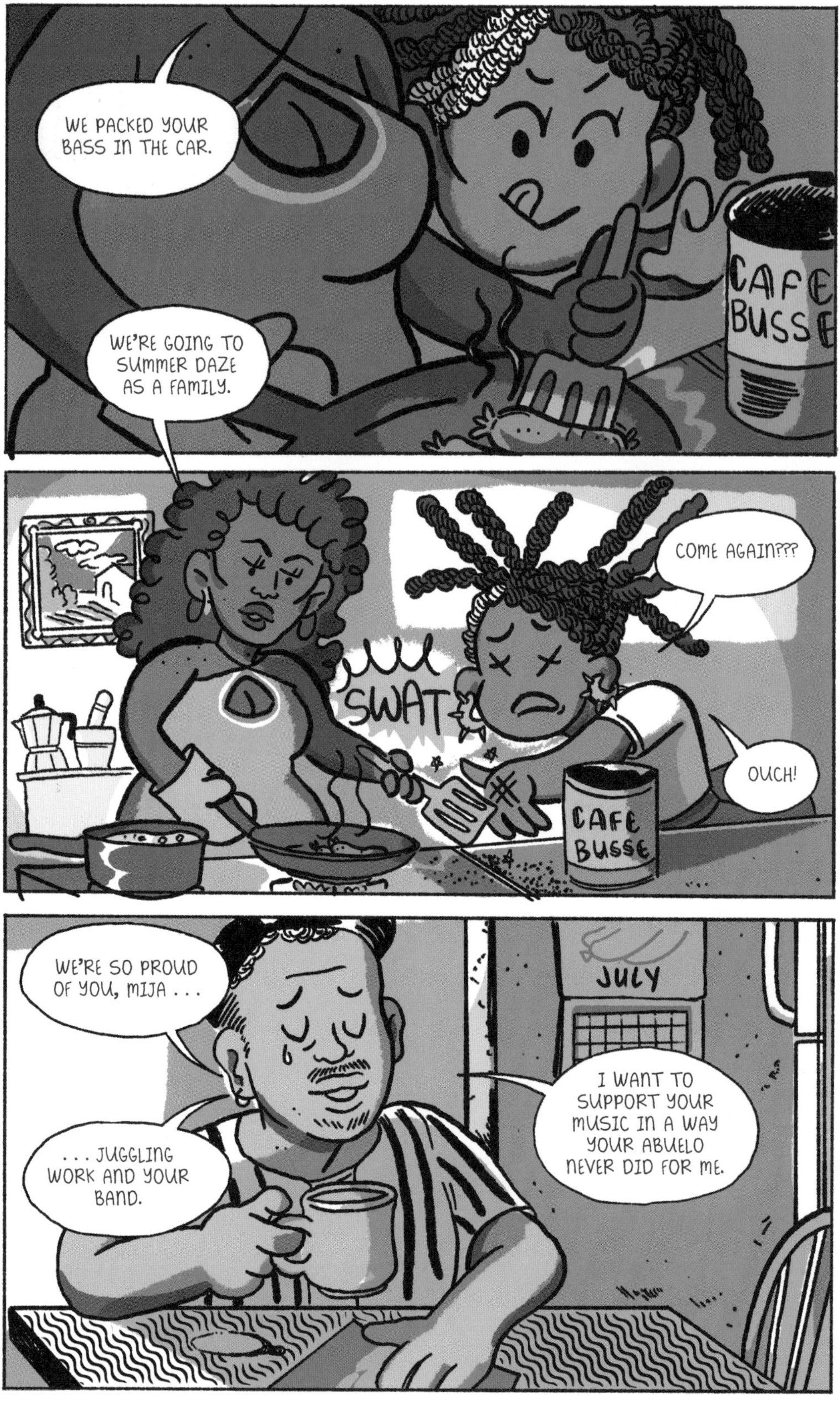
WE PACKED YOUR BASS IN THE CAR.
WE'RE GOING TO SUMMER DAZE AS A FAMILY.
CAFE BUSSE
COME AGAIN???
SWAT
OUCH!
CAFE BUSSE
WE'RE SO PROUD OF YOU, MIJA . . .
JULY
. . . JUGGLING WORK AND YOUR BAND.
I WANT TO SUPPORT YOUR MUSIC IN A WAY YOUR ABUELO NEVER DID FOR ME.

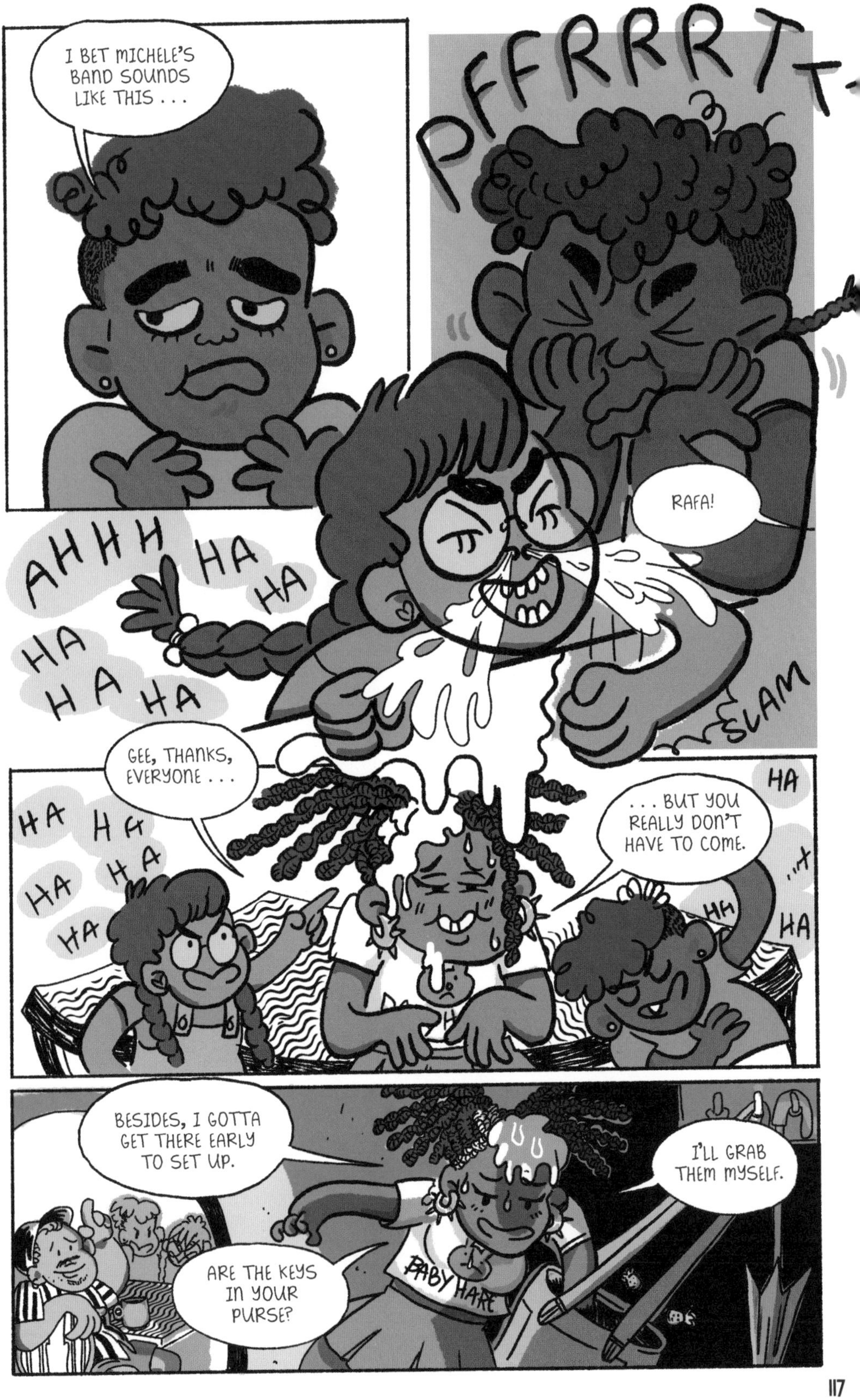
I BET MICHELE'S BAND SOUNDS LIKE THIS . . .
PFFRRRRT
RAFA!
AHHH HA HA
HA HA HA
SLAM
GEE, THANKS, EVERYONE . . .
HA H HA HA HA
. . . BUT YOU REALLY DON'T HAVE TO COME.
HA HA HA
BESIDES, I GOTTA GET THERE EARLY TO SET UP.
I'LL GRAB THEM MYSELF.
ARE THE KEYS IN YOUR PURSE?
BABY HARE

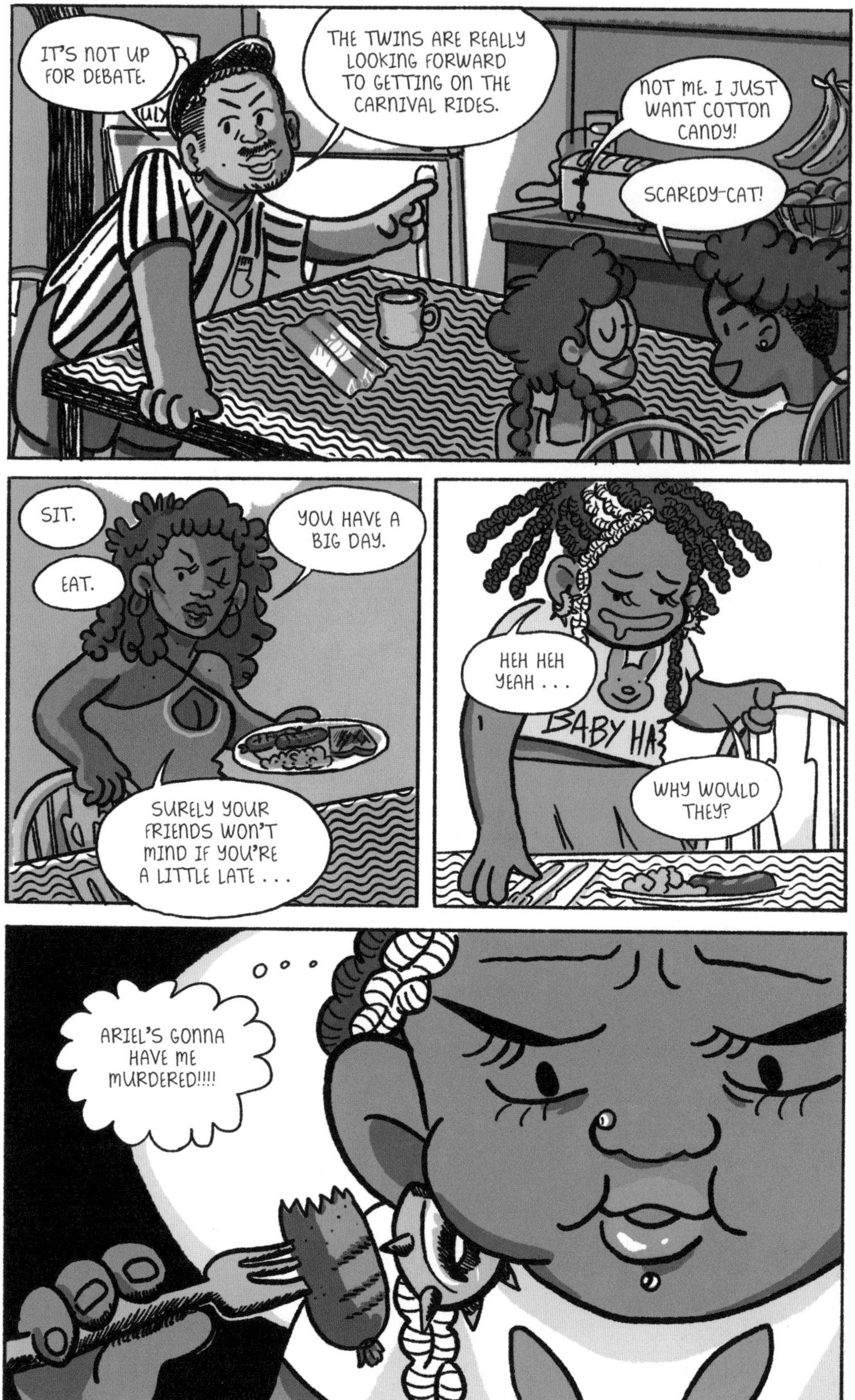
IT'S NOT UP FOR DEBATE.
THE TWINS ARE REALLY LOOKING FORWARD TO GETTING ON THE CARNIVAL RIDES.
NOT ME. I JUST WANT COTTON CANDY!
SCAREDY-CAT!
SIT.
EAT.
YOU HAVE A BIG DAY.
SURELY YOUR FRIENDS WON'T MIND IF YOU'RE A LITTLE LATE . . .
HEH HEH YEAH . . .
BABY HA
WHY WOULD THEY?
ARIEL'S GONNA HAVE ME MURDERED!!!!

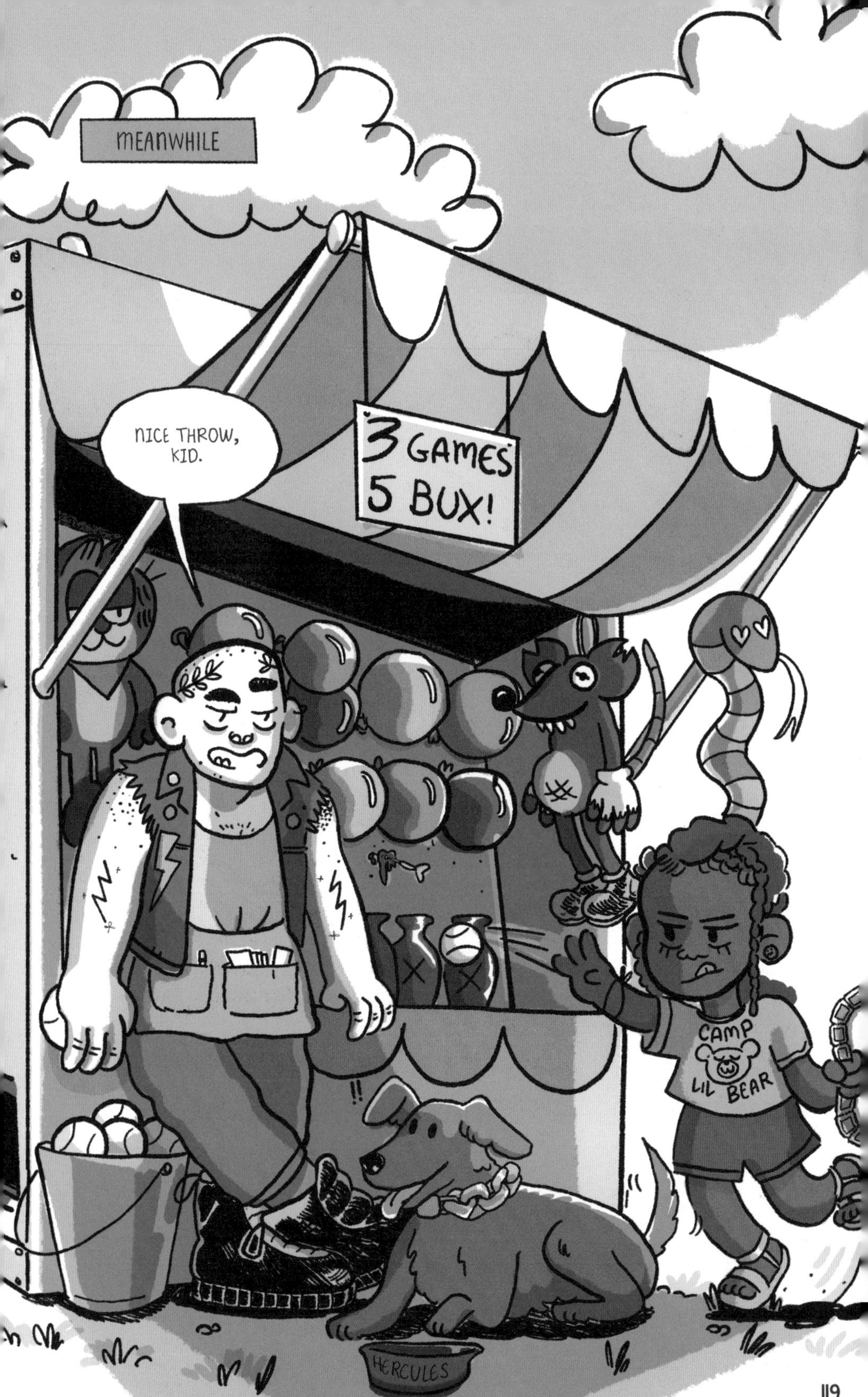
MEANWHILE
NICE THROW, KID.
3 GAMES 5 BUX!
!!
CAMP LIL BEAR
HERCULES

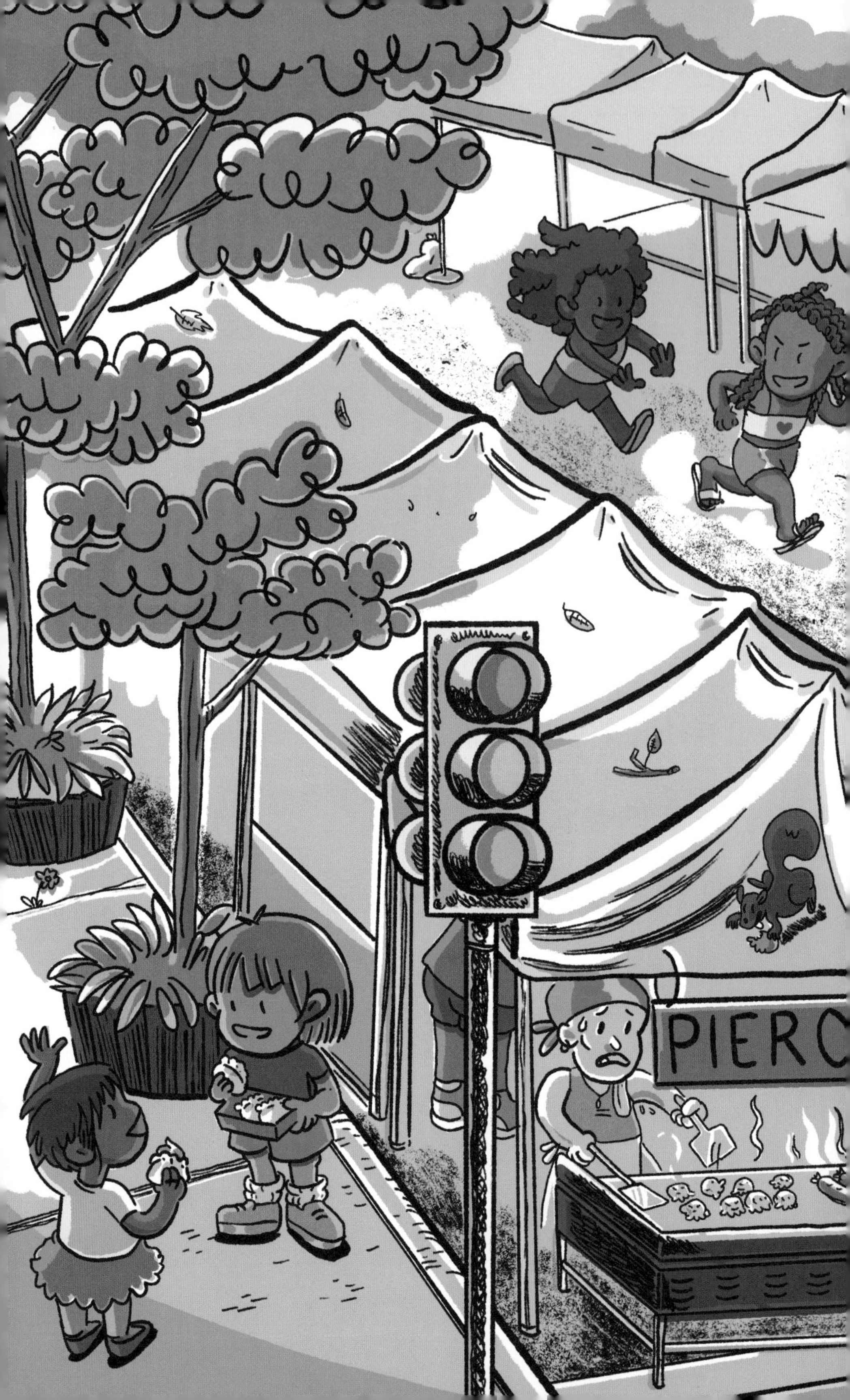
PIERC

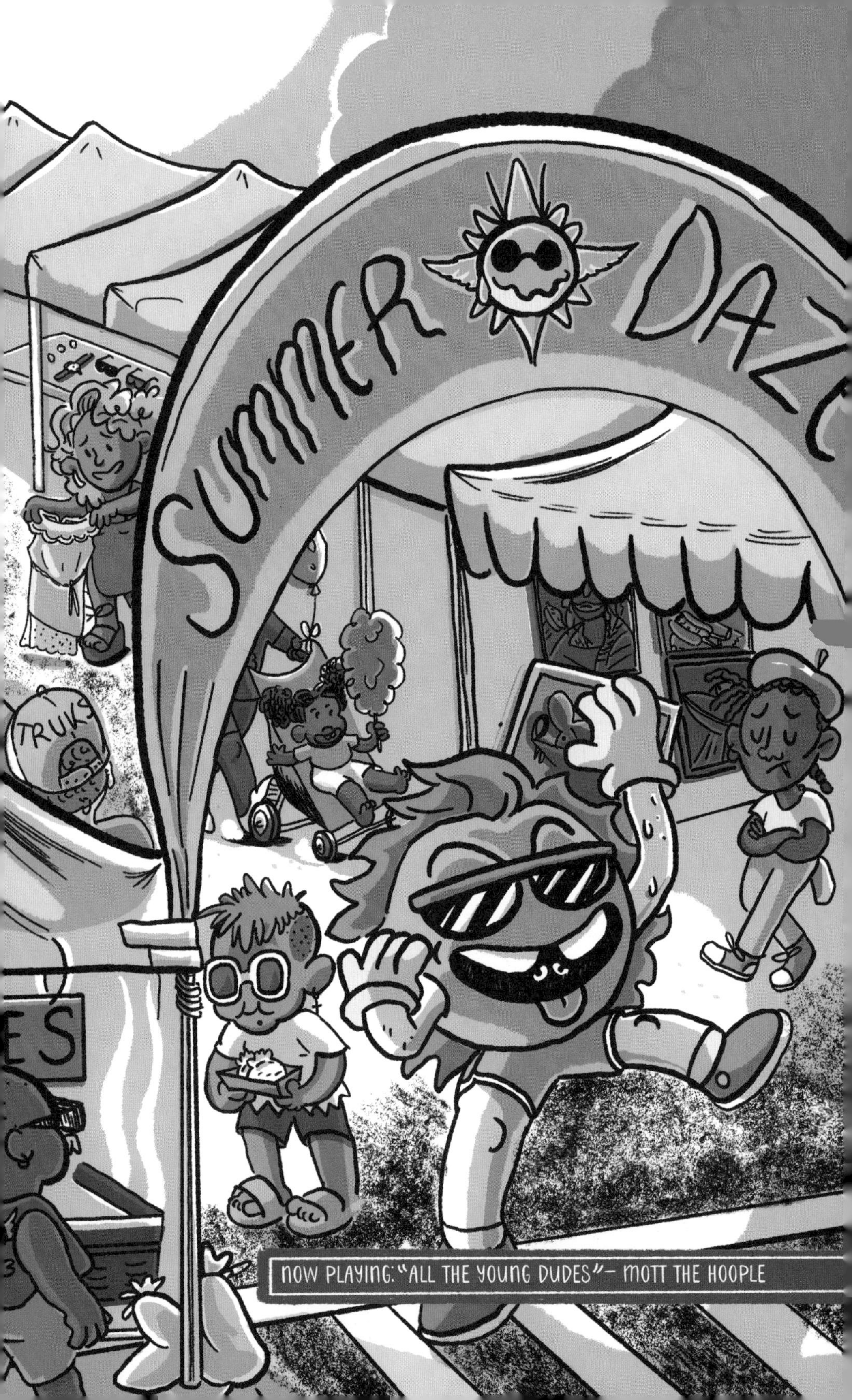
SUMMER DAZ
TRUKS
ES
NOW PLAYING: "ALL THE YOUNG DUDES"– MOTT THE HOOPLE

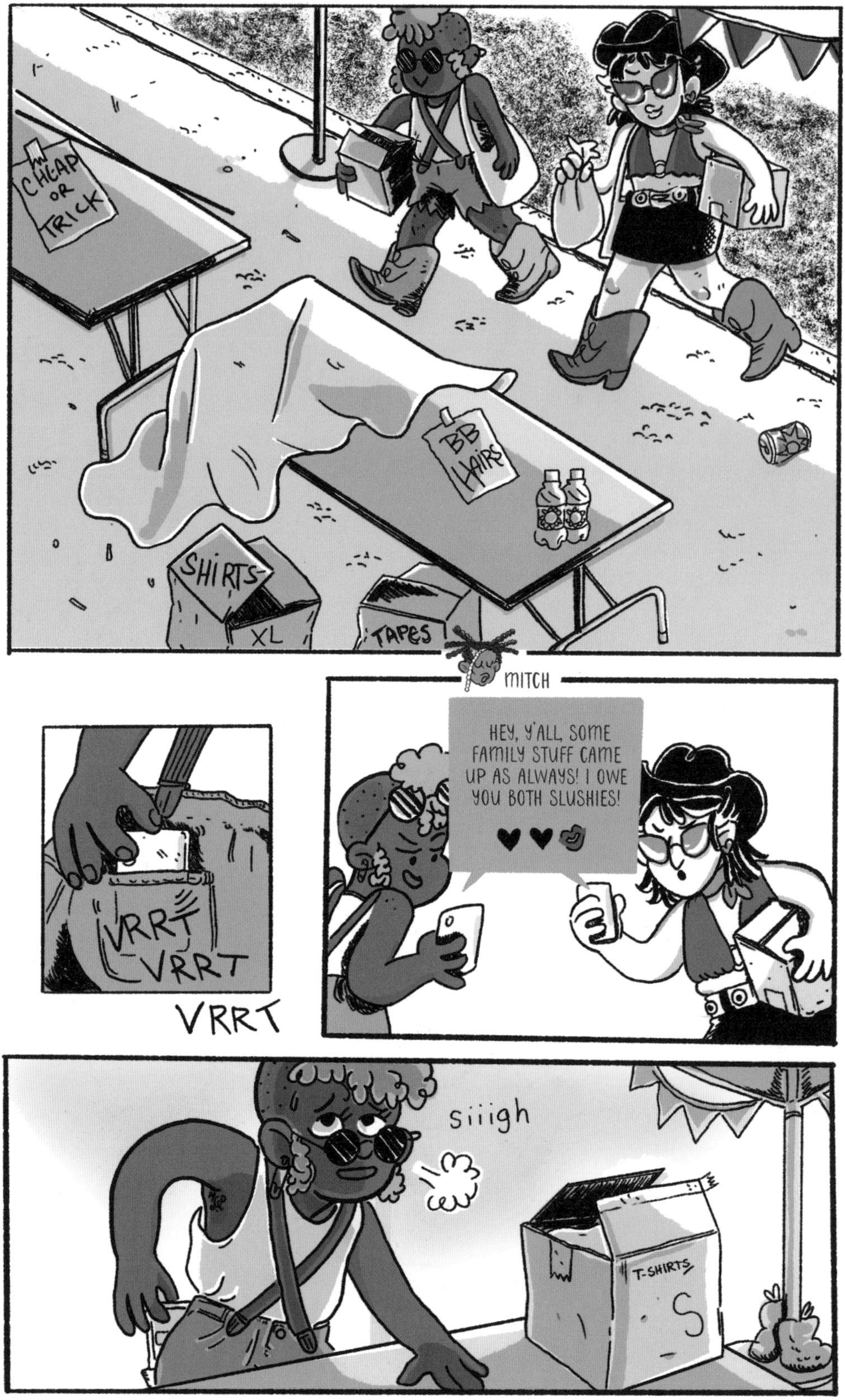
CHEAP OR TRICK
BB HAIRS
SHIRTS
XL
TAPES
MITCH
HEY, Y'ALL, SOME FAMILY STUFF CAME UP AS ALWAYS! I OWE YOU BOTH SLUSHIES!
VRRT VRRT
VRRT
siiigh
T-SHIRTS
S

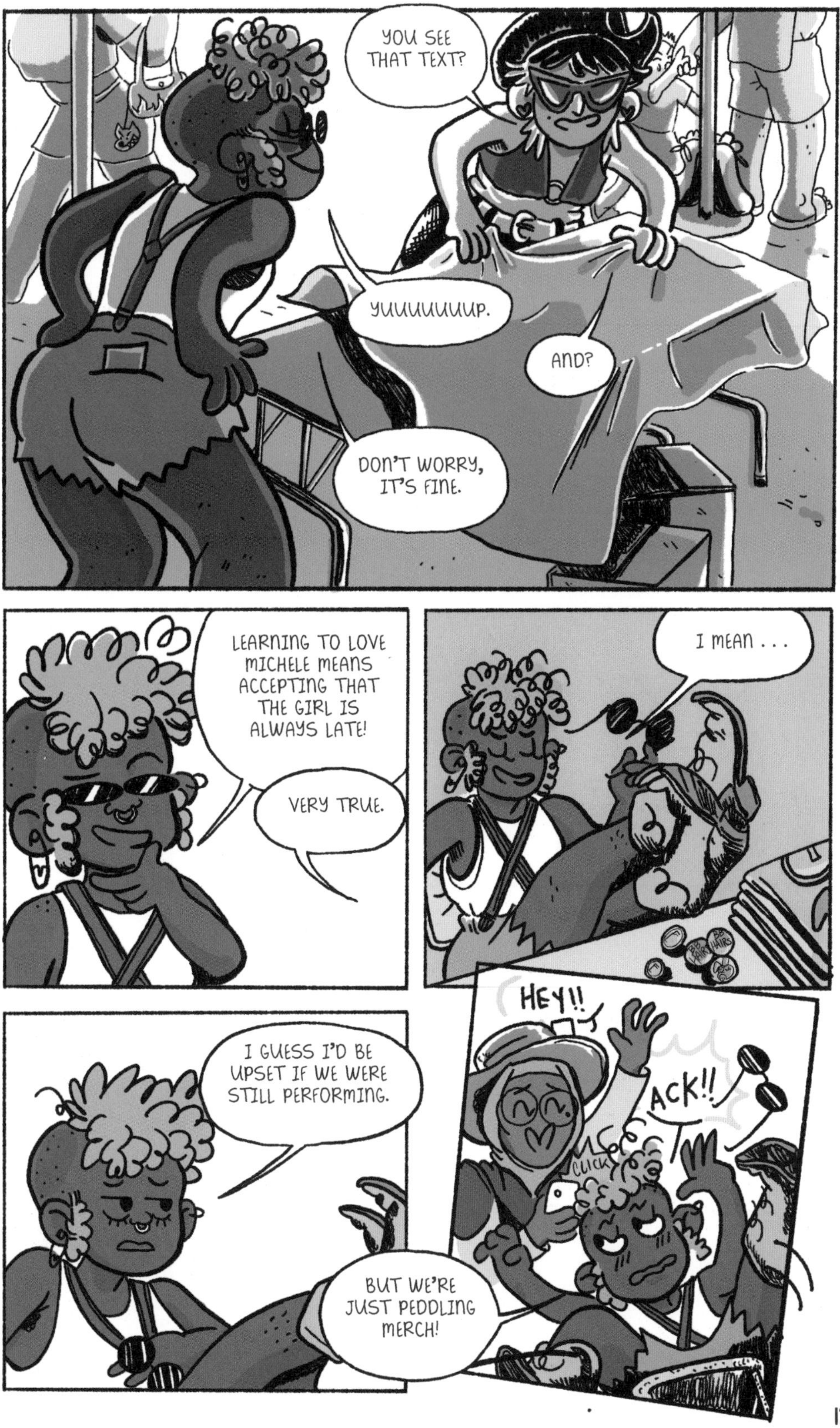
YOU SEE THAT TEXT?
YUUUUUUUP.
AND?
DON'T WORRY, IT'S FINE.
LEARNING TO LOVE MICHELE MEANS ACCEPTING THAT THE GIRL IS ALWAYS LATE!
VERY TRUE.
I MEAN . . .
I GUESS I'D BE UPSET IF WE WERE STILL PERFORMING.
BUT WE'RE JUST PEDDLING MERCH!
HEY!!
ACK!!
CLICK

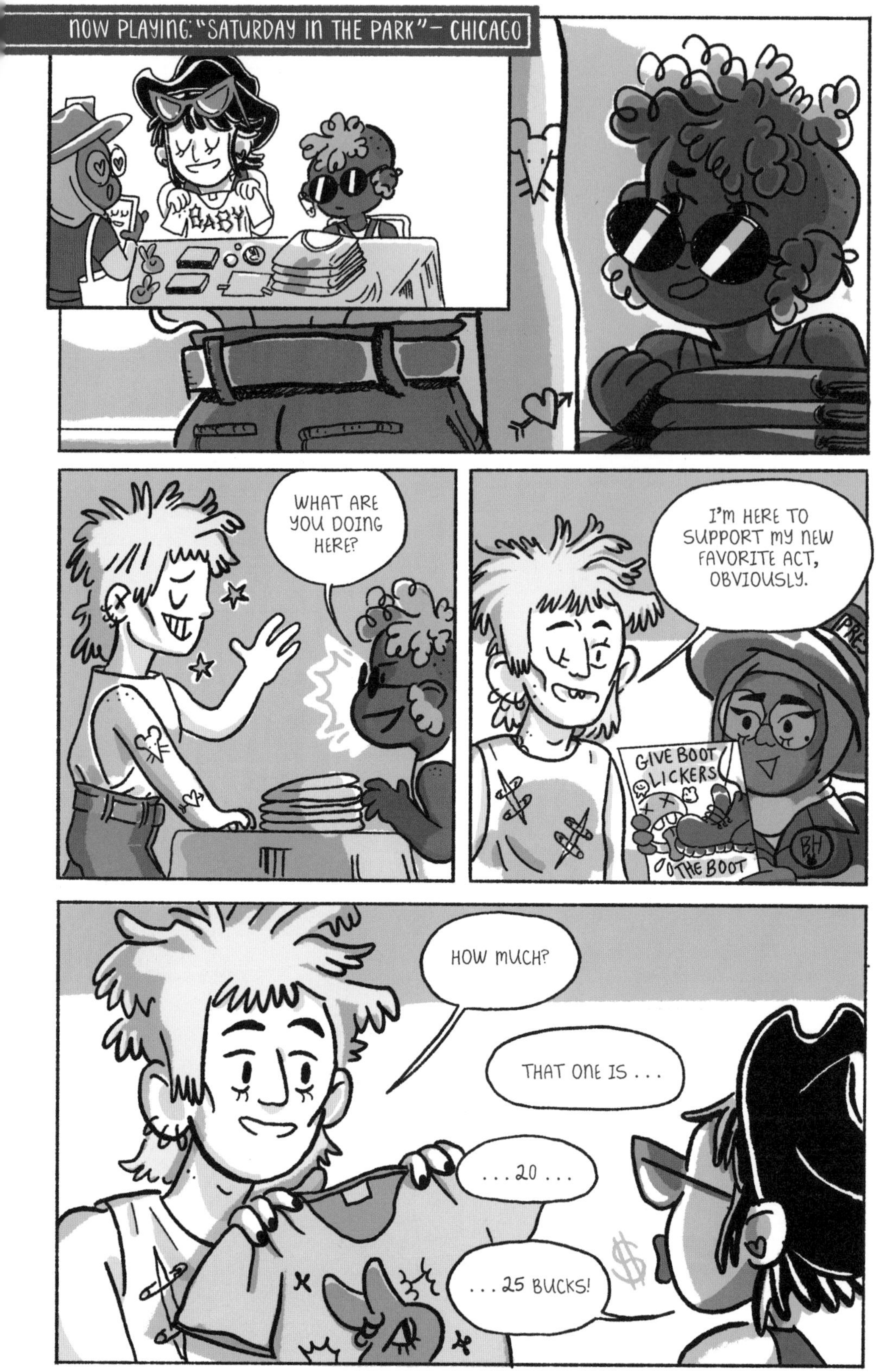
NOW PLAYING: "SATURDAY IN THE PARK" – CHICAGO
BABY
WHAT ARE YOU DOING HERE?
I'M HERE TO SUPPORT MY NEW FAVORITE ACT, OBVIOUSLY.
GIVE BOOT LICKERS THE BOOT
HOW MUCH?
THAT ONE IS . . .
. . . 20 . . .
. . . 25 BUCKS!

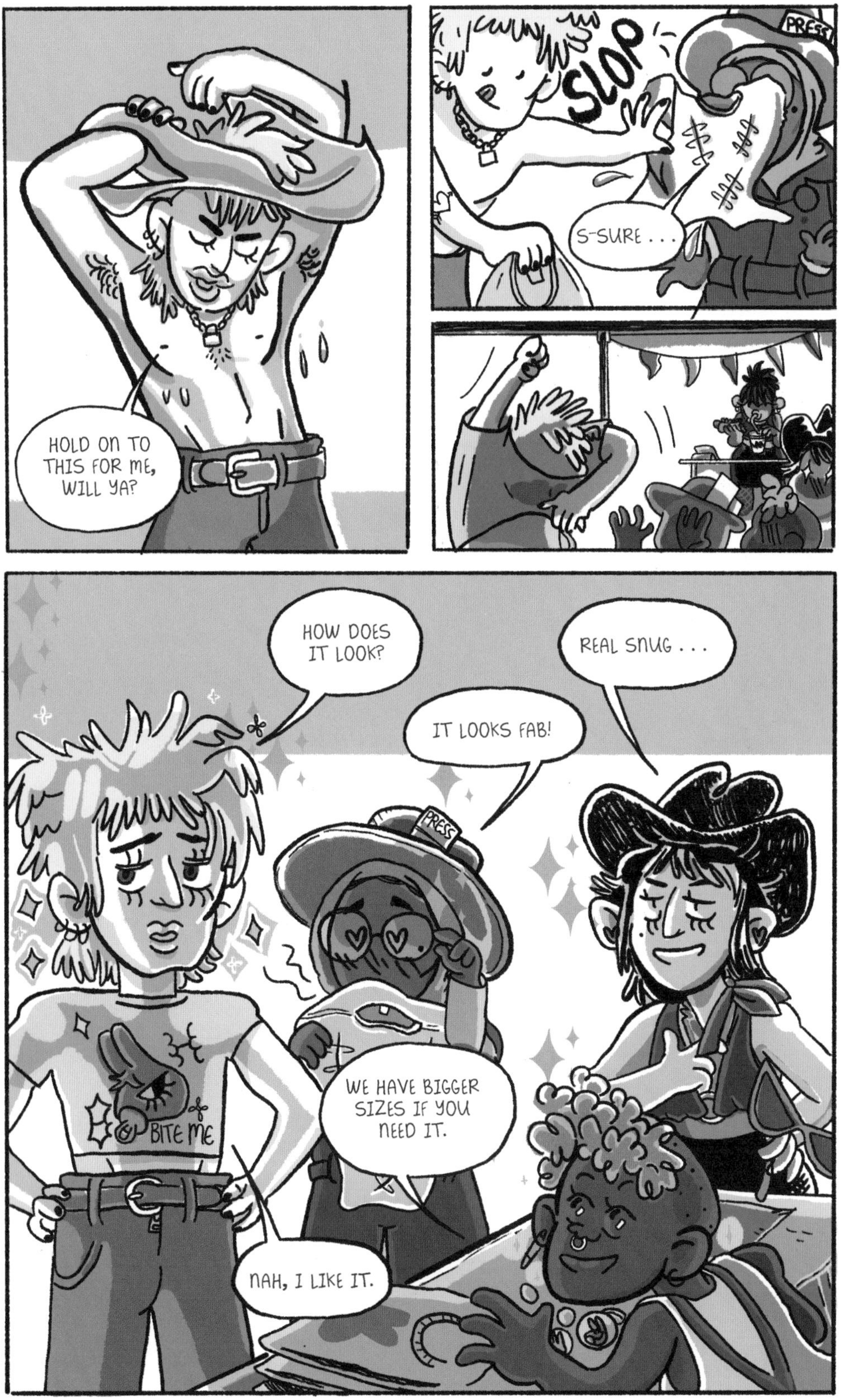
HOLD ON TO THIS FOR ME, WILL YA?
SLOP
S-SURE . . .
PRESS
HOW DOES IT LOOK?
REAL SNUG . . .
IT LOOKS FAB!
PRESS
BITE ME
WE HAVE BIGGER SIZES IF YOU NEED IT.
NAH, I LIKE IT.

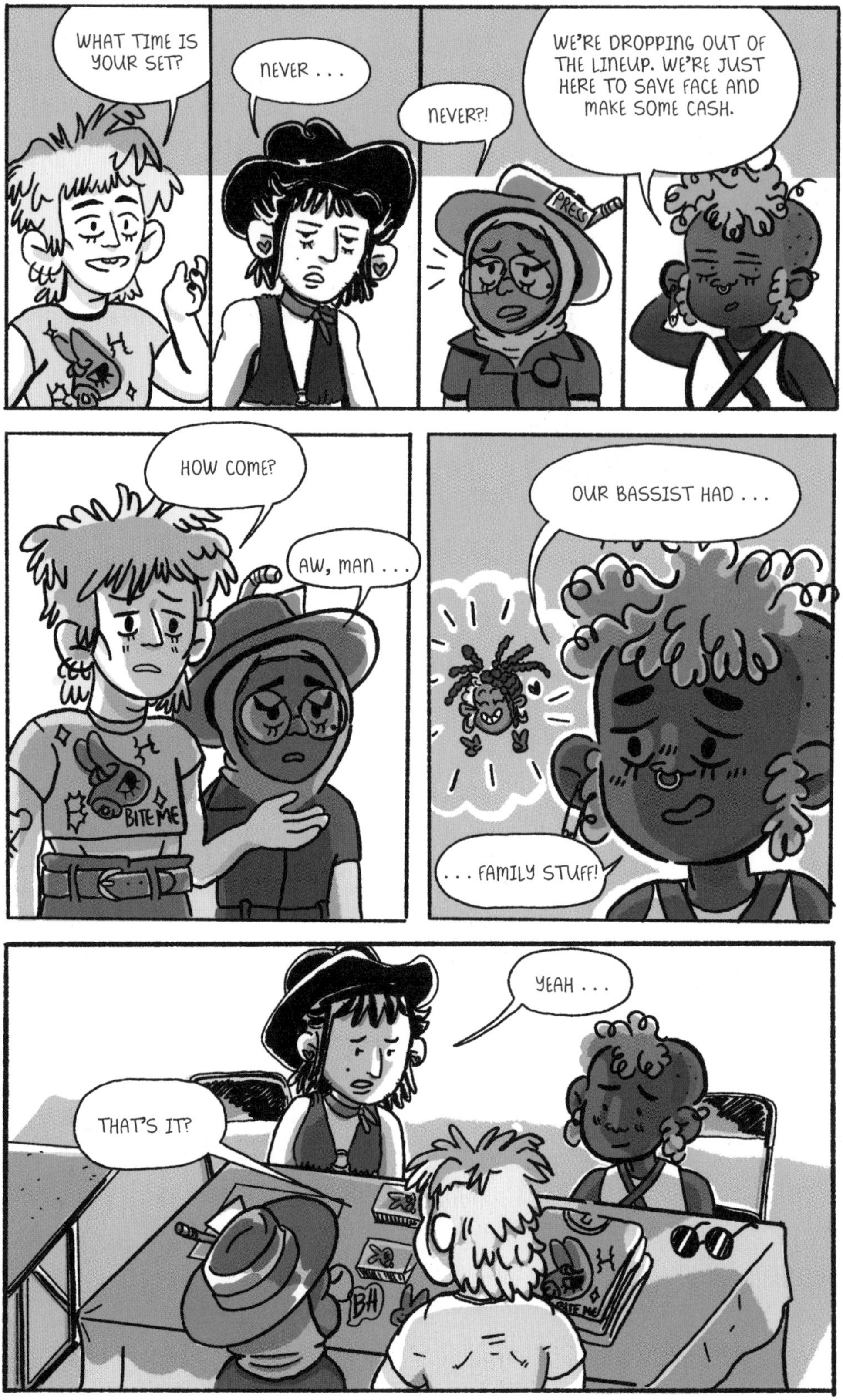
WHAT TIME IS YOUR SET?
NEVER . . .
NEVER?!
WE'RE DROPPING OUT OF THE LINEUP. WE'RE JUST HERE TO SAVE FACE AND MAKE SOME CASH.
PRESS
HOW COME?
AW, MAN . . .
BITE ME
OUR BASSIST HAD . . .
. . . FAMILY STUFF!
YEAH . . .
THAT'S IT?
BITE ME
BH

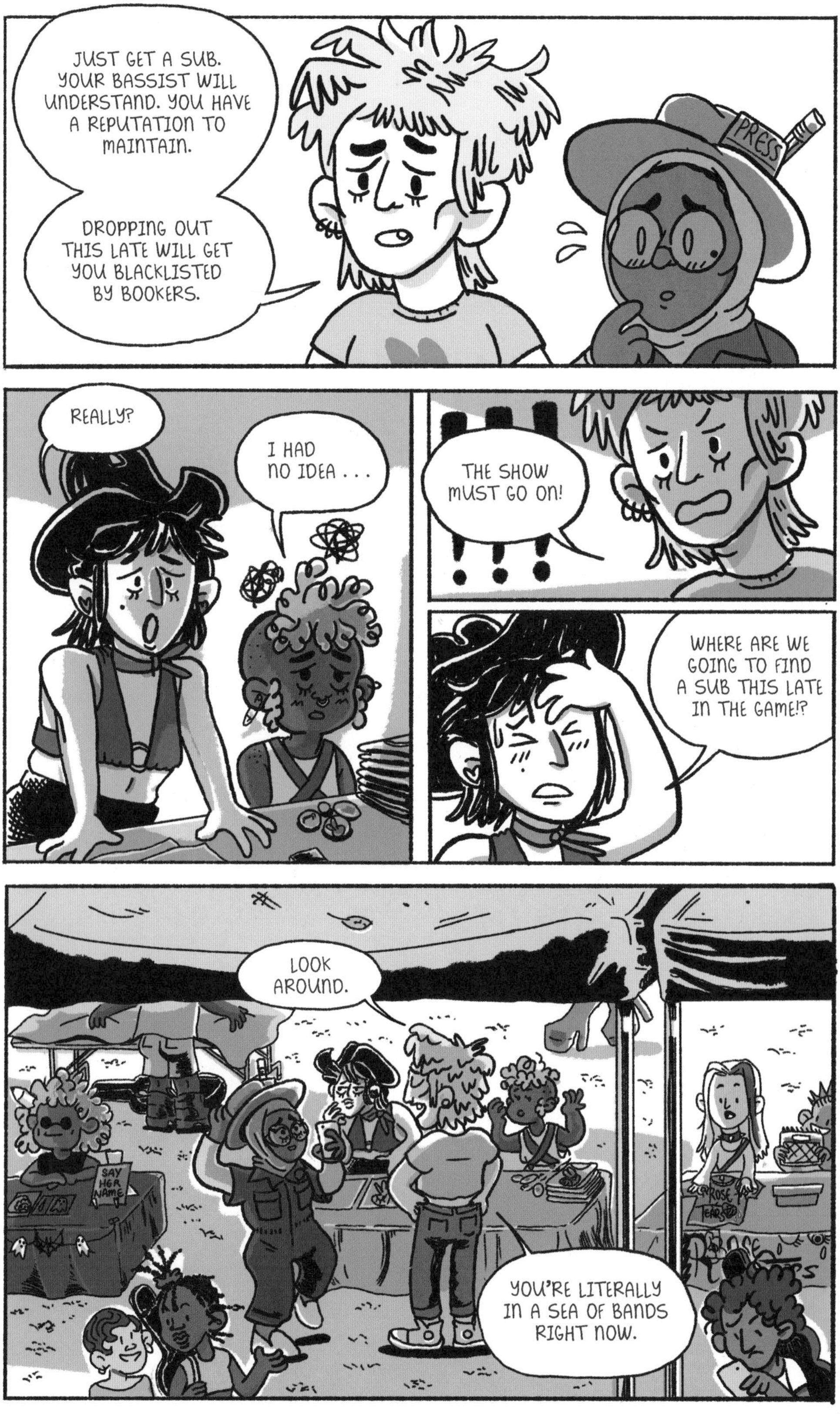
JUST GET A SUB. YOUR BASSIST WILL UNDERSTAND. YOU HAVE A REPUTATION TO MAINTAIN.
DROPPING OUT THIS LATE WILL GET YOU BLACKLISTED BY BOOKERS.
PRESS
REALLY?
I HAD NO IDEA . . .
THE SHOW MUST GO ON!
WHERE ARE WE GOING TO FIND A SUB THIS LATE IN THE GAME!?
LOOK AROUND.
SAY HER NAME
ROSE TEARS
YOU'RE LITERALLY IN A SEA OF BANDS RIGHT NOW.

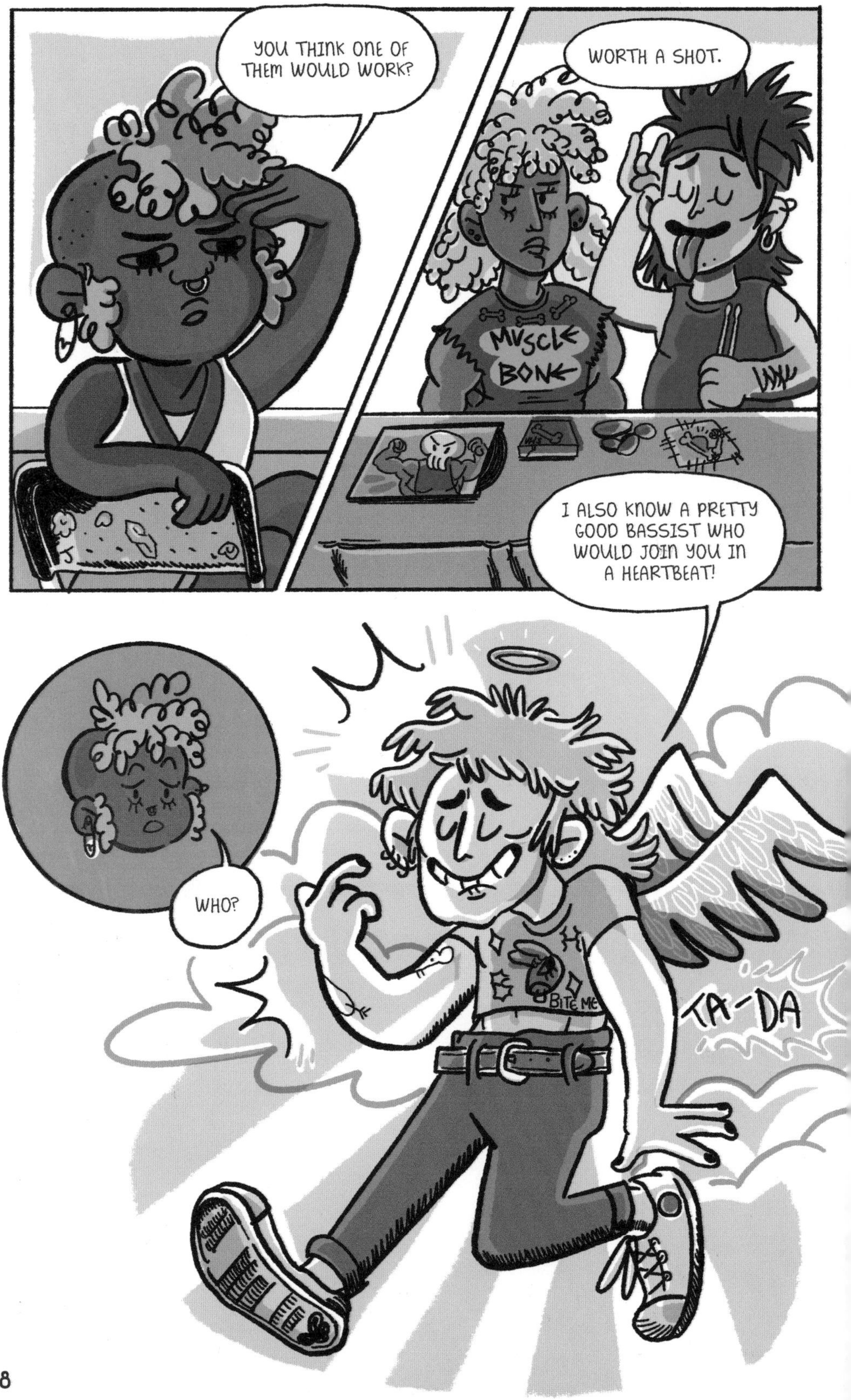
YOU THINK ONE OF THEM WOULD WORK?
WORTH A SHOT.
MUSCLE BONE
I ALSO KNOW A PRETTY GOOD BASSIST WHO WOULD JOIN YOU IN A HEARTBEAT!
WHO?
BITE ME
TA-DA

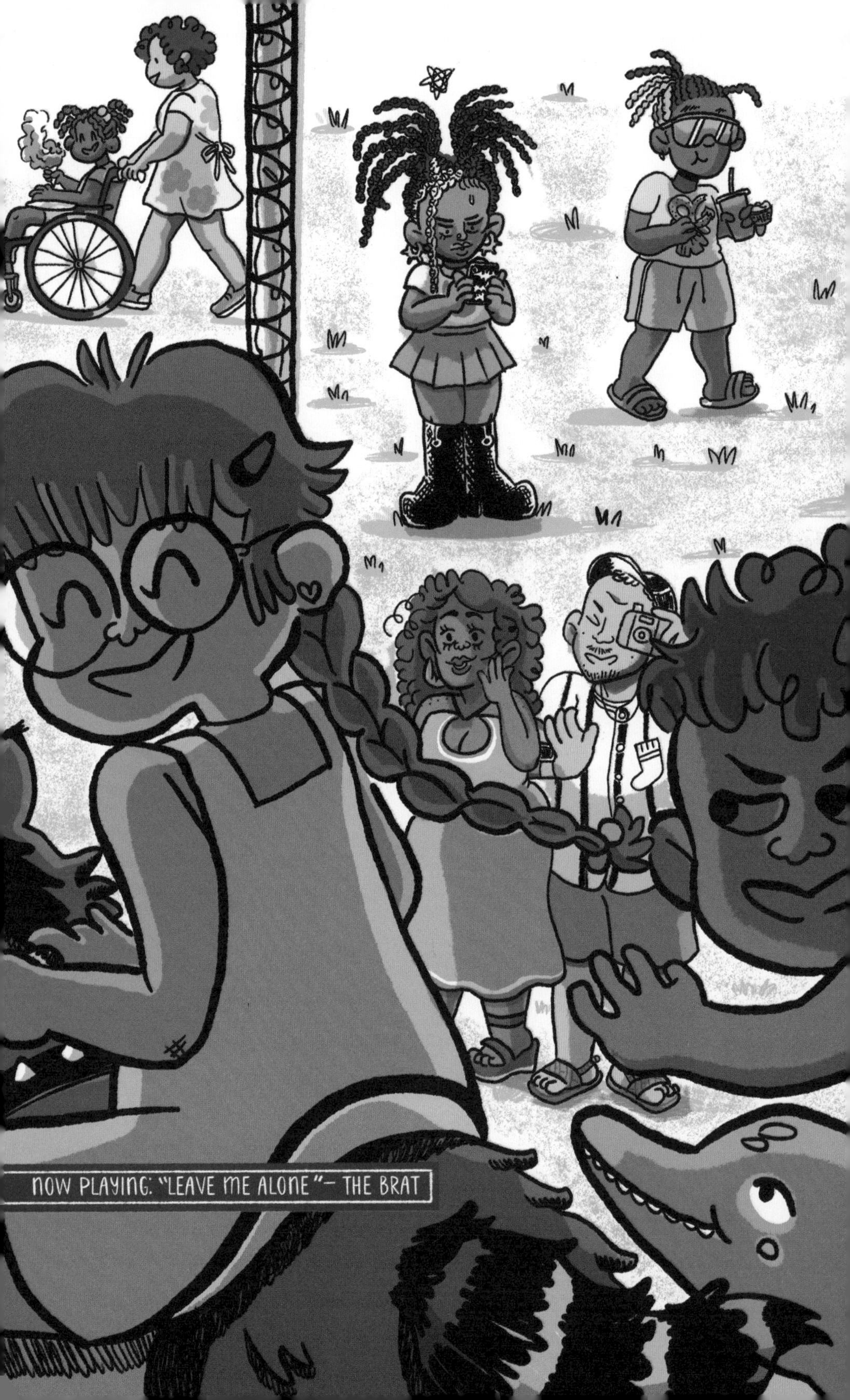
NOW PLAYING: "LEAVE ME ALONE"— THE BRAT

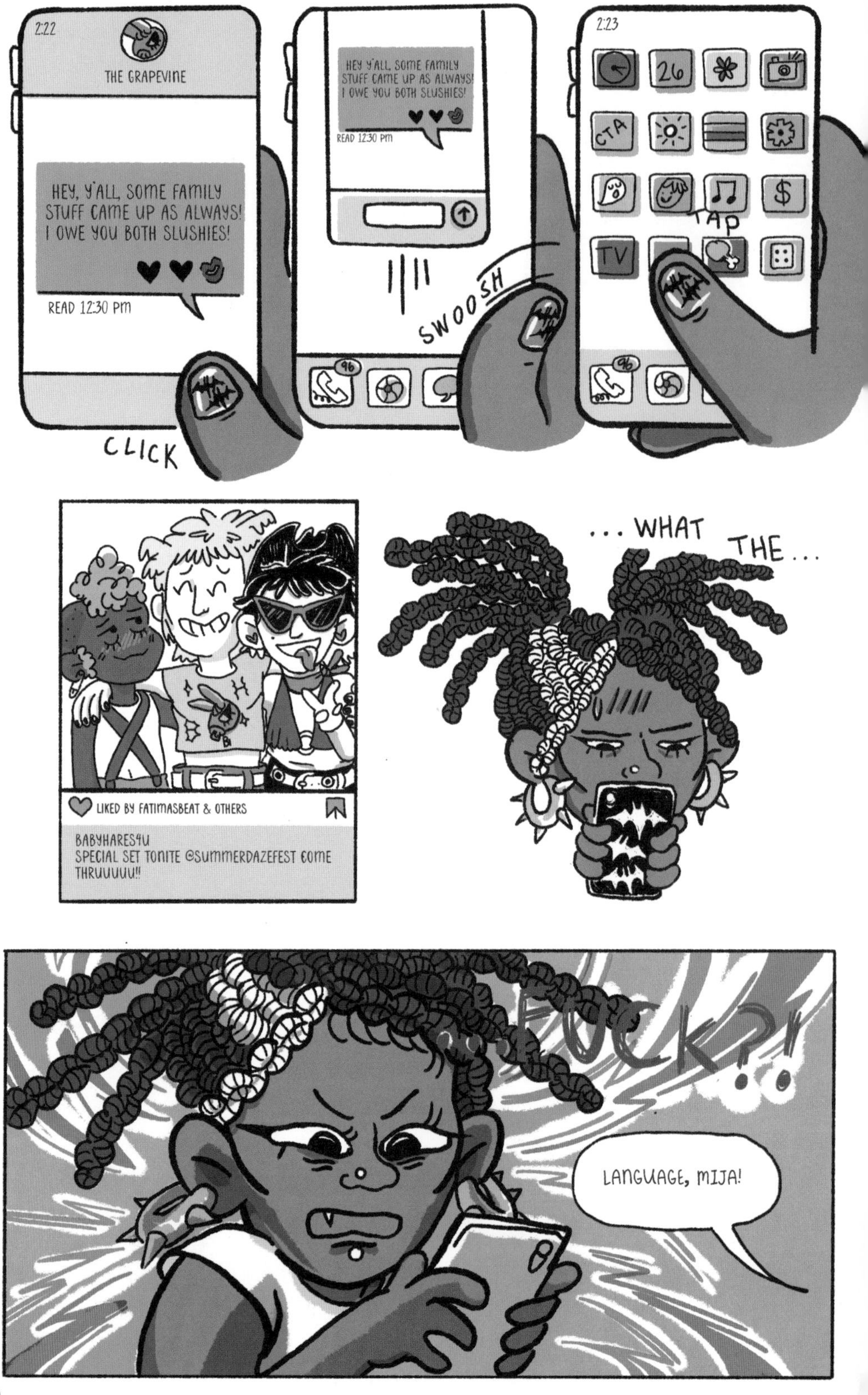
2:22
THE GRAPEVINE
HEY, Y'ALL, SOME FAMILY STUFF CAME UP AS ALWAYS! I OWE YOU BOTH SLUSHIES!
READ 12:30 PM
CLICK
HEY Y'ALL, SOME FAMILY STUFF CAME UP AS ALWAYS! I OWE YOU BOTH SLUSHIES!
READ 12:30 PM
SWOOSH
2:23
26
CTA
TV
TAP
LIKED BY FATIMASBEAT & OTHERS
BABYHARES4U
SPECIAL SET TONITE @SUMMERDAZEFEST COME THRUUUUU!!
...WHAT
THE...
FUCK?!
LANGUAGE, MIJA!

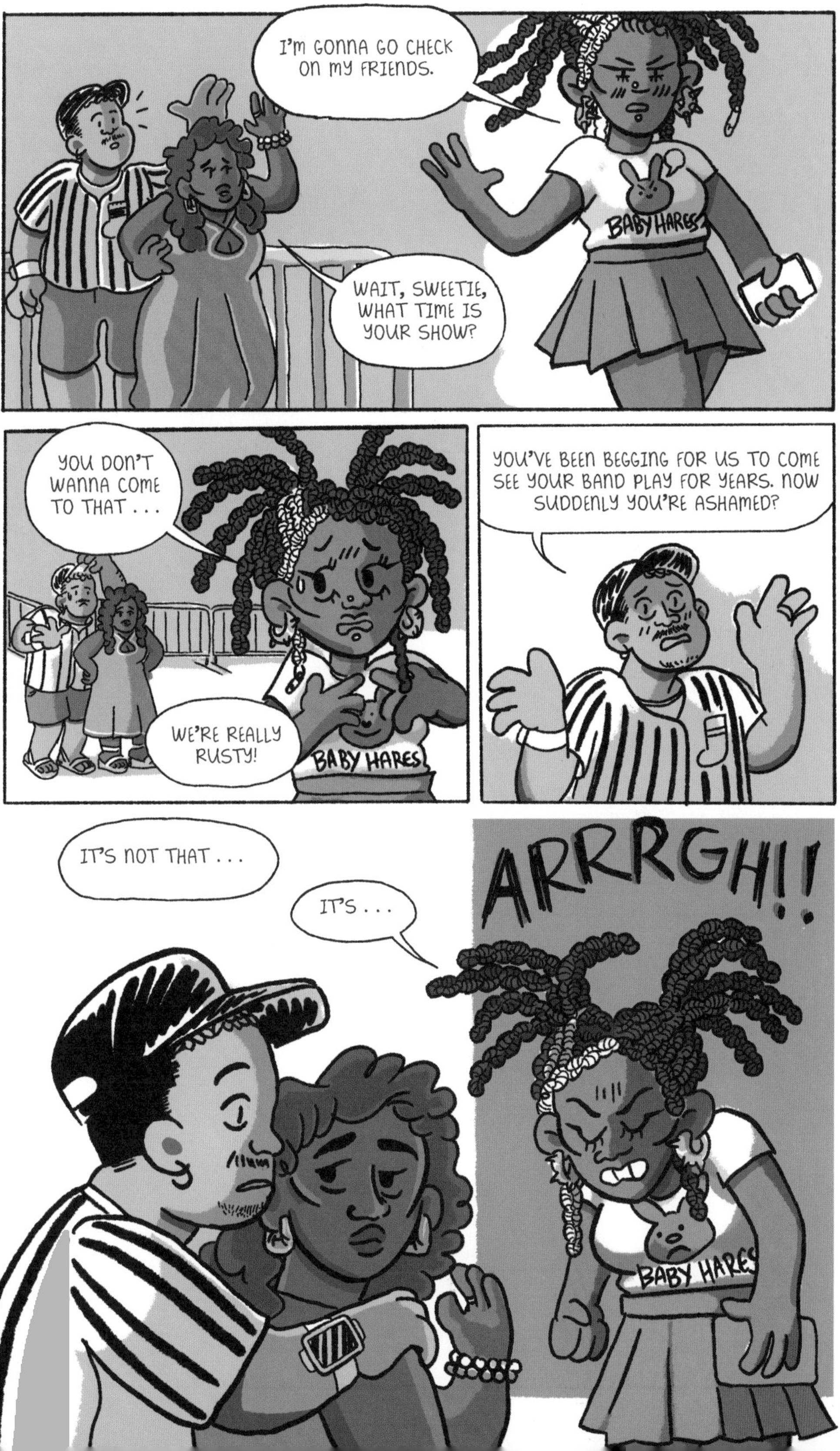
I'M GONNA GO CHECK ON MY FRIENDS.
WAIT, SWEETIE, WHAT TIME IS YOUR SHOW?
YOU DON'T WANNA COME TO THAT . . .
WE'RE REALLY RUSTY!
YOU'VE BEEN BEGGING FOR US TO COME SEE YOUR BAND PLAY FOR YEARS. NOW SUDDENLY YOU'RE ASHAMED?
IT'S NOT THAT . . .
IT'S . . .
ARRRGH!!
BABY HARES

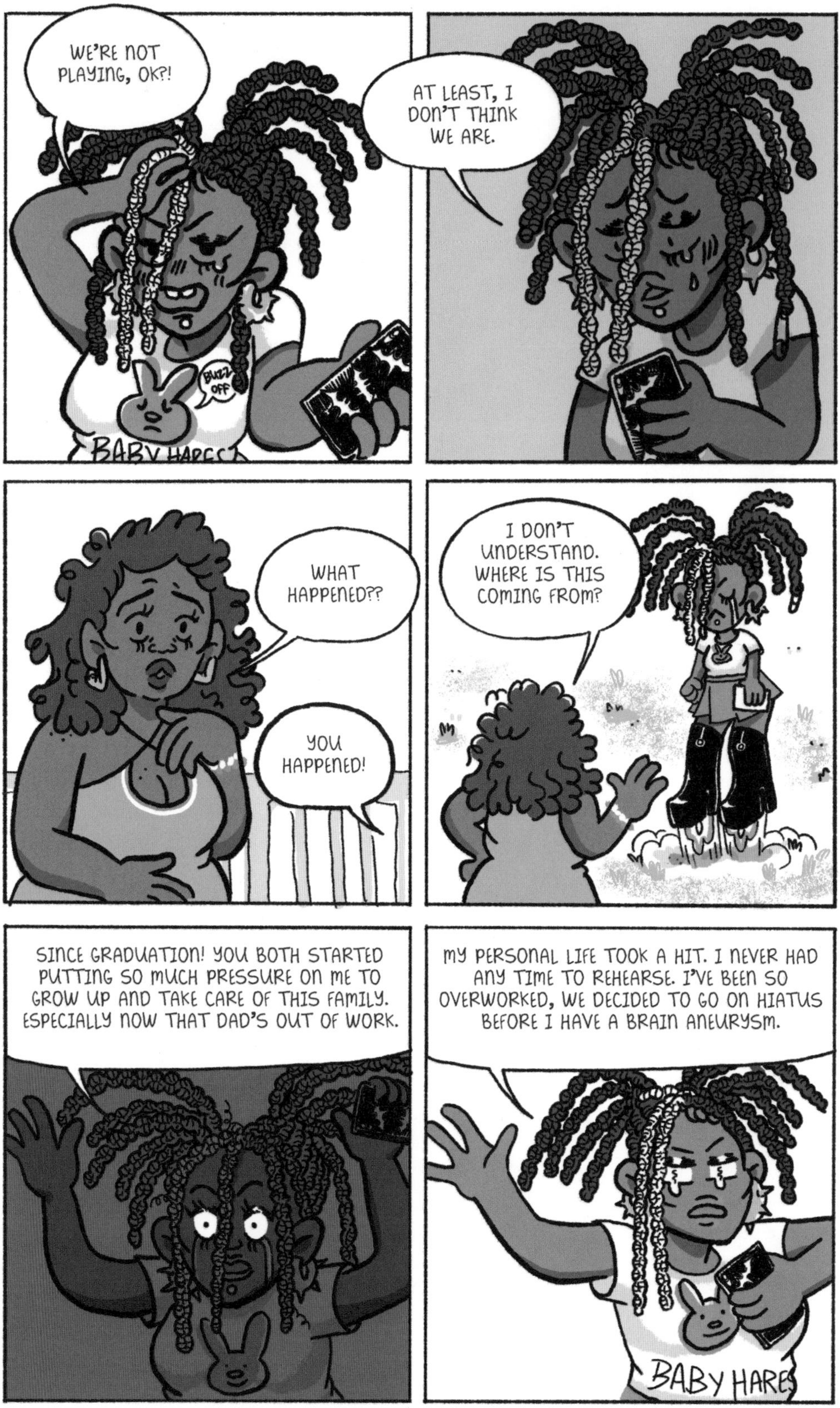
WE'RE NOT PLAYING, OK?!
BUZZ OFF
BABY HARES
AT LEAST, I DON'T THINK WE ARE.
WHAT HAPPENED??
YOU HAPPENED!
I DON'T UNDERSTAND. WHERE IS THIS COMING FROM?
SINCE GRADUATION! YOU BOTH STARTED PUTTING SO MUCH PRESSURE ON ME TO GROW UP AND TAKE CARE OF THIS FAMILY. ESPECIALLY NOW THAT DAD'S OUT OF WORK.
MY PERSONAL LIFE TOOK A HIT. I NEVER HAD ANY TIME TO REHEARSE. I'VE BEEN SO OVERWORKED, WE DECIDED TO GO ON HIATUS BEFORE I HAVE A BRAIN ANEURYSM.
BABY HARES

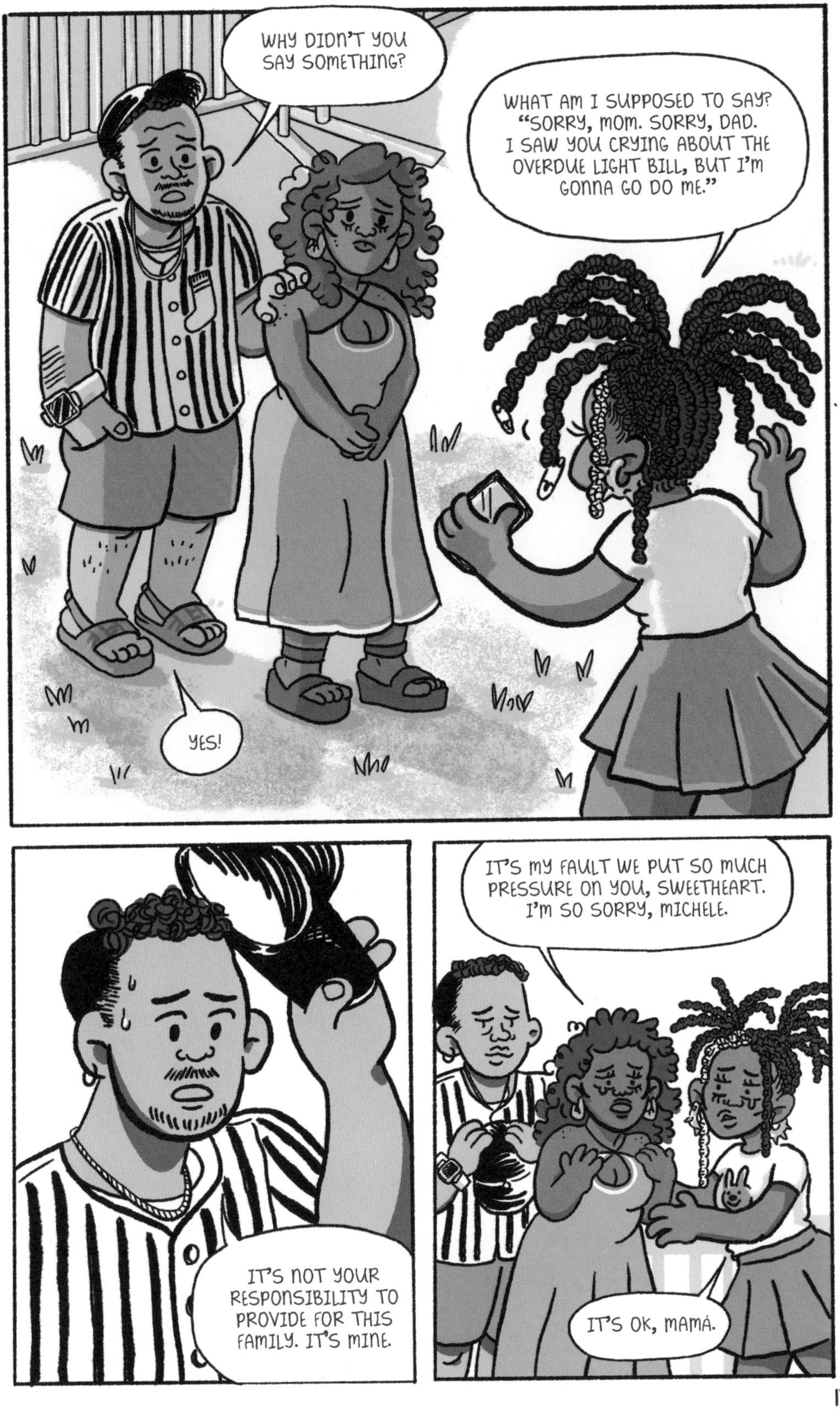
WHY DIDN'T YOU SAY SOMETHING?
WHAT AM I SUPPOSED TO SAY? "SORRY, MOM. SORRY, DAD. I SAW YOU CRYING ABOUT THE OVERDUE LIGHT BILL, BUT I'M GONNA GO DO ME."
YES!
IT'S NOT YOUR RESPONSIBILITY TO PROVIDE FOR THIS FAMILY. IT'S MINE.
IT'S MY FAULT WE PUT SO MUCH PRESSURE ON YOU, SWEETHEART. I'M SO SORRY, MICHELE.
IT'S OK, MAMÁ.

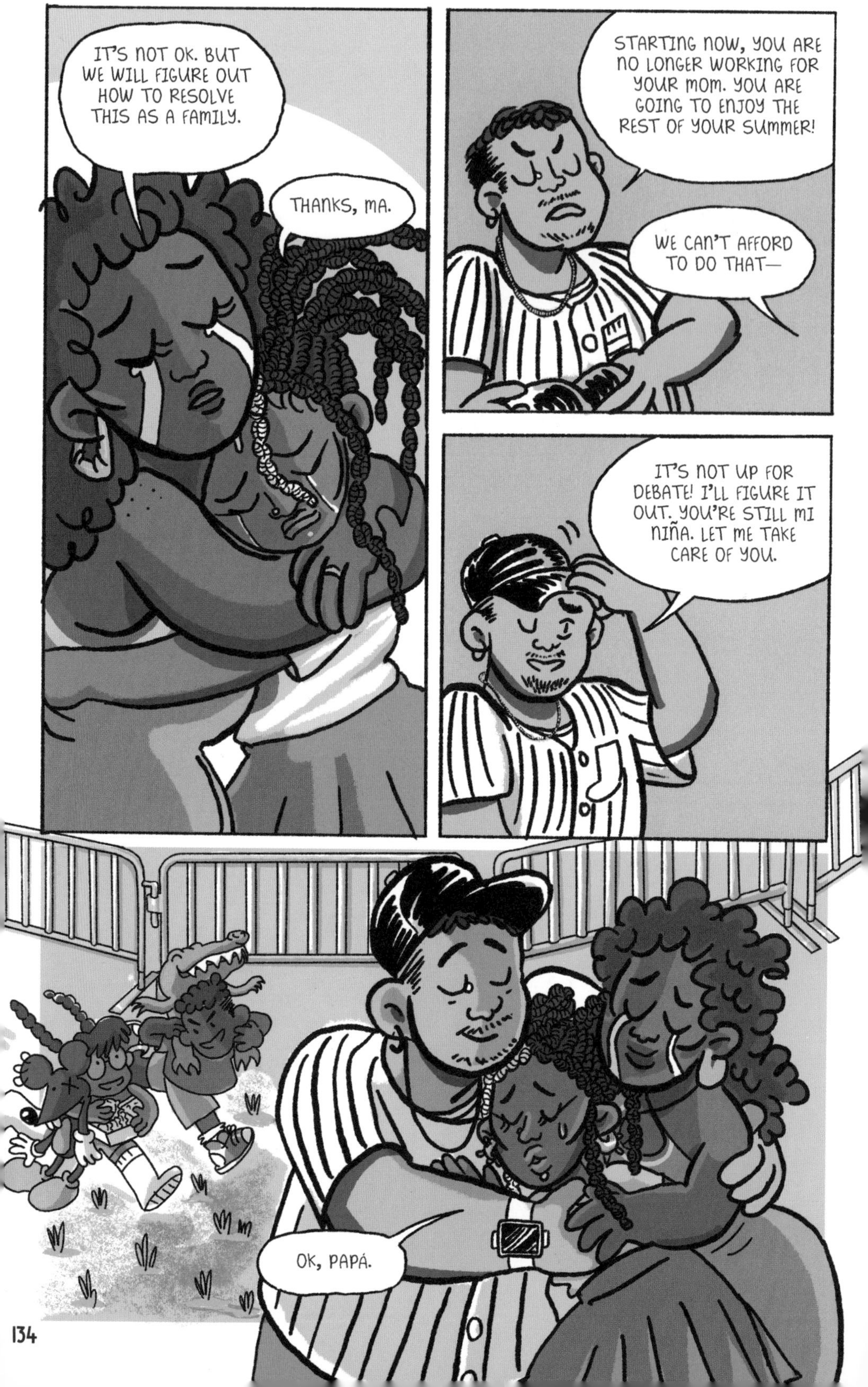
IT'S NOT OK. BUT WE WILL FIGURE OUT HOW TO RESOLVE THIS AS A FAMILY.
THANKS, MA.
STARTING NOW, YOU ARE NO LONGER WORKING FOR YOUR MOM. YOU ARE GOING TO ENJOY THE REST OF YOUR SUMMER!
WE CAN'T AFFORD TO DO THAT—
IT'S NOT UP FOR DEBATE! I'LL FIGURE IT OUT. YOU'RE STILL MI NIÑA. LET ME TAKE CARE OF YOU.
OK, PAPÁ.

TRACK SEVEN: "FAME"

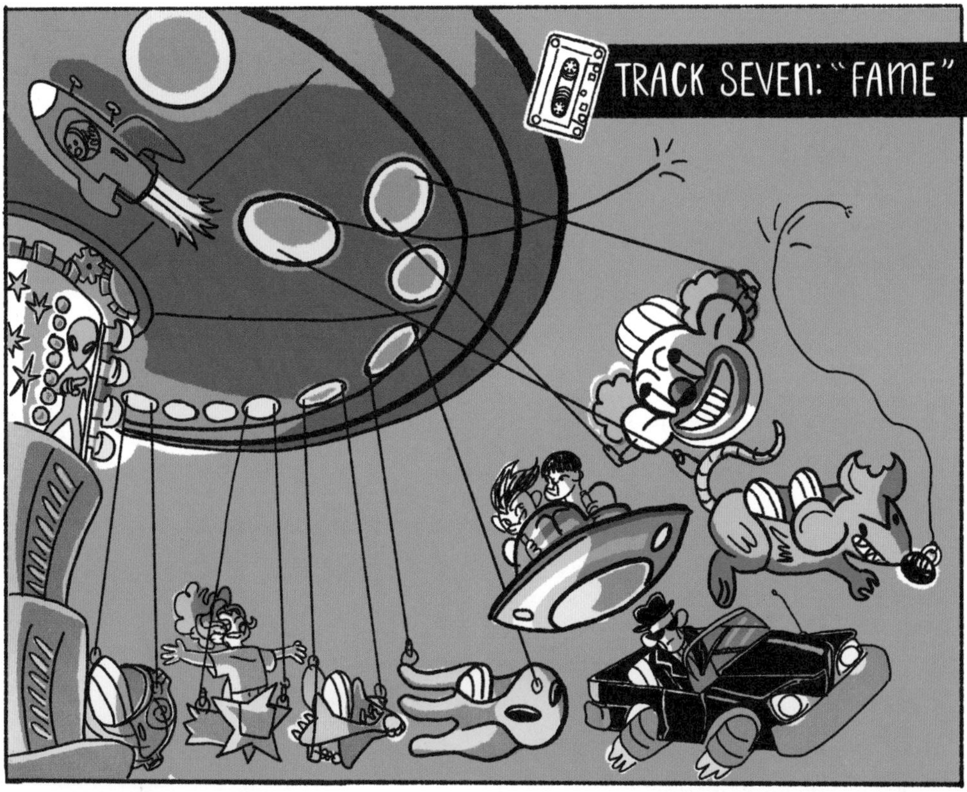

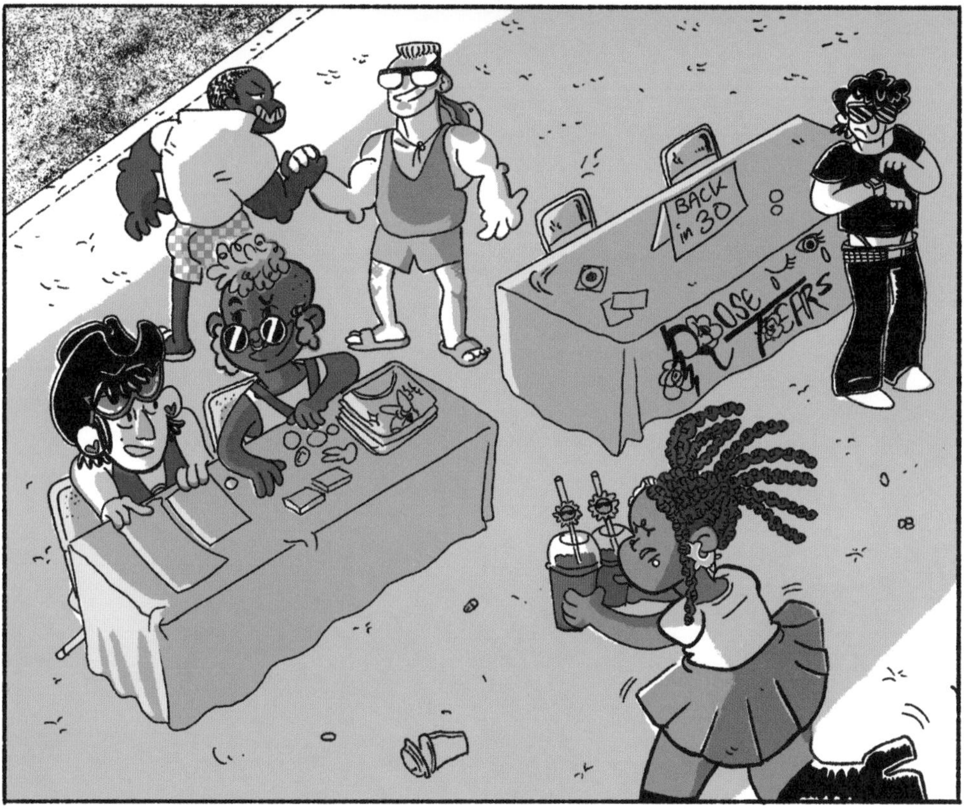
BACK in 30

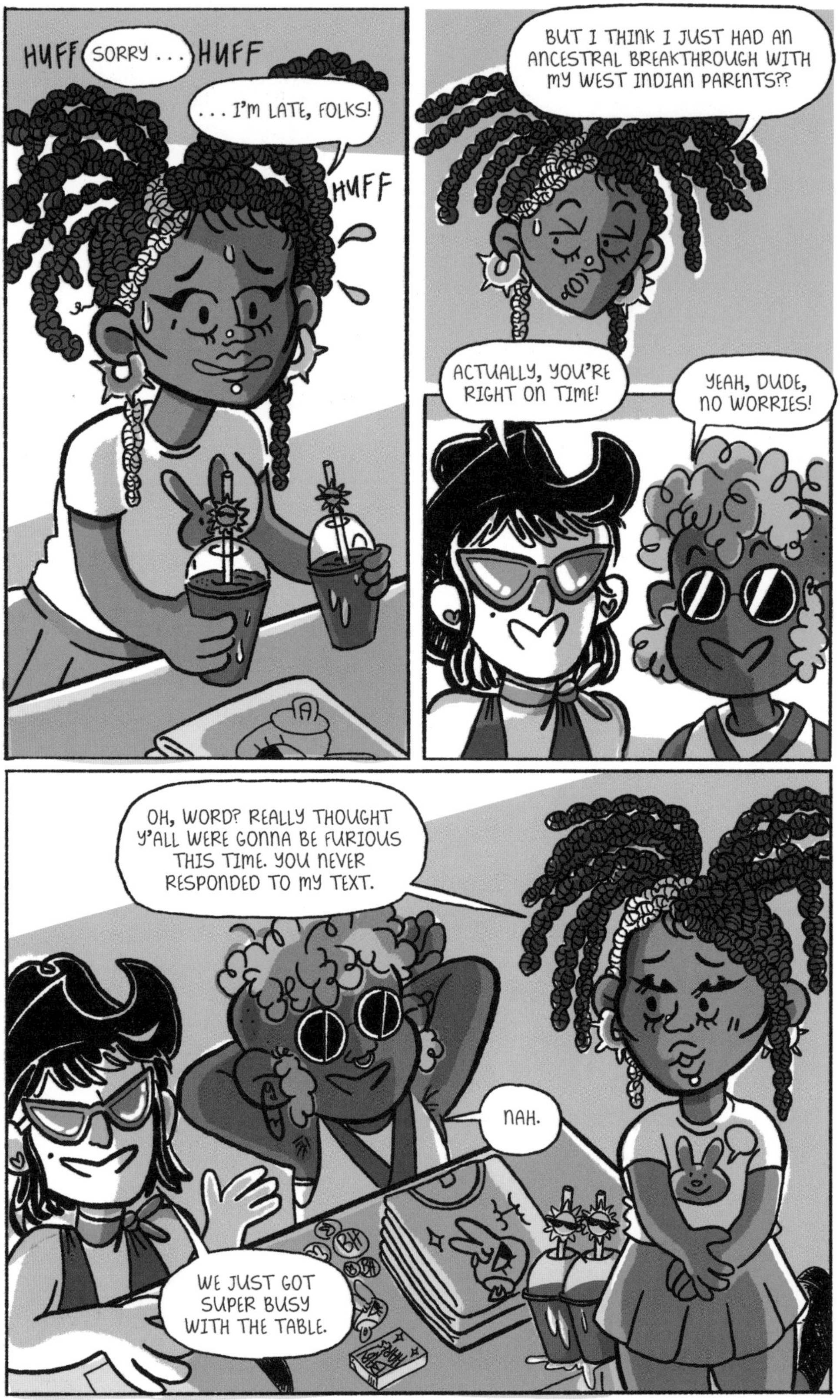
HUFF
SORRY . . .
HUFF
. . . I'M LATE, FOLKS!
HUFF
BUT I THINK I JUST HAD AN ANCESTRAL BREAKTHROUGH WITH MY WEST INDIAN PARENTS??
ACTUALLY, YOU'RE RIGHT ON TIME!
YEAH, DUDE, NO WORRIES!
OH, WORD? REALLY THOUGHT Y'ALL WERE GONNA BE FURIOUS THIS TIME. YOU NEVER RESPONDED TO MY TEXT.
NAH.
WE JUST GOT SUPER BUSY WITH THE TABLE.

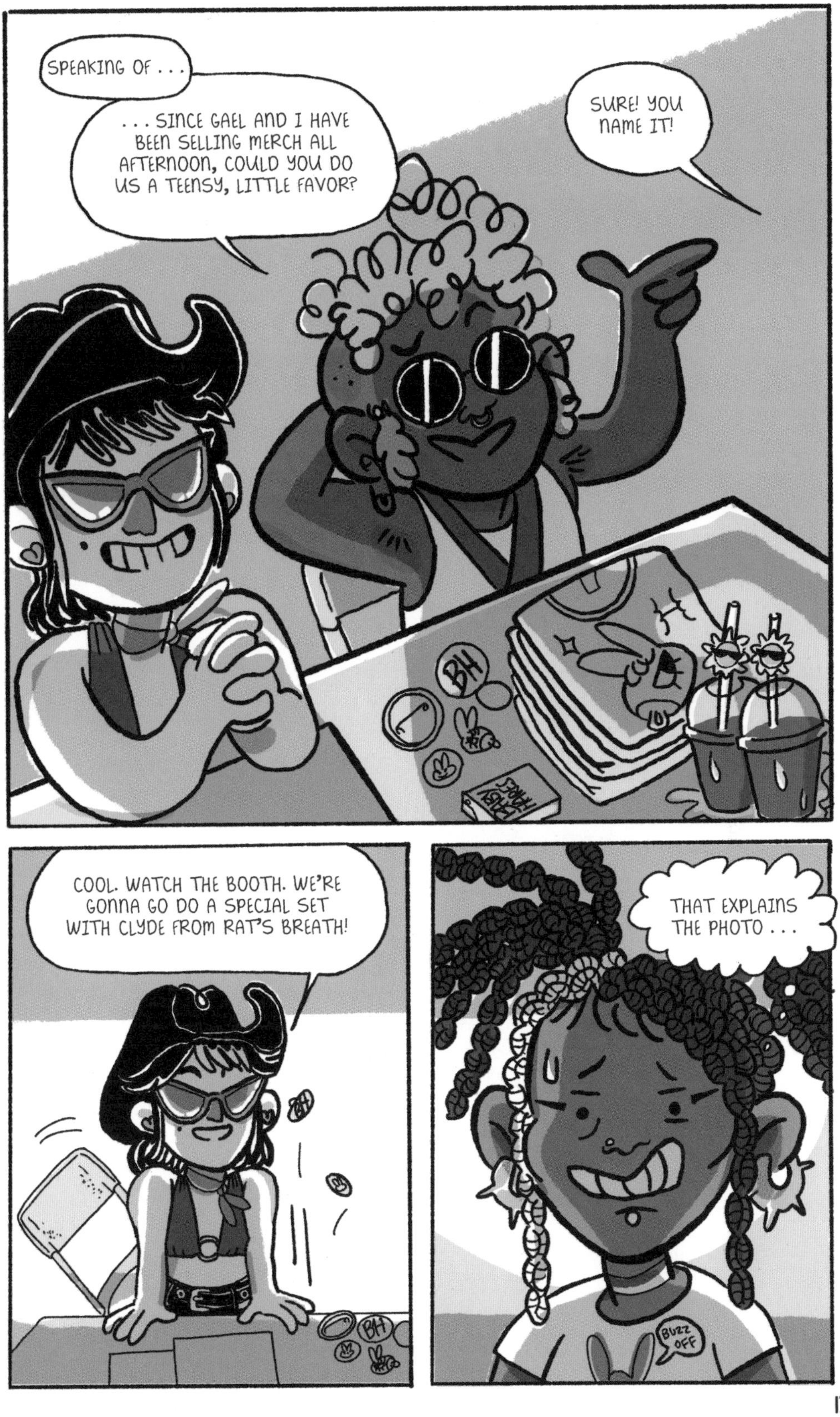
SPEAKING OF . . .
. . . SINCE GAEL AND I HAVE BEEN SELLING MERCH ALL AFTERNOON, COULD YOU DO US A TEENSY, LITTLE FAVOR?
SURE! YOU NAME IT!
COOL. WATCH THE BOOTH. WE'RE GONNA GO DO A SPECIAL SET WITH CLYDE FROM RAT'S BREATH!
THAT EXPLAINS THE PHOTO . . .
BUZZ OFF

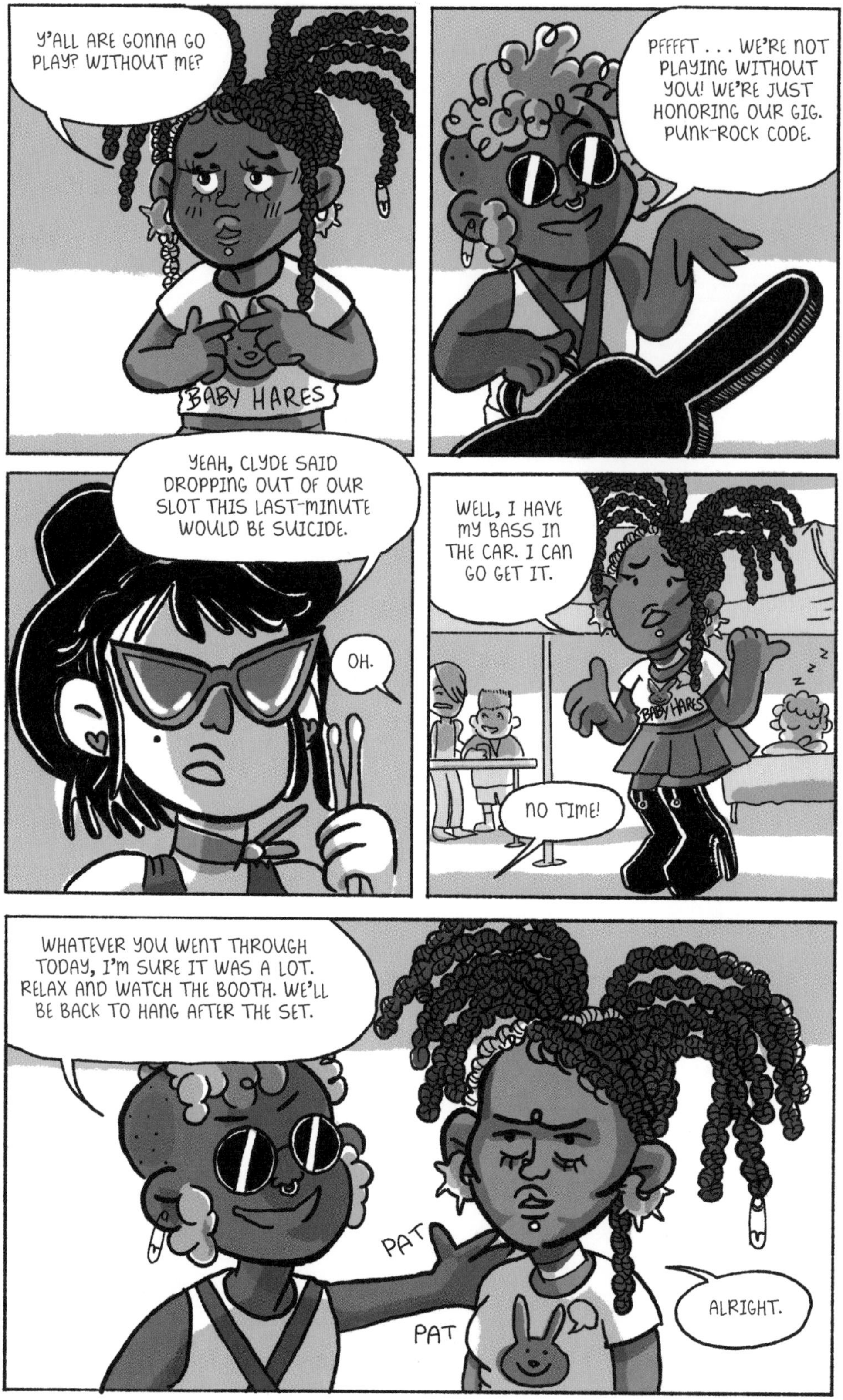
Y'ALL ARE GONNA GO PLAY? WITHOUT ME?
BABY HARES
PFFFFT . . . WE'RE NOT PLAYING WITHOUT YOU! WE'RE JUST HONORING OUR GIG. PUNK-ROCK CODE.
YEAH, CLYDE SAID DROPPING OUT OF OUR SLOT THIS LAST-MINUTE WOULD BE SUICIDE.
OH.
WELL, I HAVE MY BASS IN THE CAR. I CAN GO GET IT.
BABY HARES
NO TIME!
WHATEVER YOU WENT THROUGH TODAY, I'M SURE IT WAS A LOT. RELAX AND WATCH THE BOOTH. WE'LL BE BACK TO HANG AFTER THE SET.
PAT
PAT
ALRIGHT.

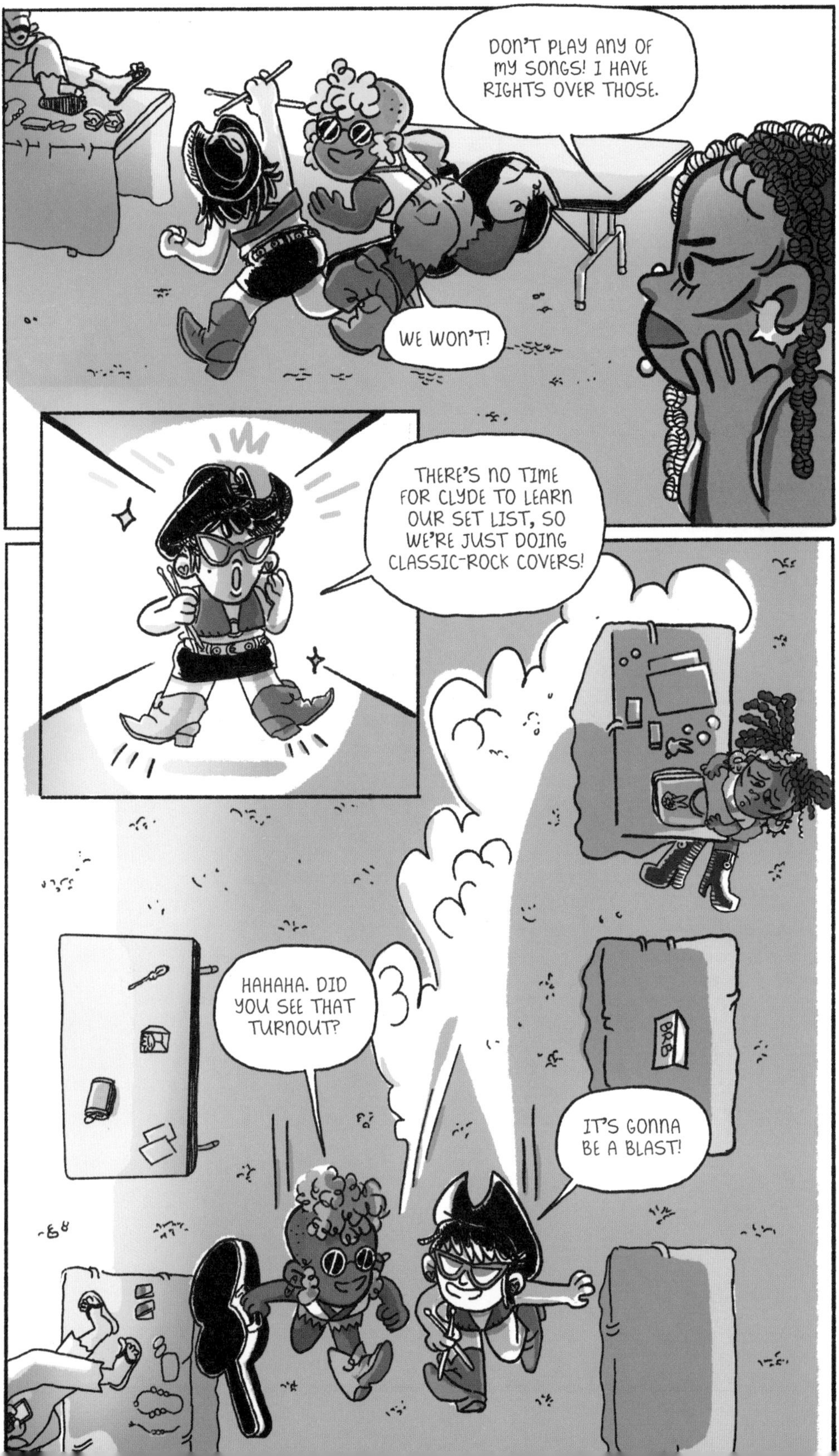
DON'T PLAY ANY OF MY SONGS! I HAVE RIGHTS OVER THOSE.
WE WON'T!
THERE'S NO TIME FOR CLYDE TO LEARN OUR SET LIST, SO WE'RE JUST DOING CLASSIC-ROCK COVERS!
HAHAHA. DID YOU SEE THAT TURNOUT?
IT'S GONNA BE A BLAST!

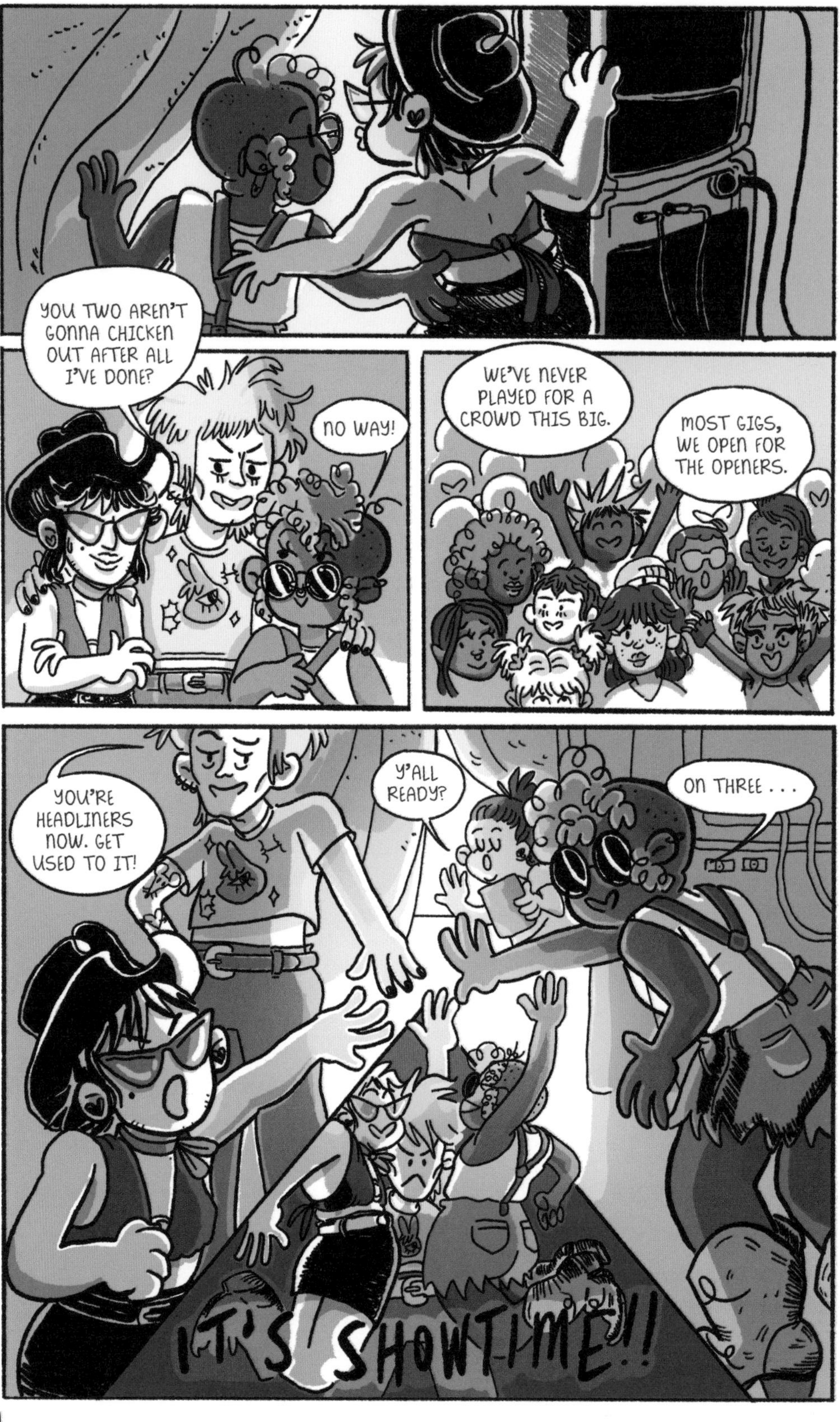

YOU TWO AREN'T GONNA CHICKEN OUT AFTER ALL I'VE DONE?
NO WAY!
WE'VE NEVER PLAYED FOR A CROWD THIS BIG.
MOST GIGS, WE OPEN FOR THE OPENERS.
YOU'RE HEADLINERS NOW. GET USED TO IT!
Y'ALL READY?
ON THREE . . .
IT'S SHOWTIME!!

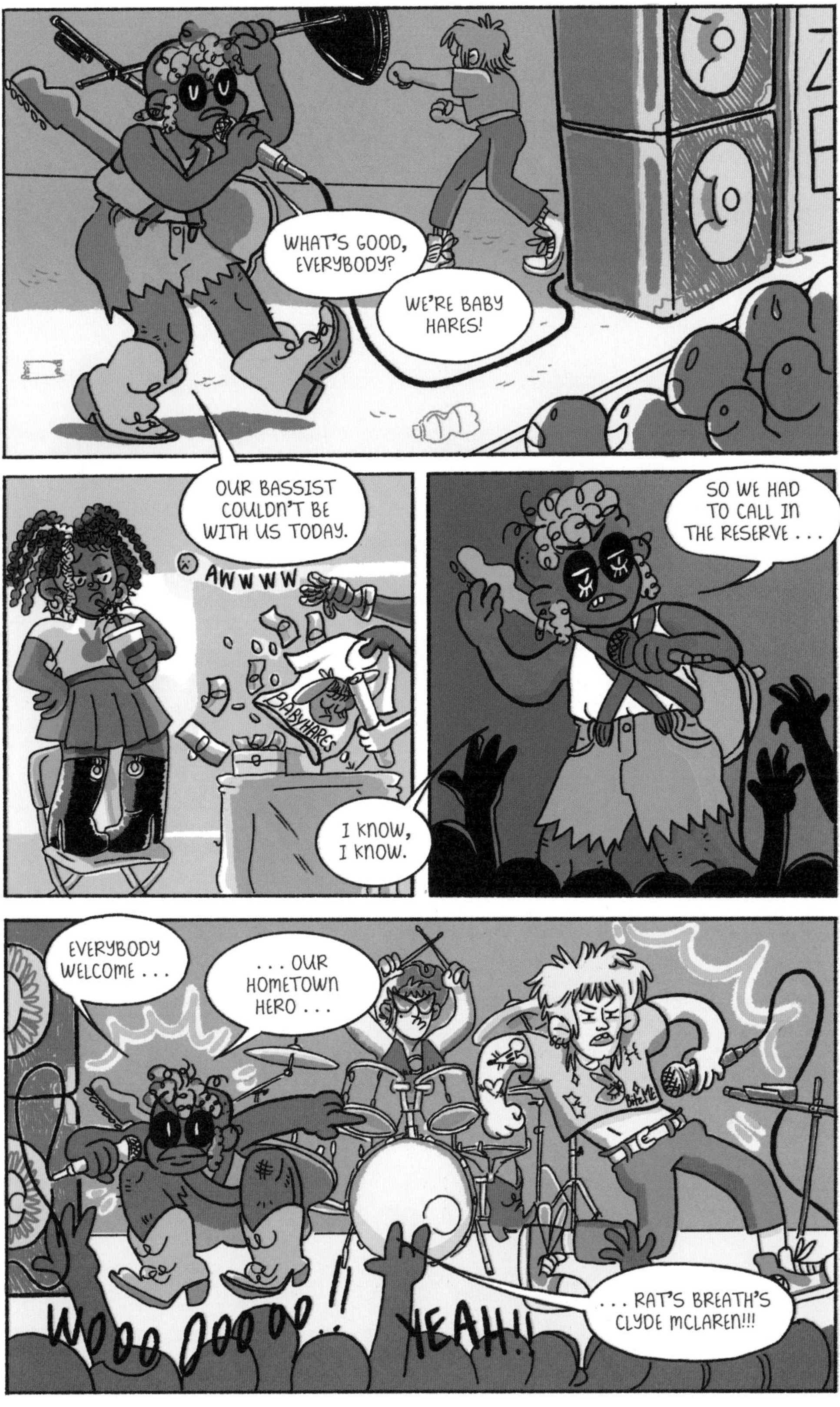
WHAT'S GOOD, EVERYBODY?
WE'RE BABY HARES!
OUR BASSIST COULDN'T BE WITH US TODAY.
AWWWW
BABYHARES
I KNOW, I KNOW.
SO WE HAD TO CALL IN THE RESERVE . . .
EVERYBODY WELCOME . . .
. . . OUR HOMETOWN HERO . . .
BITE ME
. . . RAT'S BREATH'S CLYDE MCLAREN!!!
WOOO OOO OO!!
YEAH!!

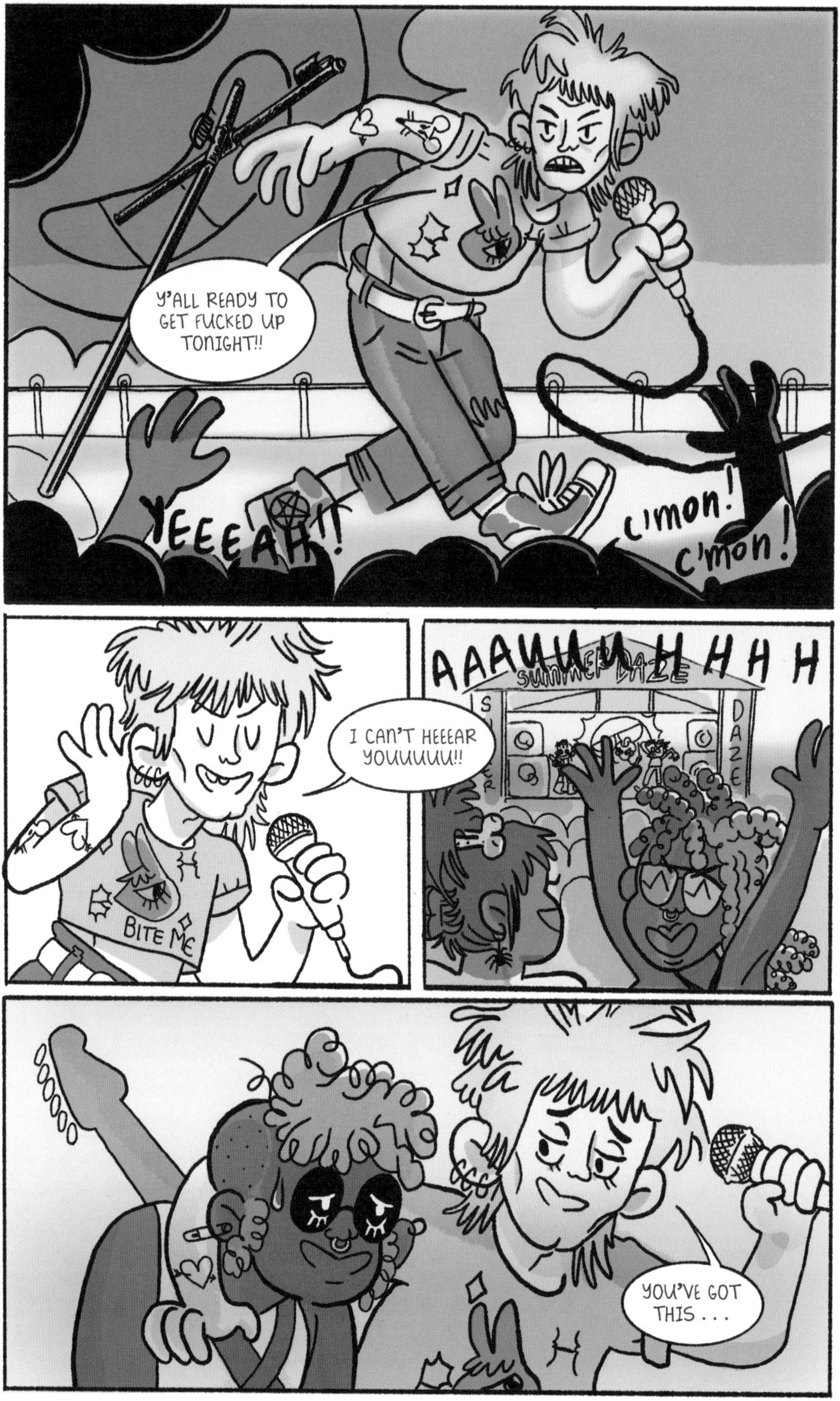
Y'ALL READY TO GET FUCKED UP TONIGHT!!
YEEEAH!!
C'MON!
C'MON!
I CAN'T HEEEAR YOUUUUU!!
BITE ME
AAAUUUHHHHH
SUMMER DAZE
SUMMER
DAZE
YOU'VE GOT THIS . . .

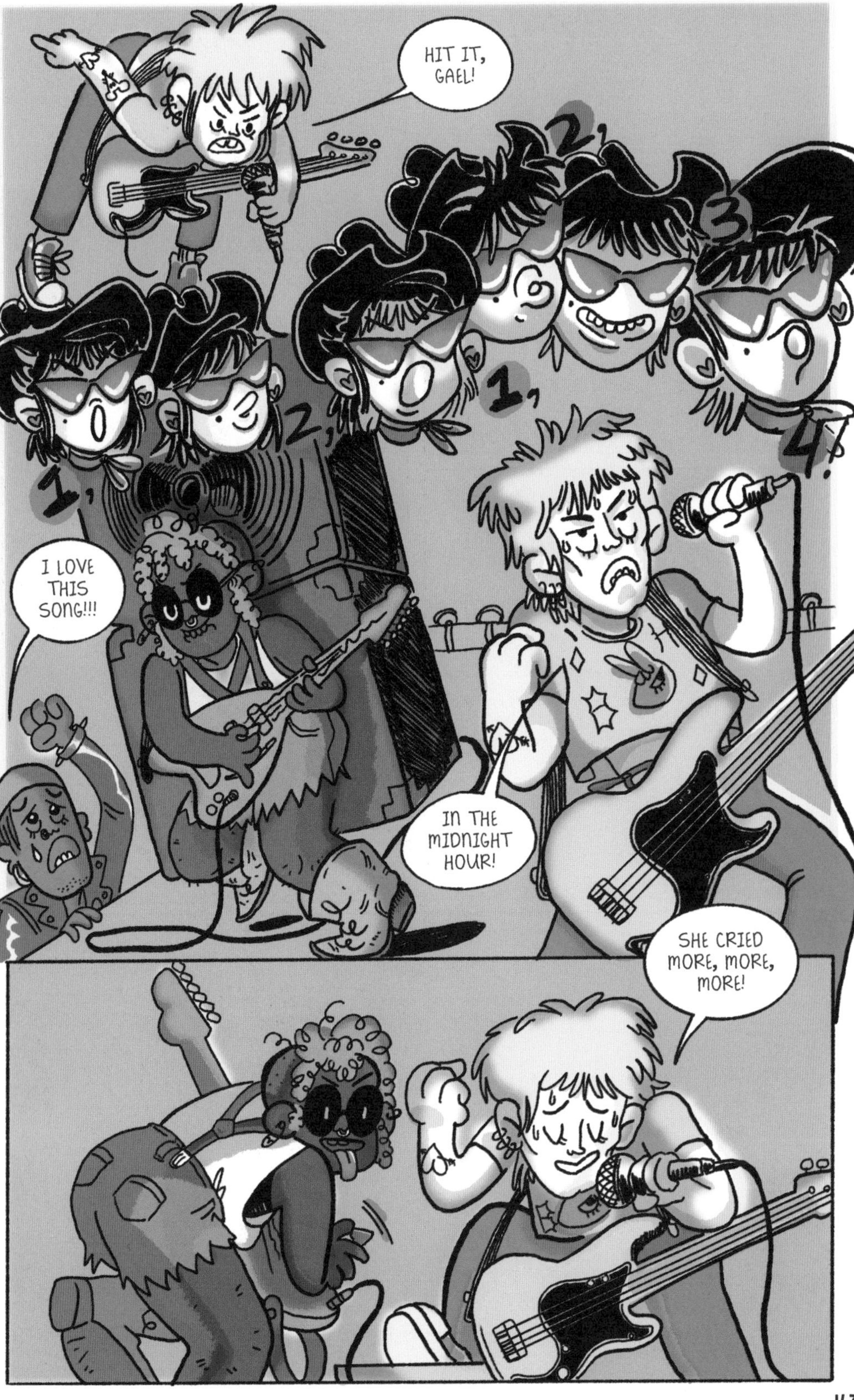
HIT IT, GAEL!
1, 2, 1, 2, 3, 4!
I LOVE THIS SONG!!!
IN THE MIDNIGHT HOUR!
SHE CRIED MORE, MORE, MORE!

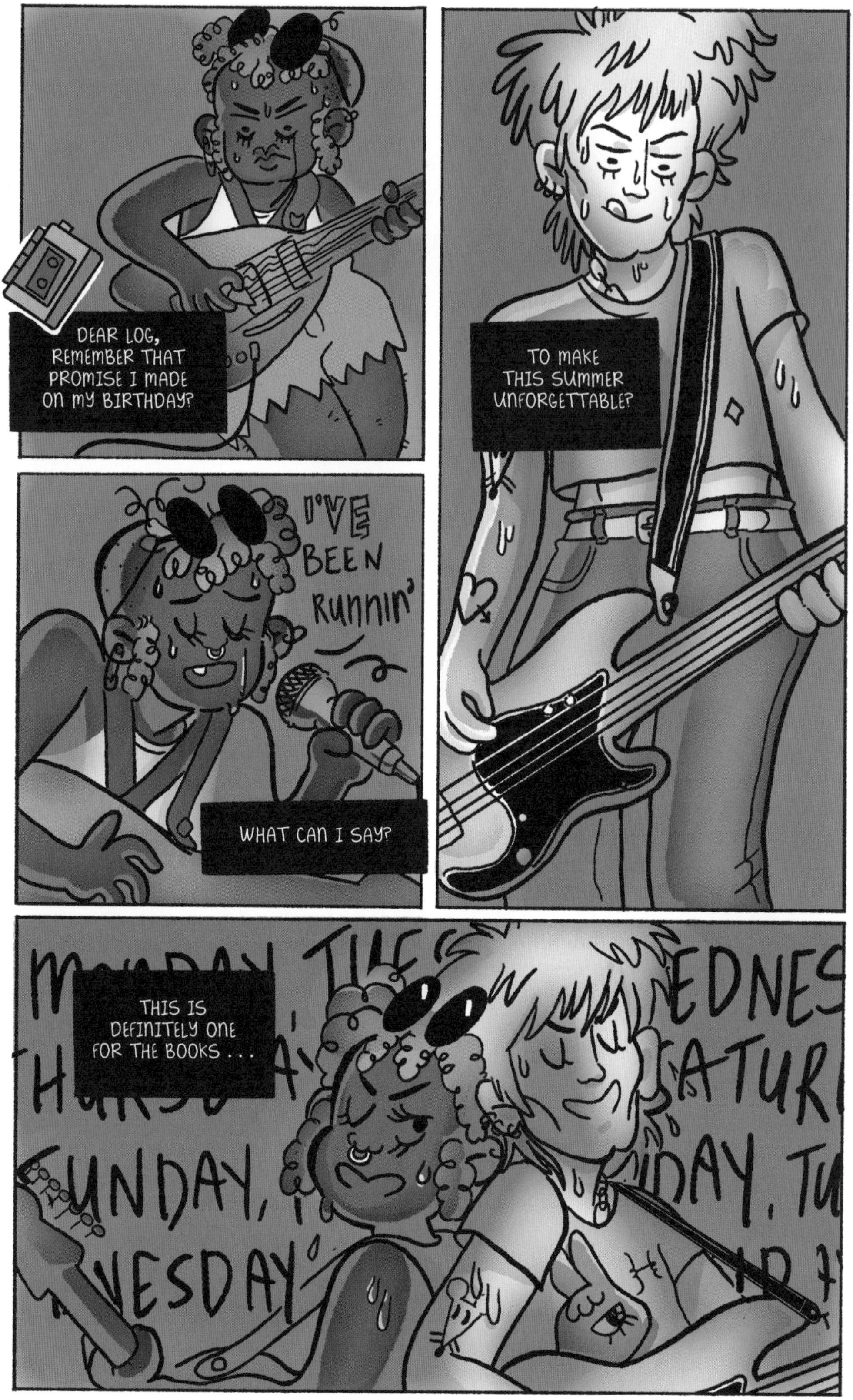
DEAR LOG, REMEMBER THAT PROMISE I MADE ON MY BIRTHDAY?
TO MAKE THIS SUMMER UNFORGETTABLE?
I'VE BEEN RUNNIN'
WHAT CAN I SAY?
THIS IS DEFINITELY ONE FOR THE BOOKS . . .

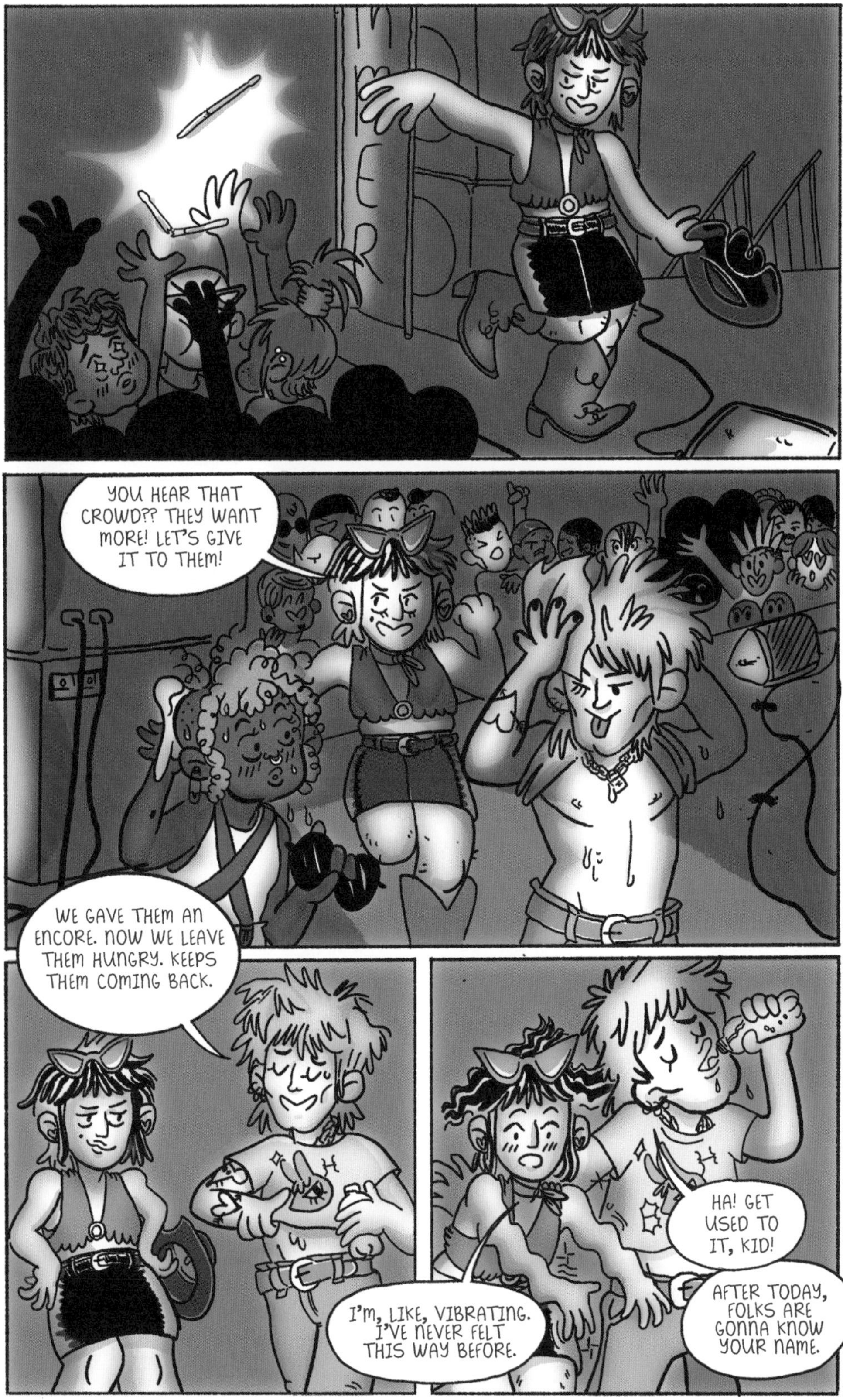

YOU HEAR THAT CROWD?? THEY WANT MORE! LET'S GIVE IT TO THEM!
WE GAVE THEM AN ENCORE. NOW WE LEAVE THEM HUNGRY. KEEPS THEM COMING BACK.
I'M, LIKE, VIBRATING. I'VE NEVER FELT THIS WAY BEFORE.
HA! GET USED TO IT, KID!
AFTER TODAY, FOLKS ARE GONNA KNOW YOUR NAME.

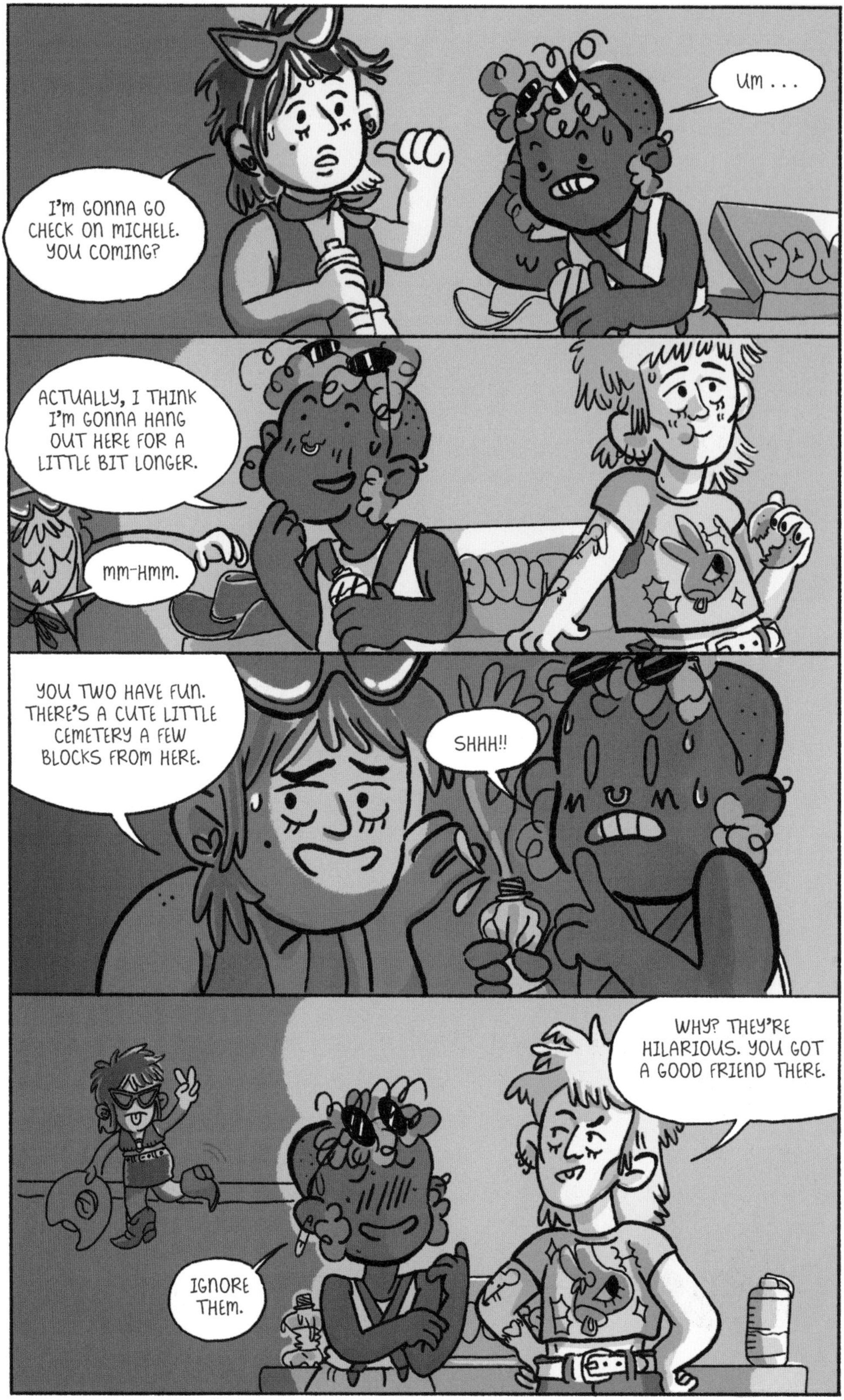
I'M GONNA GO CHECK ON MICHELE. YOU COMING?
UM . . .
ACTUALLY, I THINK I'M GONNA HANG OUT HERE FOR A LITTLE BIT LONGER.
MM-HMM.
YOU TWO HAVE FUN. THERE'S A CUTE LITTLE CEMETERY A FEW BLOCKS FROM HERE.
SHHH!!
WHY? THEY'RE HILARIOUS. YOU GOT A GOOD FRIEND THERE.
IGNORE THEM.

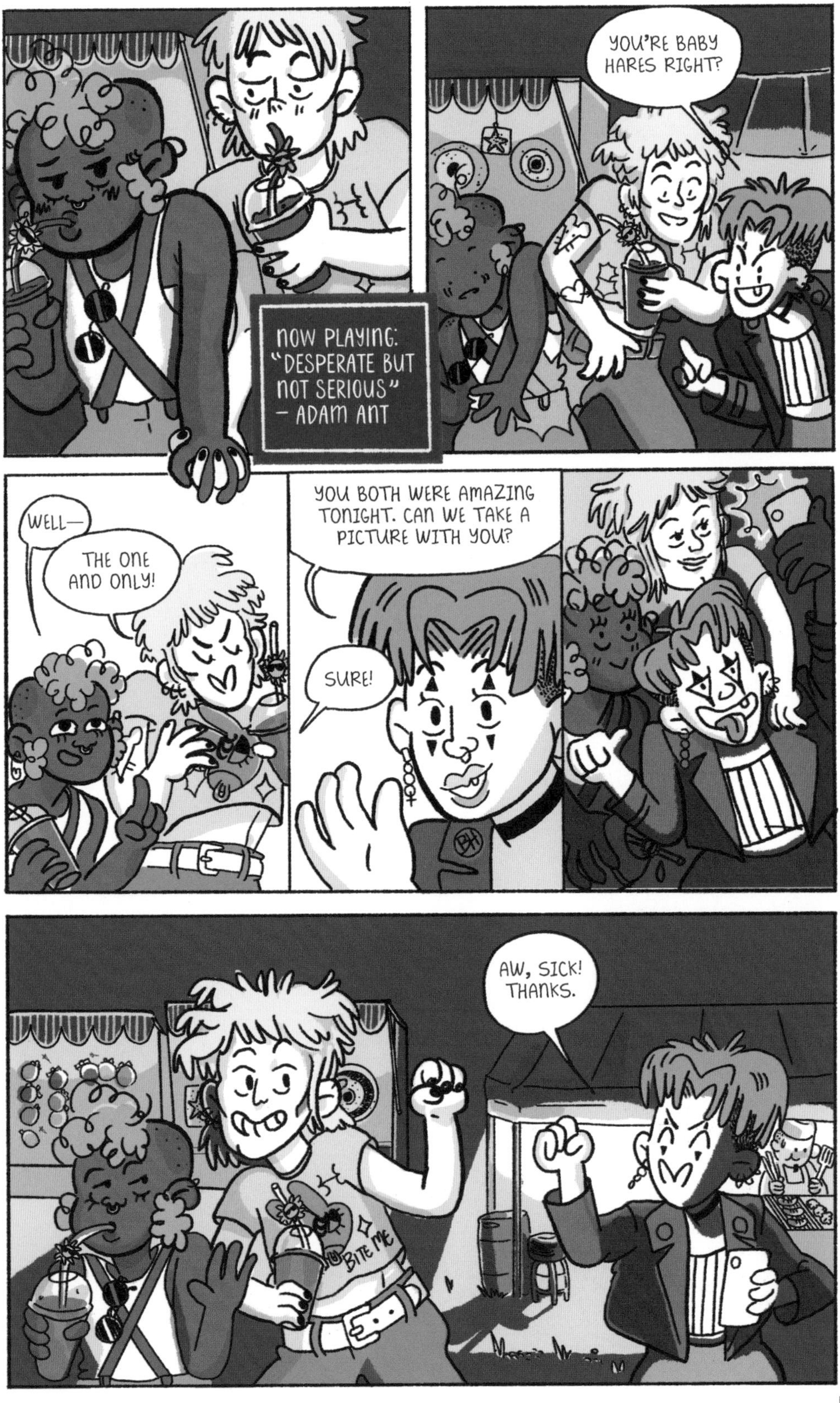
NOW PLAYING:
"DESPERATE BUT NOT SERIOUS"
— ADAM ANT
YOU'RE BABY HARES RIGHT?
WELL—
THE ONE AND ONLY!
YOU BOTH WERE AMAZING TONIGHT. CAN WE TAKE A PICTURE WITH YOU?
SURE!
AW, SICK! THANKS.
BITE ME

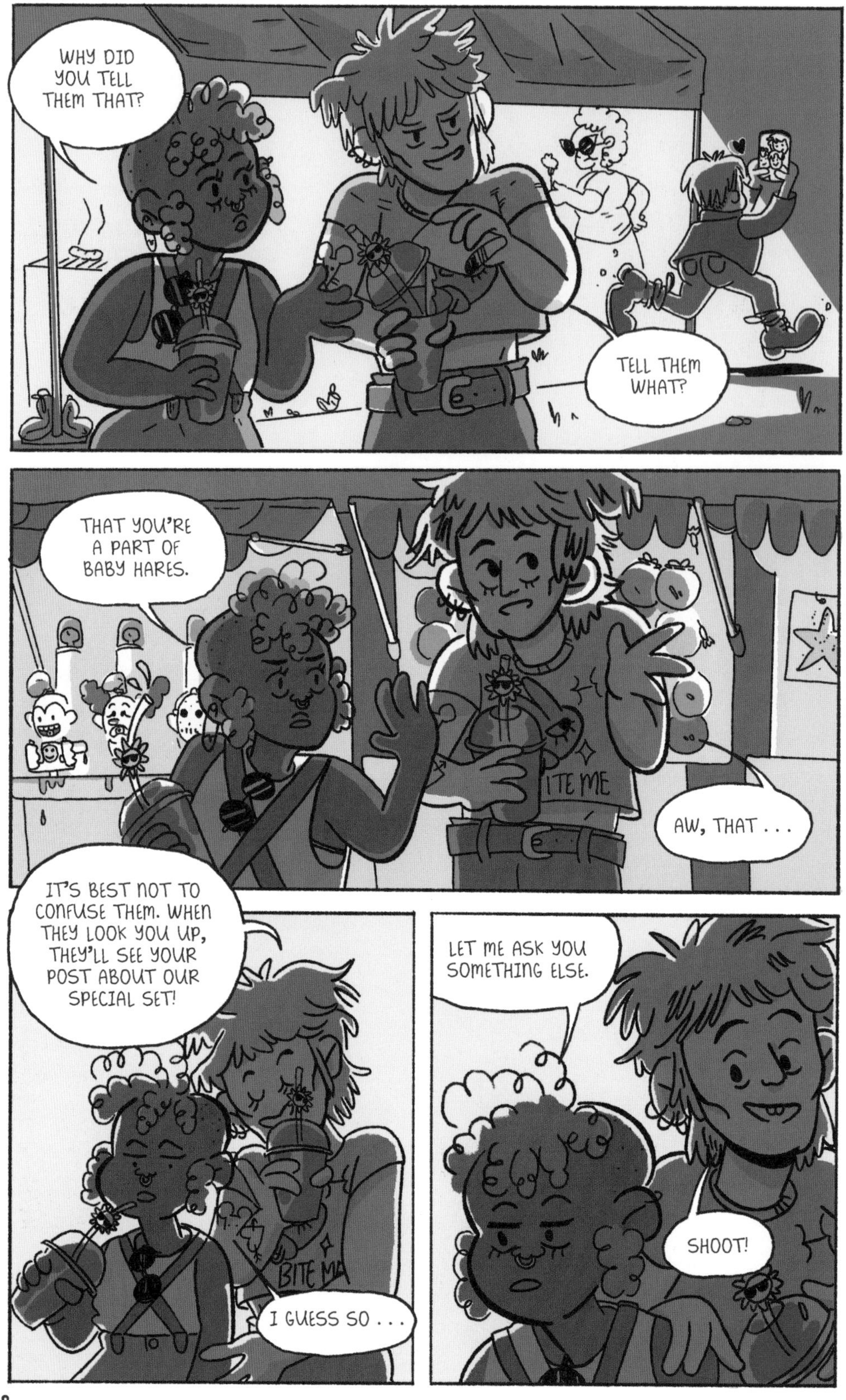
WHY DID YOU TELL THEM THAT?
TELL THEM WHAT?
THAT YOU'RE A PART OF BABY HARES.
ITE ME
AW, THAT . . .
IT'S BEST NOT TO CONFUSE THEM. WHEN THEY LOOK YOU UP, THEY'LL SEE YOUR POST ABOUT OUR SPECIAL SET!
BITE MA
I GUESS SO . . .
LET ME ASK YOU SOMETHING ELSE.
SHOOT!

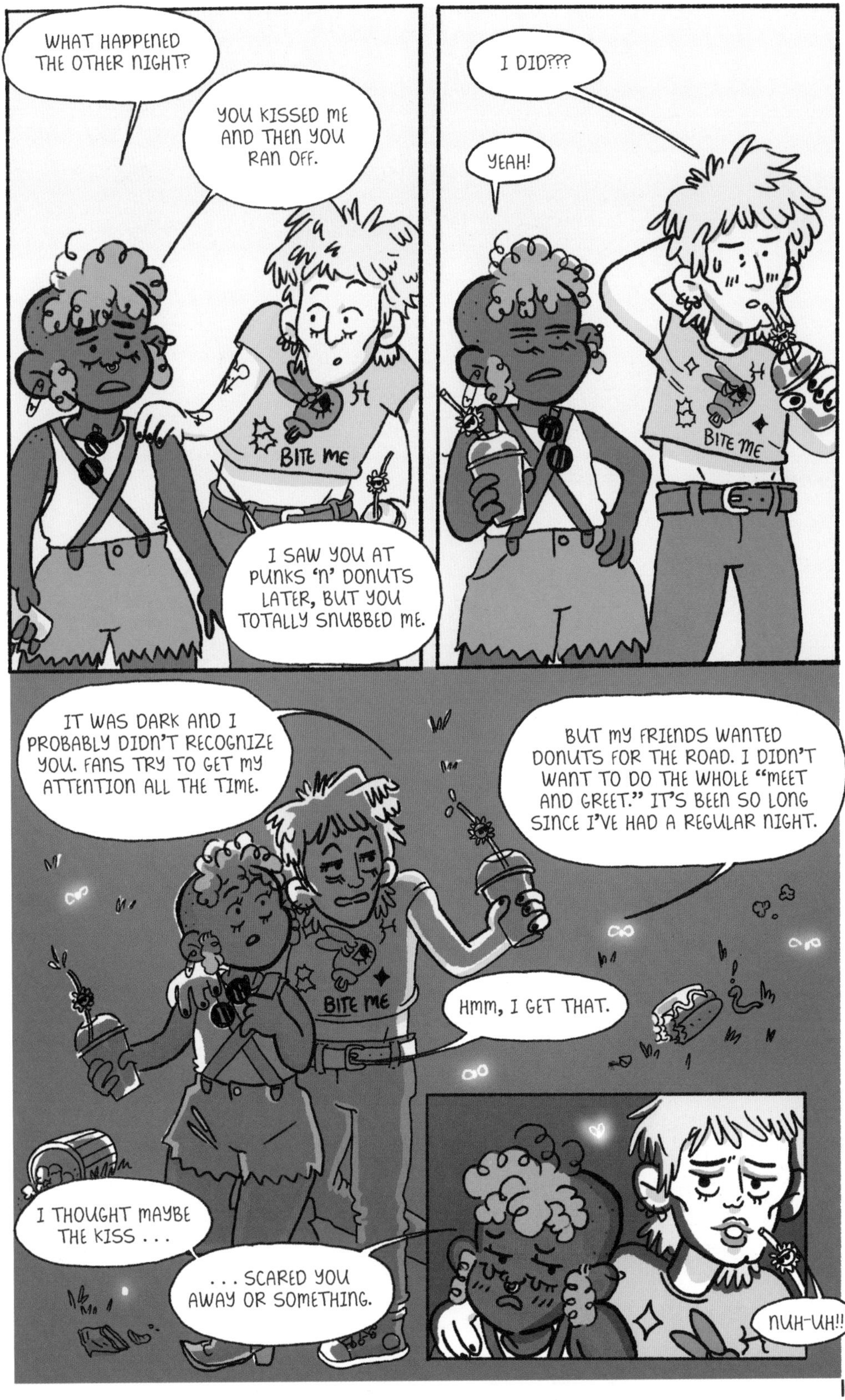
WHAT HAPPENED THE OTHER NIGHT?
YOU KISSED ME AND THEN YOU RAN OFF.
BITE ME
I SAW YOU AT PUNKS 'N' DONUTS LATER, BUT YOU TOTALLY SNUBBED ME.
I DID???
YEAH!
BITE ME
IT WAS DARK AND I PROBABLY DIDN'T RECOGNIZE YOU. FANS TRY TO GET MY ATTENTION ALL THE TIME.
BUT MY FRIENDS WANTED DONUTS FOR THE ROAD. I DIDN'T WANT TO DO THE WHOLE "MEET AND GREET." IT'S BEEN SO LONG SINCE I'VE HAD A REGULAR NIGHT.
BITE ME
HMM, I GET THAT.
I THOUGHT MAYBE THE KISS . . .
. . . SCARED YOU AWAY OR SOMETHING.
NUH-UH!!

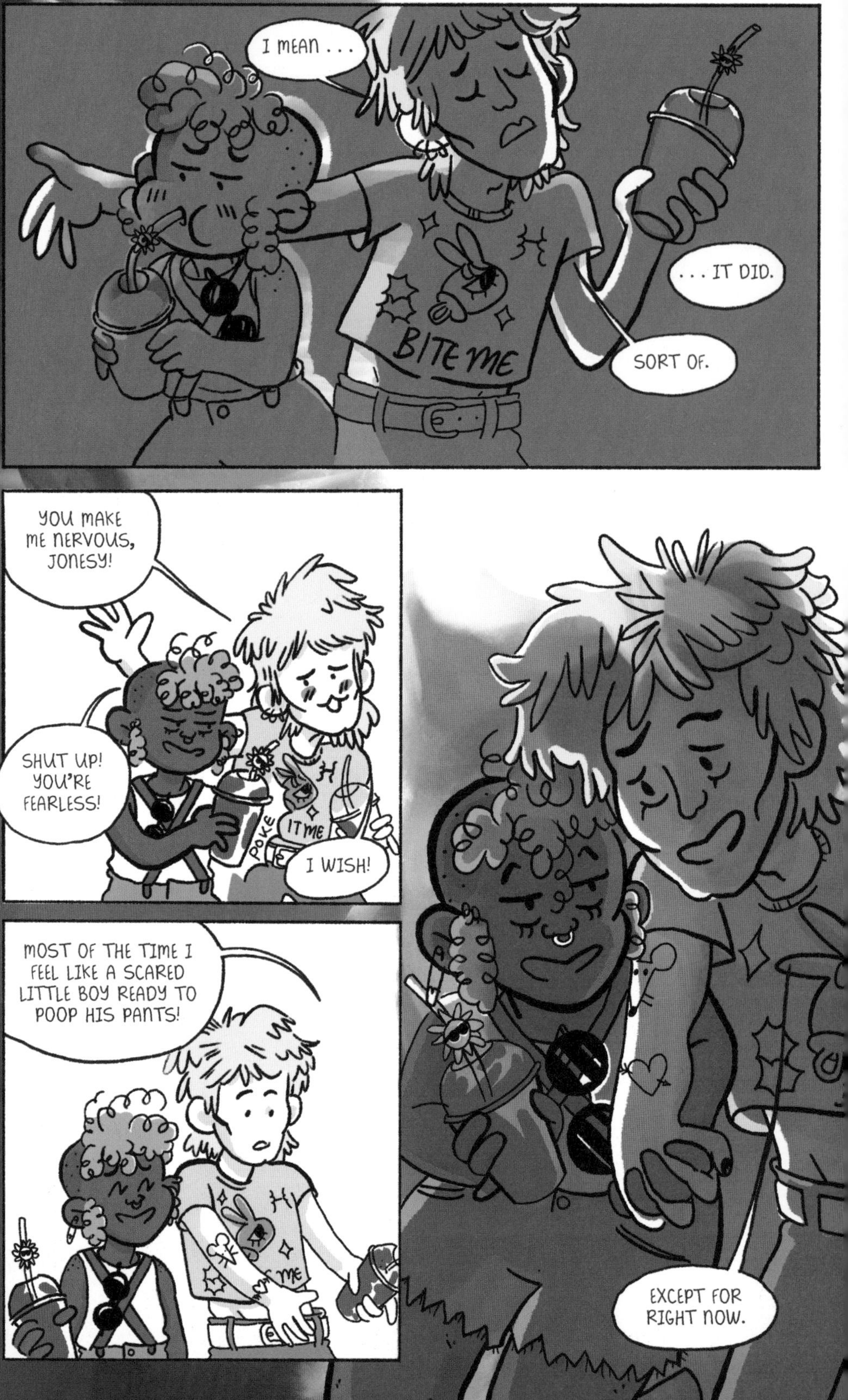
I MEAN . . .
. . . IT DID.
SORT OF.
BITE ME
YOU MAKE ME NERVOUS, JONESY!
SHUT UP! YOU'RE FEARLESS!
I WISH!
MOST OF THE TIME I FEEL LIKE A SCARED LITTLE BOY READY TO POOP HIS PANTS!
EXCEPT FOR RIGHT NOW.

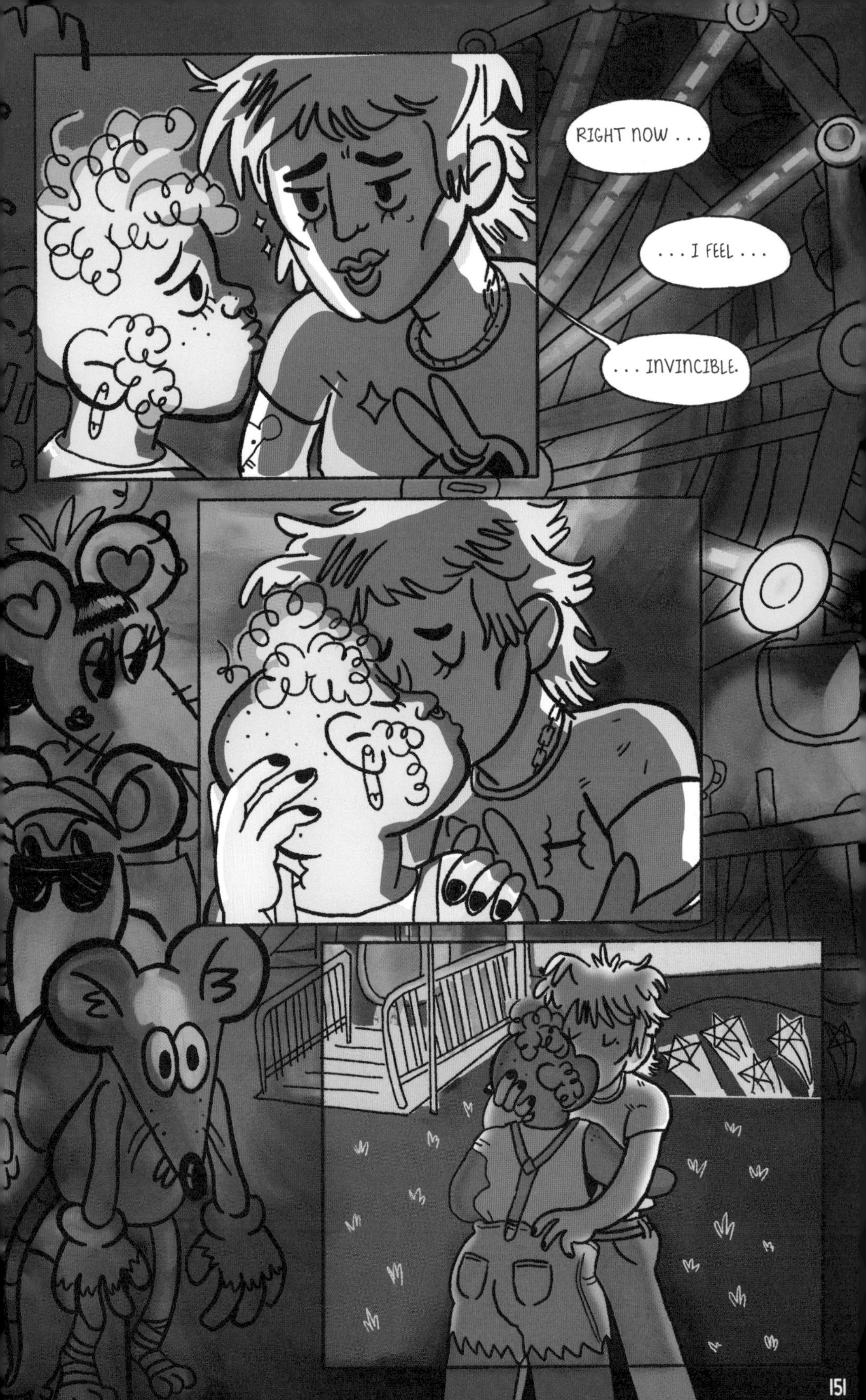
RIGHT NOW . . .
. . . I FEEL . . .
. . . INVINCIBLE.

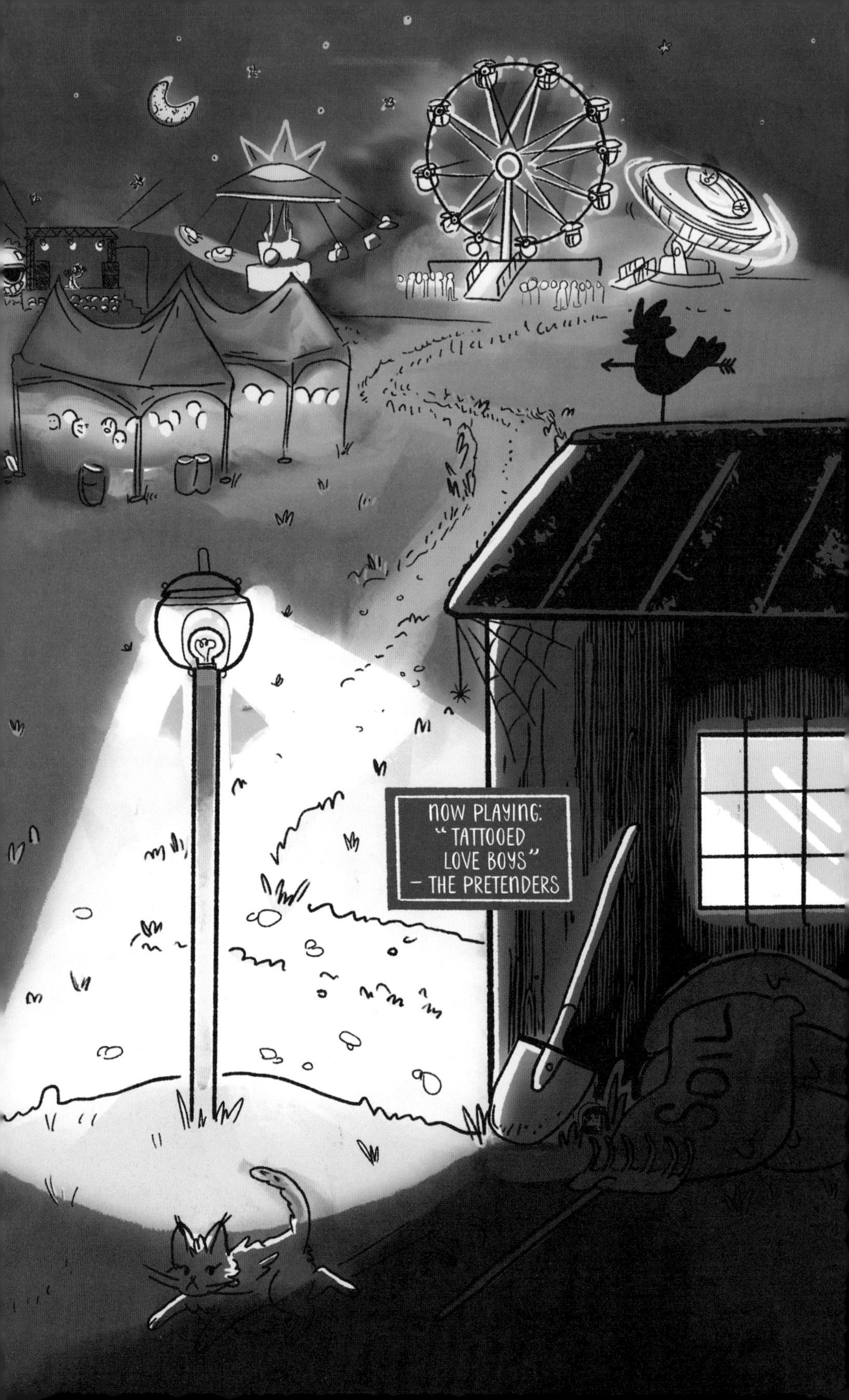
NOW PLAYING:
"TATTOOED
LOVE BOYS"
– THE PRETENDERS

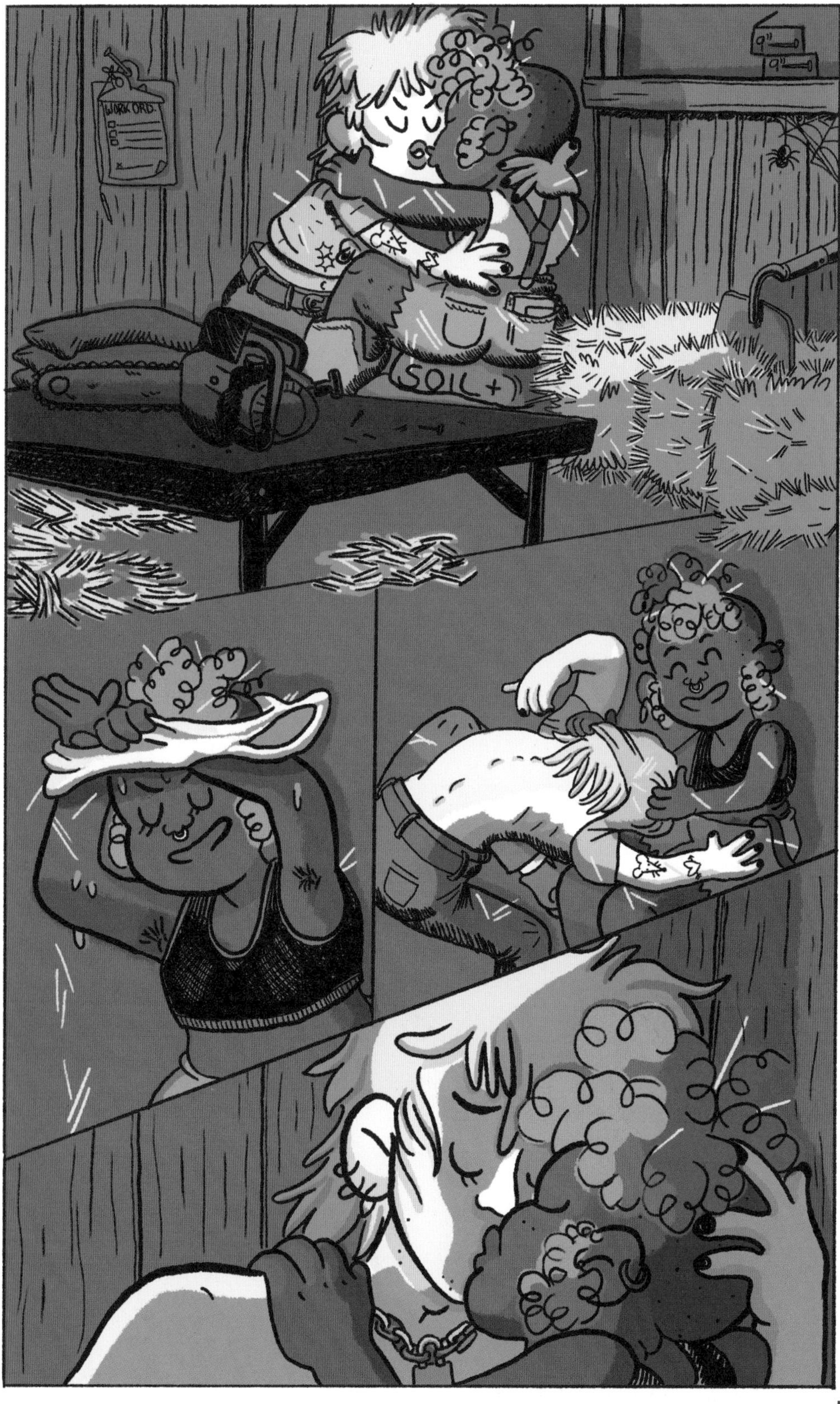
WORK ORD.
SOIL +

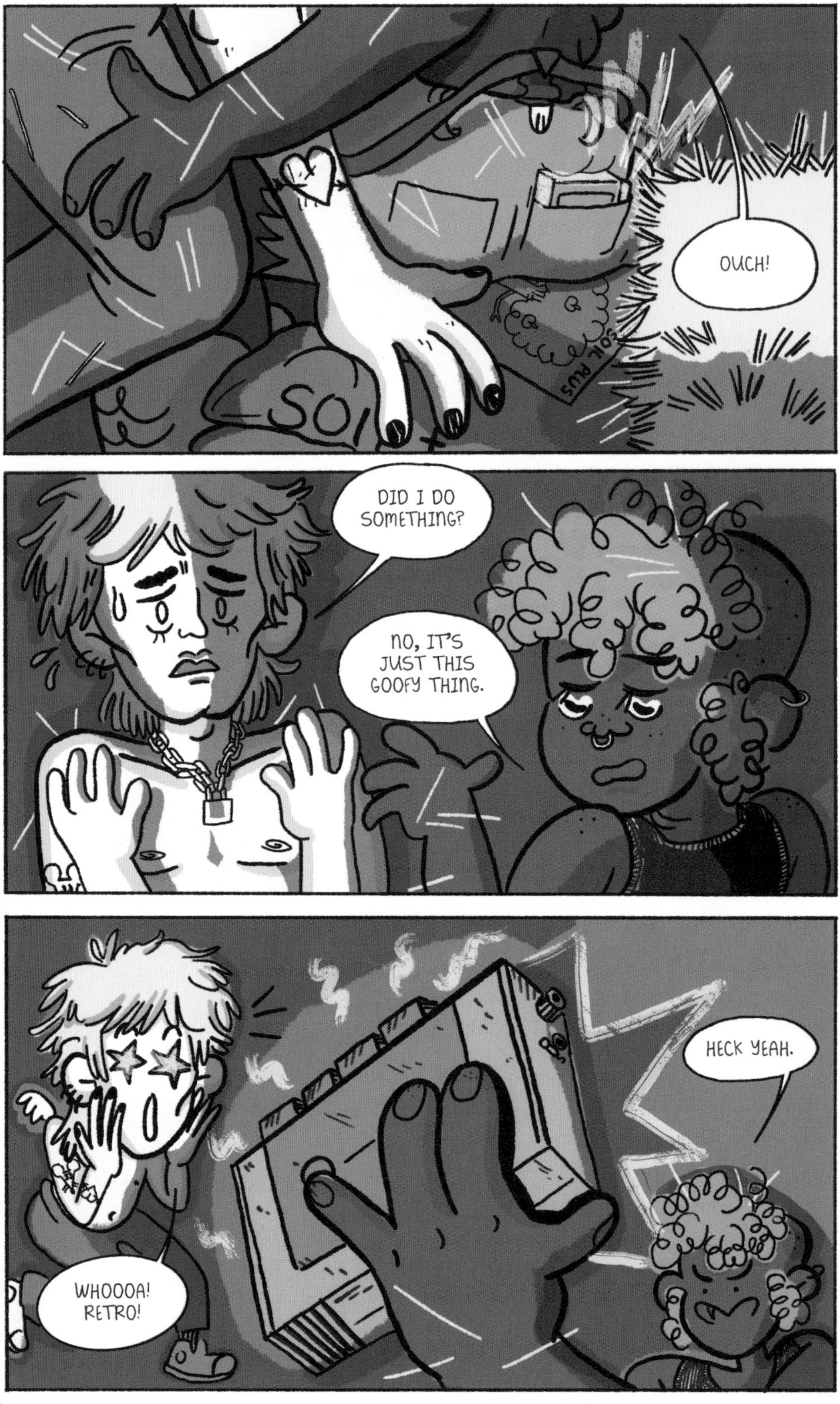
SOIL PLUS
SOI
OUCH!
DID I DO SOMETHING?
NO, IT'S JUST THIS GOOFY THING.
HECK YEAH.
WHOOOA! RETRO!

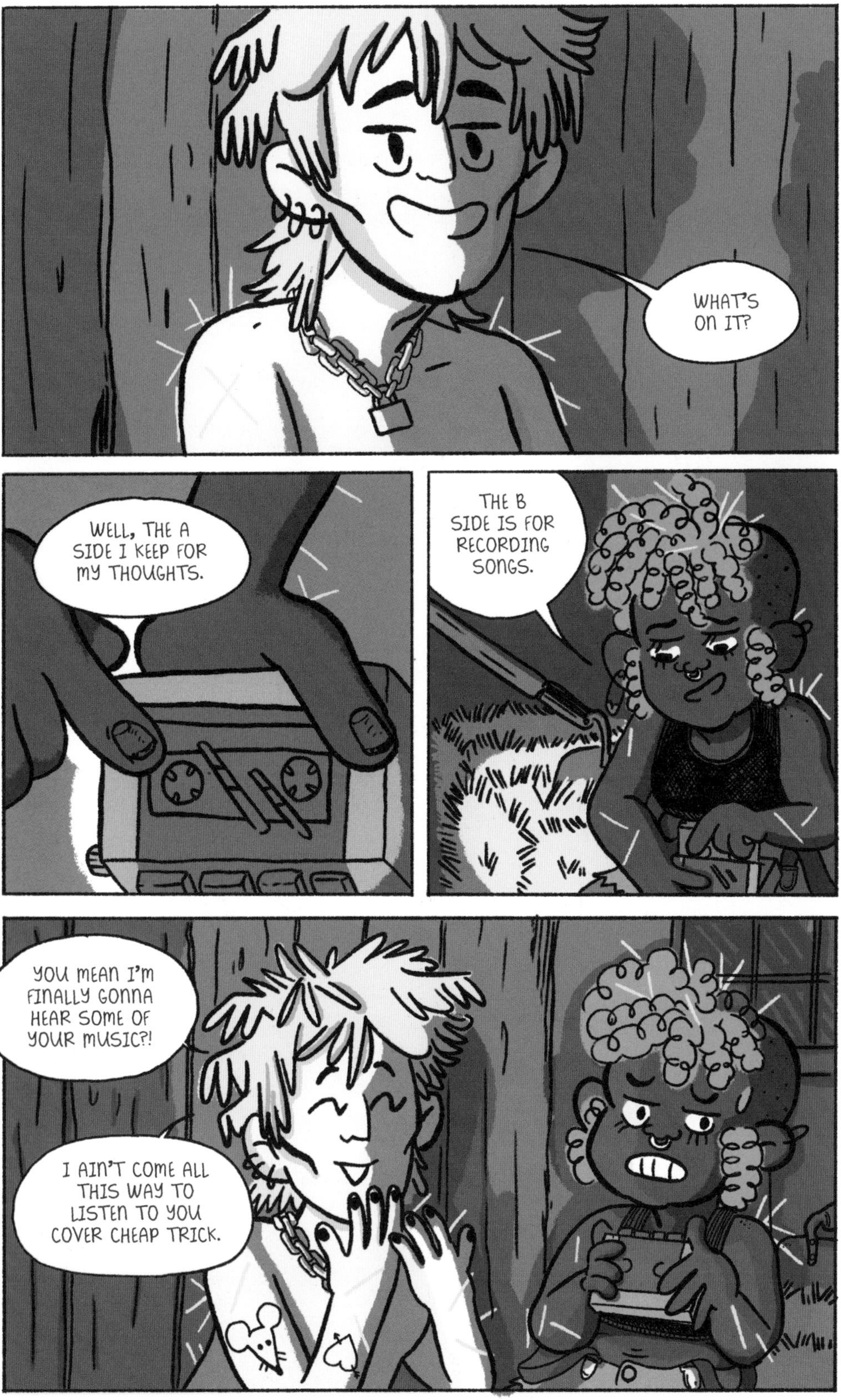
WHAT'S ON IT?
WELL, THE A SIDE I KEEP FOR MY THOUGHTS.
THE B SIDE IS FOR RECORDING SONGS.
YOU MEAN I'M FINALLY GONNA HEAR SOME OF YOUR MUSIC?!
I AIN'T COME ALL THIS WAY TO LISTEN TO YOU COVER CHEAP TRICK.

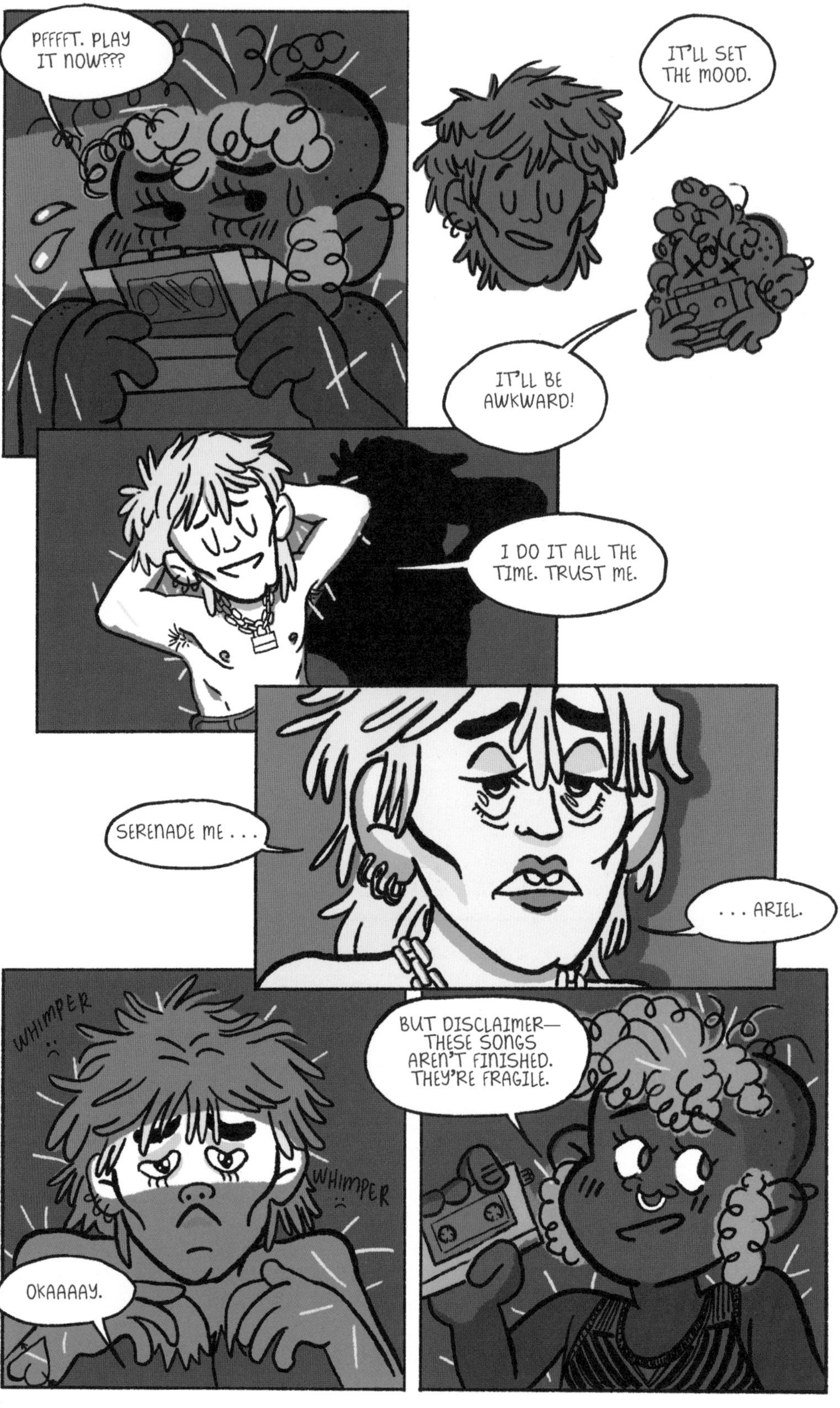
PFFFFT. PLAY IT NOW???
IT'LL SET THE MOOD.
IT'LL BE AWKWARD!
I DO IT ALL THE TIME. TRUST ME.
SERENADE ME . . .
. . . ARIEL.
WHIMPER
WHIMPER
OKAAAAY.
BUT DISCLAIMER— THESE SONGS AREN'T FINISHED. THEY'RE FRAGILE.

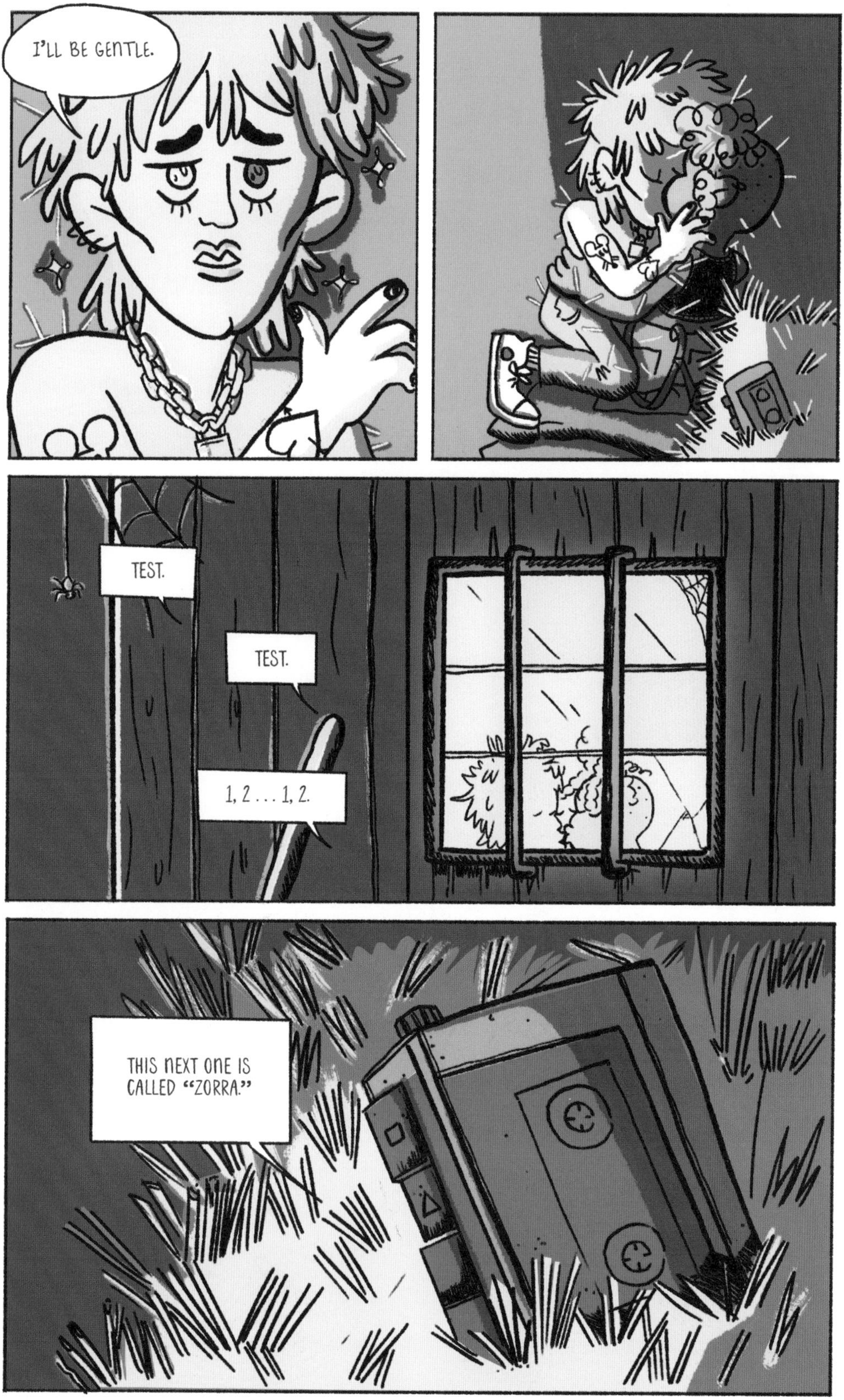
I'LL BE GENTLE.
TEST.
TEST.
1, 2 . . . 1, 2.
THIS NEXT ONE IS CALLED "ZORRA."

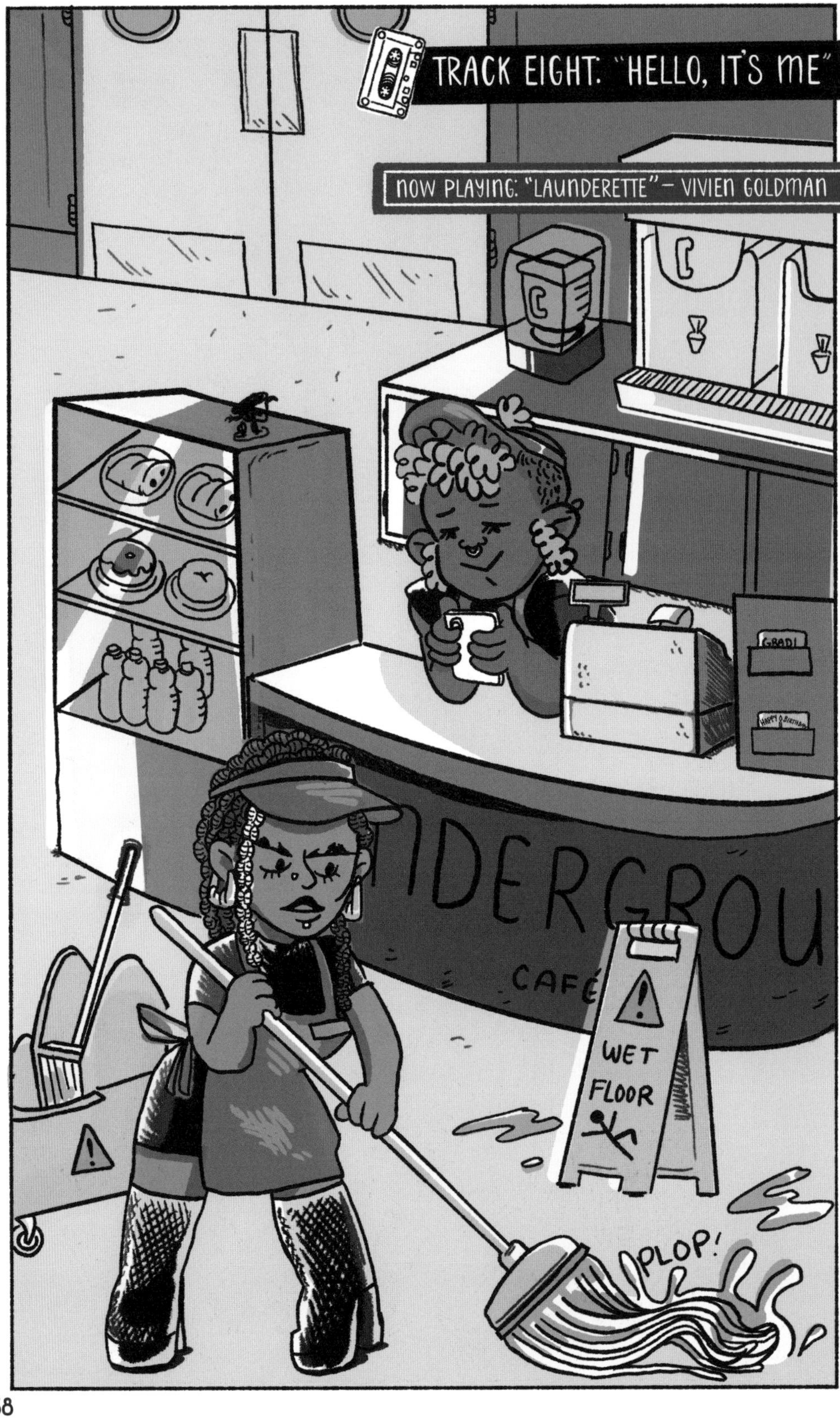
TRACK EIGHT: "HELLO, IT'S ME"
NOW PLAYING: "LAUNDERETTE" – VIVIEN GOLDMAN
GRAD!
DERGROU
CAFÉ
WET FLOOR
PLOP!

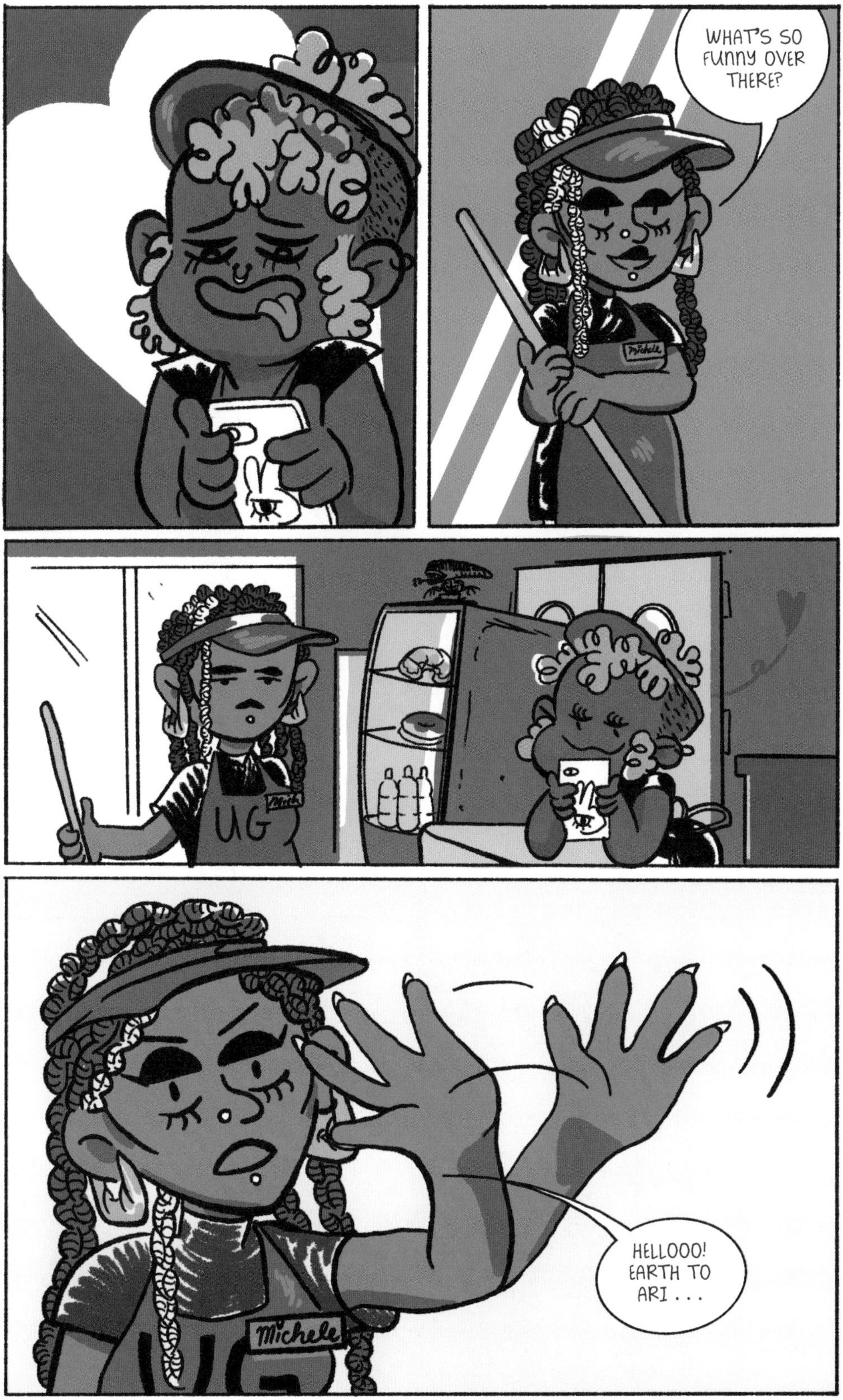
WHAT'S SO FUNNY OVER THERE?
Michele
UG
HELLOOO! EARTH TO ARI . . .
Michele

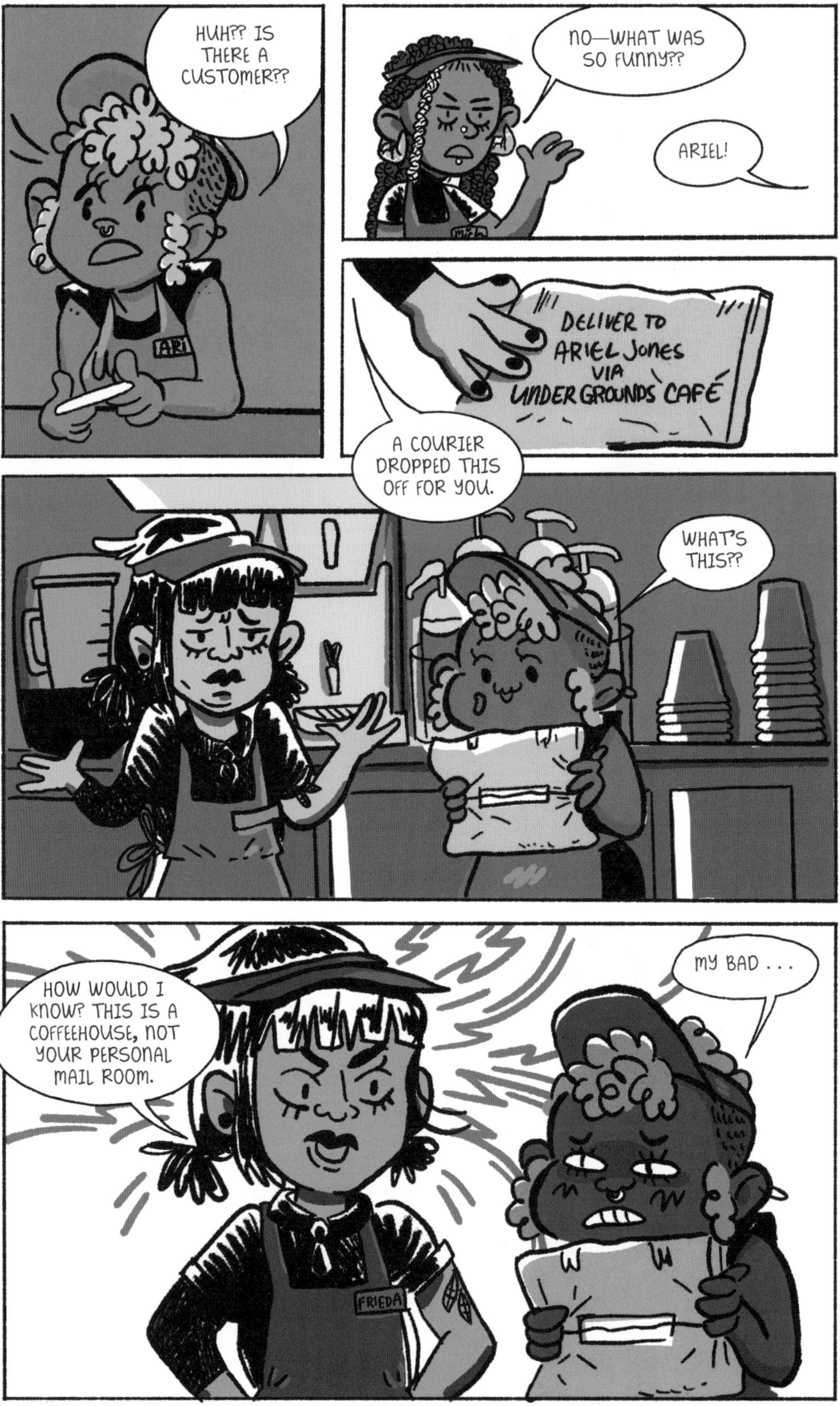
HUH?? IS THERE A CUSTOMER??
NO—WHAT WAS SO FUNNY??
ARIEL!
DELIVER TO ARIEL JONES VIA UNDERGROUNDS CAFÉ
A COURIER DROPPED THIS OFF FOR YOU.
WHAT'S THIS??
HOW WOULD I KNOW? THIS IS A COFFEEHOUSE, NOT YOUR PERSONAL MAIL ROOM.
MY BAD . . .
FRIEDA

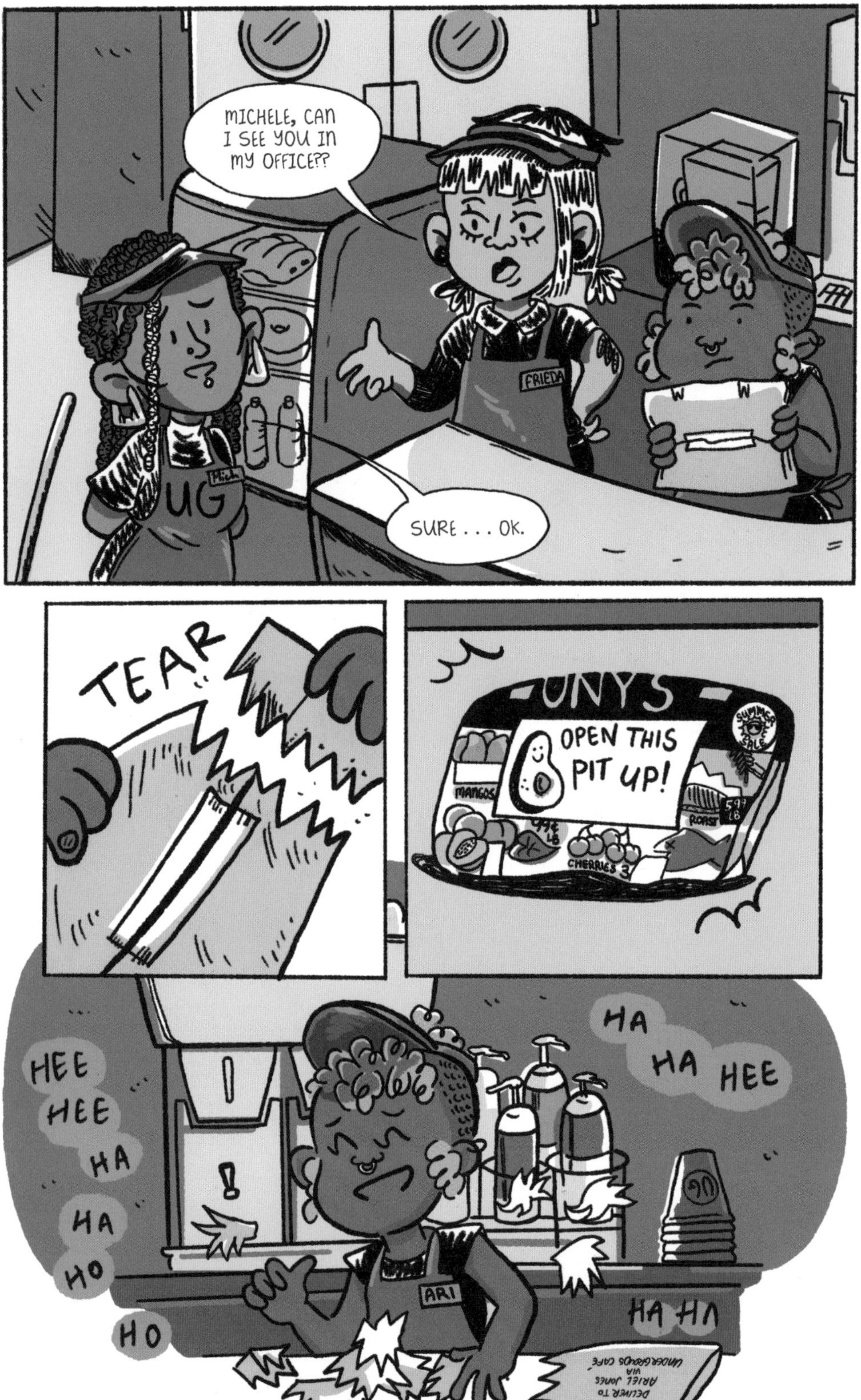
MICHELE, CAN I SEE YOU IN MY OFFICE??
FRIEDA
UG
SURE . . . OK.
TEAR
UNYS
OPEN THIS PIT UP!
SUMMER SALE
MANGOS
ROAST
CHERRIES 3
HA HA HEE
HEE HEE HA HA HO HO
ARI
HA HA
DELIVER TO ARIEL JONES VIA UNDERGROUNDS CAFE

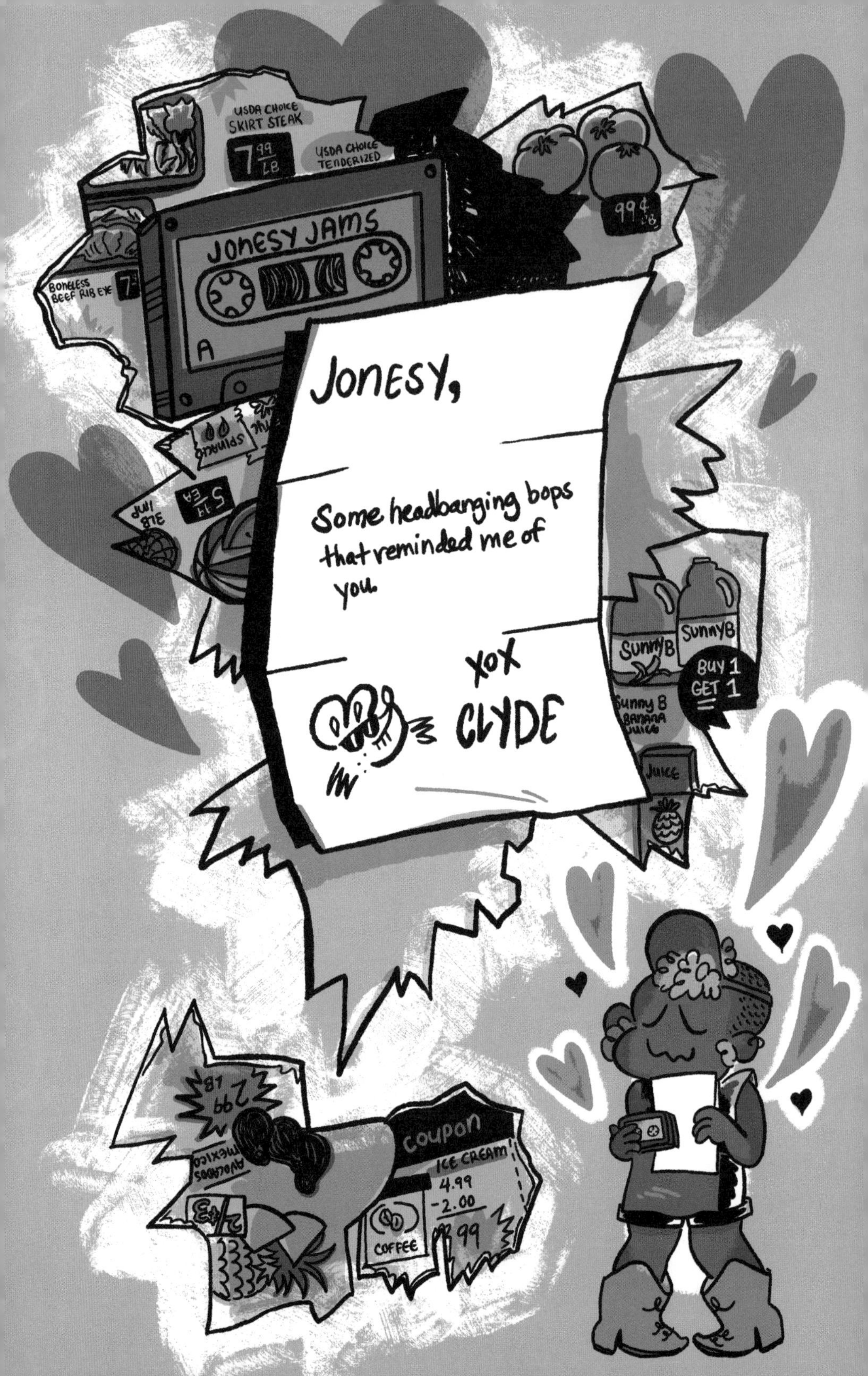
USDA CHOICE SKIRT STEAK
7 99 LB
USDA CHOICE TENDERIZED
JONESY JAMS
A
BONELESS BEEF RIB EYE
99¢ LB
JONESY,
Some headbanging bops that reminded me of you.
XOX
CLYDE
SunnyB
SunnyB
BUY 1 GET 1
Sunny B BANANA JUICE
JUICE
coupon
ICE CREAM
4.99
-2.00
COFFEE

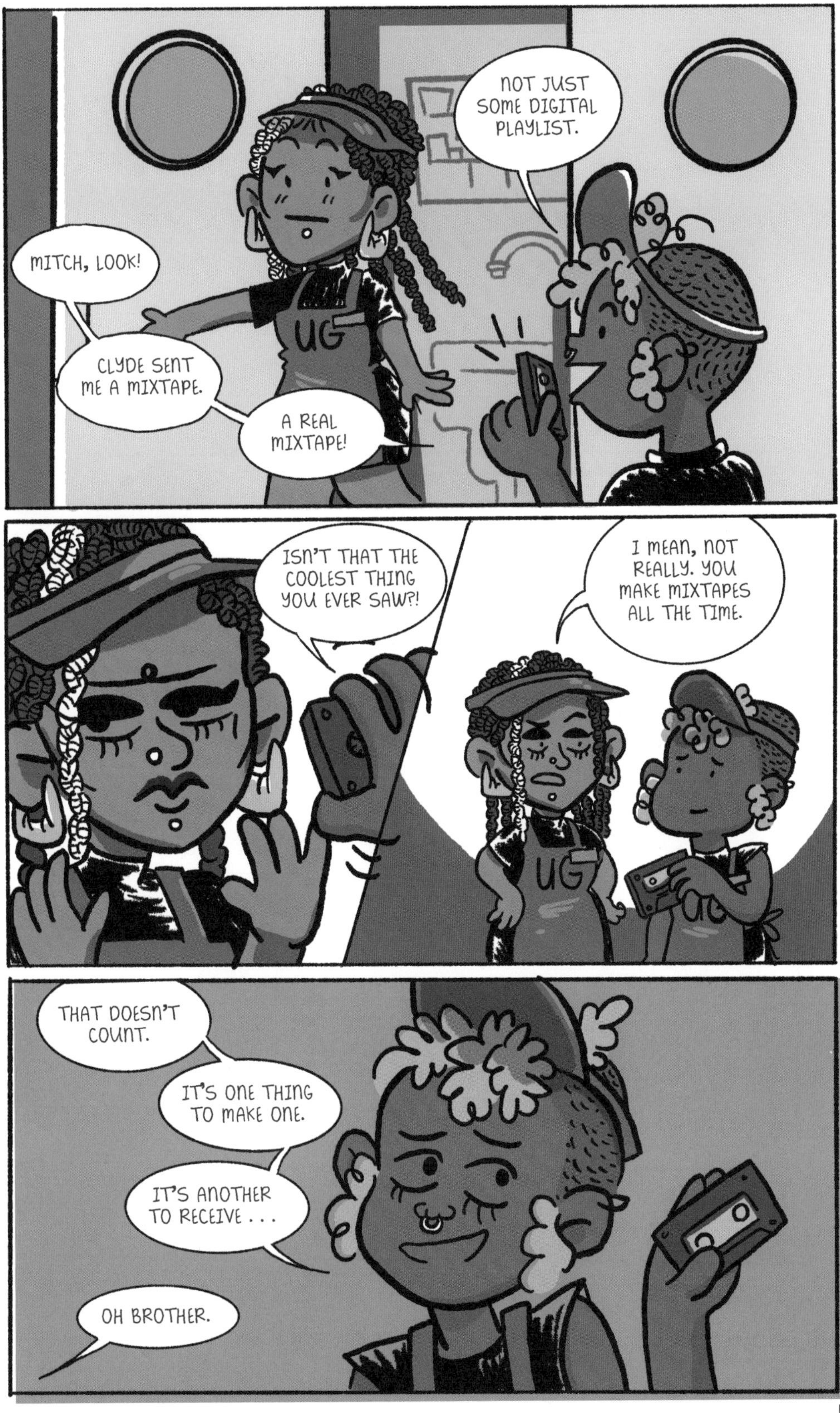
MITCH, LOOK!
CLYDE SENT ME A MIXTAPE.
A REAL MIXTAPE!
NOT JUST SOME DIGITAL PLAYLIST.
ISN'T THAT THE COOLEST THING YOU EVER SAW?!
I MEAN, NOT REALLY. YOU MAKE MIXTAPES ALL THE TIME.
THAT DOESN'T COUNT.
IT'S ONE THING TO MAKE ONE.
IT'S ANOTHER TO RECEIVE . . .
OH BROTHER.

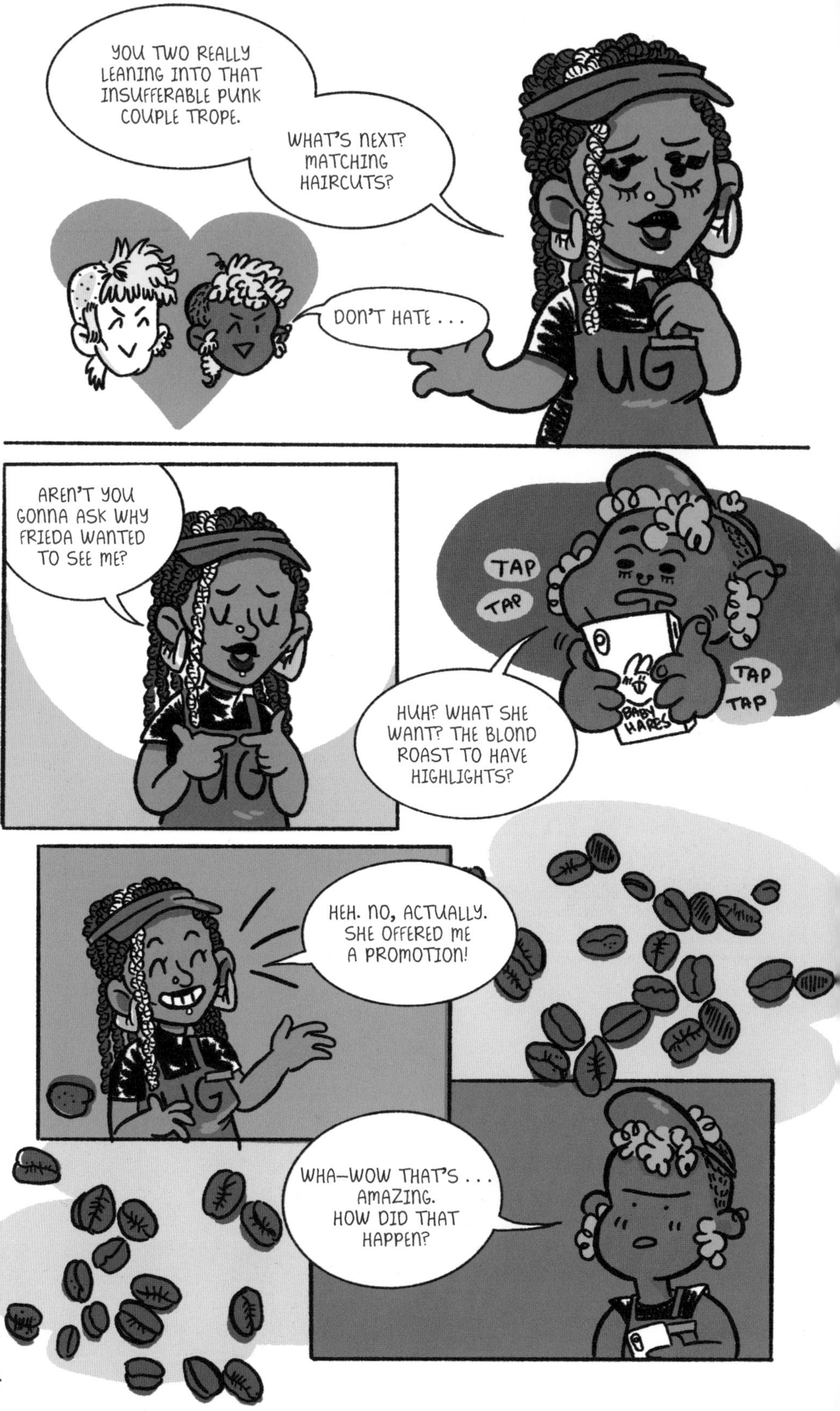
YOU TWO REALLY LEANING INTO THAT INSUFFERABLE PUNK COUPLE TROPE.
WHAT'S NEXT? MATCHING HAIRCUTS?
DON'T HATE . . .
AREN'T YOU GONNA ASK WHY FRIEDA WANTED TO SEE ME?
TAP
TAP
TAP
TAP
BABY HARES
HUH? WHAT SHE WANT? THE BLOND ROAST TO HAVE HIGHLIGHTS?
HEH. NO, ACTUALLY. SHE OFFERED ME A PROMOTION!
WHA—WOW THAT'S . . . AMAZING. HOW DID THAT HAPPEN?

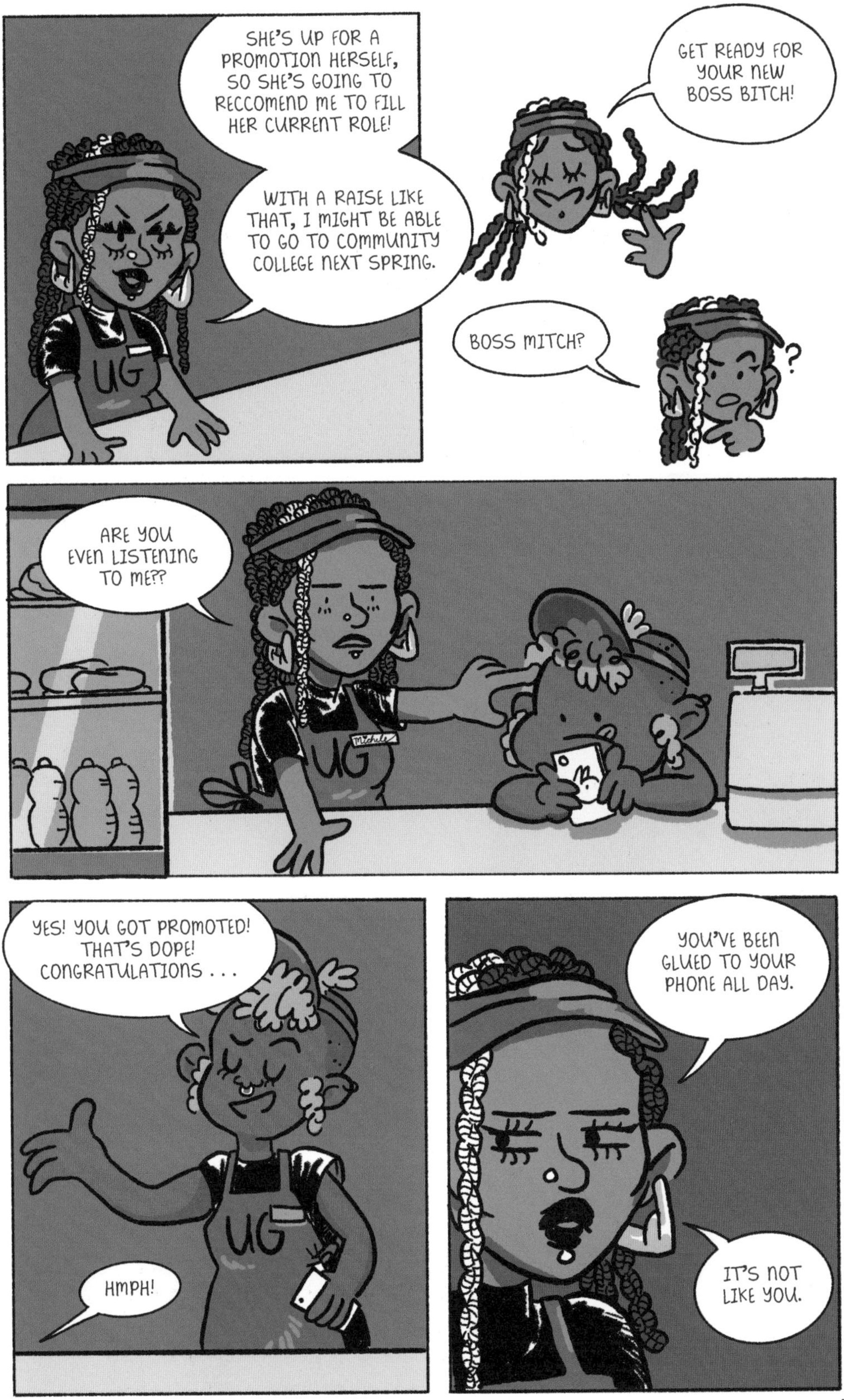
SHE'S UP FOR A PROMOTION HERSELF, SO SHE'S GOING TO RECCOMEND ME TO FILL HER CURRENT ROLE!
WITH A RAISE LIKE THAT, I MIGHT BE ABLE TO GO TO COMMUNITY COLLEGE NEXT SPRING.
GET READY FOR YOUR NEW BOSS BITCH!
BOSS MITCH?
?
ARE YOU EVEN LISTENING TO ME??
YES! YOU GOT PROMOTED! THAT'S DOPE! CONGRATULATIONS . . .
HMPH!
UG
YOU'VE BEEN GLUED TO YOUR PHONE ALL DAY.
IT'S NOT LIKE YOU.

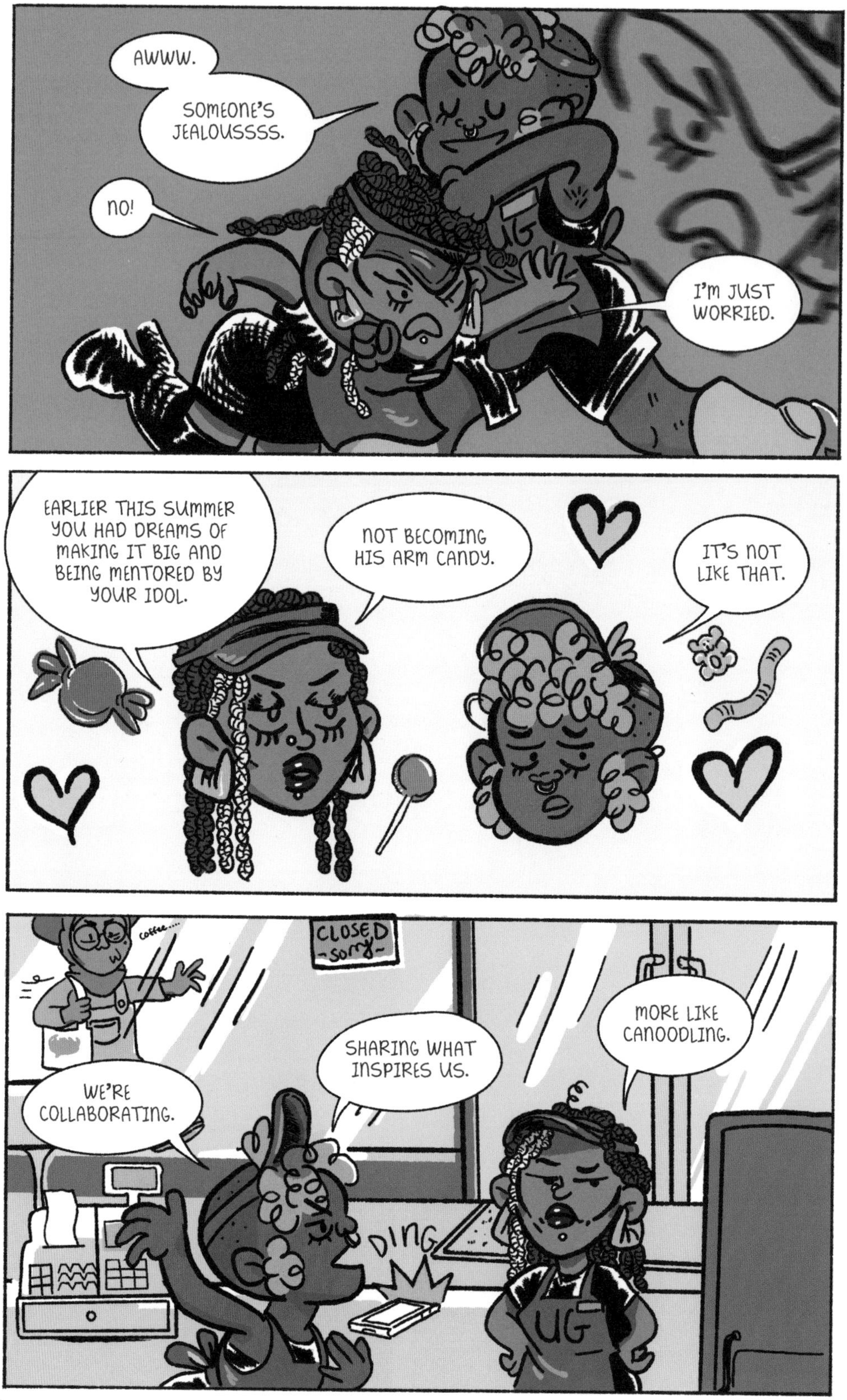
AWWW.
SOMEONE'S JEALOUSSSS.
NO!
I'M JUST WORRIED.
EARLIER THIS SUMMER YOU HAD DREAMS OF MAKING IT BIG AND BEING MENTORED BY YOUR IDOL.
NOT BECOMING HIS ARM CANDY.
IT'S NOT LIKE THAT.
coffee.....
CLOSED -sorry-
WE'RE COLLABORATING.
SHARING WHAT INSPIRES US.
DING
MORE LIKE CANOODLING.
UG

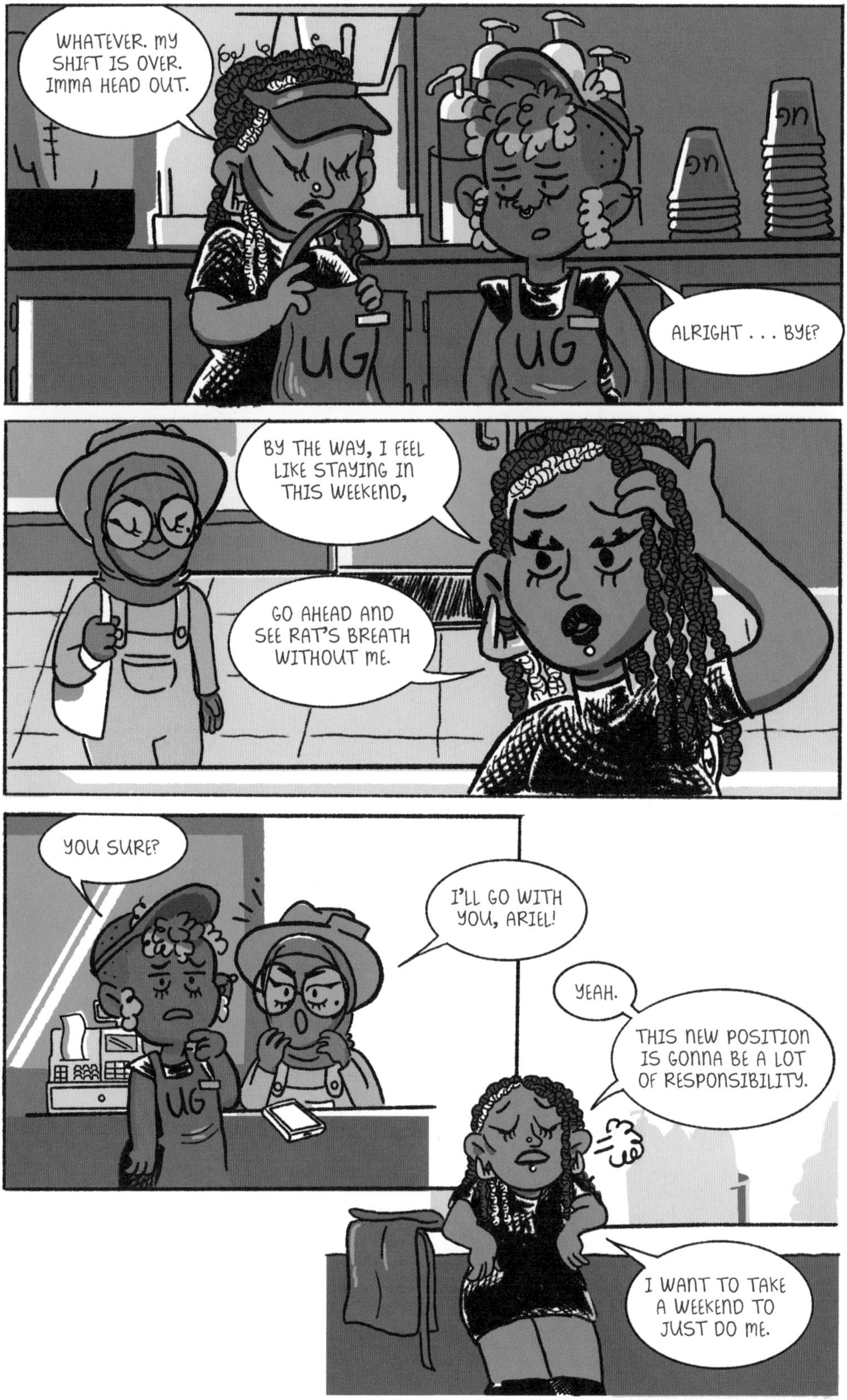
WHATEVER. MY SHIFT IS OVER. IMMA HEAD OUT.
ALRIGHT . . . BYE?
BY THE WAY, I FEEL LIKE STAYING IN THIS WEEKEND,
GO AHEAD AND SEE RAT'S BREATH WITHOUT ME.
YOU SURE?
I'LL GO WITH YOU, ARIEL!
YEAH.
THIS NEW POSITION IS GONNA BE A LOT OF RESPONSIBILITY.
I WANT TO TAKE A WEEKEND TO JUST DO ME.

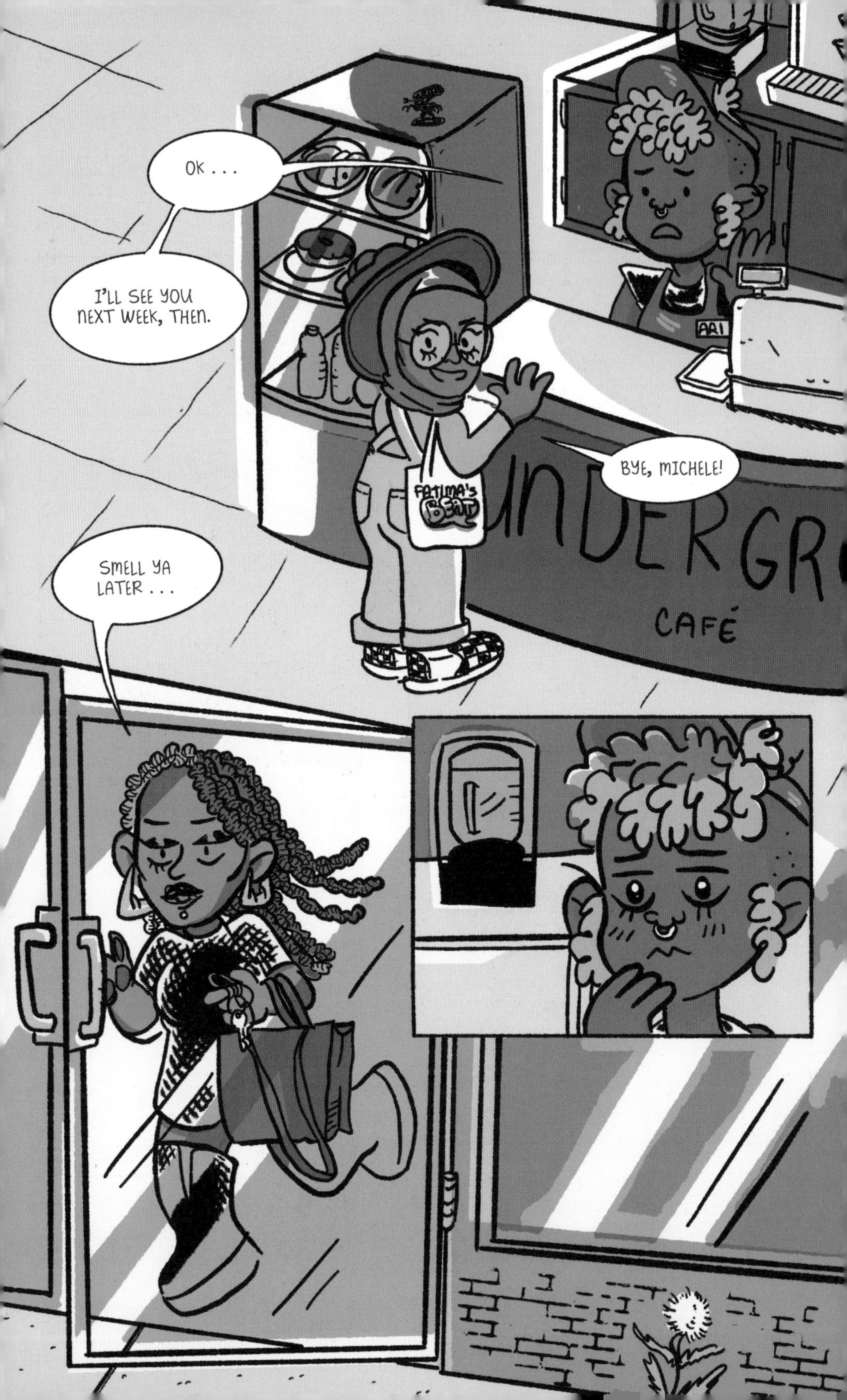

OK . . .
I'LL SEE YOU NEXT WEEK, THEN.
BYE, MICHELE!
FATIMA'S BEAT
ARI
UNDERGR
CAFÉ
SMELL YA LATER . . .

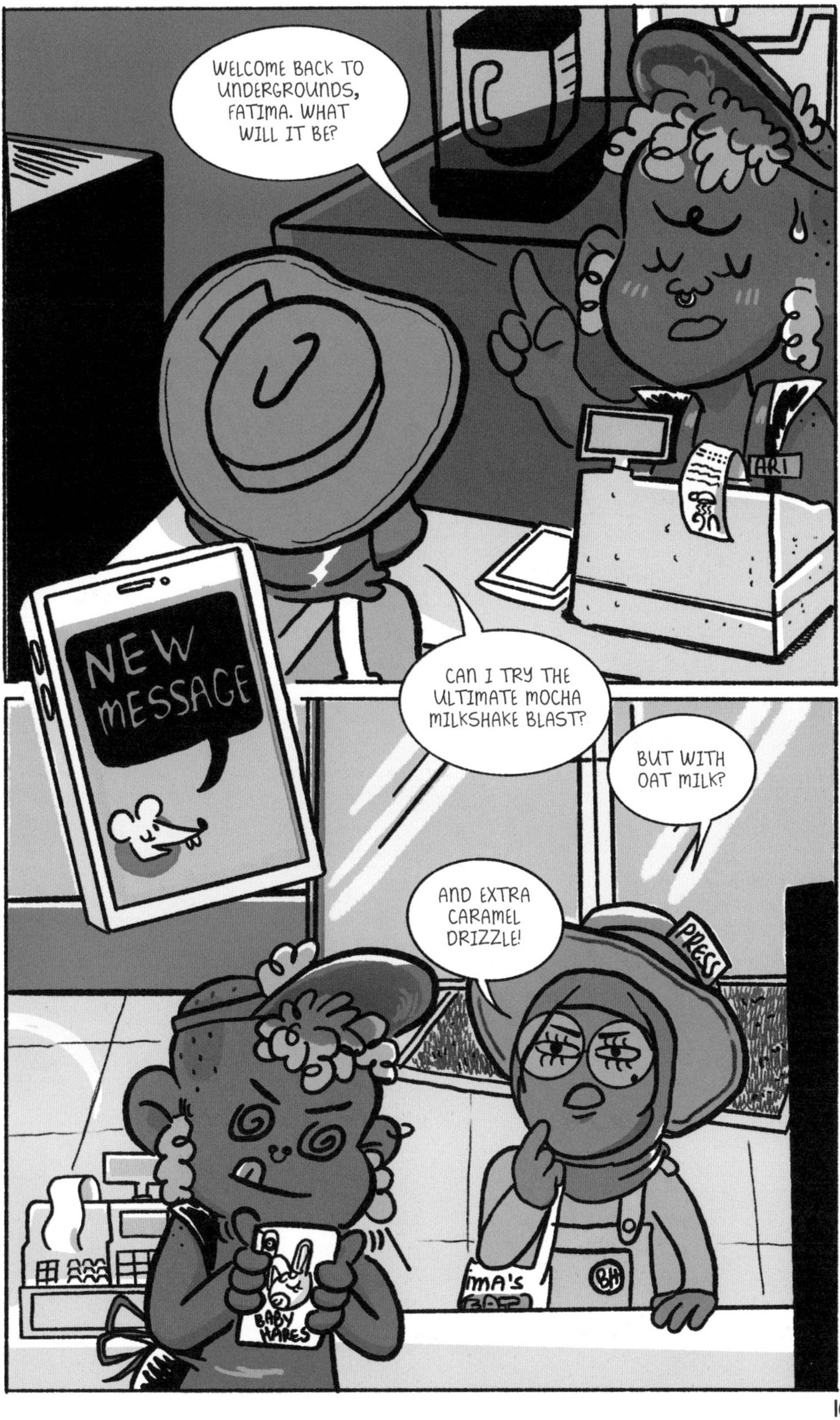
WELCOME BACK TO UNDERGROUNDS, FATIMA. WHAT WILL IT BE?
ARI
NEW MESSAGE
CAN I TRY THE ULTIMATE MOCHA MILKSHAKE BLAST?
BUT WITH OAT MILK?
AND EXTRA CARAMEL DRIZZLE!
PRESS
BABY HARES

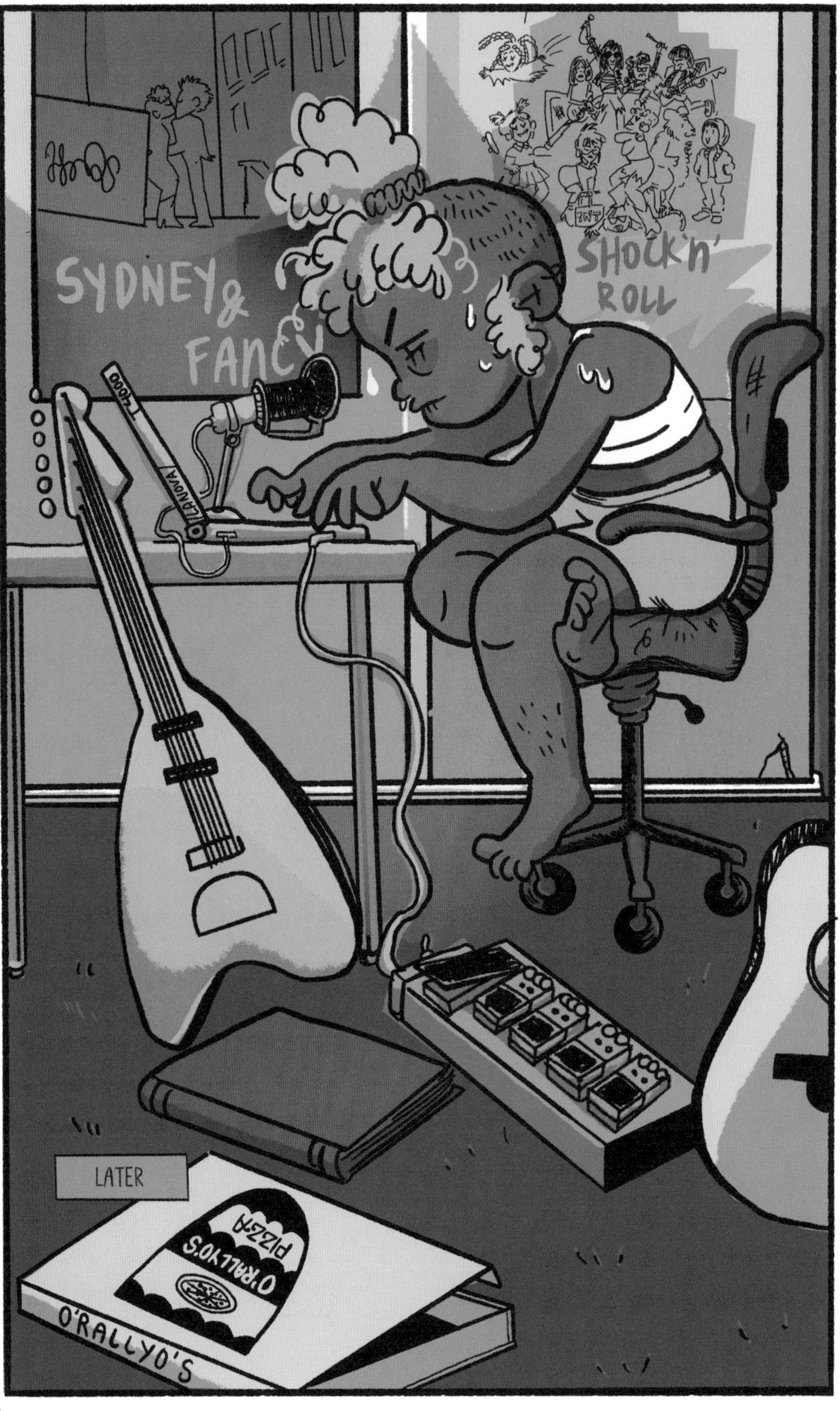
SYDNEY & FANCY
SHOCK'N' ROLL
LANOVA
LATER
O'RALLYO'S PIZZA
O'RALLYO'S

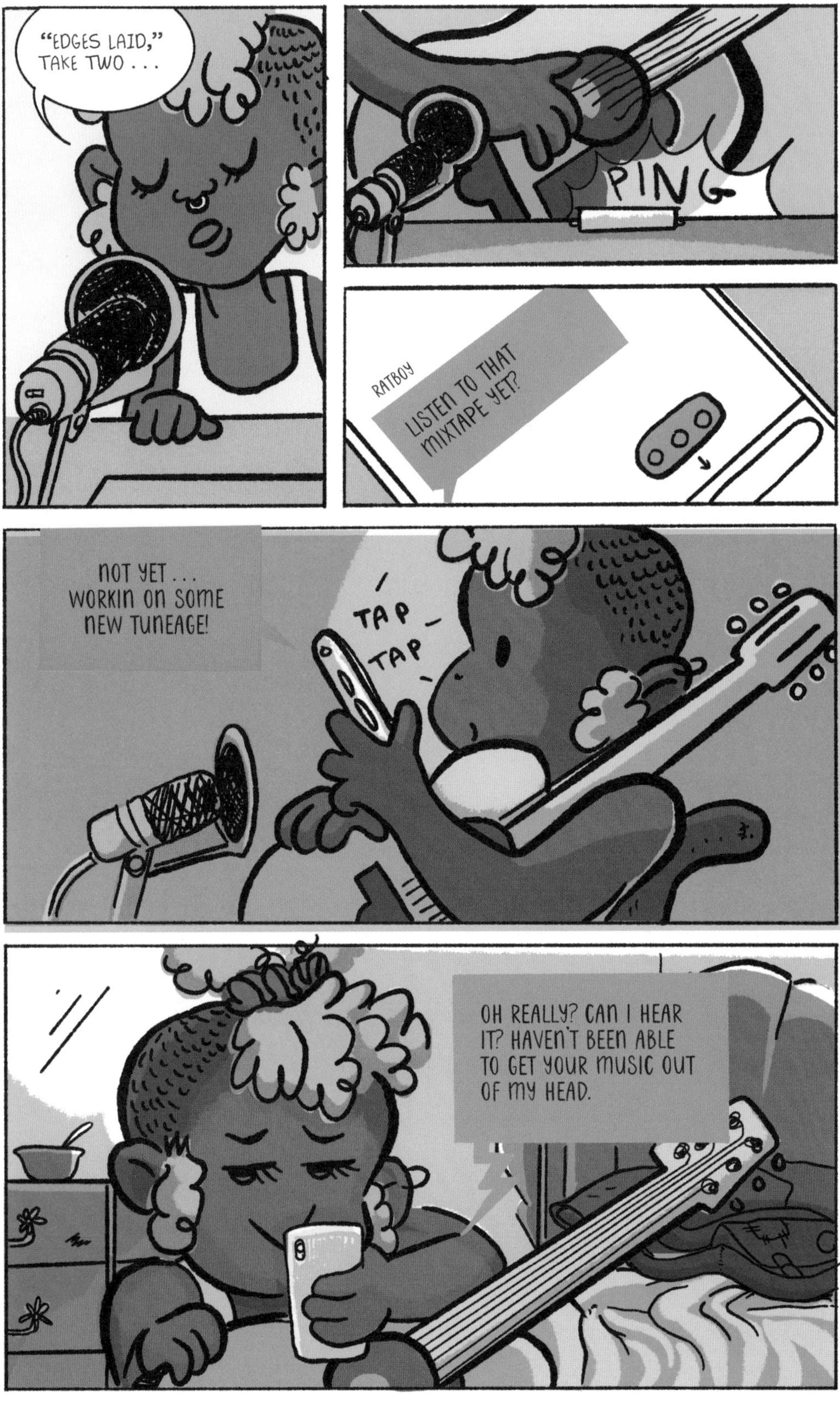
"EDGES LAID," TAKE TWO . . .
PING
RATBOY
LISTEN TO THAT MIXTAPE YET?
NOT YET . . . WORKIN ON SOME NEW TUNEAGE!
TAP TAP
OH REALLY? CAN I HEAR IT? HAVEN'T BEEN ABLE TO GET YOUR MUSIC OUT OF MY HEAD.

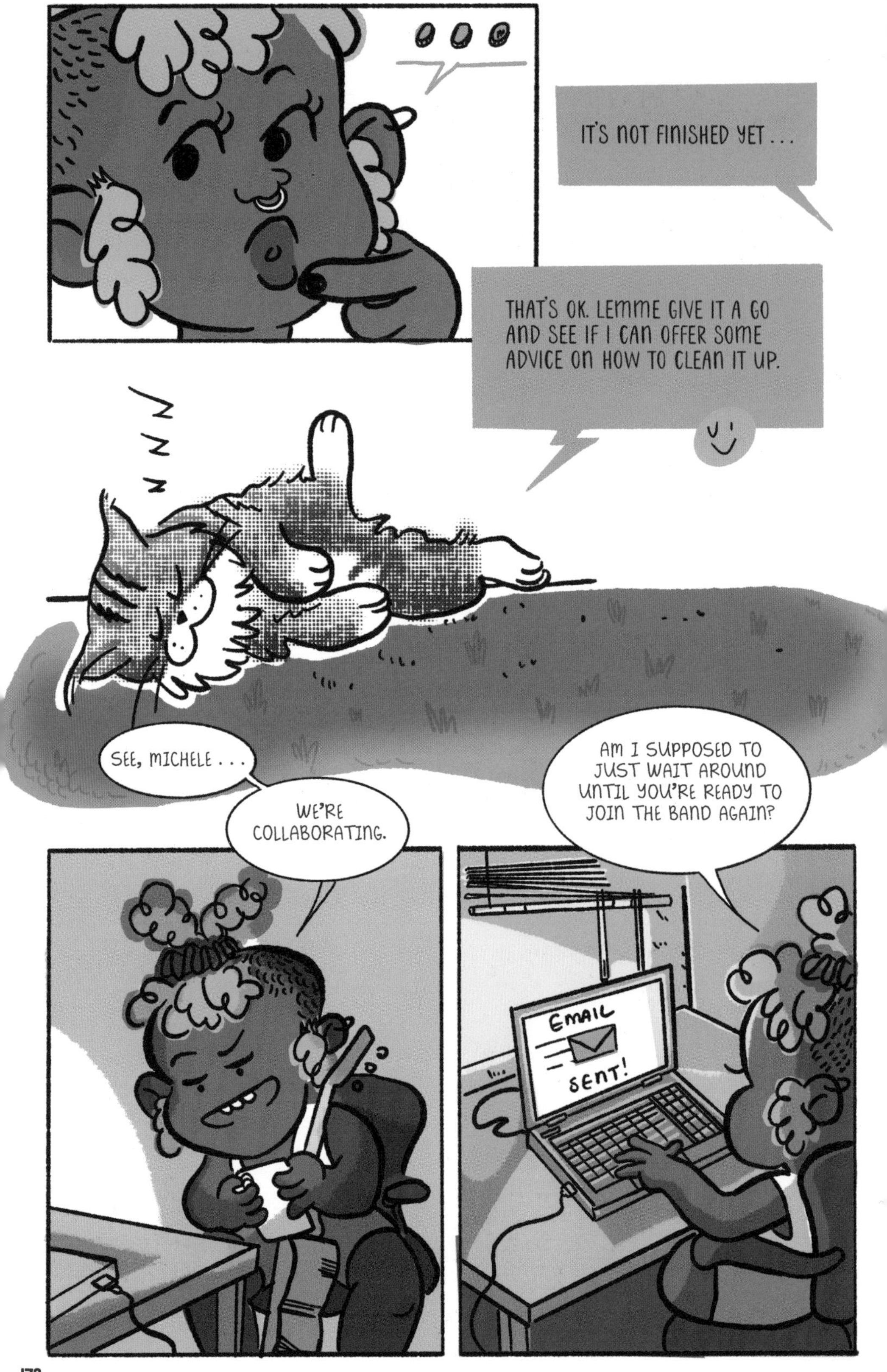

IT'S NOT FINISHED YET . . .
THAT'S OK. LEMME GIVE IT A GO AND SEE IF I CAN OFFER SOME ADVICE ON HOW TO CLEAN IT UP.
Z Z Z
SEE, MICHELE . . .
WE'RE COLLABORATING.
AM I SUPPOSED TO JUST WAIT AROUND UNTIL YOU'RE READY TO JOIN THE BAND AGAIN?
EMAIL SENT!

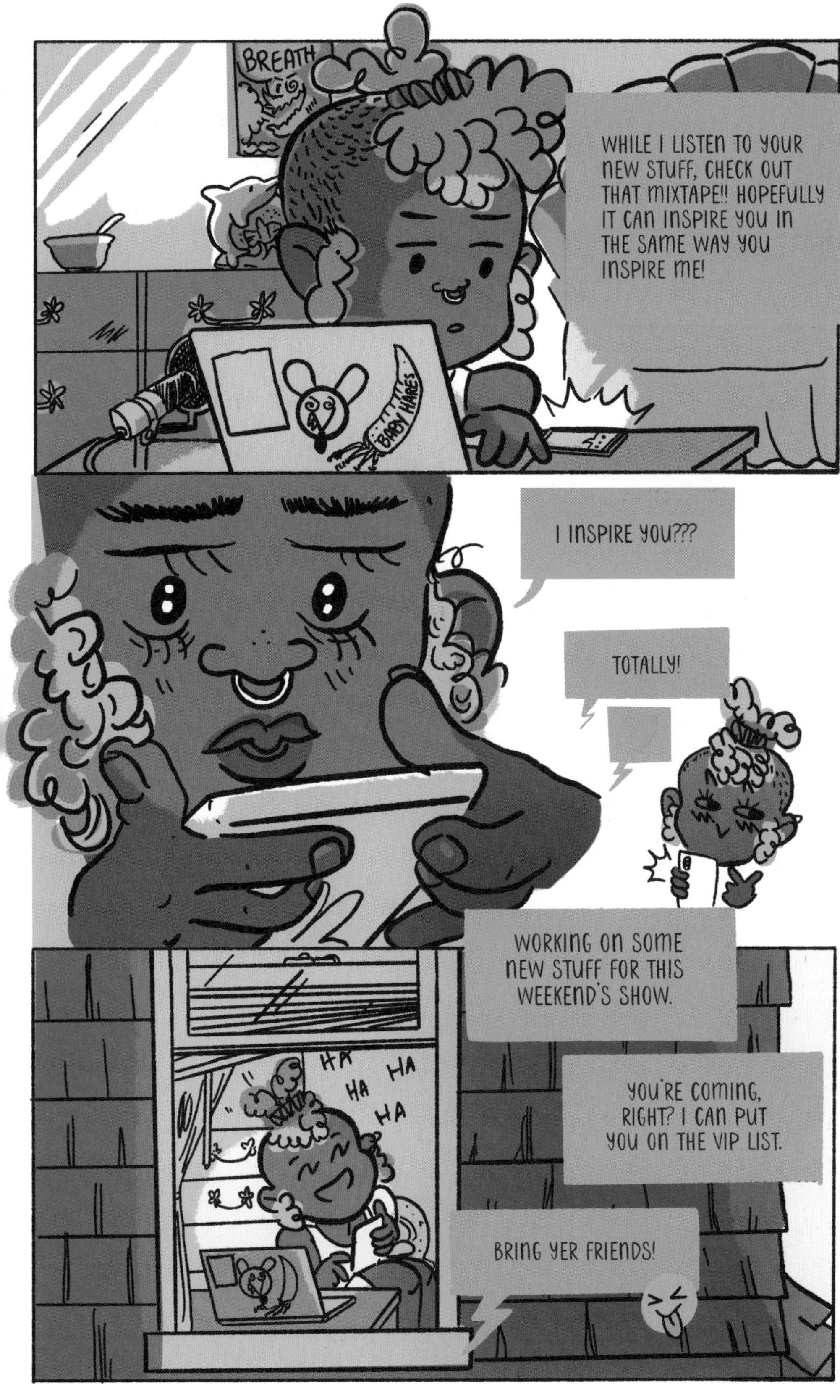
BREATH
WHILE I LISTEN TO YOUR NEW STUFF, CHECK OUT THAT MIXTAPE!! HOPEFULLY IT CAN INSPIRE YOU IN THE SAME WAY YOU INSPIRE ME!
BABY HARES
I INSPIRE YOU???
TOTALLY!
WORKING ON SOME NEW STUFF FOR THIS WEEKEND'S SHOW.
HA HA HA HA
YOU'RE COMING, RIGHT? I CAN PUT YOU ON THE VIP LIST.
BRING YER FRIENDS!

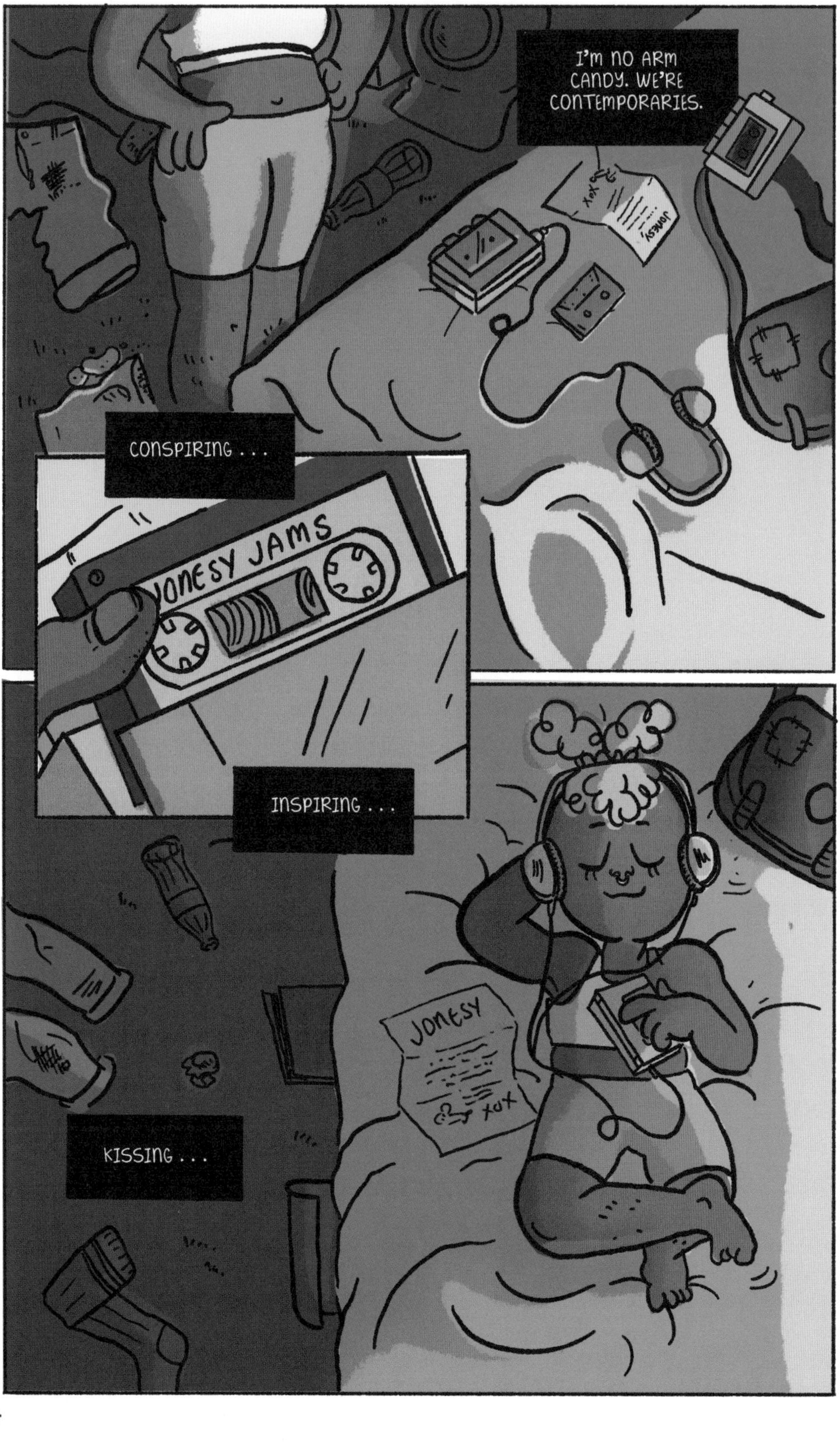
I'M NO ARM CANDY. WE'RE CONTEMPORARIES.
CONSPIRING . . .
JONESY JAMS
INSPIRING . . .
JONESY
XOX
KISSING . . .

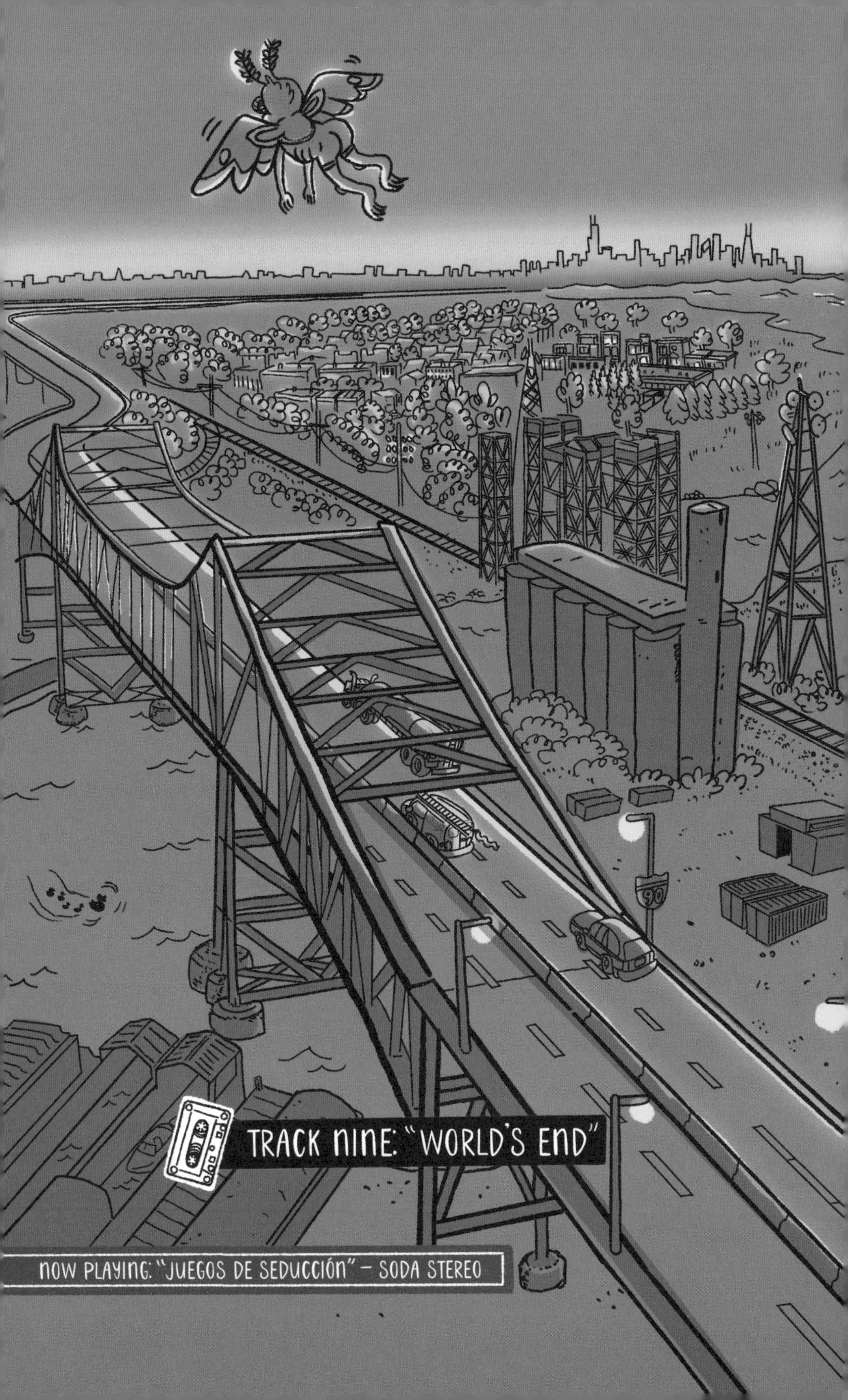
90
TRACK NINE: "WORLD'S END"
NOW PLAYING: "JUEGOS DE SEDUCCIÓN" – SODA STEREO

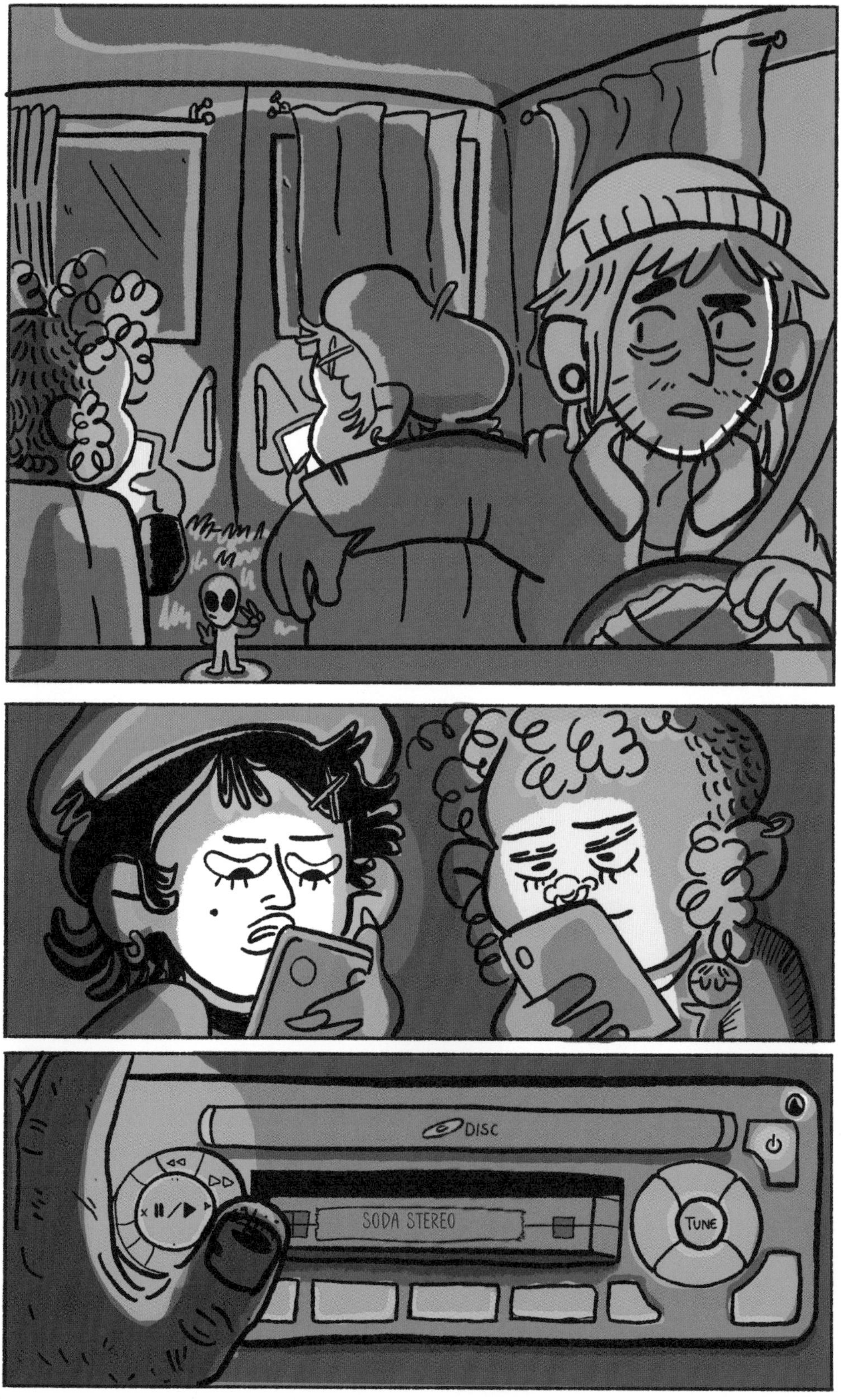
DISC
SODA STEREO
TUNE

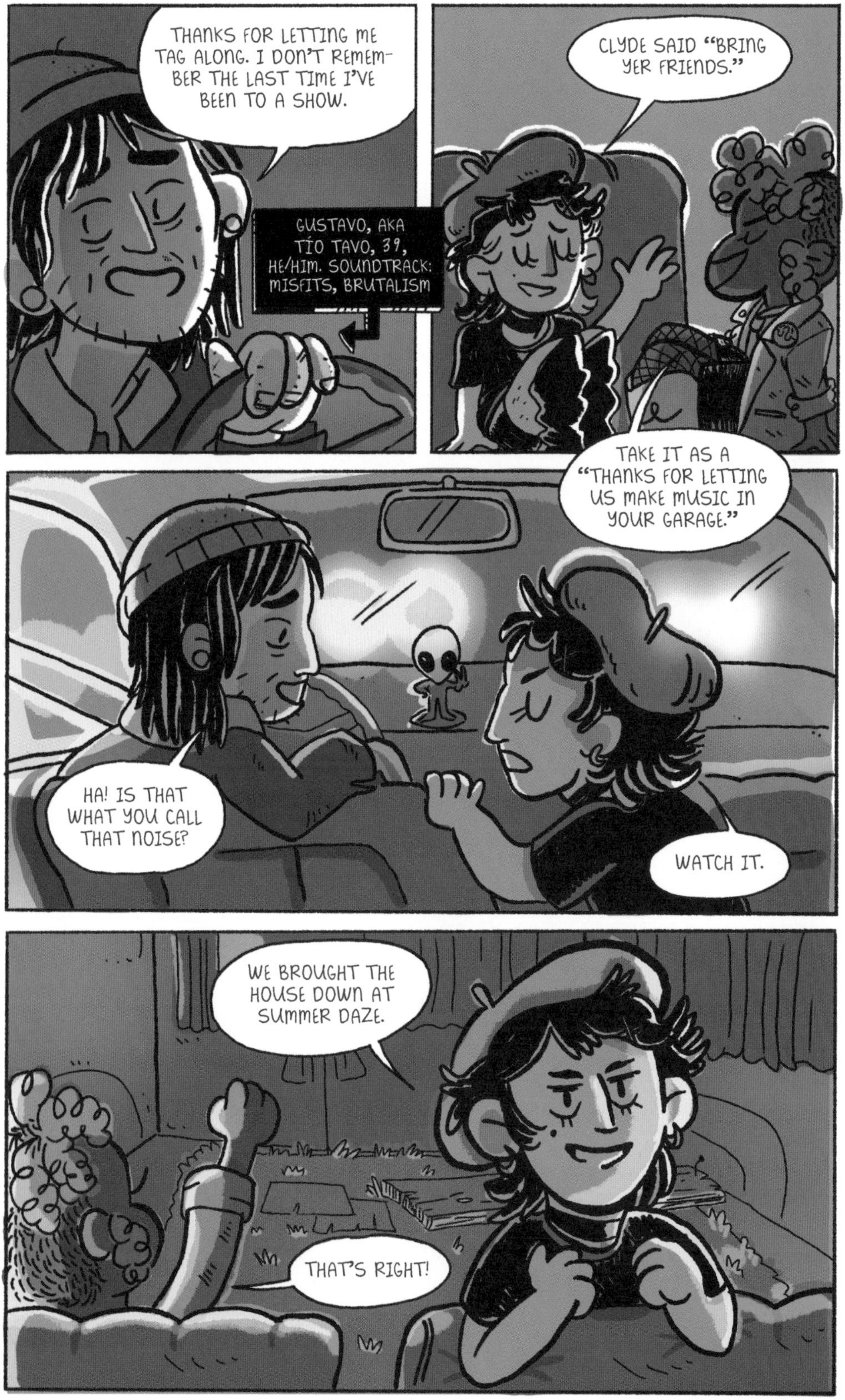
THANKS FOR LETTING ME TAG ALONG. I DON'T REMEMBER THE LAST TIME I'VE BEEN TO A SHOW.
GUSTAVO, AKA TÍO TAVO, 39, HE/HIM. SOUNDTRACK: MISFITS, BRUTALISM
CLYDE SAID "BRING YER FRIENDS."
TAKE IT AS A "THANKS FOR LETTING US MAKE MUSIC IN YOUR GARAGE."
HA! IS THAT WHAT YOU CALL THAT NOISE?
WATCH IT.
WE BROUGHT THE HOUSE DOWN AT SUMMER DAZE.
THAT'S RIGHT!

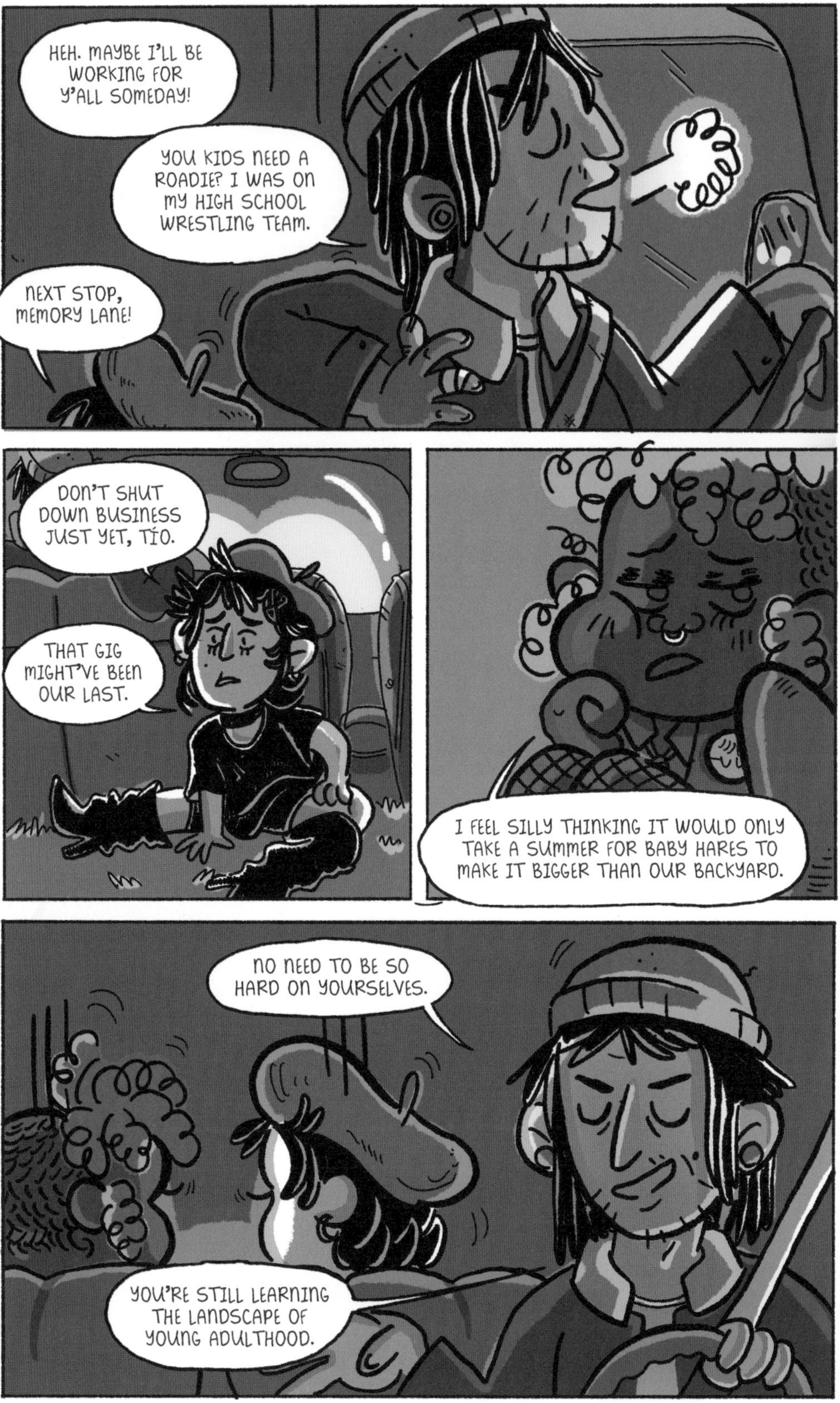
HEH. MAYBE I'LL BE WORKING FOR Y'ALL SOMEDAY!
YOU KIDS NEED A ROADIE? I WAS ON MY HIGH SCHOOL WRESTLING TEAM.
NEXT STOP, MEMORY LANE!
DON'T SHUT DOWN BUSINESS JUST YET, TÍO.
THAT GIG MIGHT'VE BEEN OUR LAST.
I FEEL SILLY THINKING IT WOULD ONLY TAKE A SUMMER FOR BABY HARES TO MAKE IT BIGGER THAN OUR BACKYARD.
NO NEED TO BE SO HARD ON YOURSELVES.
YOU'RE STILL LEARNING THE LANDSCAPE OF YOUNG ADULTHOOD.

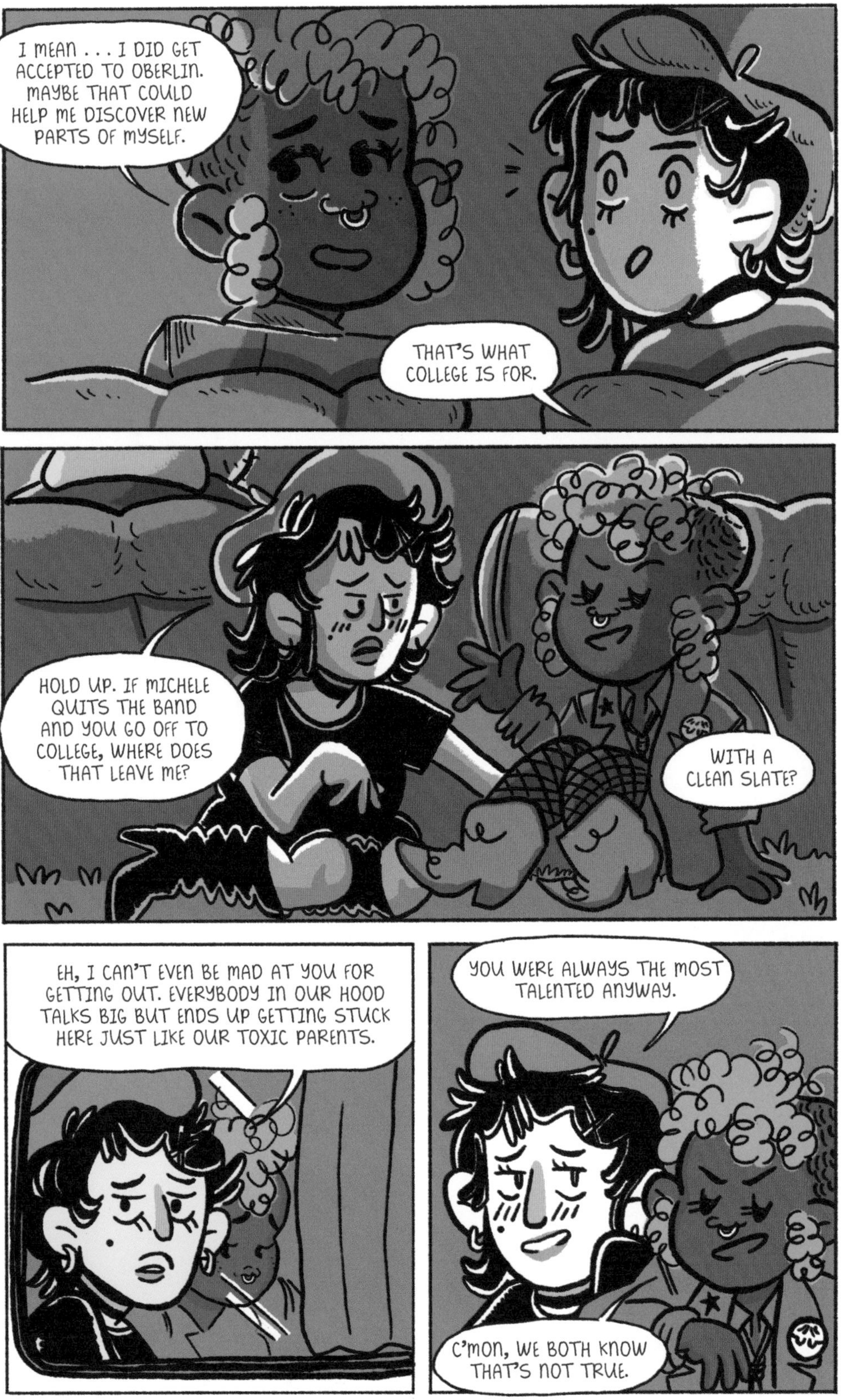
I MEAN . . . I DID GET ACCEPTED TO OBERLIN. MAYBE THAT COULD HELP ME DISCOVER NEW PARTS OF MYSELF.
THAT'S WHAT COLLEGE IS FOR.
HOLD UP. IF MICHELE QUITS THE BAND AND YOU GO OFF TO COLLEGE, WHERE DOES THAT LEAVE ME?
WITH A CLEAN SLATE?
EH, I CAN'T EVEN BE MAD AT YOU FOR GETTING OUT. EVERYBODY IN OUR HOOD TALKS BIG BUT ENDS UP GETTING STUCK HERE JUST LIKE OUR TOXIC PARENTS.
YOU WERE ALWAYS THE MOST TALENTED ANYWAY.
C'MON, WE BOTH KNOW THAT'S NOT TRUE.

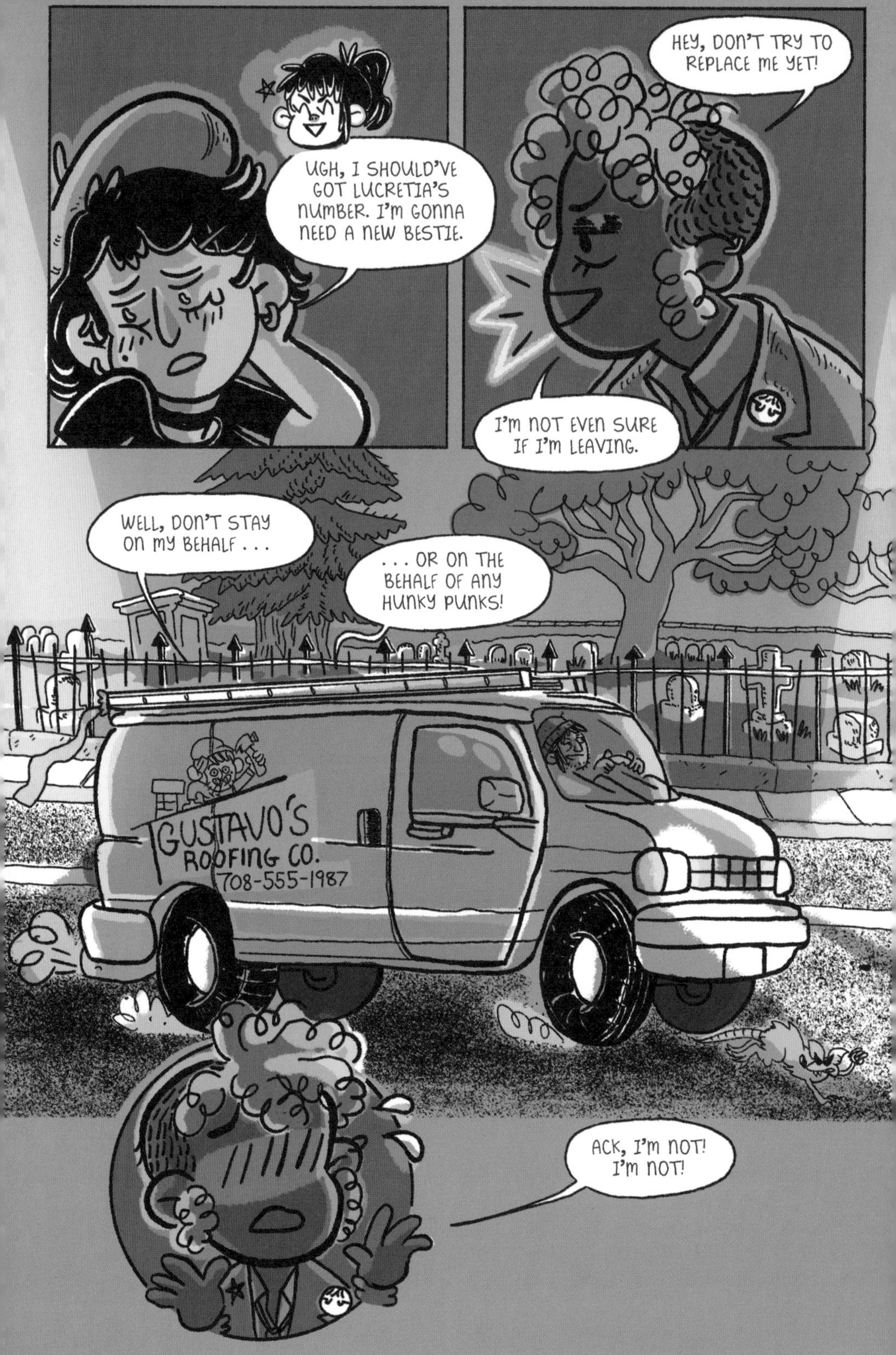
UGH, I SHOULD'VE GOT LUCRETIA'S NUMBER. I'M GONNA NEED A NEW BESTIE.
HEY, DON'T TRY TO REPLACE ME YET!
I'M NOT EVEN SURE IF I'M LEAVING.
WELL, DON'T STAY ON MY BEHALF . . .
. . . OR ON THE BEHALF OF ANY HUNKY PUNKS!
GUSTAVO'S
ROOFING CO.
708-555-1987
ACK, I'M NOT! I'M NOT!

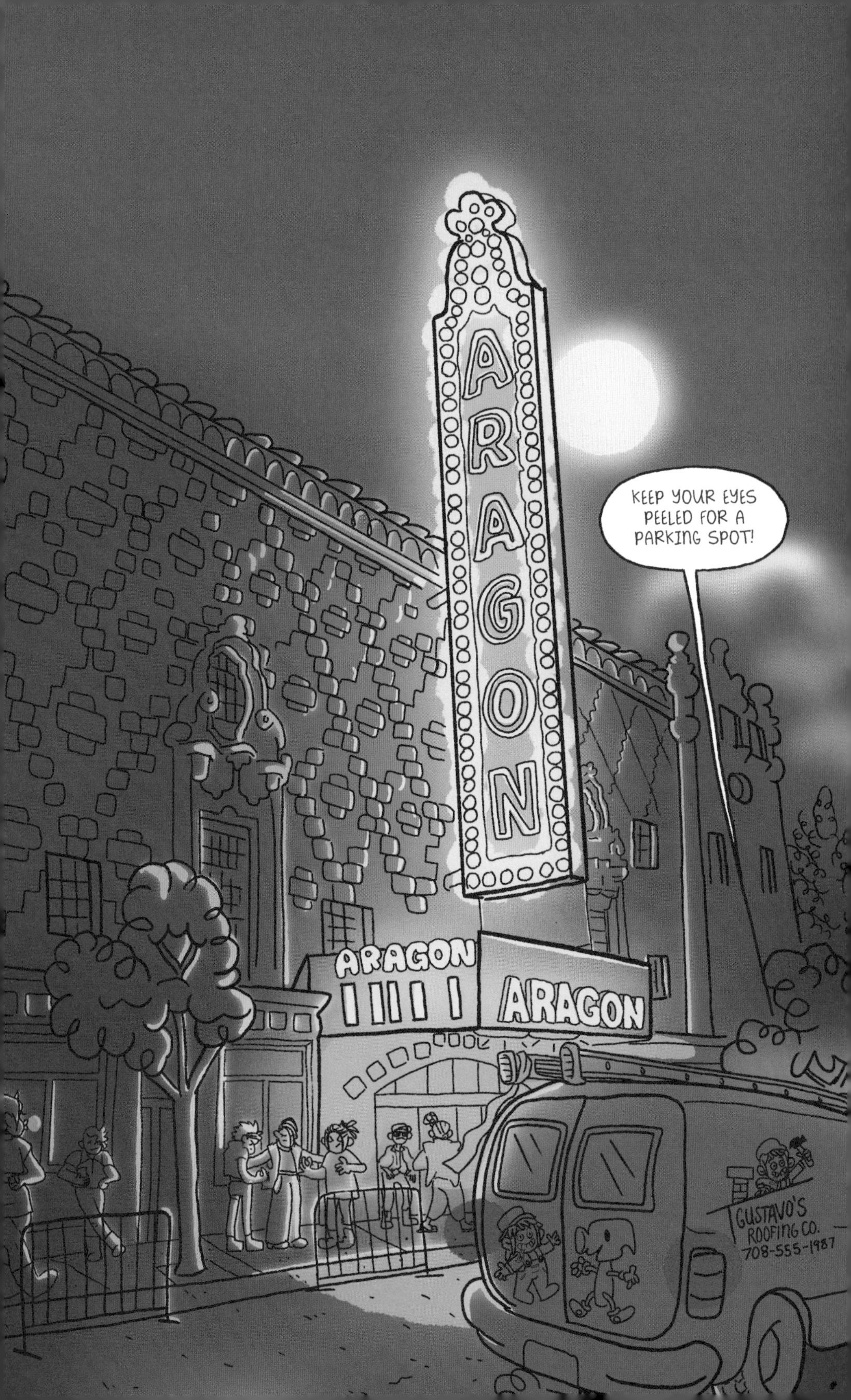
KEEP YOUR EYES PEELED FOR A PARKING SPOT!
ARAGON
ARAGON
ARAGON
GUSTAVO'S ROOFING CO. 708-555-1987

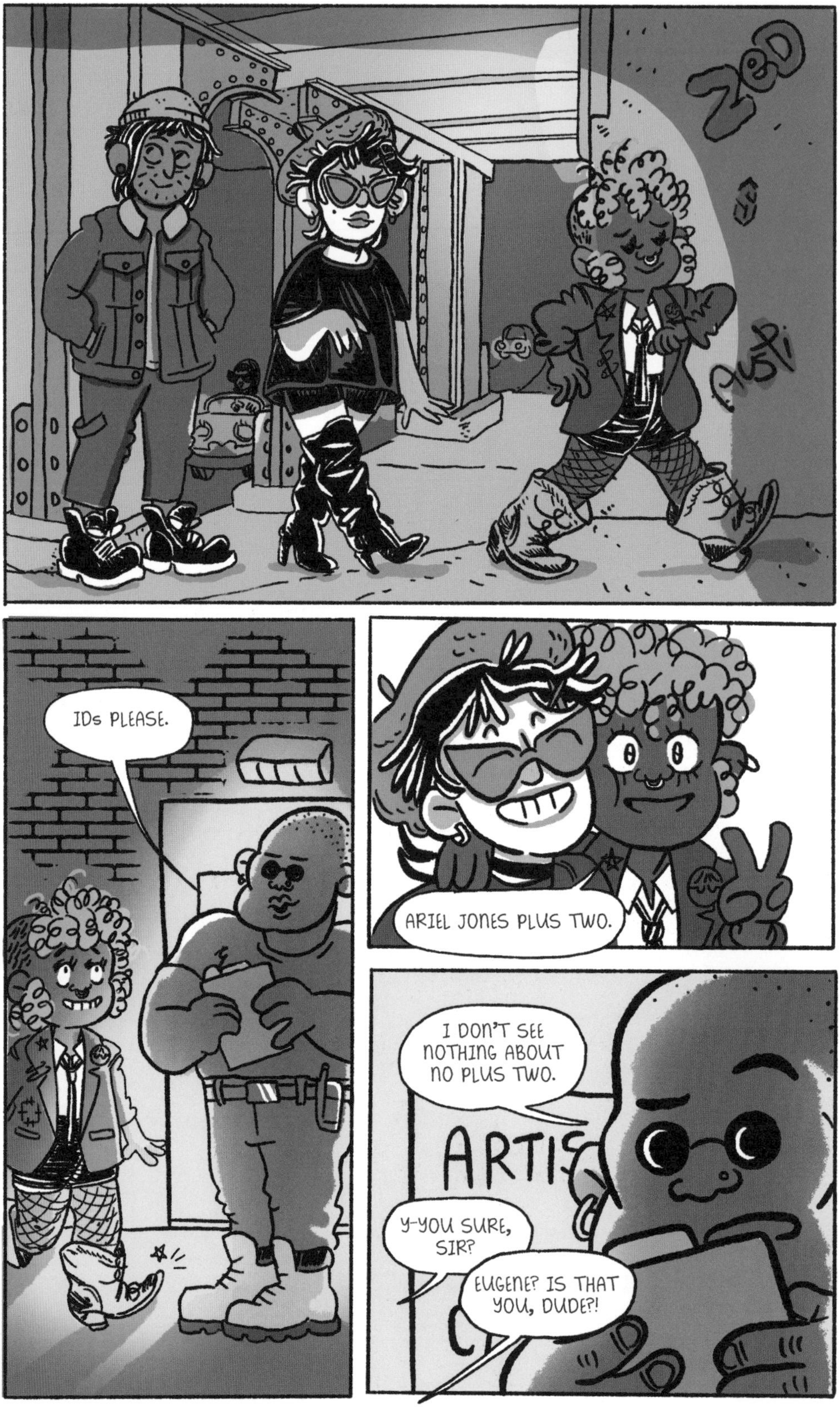
ZED
IDs PLEASE.
ARIEL JONES PLUS TWO.
I DON'T SEE NOTHING ABOUT NO PLUS TWO.
ARTIS
Y-YOU SURE, SIR?
EUGENE? IS THAT YOU, DUDE?!

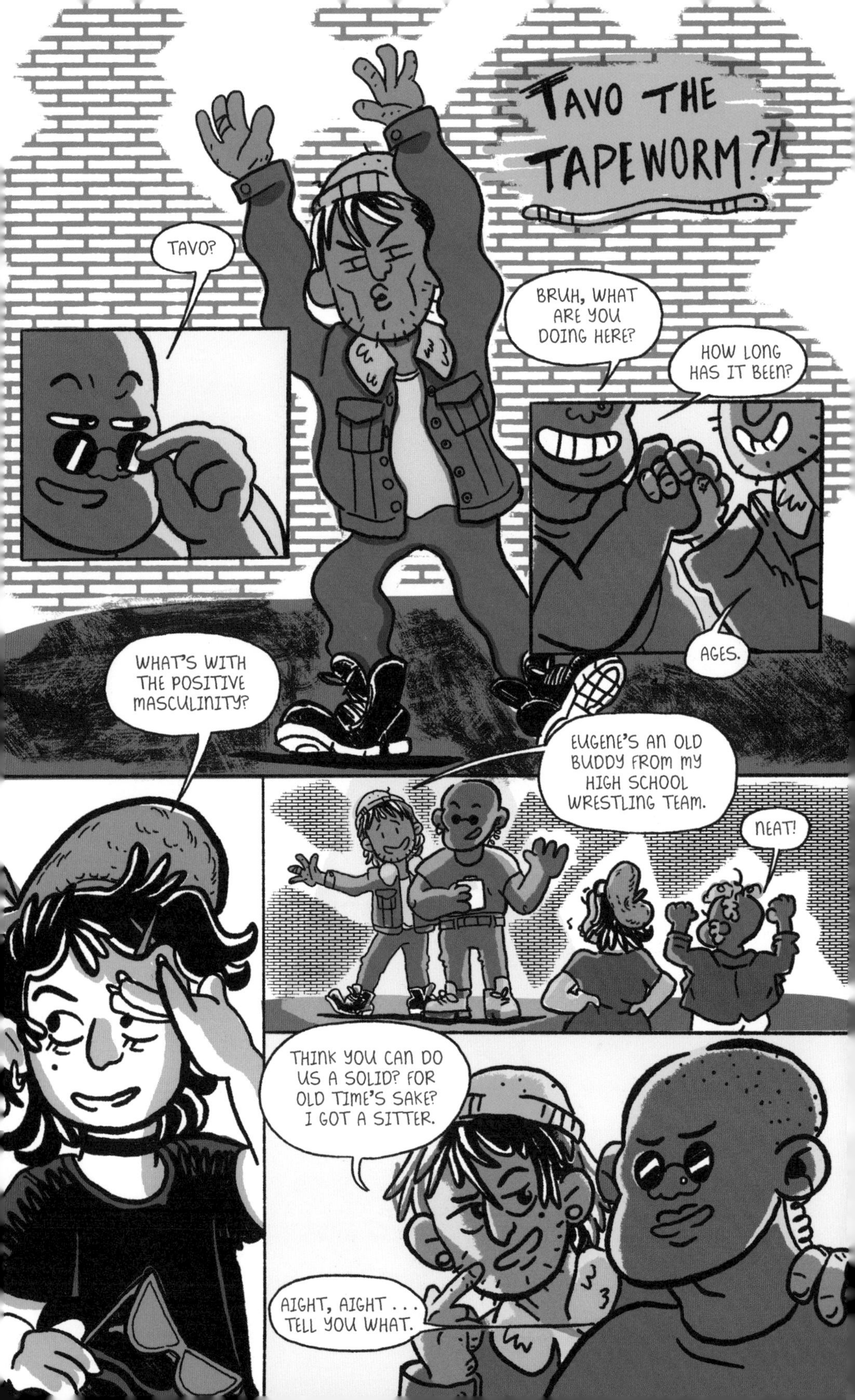
TAVO THE TAPEWORM?!
TAVO?
BRUH, WHAT ARE YOU DOING HERE?
HOW LONG HAS IT BEEN?
AGES.
WHAT'S WITH THE POSITIVE MASCULINITY?
EUGENE'S AN OLD BUDDY FROM MY HIGH SCHOOL WRESTLING TEAM.
NEAT!
THINK YOU CAN DO US A SOLID? FOR OLD TIME'S SAKE? I GOT A SITTER.
AIGHT, AIGHT . . . TELL YOU WHAT.

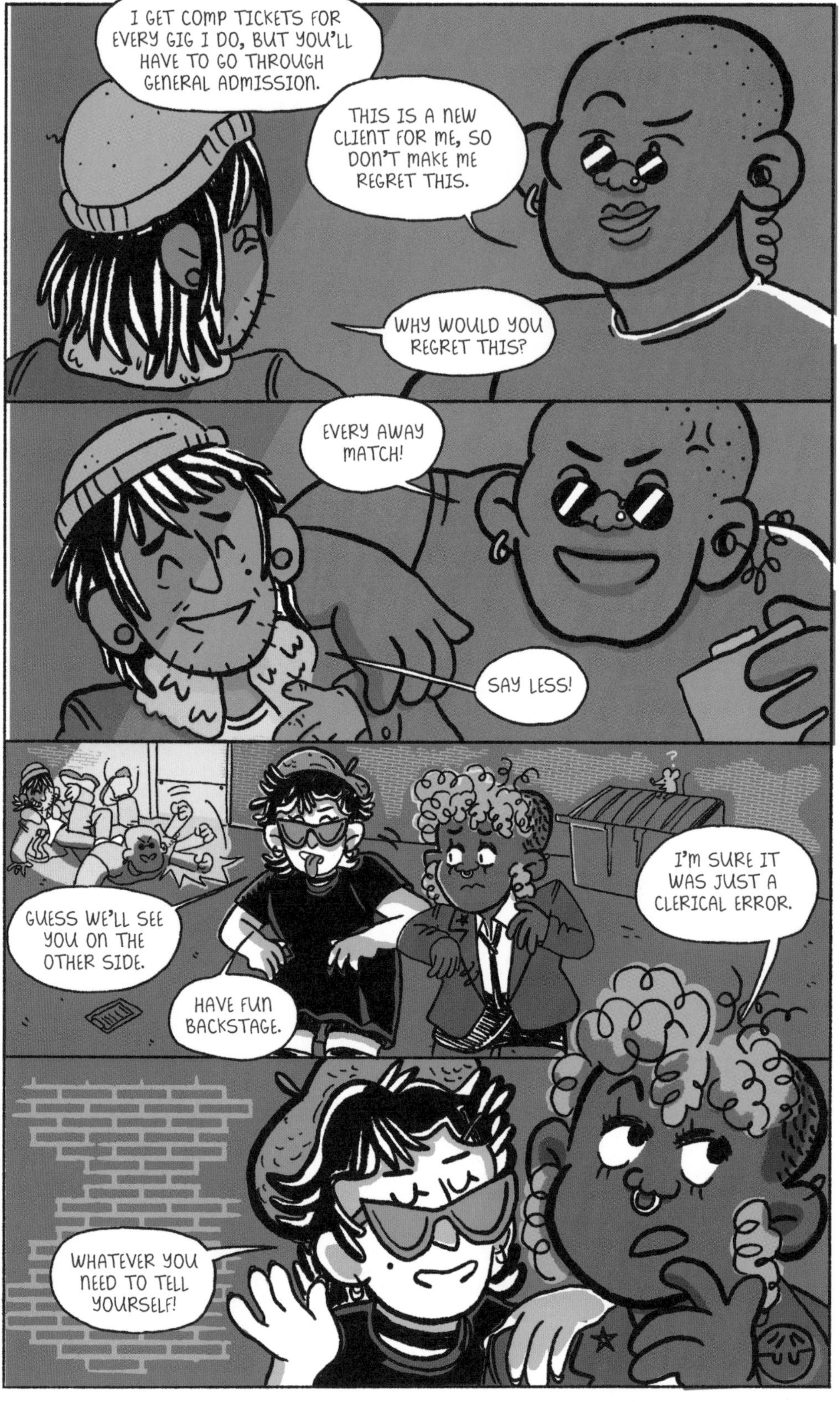
I GET COMP TICKETS FOR EVERY GIG I DO, BUT YOU'LL HAVE TO GO THROUGH GENERAL ADMISSION.
THIS IS A NEW CLIENT FOR ME, SO DON'T MAKE ME REGRET THIS.
WHY WOULD YOU REGRET THIS?
EVERY AWAY MATCH!
SAY LESS!
I'M SURE IT WAS JUST A CLERICAL ERROR.
GUESS WE'LL SEE YOU ON THE OTHER SIDE.
HAVE FUN BACKSTAGE.
WHATEVER YOU NEED TO TELL YOURSELF!

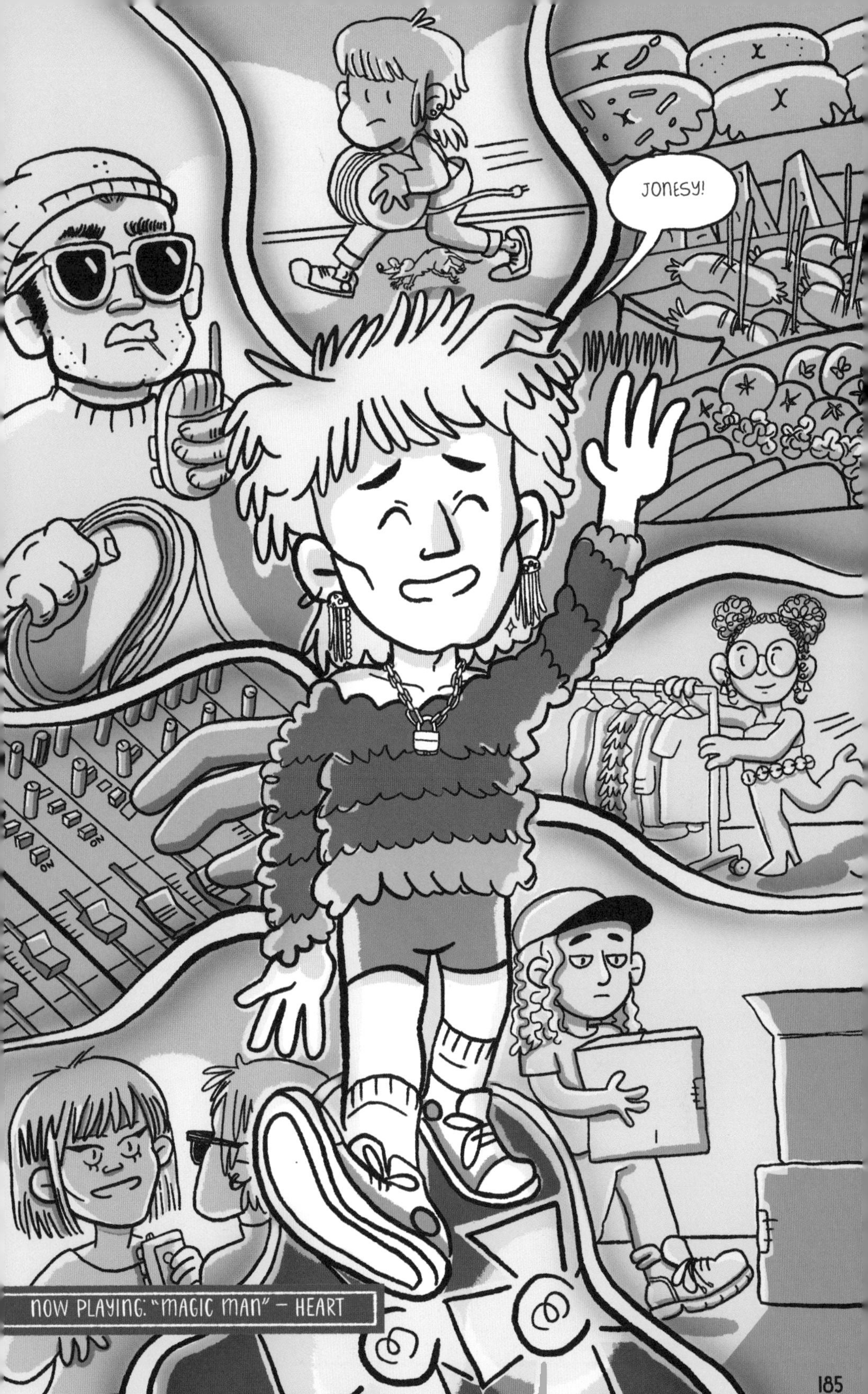
JONESY!
ON
ON
NOW PLAYING: "MAGIC MAN" – HEART

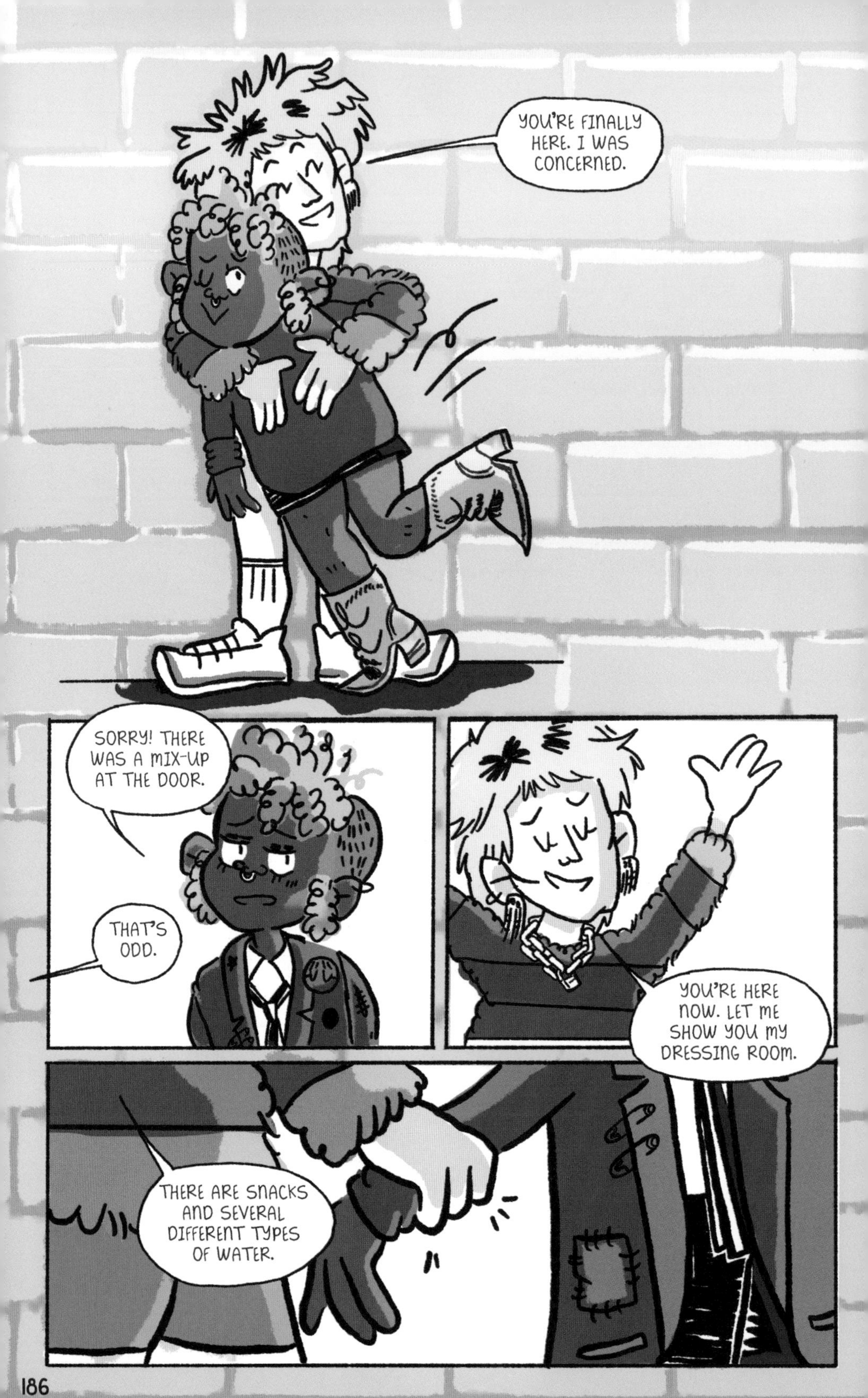
YOU'RE FINALLY HERE. I WAS CONCERNED.
SORRY! THERE WAS A MIX-UP AT THE DOOR.
THAT'S ODD.
YOU'RE HERE NOW. LET ME SHOW YOU MY DRESSING ROOM.
THERE ARE SNACKS AND SEVERAL DIFFERENT TYPES OF WATER.

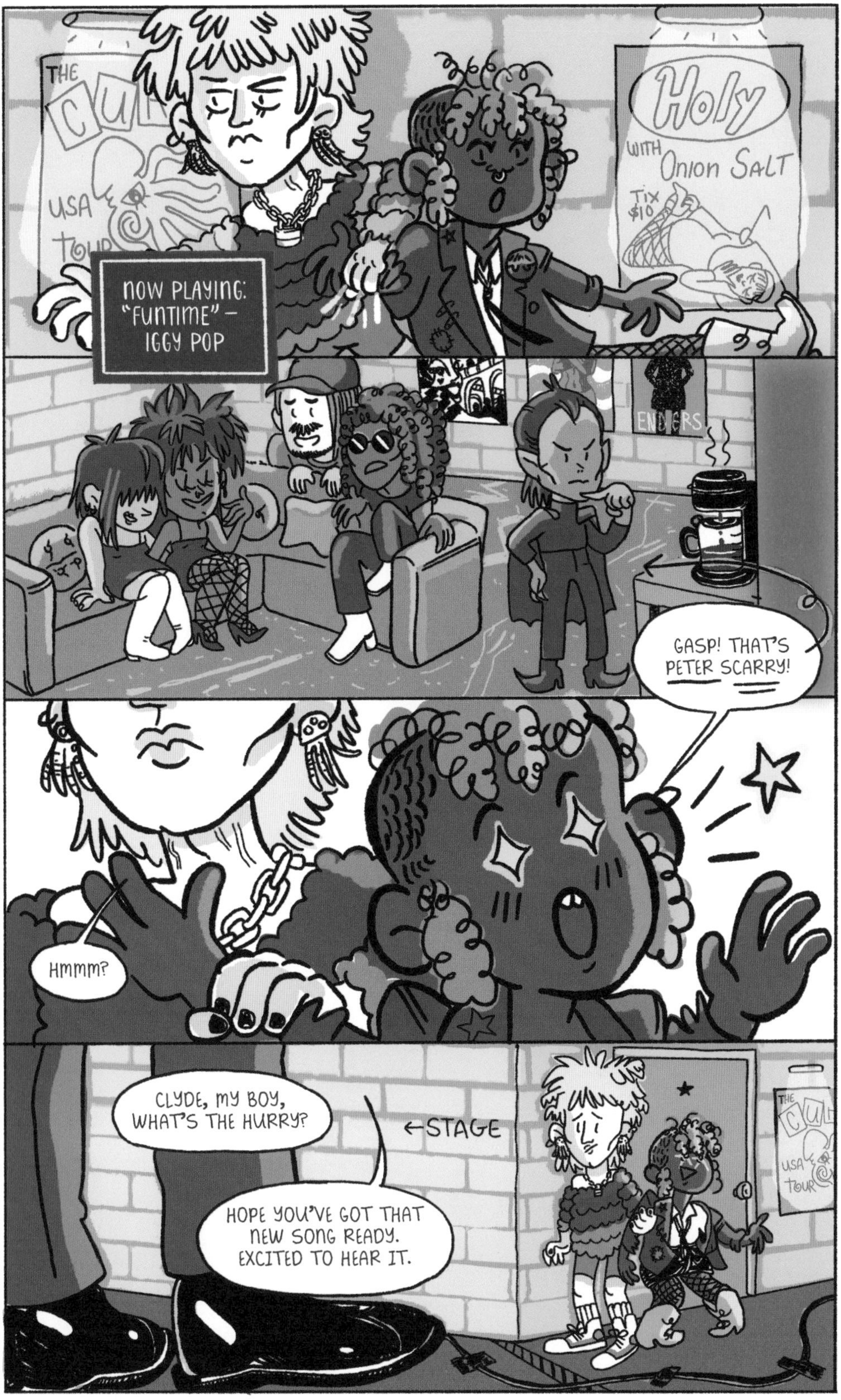
THE CURE USA TOUR
Holy
WITH Onion SALT
TIX $10
NOW PLAYING: "FUNTIME" — IGGY POP
ENDERS
GASP! THAT'S PETER SCARRY!
Hmmm?
CLYDE, MY BOY, WHAT'S THE HURRY?
←STAGE
HOPE YOU'VE GOT THAT NEW SONG READY. EXCITED TO HEAR IT.

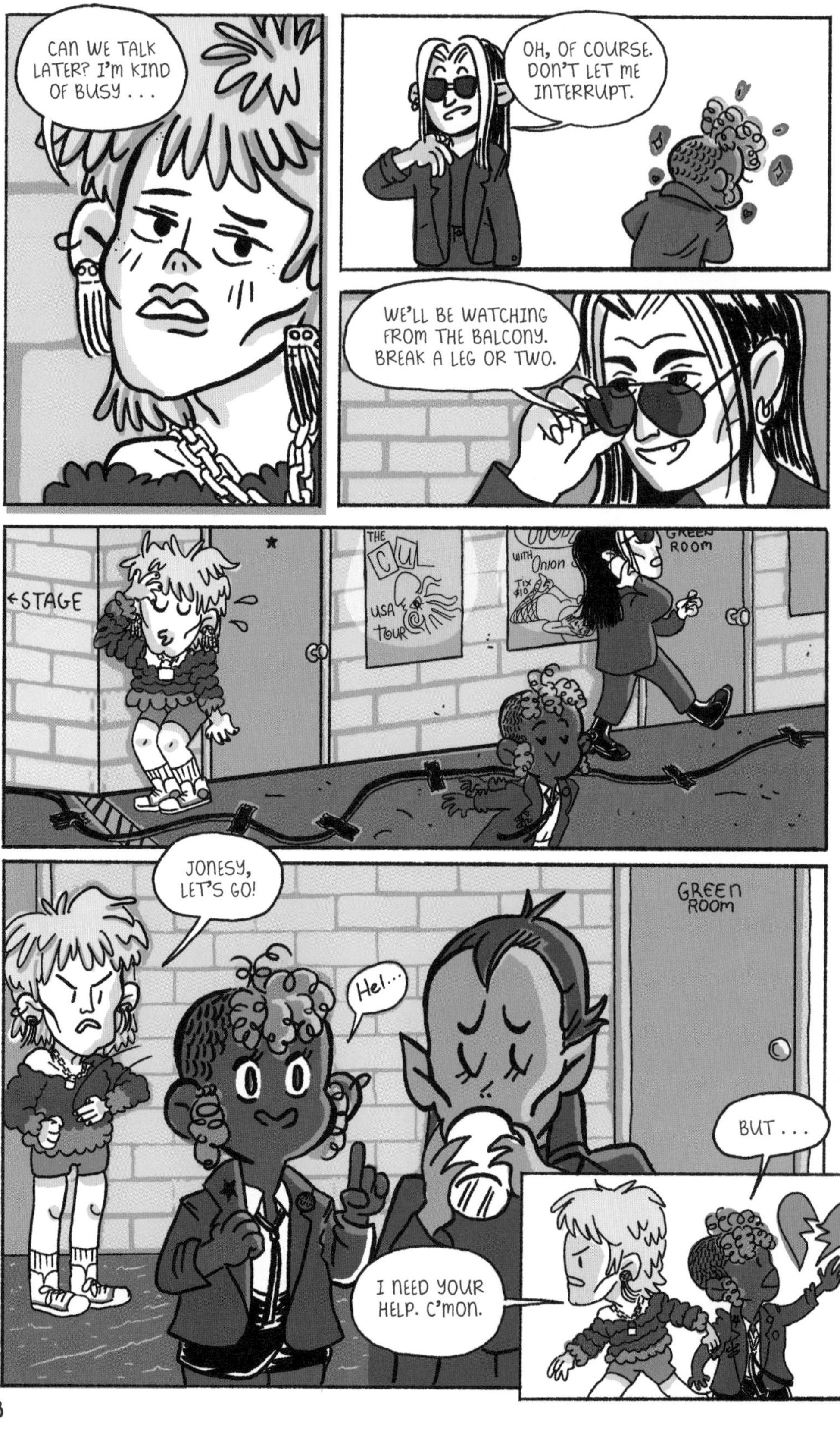
CAN WE TALK LATER? I'M KIND OF BUSY . . .
OH, OF COURSE. DON'T LET ME INTERRUPT.
WE'LL BE WATCHING FROM THE BALCONY. BREAK A LEG OR TWO.
←STAGE
THE CUL
USA TOUR
WITH Onion
Tix $10
GREEN ROOM
JONESY, LET'S GO!
Hel...
GREEN ROOM
BUT . . .
I NEED YOUR HELP. C'MON.

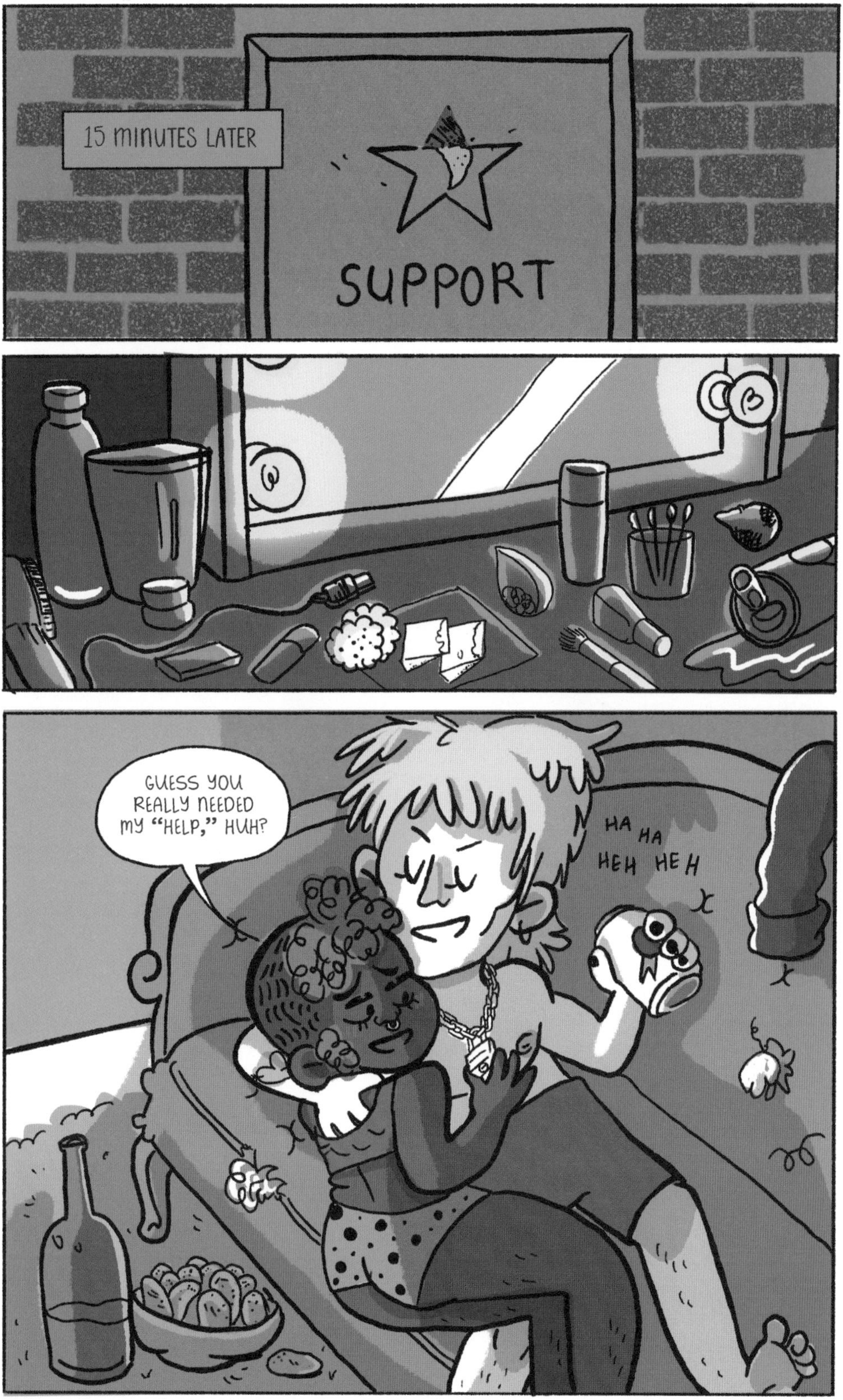
15 MINUTES LATER
SUPPORT
GUESS YOU REALLY NEEDED MY "HELP," HUH?
HA HA HEH HEH

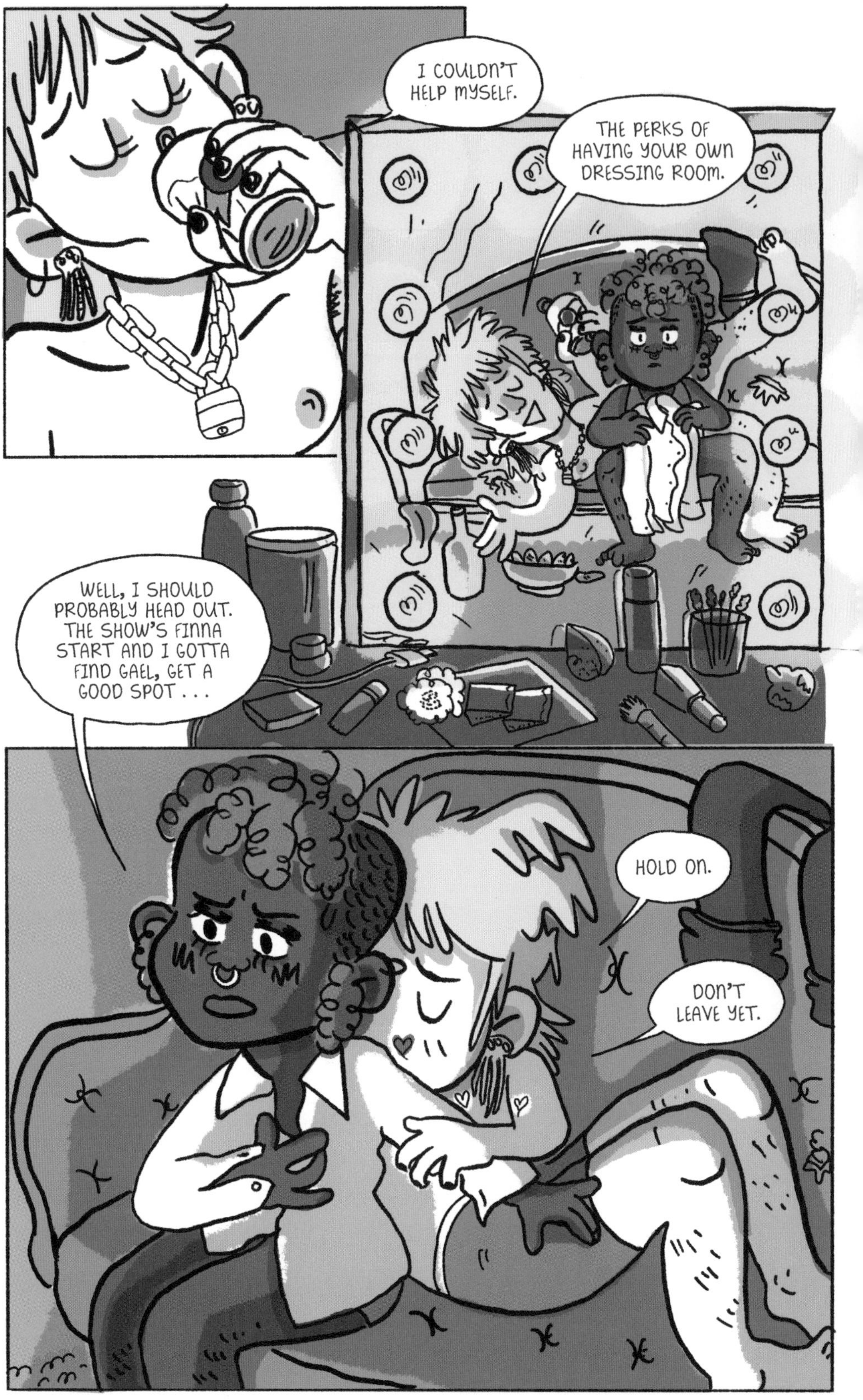
I COULDN'T HELP MYSELF.
THE PERKS OF HAVING YOUR OWN DRESSING ROOM.
WELL, I SHOULD PROBABLY HEAD OUT. THE SHOW'S FINNA START AND I GOTTA FIND GAEL, GET A GOOD SPOT . . .
HOLD ON.
DON'T LEAVE YET.

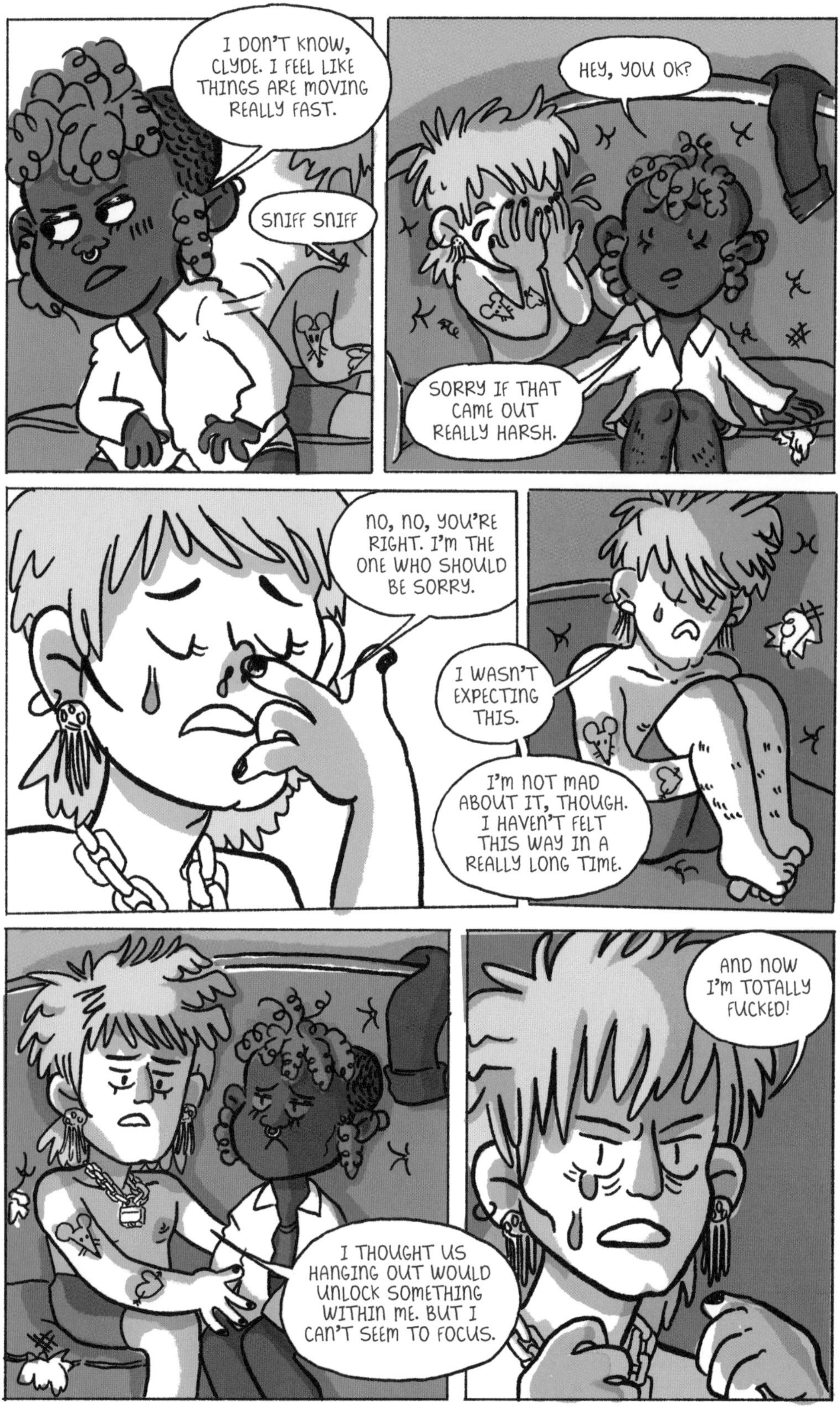
I DON'T KNOW, CLYDE. I FEEL LIKE THINGS ARE MOVING REALLY FAST.
SNIFF SNIFF
HEY, YOU OK?
SORRY IF THAT CAME OUT REALLY HARSH.
NO, NO, YOU'RE RIGHT. I'M THE ONE WHO SHOULD BE SORRY.
I WASN'T EXPECTING THIS.
I'M NOT MAD ABOUT IT, THOUGH. I HAVEN'T FELT THIS WAY IN A REALLY LONG TIME.
I THOUGHT US HANGING OUT WOULD UNLOCK SOMETHING WITHIN ME. BUT I CAN'T SEEM TO FOCUS.
AND NOW I'M TOTALLY FUCKED!

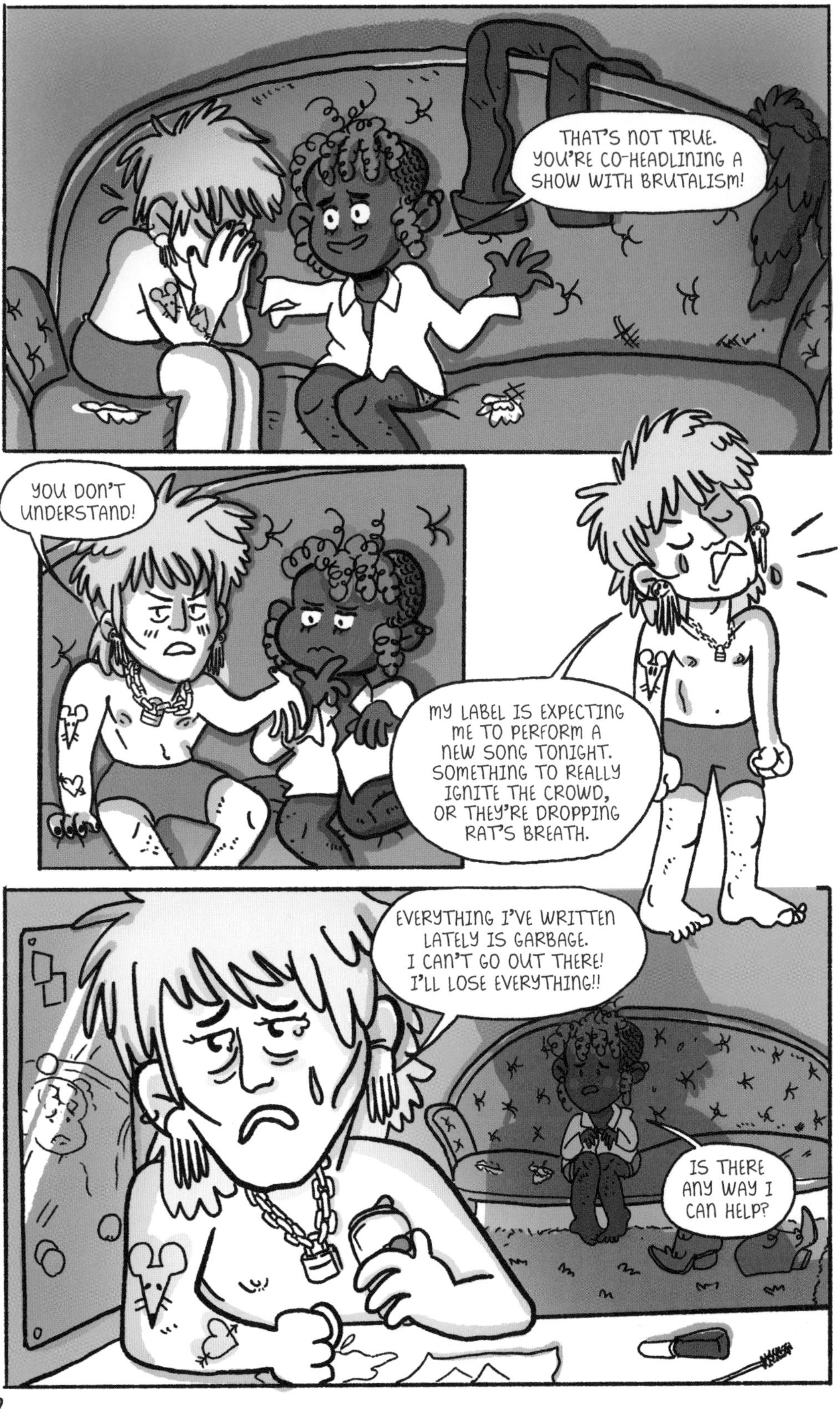
THAT'S NOT TRUE. YOU'RE CO-HEADLINING A SHOW WITH BRUTALISM!
YOU DON'T UNDERSTAND!
MY LABEL IS EXPECTING ME TO PERFORM A NEW SONG TONIGHT. SOMETHING TO REALLY IGNITE THE CROWD, OR THEY'RE DROPPING RAT'S BREATH.
EVERYTHING I'VE WRITTEN LATELY IS GARBAGE. I CAN'T GO OUT THERE! I'LL LOSE EVERYTHING!!
IS THERE ANY WAY I CAN HELP?

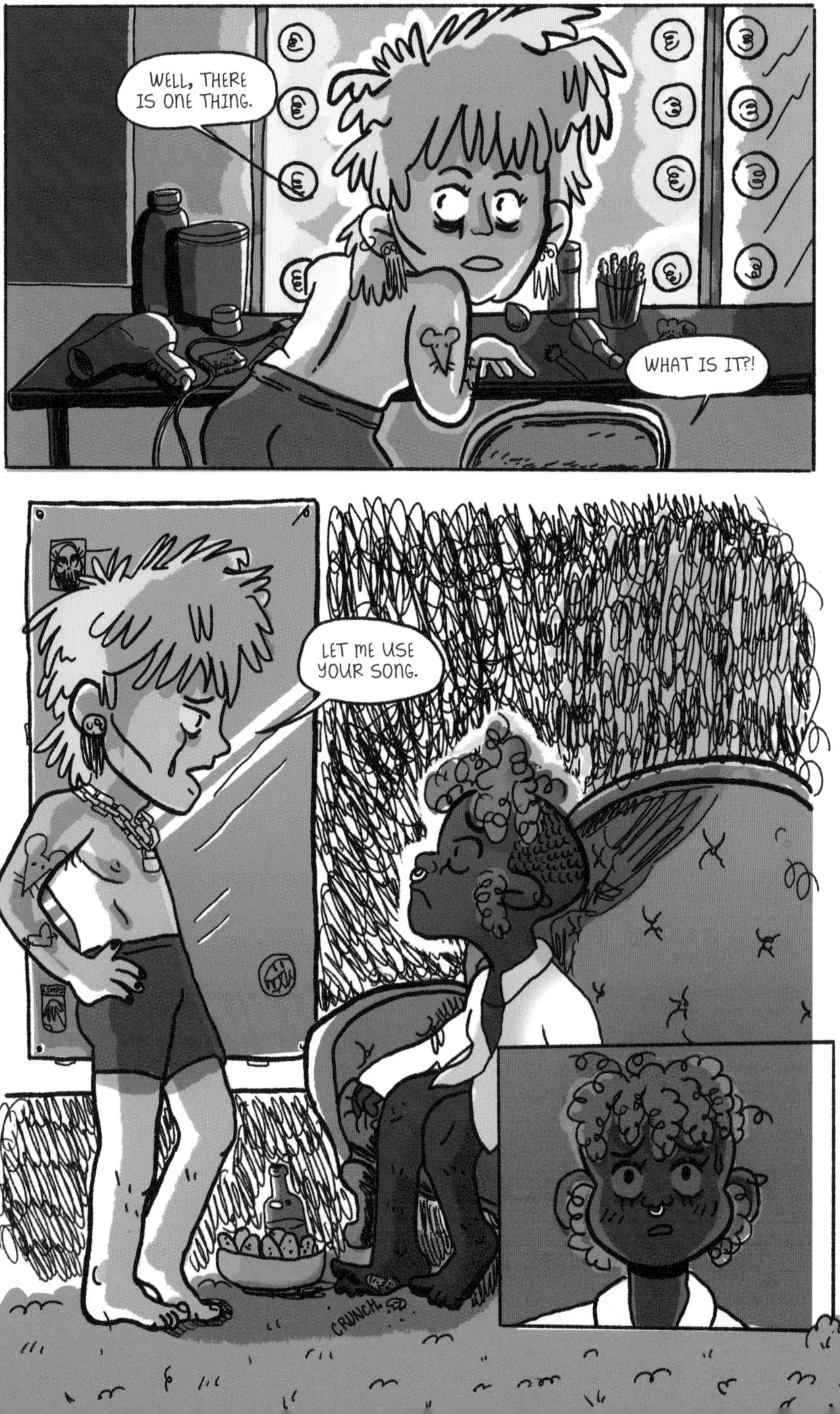
WELL, THERE IS ONE THING.
WHAT IS IT?!
LET ME USE YOUR SONG.
CRUNCH.

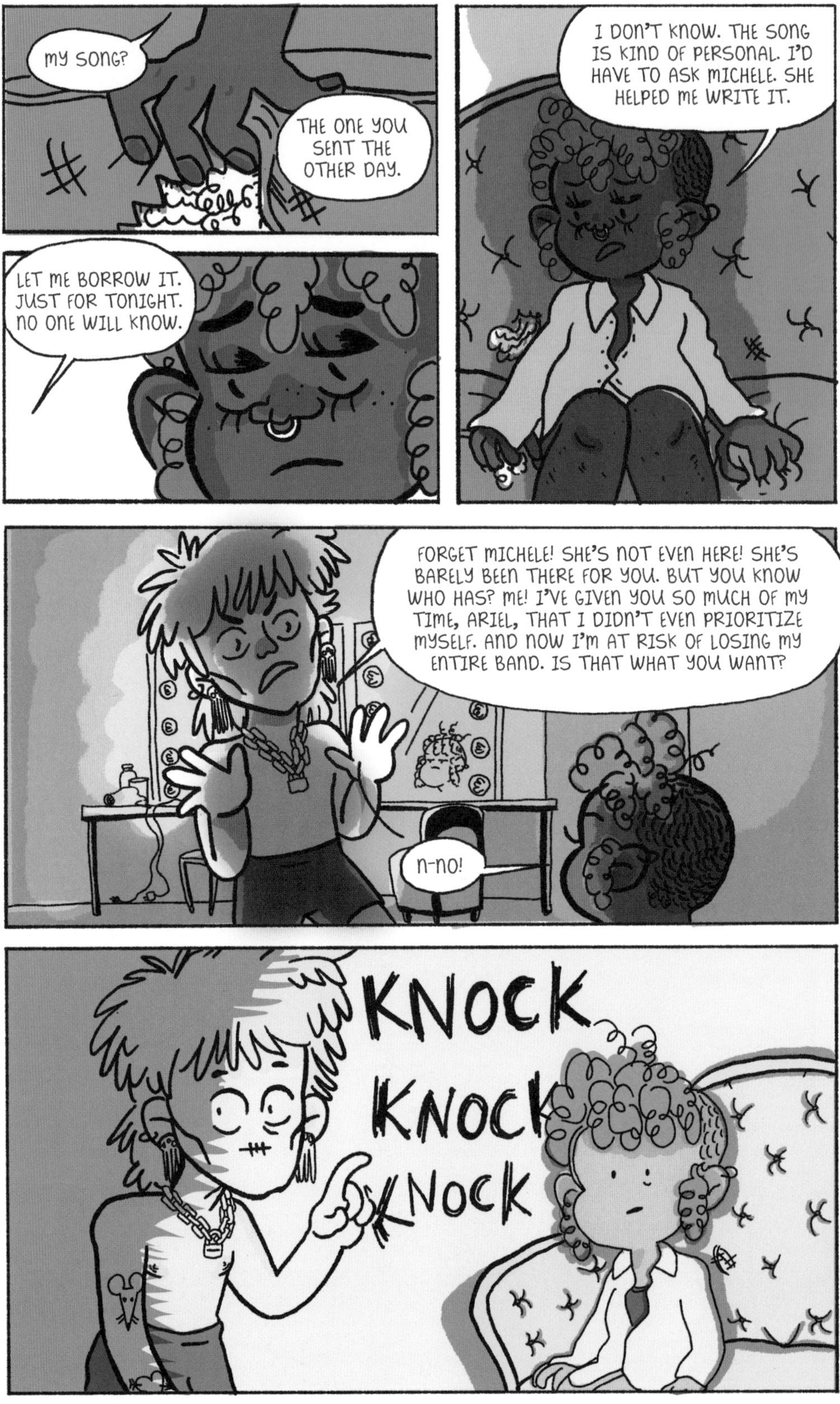
my SONG?
THE ONE YOU SENT THE OTHER DAY.
I DON'T KNOW. THE SONG IS KIND OF PERSONAL. I'D HAVE TO ASK MICHELE. SHE HELPED ME WRITE IT.
LET ME BORROW IT. JUST FOR TONIGHT. NO ONE WILL KNOW.
FORGET MICHELE! SHE'S NOT EVEN HERE! SHE'S BARELY BEEN THERE FOR YOU. BUT YOU KNOW WHO HAS? ME! I'VE GIVEN YOU SO MUCH OF MY TIME, ARIEL, THAT I DIDN'T EVEN PRIORITIZE MYSELF. AND NOW I'M AT RISK OF LOSING MY ENTIRE BAND. IS THAT WHAT YOU WANT?
n-no!
KNOCK
KNOCK
KNOCK

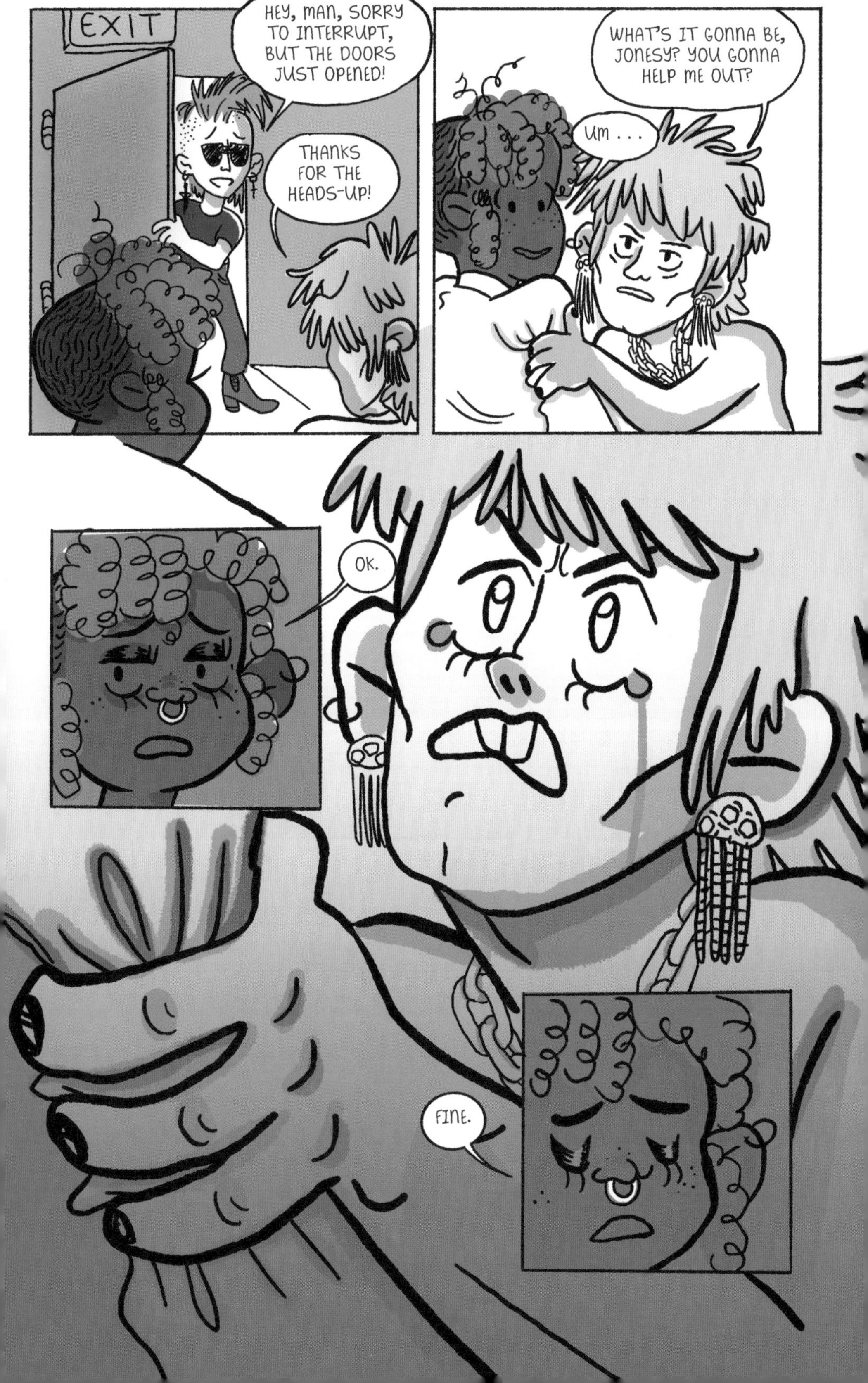
EXIT
HEY, MAN, SORRY TO INTERRUPT, BUT THE DOORS JUST OPENED!
THANKS FOR THE HEADS-UP!
WHAT'S IT GONNA BE, JONESY? YOU GONNA HELP ME OUT?
UM . . .
OK.
FINE.

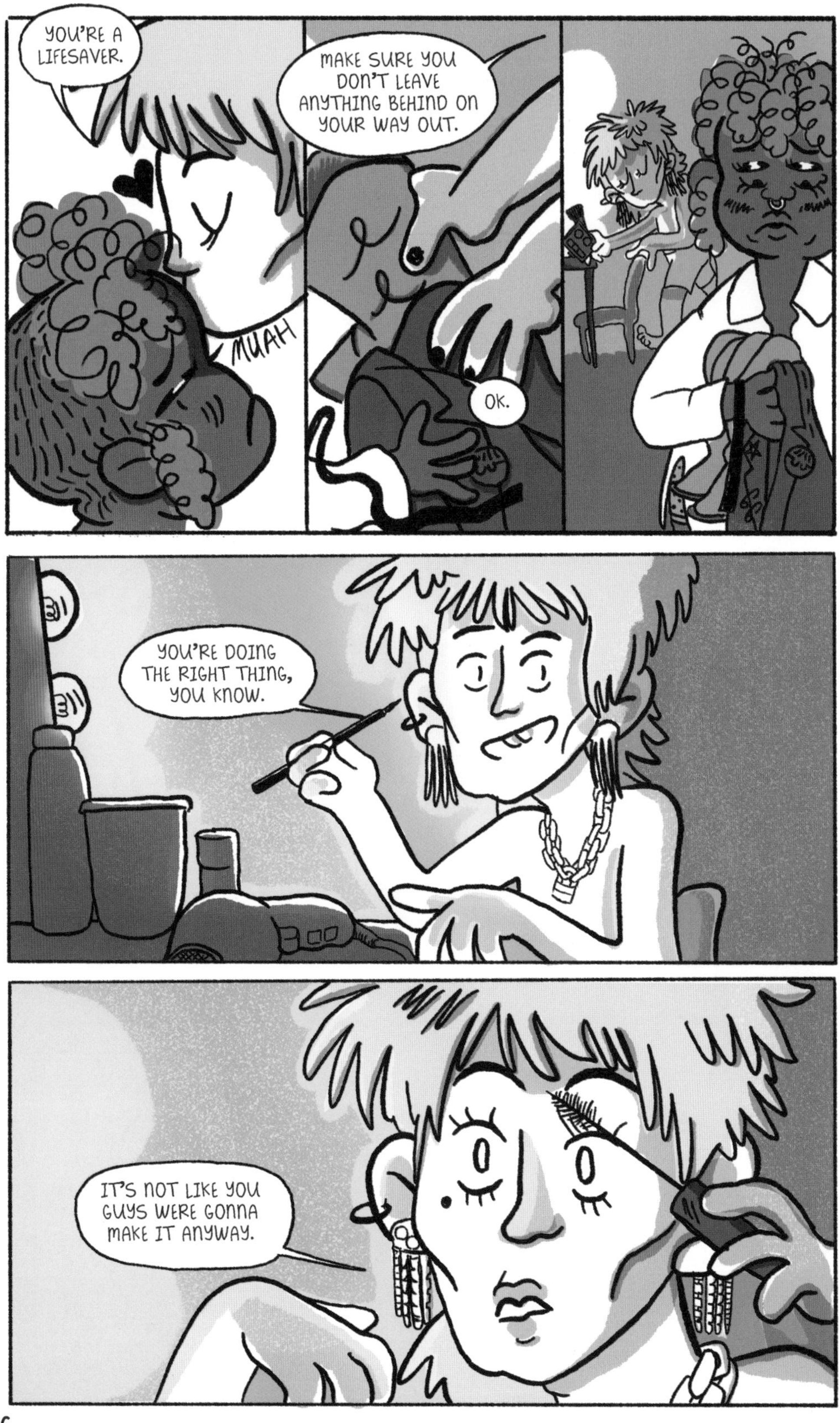
YOU'RE A LIFESAVER.
MUAH
MAKE SURE YOU DON'T LEAVE ANYTHING BEHIND ON YOUR WAY OUT.
OK.
YOU'RE DOING THE RIGHT THING, YOU KNOW.
IT'S NOT LIKE YOU GUYS WERE GONNA MAKE IT ANYWAY.

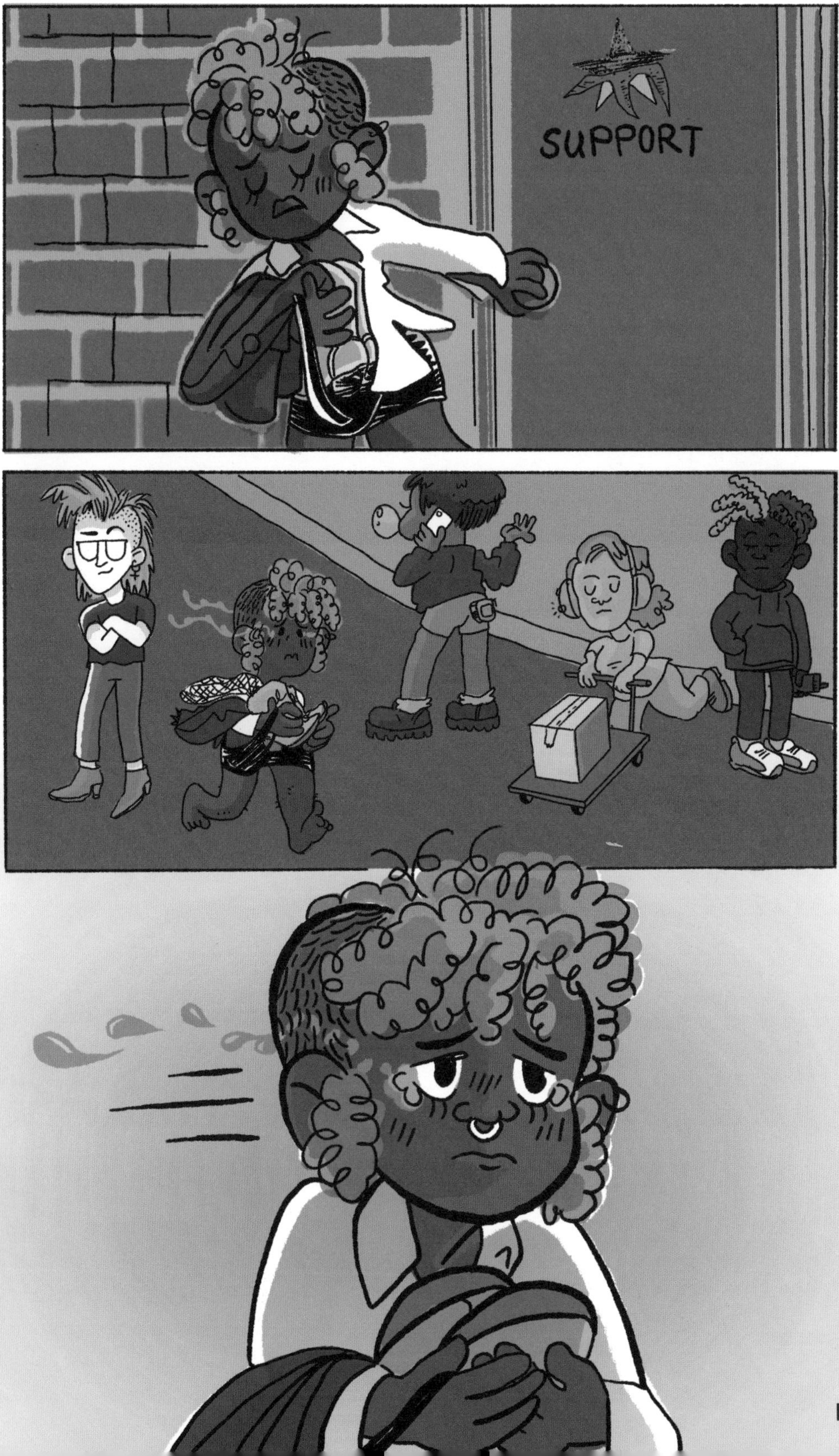
SUPPORT

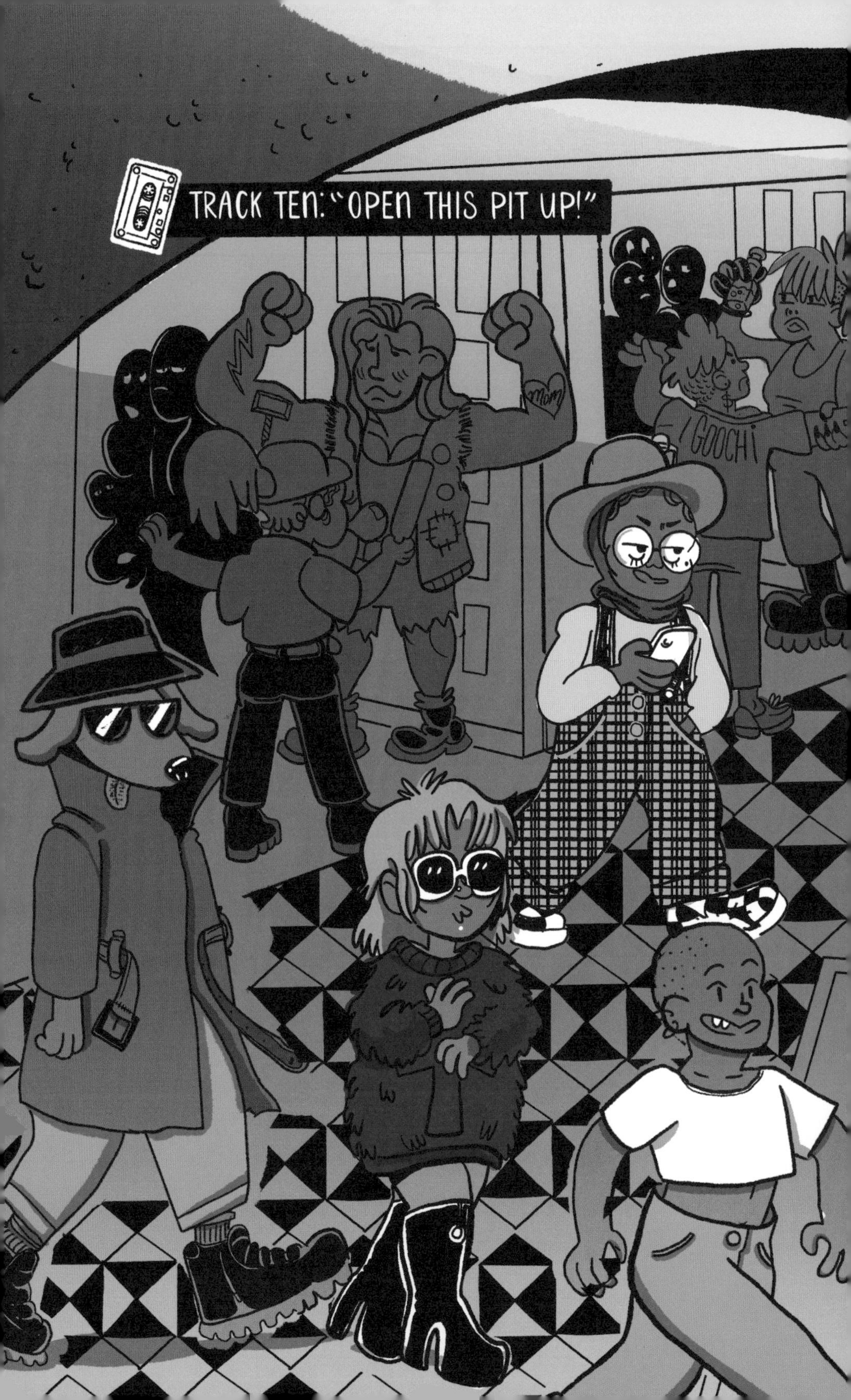
TRACK TEN: "OPEN THIS PIT UP!"
MOM
GOOCHI

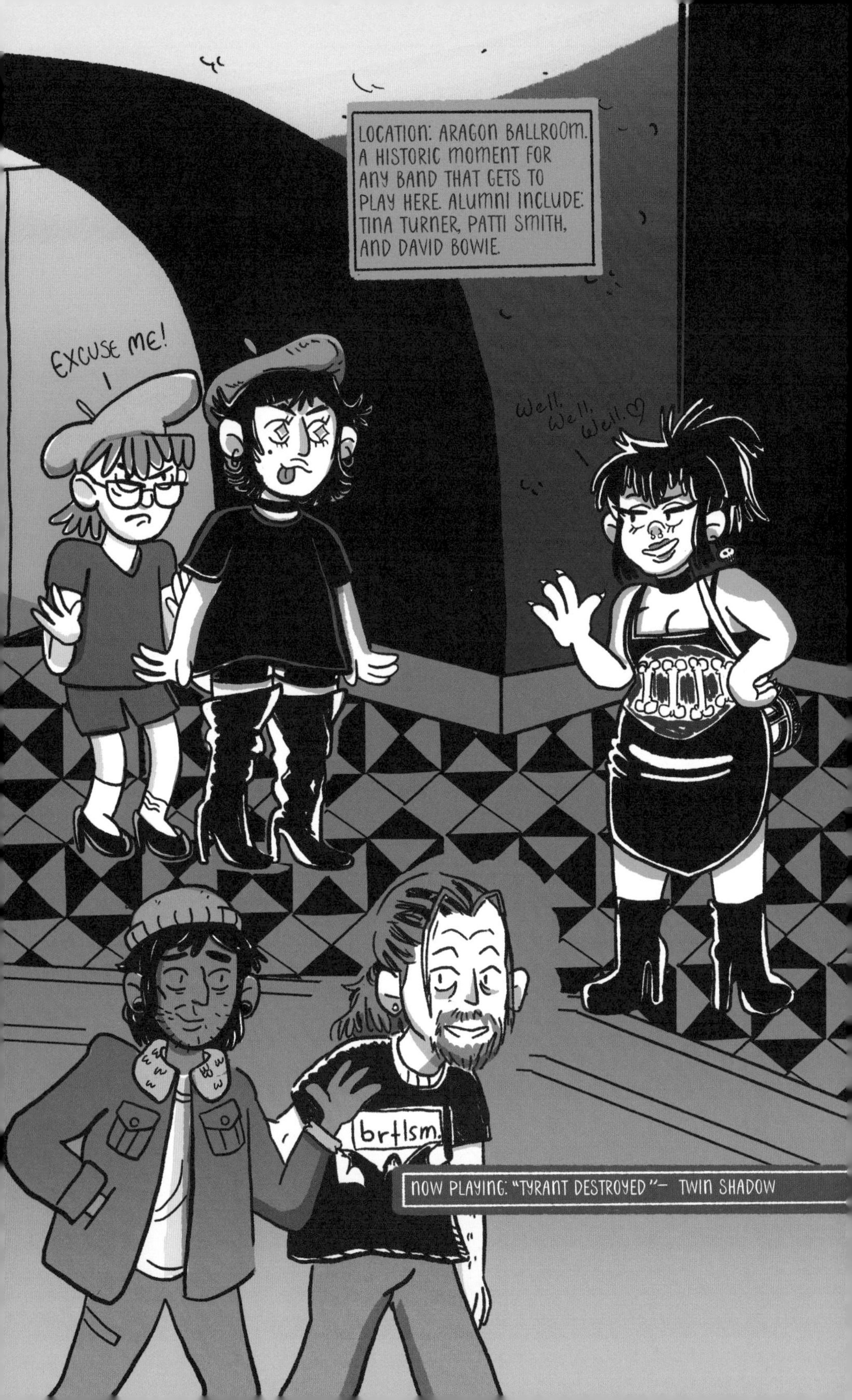
LOCATION: ARAGON BALLROOM. A HISTORIC MOMENT FOR ANY BAND THAT GETS TO PLAY HERE. ALUMNI INCLUDE: TINA TURNER, PATTI SMITH, AND DAVID BOWIE.
EXCUSE ME!
Well, Well, Well.♡
brtlsm.
NOW PLAYING: "TYRANT DESTROYED"— TWIN SHADOW

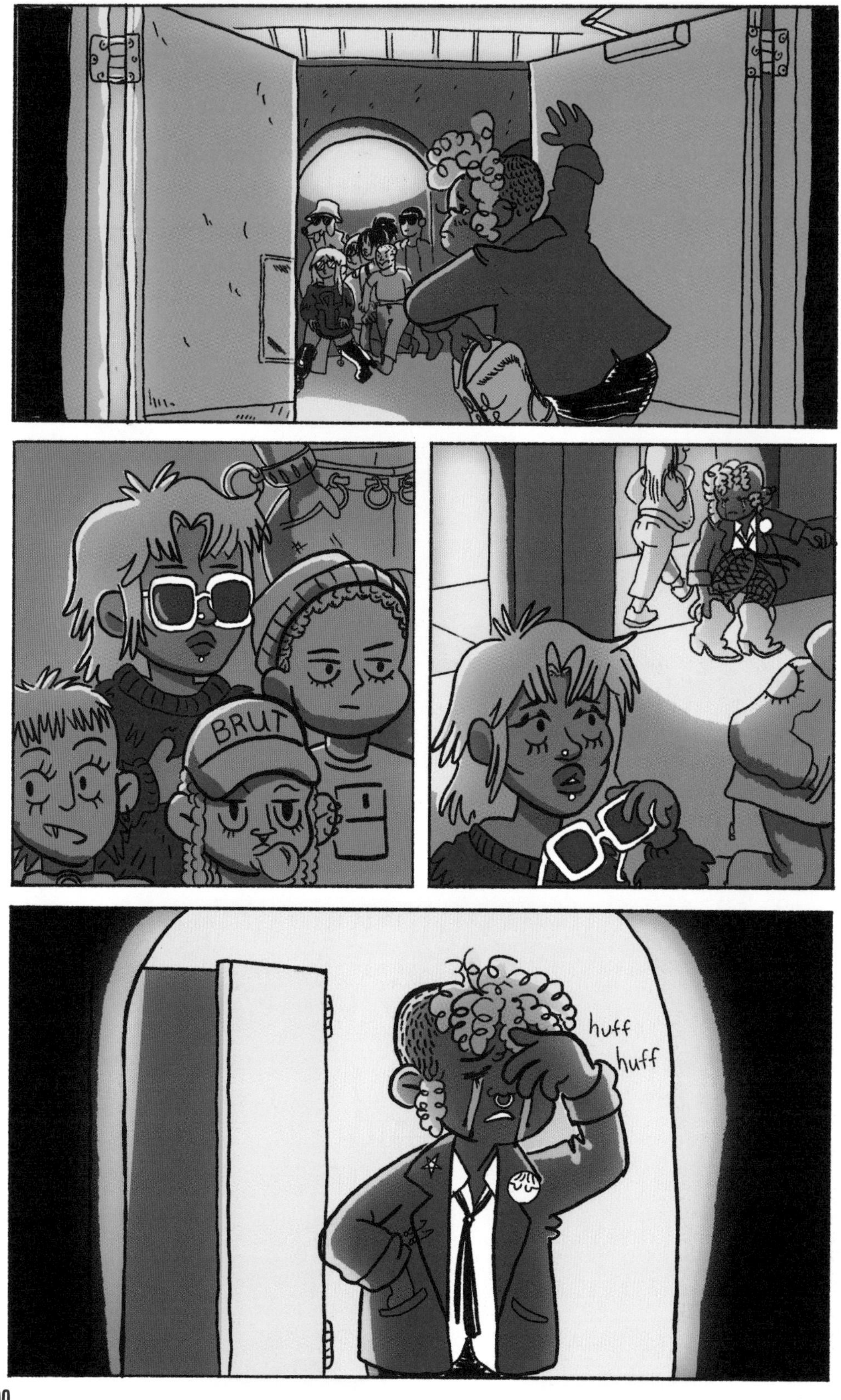
BRUT
huff
huff

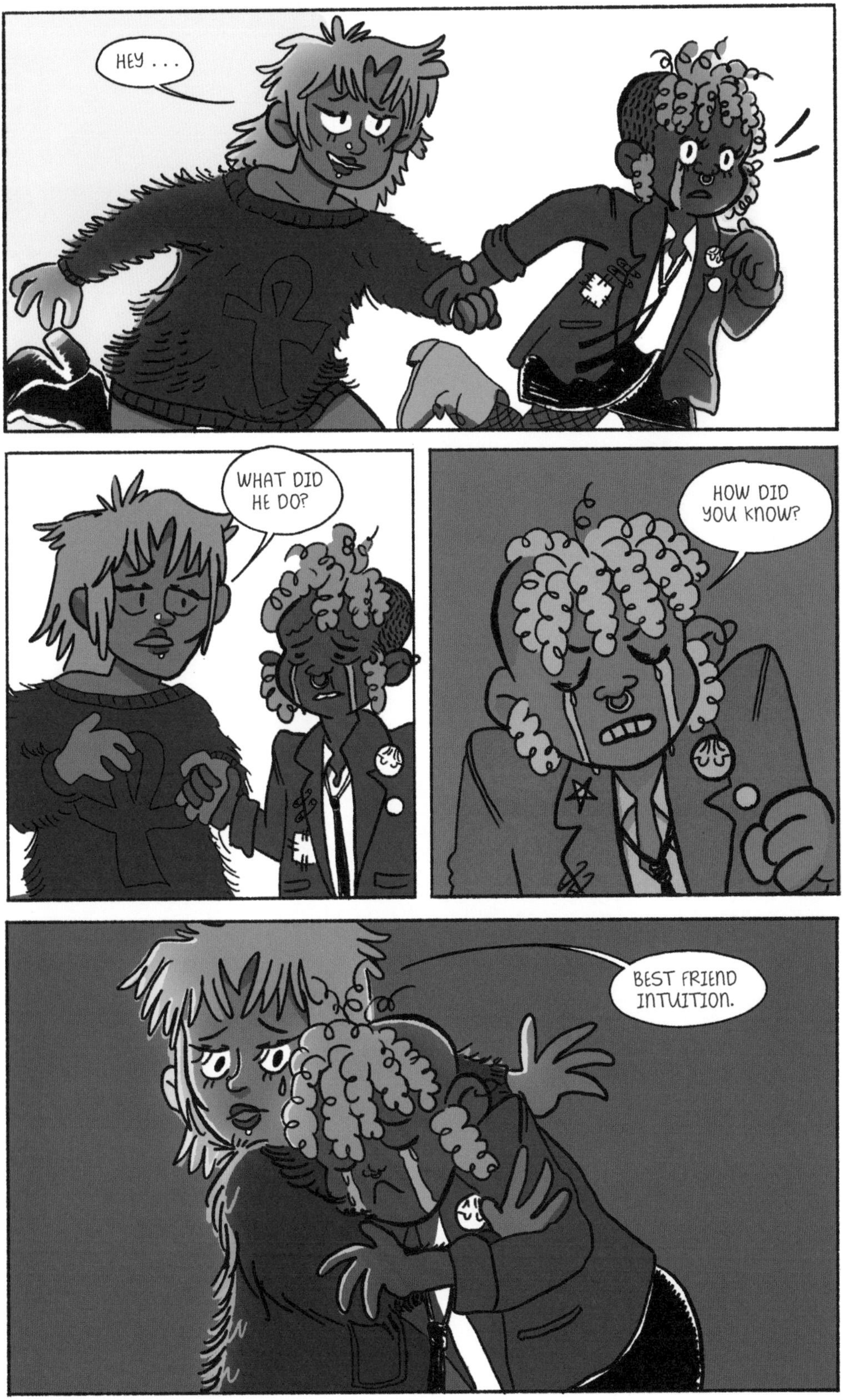
HEY . . .
WHAT DID HE DO?
HOW DID YOU KNOW?
BEST FRIEND INTUITION.

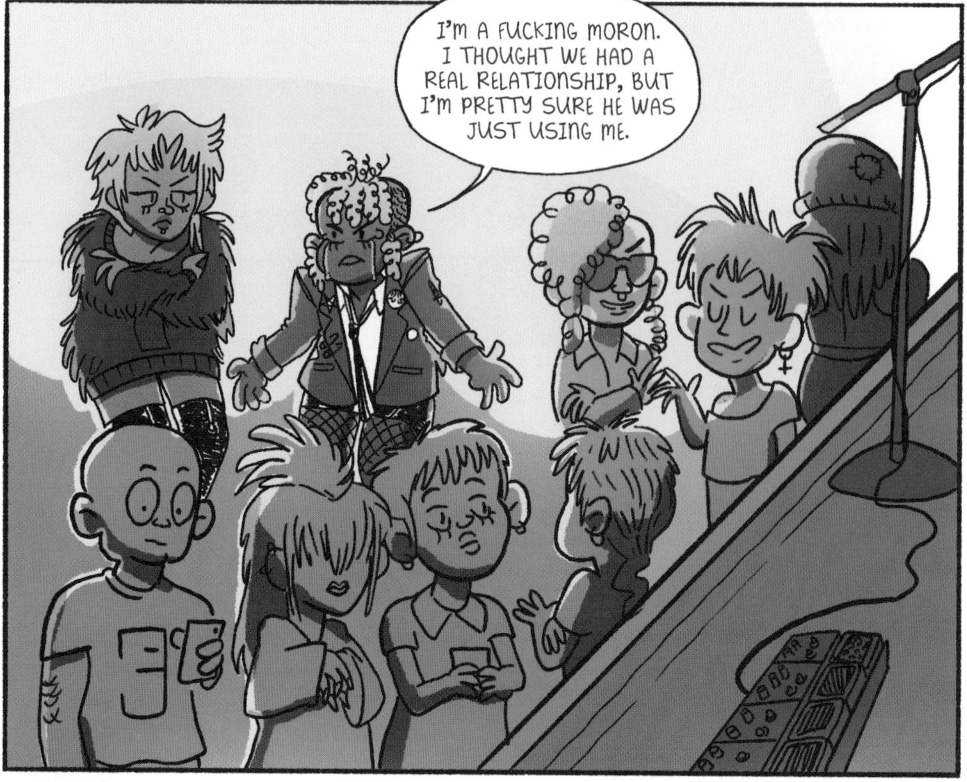
I'M A FUCKING MORON. I THOUGHT WE HAD A REAL RELATIONSHIP, BUT I'M PRETTY SURE HE WAS JUST USING ME.

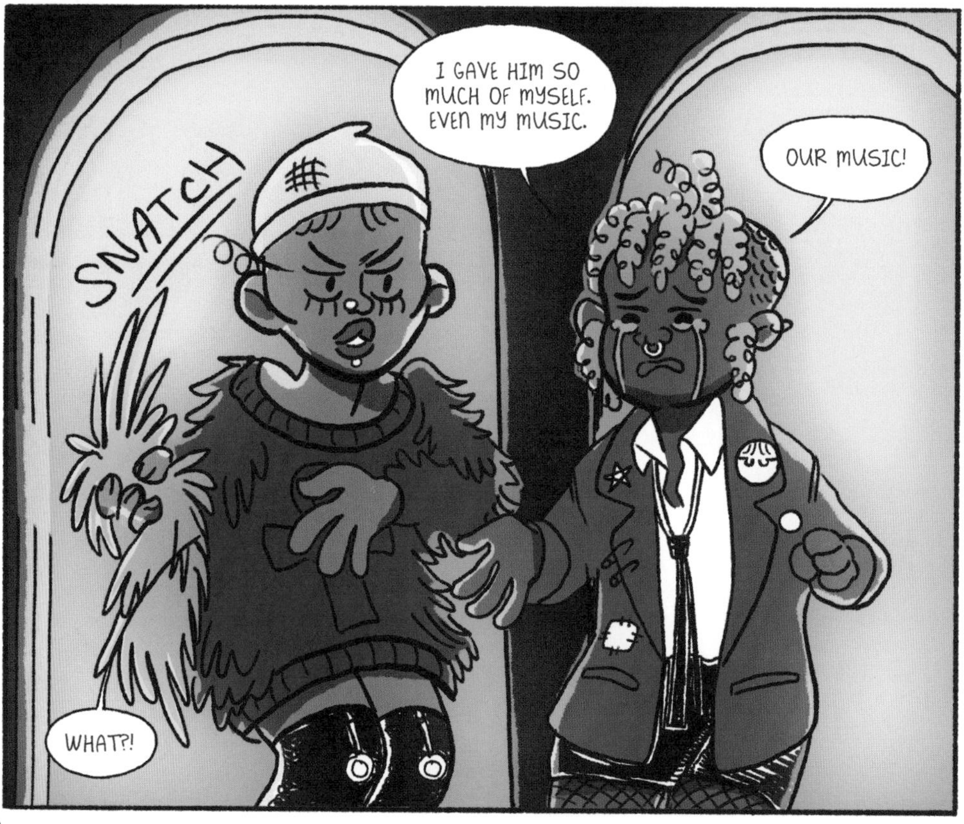
I GAVE HIM SO MUCH OF MYSELF. EVEN MY MUSIC.
OUR MUSIC!
SNATCH
WHAT?!

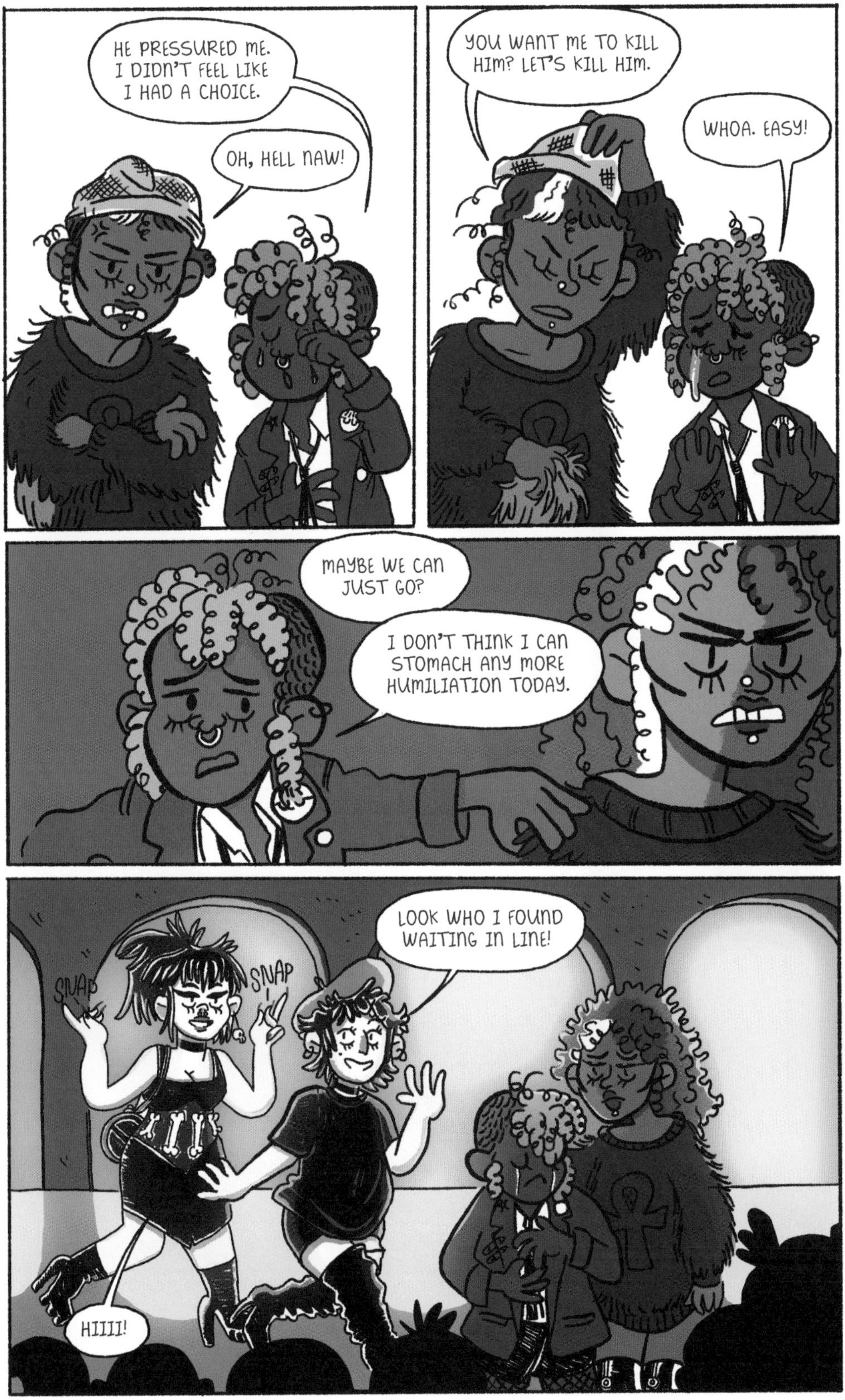
HE PRESSURED ME. I DIDN'T FEEL LIKE I HAD A CHOICE.
OH, HELL NAW!
YOU WANT ME TO KILL HIM? LET'S KILL HIM.
WHOA. EASY!
MAYBE WE CAN JUST GO?
I DON'T THINK I CAN STOMACH ANY MORE HUMILIATION TODAY.
SNAP
SNAP
LOOK WHO I FOUND WAITING IN LINE!
HIIII!

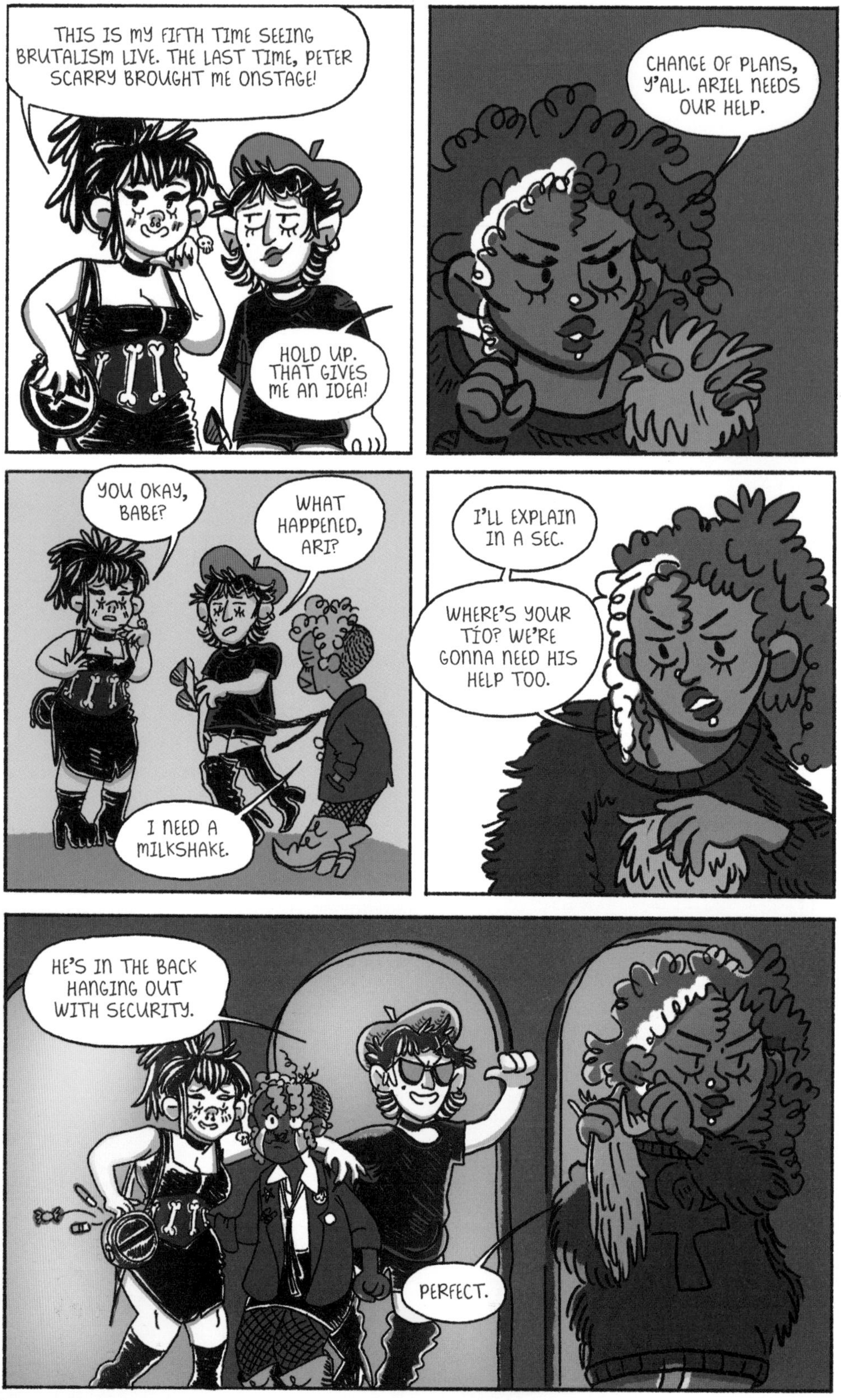
THIS IS MY FIFTH TIME SEEING BRUTALISM LIVE. THE LAST TIME, PETER SCARRY BROUGHT ME ONSTAGE!
HOLD UP. THAT GIVES ME AN IDEA!
CHANGE OF PLANS, Y'ALL. ARIEL NEEDS OUR HELP.
YOU OKAY, BABE?
WHAT HAPPENED, ARI?
I NEED A MILKSHAKE.
I'LL EXPLAIN IN A SEC.
WHERE'S YOUR TÍO? WE'RE GONNA NEED HIS HELP TOO.
HE'S IN THE BACK HANGING OUT WITH SECURITY.
PERFECT.

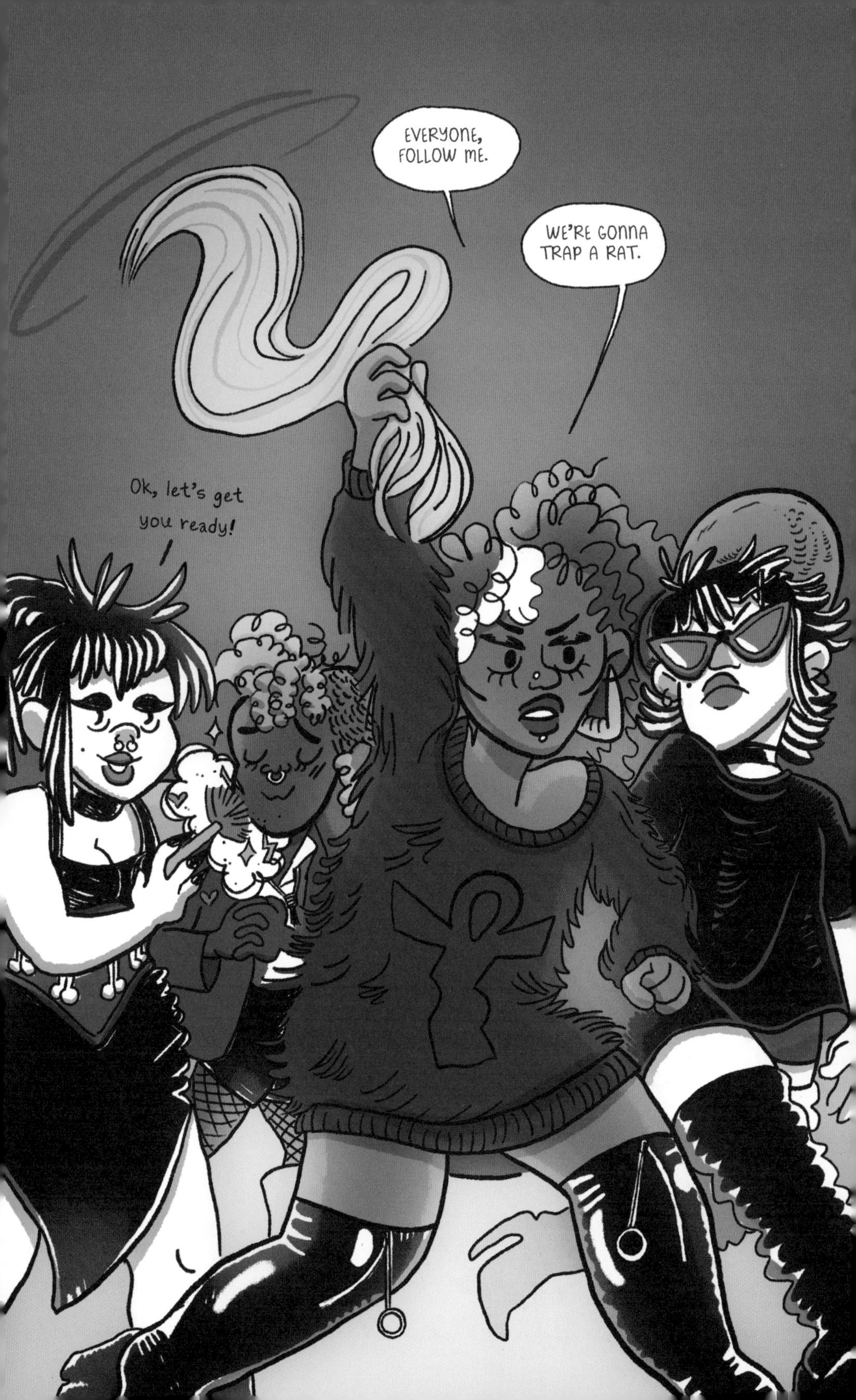
EVERYONE, FOLLOW ME.
WE'RE GONNA TRAP A RAT.
Ok, let's get you ready!

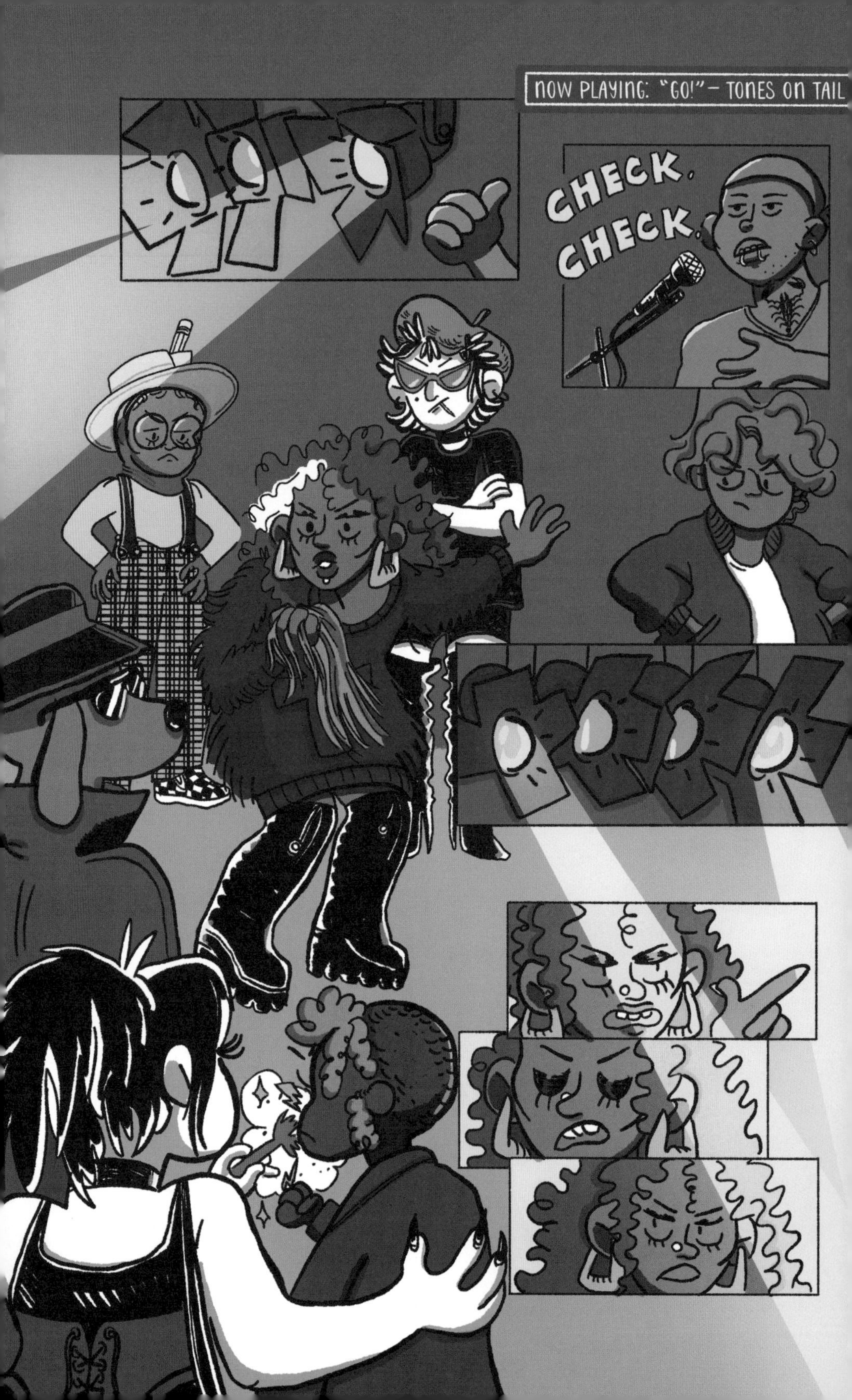
NOW PLAYING: "GO!"– TONES ON TAIL
CHECK, CHECK.

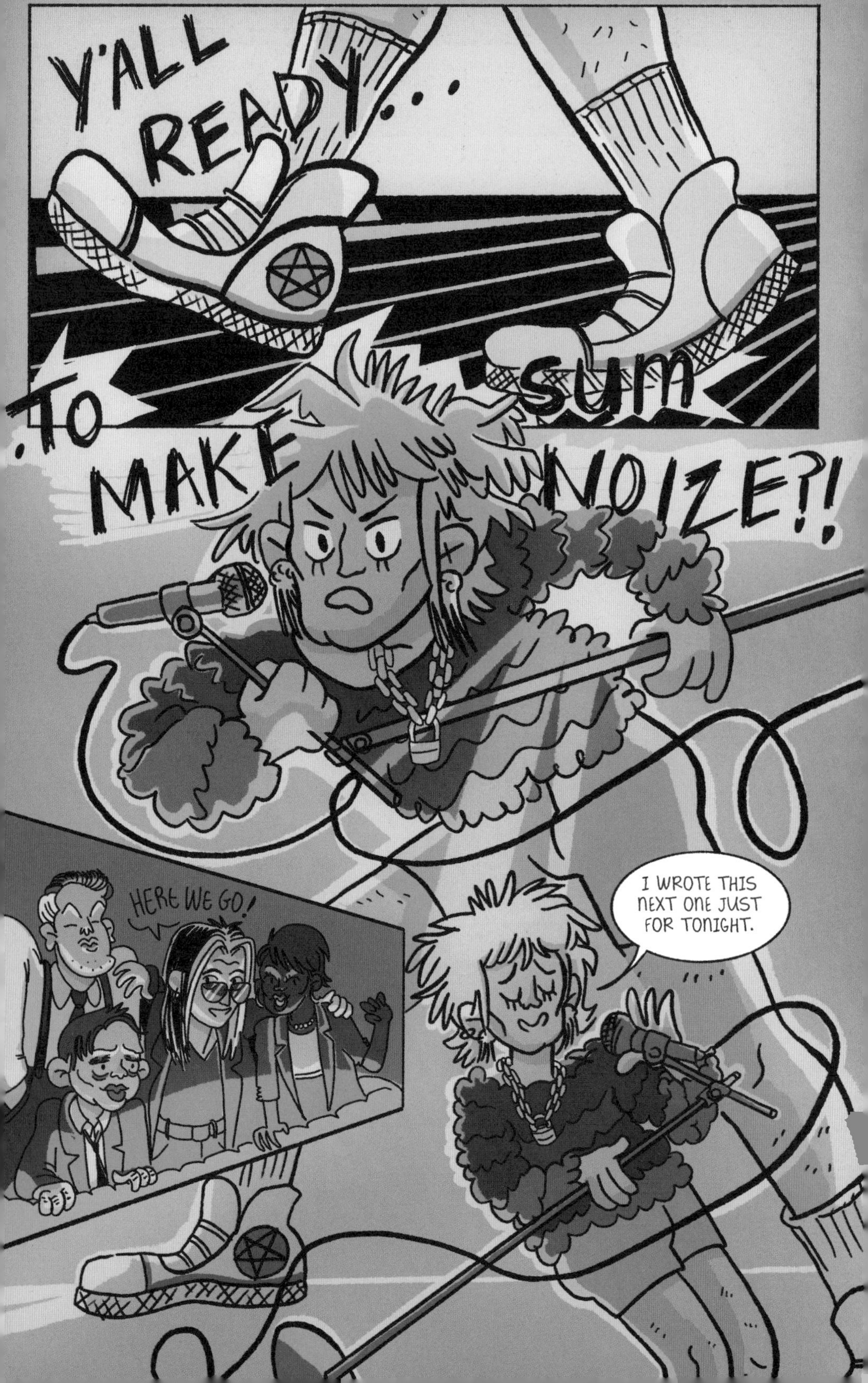
Y'ALL READY...
TO MAKE SUM NOIZE?!
HERE WE GO!
I WROTE THIS NEXT ONE JUST FOR TONIGHT.

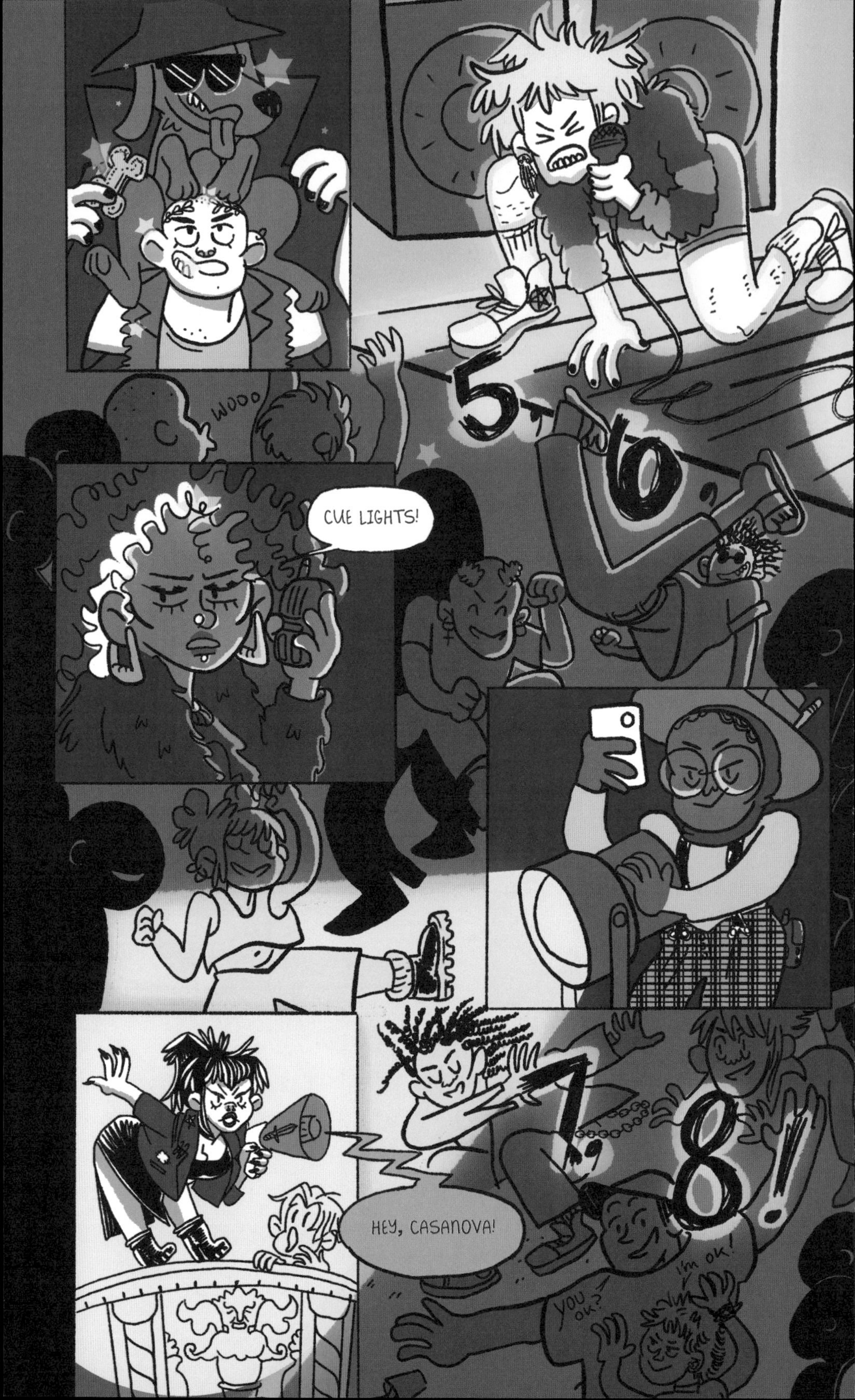
WOOO
5
6
CUE LIGHTS!
7
8
!
HEY, CASANOVA!
YOU OK?
I'M OK!

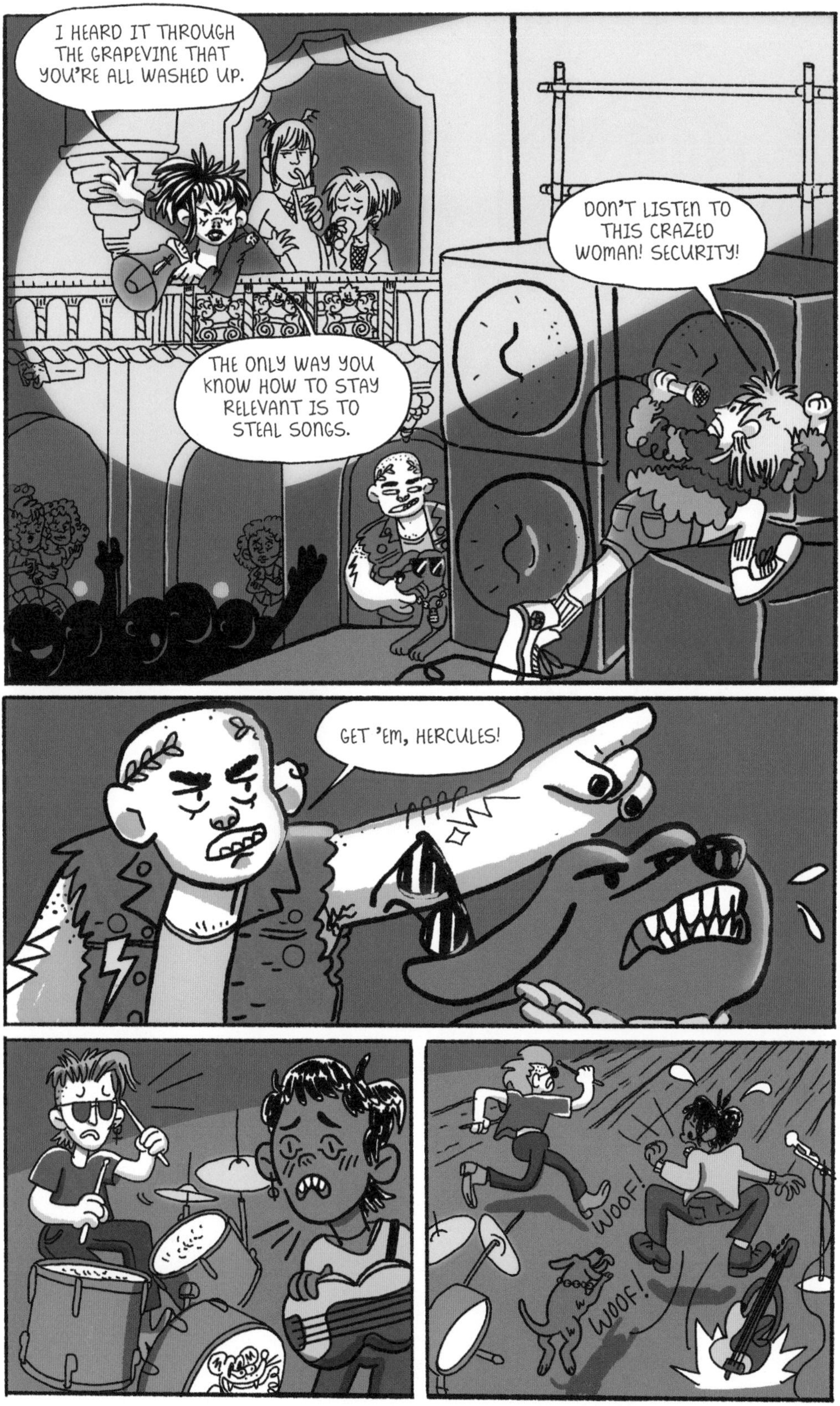
I HEARD IT THROUGH THE GRAPEVINE THAT YOU'RE ALL WASHED UP.
THE ONLY WAY YOU KNOW HOW TO STAY RELEVANT IS TO STEAL SONGS.
DON'T LISTEN TO THIS CRAZED WOMAN! SECURITY!
GET 'EM, HERCULES!
WOOF!
WOOF!

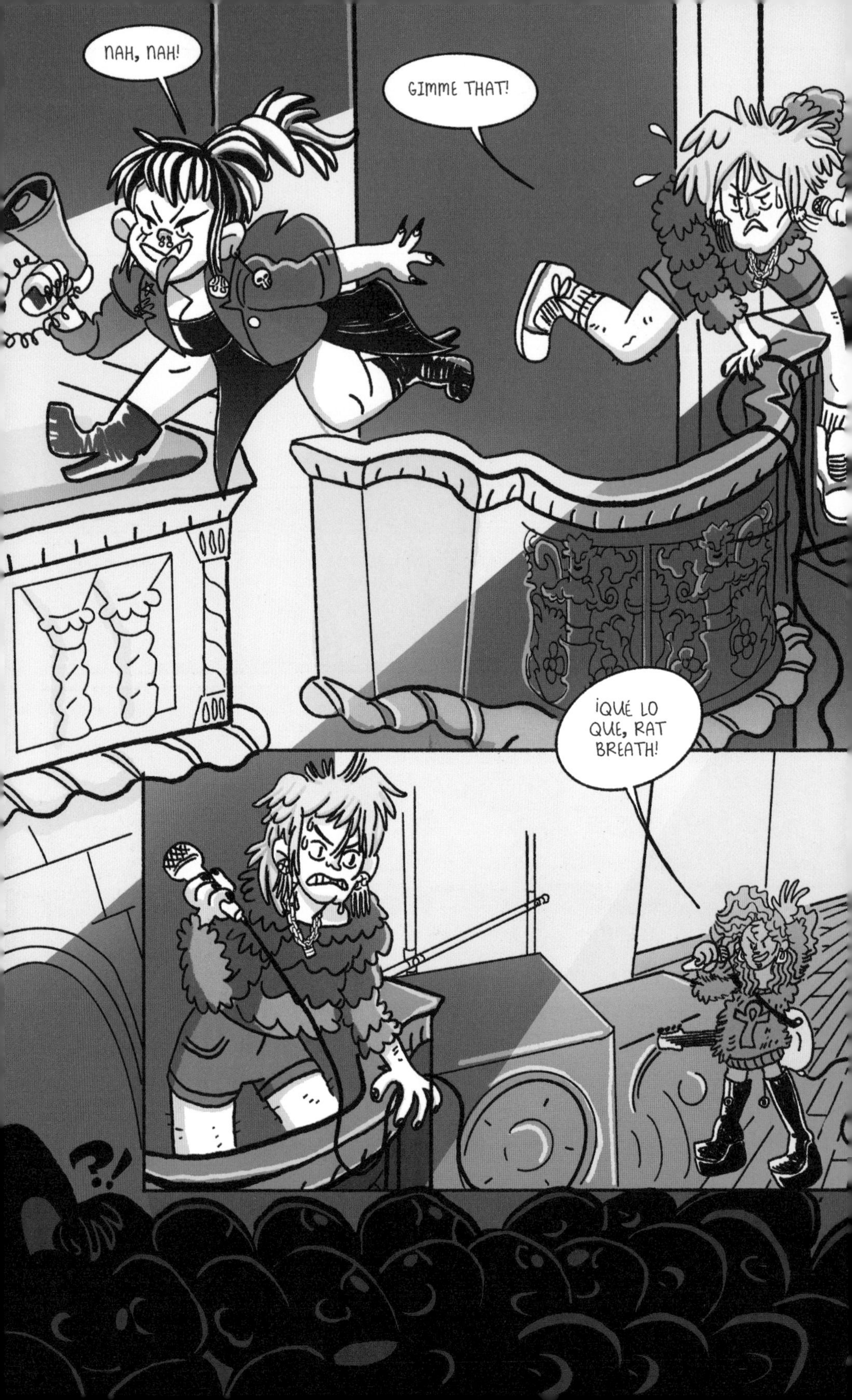
NAH, NAH!
GIMME THAT!
¡QUÉ LO QUE, RAT BREATH!
?!

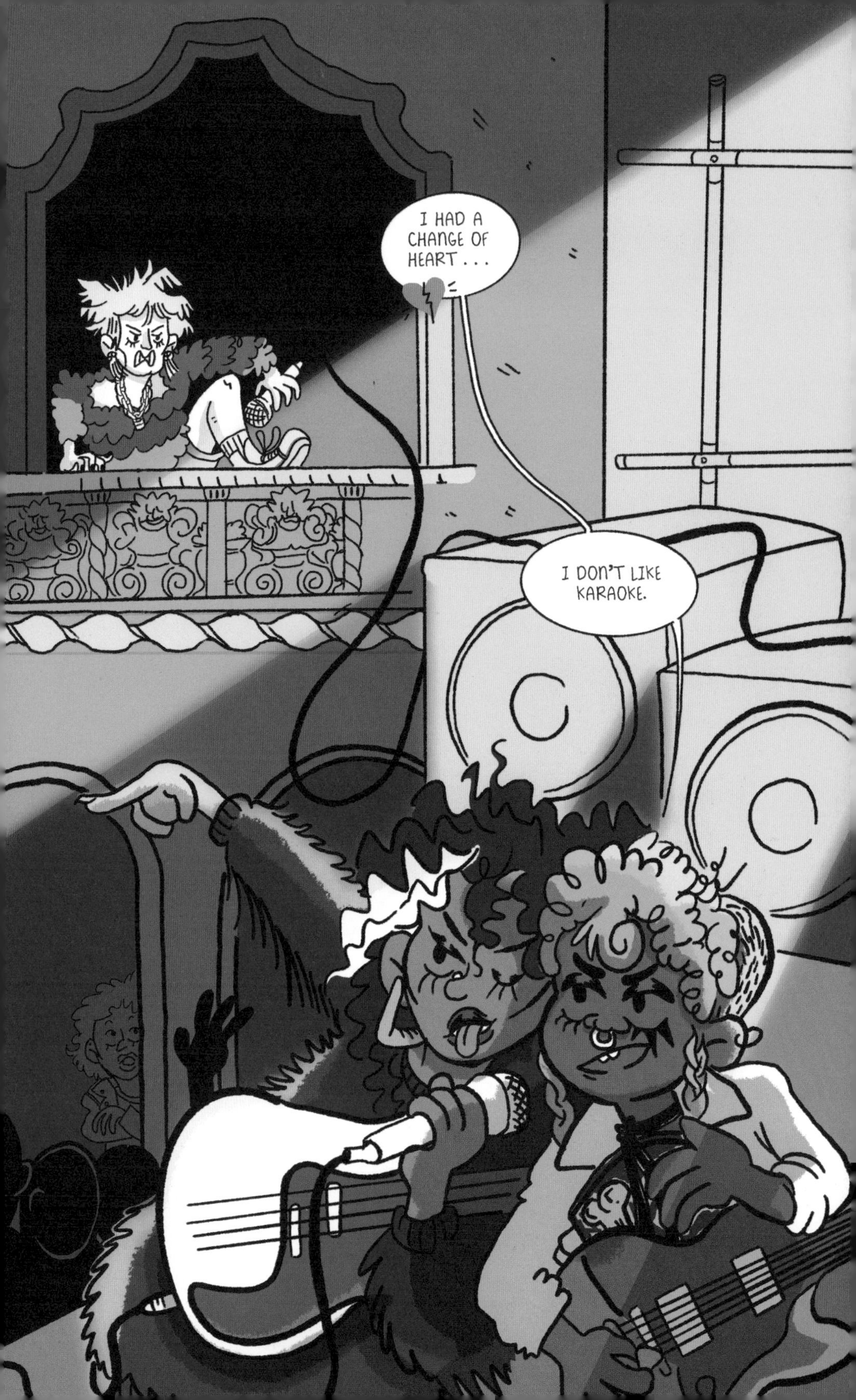
I HAD A CHANGE OF HEART . . .
I DON'T LIKE KARAOKE.

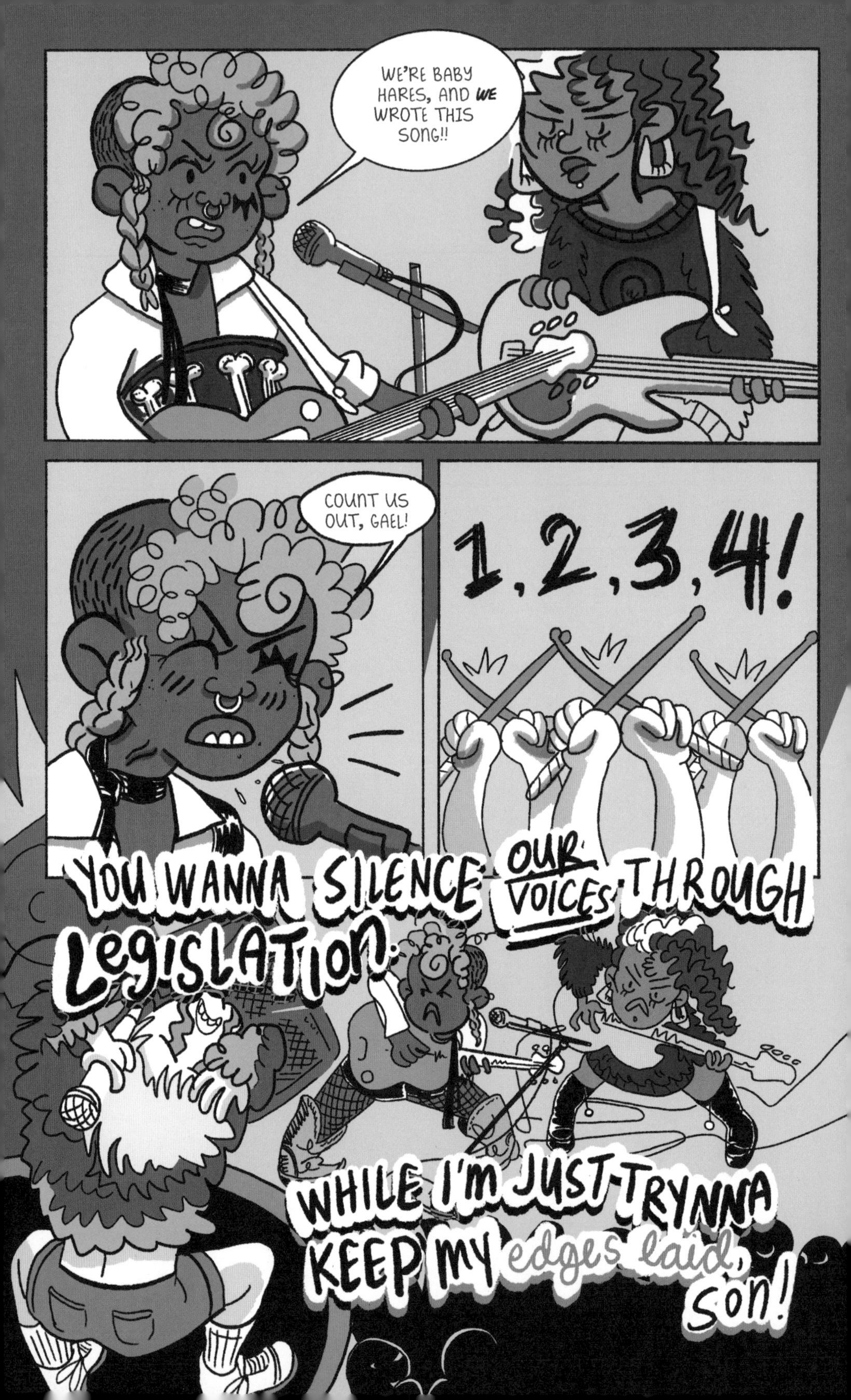

WE'RE BABY HARES, AND WE WROTE THIS SONG!!
COUNT US OUT, GAEL!
1, 2, 3, 4!
YOU WANNA SILENCE OUR VOICES THROUGH LEGISLATION.
WHILE I'M JUST TRYNNA KEEP MY edges laid, SON!

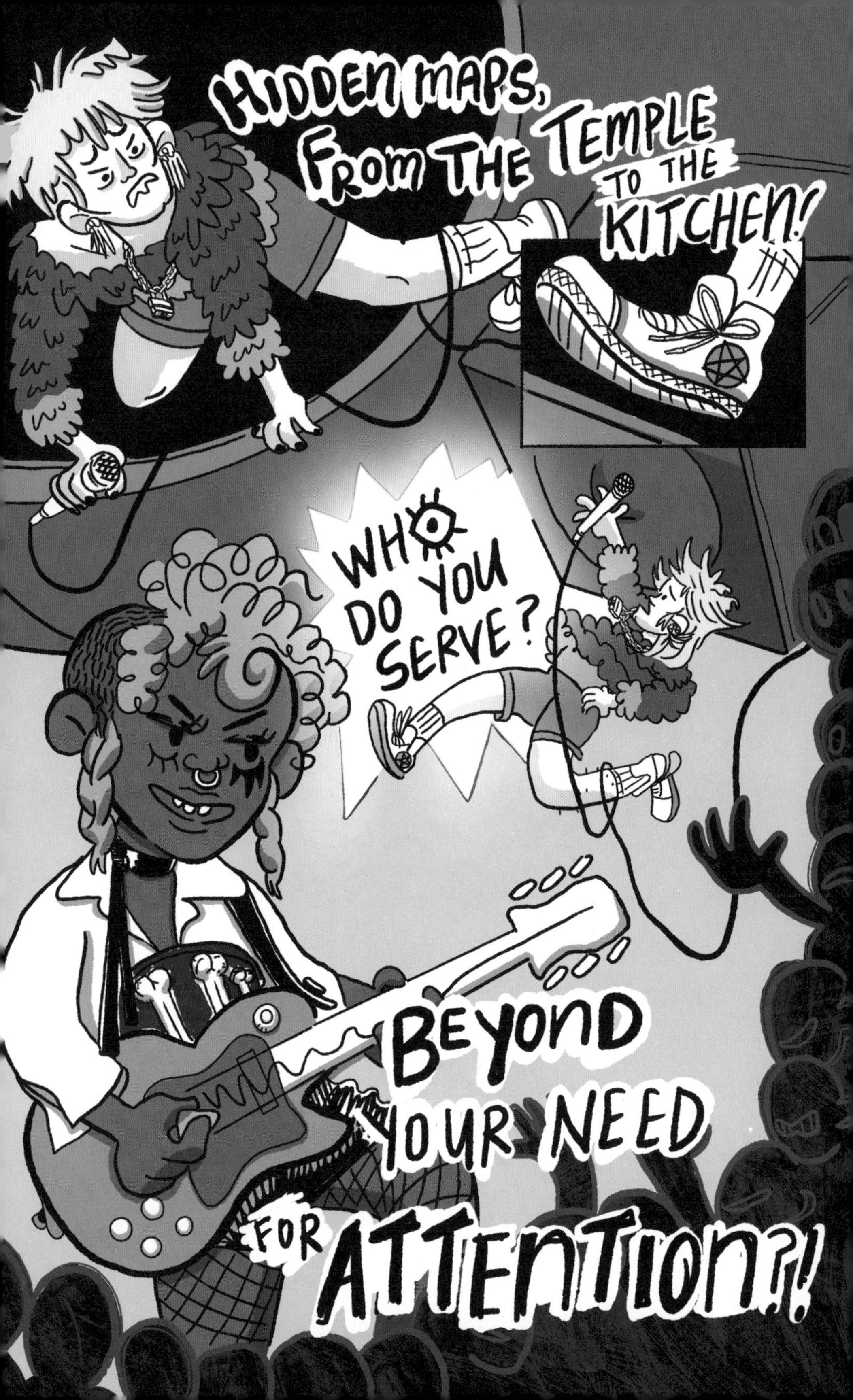
HIDDEN MAPS, FROM THE TEMPLE TO THE KITCHEN!
WHO DO YOU SERVE?
BEYOND YOUR NEED FOR ATTENTION?!

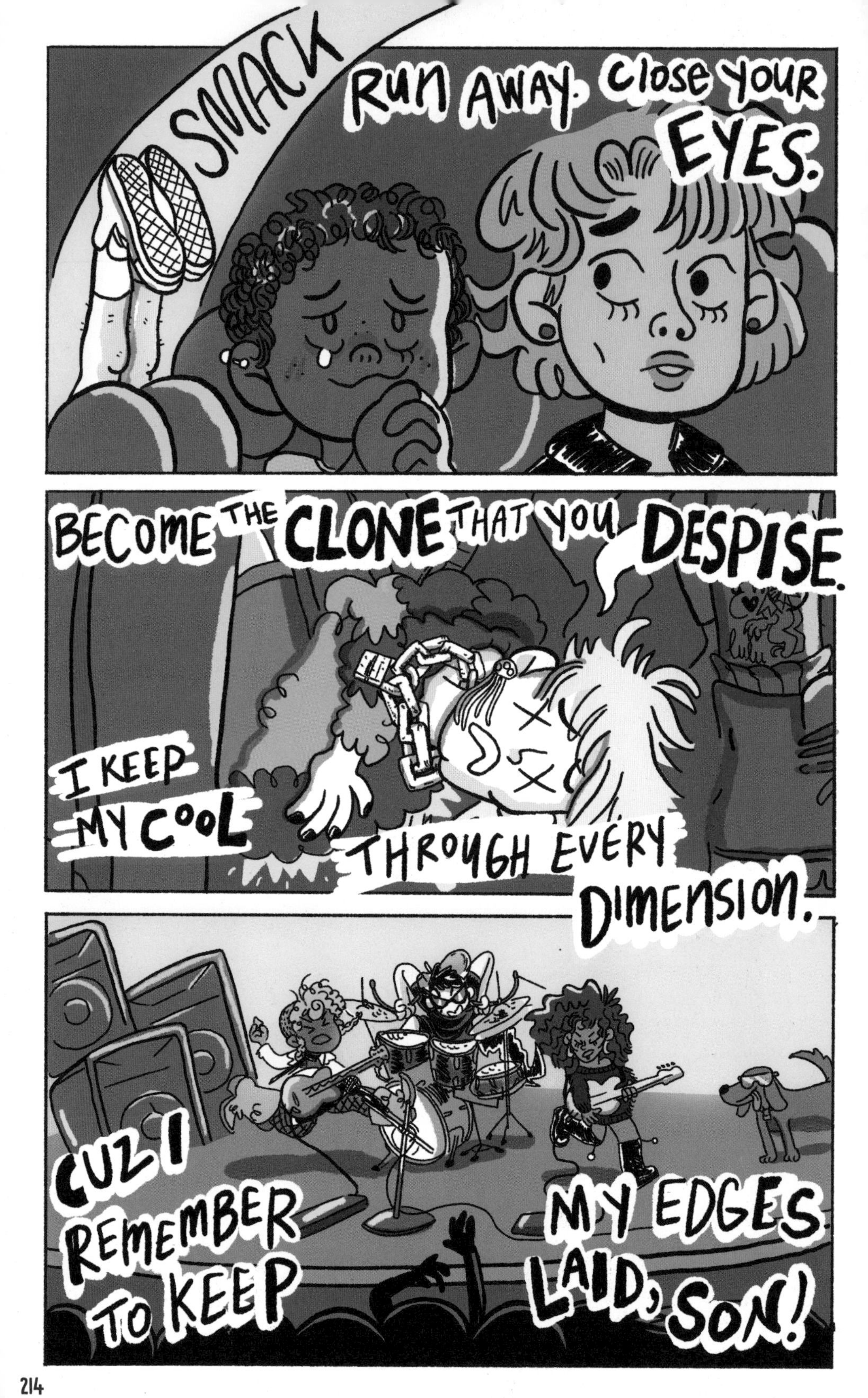
SMACK
RUN AWAY. CLOSE YOUR EYES.
BECOME THE CLONE THAT YOU DESPISE.
lulu
I KEEP MY COOL
THROUGH EVERY DIMENSION.
CUZ I REMEMBER TO KEEP
MY EDGES LAID, SON!

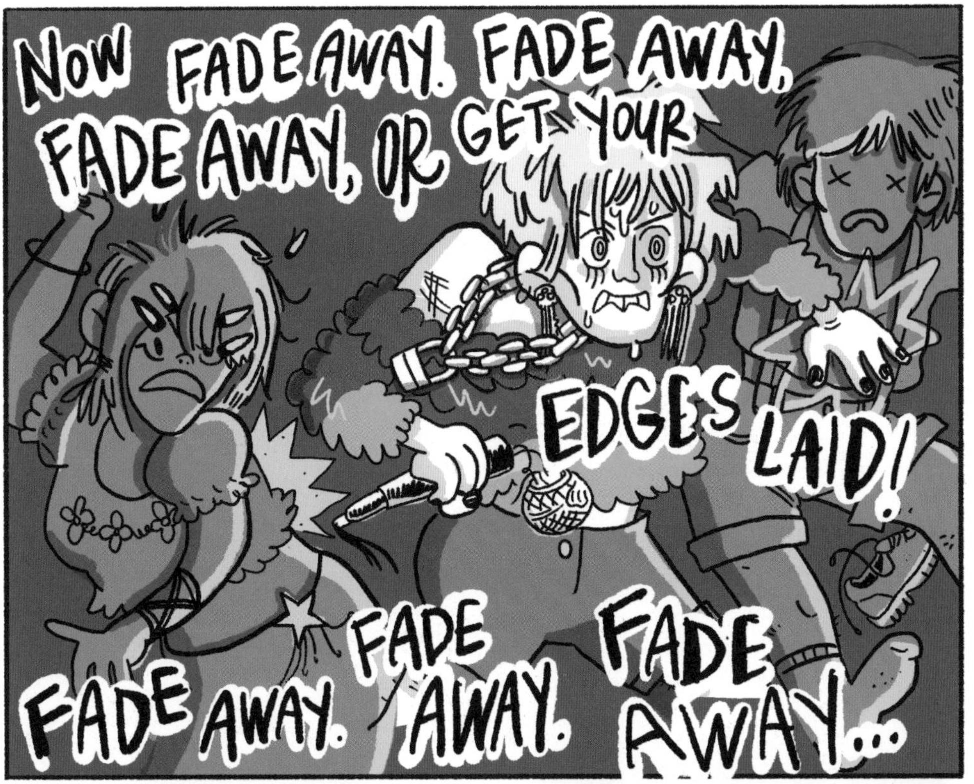
NOW FADE AWAY. FADE AWAY. FADE AWAY, OR GET YOUR
EDGES LAID!
FADE AWAY. FADE AWAY. FADE AWAY...

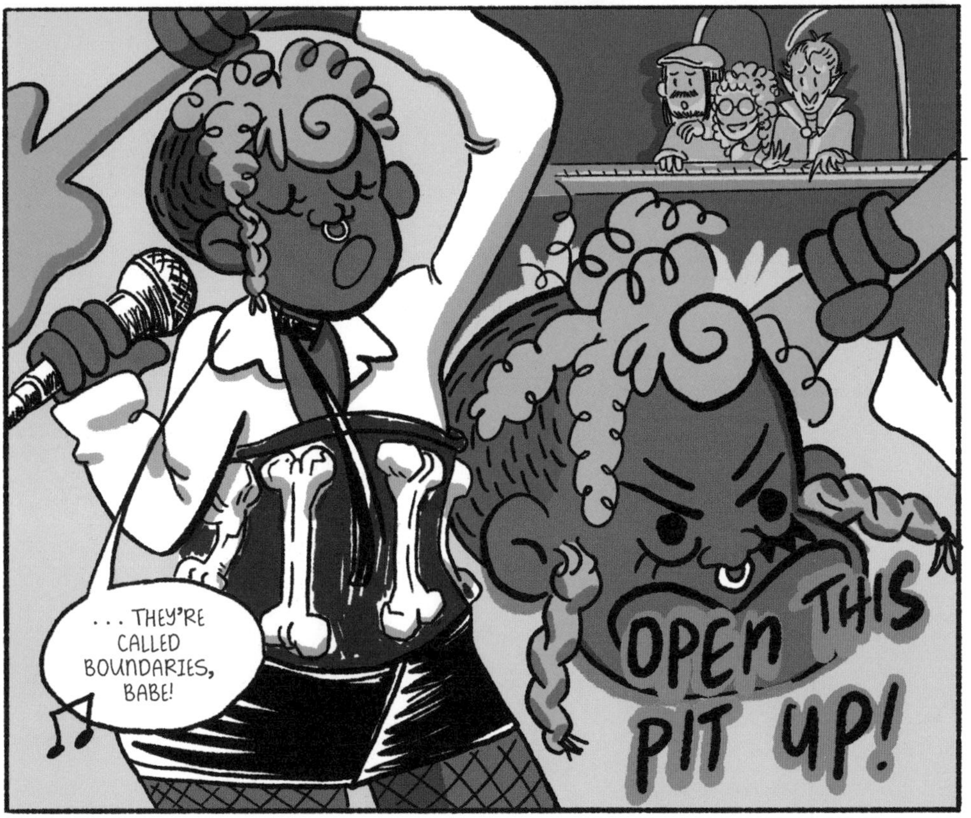
. . . THEY'RE CALLED BOUNDARIES, BABE!
OPEN THIS PIT UP!

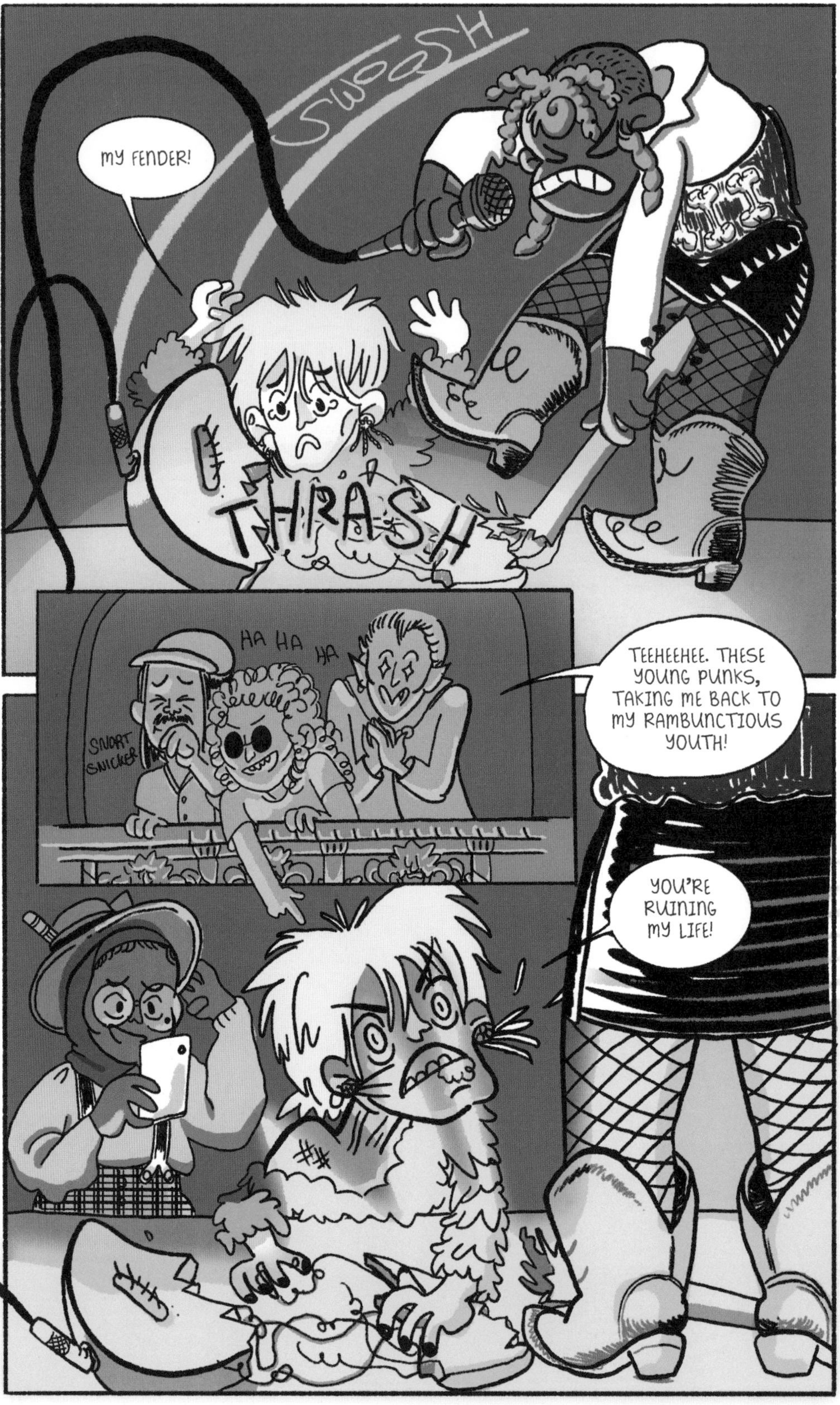
SWOOSH
MY FENDER!
THRASH
HA HA HA
SNORT SNICKER
TEEHEEHEE. THESE YOUNG PUNKS, TAKING ME BACK TO MY RAMBUNCTIOUS YOUTH!
YOU'RE RUINING MY LIFE!

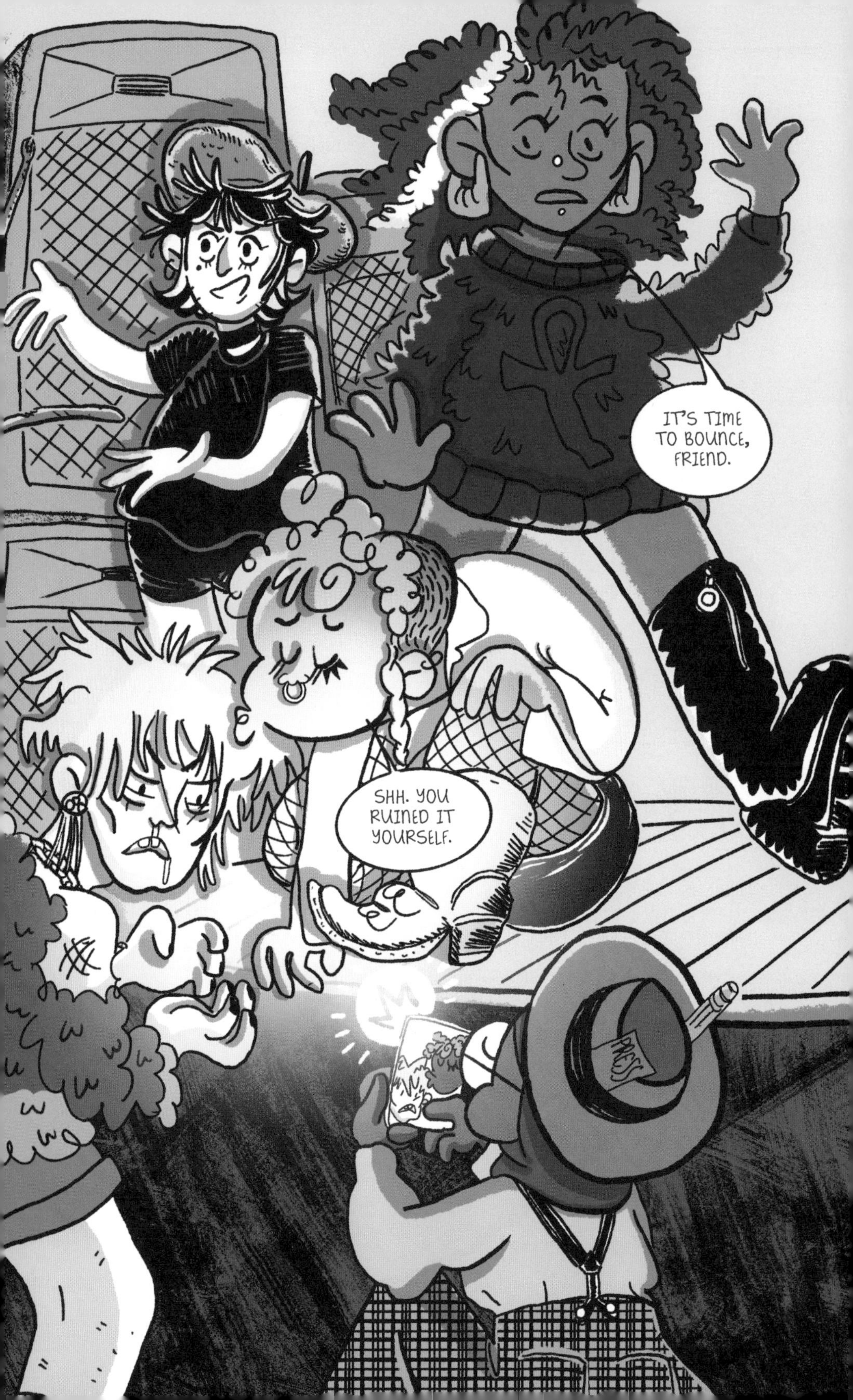
IT'S TIME TO BOUNCE, FRIEND.
SHH. YOU RUINED IT YOURSELF.

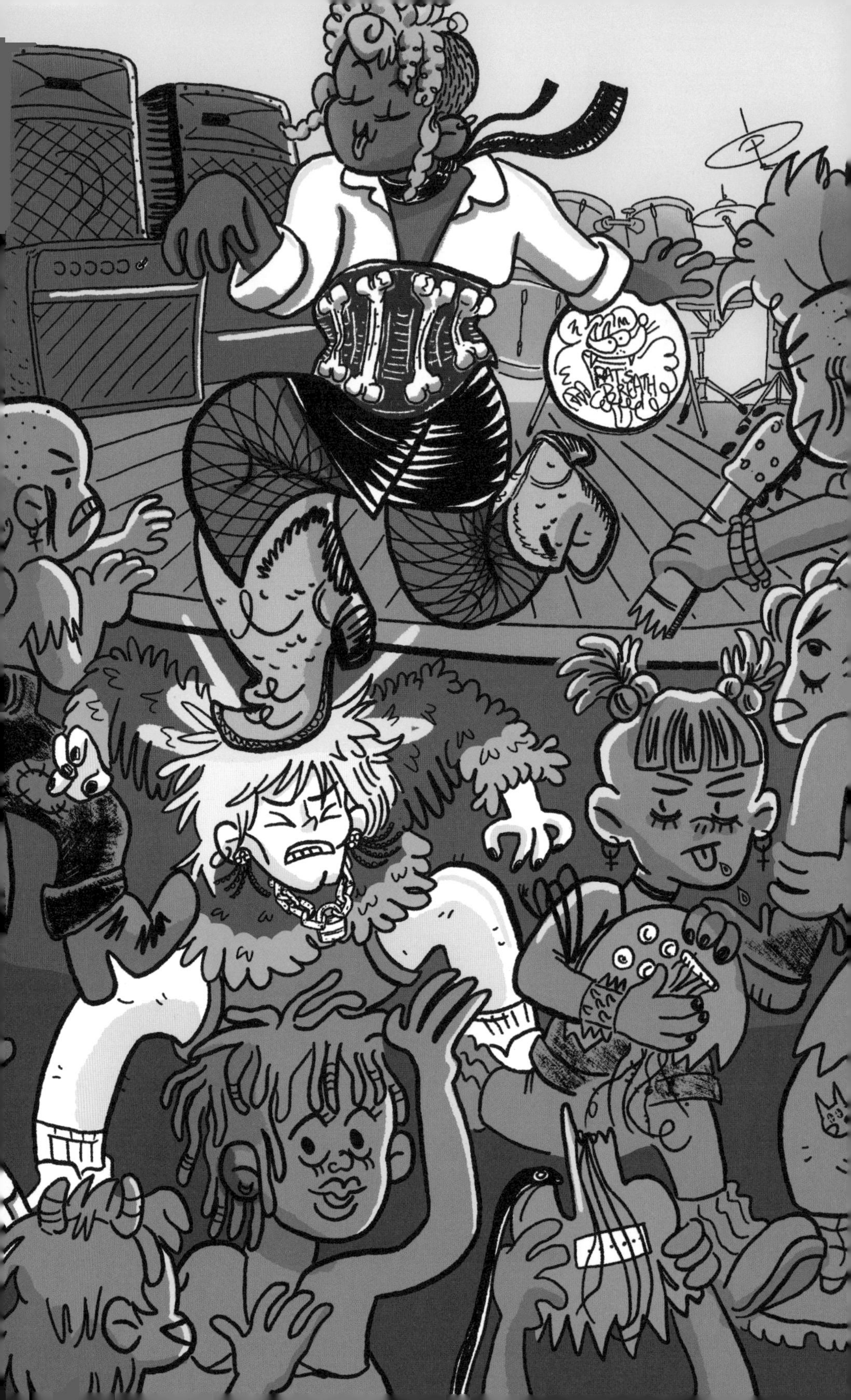
RAT'S BREATH

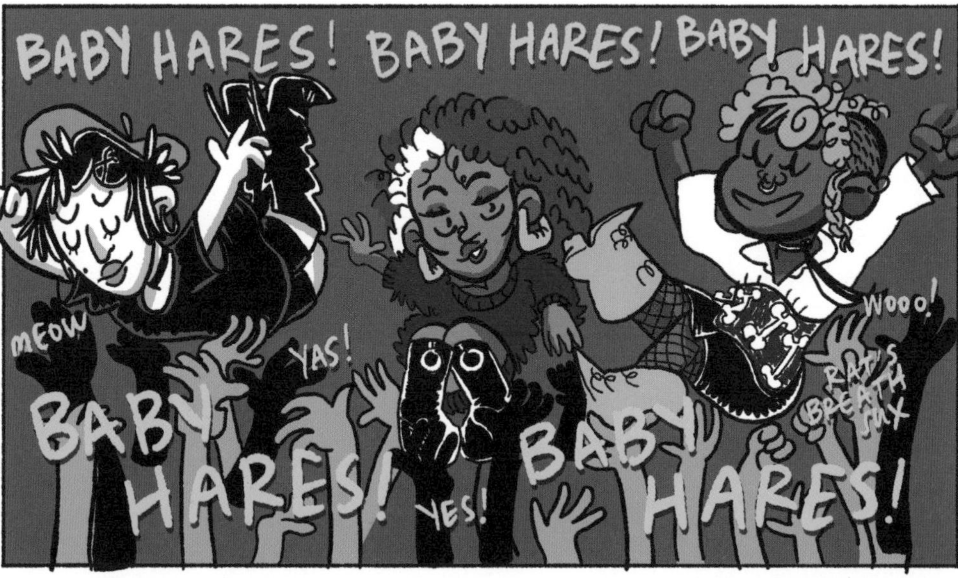
BABY HARES! BABY HARES! BABY HARES!
MEOW
YAS!
BABY HARES!
YES!
BABY HARES!
WOOO!
RAT'S BREATH SUX

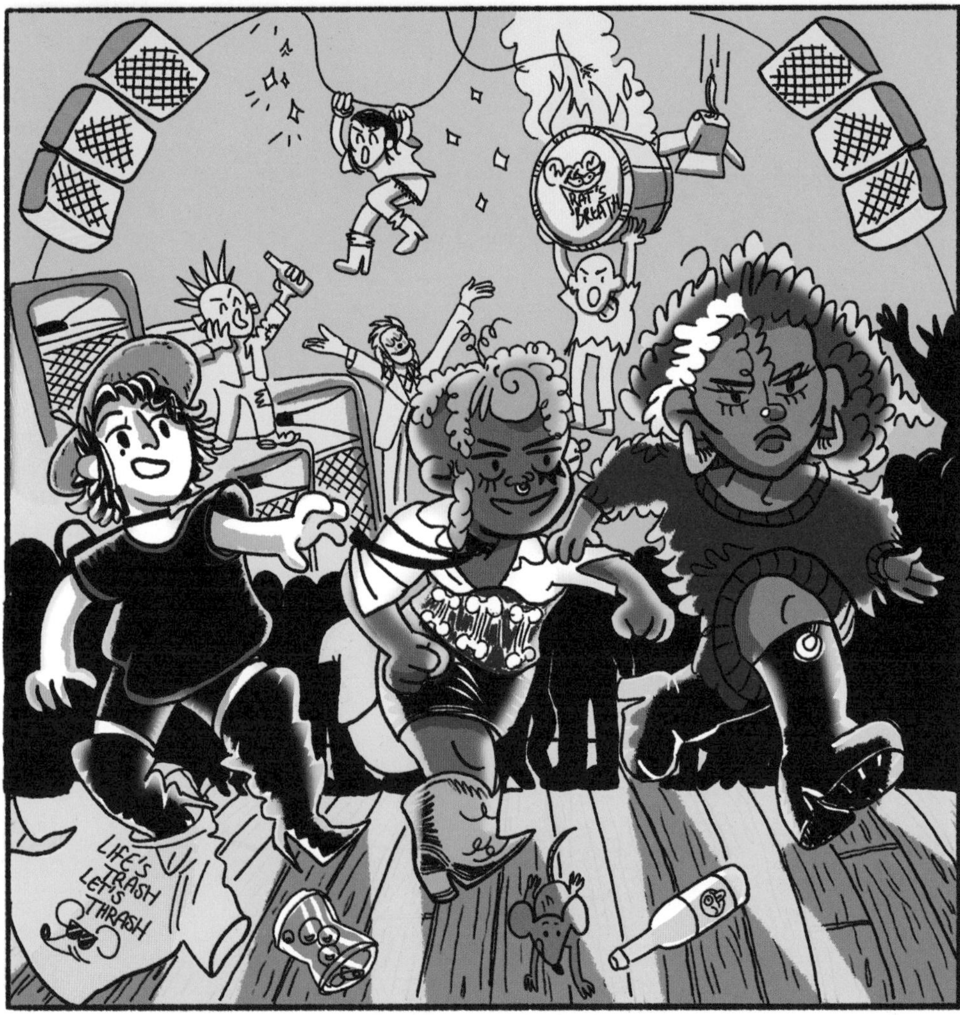
RAT'S BREATH
LIFE'S TRASH LET'S THRASH

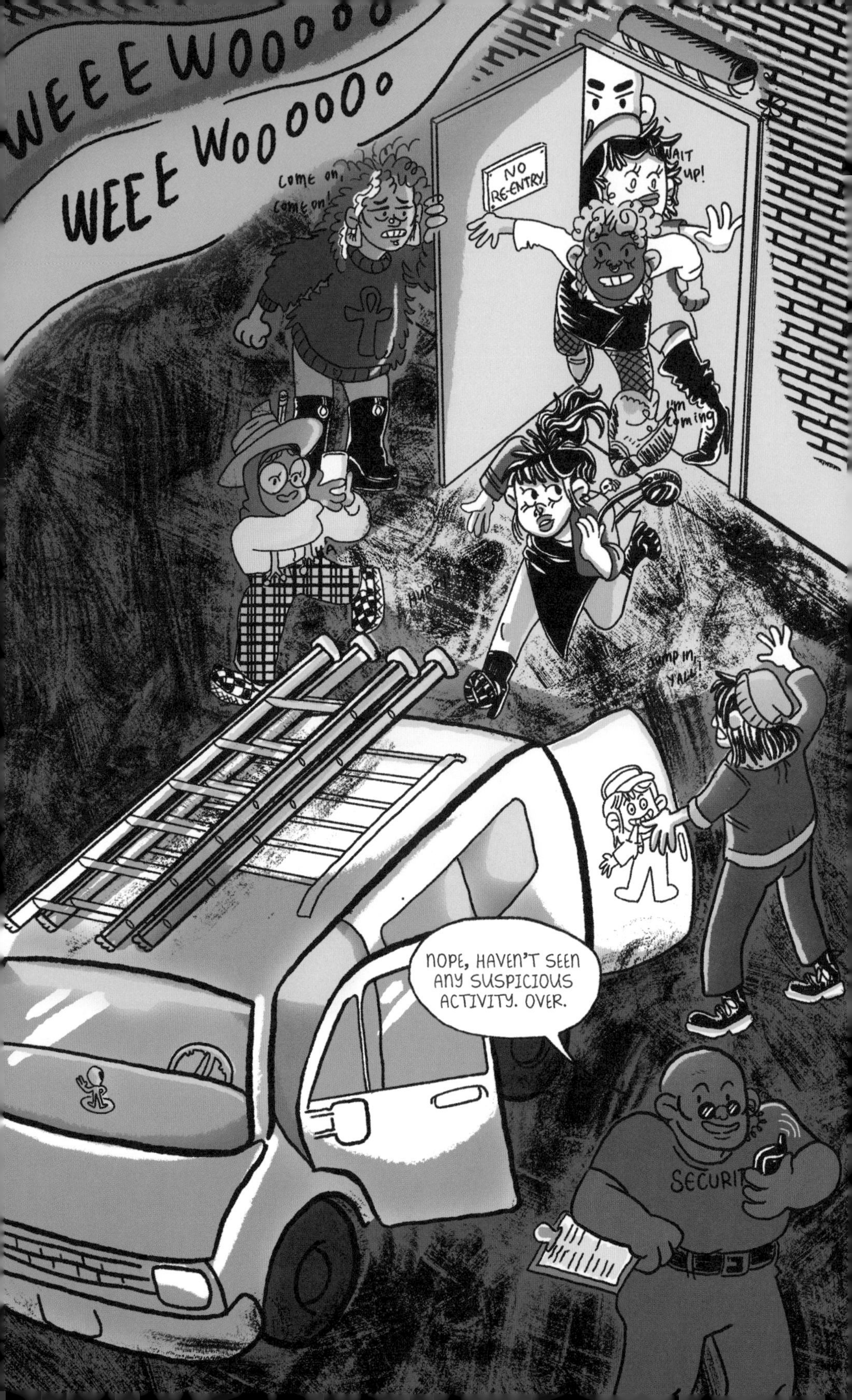
WEEE WOOOOO
WEEE WOOOOOo
come on, come on!
NO RE-ENTRY
WAIT up!
I'm coming
HURRY
Jump in, Y'ALL!
NOPE, HAVEN'T SEEN ANY SUSPICIOUS ACTIVITY. OVER.
SECURIT

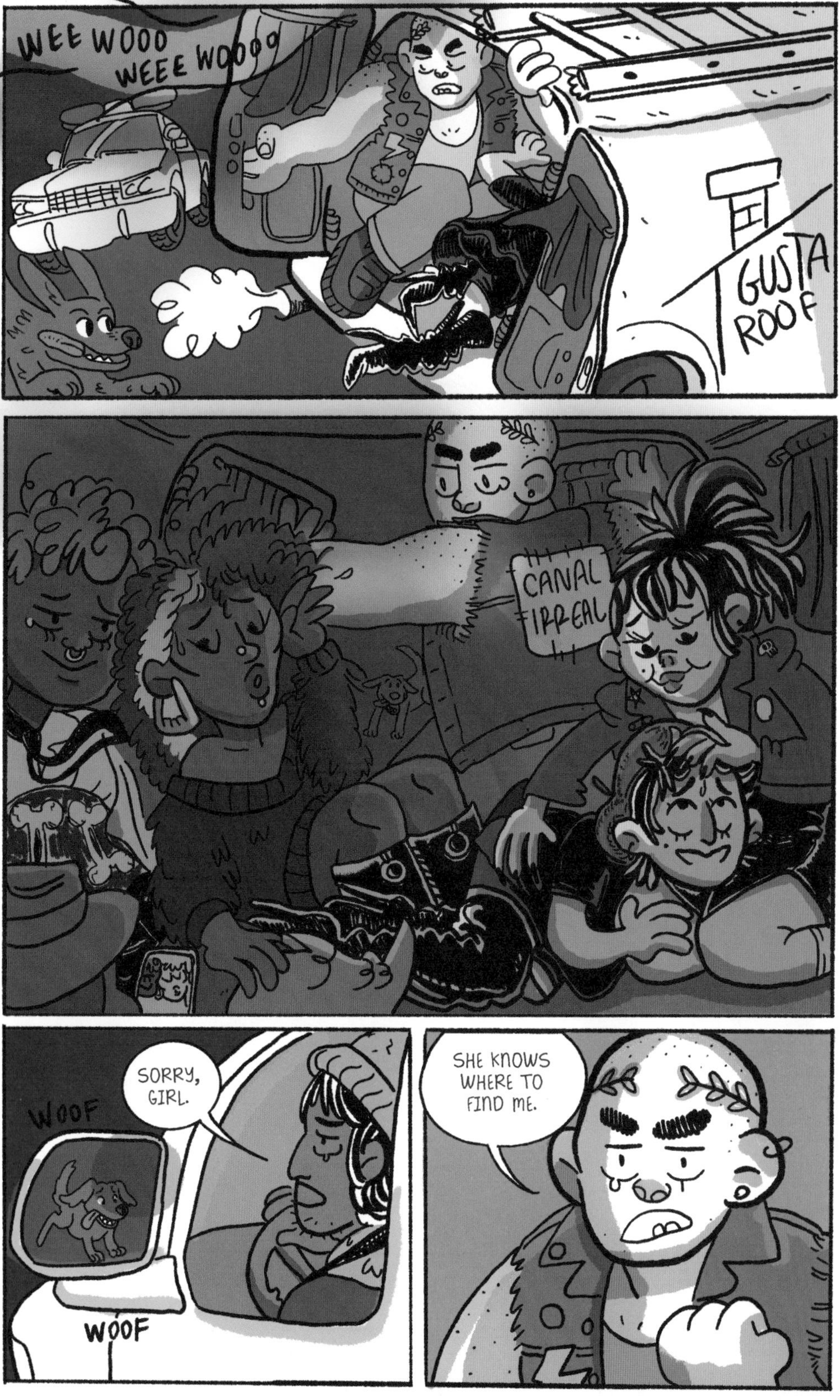
WEE WOOO
WEEE WOOOO
GUSTA ROOF
CANAL IRREAL
WOOF
SORRY, GIRL.
WOOF
SHE KNOWS WHERE TO FIND ME.

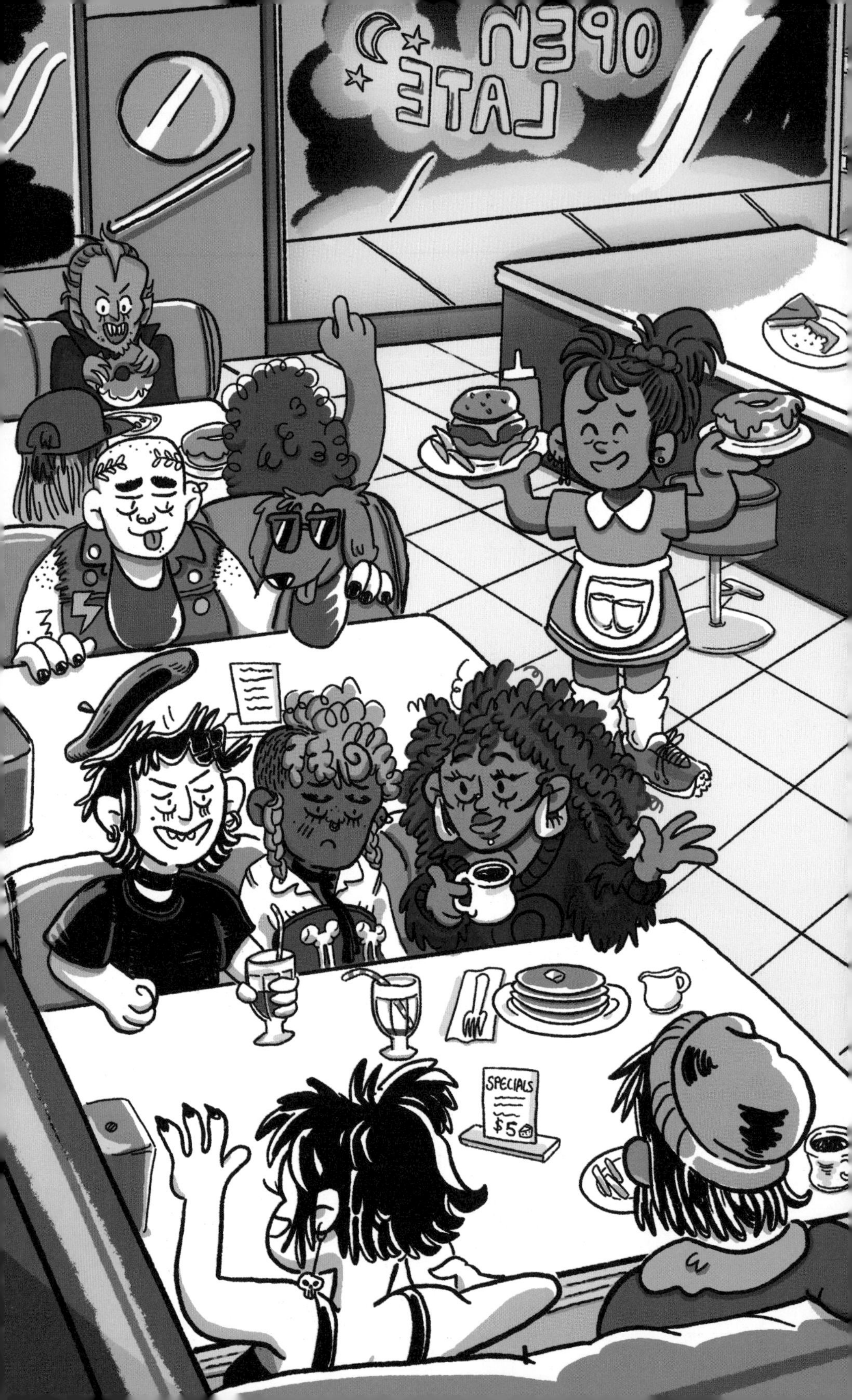
OPEN
LATE
SPECIALS
$5

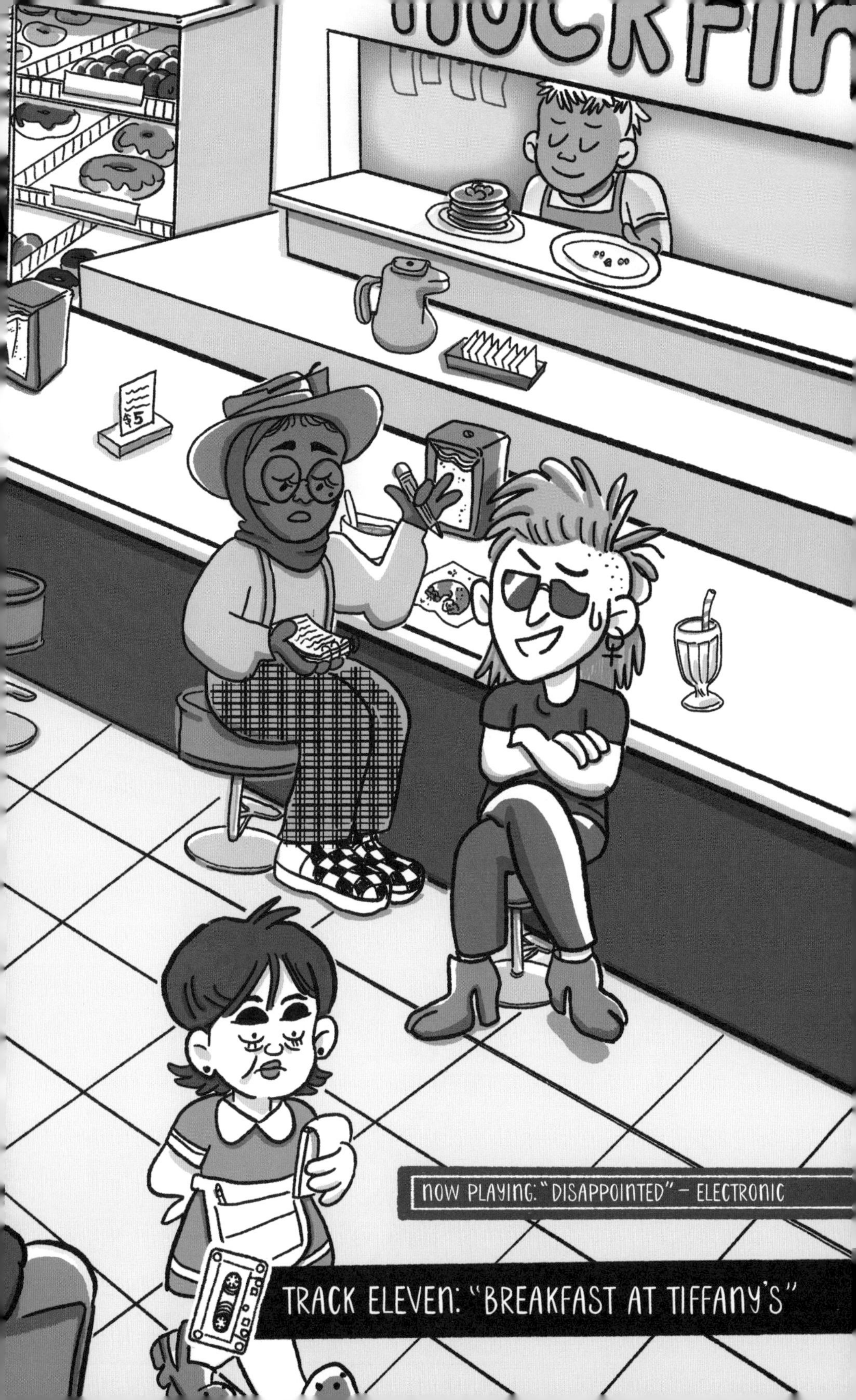
$5
NOW PLAYING: "DISAPPOINTED" – ELECTRONIC
TRACK ELEVEN: "BREAKFAST AT TIFFANY'S"

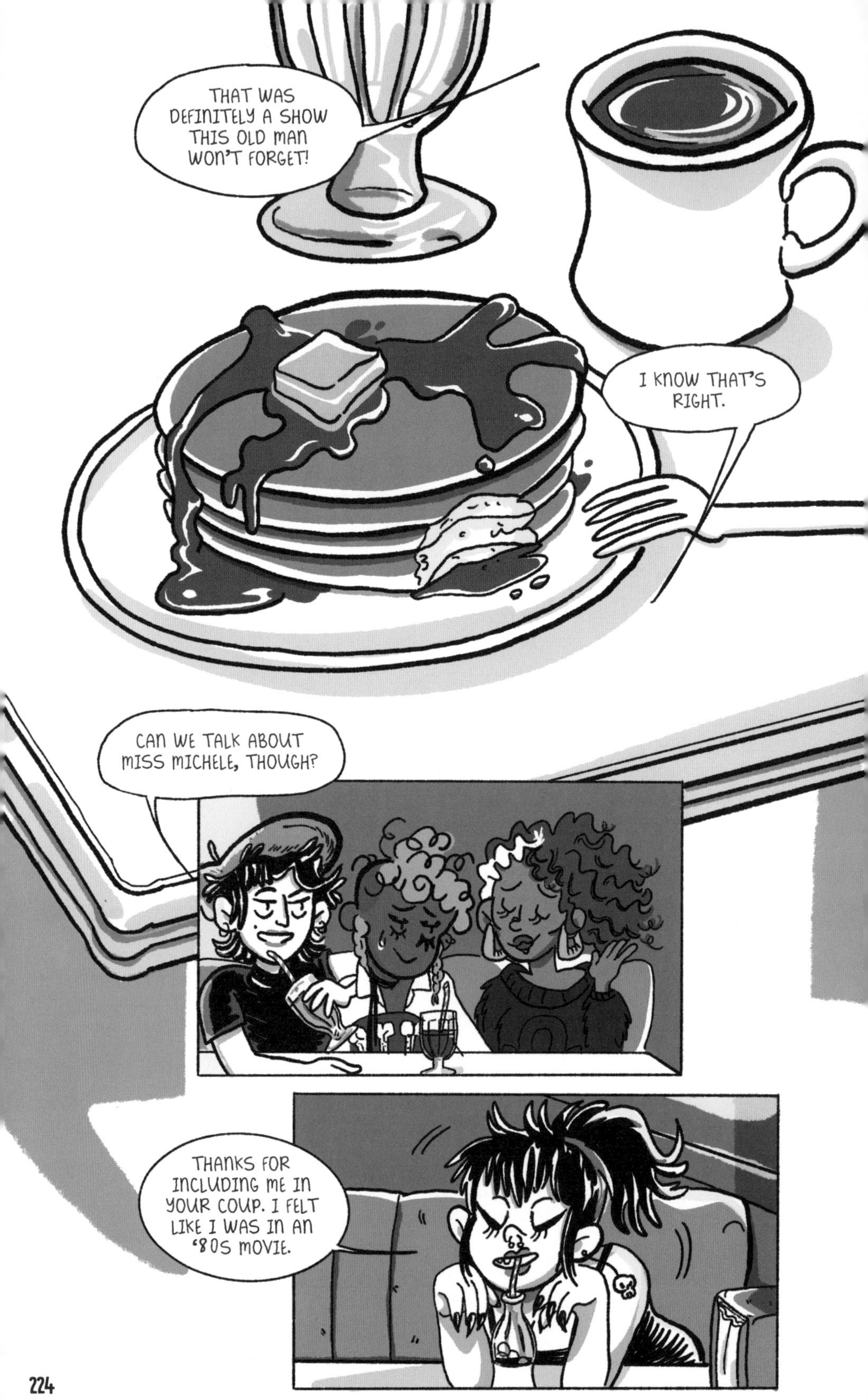
THAT WAS DEFINITELY A SHOW THIS OLD MAN WON'T FORGET!
I KNOW THAT'S RIGHT.
CAN WE TALK ABOUT MISS MICHELE, THOUGH?
THANKS FOR INCLUDING ME IN YOUR COUP. I FELT LIKE I WAS IN AN '80S MOVIE.

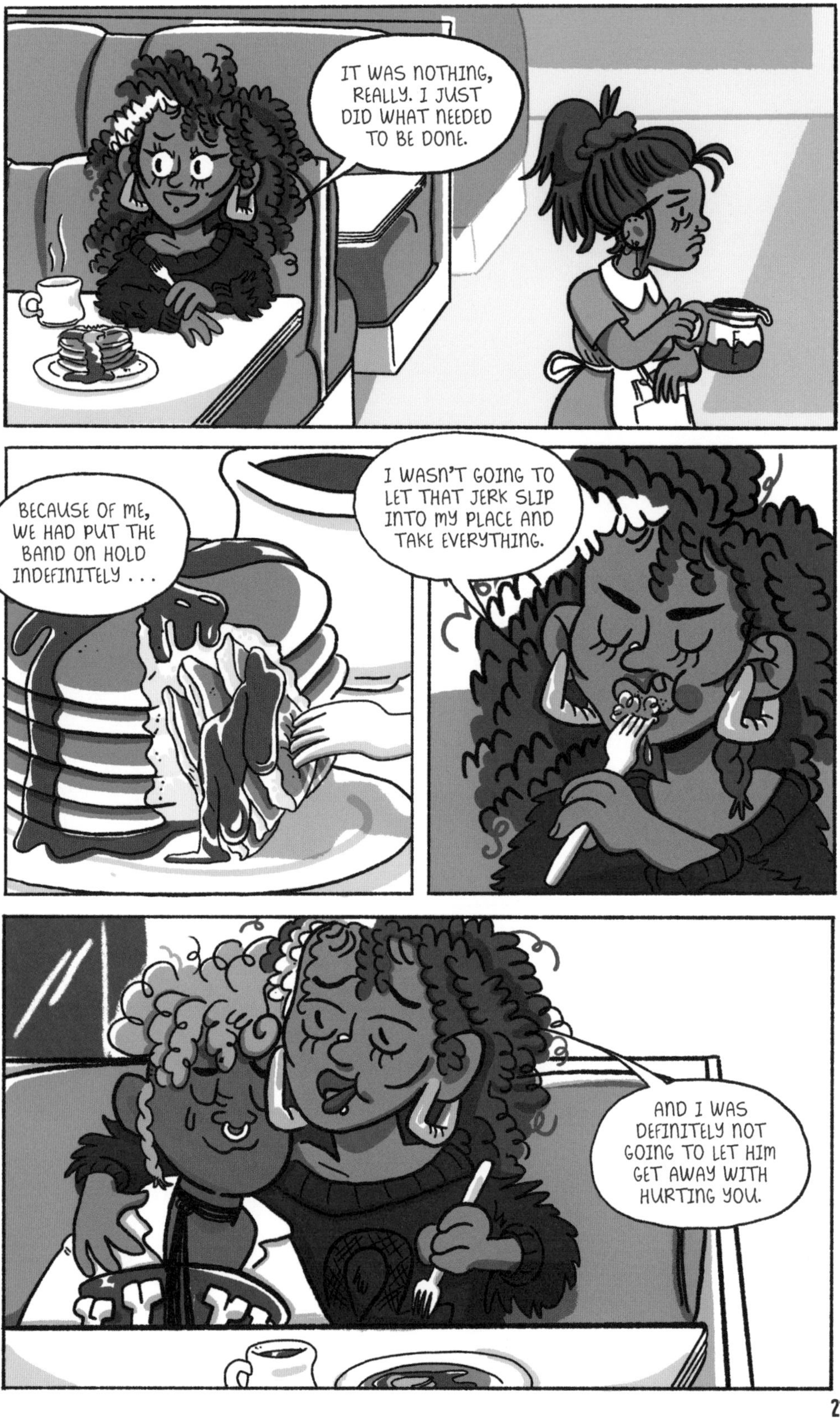
IT WAS NOTHING, REALLY. I JUST DID WHAT NEEDED TO BE DONE.
BECAUSE OF ME, WE HAD PUT THE BAND ON HOLD INDEFINITELY . . .
I WASN'T GOING TO LET THAT JERK SLIP INTO MY PLACE AND TAKE EVERYTHING.
AND I WAS DEFINITELY NOT GOING TO LET HIM GET AWAY WITH HURTING YOU.

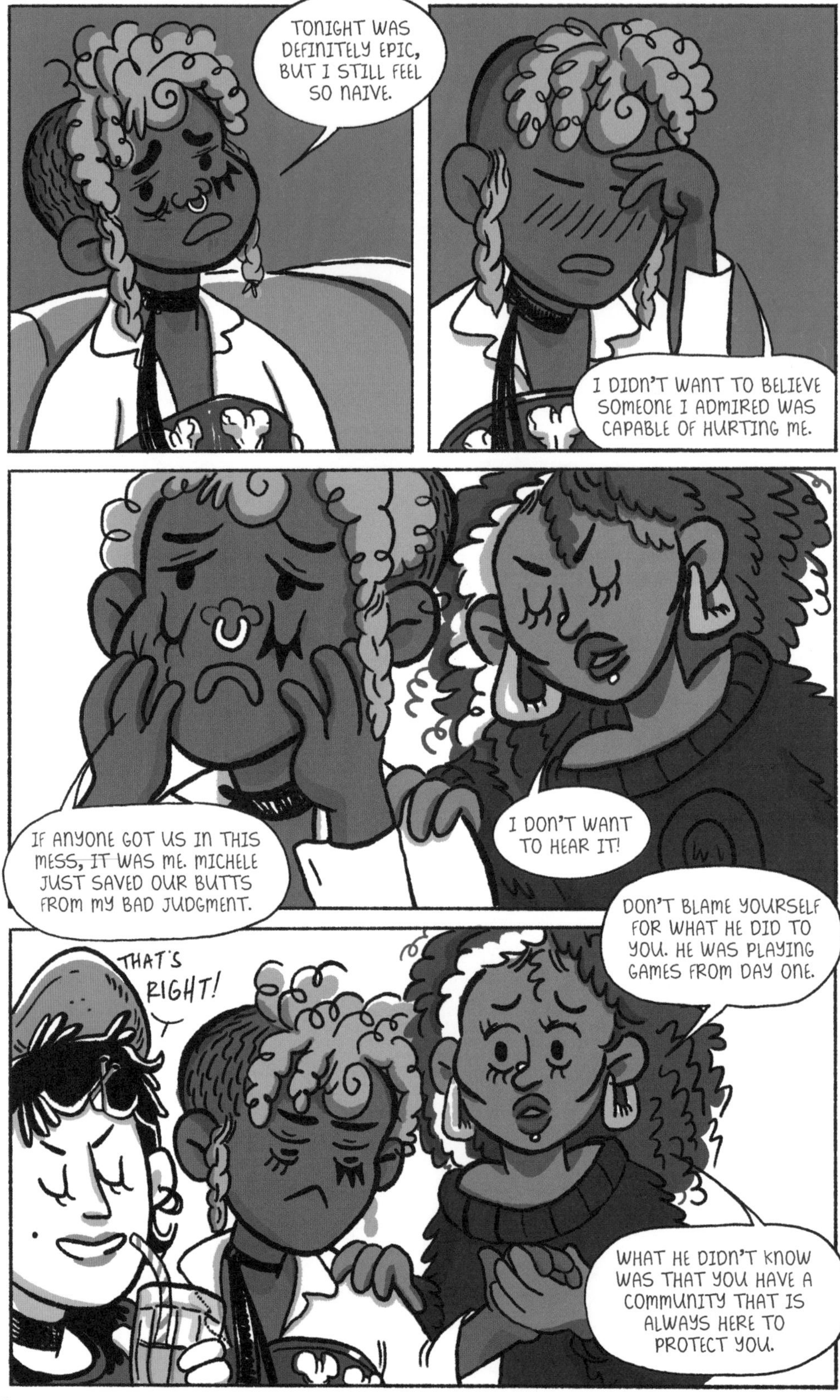
TONIGHT WAS DEFINITELY EPIC, BUT I STILL FEEL SO NAIVE.
I DIDN'T WANT TO BELIEVE SOMEONE I ADMIRED WAS CAPABLE OF HURTING ME.
IF ANYONE GOT US IN THIS MESS, IT WAS ME. MICHELE JUST SAVED OUR BUTTS FROM MY BAD JUDGMENT.
I DON'T WANT TO HEAR IT!
DON'T BLAME YOURSELF FOR WHAT HE DID TO YOU. HE WAS PLAYING GAMES FROM DAY ONE.
THAT'S RIGHT!
WHAT HE DIDN'T KNOW WAS THAT YOU HAVE A COMMUNITY THAT IS ALWAYS HERE TO PROTECT YOU.

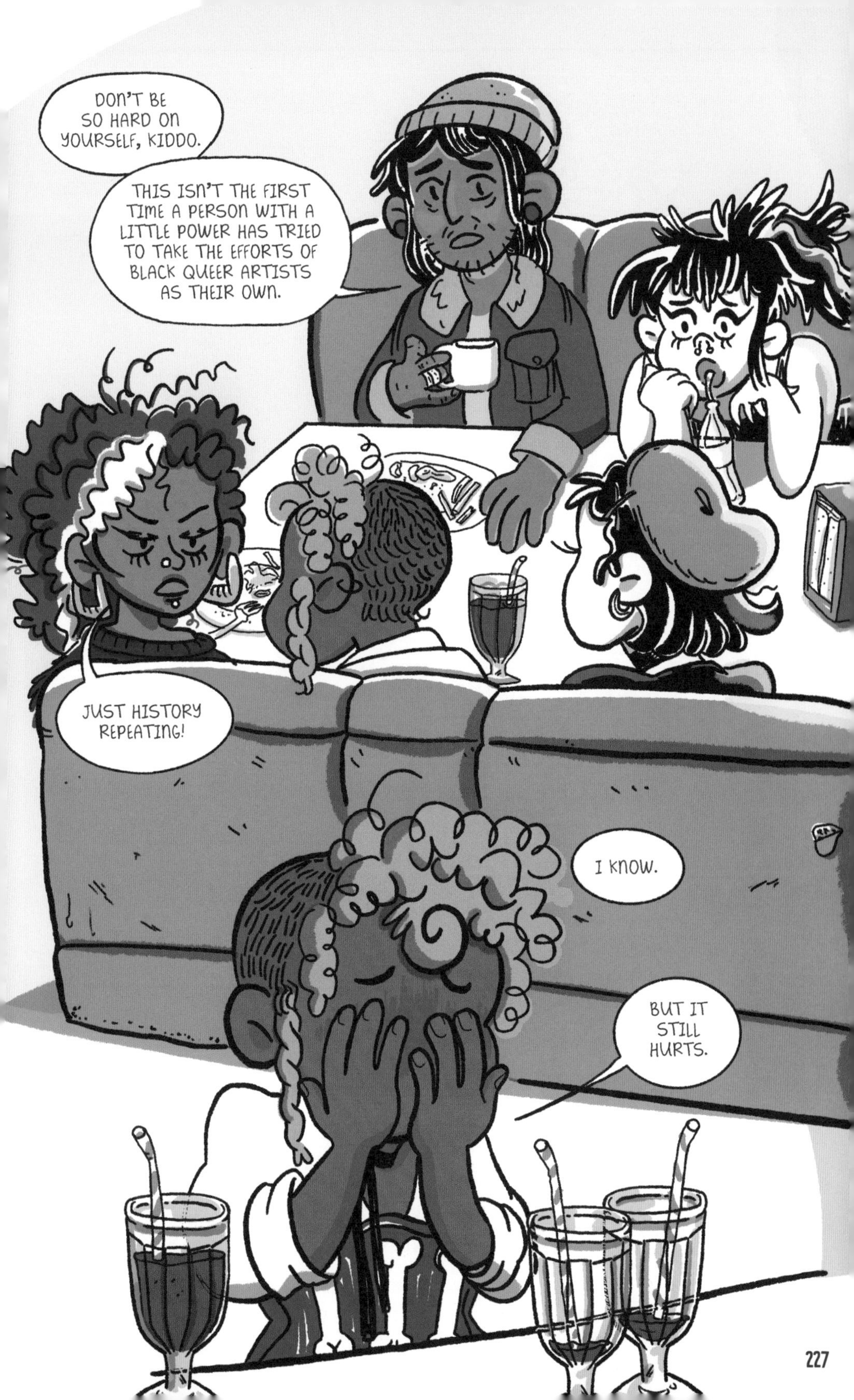
DON'T BE SO HARD ON YOURSELF, KIDDO.
THIS ISN'T THE FIRST TIME A PERSON WITH A LITTLE POWER HAS TRIED TO TAKE THE EFFORTS OF BLACK QUEER ARTISTS AS THEIR OWN.
JUST HISTORY REPEATING!
I KNOW.
BUT IT STILL HURTS.

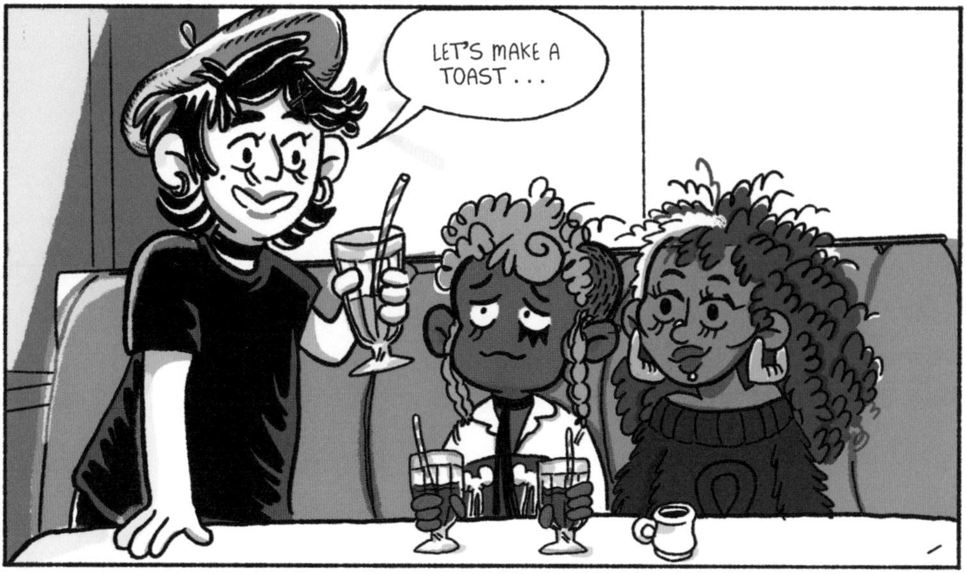
LET'S MAKE A TOAST . . .

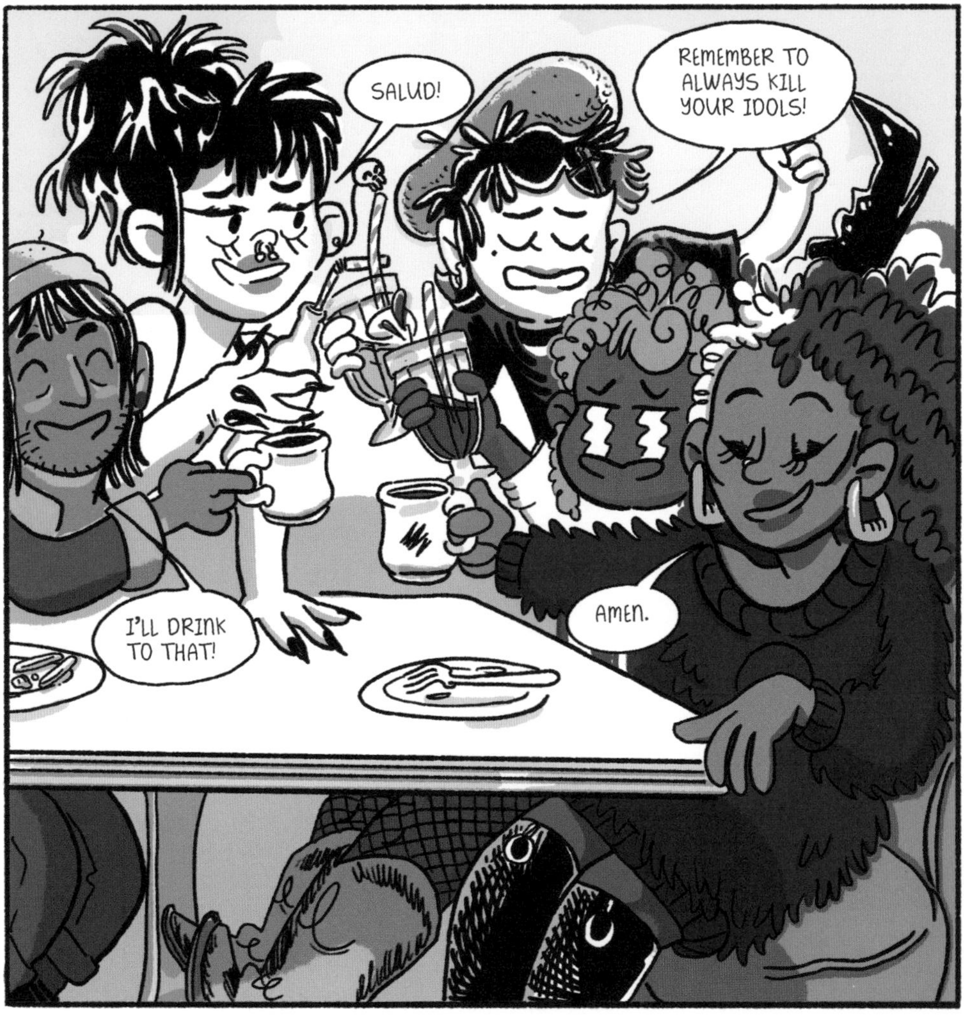
SALUD!
REMEMBER TO ALWAYS KILL YOUR IDOLS!
I'LL DRINK TO THAT!
AMEN.

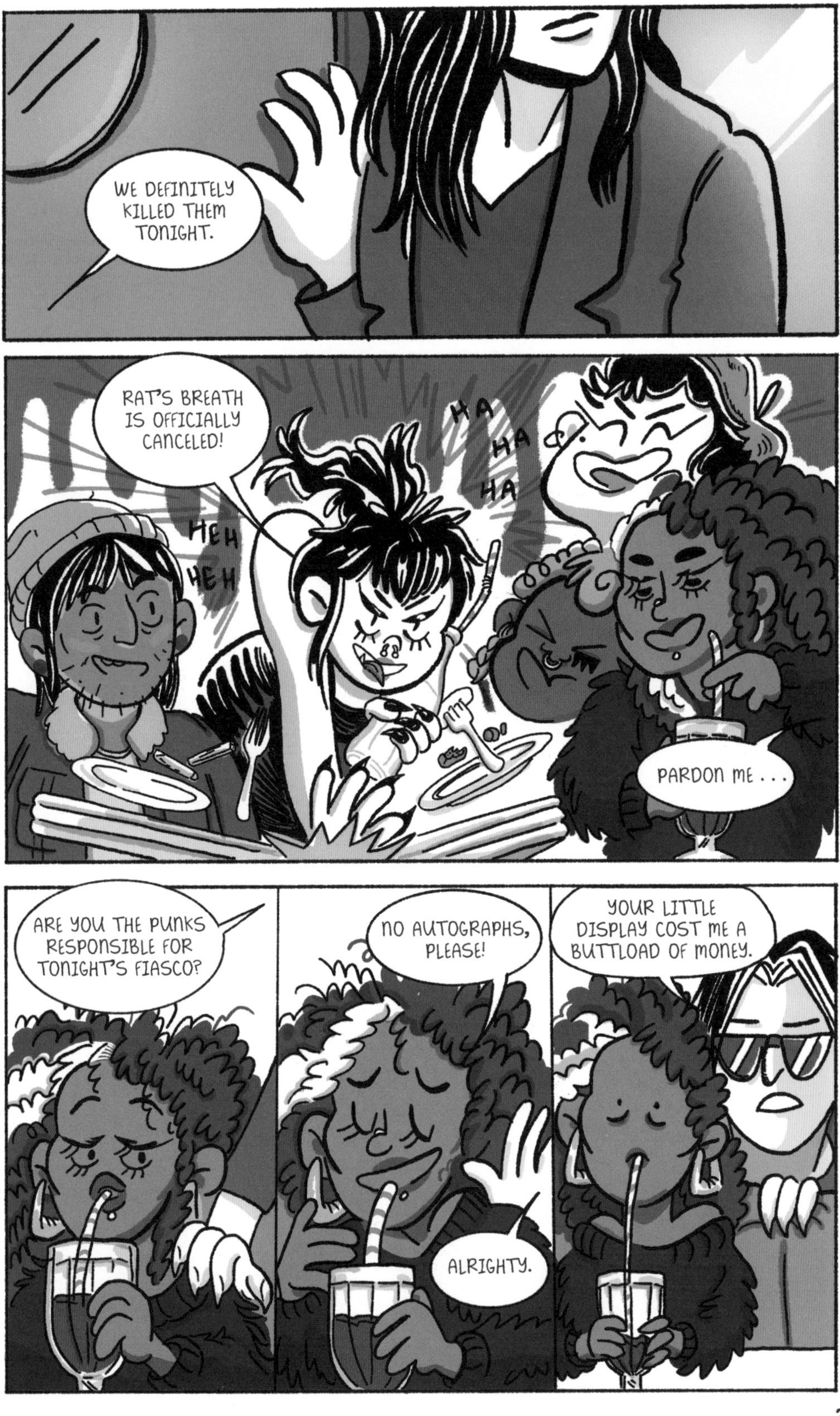
WE DEFINITELY KILLED THEM TONIGHT.
RAT'S BREATH IS OFFICIALLY CANCELED!
HA HA HA
HEH HEH
PARDON ME . . .
ARE YOU THE PUNKS RESPONSIBLE FOR TONIGHT'S FIASCO?
NO AUTOGRAPHS, PLEASE!
ALRIGHTY.
YOUR LITTLE DISPLAY COST ME A BUTTLOAD OF MONEY.

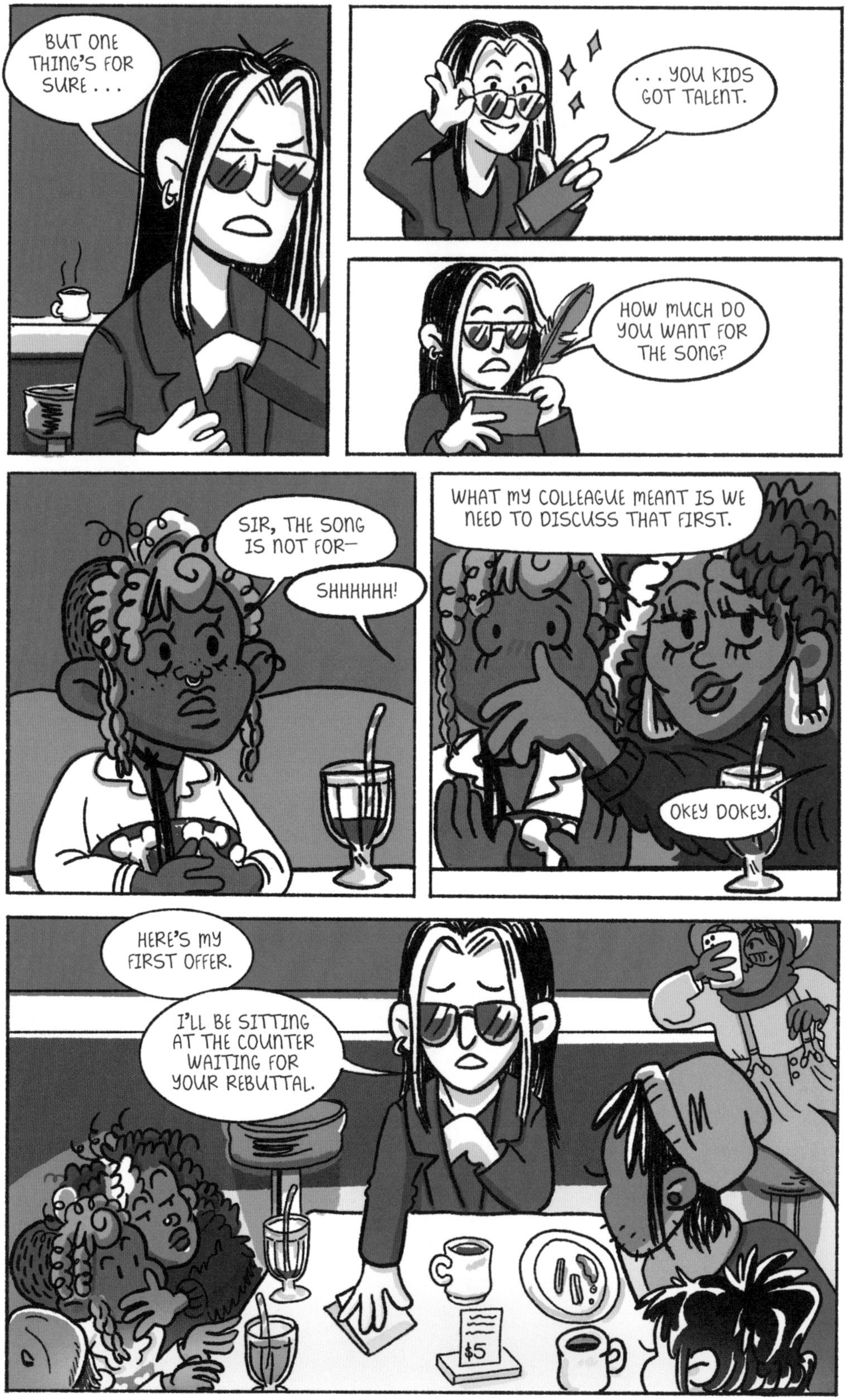

BUT ONE THING'S FOR SURE . . .
. . . YOU KIDS GOT TALENT.
HOW MUCH DO YOU WANT FOR THE SONG?
SIR, THE SONG IS NOT FOR—
SHHHHHH!
WHAT MY COLLEAGUE MEANT IS WE NEED TO DISCUSS THAT FIRST.
OKEY DOKEY.
HERE'S MY FIRST OFFER.
I'LL BE SITTING AT THE COUNTER WAITING FOR YOUR REBUTTAL.
$5

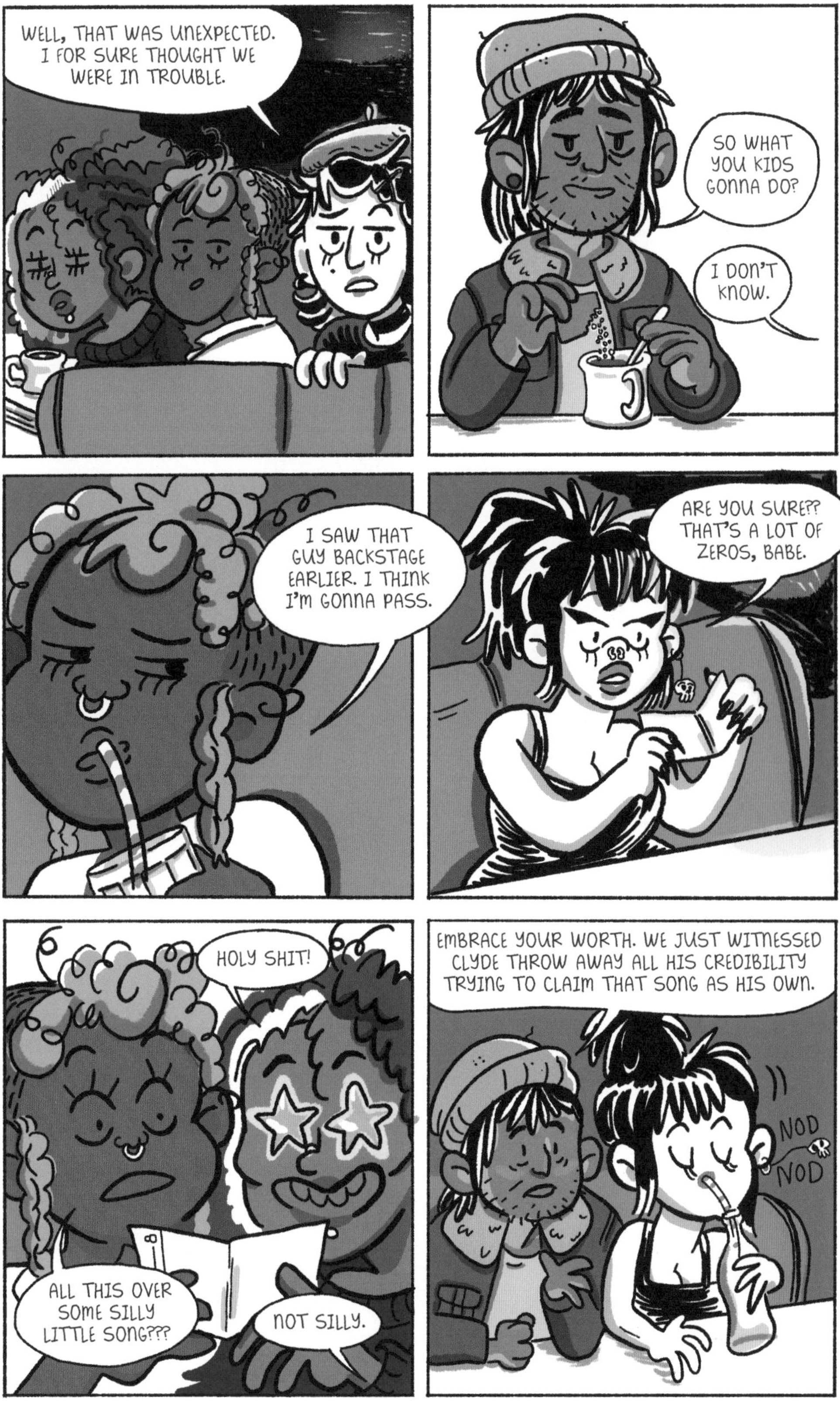
WELL, THAT WAS UNEXPECTED. I FOR SURE THOUGHT WE WERE IN TROUBLE.
SO WHAT YOU KIDS GONNA DO?
I DON'T KNOW.
I SAW THAT GUY BACKSTAGE EARLIER. I THINK I'M GONNA PASS.
ARE YOU SURE?? THAT'S A LOT OF ZEROS, BABE.
HOLY SHIT!
ALL THIS OVER SOME SILLY LITTLE SONG???
NOT SILLY.
EMBRACE YOUR WORTH. WE JUST WITNESSED CLYDE THROW AWAY ALL HIS CREDIBILITY TRYING TO CLAIM THAT SONG AS HIS OWN.
NOD
NOD

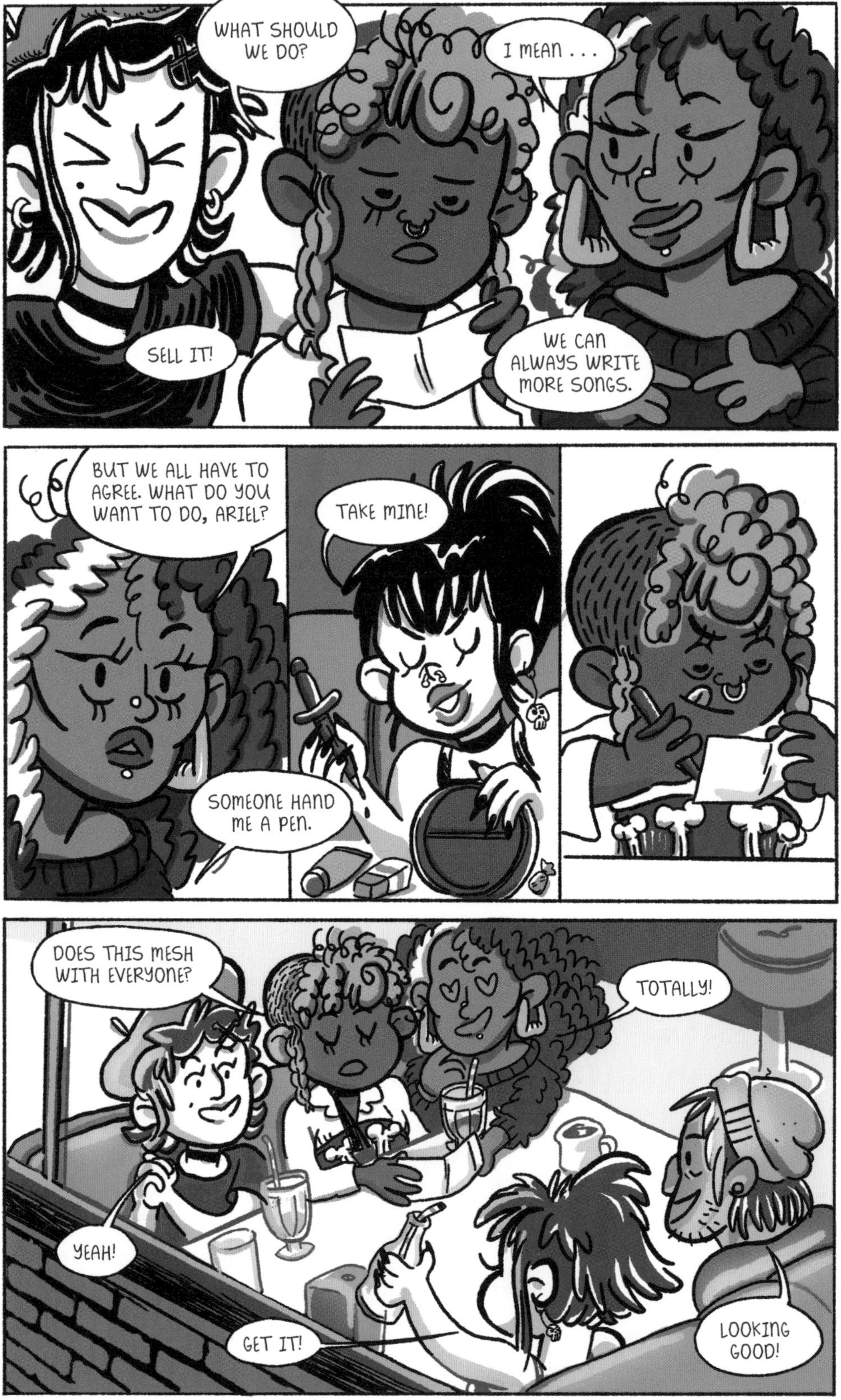
WHAT SHOULD WE DO?
I MEAN . . .
SELL IT!
WE CAN ALWAYS WRITE MORE SONGS.
BUT WE ALL HAVE TO AGREE. WHAT DO YOU WANT TO DO, ARIEL?
TAKE MINE!
SOMEONE HAND ME A PEN.
DOES THIS MESH WITH EVERYONE?
TOTALLY!
YEAH!
GET IT!
LOOKING GOOD!

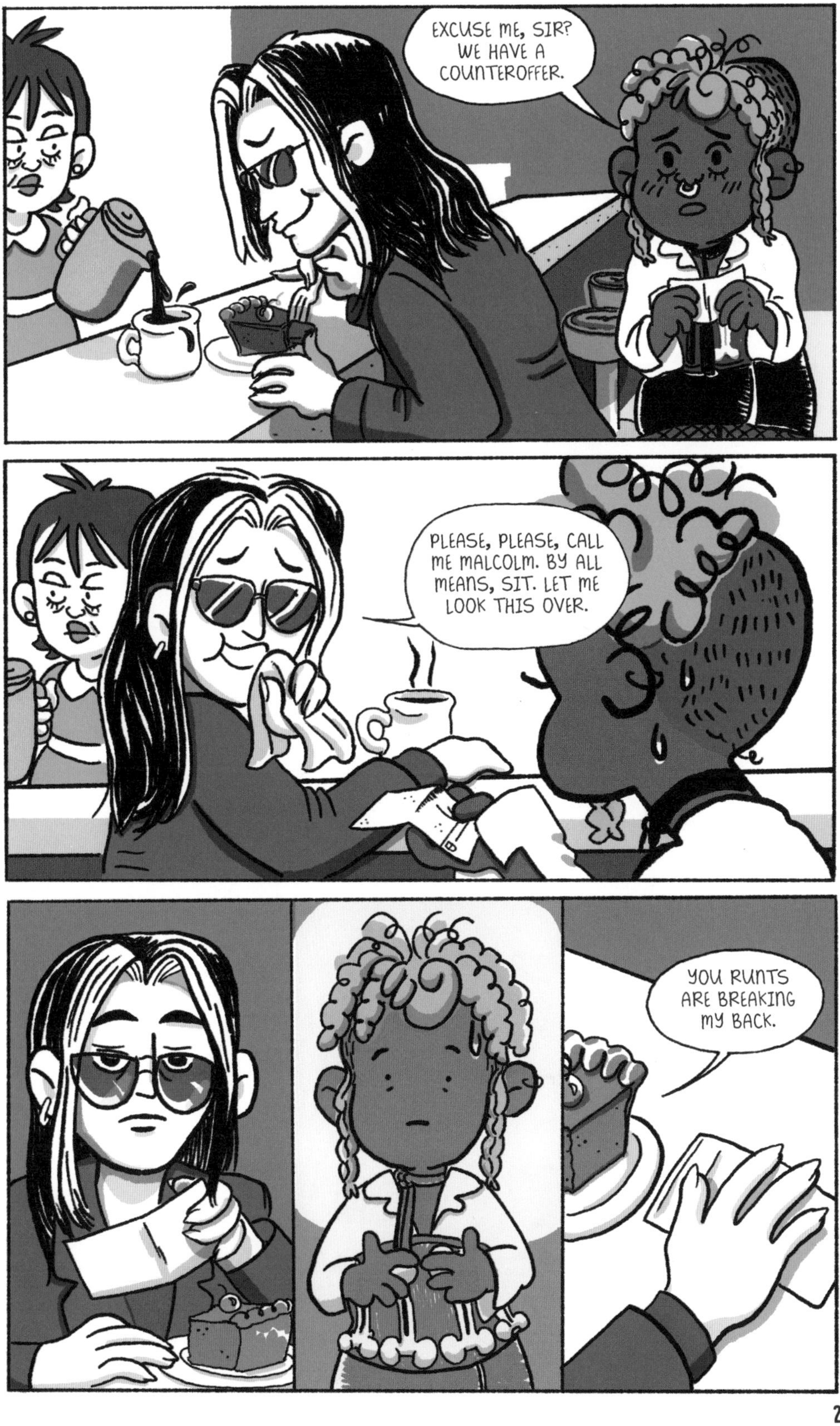
EXCUSE ME, SIR? WE HAVE A COUNTEROFFER.
PLEASE, PLEASE, CALL ME MALCOLM. BY ALL MEANS, SIT. LET ME LOOK THIS OVER.
YOU RUNTS ARE BREAKING MY BACK.

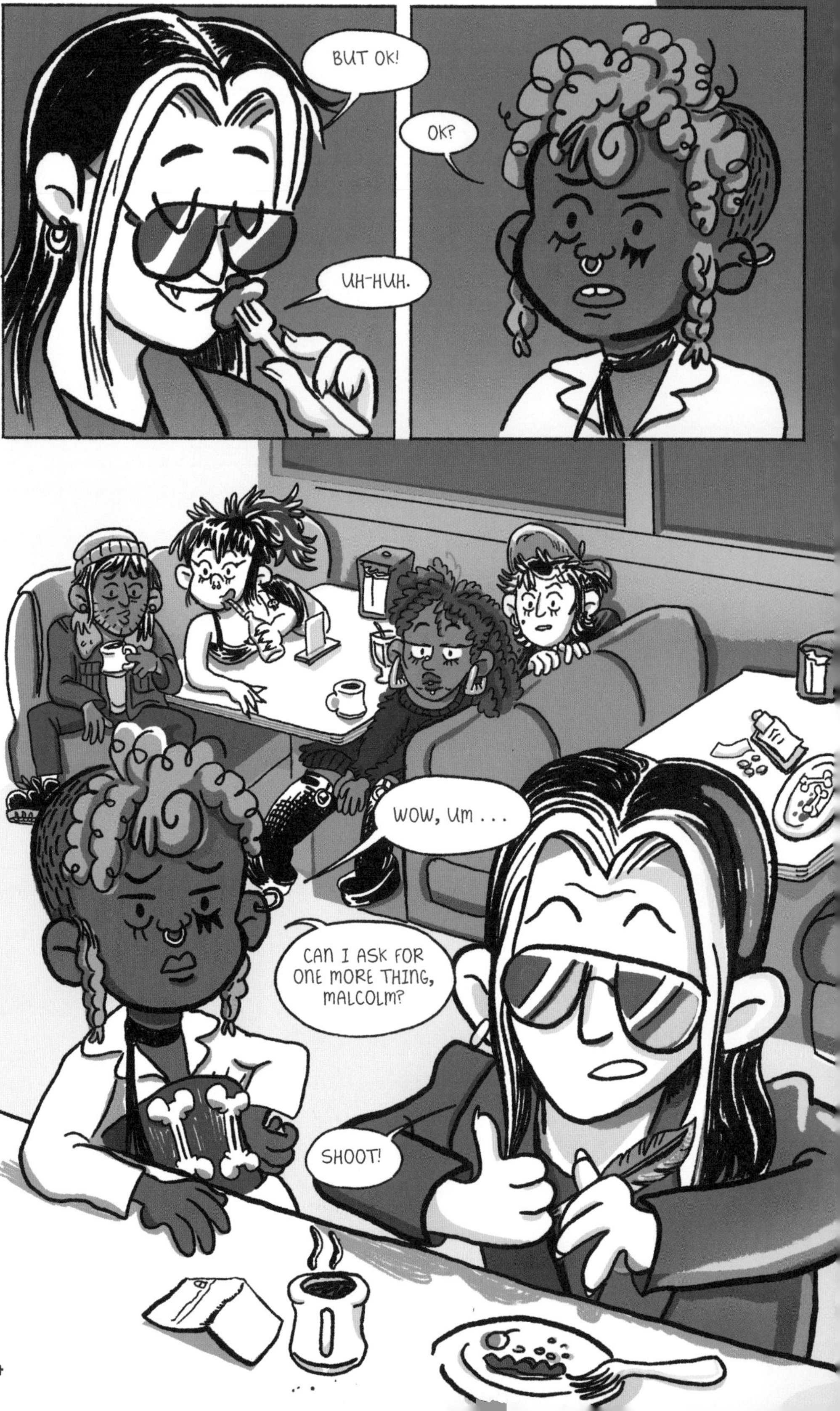
BUT OK!
OK?
UH-HUH.
WOW, UM . . .
CAN I ASK FOR ONE MORE THING, MALCOLM?
SHOOT!

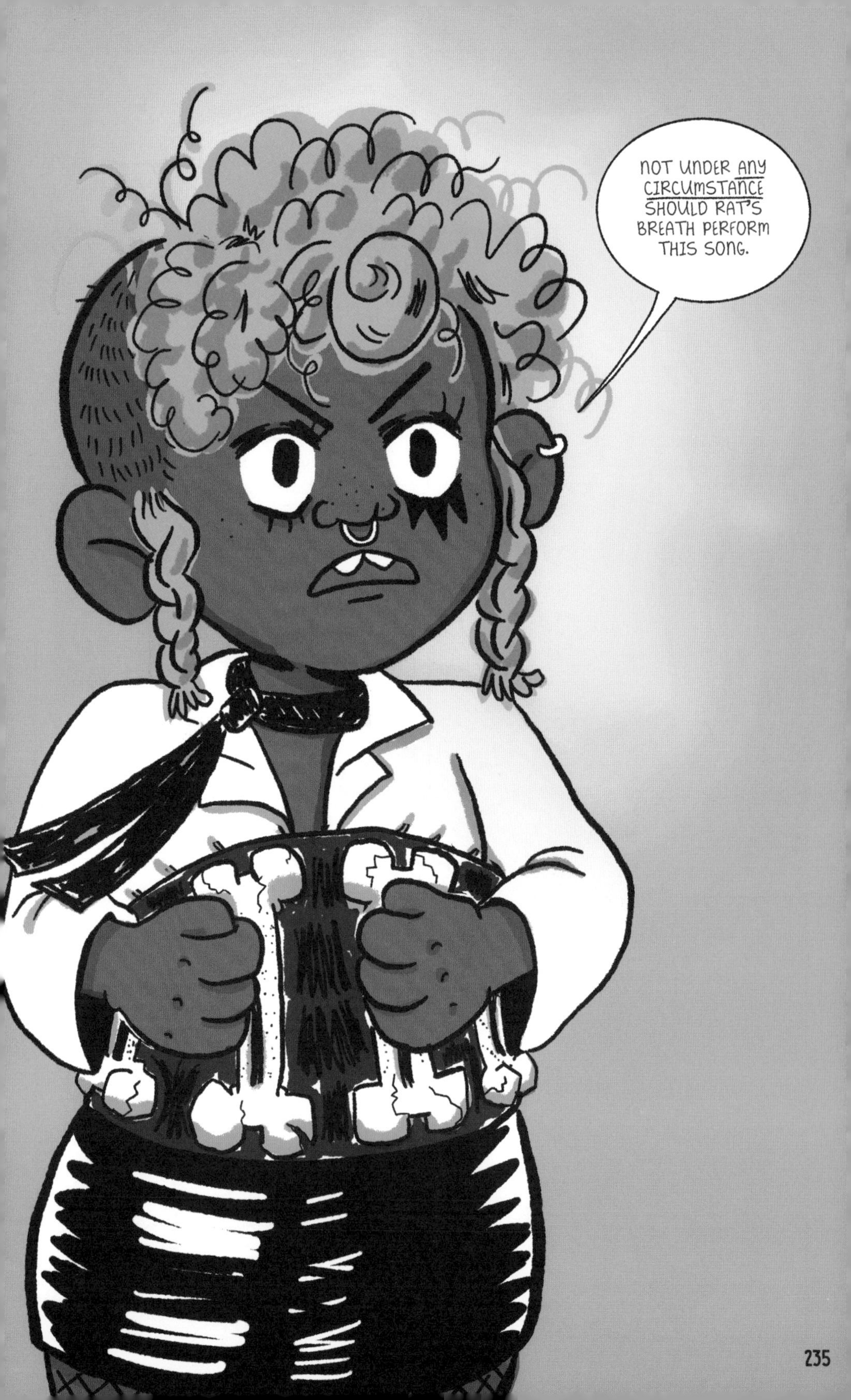
NOT UNDER ANY CIRCUMSTANCE SHOULD RAT'S BREATH PERFORM THIS SONG.

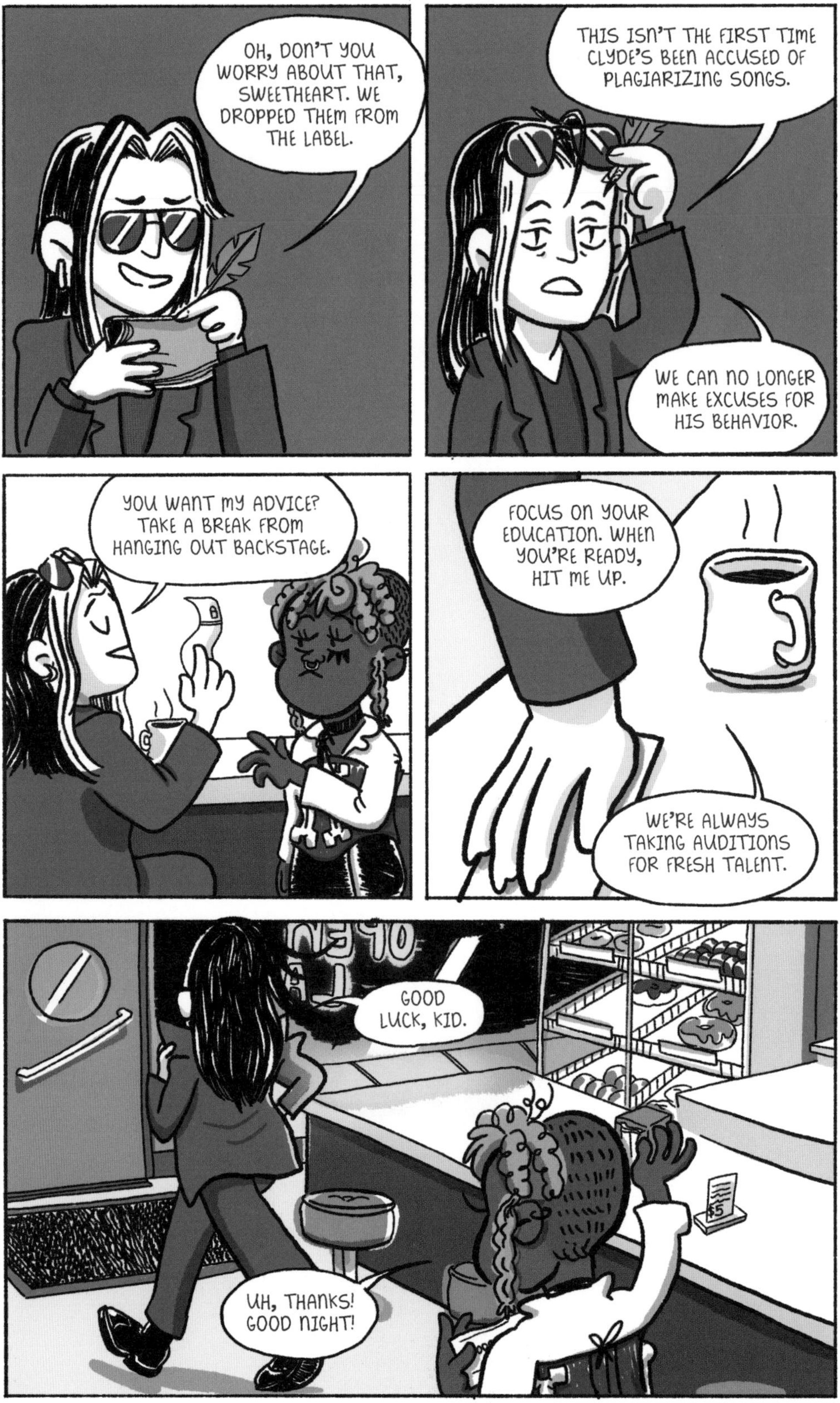
OH, DON'T YOU WORRY ABOUT THAT, SWEETHEART. WE DROPPED THEM FROM THE LABEL.
THIS ISN'T THE FIRST TIME CLYDE'S BEEN ACCUSED OF PLAGIARIZING SONGS.
WE CAN NO LONGER MAKE EXCUSES FOR HIS BEHAVIOR.
YOU WANT MY ADVICE? TAKE A BREAK FROM HANGING OUT BACKSTAGE.
FOCUS ON YOUR EDUCATION. WHEN YOU'RE READY, HIT ME UP.
WE'RE ALWAYS TAKING AUDITIONS FOR FRESH TALENT.
GOOD LUCK, KID.
UH, THANKS! GOOD NIGHT!
$5

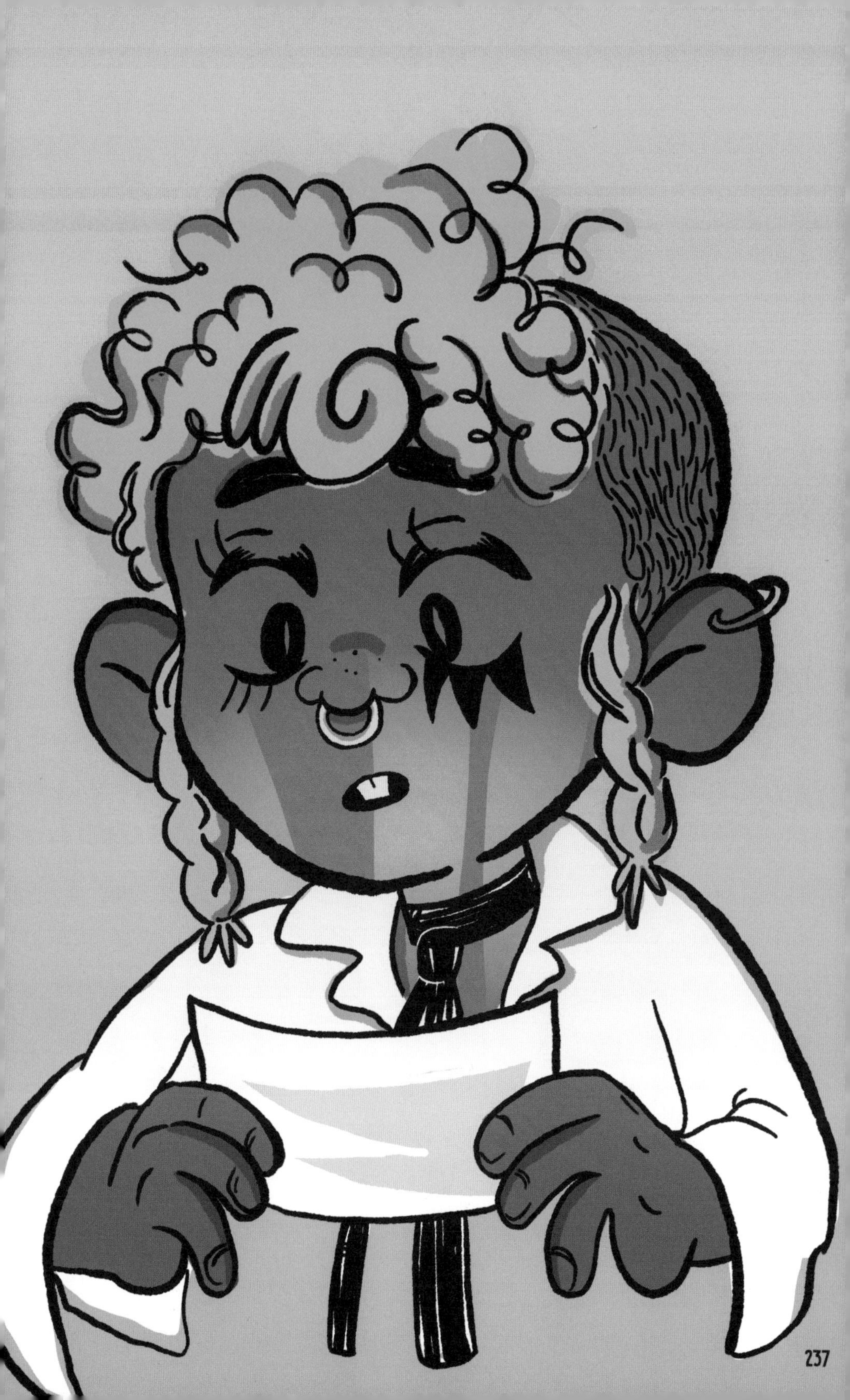

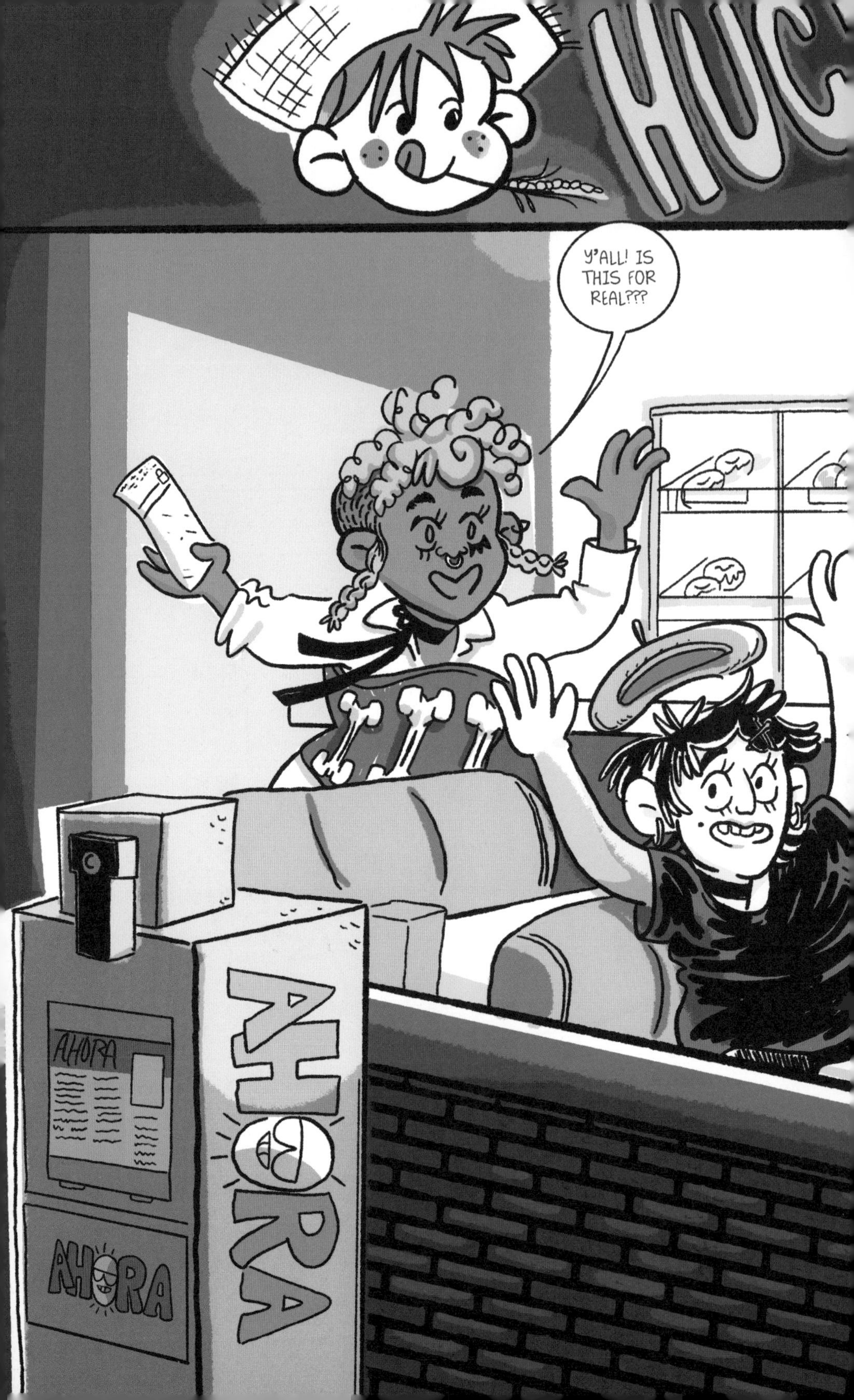
HUC
Y'ALL! IS THIS FOR REAL???
AHORA
AHORA
AHORA

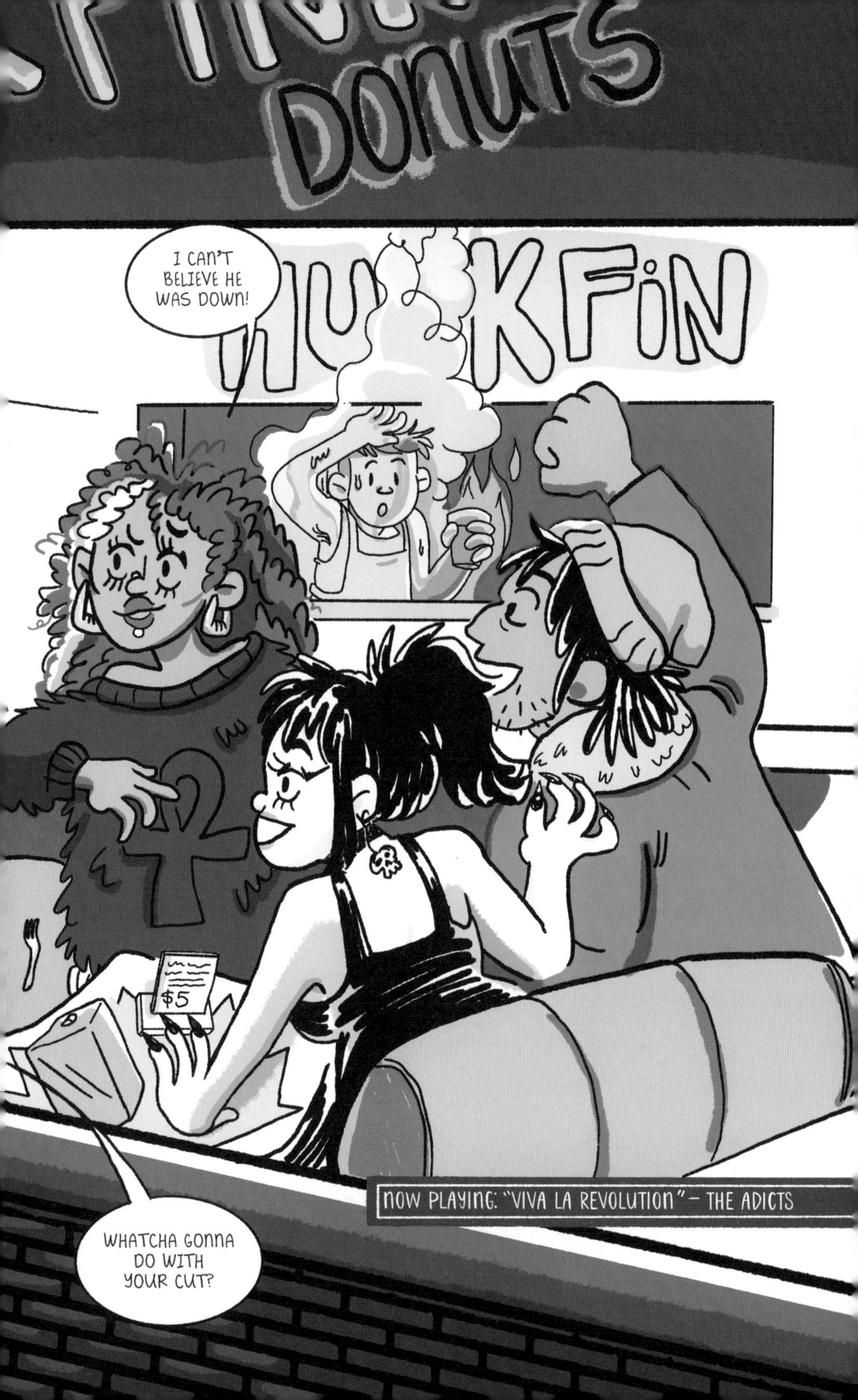
DONUTS
HU KFIN
I CAN'T BELIEVE HE WAS DOWN!
$5
NOW PLAYING: "VIVA LA REVOLUTION" – THE ADICTS
WHATCHA GONNA DO WITH YOUR CUT?

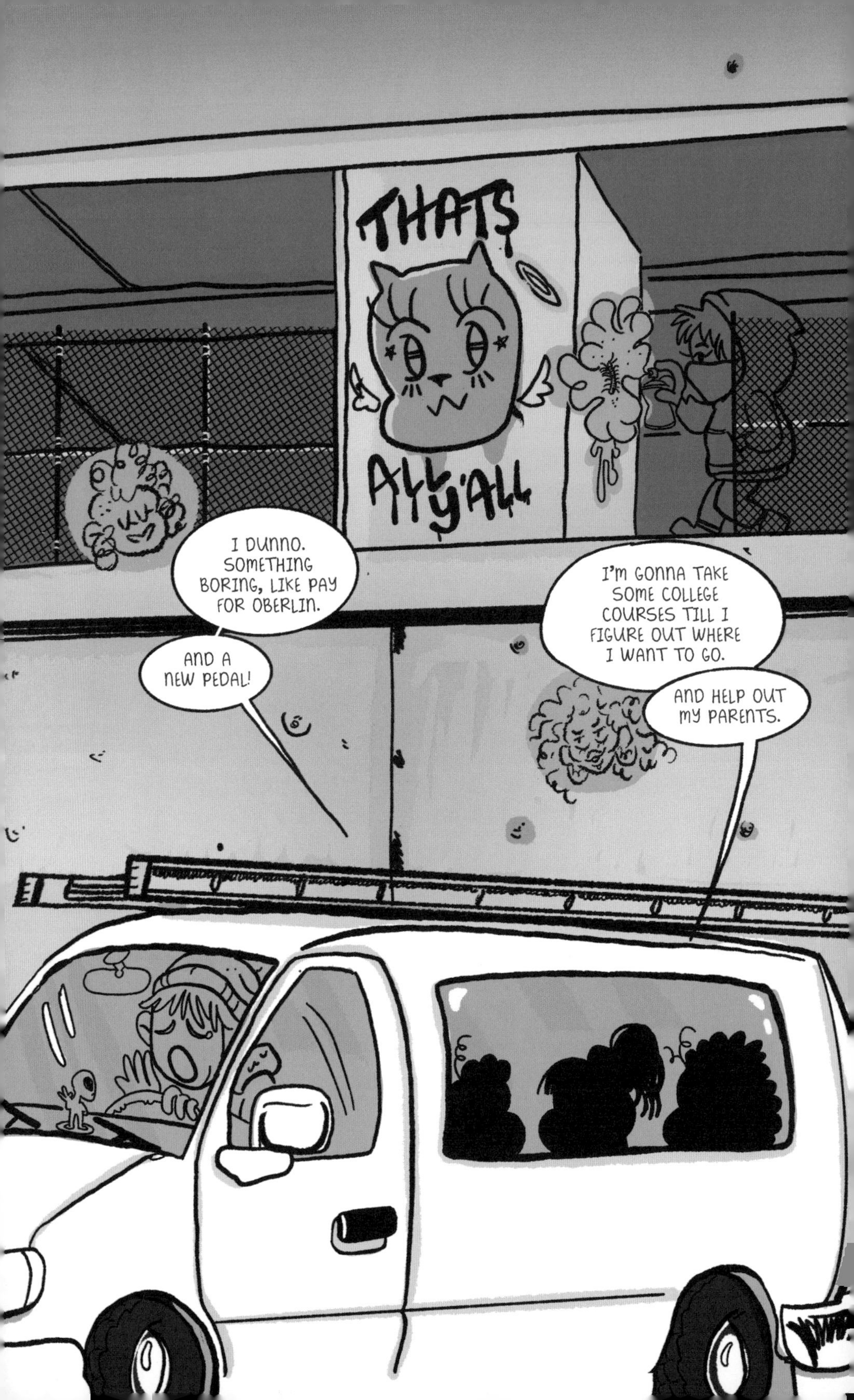
THATS ALL Y'ALL
I DUNNO. SOMETHING BORING, LIKE PAY FOR OBERLIN.
AND A NEW PEDAL!
I'M GONNA TAKE SOME COLLEGE COURSES TILL I FIGURE OUT WHERE I WANT TO GO.
AND HELP OUT MY PARENTS.

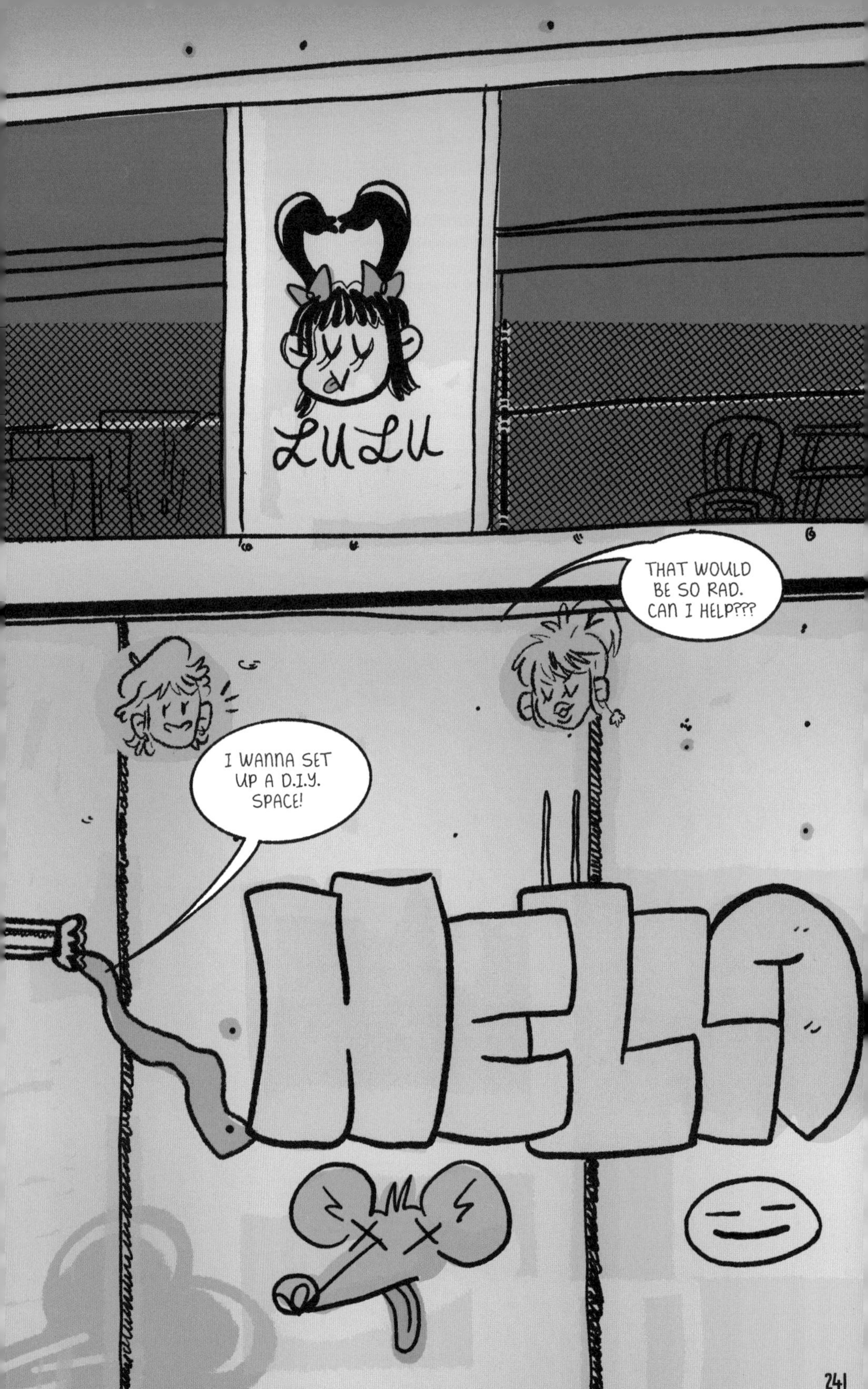
LULU
THAT WOULD BE SO RAD. CAN I HELP???
I WANNA SET UP A D.I.Y. SPACE!
HELLO

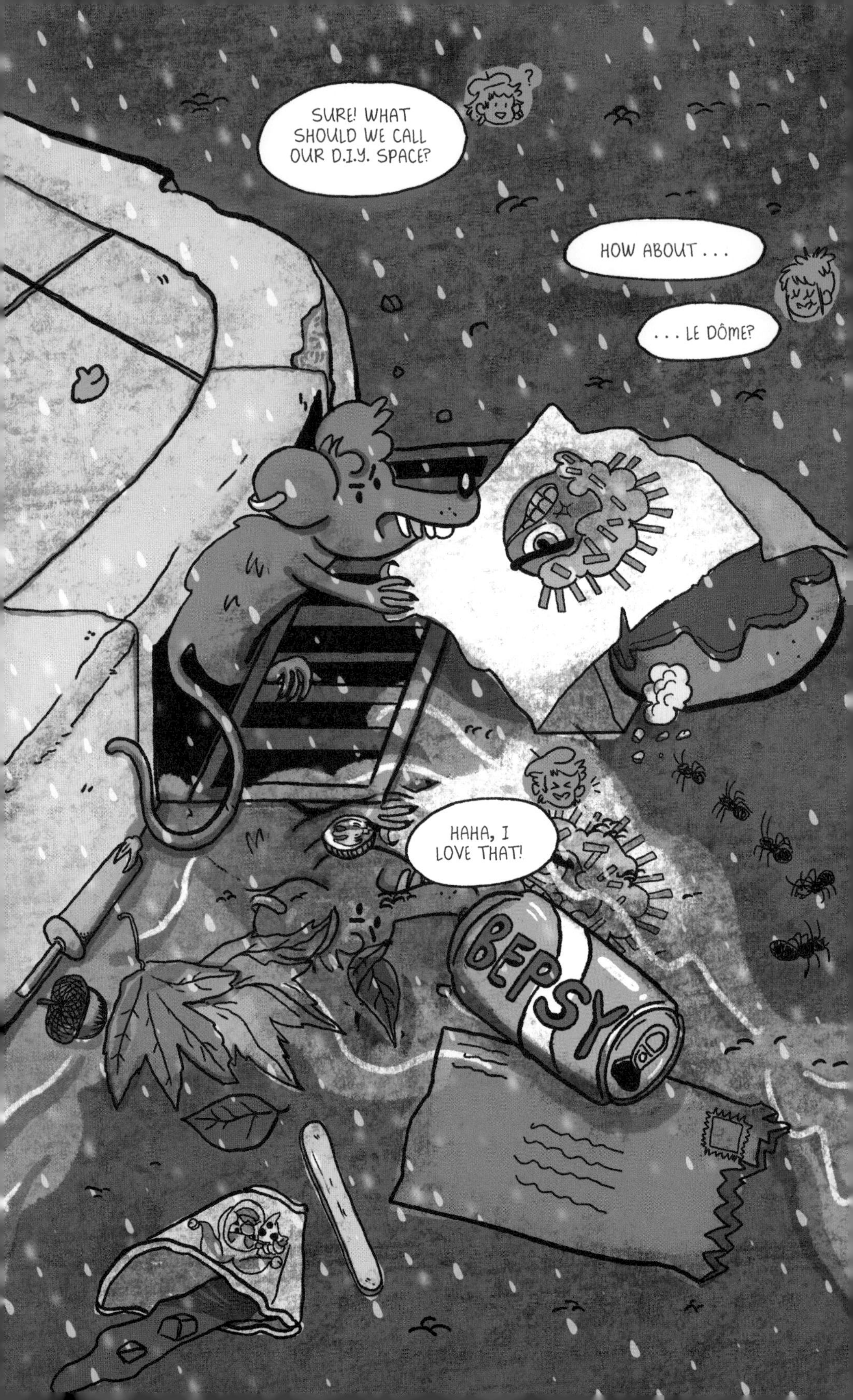
SURE! WHAT SHOULD WE CALL OUR D.I.Y. SPACE?
HOW ABOUT . . .
. . . LE DÔME?
HAHA, I LOVE THAT!
BEPSY

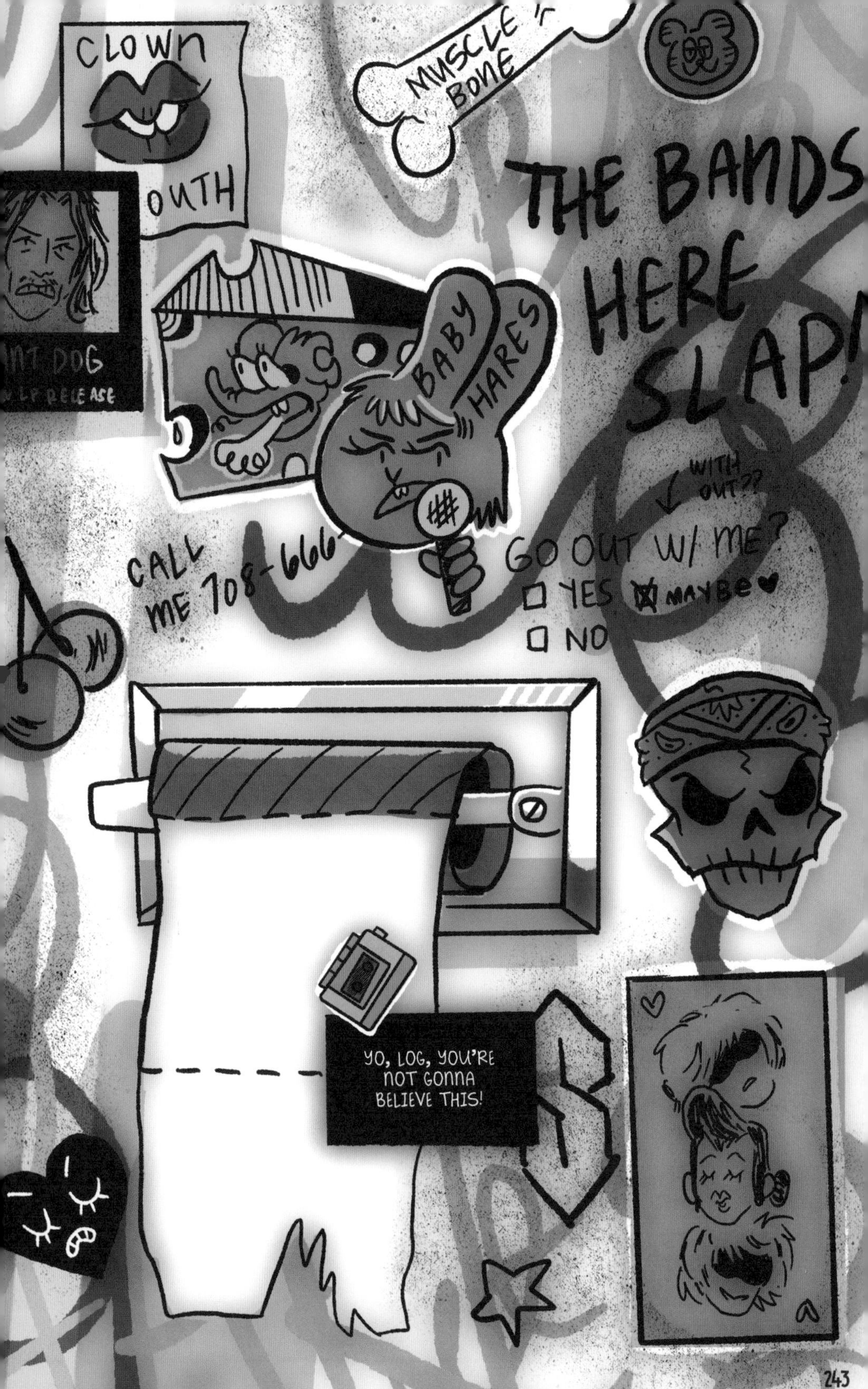
CLOWN
OUTH
MUSCLE 'N BONE
THE BANDS HERE SLAP!
BABY HARES
CALL ME 708-666-
WITH OUT??
GO OUT W/ ME?
YES
MAYBE
NO
YO, LOG, YOU'RE NOT GONNA BELIEVE THIS!

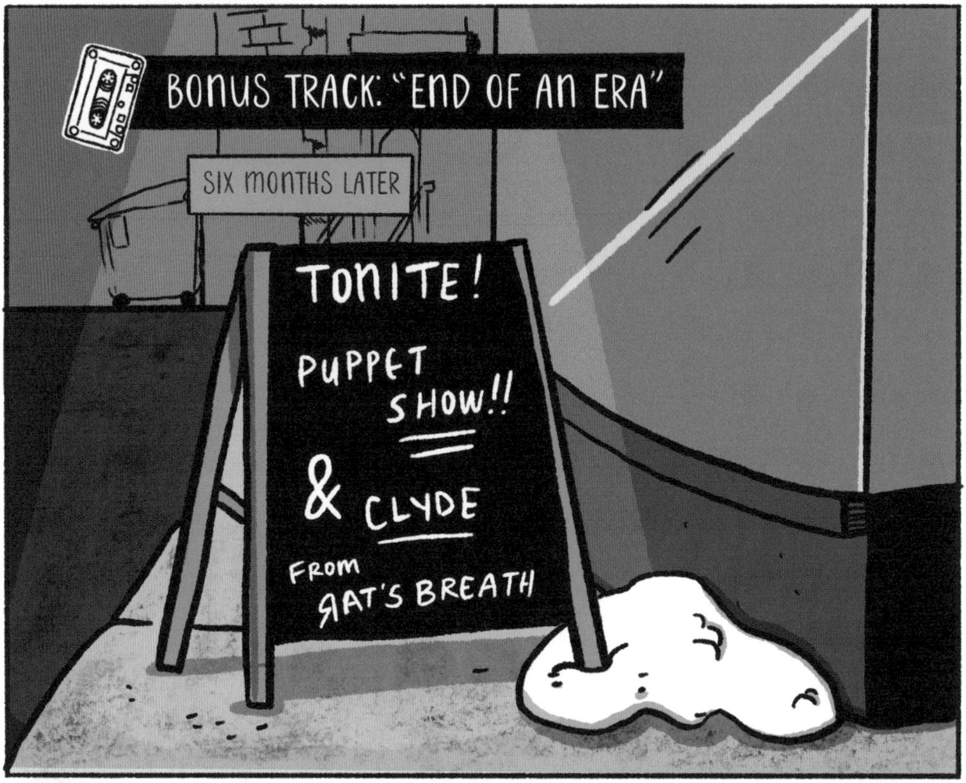
BONUS TRACK: "END OF AN ERA"
SIX MONTHS LATER
TONITE!
PUPPET SHOW!!
& CLYDE
FROM ЯAT'S BREATH

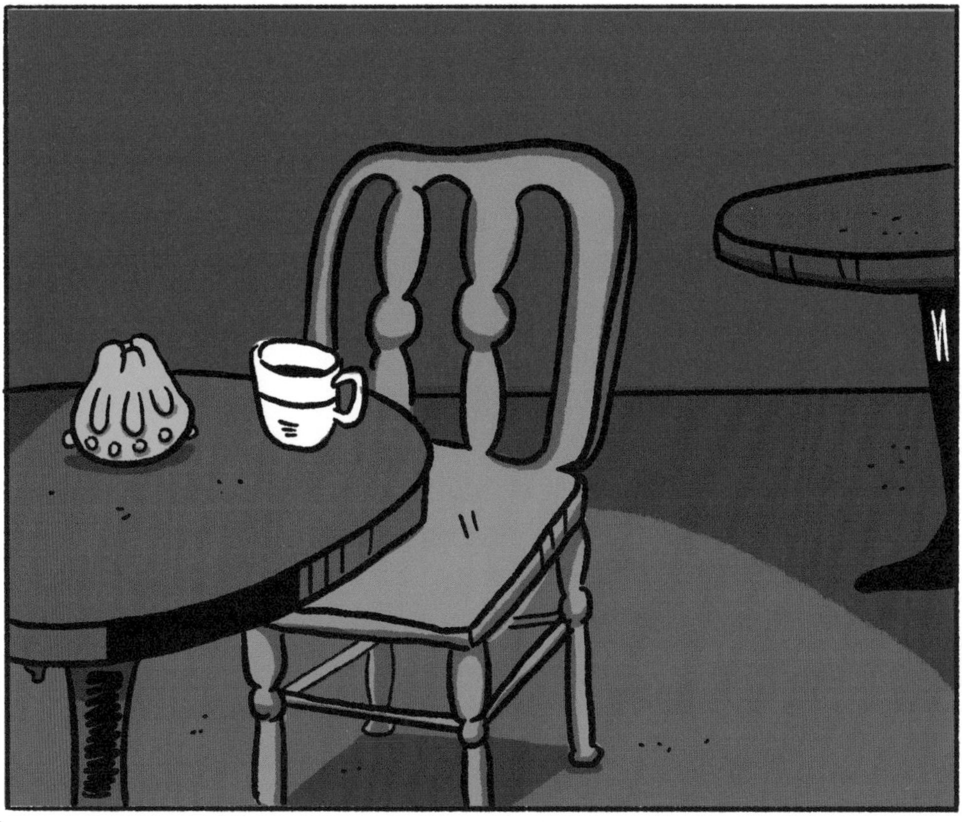

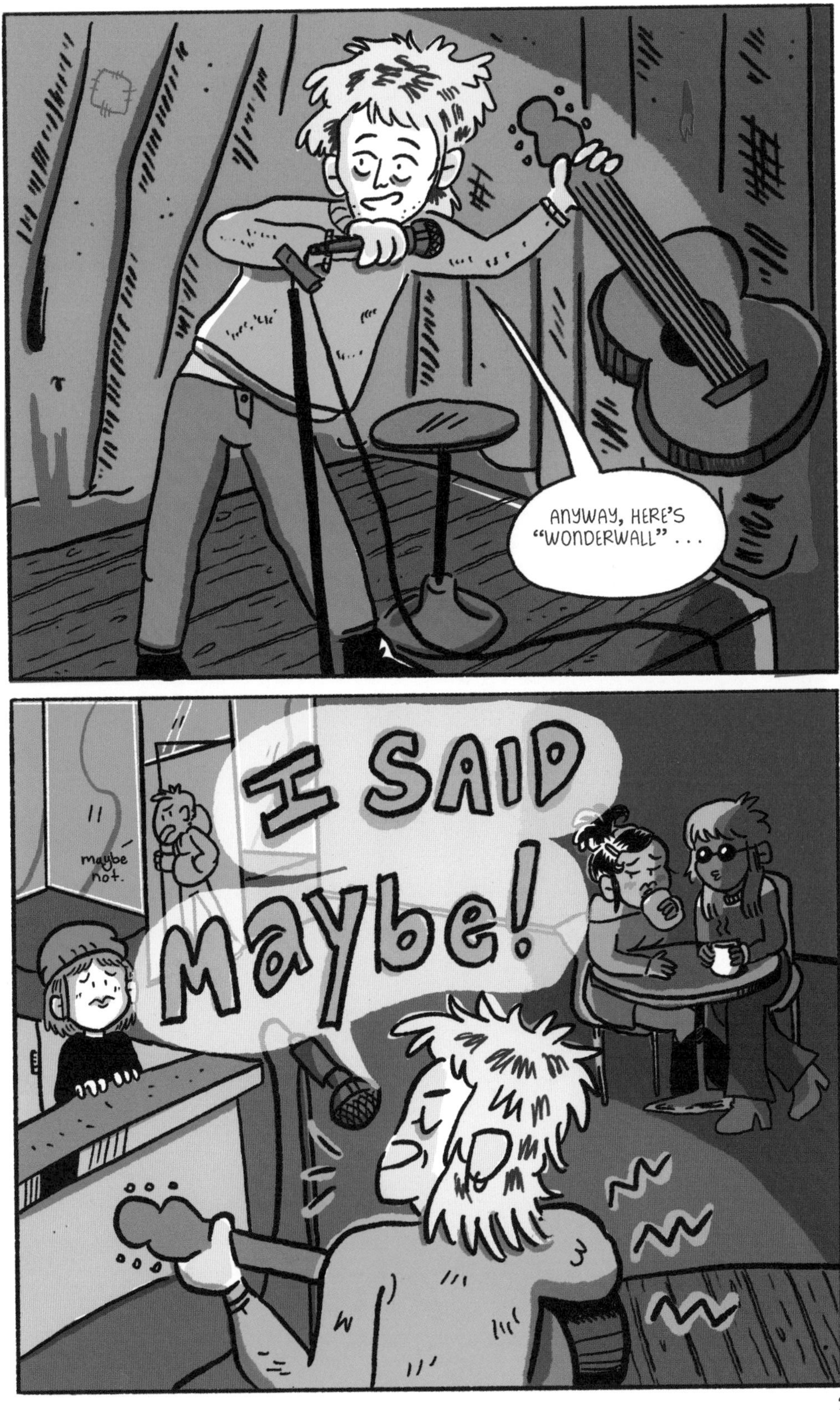
ANYWAY, HERE'S "WONDERWALL" . . .
maybe not.
I SAID maybe!

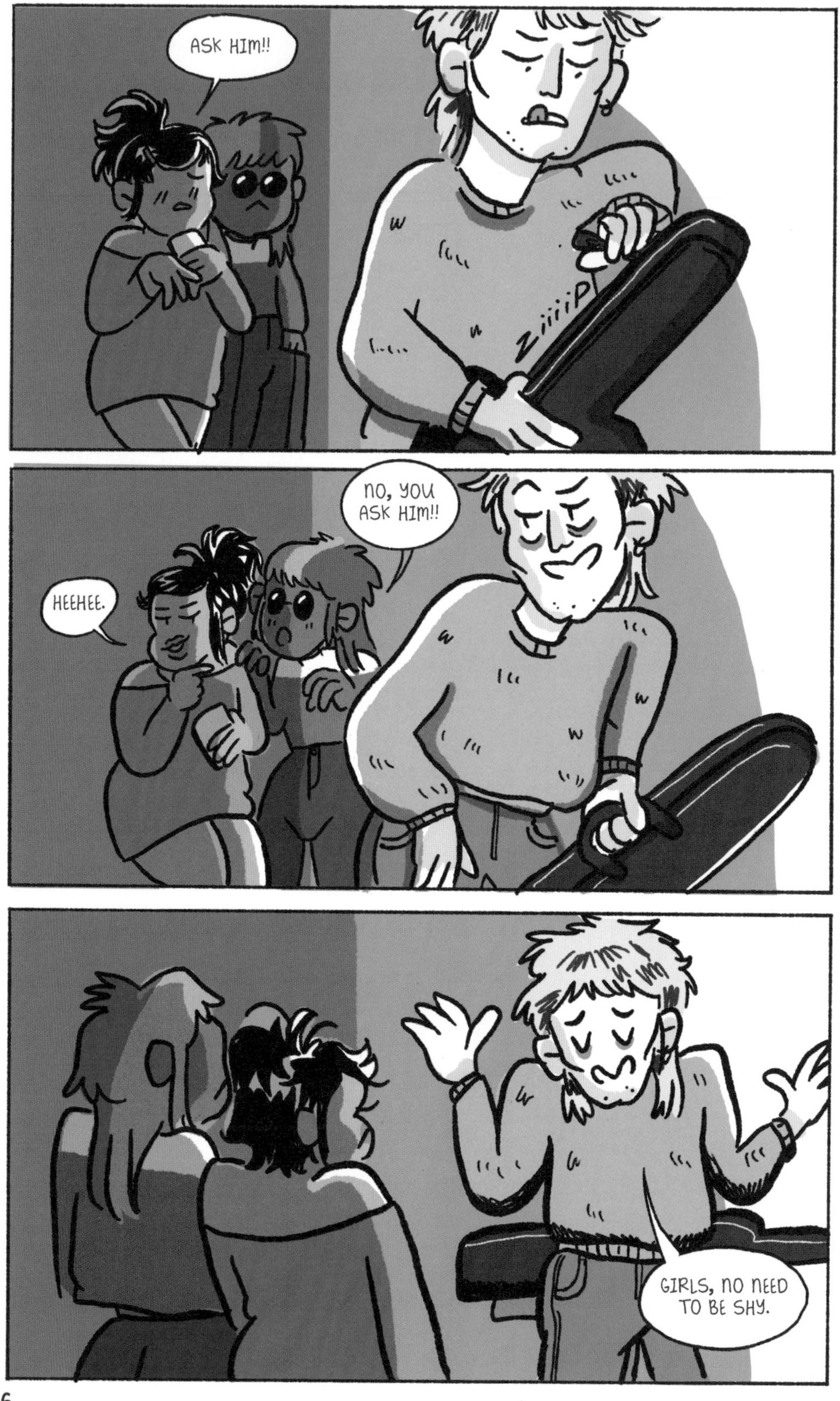
ASK HIM!!
ZIIIIP
NO, YOU ASK HIM!!
HEEHEE.
GIRLS, NO NEED TO BE SHY.

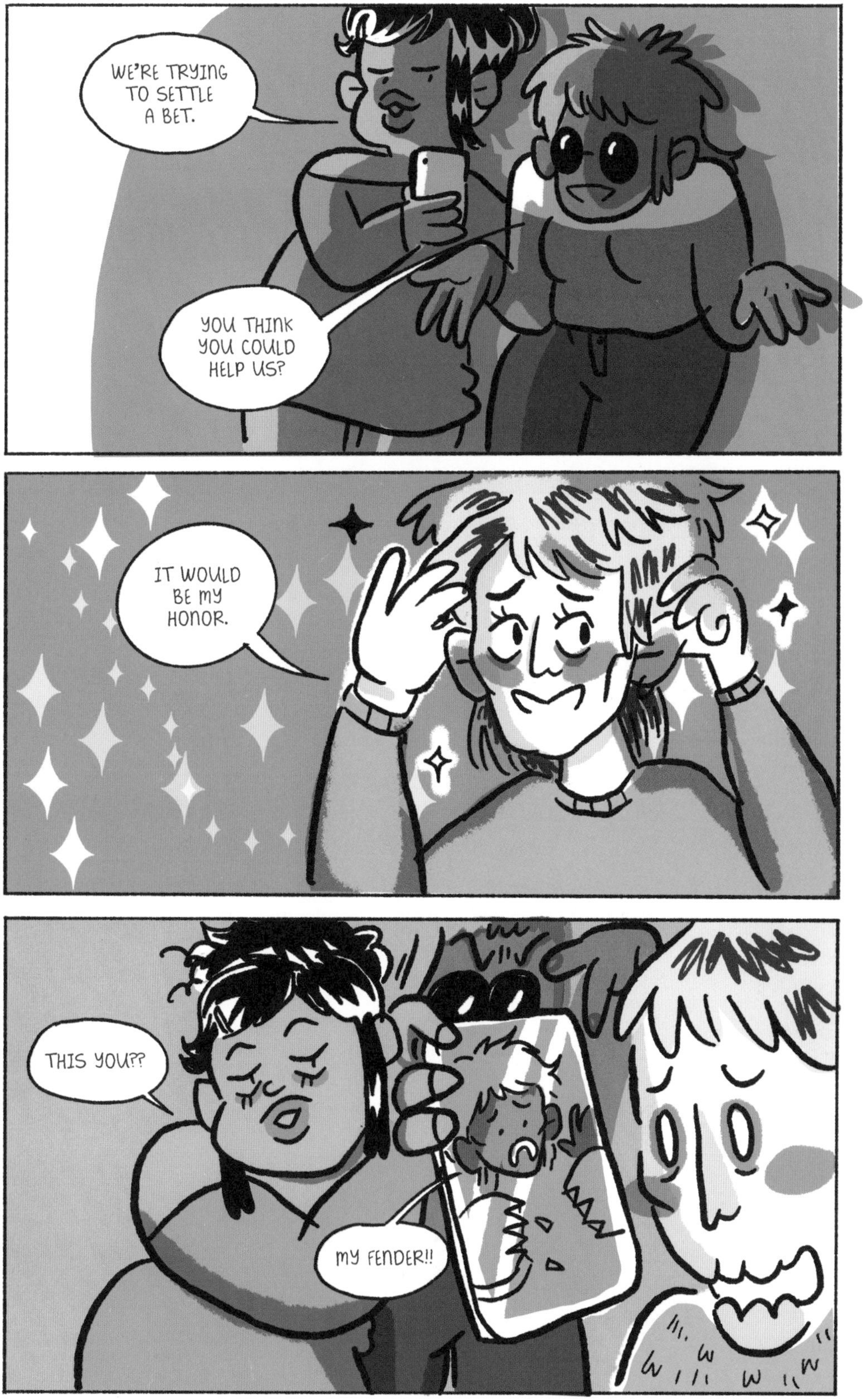
WE'RE TRYING TO SETTLE A BET.
YOU THINK YOU COULD HELP US?
IT WOULD BE MY HONOR.
THIS YOU??
MY FENDER!!

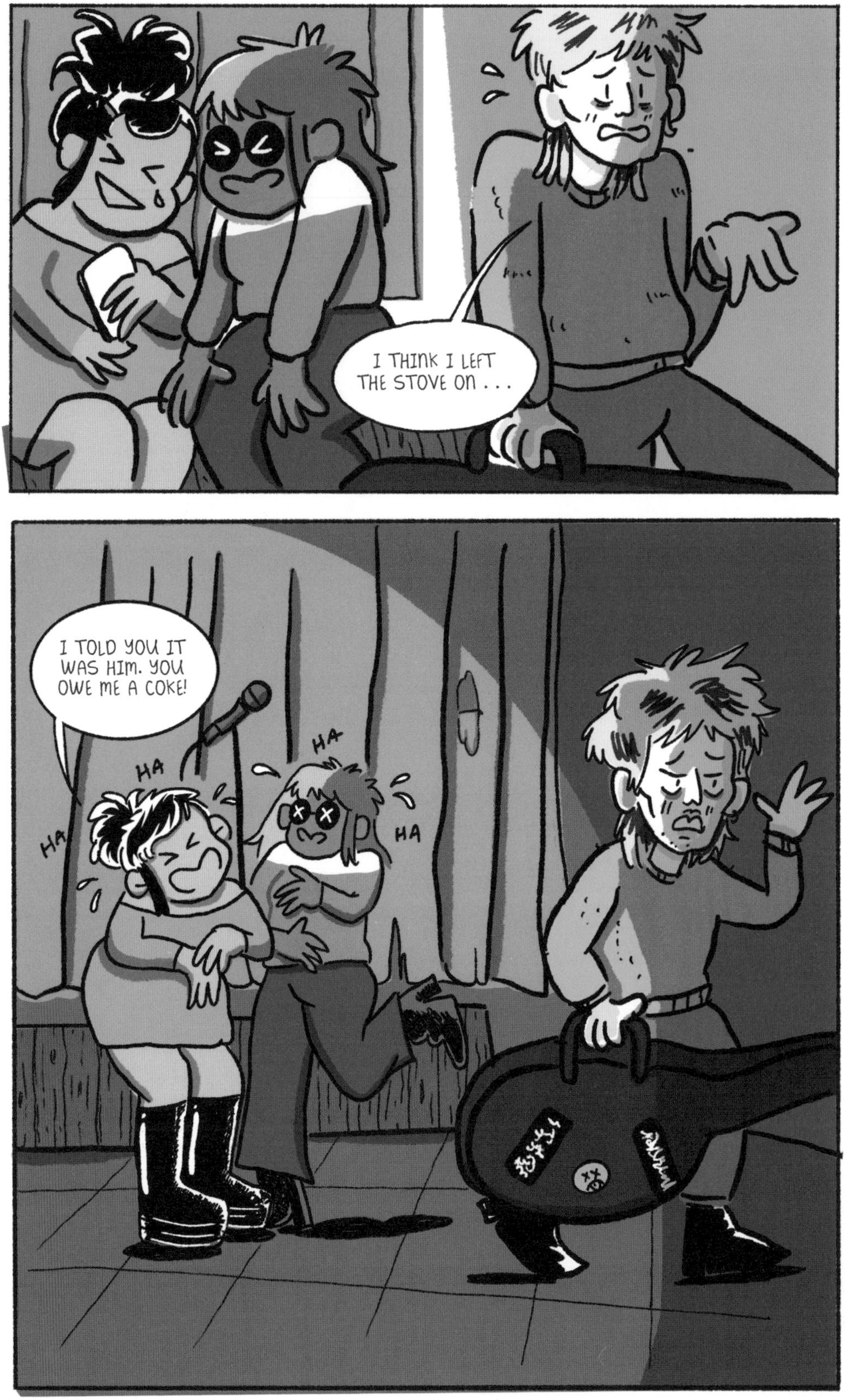
I THINK I LEFT THE STOVE ON . . .
I TOLD YOU IT WAS HIM. YOU OWE ME A COKE!
HA
HA
HA
HA

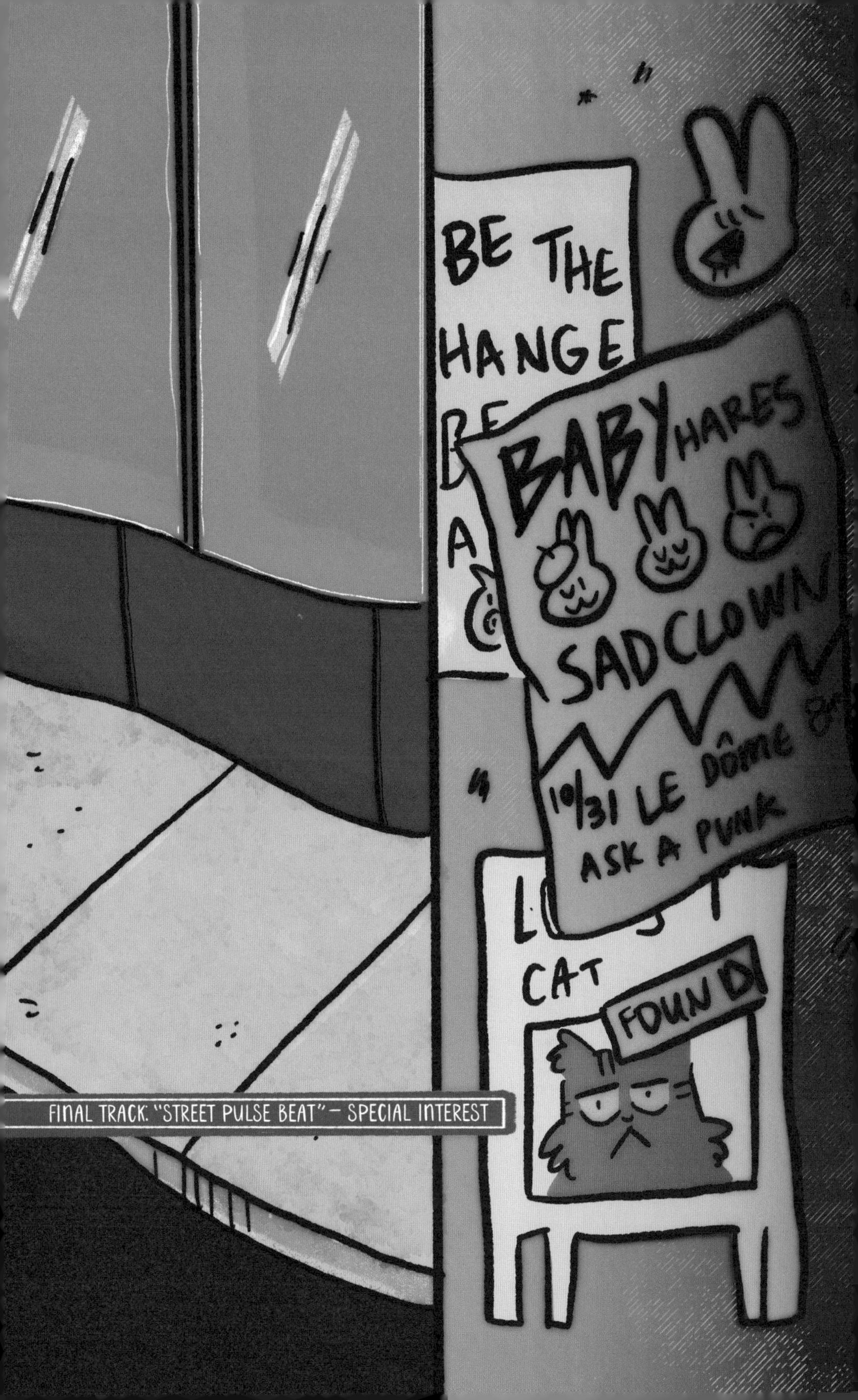
BE THE
HANGE
BABY HARES
SADCLOWN
10/31 LE DÔME
ASK A PUNK
CAT
FOUND
FINAL TRACK: "STREET PULSE BEAT" – SPECIAL INTEREST

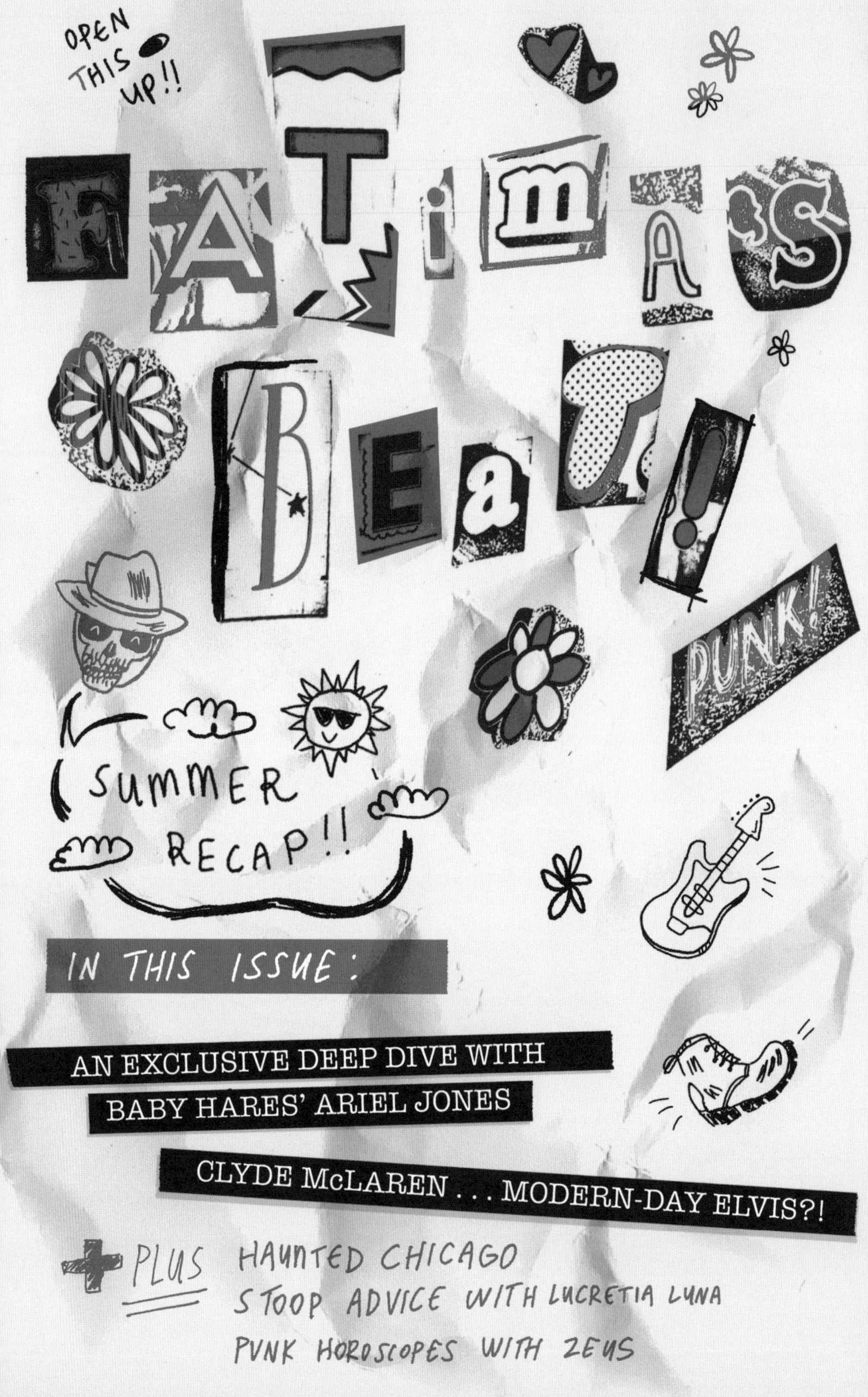
OPEN THIS UP!!
FATIMA'S
BEAT!
PUNK!
SUMMER RECAP!!
IN THIS ISSUE:
AN EXCLUSIVE DEEP DIVE WITH
BABY HARES' ARIEL JONES
CLYDE McLAREN . . . MODERN-DAY ELVIS?!
+ PLUS
HAUNTED CHICAGO
STOOP ADVICE WITH LUCRETIA LUNA
PUNK HOROSCOPES WITH ZEUS

ABOUT *FATIMA'S BEAT*

Welcome to *Fatima's Beat*. Here you'll find out the hottest news about the local underground scene. I bet you're wondering what punk rock is all about. Is it a genre of music, a counter-culture, or a call to action like "open this pit up"?

Friends, it is all of the above and so much more! If this zine made its way to you, I bet you're a punk at heart, just like me. You enjoy creating communities with your friends, marching to the beat of your own drum! Maybe you organize community service or always stick up for those who need their voices to be amplified.

This zine is for us. I poured my sweat, tears, and a few iced lattes from Undergrounds into this issue, so please enjoy! As the 1970s punk band Ramones once said, "Hey ho, let's go!"

WHAT is PUNK?

PUNK HOROSCOPES

WITH ALL-KNOWING ZEUS

WATER SIGNS

YOU MAY FEEL LIKE YOU'VE FALLEN IN THE PIT, BUT YOU CAN ALWAYS SURF YOUR WAY TO THE TOP.

AIR SIGNS

DON'T GO THROUGH LIFE WITH A ROCK IN YOUR ~~BOOTerrible~~ BOOT — SHAKE THAT SHIT OUT!

FIRE SIGNS

NOT ALL YOUR TRASH IS THRASH AND NOT ALL YOUR THRASH IS TRASH.

EARTH SIGNS

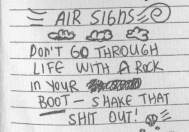

THE 2 FOR $3 VEGAN DOUBLE-DOG ~~SPECAIL~~ SPECIAL MAY NOT FIX ALL YOUR WOES, BUT YOUR BRAIN CAN'T FUNCTION ON AN EMPTY STOMACH.

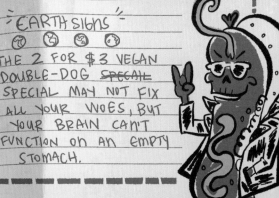

BRING ON THE
MACABRE

ETERNAL SILENCE 😐

The spooky isn't just for Halloween. Did you know goth is the spine-chilling sibling to punk rock? Set your sights on the supernatural lore that makes Chicago tenebrous.

ARCHER BALLROOM (PAGE 2 IN *PUNK ROCK KARAOKE*) ISN'T JUST A DIY SPACE TO SEE RAT'S BREATH. IT'S ALSO RUMORED TO BE THE LOCATION WHERE THE DEVIL ONCE DANCED IN THE PIT HIMSELF.

WHO IS RESURRECTION MARY (PAGE 81 IN *PRK*)? WHILE MANY CHICAGO-BASED CEMETERIES CLAIM TO HAVE SEEN HER, MARY IS THE GHOSTLY GATEKEEPER AT RESURRECTION CEMETERY, WAITING FOR SOMEONE TO GIVE HER A RIDE HOME AFTER DANCING IN THE DARK.

GOTHS AND PUNKS ALIKE LOVE A CEMETERY PICNIC UNDER THE STARS, BUT BE CAREFUL NOT TO LOOK IN THE EYES OF *ETERNAL SILENCE* (PAGE 81 IN *PRK*) AT GRACELAND CEMETERY AND ARBORETUM. LEGEND SAYS HE CAN PREDICT THE MOMENT YOU LEAVE THIS MORTAL COIL.

SEE SOMETHING UNUSUAL FLYING AROUND CHICAGO AT NIGHT? COULD BE THE MOTHMAN (PAGE 175 IN *PRK*). MOTHMAN IS AN AMERICAN CRYPTID THAT CARRIES FOREBODING NEWS UNDER HIS WINGS. IF YOU SPOT HIM, HE MAY BE BRINGING NEWS OF A MAJOR UPSET IN YOUR LIFE, OR JUST SAYING HOWDY.

STOOP ADVICE
WITH Lulu

OPEN THIS PIT UP? OPEN YOUR HEART UP? EITHER WAY— CONSENT.

Dear LULU,
I'm going to my first basement show!! What should I wear? I'm worried I'll look like a poseur and not be invited back
— Punk Baby

Dear Baby,
Come as you are! The punk scene is for everyone, no matter what you wear. But might I suggest clothing you don't mind getting a little dirty, comfy shoes to help you stomp, and a satchel to carry all the essentials. Leave the fancy fits for the goth club.

Dear Lulu
There's a shaggy haired boy I like. But my friends are not impressed. What should I do?
— Lost in Feathered Hair

Dear Lost,
Sometimes when we have hearts in our eyes, we can't see very clearly. Let your buds guide your way. Cute boys shouldn't make you choose.

EX-RAT'S FINAL BREATH

I got a chance to sit down with Rat's Breath drummer Joey Bones over milkshakes to discuss Rat's Breath's recent demise. Here's what he had to say about their final show.

Joey Bones: Clyde was a poet like Morrissey, but his ego would get in the way. What happened tonight was a long time coming. Can't say I didn't have fun, though.

Fatima: Did you know Clyde was stealing songs?

Bones: He would claim they were "collabs," but that always seemed fishy.

Fatima: Would you say he's like a modern-day Elvis?

Bones: I don't know, I guess he was always gyrating on stage, so yeah.

Fatima: Heh...what's next for Joey Bones?

Bones: I think I want to switch things up, be the lead singer for once! I'm tired of sitting in the back being attacked by dogs. I'm pushing my drum kit to the front of the stage!!

Fatima: Thanks, Bones, for your time.

Bones: This milkshake is comped right?

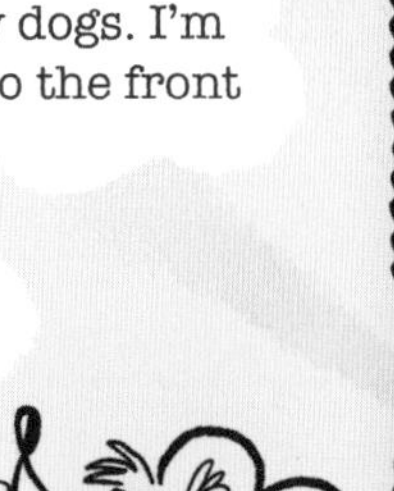

EXCLUSIVE...

I AIN'T NUTHIN' BUT A HOUND DAWG!

CLYDE McLAREN MODERN DAY ELVIS?!

As a punk it's pivotal to know your roots. Within history we can always find our truths. Punk rock is a genre of rock 'n' roll, but who was the first rock 'n' roller?

Some would argue Elvis Presley. But did you know Elvis got his rise to fame by cherry-picking songs that were originally performed by lesser-known Black musicians? His hit "Hound Dog" was initially sung by Big Mama Thornton, who never received the same level of recognition or notoriety. Elvis isn't the only musician to rise to explosive success after covering Black artists. The Clash, Rolling Stones, even goth favorite Soft Cell all had smash hits that were actually covers of the Equals, Eric Donaldson, and Gloria Jones respectively.

In the modern landscape of music, doing a cover of your favorite song isn't taboo. But taking all the glory in the same way Clyde tried to take from Baby Hares is a total prick move. Remember, punks, amplify the voices of the unseen, but don't steal from them. Only poseurs plagiarize.

ARIEL'S DEEP DIVE

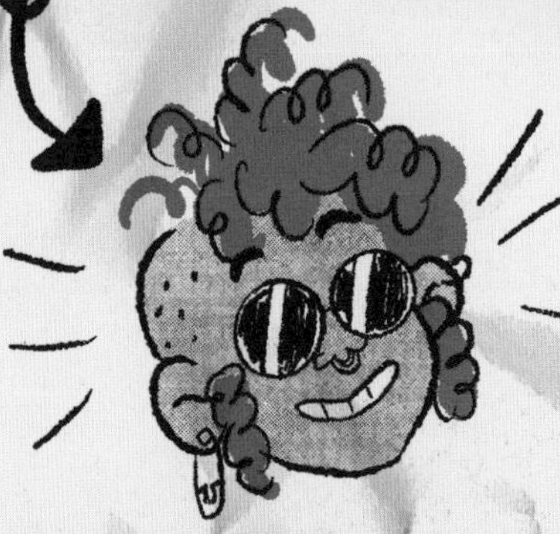

Yo, what up, Ariel here! Fatima was dope enough to let me geek out in this issue and talk about my favorite thing ever. PUNK MUSIC. But not just any genre of punk, women in punk!! There's so many bands that inspire me and Baby Hares. The Slits, the Muffs, even Hole, just to name a few.

When Michele and I first met in our elementary school uniforms, we'd always dreamed of being in a band together like the Runaways. Who are the Runaways, you might ask? It's the all-girl band where Joan Jett got her start, and she later became the first female recording artist to start her own label. United by their love for David Bowie, the Runaways were one of the first bands to shake up the scene, after the Ramones, of course. But we wouldn't even have the Ramones if it wasn't for all-girl groups like the Ronettes, who inspired the Ramones' whole getup.

Black women are often the unsung heroes of rock 'n' roll, inspiring a plethora of genres without the deserved credit. I am honored to pull inspiration from pioneers such as Sister Rosetta Tharpe, heralded as the inventor of Rock 'n' Roll, and Tina Turner, who modernized the sound. I also adore legends like Betty Davis, Grace Jones (who I was named after!), Tina Bell, and of course the GOAT—Poly Styrene.

Don't ever let anyone tell you that rock 'n' roll isn't for Black kids and queerdos, because we are the secret ingredient! If only there was some way to stop the poseurs who try to repackage our cool as their own. A friendly reminder that if you ever feel like an outsider, you actually might be the coolest person ever. Just lace up your boots and channel some energy from the misfits who paved the way for us to rock on.

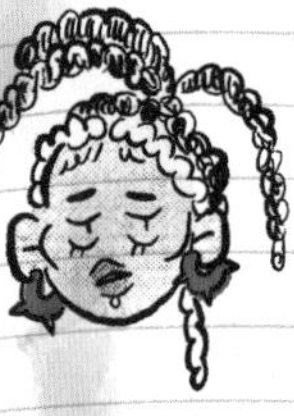

MICHELE: I listened to "Fast Car" by Tracey Chapman on my way here. It makes me feel better whenever I feel sad. It's like a lesbian national anthem.

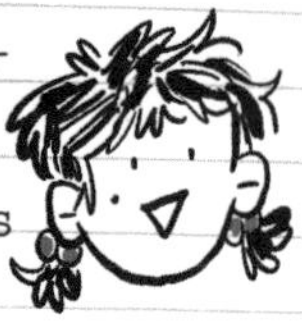

GAEL: I love going to *Rocky Horror Picture Show* screenings at the movies. The best part, everybody dresses up like the characters and sings along with the musical!

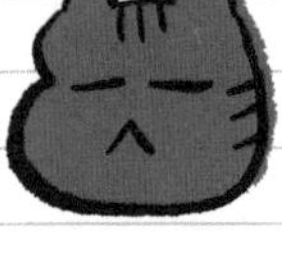

GATA: Mrrreow-ow. (Translation: I hope Tavo BBQs some chicken later.)